Through Castle Windows

VOLUME FIVE OF THE
HORSTBERG SAGA

Books by Elizabeth D. Michaels

Horstberg Saga
Behind the Mask (Volume One)
A Matter of Honor (Volume Two)
For Love and Country (Volume Three)
The Tainted Crown (Volume Four)
Through Castle Windows (Volume Five)

Through Castle Windows

VOLUME FIVE OF THE
HORSTBERG SAGA

Bestselling author Anita Stansfield writing as

Elizabeth D. Michaels

WHITE
STAR
PRESS

This is a work of fiction, and the views expressed herein are the sole responsibility of the author. Likewise, certain characters, places, and incidents are the product of the author's imagination, and any resemblance to actual persons, living or dead, or actual events or locales, is entirely coincidental.

Through Castle Windows: Volume V of the Horstberg Saga

Published by White Star Press
P.O. Box 353
American Fork, Utah 84003

Castle painting copyright © 2015 Anna C. Stansfield
Cover and interior design by Epub Masters

Print ISBN: 978-1-939203-63-2
Printed in the United States of America
Year of first printing: 2015

To M

Prologue

Erich du Woernig came awake with a start. He sat upright in bed, sweat beading over his face. The dream that had awakened him was familiar—eerily familiar. He could hear glass breaking, and at the same time, a loud boom, as if a gun were fired, and the force of the shot threw him against a wall.

Erich groaned and pressed his face into the pillow. Surely the repetition of this dream was simply a hangover from the fears he'd just recently come to terms with. Those who had wanted him dead were no longer a threat. Surely it was nothing.

When Erich couldn't go back to sleep, he rose at dawn and went riding. The fresh air of late summer cleared his senses and gave him the peace he was looking for. He kept busy through the remainder of the morning, attempting to get everything in order for the busy week ahead.

Erich hurried into the dining room late to find the entire family already seated for lunch. He tossed his gloves aside and took his usual place, glancing around the table at those he loved. Maggie, his sister. Han, her husband and his closest friend. Their children, Hannah, Gerhard, and of course, Stefan. Stefan was seven years old and one of the most important people in Erich's life. The boy was going to be great one day. Erich just felt it. Then there was Georg, Han's father and an integral part of all their lives. He was the man who kept this place running, and everyone knew it. Sonia, his youngest sister, and her family were also here.

They lived elsewhere, but they'd come for the wedding. And then there were Erich's parents.

"Is everything all right?" Abbi du Woernig asked. His mother always had a sixth sense about his emotions, but today there were no hidden concerns. Even his nightmares seemed petty and insignificant.

"Oh yes," he assured her. Then he laughed. "Everything is perfect. I'm getting married in four days, remember?"

"Oh, so that's why you've always got that silly grin plastered on your face," Cameron du Woernig said. Erich grinned at his father as if to demonstrate.

"I'd say he's earned the right to smile," Abbi said. "After what he's been through to get to the altar, let him smile."

Cameron chuckled and focused his attention on his wife. "You think I don't know what it's like to have to fight to marry the woman I love?"

Erich saw his parents' eyes meet across the table, and something tangible seemed to pass through the air between them. He knew their own history was filled with struggle and heartache. They were the Duke and Duchess of Horstberg. Their lives were tangled into the responsibilities of ruling a nation. But the joy they shared was evident, and the legacy of love they'd given him was priceless. There had been a time when he'd envied what they shared but not anymore. Now, he understood it. Kathe Lokberg was everything he'd ever wanted, and in four more days, she would be his wife—at last.

The wedding had been postponed due to a political uprising that had put the entire family in danger—most specifically him, being the heir to Horstberg. But that was over now. The danger was past. He was free to make Kathe his wife without the fear of making her a widow. For months he'd had feelings that had nearly convinced him his life would be cut short. He'd come to believe that their time together would be brief, and they had learned to make the most of the present. Of course, having his life regularly threatened had certainly contributed to his fears. He'd felt prepared to die, in spite of his heartache at the thought of not having a lifetime to share with Kathe. But now he was prepared to live, knowing his life was in order and all was well.

The meal proceeded with talk of the wedding and plans for the afternoon. Cameron was the first to push back his chair and stand. "Come along, Han," he said. "We've got work to do. Georg?"

"I've got to get that report from the captain, then I'll be in."

Han stood and kissed Maggie, as he always did. The love they shared was also evident. "Are you coming, Stefan?" Han asked his oldest son. Erich smiled at the boy. Unlike the other children, he preferred to sit in the office with the men, as if the ducal business actually meant something to him.

"I'm going riding with Erich," Stefan said. "He promised."

"That's right," Erich said. "But not until I get the dungeon cleaned out. You go ahead and I'll find you in the office when I'm finished." Stefan smiled and hurried after his father.

While Han and Stefan hovered in the doorway, Cameron walked the length of the table and bent to kiss his wife. Erich couldn't help watching them, his thoughts with Kathe. It wasn't unusual for his parents to kiss, but everyone in the room was a little surprised at the way this particular kiss went on and on.

"What was that for?" Abbi asked with a soft laugh. She glanced briefly down the table and blushed slightly at the evidence that they were being watched.

"It was for thirty-two years of life with you, Abbi girl. I just wanted you to know that I love you, and I'm grateful for every minute we've had together."

Abbi's embarrassment turned to emotion as she looked into her husband's eyes. It was difficult to tell if she was simply touched by his sentiment or somehow concerned as she rose to her feet and embraced him. They held to each other a long moment, and then he kissed her again and hurried to where Han and Stefan were waiting. He paused and glanced back at Abbi, who was still watching him, and they exchanged a warm smile before the men left the room. Maggie rose from the table and took the other two children, leaving Erich alone with his mother. Abbi sat back down as if she'd suddenly come out of a trance, and she passed him a warm smile, not unlike the one she'd just given his father. But there was a sadness in her eyes that chilled him.

"What is it, Mother?" She looked suddenly guilty, as if he'd caught her at mischief.

"Nothing," she insisted with a smile. Erich forced any negative feelings away, concentrating instead on all that was good in his life. Following his father's example, he rose from the table and approached his mother. Taking her hands, he urged her back to her feet, holding her tightly in his arms.

"I love you, Mother." He kissed her with a loud smooch that made her laugh. "That's for thirty-one years of life. The best life a man could ever want."

Abbi looked into his eyes and touched his hair. "I love you too, Erich. You've given me such joy." He eased away, and she added, "You be careful, now."

Abbi left the room through a different door, and he knew she would likely spend the afternoon painting. Later he would find her and pretend to know what he was talking about when he told her that her latest painting was the best so far.

Spurred on by his desire to see Kathe this evening, Erich hurried toward the dungeon to complete a necessary task. His hobby of chemistry had accompanied him all the way through his youth. It had always fascinated him, and he'd spent many long days in the dungeon playing with his chemicals. But through the recent threats against his life, the dungeon had become a trap. The last time he'd gone there, he knew someone had been in the room, tampering with the chemicals. He'd decided to clean everything out and start over, and his father had insisted it be done before the wedding. Georg had suggested they get someone else to do it, but Erich had assured them he preferred to do it himself. He knew what he was doing, and he would be careful. He didn't have to fear that there was someone lurking in the shadows down there, waiting to do away with him, as there had been in the past.

Erich was nearly to the door that led to the dungeon when he passed Georg, on his way to find the captain.

"Hey, Georg," he teased, "why don't you come down with me? We could concoct a potion to enhance your looks."

"It would be just my luck," he said lightly, "if it blew up in my face."

"It could still enhance your looks," Erich joked.

Georg laughed heartily, a rare thing to see since his wife's death seven years earlier.

"You insolent pup," Georg said with mock anger. "Just get out of here."

"I am *not* an insolent pup." Erich feigned indignation. "And when I take over this country, I'm going to remember you said that."

"Perhaps you should also remember that I bounced you on my knee before you could even walk. When you take over this country, you're going to need *me* to tell you how to do it."

Erich smiled and approached the door. "Yes, Georg, you're right, I know. You usually are." Erich turned to the two officers waiting at the door that led from the hallway down to his dungeon. "Hello, gentlemen. I assume my father sent you to keep an eye on me."

"In a roundabout way, sir," one of them said. "We're just here to help, and we all want you to stay safe."

"Of course." Erich tired not to take the implications too seriously. He also tried not to feel the habitual concern that he was in danger, and he forced away the memory of that recurring dream.

Erich took the key out of his pocket and unlocked the door. "Just wait here with the door open," he said to the officers. "I'll keep the door open down there, as well. And I'll yell if I need you."

"Very good, sir," the other officer said.

Erich thanked them and hurried down the winding stairs and into his chemistry room. He stood for a minute in the center of the room, wondering where to start. Then with purpose, he reached up to take some little bottles of chemical down from a crowded shelf. As he took hold of the first one, all the others moved slightly, and he realized that a tiny bottle sitting precariously at the edge of the shelf was going to fall. And there was nothing he could do to stop it. He watched it plummet toward the floor, as if time were moving more slowly. Just before it hit, the memory of his dream plunged into his mind. *Glass breaking. A loud boom.* And then the world ended.

Feeling unusually tired, Kathe Lokberg took down her dark hair and stretched out on the bed. The warmth of the afternoon sun sprayed through the corner window of her bedroom, adding to her contentment. As always, her mind wandered to thoughts of Erich.

Erich. His name alone sent shivers of delight through every part of her. She marveled at how he'd changed her life, and more so at the intensity of their love. It was difficult to comprehend everything that had happened since they'd first met. But she felt peace in knowing they would be married soon. The thought intensified her contentment, and she nearly laughed aloud as she settled more comfortably against her pillow.

At first the rumbling seemed a part of Kathe's dream. Certain it had to be thunder, she reluctantly opened her eyes, wondering if it might rain. Her heart quickened as she absorbed the sunlight, and her surroundings briefly trembled, as if the earth itself had opened up.

"What in the world?" she gasped, hurrying to the window. Fear gripped Kathe's heart as something died inside her. She cried out in horror to see black smoke billowing up behind Castle Horstberg. It only took a moment for her feelings to take hold. She could never explain it, but she knew something horrible had happened to Erich.

Oblivious to her surroundings, Kathe fled to the stable and mounted bareback, riding across town as fast as the mare would go. Her thoughts flitted through the difficulties Horstberg had just emerged from. They had endured revolution and come through triumphant. Being engaged to the next Duke of Horstberg, she had almost become accustomed to Erich's life being in danger. But the war had ended almost as soon as it began. The royal family had all survived, and Erich's father had assured them all was well. They had finally been able to set a date for the wedding, and Kathe truly felt like a part of the family.

Coming into the castle courtyard, Kathe immediately sensed the havoc. Her fears settled a little deeper, gathering in the pit of her stomach until they threatened to devour her. Reminding herself that she was practically family, she entered without knocking and ran down the long main hall. Her fear knotted into tangible pain as a charred smell struck her senses and the air became hazy with smoke.

Turning the corner near her destination, Kathe stopped cold. Her eyes quickly surveyed these people she had come to know and care for. Erich's mother, Abbi, was sitting on the floor sobbing. The dignity Kathe had always seen her bear was completely absent. Georg, the duke's highest advisor and a close family friend, knelt with his arms around Abbi, shock and horror carved into his expression. And Georg's son, Han, sat on the floor nearby, leaning against the opposite wall. He appeared dazed and in shock while a doctor knelt beside him, administering to blatant burns over his left shoulder and arm.

Erich's young nephew, Stefan, stood looking on, his eyes wide with fear. Kathe's heart went out to him as he stared toward the body on the floor that was just now being covered by an officer of the Guard—the body of Cameron du Woernig. With the finality of the gesture, Abbi cried out her husband's name in anguish.

Kathe wanted to ask what had happened, but the words wouldn't come. She wanted to ask where Erich was, but in her heart she knew. As if her ignorance would keep her from the pain, she instinctively pushed her questions aside and moved to Stefan. The moment she put her arms around him, the pride of the young prince dissipated, and he clung to her and cried.

Sounds emitted from the stairwell nearby where hazy smoke still rose. Han suddenly became alert as Abbi's eyes shot toward the door.

"Get her out of here!" he demanded, struggling to his feet.

Georg reacted immediately and attempted to move Abbi down the hall.

"No!" she screamed, reaching toward her husband's body. Georg pulled her into his arms and carried her up the stairs.

Han's head swung toward Kathe as he became aware of her presence. For a moment she could almost read his thoughts. He was Erich's closest friend, and she had come to love him as Erich did. But something in Han's eyes had changed. He had seen something unspeakably horrible.

"Get them out of here!" Han ordered an officer standing nearby. She'd never seen him behave so brashly.

Two men in uniform gently urged Kathe and Stefan down the hall. Kathe stopped them briefly and turned toward Han, her eyes full of question. She needed to hear it.

"He's gone, Kathe." Han's voice trembled and tears brimmed in his eyes. "You can't see him. Please trust me. You wouldn't know him."

The pain of reality deepened as Kathe let the officers move her away. She was aware from a quick glance over her shoulder of a body, already covered, being brought from the stairwell and laid with the other.

For Stefan's sake, Kathe fought to remain calm. Everything inside of her screamed in silent anguish. But she was grateful for Stefan's need for comfort as she took him to his room and helped him to bed, staying with him until his mother came. Then Kathe quietly returned home to mourn in private.

The funeral was torturous for Kathe. On the day she should have been married, the sky hung gray while Horstberg mourned its loss. The duke and his heir were both dead. The funeral procession moved through the beautiful village like a shrouded black serpent. Kathe managed to maintain her dignity, while inwardly she cursed fate for its cruelty in taking Erich from her this way—the same fate she had so recently blessed for sending him into her life.

Though Kathe's pain ran deep, she felt hesitant to lean on these people she had come to love. Their wounds were as fresh as hers. No one intended to push Kathe away. She chose to remain in the background. Without Erich, she simply didn't belong anymore. If they had married, it might have been different, but that would never come about now. Her life was over.

Kathe's brother, Theodor, took her home after the funeral and put her to bed where she mourned herself sick over the next several days. Her father was always close by, but there was nothing anyone could do. She finally convinced herself that she had to go on living. On market day she went into town, just as she'd done hundreds of times in her life. But nothing was the same. The black she wore didn't begin to express the hole in her heart. It hadn't been so long since she had been here with Erich. All eyes had watched them, marveling that the prince had finally fallen in love. Now Kathe felt those same eyes on her as she quietly went about her business. Everyone knew she had almost become a du Woernig. And the pity in their expressions made her tangibly ill.

Kathe hurried home and went back to bed, staying there for days. Eventually instinct told her that something more was making her ill. A deep mixture of emotions accompanied the realization that she was going to have a baby. *Erich's baby.* They had never intended to allow such a thing to happen outside of marriage, but his life was being threatened and the wedding had been postponed. Desperation had driven them into each other's arms. She wondered how many illegitimate children had been conceived in times of war throughout the history of the world. But knowing it had happened to others didn't make it any easier.

Once Kathe adjusted to the idea, she felt grateful to have this part of Erich with her. It gave what was left of her life some purpose. What she had shared with Erich was too powerful to regret, and she believed in her heart that he would be pleased to know that a child remained in his stead.

Kathe nearly went to tell Abbi, but an unexplainable fear stopped her. She knew the du Woernig family didn't need the burden of this to add to their grief. It would not be joyous for them. It would only be a stigma, a painful reminder of Erich's absence.

When Kathe told Theodor and her father, they were not as

shocked as she'd expected them to be. Of course, they had been well aware of the duress she and Erich had been under. But her father brought another problem to light. Erich's life had been precarious. The country had just emerged from revolution. The heir to the throne was dead. Were there still revolutionaries out there who would not want Erich du Woernig's child to exist? Legitimate or otherwise? Unlikely perhaps, but possible enough to make Kathe's decision clear.

Kathe's father said nothing when she told him she was leaving Horstberg. Somehow she knew he understood her need to go, even though it broke his heart. But he promised to visit often, and she knew he would always be there for her, in spite of the miles that would now exist between their homes.

Theodor, however, protested her leaving strongly. He begged, pleaded, and ordered her not to go. But her mind was made up. And reluctantly he swore to never tell a soul what he knew.

One last time, Kathe wandered through town on market day. Still wearing black, she was almost becoming accustomed to the pitiful stares of those she passed. But she couldn't bear the thought of how they might look at her if they realized she was pregnant with Erich du Woernig's child.

The morning Kathe was scheduled to leave, she walked with purpose to the cathedral where she and Erich should have been married. The huge edifice served as the north boundary to the cemetery. She walked a familiar path through the gate, toward the section in the center surrounded by a high wrought-iron fence, where members of the royal family were buried. The trees that shaded the graves were nearly bare; their leaves crunched beneath her feet as she walked. The huge marble stones that marked the graves of Erich and his father had a new, polished appearance that made them stand out among the others.

With hesitancy, Kathe reached out to touch the words carved in stone. *Erich Cameron Georg Gerhard du Woernig. 1818 – 1849.* And etched below the name and date were the words to a song that Erich's father had written for him before he was born. Kathe touched each word, one by one, clearly hearing in her memory the way Erich had taught them to her. She managed to hold back her emotion until her fingers traced over the final lines. *I know my love is here with me. A fire burns in my heart.*

The full extent of Kathe's pain rushed out of the numbness that held it bound, burning through her chest before it came into the open with an anguished howl. She sunk to her knees and pressed her face to the cold stone that bore Erich's name.

"How can I go on?" she cried as if he could hear her. "How can I bear this child alone? I can't!" she sobbed and pressed herself closer to the marble slab. "I can't!"

Kathe felt warm hands on her shoulders, but she paid no attention. It wasn't the first time her father had found her here and forced her to come home. She expected his grip to tighten and urge her to her feet. But instead his arms came around her, holding her tightly. And with his embrace, a tangible warmth filtered through her entire being. The intensity of the feeling made her gasp and lift her head, glancing briefly over her shoulder. Then she caught her breath and held it. *She was alone.* But she *wasn't.* She forced the air out of her lungs when they began to burn, and her breath carried his name into the open air. "Erich."

The undeniable sensation of his embrace only deepened. Her tears turned to laughter. "Erich," she said again, closing her eyes to savor the feeling, knowing she couldn't expect it to last any more than a long moment.

Kathe expected to feel emptiness and despair in the absence of what she'd experienced. But she rose to her feet with hope and determination. In her heart she knew that he *was* with her, as much as he possibly could be. She felt the fire in her heart. And she knew that one day they would be together again. But not until she carried out her mission in this world, to raise his child with the legacy of love that he had given to her. And she *would!*

Kathe Lokberg's absence went generally unnoticed, even by many who knew her well, until their mourning had subsided enough for them to think clearly. By then she was nowhere to be found.

The people of Horstberg would likely never forget the explosion of 1849. It inevitably affected their lives. But much like other stories of interest in the history of their small country, it was put to the back of their minds. And life continued. Time naturally made the loss feel less significant, and what had once seemed unbearable to face was eventually taken for granted.

Kathe Lokberg's own death some eighteen years later left her daughter with no choice but to return to Horstberg, with little more than her mother's dying promise that it was beautiful enough to be heaven on earth. And much like Kathe's departure, Ericha's return went generally unnoticed.

Chapter One

RETURN TO HORSTBERG

Bavaria—1867

A misty rain shrouded the valley of Horstberg when Ericha first saw it. Wiping her hand over the steamy train window, she peered through the haze, willing her heart to stay calm. It was difficult to see the mountains surrounding her, but she knew from her mother's stories that they were there, standing like ominous protectors of the fair valley below.

Ericha caught her breath and held it when the high turrets of Castle Horstberg appeared, surrounded by floating wisps of low clouds that seemed to hold the castle suspended from the rest of the world like a fairy-tale edifice resting in the sky. Though Ericha had never seen it before, the sight felt somehow familiar. She credited her mother's vivid descriptions for making her feel as though she was returning home.

The sadness Ericha felt over her mother's recent death became buffered by expectation as the train came to a grinding halt. The conductor called in a voice resembling the train whistle that they had arrived in Horstberg.

Rising from her seat, Ericha adjusted her hat, hoping that she looked presentable after the journey. In one hand she clutched her valise. In the other she carried a letter that had come in response to the notification she'd sent her uncle that his sister had passed away. With courage, she moved deftly toward the end of the car, wondering what she would do if no one had come to meet her.

Stepping from the train, Ericha glanced around expectantly. She had barely absorbed her surroundings when a young man approached. Apparently in his mid-twenties, he was slender and tall, with dark hair and smiling eyes.

"Ericha," he stated with confidence, rocking on his heels as he stood before her.

"Yes," she said hesitantly, "how did you know?"

He smiled carelessly. "You're the only one who got off the train that looked like you didn't know what to do." He chuckled. "Also, my father told me you would have red hair."

"And you are?" she asked.

"Karl." He held out his hand, and Ericha set down her bag to take it.

"Just Karl?"

"Lokberg of course." He smiled, and she decided then that she liked him. "I'm your cousin."

"I'm pleased to meet you," she said while he squeezed her hand, then surprised her with a warm embrace. Their eyes met and Ericha smiled at him as he pulled away.

"Let's get your baggage and start home before it rains again." Karl picked up her valise, and they walked alongside the parked train.

"I don't have any more baggage."

"This is it?" His tone was skeptical.

"I brought everything I had that was worth keeping," she replied apologetically.

"Well, then." He glanced toward the bag in his hand, dubious that something weighing so little could carry a young lady's entire belongings. "I suppose we can go."

"No, we can't," Ericha protested, and Karl looked baffled. "I don't have any more baggage, but there is something I need to get. Wait here." She glanced toward the baggage car. "I won't be long."

Karl smiled and motioned her away with his arm. She returned a few minutes later with a large, well-groomed dog on a leash. Karl's eyes widened. "Is it a dog or a bear?" He chuckled.

Ericha became alarmed. "Is it all right?" she asked. "I mean . . . I don't want to cause any inconvenience. It's just that he's been with me a long time. He's very well behaved. I couldn't just leave him, and—"

"I'm certain we'll manage fine," Karl said with another chuckle. But he seemed hesitant to get too close to the dog as they walked away from the train.

It began to rain slightly as Karl helped Ericha into a trap, and the dog settled around her feet. Seating himself next to her, Karl took the reins and they moved forward.

"What's his name?" Karl asked, glancing dubiously at Ericha's furry companion.

"Job," she stated. Karl's brow went up, and she clarified, "Like Job in the Bible. He started out as a stray. But he proved himself very faithful, in spite of many struggles."

Karl nodded his understanding and turned the trap toward town. Ericha absorbed the scenery as they went at a slow pace, noting the narrow cobbled streets edged by high store fronts on each side. Doorways opened onto the road with signs hanging out above them. Again her mother's descriptions came back to her, and she felt as if she'd been here before.

Wanting to be certain where she stood with Karl, Ericha felt it necessary to say, "If you prefer that Job not stay in the house, I'm certain we can adjust. He's clean and well trained, but it's your home and I don't want to—"

"I'm sure it will be fine." Karl's good-natured smile put her at ease.

"How far is it?" she asked to make conversation. No sooner than she asked, Karl turned the trap down a drive next to a white stone house, much more substantial than what Ericha was accustomed to. It was surrounded by a stone fence with an arched gate in the front that was covered by vines. The entire structure seemed mostly overgrown with foliage of one sort or another.

Karl drove the trap into a stable, dismounted, and helped Ericha down.

"We're home," he said proudly. "I do hope you like it."

"It seems very nice." She waited a couple of minutes while he unharnessed the horse and put it into a stall. She then followed him out of the stable and through the rain, along a narrow stone path nearly overgrown by the enchanting garden through which it wound. There were flowering bushes of every kind that seemed overpowering. But they helped Ericha feel at home already, and she wondered if it would be all right for her to groom this garden.

Karl opened a side door, and she entered the house. "I'll show you your room," he said, starting down the hall. "I'm certain you're tired. That's the kitchen." He pointed idly to his left, not allowing time for a peek. They continued down a long hall, and he added, "There's the dining room. Over there is the parlor. And that," he pointed to French doors near the foot of the stairs, "is the library."

Karl walked briskly up the stairs, and Ericha followed as they curved gracefully onto a landing where a window looked to the street below.

"I thought you could use your mother's room," he said, his boots echoing against the polished wood floors. "Nothing's been done with it since she left here; at least that's what my father told me."

"Where is your father? Theodor, isn't it?"

"Yes." He glanced over his shoulder and smiled. "Your Uncle Theodor doesn't live here."

Ericha looked surprised.

"He lives at Castle Horstberg."

"Really?" she said, fascinated.

"It's not that exciting." Karl gave a wry smile as he paused in front of a door. "Actually, he's the duke's valet. He rather enjoys it. You'll meet him soon enough and he can tell you all about it. I'm sure he will. He often comes for Sunday dinner, and his favorite subject is his work."

A smile passed between them as Ericha caught Karl's impish undertone. Again she thought that she liked him.

Karl opened the door and motioned for Ericha to enter. Job settled immediately on the rug at the foot of the bed, as if he had no trouble feeling at home. Ericha felt a subtle permeation of the past as she quickly surveyed the room, while Karl waited expectantly for her reaction.

The first thing she noticed was the window. Built into the corner of the room, it overlooked the street, and she could almost see into town from here. The room seemed dusty, but it was much bigger than what she'd been accustomed to. Decorated attractively in warm hues of green and cream, it actually reminded Ericha of her mother. She immediately liked the mood.

"It's beautiful," she said.

"It could use a little work," he apologized. "I tried to get Miss Busch to clean it up some, but she can be a procrastinator, and—"

"Who?" Ericha asked.

"Miss Busch. She's the maid." He smirked. "At least that's what she's supposed to be. She's more like a . . . well . . ." He laughed. "I'll let you find out for yourself. You've got to know her to believe she's real."

Ericha wondered what he meant, but she felt certain she would find out soon enough.

"Does anyone else live here?" She sat on the high, curtained bed to test it.

"Just me," he said. "But I am engaged to be married."

"Really?" She smiled at him.

"A man my age should have a wife. Don't you think?"

"You don't look so old." She laughed, but Karl tipped his head to the side as his thoughts obviously changed.

"You don't look like a Lokberg," he stated.

Ericha glanced down briefly, and then she looked up at him and drew back her shoulders. "I should not have been a Lokberg," she said, revealing a hint of defensiveness.

Karl's eyes narrowed, but his voice was kind. "There's no need to apologize for—"

"I was not apologizing," she said straightly. "It was not my fault that my mother never married."

"It makes no difference to me," he said with an easy smile.

"Good." Ericha stood and took her valise from him to put it on the bed. "Because it makes no difference to me."

Karl laughed, and without knowing why, Ericha laughed with him. He didn't seem to want to leave, so she began unpacking.

Karl watched with interest at what she might bring forth from the little bag. "That's really all you brought," he said as if reassuring himself.

"I brought Job," she replied.

He chuckled and watched as she pulled out two dresses of calico that were rather plain, in his opinion. There was one night-gown, and a wad of white that she discreetly set aside, which he assumed to be underclothing. Other than a hairbrush, and what appeared to be some sewing things, that was the entire contents of her valise—except for a little wooden box.

"What's that?" he asked, noting the way she eyed it wistfully while opting to set it in the center of the bureau.

"I'm not certain, really," she said, perhaps sadly. "My mother gave it to me before she died."

"May I?" he asked, motioning toward it.

"Of course," she replied, and he picked it up, turning it over in his hands.

"I was sorry to hear about your mother," Karl said with compassion while his fingers explored the fine carvings of the little box. "My memories of her are vague, though my father and grandfather spoke of her a great deal."

"She was a great lady," Ericha stated with conviction.

Karl turned to watch Ericha, absorbing the strength of her aura and the vibrancy of her eyes that seemed to defy her petite frame. "I dare say she was an excellent example."

Ericha glanced away, not knowing how to take the comment. She turned toward the mirror while removing her hat pin.

Karl watched with interest as she set the well-worn hat on the bureau. With little effort she pulled only a few pins from her hair to let a loosely woven red braid fall gracefully down her back. There was something intriguing about this cousin of his. Despite what little Karl knew of her, he admired her instinctively and was glad to have her here.

Ericha turned toward Karl, not feeling uncomfortable with the silence. She watched as his attention turned back to the little box in his hands. He squinted to scrutinize the bottom of it and smiled.

"What?" she asked curiously.

"Come with me." He took her hand easily.

Job followed at Ericha's heels as Karl led her down the stairs and toward the back of the house. Ericha wondered if it was the binding of their blood that made her feel so at ease with him; it was as if they'd been friends forever. And he seemed to feel the same way.

Karl led her out a different door and through a corner of the garden to a structure built of the same stone as the house. He opened the door and entered with Ericha and Job close behind.

Ericha realized immediately it was some kind of workshop with tools of many kinds, a long work bench, and pieces of wood in all stages of creation. The completed projects lined against one wall varied from a baby cradle to a chair to carvings that could only be called works of art. But her eye caught an assortment of carved boxes.

"This is where I work," Karl announced. "Of course, you haven't been here long, but if you had, you would know that Karl Lokberg is known for his craftsmanship." He smiled sheepishly as he sat on a stool that was obviously accustomed to him.

"I am impressed." Ericha glanced around before turning her attention back to the familiar-looking boxes.

"This box," he said as if reading her mind, "is marked here." She moved closer to see where he pointed in the center of the bottom.

"K.L.," she read. "I always thought they were my mother's initials."

"They are, but that particular K.L. is for Karl Lokberg. Not me. My grand . . . No, *our* grandfather. He made that box—just like he taught me to do this." He elaborately held up his arms to indicate the contents of the room.

Ericha gave a soft laugh as she rubbed her arms and absorbed her surroundings again. She could almost imagine her grandfather here as she thought of the stories her mother had told her about him. She felt as if she'd come home.

"I remember my grandfather," Ericha said. "He came to visit us a few times. I often wished that we might have had the opportunity to be closer." She glanced around again, then looked at Karl. "How long has it been since he passed on?"

"Nearly three years now." He gave a sad little smile.

"You miss him still."

"Yes," Karl admitted. "He practically raised me, you know. My mother died giving birth to me, and my father's work always kept him busy."

While Ericha tried to recall what her mother had told her about Karl, he changed the subject. "What's in it?" he asked, examining the box again.

"I don't know," she stated, and he looked surprised.

"Well, where's the key?"

"There isn't one. At least not that I know of. My mother said that it was my heritage, but she told me to never open . . . no," Ericha corrected, "she said she felt it might be better left locked."

"Really?" Karl grinned. "How very exciting!"

"I suppose," Ericha said, not sharing his enthusiasm.

"Do you like to ride?" he asked.

She smiled. "I do, though I've had little opportunity to do it. We didn't have a horse of our own."

He looked surprised, and then his expression quickly changed. Ericha caught something perhaps mischievous in his eyes. Looking around again, she noted a guitar leaning against the wall near a chair.

"Do you play?" she asked, nodding toward it.

"I try." Karl laughed. "A friend taught me, mostly because he doesn't like to play alone. I enjoy it now and then."

"I would like to hear you some time," she said earnestly.

"Some day when you are very bored." He grinned.

A clock on the wall startled Ericha when it chimed. Karl nearly jumped from his seat and shoved the box into her hands.

"Good heavens. I'm supposed to be at the pub."

"What for?" Ericha followed him out to the garden, amused by his apparent urgency.

"I'm to see a friend there." He moved quickly toward the stable. "We've been meeting every day since we were old enough. And I mustn't miss him today. I've just realized there's something very important I have to ask him."

"What?" She followed him into the stable to watch while he saddled a horse with near frenzy.

"That's a secret," he said, and again she noted mischief in his eyes. "Make yourself at home." Karl grinned as he mounted. "I won't be terribly long."

Ericha smiled and waved as he rode out, and then she went slowly back to her room with Job close behind, taking time to absorb her surroundings. She liked the house. It had a mood that was endearing. Compared to the cottage she had just left, it was large and elaborate. Though it was still smaller than many homes she had seen while accompanying her mother who had mostly made her living as a seamstress.

Ericha couldn't suppress the ache that came with thoughts of her mother. She missed her. And in a way, she missed the three-room cottage where they had spent their secluded life. But she had no real bonds there, so it had not been difficult to leave. Beyond her mother's absence, she felt this was very much home to her already.

Lying back on the bed, Ericha pondered over what her mother's life might have been like before she left here. This room had been hers. It seemed strange to try and imagine such things. Though Kathe had told her much about Horstberg, she had been vague about her personal life. Ericha knew little about her mother in that respect.

Recalling that Karl had said this room had been left as it was, Ericha jumped from the bed and opened the closet. She caught her breath to see dresses and a long, gray cloak hanging there. She pulled them out one at a time to admire. Though they were a bit old fashioned, Ericha liked them and decided they would do nicely. They were perhaps slightly long, but she had worn her mother's clothes before with little alteration, and was certain she could make them work. It gave her a great deal of excitement, and perhaps comfort, to have these tangible remnants of her mother. Everything else had been sold to settle her mother's debts and make the journey to Horstberg.

Ericha found the drawers of the bureau empty. She put her things into them and dusted the room. Deciding that fresh flowers would help a great deal, she started for the door but paused at the corner window of her room, noticing that the mist was clearing. In the distance she could see Castle Horstberg at the opposite end of the valley, sitting majestically against the mountainside. She wondered for a moment if someone really lived there, and then recalled that Karl had said her own uncle did—a servant to the duke. She knew from what her mother had told her that the Duke of Horstberg was much like a king in this small country. She wondered if she would ever have a chance to see him. Most likely not.

Admiring the beauty of the castle, Ericha nearly felt chills rush through her from the sight of it. Moving on to the garden, she found it incredible to think that people really lived in such places.

Karl hurried through the door with the swinging sign above it: *The Red Lion.*

"You're late." Stefan's deep voice was stern as Karl sat at a corner table where a tankard of beer waited for him.

Karl grinned at his friend. "It'll keep you humble. Besides, I have a good excuse. I met my cousin at the station."

"I didn't know you had a cousin." Stefan took a long swallow of his drink. "In fact, I didn't know you had any relatives at all."

He chuckled. "Except your father, of course. And he's always so occupied attending to that ogre who rules this dreadful place."

"He is indeed." Karl laughed in return. "Now you know. I have a cousin. And she's very charming."

"Hmm." Stefan made a disinterested sound.

"By the by, my friend," Karl said, "have you any horses you'd be willing to sell right now? A good high-spirited one—from the famous line, perhaps," he finished with a sing-song lilt in his voice.

"You're asking a lot," Stefan said. "I have one. But I'm not certain you can afford it." There was humor in Stefan's eyes, though Karl was one of the few people who knew him well enough to catch it.

"I'll pay anything," Karl said adamantly.

Stefan lifted his brows at the seriousness of Karl's tone. "Just what are you going to do with this high-spirited horse?"

"A gift. Ericha's never had a horse."

"Who?"

"My cousin."

Stefan paused thoughtfully. Knowing the animal would remain in Karl's family made a difference.

"Well," he said at last, "if you want a horse, let's go see what we've got."

"I haven't finished my drink yet."

"Hurry it up," he said in good humor. "I've got things to do before I go."

"Go?" Karl asked between gulps.

"I thought I'd spend a few days at . . ." He glanced around, then added more quietly, "I just need some time away."

Karl watched Stefan carefully, sensing something deep in the statement. "You've been spending a lot of time away lately."

Stefan's eyes lost all enjoyment. "Yes, well," he replied, "there's little to stay around for these days."

Karl lightened the mood by acting insulted. "I'll remember that next time you want me to buy you a drink."

"Don't take it personally." Stefan chuckled. "But life can hardly be sustained by a daily meeting at the pub."

Karl sobered as he asked, "Is it really so bad?"

He wished he hadn't when Stefan's eyes bored into him with a familiar burning intensity. "Yes," he replied, "it really is."

Silence reigned until Stefan broke it with a phony laugh. "Are you finished yet?"

"Yes, Stefan," Karl said. "I'm finished."

"Then let's go look at a horse."

"I want it today. Can I have it today?"

"Maybe." Stefan gave a subtle smile. "It's your turn to buy."

Karl paid for the drinks, and together they left for Stefan's stables.

The clouds were low and heavy as Ericha picked a satisfactory bouquet of flowers. She felt a strong urge to care for this garden, and paused to imagine its potential. Sitting for a few minutes on a little bench, she recalled her mother talking of the hours she'd spent here. The roses had been Kathe's favorite, and she felt close to her mother in spirit as she tried to imagine her in this very garden as a young woman.

Going inside, Ericha wondered where she might find a vase, and she set the flowers on the kitchen counter to go and look. She opened a closet in the hall near the kitchen, only to have a pile of linens fall out on the floor.

Ericha sighed and stooped to pick them up, but she had no idea where to put them. The closet was a disaster. She stuffed them back and closed the door quickly, and then she moved on to another cupboard and held her breath as she opened it. Ericha laughed to see an assortment of vases along with a number of distasteful looking objects that she assumed were meant to be centerpieces.

Choosing an appropriate vase, Ericha took it back to the kitchen. She entered just in time to see an almost plump woman, with scraggly blonde hair pulled back in a ribbon, throwing the flowers into a sack that was obviously intended for trash.

"What are you doing?" Ericha demanded.

The woman turned in apparent surprise. "Who are you to be askin' me what I'm doin'?" Her voice seemed deep for a woman.

"I'm Ericha Lokberg. And I don't care who you are, you're not going to throw away my flowers."

"Well," she huffed, eying Ericha speculatively, "I don't want those noxious . . . *weeds* in here. They make me sneeze."

"I will take them to my room, and you won't know the difference," Ericha retorted.

"Your room won't get cleaned if they're goin' to be in there." She wrinkled her nose as Ericha retrieved her bouquet and made an effort to recover it.

"I'll keep that in mind, Miss Busch," Ericha stated with confidence. She not only knew who this was, but she could also see what Karl had meant when describing her. If she was the maid, the term was used lightly. Her housekeeping abilities were obviously poor, and her attitude was dubious. But Ericha didn't care. Accustomed to taking care of herself, she wasn't going to let Miss Busch interfere with her life one way or the other.

Ericha nearly laughed out loud when the maid's eyes were drawn to the dog sitting at Ericha's feet.

"What is *that?*" she gasped.

"His name is Job," Ericha said. "I can assure you he's harmless, and he'll cause you no extra work."

Miss Busch gave an indiscernible noise as Ericha left the room and Job followed. She wondered why on earth Karl would keep someone like her. Perhaps she was all he could afford.

Ericha arranged the bouquet and glanced at her new bedroom, feeling satisfied and content. She was speculating again over her mother's past when a door slammed somewhere below.

"Ericha!" Karl called as footsteps bounded up the stairs.

"What is it?" she asked, coming into the hallway to meet him.

"I have something to show you." He took her hand and led her to the stable, rambling something about what every young lady needed.

"Ta-dah!" he said, throwing the stable door open.

"What?" she asked, seeing nothing but horses.

"Don't you like him?" he asked, seeming deflated.

"What?" She laughed.

Karl stepped toward a fiery stallion, patted his neck carefully, and said, "This is Pegasus. He comes from a long line of great horses—cared for by a long line of people who know how to raise them."

"He's very nice," she stated.

"He's for you," Karl said, feeling gratified when her eyes widened incredibly.

"Karl," she gasped, "how can I . . . I . . ."

"Listen, Ericha." He came close to her. "I know what kind of life you've lived. And I know why." She drew back her shoulders, but he touched her chin, and her expression softened. "We are family. You and I belong together. Can't you tell?" He grinned, then quickly became serious again. "And I want to do what I can to make up for what you haven't had."

"But Karl . . . I don't need anything. I feel grateful just to have a roof over my head and food to eat. You don't need to—"

"Hogwash!" He laughed. "Didn't I tell you? Karl Lokberg is the finest craftsman in Horstberg. He can afford to buy you a horse. And you'd best love it or I'll be insulted." He grinned sheepishly. "And so will the man I bought it from."

"Just today?" she asked, feeling awkward about taking such a gift.

"Yes," he replied, "and I caught him just in time. He's leaving town for a few days."

Ericha looked the horse over, and he saw her eyes sparkle unwillingly. "You do like him," he stated.

"I do," she said, "but I—"

"No buts," he interrupted firmly.

"Thank you." Ericha smiled at last and took his hand, not wanting to be ungracious.

"You're very welcome," he said. "Now let's see if you can ride him."

"Right now?" she asked.

"Of course." Karl began to saddle the stallion. "I've got a project to finish up, but if you don't mind going alone, then . . ."

"I don't mind." She smiled.

"I dare say you're used to being independent."

Ericha nodded slightly in agreement. "What did you say his name was?" she asked, nuzzling against the horse.

"Pegasus," Karl said. "His name likely fits. He's well trained. But he'll fly like the wind if you let him."

Ericha laughed, feeling more happiness than she knew what to do with. "Thank you, Karl."

"For what?" he asked, tightening the strap beneath the horse's belly.

"Everything. I had no idea what to expect in coming here," she admitted, "and I was a bit wary. But here in one day you've made me feel so at home. And this." She laughed. "I can't believe it. Thank you."

"It's my pleasure." He gave a gratified chuckle. "Actually," he added, "my motives are purely selfish. It can get lonely around here. It will be nice to have some company."

"I thought you said you were engaged."

"I am." Karl grinned proudly. "But she works at an inn, and her father is in poor health. We won't be able to marry as long as he needs her. I don't see her as much as I'd like to."

Ericha asked in a teasing tone, "What about Miss Busch?"

Karl laughed. "So you've met her."

"I have indeed."

"She is entertaining," he smirked, "but that's about it."

"Is that why you hired her?"

"I hired her because I hate to cook. And that's one thing she *can* do. I keep her around because she keeps me humble," he admitted with a smile that Ericha was realizing came often. "Actually," he added more seriously, "I know where her loyalties are, and she doesn't gossip. Her discretion is worth more to me than her housekeeping abilities."

Ericha felt tempted to question him on that, but he quickly added, "There you go." He held out his hand to help her mount.

"Hey," he said when she was seated, "that horse has the same color of hair that you do." He glanced toward the red braid that hung down Ericha's back. "The color of fire." He raised his brows, and she smiled. "Now you be careful."

Karl moved aside, and the late afternoon sun burst through the clouds as Pegasus heeded his new mistress's heel, trotting into the open air. Karl waved and watched them move down the long drive, onto the street.

It took only a few minutes for Ericha to feel confident on Pegasus. Despite her minimal training, she felt a natural rapport with the horse, and she immediately enjoyed the freedom and enjoyment he offered. Though she didn't stray far from home, Ericha enjoyed the prospect of exploring Horstberg.

The following day, she asked Karl if he would teach her how to saddle the horse. He gladly complied.

"How are you liking this place so far?" he asked.

"Fine," she said.

"Do you have what you need?"

"Oh, yes."

"If you need anything—anything at all," he said, "you'll have to speak up. Understood?"

"Yes," she answered gratefully.

Karl smiled at her as she mounted, and Ericha felt grateful for his friendship.

"I'll see you at dinner," he called after her. She waved and was quickly out of sight.

Today Ericha ventured farther from home. With the freedom that Pegasus offered, she felt a desire to see all of the places her mother had spoken of. Observing the mountains around her, Ericha recalled vividly the description of the mountain meadow where her mother and father had often met to be alone. Gazing in the direction she knew it must be, Ericha almost headed there. But it began to rain, and she turned hesitantly toward home, thinking perhaps it was best to become more familiar with her surroundings before venturing so far.

Her second night in Horstberg, Ericha awoke to thunder.

The rain came down hard and strong, while the sky lit up in white flashes, and thunder crashed far too closely. It was the first severe storm since her mother's death, and Ericha felt the loneliness keenly. She hugged her pillow tightly and cried, allowing the memories to absorb her. She could almost feel her mother's presence as the storm persisted. Kathe Lokberg hated thunderstorms, and Ericha had naturally followed her example. How she longed for the comfort she and Kathe had given each other as they had endured their mutual fear!

Ericha wondered, as she often did, what had made Kathe so afraid. It seemed to go against her mother's character. Longing for Kathe only seemed to intensify Ericha's fear, and she was relieved when the rumbling finally dissipated in the distance. Gradually it was replaced by a peaceful sprinkling of rain that sang her back to sleep.

It didn't take long for Ericha to settle into her new lifestyle. She took the opportunity to ride Pegasus often and relished finding the many places her mother had told her about, feeling a new kinship with Kathe as she did.

Four days after her arrival, the rain was still persisting much of the time, and Ericha began to wonder if she would ever see Horstberg with fair weather. But she donned the hooded cloak that had been her mother's and felt quite impatient while Karl saddled the stallion. She had made up her mind that today she would find that meadow where her mother—and the father she had never known—had gone together to be alone.

"I had you teach me how to do it," she said, "so that you wouldn't have to."

"I like to," Karl said, and Ericha smiled. "You be careful now," he admonished, helping her into the saddle.

She smiled again at him and rode out, immediately exhilarated by the brisk air and the smell of rain that struck her senses. With her mother's cloak around her shoulders, Ericha could almost imagine herself being the woman who had been here many years earlier, riding up the mountain to meet the man she loved. She wondered, as she often did, what her father was like. And what had happened to him. It was something Kathe Lokberg simply never talked about.

Ericha felt certain that she was much like her father—mostly because she was so unlike her mother. As her speculations gained momentum, her desire to find this place become more vivid, as if going there might answer some of the questions that had always existed deep within her.

Pegasus was indeed high-spirited, but Ericha liked the way he almost went by his own will. She relished the wind in her face as they moved together across lush, green countryside and through a covered bridge toward the steeply rising mountain.

Following the memory of her mother's vivid instructions, she went past a covered bridge and through a clearing where a tree had fallen. Then with little trouble she discovered the forest trail that barely existed between the closely rooted pines. Pegasus galloped up through the trees at a dangerous pace, while Ericha felt a growing anticipation to see what she knew lay at the other end. The trail was narrow and dark, but Ericha bent low and wrapped her arms around the stallion's neck, caught up with the idea that the past was pulling at her, taking her somehow to the beginning of her own life.

Ericha had no warning that a rider was approaching from the other direction at an equally vigorous speed. She hardly realized what was happening before Pegasus reared back to avoid colliding with the other horse. Ericha landed flat on her back in the trail. A ringing sounded through her ears, and she squeezed her eyes shut in an effort to avoid the stars swimming above her. The fall forced the air from her lungs, and she gasped painfully, fighting to catch her breath.

"Good heavens!" a deep voice said somewhere at the edge of her coherency. "Are you all right?"

Ericha felt herself being pulled to a sitting position, but her eyes remained closed as she concentrated on regaining her breath.

Stefan didn't have any idea why this girl was here, but he felt frustrated by his inability to help her recover. Silently he held her shoulders until her breathing regained some normality.

Ericha's hand went over her eyes as she felt herself coming back to life. She moaned from the pain permeating against the back of her head.

"Are you going to be all right?" that voice repeated.

"Eventually," she replied and pushed the hood of her cloak back, tilting her head skyward to breathe easier.

Though he tried, Stefan couldn't deny that he was intrigued by the fair skin that appeared when the shadow of her cloak fell away. A long red braid came naturally over her shoulder as she bent forward to take a deep breath, moving her hand away from her eyes.

"I think I can breathe now," she said, though still slightly unsteady. Then she looked up to see the man who had unwittingly caused this calamity.

Something intangibly haunting struck Stefan when the bold, green eyes caught him. He felt briefly frozen, searching for the reason behind what he was feeling. Trying to hide his interest, he abruptly let go of her shoulders and stood.

"Are you all right?" Ericha came slowly to her feet, aware of this man's distressed expression.

"Of course I'm all right," he said sharply, "but you're lucky you didn't get yourself killed. What are you doing riding up here anyway—and at such speed?"

"I wasn't going any faster than you were," she replied in her defense.

"Well, at least I stayed in my saddle," he argued.

"I would have far preferred to," she retorted, scrutinizing him briefly as she wondered why he was so angry with her.

"Next time I suggest you go slower, hold on tighter—and ride elsewhere."

"I will ride how and where I please, sir."

"And you might find yourself in trouble, young lady."

"This is not private ground," she argued. "I was—"

"This trail," he interrupted, "leads to private ground—and nothing else. You'd do best to ride elsewhere."

Ericha couldn't think of a reply to that one. She found herself facing him silently for a long moment, as he apparently had nothing else to say either. Despite the shadows of the hovering trees, she could see that his hair was thick and dark, combed off his face and hanging in loose waves, well over his collar. He was not quite as tall as Karl, and his build was lean. But there was something about his stature that she found intimidating. His features were firm and chiseled, and she noted something burning and fearless about his eyes, contrasting with an aura that was almost sadly timid.

"Why are you looking at me that way?" she asked curtly when the unblinking intensity of his eyes unnerved her.

"If you've recovered sufficiently," he said without even a trace of concern, "you'd best turn yourself around so that I can be on my way."

"Fine!" she retorted, fighting to keep her equilibrium as she caught Pegasus's reins and turned him homeward on the narrow trail.

Setting her foot in the stirrup, Ericha felt unsteady as the pounding in her head increased. She glanced warily toward this man, wondering if she should hate him or like him. She leaned toward hating him until he stepped forward and nearly lifted her into the saddle.

"Hold on tight now," he said blandly. Their eyes met briefly, and then Ericha started down the trail, aware that he was following close behind.

When she finally emerged from the forest and paused, he came beside her and asked, "Will you make it home all right?"

"Yes," she said, "I'm fine."

Those fearless eyes caught her again, and Ericha felt both unsettled and intrigued. He nodded very slightly and galloped away, leaving Ericha baffled by the experience altogether.

She was grateful to arrive home, but she wished that Karl was there when she attempted to dismount and nearly fell. Steadying herself, Ericha wondered if her weakness was a result of her fall—or of her meeting in the forest.

Ericha went to bed despite it being the middle of the afternoon. But she found herself restless. For reasons she couldn't decipher, she was unable to stop thinking about her bizarre encounter in the forest. Those fearless eyes haunted her. She felt changed somehow and wondered if she would ever see him again.

Stefan entered the dining room late, and Johanna looked up, briefly startled by his entrance. Their eyes met and she smiled, but Stefan remained expressionless.

"Hello, my dear," she said warmly. "I didn't know you were back."

"I'm back," he said blandly. Seating himself, he glanced around the room. "Where is everyone?"

"I suppose they've all taken to eating in their rooms," Johanna said. Stefan wished he had thought of that. "Your grandmother's not feeling well and—"

"What's the matter?" He looked up sharply from his meal.

"It's nothing serious. Just a little under the weather, I believe. You should go and see her. She's always positively overjoyed by your presence." Her sarcasm was subtle but true. Stefan passed her a brief look that she could only interpret as disgust, and then he turned his full attention to his meal.

"I've missed you," Johanna said when the maid brought in dessert. "Why must you insist on hiding away in that dreadful lodge with your paperwork when it would be just as easy, if not more so, to do it here?"

"I've told you before," his voice was monotone. "I can concentrate better there."

"Well, I'm glad you're back." She smiled expectantly toward him, but he answered with a sober glare that seemed to momentarily disturb her.

Johanna's distress quickly faded as she lifted her chin saucily and the lamplight caught her flaxen hair. Stefan noticed the brilliant emeralds hanging from her ears and knew well what kind of mood she was in, which made her attention all the more distasteful.

"Is something disturbing you?" she asked.

"What difference does it make to you?" he retorted. His eyes briefly penetrated her.

"I was merely inquiring," she stated defensively.

"Nothing is disturbing me, Johanna," he said with no inflection in his voice. "Please don't concern yourself."

"You are my husband," she said as if to convince him. "Should I not concern myself?"

"Perhaps you should." He stood and threw his napkin to the table. "But I won't lose any sleep over whether or not you do."

"Where are you going?" she asked tensely. "You hardly touched your dinner."

"I don't seem to have much of an appetite." He walked briskly toward the door. "I'm going to bed."

"Wait," she said. He stopped but didn't turn. "You've been gone for days. I had hoped that . . . well, you've not come to my room for so long and . . ."

Stefan turned to look at his wife with a dubious glare. He wondered over her motives until he realized a maid was hovering in the doorway. He focused his glare on the maid, and she scurried away.

"Do you prefer to spend your nights alone?" Johanna asked, and her lip quivered.

"Either way," he said blandly, "it's still a cold bed."

"Stefan!" She stood abruptly, and tears came to her eyes. She looked pointedly downward and apparently made an effort to blink them back, then lifted her chin proudly to face him.

"What?" he asked with no expression.

"How can you say that? How could we have known there would be no children? You can't blame that on me, Stefan. I . . ." She broke off with a gentle sob.

"Good-night, my dear." Stefan quietly left the room and

forced the episode out of his mind. He walked briskly up the stairs and down a long hall. Rapping lightly on his grandmother's bedroom door, he couldn't help but smile when she called for him to enter.

"Stefan!" She held out her arms, and he moved to the side of the bed to embrace her. "Oh, I've missed you," she said. "Are you well?"

"I'm fine, but I hear you're not feeling so good."

"I've never felt better," Abbi du Woernig replied. "I just didn't feel like eating downstairs, that's all."

"Are you certain?" he asked shrewdly.

"Yes, of course." She moved out of the bed and pulled a wrapper around her. "Is it still raining?"

"A little here and there, I think." He sat down and crossed his ankles, relaxing his head against the back of the chair.

"You know," Abbi said, standing near the window with her back to him, "I was thinking today about your parents—more so than usual. Aren't they due back soon?"

"I think so. Next month some time is what I gather from the last letter."

"It will be good to see them again."

"Yes, it will."

"And how is the lodge these days?"

"Still the same."

"Tell me . . ." She laughed softly. "Have you gotten to the bottom of your grandfather's woodpile yet?"

Stefan chuckled. "Not yet, but it's getting close."

A long moment of silence followed. "Is something wrong?" she asked, turning toward him with those discerning green eyes.

"No, why?"

"You seem . . . sad for some reason."

"I'm fine." He forced a chuckle, but he knew she didn't believe him. Yet he didn't know himself why he felt the way he did. It would be impossible to try explaining it to her.

"If there's something you'd like to talk about," Abbi offered softly, seating herself in front of the mirror.

"Really, I'm fine; perhaps tired."

"You look tired." She glanced toward him, then pulled the pins from her hair. He enjoyed watching as it fell around her shoulders and she brushed it through. He marveled at its thickness, and despite touches of gray, the deep red was still vibrant. For a woman approaching seventy, she looked remarkable.

"Have I ever told you that you're beautiful?" he said, coming behind her and meeting her eyes in the mirror.

"Too much." She laughed. "Now run along to bed, Stefan. It's getting late and I know you have a busy day tomorrow."

"How did you know that?"

"You always have a busy day."

"Yes," he said, "I suppose I do."

"Have you seen Georg since you returned?" she asked.

"No."

"He needs to talk to you, I believe."

"I'll see him early," he promised, bending to kiss her cheek. "Good-night, Grandmama," he said gently. "Sleep well."

"And you." She smiled. "I'll see you at breakfast."

He nodded and left the room quietly.

Stefan opened all the windows in his bedroom, but the heavy air left him feeling sultry as he climbed between the sheets and sprawled himself in the center of the huge bed. He was only there a minute before the dogs jumped up and settled themselves near his feet.

Physically, Stefan felt exhausted. It seemed that more and more all he ever did was work himself to the limit, and he knew it was catching up with him. But despite the tired ache, his mind kept him awake far into the night. Staring into the darkness above him, Stefan wondered why he suddenly felt more discontent and unhappy than he ever had in his life.

Chapter Two
STOLEN MOMENTS

Ericha was grateful that Karl had gone out for the evening. She had no desire to get out of bed and felt little appetite. Knowing Karl's perception and the kindness he'd shown her, she was sure he would have taken notice of her unusual behavior.

Ericha finally fell asleep, but she awoke somewhere in the night feeling more drained than when she'd gone to bed. Lying in the darkness, her mind relived the dream she'd emerged from. In it she saw a man with no face, and his form was elusive. His only recognizable feature was his hair, deep red and full of curls, much like her own. And there was a woman, with dark, straight hair, riding with purpose up through the forest to meet this man. Then the image of Kathe Lokberg turned into Ericha. And the face of the stranger in the forest merged into the formless blur of Ericha's father.

Ericha's dream left her feeling cold and alone, and she lay gazing upward while the room lightened with the day. She felt unsettled by the face in her dreams: vague and shadowed, just as it had been those brief moments in the forest.

Hoping to divert her thoughts, Ericha got out of bed, fighting to ignore the aching muscles that reminded her more vividly of yesterday's brief encounter. She dressed and went out to work in the garden, and was pleased to see the day coming forth with cloudless skies and a pleasurable warmth in the air.

The garden brought Ericha satisfaction as she observed the

changes she'd made in the few days she had been working in it. She was pleased by Karl's comment when he came out to greet her, glancing around with interest as he scratched Job behind his ears. "I didn't realize this place was so nice."

"I'm glad you don't mind my working here," she said, kneeling near a rosebush to remove the weeds from around it.

"Mind?" He laughed. "I think it's great. This poor place has been neglected as long as I can remember." Ericha smiled at him, and he added, "Breakfast's ready. Are you hungry?"

"I am." She stood and brushed her hands on her skirt.

"Is something wrong?" Karl asked suddenly.

"No." She moved toward the door, and he followed.

"Then why are you walking like a . . . well, why are you walking like that?"

"It's nothing serious," she said. "I just had a little fall yesterday . . . that's all."

"What kind of a little fall?" His eyes narrowed in concern.

"It's nothing to worry about." She laughed while he watched her wash her hands. "Pegasus got spooked, and I wasn't holding on tightly enough."

"Are you going to be all right?"

"Of course. I'm just a little stiff. I'll be good as new in a day or two."

"Perhaps I should have the doctor come and—"

"Heavens, no!" she insisted, leading the way down the hall.

"Are you certain? Maybe you broke something or—"

"Karl," she turned with a laugh, "I'll be fine."

Karl grinned sheepishly and shrugged his shoulders. "I'm just making certain."

Ericha smiled in appreciation for his concern, and they moved into the dining room as Karl said, "By the by, after breakfast you are going into town."

"Whatever for?"

"To get yourself a few things." He glanced toward the old calico dress she was wearing as he pulled out a chair for her to be seated.

"I don't need anything," she stated strongly.

"Nonsense." He laughed. "I know for a fact that you have almost nothing. And a lady so pretty ought to dress like a lady."

Ericha glanced down at her dress and hardly knew what to say. She knew he was right, but she found it difficult to accept what he was offering.

"Don't you want some new things?" he asked when she made no response.

"Oh, that would be fine," she said, not wanting to be ungracious, "it's just that, well . . . I don't really need them. I've always had what I need and—"

"Nonsense," he said. "You're just used to being poor. You handle it very graciously, I must say, but—"

"What do you mean by that?" she interrupted.

"There's no need to be upset, little cousin." He smiled endearingly. "I know your mother was a proud woman. She rarely accepted any help we offered her. But I'm your guardian now, so to speak, and there is no reason why you should go without.

"Now as soon as you've eaten I want you to walk into town to a little shop on Herger Street called Frieda's. Tell her that I sent you and order whatever you need."

"But Karl, I—"

"No buts." He grinned. "Give me the pleasure of putting some of my money to good use."

Ericha managed a smile, not knowing what to say. But Miss Busch entered the room with their breakfast and Karl's attention was diverted.

"Ah," he said to her, "how nice it is to see your lovely, shining face this morning."

"As long as you're in a good mood," she said, setting the plates on the table, "let's talk about a raise in my wages."

"Miss Busch, you know I can't afford to—"

"If I'm workin' to feed and pick up after two," she insisted. "I think it's only fair that I get paid what it's worth."

"No," Karl said thoughtfully, looking toward the ceiling, "I think that now perhaps you will have the opportunity to earn the generous salary you've been getting for years."

Miss Busch only grunted in defeat and left the room. Karl laughed before proceeding with his meal, and Ericha hardly gave the encounter a second thought. She'd become quickly accustomed to their bantering and had realized that Miss Busch was not nearly so brash as she pretended to be.

"I wonder if you could tell me something," Ericha said, and Karl gave her his attention. "I would like to go to service on Sunday, and—"

"That's not a problem," he interrupted. "The main service is held at the cathedral, but there are smaller services held for those who don't want to travel so far. The closest church is within walking distance. We passed it on our way in from the station."

Ericha nodded, recalling the moderate steepled structure.

"I don't go often myself." He smiled wryly. "But I'd be happy to take you if—"

"I'm certain I can manage," she said, and hurried to finish her breakfast.

Ericha couldn't deny feeling excited as she set out on foot toward town, enjoying Horstberg with cloudless skies. The narrow cobbled streets were charming, and she loved looking into the store fronts as she walked slowly.

It was easy to find the little shop on Herger Street, and Ericha waited only a few moments while the woman called Frieda finished helping another customer.

"Can I help you, miss?" she asked.

"My name is Ericha Lokberg. I am Karl Lokberg's cousin and—"

"I've not seen you in here before," she said curiously.

"No. I just moved here, to stay with him and—"

"Oh, that's lovely." She smiled. "What can I get for you today?"

"Karl insisted that I come to get some new things and—"

"What a splendid idea." Frieda took Ericha's arm and led her to the back of the shop where more items were displayed. "That Karl is a sharp one, he is. Comes in often buying gifts for that Miss Hilgendorff. Now, what kind of things do you need?"

"Well, I—"

"Day wear? Night wear? A riding habit perhaps? Stockings? *Underclothing?*" she finished in a whisper.

"Actually," Ericha glanced around, feeling overwhelmed, "I suppose I need a little of everything. But I don't know where to begin. I've never been in a shop like this before and—"

"You haven't?"

"My mother was a seamstress," Ericha said quickly, with pride in her voice. "We rarely purchased anything that was—"

"Don't you worry about that. You just let Frieda take care of you." She stood back to scrutinize Ericha, absorbing Ericha's size and coloring as she added, "I know just what you need."

Frieda proceeded to show Ericha everything from the bare necessities to the finest gowns, with a great deal of pomp. But Ericha left the shop with her order consisting of cotton chemises that could double for nightgowns, cotton stockings of fine quality, and some petticoats and underthings. She ordered three simple dresses to be made of calico, and a wool cloak. Frieda seemed frustrated by Ericha's conservative nature; Ericha would not be persuaded into buying things that went beyond practicality.

The order was to be delivered upon completion, but Ericha opted to take with her a hat that caught her fancy. It was wide-brimmed straw hat with the crown cut out, and she thought it would do well for working in the garden.

Wearing the hat, Ericha emerged from the shop, exhilarated by the freshness of the day. She walked home in a roundabout way that took her through the center of town where all of the streets met in a large square filled with open markets. She remembered Karl telling her that today was market day, when the vendors came out to sell and trade their wares.

She was intrigued by the noise and bustle. But she found the solace of a nearby park more relaxing, and she stopped briefly to sit on a bench before returning home.

The spot came to be one she liked well, and as going into town on market day became a habit, so did sitting on the bench to rest each time before returning home.

Life in Horstberg was good for Ericha. Instinctively, she loved this fair valley, and she was grateful to be home.

On a warm Sunday, Ericha returned from church service to find dinner on the table and Karl already seated there with another man. It was the first time she and Karl hadn't dined alone. She was caught briefly off guard, as Karl had said nothing to warn her.

"Ah, here she is." Karl rose from his chair and took her hand. "Didn't I tell you she was beautiful?"

The other man stood to greet her, and Ericha felt tense as he scrutinized her closely, seeming almost dazed.

"Ericha," Karl said, apparently unaware of the tension, "this distinguished gentleman is none other than my father."

"Theodor," she said, feeling more at ease as he took her hand into his. Despite his receding hairline and sturdy build, Ericha could now see a slight resemblance to her mother.

"Ericha," he said gently, "you look exactly how I pictured you."

Ericha's eyes widened. She was certain she looked like her father. Had Theodor known her father? She wanted to ask but only said, "Why do you say that?"

"Uh . . ." He chuckled. "Well, from your mother's letters, of course. She spoke of nothing but you."

Ericha smiled. "She spoke very highly of you."

"I was so sorry to hear of her death," Theodor went on kindly, ushering Ericha to her chair. "But it is such a delight to have you with us. I trust Karl is taking good care of you."

"Very." She smiled toward him, and he grinned. "In truth,

he's taking such good care of me I hardly know how to act. He practically treats me like a queen."

Theodor raised his brows and almost smirked. "I must apologize," he said, "for not coming to see you sooner. Things have been busy lately. It seems the duke has had something important going on nearly every day this last while."

"Karl tells me you enjoy your work very much," Ericha said.

"I must admit," he replied, "His Grace treats me well."

"How long have you worked at Castle Horstberg?" she asked.

"I started before Karl was born," he stated, then he glanced wryly toward his son. "Seems like forever."

"I am getting old," Karl retorted. "But you'll always be older."

"Don't remind me," Theodor came back, and then his attention turned again to Ericha. "So, you must tell me about yourself, my dear. What sort of things do you enjoy?"

"She loves the garden," Karl answered for her. "And a day hardly passes when she doesn't ride. When she's not doing that, she's always working hard at doing that . . . now what did you call it?"

"Tatting," she replied.

"Yes," Karl said, "that's it."

"Kathe must have taught you," Theodor said.

"Yes," Ericha replied brightly. It felt good to talk to someone who had really known her mother. Kathe had been well skilled in creating the intricate lace with the tiny, hand-held shuttle. And Ericha was grateful for her mother taking the time to pass the knowledge down.

"I would like to see what you do," Theodor said.

"It's quite fascinating," Karl inserted. "I've told her, you know, that Lokbergs must have craftsmanship in their blood."

Theodor nodded toward his son. "I dare say you're right, though it must have skipped me."

"Karl suggested I try and sell it," Ericha said to her uncle. "I'm certain my work wouldn't compare to Mother's. Of course, she practically made our living from it. I took some samples into the dress shop, and Frieda did agree to buy some."

"She's being humble," Karl said. "Frieda nearly swooned when she saw Ericha's work. She was also quick to notice the lace collar Ericha had added to one of those dreadful dresses she ordered. Frieda declared she would make it fashionable for the ladies of Horstberg to wear the lace on their gowns."

"That's wonderful," Theodor said, and Ericha glanced down, blushing slightly.

"Well, it will help out. Karl has already spent so much on me. At least with this I can—"

"Oh, bother." Karl pushed his hand through the air. "You know I'd get you anything you want."

"I know," Ericha said warmly, "and I do appreciate it; nevertheless, I—"

"Proud like her mother," Theodor declared.

Ericha wanted to say something in her mother's defense, but Theodor smiled and she believed he was mostly teasing. She opted to change the subject by attempting to satisfy her curiosity a little further. "Is Castle Horstberg really as big as it looks?"

Theodor chuckled. "It's bigger. I nearly get lost there myself at times."

With the conversation open, Theodor proved what Karl had said about him. His favorite subject was his work.

After this visit, Theodor came often for Sunday dinner, and with each visit, Ericha learned a little more about the Duke of Horstberg. She had never seen the duke, but she'd caught a glimpse once of a tall, blond man in an elaborate uniform, riding through the crowds in the market square. By the way people hovered around him with awe and respect, she was certain he must be the duke.

From what Theodor had told her, Ericha knew that the ruling family of Horstberg was well liked and respected for the most part. Not that Horstberg didn't have problems, and Theodor was well aware of these. But still, Ericha sensed that the duke and his family were good people who were doing their best. She became familiar with them through Theodor's constant rambling, though she only knew them as: the duke, the duchess, the grand duchess, the princess, and so on. The only one she knew by name was Rusty, the duke's secretary and highest advisor, who worked with him very closely.

It all sounded intriguing to Ericha. She looked forward to Theodor's visits and the reports that came along with them. She often gazed out her window toward the magnificent structure that housed the royal family and tried to imagine Theodor there, caring for the duke's personal needs. What would it be like, she wondered, to mingle so closely with royalty and to be a part of their lives?

Ericha and Karl became closer as the weeks moved on. She appreciated the way he cared for her—much like a brother. He spent a great deal of time in his workshop, and people would often come to purchase things or place orders. Each day except Sundays, at the same time, Karl rode into town for a drink at the pub. Ericha wondered about this friend he met. As far as she knew, he never came to the house. But then, this woman who Karl was to marry hadn't come to the house either.

When Ericha was not riding, tatting, or working in the garden, she began occupying her time by cleaning. She had to be careful to avoid Miss Busch when she was at it. And she almost made a game out of cleaning a closet or polishing in a room without Karl or Miss Busch noticing. Ericha was certain that eventually the tidiness and organization of the house would be realized. But her greatest reward was the gratification of her results and the lack of idleness it offered her.

In quiet moments, Ericha would take out her tatting and her thoughts would go to Kathe. As the pain of her mother's death gradually eased, Ericha's contentment deepened. She often stopped to admit that her life was good, and she had much to be thankful for. But still, there was something inside of Ericha that ached. It would start with a subtle twinge of missing her mother, which inevitably brought on musings about her father. She wondered where he was—or if he was still alive. Did he know she existed?

Ericha often felt unsettled thinking of her father. In spite of her mother's obvious love for him, Ericha wondered if she should resent the fact that he'd never married her mother. What kind of man would father a child and leave it to suffer the taunting and persecution she had endured throughout her life? Of course, her mother had worked hard to compensate for all that, and she had never wanted for love and security. But how could Ericha not wonder why she had been born illegitimate when her mother was a woman who greatly respected right and wrong?

There was a memory of something in Kathe Lokberg's eyes that haunted Ericha. And she had an instinctive desire to know who she belonged to. Yet combined with her desire was fear. She would often hold the little wooden box and wonder if she really wanted to know what was inside. Her mother had said it was perhaps better left locked—and she trusted her mother's judgment implicitly.

Each time Ericha took Pegasus out to ride among the foothills, she felt Kathe's memories absorb her—as if this had always been home. The ache she felt made her want to find the meadow that Kathe had spoken of, but recalling her previous attempt only deepened the formless longings.

Often Ericha's mind unwillingly contemplated her brief encounter in the forest, and she wondered why it had left such an impression on her. There was something almost frightening in the feelings stirred by her memories of the incident. Yet intrigue would often override her fear and make her long to go up that trail—not only to see, but to feel, what lay beyond it. Instinctively, Ericha was certain that something very real from her past—or perhaps her mother's—was willing her there. But still she avoided it, and not unlike many times in the past, she returned from riding without any attempt to ease her desires.

Ericha galloped Pegasus into the stable and dismounted. She found a note from Karl tacked to the wall saying that he'd gone to accompany his father to an appointment with a solicitor, and he would be back for dinner.

Stuffing the note into her pocket, Ericha pulled the saddle off Pegasus's back. She led him to his stall where he could eat while she brushed him down, humming as she did. The simple melody reminded Ericha of her mother, who had often sung the words while she worked. But Ericha's memories were peaceful as she recalled the happy times they had shared.

"Hello, Job." She paused to scratch the dog's head as he nuzzled against her in greeting. Apparently assured that she was well, Job plopped himself into the straw and yawned noisily.

Pausing to lift her hair off her neck, Ericha wished that she'd taken time to braid it. The warm sun had made her sweat, and the heavy hair didn't help.

Ericha heard a horse come in as she returned her attention to brushing Pegasus. She couldn't see above the stall, but she assumed it was Karl until a man's voice called out, "Karl? Are you here?"

"No, he's not," she answered without moving from her chore.

"Do you know where he . . ." the voice began, then paused. "To whom am I speaking?"

"To me." She popped her head around the corner, then felt compelled to take a second look as something familiar struck her.

"Do you know where he is?" the man asked as she stepped out of the stall, holding the brush with one hand and wiping sweat from her brow with the back of her other sleeve.

"Yes," she stated, and silence fell as the familiarity took hold. Ericha had no doubt this was the same man she'd encountered in the forest. Despite continued efforts, she had been unable to erase him from her memory. She was immediately aware of that same unblinking intensity in his eyes.

Taking in his appearance, Ericha wondered if this was the friend Karl met daily. He wore dark breeches, high black boots, and a white muslin shirt, topped by dark braces. His manner, as well as his dress, simply reminded her of Karl. Their eyes met. And despite his lack of expression, Ericha could almost feel his mind racing with a thousand thoughts.

Stefan watched this girl expectantly, trying to rationalize away his reaction to just seeing her. While he'd allowed himself to indulge in senseless fantasies about the woman he'd met in the forest, he'd considered it a safe pastime, certain he'd never cross paths with her again. Waiting for her to explain, he wondered what she was doing *here,* of all places. When she said nothing more, he asked, "Could you tell me?"

"I could," she said, feeling upset for some reason that he made no acknowledgment they'd met before.

"Well, out with it," he demanded arrogantly. Then Ericha realized she probably looked no better than a stable girl, dressed as she was in her oldest calico with her hair hanging loose and mussed from her ride. But then, he hardly looked high society.

"May I ask who's inquiring?" she asked him.

"A friend," he stated.

"I already figured that much," she replied.

Stefan tilted his head to scrutinize her more closely. He told himself he should turn around immediately and ride out of here. "You look different," he said as he dismounted.

"So do you," was all she could think to say.

"Your hair was braided before," he said, "and your dress was blue."

Ericha was surprised by the clarity of his memory. She couldn't help hoping that their previous meeting had left an impression on him, as well.

"You look much . . . kinder," she stated with no expression.

Stefan showed a subtle smile and folded his arms, leaning against his horse. Movement caught his eye, and he looked down into the face of one of the biggest dogs he'd ever seen. Its size might have made him wary, but the animal's demeanor was completely affable.

Ericha watched in surprise as this man squatted down and ruffled Job's ears affectionately. Most people either ignored the dog or gave him a patronizing pat on the head.

"His name is Job," she informed him.

"Hello there, Job," he said to the dog. Job licked his face in response. Ericha grimaced in embarrassment, but he only chuckled and gave the dog some semblance of a hug. She felt his attention shift back to her before she willed herself to meet his eyes. Ericha became almost frightened by what she felt as he stood straight again and slapped his hands on his breeches. Job plopped down at his feet, indicating he'd made a new friend.

"Why is it that I have come here often, and I've never seen you before?"

"I probably wasn't here," Ericha stated. Feeling uncomfortable under his obvious gaze, she pulled Pegasus out of his stall so that she could brush him.

Stefan took notice of the horse. "How long have you been here?" he asked.

"Not long enough," she answered, and his eyes narrowed, trying to perceive a deeper meaning to her words.

He put his hands into his pockets and watched her until she glanced toward him and stated, "You were asking about Karl."

"Yes," he said. She thought he should have been embarrassed by his overt interest in her that distracted him from his intentions, but he didn't seem to be. "Do you know where he is . . . or when he'll be back?"

"He said he'd be back before dinner," she replied. "He's with his father."

"I see."

Ericha expected him to say something else, but he only stared at her, seeming perhaps dazed.

"Is something wrong?" she asked at last.

"Uh . . . no . . . I was just wondering your name. May I ask?"

"Ericha," she said, assuming he knew the rest.

"Ericha what?"

"Lokberg, of course."

He chuckled. "Of course. You must be Karl's cousin."

"Yes."

"I wasn't aware that Karl's father had a brother."

Ericha took a deep breath and drew back her shoulders. "He doesn't." There was a long pause before she added, "My mother is his sister."

As he apparently grasped her meaning, Ericha looked into his eyes for a reaction. She felt relieved to see more intrigue than disapproval.

"And where is your mother now?" he asked.

"She passed away not long ago. That is why I came to live with Karl."

"I'm sorry," he said, then looked briefly alarmed, "about your mother's death, I mean."

Ericha smiled and glanced toward Pegasus.

"If you are Ericha Lokberg," he said, "then Pegasus must be yours."

"That's right," she replied, and he stepped forward to pat the horse's neck in a gesture of greeting.

"Karl told me the horse was for his cousin." He looked more at Pegasus than Ericha. Then his eyes shifted abruptly, and Ericha felt weak as they seemed to hold some power over her. "Lucky horse," he stated, and a brief sparkle in his eyes was the only hint of amusement. "I assume," he went on, "that he's the one who threw you when we last met."

"Yes," she said with no inflection in her voice.

"Stupid horse," he said more to Pegasus.

"But it wasn't his fault," she replied.

Stefan looked at her in surprise as he realized she was blaming him.

For a moment Ericha thought he was going to argue or yell at her again, but he only bowed slightly and said, "You must forgive me, Miss Lokberg."

"Only if you will introduce yourself," she said, showing a hint of a smile as they stood with Pegasus between them.

"Uh . . ." he stammered. Stefan hated telling people his name. It always made them behave differently toward him. He was tempted to make up something, but his sense of honesty overruled. "My name is Stefan," he said, hoping to avoid the rest.

"Just Stefan?"

"Heinrich." He waited for the inevitable reaction, but she only smiled, revealing deep dimples in her cheeks. He felt certain she recognized the name, as anyone in Horstberg would. But she obviously didn't care, and he had to smile back.

"I'm pleased to meet you, Stefan Heinrich." She held out her hand over Pegasus's back. She expected him to shake it, but instead he took it slowly, sending a tingle through her from his touch. He brought it to his lips, and the tingle increased.

"The pleasure is mine," he said, then silence took hold as he seemed hesitant to let go of her hand, and their eyes met intently.

Reality intruded upon Stefan's thoughts, and he shook his head. "I should be going."

"Would you like me to give Karl a message?" she asked, trying not to betray her disappointment.

"No, I'll . . . well, tell him I stopped by and I'll come back later."

"Do you want him to meet you at the pub?" she asked as he walked toward his horse.

He turned back briefly before mounting. "Uh . . . no. I'd like to talk to him here."

"Very well." She smiled.

Stefan paused to soak in her appearance once more, and then he nodded slightly and rode out.

Ericha stood motionless for several moments, feeling all over again the way she'd felt on the day they'd first met. What little success she'd had in trying to forget the brief meeting in the forest had just fallen through. Her thoughts were absorbed freshly with Stefan Heinrich. She liked the name.

When Karl returned, she gave him the message, hoping to glean some information.

"A friend stopped by to see you," she reported.

"Must have been Stefan," he said absently, hovering over his workbench.

"How did you know?" she asked.

"He's the only friend I've got." Karl chuckled. "Did he say what he wanted?"

"No. He just said he would come back later."

Karl said nothing more.

"Is he the one you meet at the pub?" she asked.

"Like I said, he's the only friend I've got."

Again silence fell.

"He's very nice," Ericha said, and Karl glanced up sharply.

"Yes, he is," Karl replied with a suspicious tone.

Ericha wondered if her motives were so transparent, and she opted to say nothing more for the time being. If Stefan did return later, Ericha wasn't aware of it. But she was intrigued by the memories of his gaze and his touch. And she found herself absorbed by them, almost against her will.

Ericha's thoughts continued to be monopolized by Stefan Heinrich, and her sparse knowledge made him all the more intriguing. She wondered if he would ever come again when she might have the opportunity to see him. But when days passed and he didn't, she fought to steer her mind elsewhere.

The garden continued to be a release for Ericha, and the time she spent there helped clear her mind. She thought less of Stefan when she kept busy. And this was helped along by Mrs. Burger, whose garden across the fence was in close competition to Ericha's.

Ericha had come to know Mrs. Burger through much chatter over the fence, and occasionally she invited Ericha into her cottage for wine and cinnamon cakes. Eventually she learned that Mrs. Burger was a widow of many years, whose only son had been killed. But she seemed happy, and Ericha enjoyed listening to her disjointed chatter. One of her favorite subjects was her garden, which was one of the few things they had in common.

Today Ericha was glad to have Mrs. Burger as a distraction. As they relaxed and talked in the tiny parlor, she thought how ridiculous it was to let her mind become so absorbed with a man she hardly knew.

"You know," Mrs. Burger commented as Ericha poured the wine at her request, "you've got some of the prettiest hair I've ever seen."

"Thank you." Ericha smiled timidly. "But actually it's very difficult to manage."

"Oh," Mrs. Burger said dubiously, "that's what makes it unique. Why, be glad your hair's not so thin and fly-away as mine.

Hair as thick as that would look pretty no matter what you did with it."

Ericha smiled graciously as Mrs. Burger rambled on. "I'd swear your hair reminds me of someone else's—if I could only think who. Hmm." She set a finger against her temple. "I just can't think. But I know I've seen somebody somewhere with hair that reminds me of yours. Oh, well. It'll come to me."

Ericha's smile widened at the statement that was typical of her, then Mrs. Burger went on with a new subject. "You know, my parsnips are doing well this year. Have you ever had parsnip wine, my dear?"

"No," Ericha replied, certain she'd not want to.

"If the parsnips keep up, we'll have parsnip wine aplenty this year. Oh, I know who it is," she added exuberantly. "It's Abbi du Woernig."

Ericha felt certain Mrs. Burger would start rambling about one acquaintance or another from years gone by. But she responded to Ericha's questioning gaze by saying, "Now, don't tell me you don't know who that would be!"

"I'm afraid I don't," she apologized.

"I keep forgetting you weren't raised here; seems like you were. Anyway, Abbi du Woernig is the grand duchess, of course."

Ericha leaned forward eagerly as Mrs. Burger continued. "She's a beautiful woman. Must be getting old now, though; about my age. But she had the most beautiful red hair—not unlike yours. When she was younger and her husband was alive, I would love to see them together at the market or when they'd have a procession."

"Do they have them often?" Ericha asked, wondering if she might get a chance to see these people of interest.

"At least once a year on Reclamation Day." To Ericha's questioning look, she clarified, "That's when they have the fair. Oh, they've been having that for centuries I would guess, but they only started calling it Reclamation Day when Prince Cameron came back and reclaimed the duchy from his evil brother, Nikolaus."

Ericha's interest escalated as Mrs. Burger went on to tell the fine details of the story. But it all seemed so fantastic that Ericha felt certain it had been distorted by time.

"So," Mrs. Burger said in a tone to indicate she was summing up, "it was on the day when Prince Cameron married that Prince Nikolaus was killed, and that was the first day I noticed Abbi du Woernig's hair."

"You mean you were there?" Ericha asked, thinking all of this was merely legend.

"Of course I was there," she said proudly. "I was with those waiting outside the grand cathedral when the prince emerged with his new bride. She was crowned duchess that day. How beautiful she looked!"

Mrs. Burger took on a dreamy look, apparently lost in days gone by, until Ericha asked, "How many years ago was it?"

"Oh," she thought a moment, "about fifty—give or take a few."

"Is she still alive?"

"Of course she is. And she has quite a posterity, I'll tell you. I admire the woman a great deal. What I wouldn't give to talk to her for a day—the stories she must have to tell."

"Like what?" Ericha asked intently, hardly conscious of the time drifting by.

"Surely she's been there amidst all of it. They say she delivered the princess's baby while the castle was being overtaken by revolutionaries. And of course, she was there the day of the explosion, but . . ." Mrs. Burger looked briefly sad, but Ericha waited patiently for her to go on, knowing that she would. "She most likely wouldn't want to talk about that. But I dare say she'd be willing to talk about how she met the prince when he saved her life on the mountain. Why, that story's almost a legend around here."

"Tell me," Ericha urged, fascinated for reasons she couldn't explain.

"It was said that she died one winter. I remember that blizzard—one of the worst I've seen in all my years. All anyone knows for certain is that she disappeared in the storm and came home in the spring—none the worse for wear. Soon after that, Prince Cameron came back, when everyone thought he'd been dead for years. He married her, reclaimed the duchy, and life has been better for all of us ever since."

"And that's all you know?" Ericha asked, disappointed.

"I suppose that's why I'd like to talk to her. What she couldn't tell me!"

Ericha smiled, and then she felt the passing of time and glanced at the clock. "Good heavens!" She stood abruptly. "Karl will wonder what's become of me. Thank you for the stories," she added. "They were wonderful."

Mrs. Burger followed her to the door. "Thank you for the visit, dear. I'll most likely see you tomorrow." She waved at Ericha as she disappeared up the walk, coming around the fence into her own yard.

Ericha found Karl in his shop. Just as she expected, he glanced at the clock and gave her a glare of mock disapproval, which made her laugh.

"That old woman will just fill your head with nonsense," Karl said impishly.

"She's a better storyteller than you are," Ericha teased. "If I had to depend on you to keep me entertained, I'd die of boredom."

"Most likely," Karl agreed with a smirk.

"And you've not once played for me since I've come," she added. "That guitar has so much dust on it, you probably couldn't pick it up."

Karl laughed. "Well, one of these days I might surprise you. Just wait until—"

He was interrupted by a knock at the door.

"Come in," Karl called.

Ericha caught her breath when Stefan Heinrich entered, wearing a jacket that looked as old and comfortable as his boots. His shirt was left untucked and hung below the jacket's edge. But she liked the common way he dressed, which somehow defied an unspoken air of dignity about him.

"Hello, my friend," he said to Karl, and then he noticed Ericha and was silent a moment. "Miss Lokberg." He nodded toward her. Their eyes met as she nodded in reply.

"Stefan," Karl said easily. "What can I do for you?"

"I gave you those . . . uh," he glanced toward Ericha, perhaps nervously, "papers . . . and . . ."

"You need them?"

"Need to see them. I'll let you hang on to them."

"I'll be right back." Karl stood and went into the back room, leaving Ericha alone with Stefan.

Ericha remained silent, not knowing what to say since she felt far from indifferent in his presence. She glanced up to find him staring at her, and she felt her heart quicken.

"Is there a reason you're looking at me that way?" she asked boldly. But Stefan didn't mind the question. He didn't see any reason to not be honest with her.

"I'm weighing things in my mind," he said.

Her eyes widened in question. "What sort of things?"

"There's a scale, you see." He smiled slightly, but the severity in his eyes deepened. "I can see you on one side, and on the other is—"

"Here they are," Karl announced as he came back in and handed Stefan a packet of papers.

Stefan turned his back as he opened them and apparently found what he was looking for. He read for a moment before handing them back to Karl.

"Thank you," he said. "You keep those well hidden now, my friend."

"No problem," Karl smiled and left to return the papers.

"You were saying," Ericha stated, intently curious over his remark about the scales.

"Yes," he chuckled, "well . . . it was a ridiculous analogy, not worth mentioning."

"On the contrary," she replied, "I'd be very interested to hear it."

"You would?" He lifted his brows, feeling a brief sense of

hope. But reality quickly pushed it away. "I must be going. I have an appointment and . . ."

Karl came back into the room glancing toward Ericha and then Stefan, as if he sensed something unusual.

"Is there anything else you need?" Karl asked Stefan.

"Uh . . . no, thank you. I . . ." He paused as Ericha stood and sauntered out of the shop. She sensed there was something he wanted to say to Karl, but he wouldn't in her presence.

Ericha went into the stable to see Pegasus, secretly hoping she would have a chance to speak to Stefan again before he left. She was relieved to see his stallion there. Affectionately, she stroked its withers, feeling somehow closer to Stefan. Noting it had a similar stature and color as Pegasus, she put the pieces together. It must have been Stefan that Pegasus had been purchased from.

"His name is Fire," Stefan said from behind, and Ericha turned, startled.

"He's beautiful," she replied, wondering why Stefan's mere presence caused her heart to nearly leap.

Ericha turned her attention back to the horse, wanting to hide the feelings she knew her eyes would betray. She glanced up to see Stefan standing close to her as he put his hand on the saddle near her own.

Stefan quickly tried to squelch the idea formulating in his mind. He'd nearly talked himself out of it when Ericha looked up at him. Seeing his emotions clearly mirrored in her eyes, he let all reason dissipate.

"Ericha," he whispered as if the walls might overhear. "Do you know where the road forks just below the trail where you once met a strange man in the forest?"

"Yes." She smiled.

"There is a clearing where a tree has fallen."

"I've been there," she stated, and one corner of his mouth twitched upward.

Ericha felt his hand come over hers in a warm, possessive gesture. "Would you meet me there?" he asked with no inflection in his voice. Ericha held her breath as she realized he too was aware of these feelings.

"Are you against calling in drawing rooms?" she asked in an effort to ease the tension.

But it only intensified as he replied severely, "Yes."

Taken off guard, Ericha looked up at him, trying to perceive his intentions. His eyes burned through her, compelling her to answer, "I could meet you there."

"Right after dark," he stated.

Ericha nodded. Stefan mounted and rode away, slowing his pace once he came onto the street and turned the corner. Something about Ericha Lokberg made him not want to go home. He wanted to just be in the same room with her and absorb the reality of her presence. He wondered if he had done the right thing in asking to meet her. But thoughts of it made his heart quicken, and reasoning was thrown over. From that first moment he'd met her eyes, his mind had been clouded with an impression that time had not dispelled. He had made up his mind long ago to spend his life alone and be content. But that had changed now. His facade of contentment had disappeared the day he met Ericha Lokberg.

Did she have any idea how many times he had awakened with her name on his lips? In his mind he had held her a thousand times, and his thoughts were getting the better of him. He had to know the reality of it in order to go on living. *He had to!*

Ericha felt both puzzled and excited as she anticipated her meeting in the forest. For whatever reason that Stefan seemed to want his interest in her to remain unnoticed, she opted to not tell Karl.

As soon as the sun went down, Ericha rode with purpose to the specified place. She waited until it had been dark a long while, wondering if Stefan would show up. When she heard a horse coming through the trees, her heart raced unwillingly. She took a deep breath to keep it under control as a figure in a dark, hooded cloak dismounted and stood before her. He pulled off the hood and pushed the cloak behind his shoulders. In the moonlight she could pick out the strong cheekbones and firm jaw.

"Ericha," Stefan said softly. "May I call you Ericha?" he added as an afterthought.

"You may," she said, following the same impetuous mood that had urged her to agree to this meeting.

"Come, walk with me," he said, holding out a hand toward her. Ericha slipped her hand into his, feeling the warmth of it through the soft leather of his glove. A full moon guided them through the trees as they walked slowly with no apparent purpose or destination.

"So," he said at last, "you've only recently come to Horstberg. What do you think of it so far?"

"I love it," she replied eagerly.

"Really?" He seemed surprised.

"Don't you?" she asked.

Stefan stopped walking, wishing he could see her eyes through the darkness. Did she have any idea how deeply that question struck him? "As a child I loved it," he said. "But I must confess there are times when I wish I could leave here and never come back."

"Why?" she asked with an innocence that warmed him.

Stefan chuckled and began to walk again. "I did not meet you here to discuss such things, Ericha."

"Why *did* you meet me here?" she asked.

Stefan found her directness alluring. Everything about her was such a refreshing contrast to the manipulation and tawdriness he'd become accustomed to.

"Well?" she asked when he didn't answer right away.

"Don't beat around the bush, Ericha. Just get past the small talk and get to the point."

Ericha stopped walking, not certain how to take him. He chuckled, and she realized he was teasing her. She laughed with him. "I'm beginning to think you're a scoundrel, Stefan Heinrich."

"Maybe I am," he admitted. "So, what is an incredible young woman like you doing in the forest at night with a scoundrel?"

"*Are* you a scoundrel?"

"Does it make a difference?" he asked.

Ericha quickly evaluated her feelings and answered firmly, "No."

He took hold of her other hand, and she wished she could see his eyes. "You didn't answer my question," she stated. "Why did you want to meet me here?"

"I'm not certain," he said in a tone of confession. "I only know that I had to see you . . . to talk with you . . . alone."

"What did you want to talk about?" she asked calmly while her heart moved into her stomach with a fluttery rush.

"I'm not certain of that either," Stefan admitted.

"What are you certain of?" she asked, laughing slightly.

She heard him sigh in the darkness, and then he said, "I'm certain of what I'm feeling."

Ericha thought she'd go mad as she waited for Stefan to go on. When he didn't, she asked, "And what is that?"

"Ericha." He ignored her question and squeezed her hands. A bitter memory flashed through his mind. He had opened his heart to a woman only once, and it had been carelessly trampled upon. But it had never felt this way. Surely this was different. Needing a minute to think, he began to walk again, keeping her hand securely in his.

"You're not saying much," Ericha said, if only to break the unbearable silence.

"I'm thinking," he said. Ericha heard the movement of the horses and realized they had come back to the clearing. "Let's sit," he said, motioning toward the fallen tree.

Ericha sat down and watched as he removed his gloves and tucked them into the waist of his breeches. He straddled the tree trunk and sat close to her, but still he said nothing. She turned to look at him and found his face so near she could almost feel his breath. He shifted slightly and his chest briefly brushed her shoulder.

"What are you thinking?" she finally asked.

"I was wishing I could be as direct with words as you are. Actually . . . it's not usually a problem for me. But right now . . ." Trying a different approach, Stefan said, "Tell me what you are feeling, Ericha. I sense something, but I . . ." He wondered if he had ever stammered so much in his life.

There was a moment of silence. "I couldn't possibly."

He felt certain her voice had quivered. "Why not?"

"There are no words," she whispered.

Stefan's only reply was his arm coming around her waist to pull her against him. His fingers were on her face, smelling of warm leather, and then they pushed into her wild hair. Ericha felt them against the back of her head, holding her in a grip that left her powerless. She sighed when his lips came against her face. She didn't understand what was happening, but she wasn't about to deny herself of it. She believed she had wanted it from the moment she'd laid eyes on him.

"Ericha," he whispered, and his breath was warm against her skin. "My sweet Ericha. Where did you come from?"

Attempting to ease the tension, Ericha answered matter-of-factly. "It was a little village up north. You've probably never heard of it. It took me days to get here by train, and—"

She stopped when he laughed softly and buried his face into her hair. "It doesn't matter where you came from." He touched her chin with his finger. "You're here now."

Ericha could hardly breathe as Stefan's lips came over hers. He kissed her softly at first, and then a fervency seeped into it, sweeping Ericha into sensations so pleasurable, she wanted never to let them go.

"Ericha," he repeated, pulling his lips away. "Forgive me." He tightened his embrace as if to defy his words. "I shouldn't have done that, but I . . ."

"You what?" she urged when he didn't finish.

"I had to know . . . what it would be like if . . ." Again he paused, and he embraced her desperately. "I must go," he whispered, but Ericha protested.

"Why? You only just got here. Stefan, I . . ." She faltered, but he pulled her closer.

"Ericha." Her name came from his lips with intense emotion, and then he was kissing her again. Ericha sensed from his attitude that these were stolen moments—but she didn't care. Instinctively she turned toward him. Her arm went beneath his cloak and moved over the soft muslin shirt that covered his back. The fingers of her other hand threaded into his hair. She marveled at the reality as his kiss turned warm and moist, and he eased impossibly closer.

Ericha began to believe it could last forever. Then something changed abruptly in Stefan. His lips came hesitantly from hers. "Tomorrow," he said and moved away. "Here . . . same time."

Ericha wanted to protest his leaving, but every nerve was taut with the memory of his touch. How could she speak when she could barely breathe?

She heard him mount and saw his shadow on the stallion. "I love you, Ericha Lokberg," he said and was gone.

Ericha didn't know how long she stood in the darkness, wondering. She wondered who he was, where he had come from, why he was intent on meeting her secretively. And why she was in love with him. Reason told her she was mad. She couldn't think of one logical point to any of this. But her heart told her it was joyous, and she rode home feeling happier than she believed she ever had.

"Where have you been?" Karl asked from the darkness as she rode into the stable.

Ericha made no reply, but she was certain he noticed the weakness in her knees that made her lean heavily against him as he helped her dismount.

"Well?" he asked.

"Riding," she replied with a lilt in her voice.

Karl wanted to insist she tell him the truth, but he only admonished her about riding alone after dark.

Ericha bid him good-night and nearly sailed through the house and up to bed, still absorbed in the heavenly kisses she'd received in the forest. There was something about Stefan's brief presence in her life that eased the ache in Ericha. He somehow made up for the void that had come from her circumstances.

The following evening, Ericha was glad that Karl went out so he wouldn't notice her disobeying his admonition. But after waiting for what seemed like hours in the forest, Ericha had to admit that Stefan was not coming.

Her feelings as she went home to bed were such a contrast to the previous evening that she thought she would die from the lonely ache. Analyzing her circumstances briefly, Ericha realized that despite how good Karl and Theodor were to her, there was little else in her life except her friendship with Mrs. Burger. There was something in Stefan Heinrich that she needed. And she wondered far into the night why he'd not come.

Rationalizing that something had come up, she went to the same place the following evening. But still he didn't come. She knew that he could find her if he wanted to, which made her realize after several days passed that for some reason he didn't want to.

Ericha asked Karl about Stefan, but he said almost nothing, and his tone discouraged her interest. She wanted to send a message to the pub with Karl but knew it would make no difference. If Stefan wanted to see her, he would. After all, he had told her that he loved her.

"You've certainly been gone a lot lately," Ericha said to Karl as he plopped into a chair and put up his feet. "Spending time with Luise?" she added, and he smiled. "When do I get to meet this famous bride-to-be?"

"You've not met her?" he asked, astonished.

"To my knowledge you've never brought her here." She gave a teasing smile. "Are you ashamed of me, Karl?"

"Hardly. Luise is simply a very busy woman. She loves her job, and her father isn't well. I often go there to be with her so that she can be with him at the same time."

"That makes sense," Ericha replied and returned her attention to her tatting.

"I can't believe you haven't met her," Karl said. "I must be getting senile."

"Why don't you do something about it?"

"I believe I will. Tomorrow evening you and I are going out. I'll tell Erma she gets the night off."

"Erma?"

"Miss Busch, of course," he said. Ericha had never heard the maid's given name.

True to his word, Karl took Ericha out the following evening. They went to the *Horstberg Inn,* and Karl declared it was the finest in the country. They were barely seated when a bustling woman with brown hair and a full figure approached and bent to kiss Karl on the lips. She said something to Karl that Ericha didn't hear. Her mind had turned abruptly to a kiss that had left her feeling more discontent than she ever had in her life.

"Ericha," Karl said, startling her from her thoughts, "this is Luise soon-to-be-Lokberg. Luise, meet my cousin."

"What a pleasure," Luise replied giddily, sitting close beside Karl. "Of course I've heard nothing but wonderful things about you, Ericha."

Ericha smiled toward Karl. He told Luise what they would have for dinner, and she bustled off to the kitchen. She returned with their meal and sat down to take a break and eat with them.

Ericha was at first surprised by Luise; she seemed initially to be so different from Karl. But as she had a chance to observe Karl and Luise together, she found the woman endearing, and she could see why Karl loved her.

It felt good to be out. The inn was quaint and the food delicious. But Ericha's mind kept wandering. On the way home Karl said, "You seem down—more so tonight than usual. Is something wrong?"

"No," she insisted with a convincing smile. "I'm fine, really."

Karl doubted she was telling him the truth, but he tried not to be nosy, knowing it was one of his weak points.

"You like Luise," he stated.

"Yes," she replied with enthusiasm, "I do. I can see that the two of you are very happy together. And that makes *me* happy."

Karl smiled, and his eyes turned wistful. Ericha looked distantly ahead, her heart aching. She realized then that seeing Karl and Luise together made her long for such companionship in her own life. But she wondered if it would ever be.

Chapter Three

THE MOUNTAIN LODGE

It took great effort for Stefan to concentrate on his work. He was just beginning to make some headway when Johanna erupted into his office as if the world were about to end.

"I simply cannot take it anymore!" she snarled. The look in her eyes clearly indicated that whatever she couldn't take, she was deeming it *his* problem.

"What?" Stefan asked blandly.

"I will not tolerate that maid's impudence another day. If you don't see that she's dismissed, I'll—"

"You'll what?" he interrupted, removing his glasses. He leaned toward her, and she took a step back. "Has it ever occurred to you that you are the only one in this household who has trouble with the servants? Forgive me if I don't jump out of my chair and challenge the poor girl to a duel, my dear, but I have *important* matters to deal with. Try treating the servants civilly for a change, and see if you don't get different results."

Stefan put his glasses back on and looked pointedly to the papers on his desk, indicating that was all he had to say.

"I don't know what's gotten into you lately, Stefan." Johanna's voice turned acrid.

Stefan leaned back and sighed. She hadn't gotten his ire up over impudent servants, so naturally she would resort to *his* unfair behavior.

"And what is that?" He tossed his glasses on the desktop, knowing if he didn't humor her a little, this could go on all day.

"Sometimes you're almost . . . *cruel* to me. I just don't—"

Stefan shot out of his chair, and she retracted further. He cautioned himself to remain calm, as difficult as it was. "You're the one who started this cruelty thing, Johanna. You started twisting the knife years ago. Don't misinterpret my not putting up with it for cruelty."

Johanna started to cry. Stefan shook his head and sighed. "You've always got an ace up your sleeve, don't you," he stated. "Give it up, wife. Your tears stopped affecting me a long time ago."

"But . . ." she sniffled and dabbed at her eyes, "you've not even touched me for months, and . . ." She broke off with a gentle sob.

"Nearly a year, to be precise," he stated. "Funny that you should notice *now*. What's *really* bothering you? Shortage of available lovers this week?"

Stefan almost smiled as her eyes turned cold and hard. It was what he'd expected. Eventually the *real* Johanna always came out. And it usually happened when he got too close to the truth.

"You're an arrogant bastard," she hissed.

"Coming from you, my dear, that's music to my ears. I wouldn't want to be the kind of person that someone like you would actually enjoy being with. Now, I think I've had enough of your antics for one day. If you would do me the honor of leaving my office so I can—"

"I'm not going anywhere until—"

"Fine," he brushed past her, "I'll leave. Careful you don't mess anything up, or you might feel a great deal of empathy for the maids."

Stefan resisted his temptation to slam the door and instead left it open so that the officers of the Guard standing there could keep an eye on his wife. He knew they had standing orders to do so, since this was far from the first time such a scene had occurred in the office. He barely exchanged an apologetic glance with the officers, glad to see in their expressions that they seemed to understand. It eased his embarrassment slightly. Hurrying away, he pushed his hand brutally through his hair, but it did little to ease his frustration. Instinctively, he headed down a couple of long halls and up the stairs, his boots echoing against the stone as he took them three at a time. Coming into the hall where the family portraits were displayed, he slowed and approached the gallery with reverence.

Desperately needing the solace that his forebears seemed to offer, he glanced wistfully across the row of paintings. Each portrait seemed to tell a life story with its expression. Concentrating on warm, childhood memories, Stefan fought to push away the disturbing scene with Johanna.

With longing, Stefan focused on the portrait of his uncle. The artist had captured well the sparkle in his eye, and the zest for living that Stefan remembered so well. He envied the training and experience that had existed inside of his intricate mind. And he cursed the day that fate had taken his uncle's life and left Stefan to face the burdens of this position. Looking into the lifeless eyes that were nothing more than a mixture of oils and canvas, Stefan's mind wandered. He recalled all too vividly the day that had changed his life—and the lives of those around him. Nothing had ever been the same after the explosion, and the reality made him hate his position all the more. The whole thing was distasteful simply because of the reasons it had come about.

The faces surrounding Stefan seemed to speak of the past, and he ached to have things as they once were. He knew there was a time when life had been better in this wretched place. Occasionally he found traces of the happiness that had once existed. But something had been absent since that day in forty-nine, and Stefan felt certain it was gone forever.

The realities of the present became overwhelming, and the permeation of the past filtered around him. Rather than drawing the desired comfort, Stefan could only feel the pressure to uphold what had been left to him. He turned away and nearly ran back down the stairs, out the door, and to the stables. He needed peace and solitude. He needed to escape all of this, if only briefly. And there was only one place he could go.

Ericha made every effort to become lost in her trivial pastimes, hoping to distract herself from this relentless lonely ache. But it only worsened daily.

She went to the garden to pull weeds but ended up just sitting on the ground. She stared blankly toward the sky as dark clouds seeped into it, and the breeze pulled wisps of hair from her braid. But Ericha hardly noticed.

Her mind turned to her mother. Lately she had missed Kathe more than ever. She longed for the comfort Kathe had given her in troubled moments, and her heart ached for the life her mother had lived. Ericha wondered if she would be doomed to the same loneliness her mother had dwindled away in—longing for a man who wasn't there, and not satisfied with any other.

"Stefan." She whispered his name into the breeze and closed her eyes. While she blessed the memories of being in his arms, she cursed him for coming into her life at all. She thought back to the trivial encounters she'd had with men prior to her mother's death. It took no effort to admit that what she felt for Stefan was beyond compare.

Hoping to distract her thoughts, Ericha went aimlessly back to her room. Job was there to greet her, and she appreciated the way he nuzzled against her legs, as if he could sense her emotion. She gazed out the window while she unbraided her hair and brushed it through. When that became tiresome, she went to the closet and fingered the dresses and cloak that Kathe had worn. Kathe's belongings gave her a degree of comfort, but Ericha's thoughts shifted when her eye caught something flat leaning on the closet floor to face the wall.

Ericha went to her knees and struggled to bring it out where she could see it. Blowing on it, dust flew from the back of what appeared to be a painting. She coughed slightly and turned it over to see what it might be. Not knowing what to expect, she was surprised to see a pencil drawing of a man. Immediately logic insisted it was her father. Her emotions confirmed the truth as she scrutinized it more closely and the evidence deepened.

The size of the drawing and the way it was framed constituted a portrait, but it was far more casual. The expression was a genuine smile, and the eyes seemed to sparkle. There were deep dimples in the cheeks, strength in the square jaw, and the curly hair was combed back uniquely over the ears. Though the drawing was done in charcoal-colored pencil, Ericha knew that hair was red.

She squinted to read the tiny signature. It simply said: *Maggie*. Looking again at the face, Ericha recognized her own features and swallowed hard. Reaching out to touch it, her fingers trembled as reality told her it was a lifeless surface. Ericha pressed her hand longingly over the glass that protected the work, and her many emotions combined, becoming suddenly unbearable.

She knew why this was hidden deep in the closet. For some reason, Kathe had been unable to bear looking at it, and she had chosen to leave it behind when she'd left Horstberg. The picture provoked pain in Ericha, but she could neither hang it nor put it back. Instead she leaned it to face the wall.

Impulsively, Ericha grabbed her mother's cloak and wrapped it around her. She swept down the stairs and out to the stable, as if her emotions might catch up and smother her. Urged on by a formless desperation, Ericha mounted Pegasus without a saddle. Almost by his own will, the stallion thundered down the drive and toward the covered bridge.

Driven by an intangible force, Ericha headed toward that meadow she hadn't yet found. As if her mother's will were inside her, Ericha ached to be there, perhaps believing it would help ease this torment within.

Ericha bent low and wrapped her arms around Pegasus, galloping at a dangerous pace between the closely rooted pines. She thought of meeting Stefan the last time she'd attempted this, but the ache deepened so intently, she forced her mind away from him. Her emotions swept high and the wind whipped against her face as she rode with everything she had up the forest trail. Her imagination ran wild from an intangible sensation that the past was grabbing at her from all sides. It seemed that something very real was drawing her toward the meadow that she knew existed at the end of this trail.

Ericha caught her breath as the trees moved behind and a spacious field opened up before her. It seemed immediately familiar, as if in her mind she had been here hundreds of times. Again the past consumed her, and she nearly felt a kinship with this place. The wind increased with her emotions. The sky darkened with her mood. Ericha felt an unbearable sadness as she galloped the circumference of the meadow, noting the foliage-covered rock wall that rose steeply against the uphill side, and the thick trees surrounding her otherwise. She thought of her mother and missed her desperately. The stories Kathe had told her about this place became vivid, and she wondered about her father as she stopped Pegasus to glance nostalgically at her surroundings, feeling lonely and sad as she yearned for something from her past.

Ericha had not been thinking about Stefan when he emerged from the forest at a full gallop. She caught her breath sharply and waited only a moment before he saw her and pulled his stallion to an abrupt halt. The wind whipped at her hair, and she gathered it into one hand to keep her view of him uninhibited. She thought it funny to recall in that moment one of her mother's adages. *The feelings that lead to fate are feelings that won't negate.*

Ericha's heart raced as he watched her. If not for the wind, she might have believed that time had stopped. He was too far away for her to see his expression, but she could almost feel his anxiety. She wondered if she was the cause. Wondering how to react, Ericha wanted to both run into his arms and run away. Feeling helpless to do either, she was relieved when he trotted slowly toward her, the wind playing havoc with his hair.

Ericha's emotions swept higher as he reined the horse in close to her. She could see now that he looked more sad than upset. That timeless, dreamlike quality persisted as she tried to absorb the reality of his presence. What kind of coincidence could have possibly put them both in this place at this moment? It seemed impossible! Yet, here they were. There was something formlessly comforting in the way his eyes delved into her. She could almost believe from the look alone that he had missed her as much as she'd missed him. Questions of his absence intruded upon her relief of seeing him, creating a storm within to match the one threatening around them.

"Miss Lokberg," he said at last, nodding slightly.

Ericha nodded in reply, not liking the formality of his greeting. It seemed so incongruous with the apparent yearning in his eyes. Thunder sounded in the distance, and Ericha couldn't help being startled by it. She glanced around to realize the sky was almost black, and the wind had increased dramatically.

"I must go," she said, overwhelmed by her fear of storms. Stefan's eyes narrowed, but he made no reply. Thunder sounded again, and Ericha started across the meadow.

Stefan turned to watch her go while a decision worked unwillingly in his mind. In the breadth of a moment, he contemplated everything in his life that had made him what he was. Looking back, he could almost believe he'd been somehow predestined to misery and grief. And now a choice lay before him. His heart battled with his head. But the battle was brief, and the victory somehow bitter. His head had been ruling for as long as he could remember. It was just too weary to put up much of a fight.

"Wait!" Stefan called.

Ericha turned back. The expectancy in her countenance warmed him. It was in her hands now. For him, there was no choice to be made. He'd made his decision long ago, the first time he'd allowed his mind to wander into the paths of wanting to be with her. Wrong and right simply had no bearing. His heart had been torn apart too many times to know the difference.

Ericha's heart beat almost painfully as she wondered over his purpose. "It's too far," he called. She could barely hear him above the wind. "You'll catch your death before you get home."

Ericha wondered what her options were, but she didn't have time to contemplate it as he waved his arm to indicate she follow him. Instinctively trusting him, and feeling a degree of relief from her emotions, Ericha rode back toward Stefan. He dismounted near the ridge, and she was surprised to see him pull the thicket away to reveal an opening in the rock wall. He took his horse by the reins and urged it to the foot of the crevice. He slapped the animal lightly, and it disappeared into the ridge.

"Come here," he shouted, bracing his feet apart to withstand the wind. Ericha dismounted with his hands at her waist. Their eyes met as a hearty gust swept her against him. Warmth surged through her from the contact, and she could almost believe she had been born to be part of this man's life. Unnerved by the enormity of her feelings, she stepped back and glanced toward the opening in the rock, silently questioning what lay beyond it. Fighting to stand on her own, she pulled her cloak tightly around her. Stefan led her horse to the opening, and it too disappeared at his insistence.

"Come along," he said and took her arm into a firm grip. The wind was less fierce as they came together into a narrow crevice. Stefan let go of her only long enough to turn back and cover the entrance in order to keep it hidden.

Ericha's mind raced with questions as she moved carefully through the ridge with his help. She wondered where she was going and why Stefan came often to wherever it was. When they had nearly reached the top, she slipped slightly and almost fell. But Stefan caught her with his arm around her waist. Thunder rumbled, but she hardly noticed. As their eyes met again, that intangible sensation of the past overwhelmed her.

The wind nearly swept Ericha off her feet as she emerged from the crevice onto the plateau. Stefan caught the reins of the waiting horses and helped her mount, and then he shouted above the wind as he pointed, "Ride that way. I'll catch up."

Ericha did as he said, bending low over the horse to avoid the wind as much as possible. She was surprised to see the lodge appear in front of her, then wondered what she'd expected. At first she assumed this might be where he lived, but reasoning it out, she felt certain it was merely a place for respite. Ericha dismounted near the door, and rain began to fall. Thunder broke the air again, more loudly now, and she was grateful to be near shelter.

The rain came down hard and strong as Stefan took Pegasus from her and shouted, "Go on inside. I'll see the horses to the stable and be right in."

Ericha pushed the door open, grateful to leave the biting storm behind. Glancing around to take in her surroundings, she felt something close to homesick. A dusky light filtered through high windows from the cloud-obstructed afternoon sun. Ericha almost held her breath as she admired the lofty ceiling of log beams and the simple furnishings of the common room in which she stood. She was aware of heavy rain beating on the roof, and a loud crack of thunder made her shudder. Before it resonated into the distance, the door came open behind her.

Stefan entered, shaking the rain off as he exclaimed, "It's coming down like mad!" He pushed dripping hair back off his face and glanced toward her. "Make yourself comfortable. I'll change and build a fire."

Ericha watched as he bounded up the stairs and across a landing, disappearing through a door at the top. She was intrigued by an inviting bearskin rug in front of the fireplace and felt compelled to sit there.

"That's quite a storm," Stefan said, coming back into the room with a towel flung over his shoulder. He squatted near the fireplace, wearing dark breeches, a white shirt left untucked, and nothing on his feet. She noted how wet his hair was, as water soaked into his shirt where it lay over the collar. It had grown longer since the last time she'd seen him.

"Yes it is," she answered. "You were right. I would have been very wet and cold by the time I got home."

Stefan glanced toward her. His heart quickened a little as her reassurance was somehow comforting.

"Is this place yours?" She looked around again and hugged her knees to her chest, feeling chilled.

"It's been in the family for generations," he stated coolly. "I believe it was my great-great grandfather who built it—or something like that."

"It's very nice, but why so secluded?"

"I suppose he had his reasons," Stefan stated. "Personally, I like to be alone," he added almost defensively. Then he looked quickly back to the fire as the flames in front of him began to build.

"Do you spend much time here?" she asked, wondering perhaps if he *did* live here.

"Only when I can manage to get away, though it's not nearly often enough."

"Do you think the storm will last long?" Ericha asked, wondering how long she would be staying.

"It's hard to say." He stood up and brushed his hands on his breeches.

"You look angry," she said, noting the distress in his eyes. "Are you afraid I will spill your secret?"

"You won't, will you?" he asked.

"Of course not," she said. Stefan's expression softened, but he remained standing.

"I'm not angry," he apologized. "I've just had . . . a bad day."

"Me too," she said, and he made no further comment.

Ericha watched as he fluffed his hair with the towel and then tossed it over the arm of the sofa. He pushed both hands through his hair in an attempt to straighten it. She noticed how the waves had tightened, being wet.

"Make yourself at home." She motioned comically for him to sit down.

Stefan's eyes smiled as he sat down a short distance away from her on the rug. "So," he said, "what is it that compelled you to ride to this meadow—twice?"

"Only once," she said. "I tried before but met with an obstacle on the way."

Stefan felt as warmed by the memory as he was by the fire in front of them. "Fine," he conceded, "once."

"My mother told me about that meadow," she said, and he looked surprised. "She and my father used to meet there. She's told me so much about it that I almost felt as though I'd been there before." She stared thoughtfully into the flames and added, "Would you think me strange if I said that I could feel the past there with me?"

"No," he replied.

Ericha glanced around and rubbed the chill from her arms. "Do these walls speak to you of times gone by and the generations of your family that have come here to find seclusion? Do you find comfort feeling their presence surrounding you here?"

A wave of goose-bumps seized Stefan. She had just managed to describe in two sentences the almost eerie sensations he'd always felt in this lodge. "Can you read my mind?" he asked.

"No, that's what I was feeling. I don't know why," she laughed, "but I was."

They watched each other for several moments. The fire hissed and crackled. The rain pounded relentlessly. Ericha found herself remembering those brief moments she had spent in his arms, consumed by his kiss. How long had it been? How many times had she longed to be with him again—wondering if she ever would? She felt almost frightened by the intensity of her feelings for this man. Yet, she hardly knew him. Stefan's lips parted subtly, but he said nothing. She wondered over his thoughts. The tension between them mounted. Needing to know where they stood, she guessed cautiously, "You're wishing you hadn't brought me here."

"At least I know you can't read my mind," he came back quickly.

"No, I can't read your mind, so you'll have to tell me what you're thinking." He made no response, so she asked, "Why *did* you bring me here?"

Stefan looked directly at her. Again she felt that tension. But his genuine words eased it somewhat. "I wanted to be with you alone."

"You likely could have arranged that without a storm," she

said, unable to help the curt tone. When he made no reply, she added, "I expected to see you again before now."

"I've been busy," Stefan said blandly.

"And avoiding me."

Stefan met her eyes, marveling at her perception. She could see right through him, unlike Johanna, who couldn't even *see* him.

"I've missed you," he retorted in his defense.

"I think about you every day. No," she corrected, a slight tremor in her voice, "constantly."

Thunder sounded above them, and Ericha jumped slightly, grateful that she wasn't alone. Her attention turned back to Stefan as the rumbling subsided in the distance.

"It's quite a storm," he said.

"Did you want to talk about the weather?"

"No," he admitted readily. Her candor inspired him to be honest. "I just want to be with you, Ericha."

Ericha smiled and turned to gaze at the fire. "Did you mean what you said?" she asked, deciding to get to the point.

"What did I say?"

She met his eyes. "You told me that you love me."

Stefan looked at her in surprise before turning toward the fire. For a moment logic intruded, reminding him of reality. He'd actually forgotten that he'd admitted it aloud. He'd spent so much time trying to convince himself that he had no right to feel this way. He was taken off guard to hear it voiced. "I shouldn't have brought you here."

"But you did," she countered. "You wanted to be with me alone."

Stefan looked back at her, his eyes narrowing intently. Ericha wondered if her boldness was making him angry. But she held his gaze firmly, attempting to convey that there was no hiding from these feelings. She saw him swallow hard, and then his eyes softened and the tenseness dissipated from his jaw.

As Stefan absorbed the unmasked emotion in Ericha's face, he felt something change inside him. It was increasingly evident that she would not tolerate pretenses. She was demanding his honesty.

But before he could give it to her, he had to be certain he was being honest with himself. As if he only needed permission to admit fully to his feelings, the pretenses within him fled. His love for her that he'd tried so hard to bury now overflowed from his heart, drowning the logic. He couldn't deny it. "I meant what I said," he whispered.

"You've said a lot of things."

"I said that I love you."

Ericha smiled breathlessly, and a tone of relief bathed her confession. "I love you too, Stefan Heinrich."

Ericha saw Stefan's lips part to draw a deep breath. She wanted to tell him that they were alone and they were in love. And she wanted him to kiss her. The moment she thought it, he bent slowly toward her. The distance between them was awkward as he brought his lips close to hers, kissing her meekly.

Lightning flashed, and thunder cracked in the same instant above them. Their kiss was interrupted by a fearful gasp as Ericha glanced skyward with wide eyes.

"It's all right," Stefan said as the resounding crash dissipated in the distance. Ericha looked away from the sky to meet the comfort in his eyes. He'd moved closer, and his arms were protectively around her.

"I dare say," he said softly, and a hint of a smile touched his lips, "this lodge has seen many thunderstorms. It stands to reason that it will survive one more."

Ericha smiled, but her eyes remained intent, reflecting Stefan's as he gazed at her vividly. Her hand came against his chest as he brought her closer, and she was surprised to feel his heart beating hard and fast when his expression didn't betray it. Ericha's heart raced to meet his as he bent to kiss her again. And with his kiss she almost felt drawn with him to another time. The past absorbed her, and she succumbed to the pleasure of being in his arms, letting his kiss gain fervor.

Stefan drew back briefly to check Ericha's expression. Her innocence warmed him, but with it came a fresh reality. Logic resurfaced harshly, and he shot to his feet. He knew his reasons for being here. He had made a choice, and he was willing to face the consequences. But what of Ericha? While she had an apparent wisdom beyond her years, she was too young and innocent to comprehend the full impact of his circumstances. He had no right to make choices for her.

Stefan took hold of the mantle and gazed down into the flames. He sensed Ericha's distress and searched for the words to console her. How could he explain? Where could he possibly begin? In that moment, he could think of nothing in his life worth holding onto beyond the love of his parents and grandparents. His parents had chosen a life that he wished was open to him. They avoided Horstberg as if it were somehow cursed. Perhaps it was. His grandparents were there for him. But they were incapable of giving him any more than they already gave. Plain and simple, Stefan had little—if anything—to live for. It would be just as easy for him to jump off a cliff as it was to follow his desire to be here with Ericha. There was something almost fatalistic in his willingness to abandon everything he'd been taught—everything he believed in—just to have a few precious moments with her. Stefan didn't believe it was in him to end his own life. He respected life too much, even as tarnished as his seemed to be. But there was a time, not so long ago, when he never would have believed he was capable of feeling what he felt now.

"Are you all right?" Ericha asked gently. He glanced toward her, grateful for the intrusion on his troubling thoughts. It took Stefan a long moment to gather his answer, but he sensed her patience as she waited.

"There is something I need to say, Ericha," he finally managed. "It's difficult to put so many thoughts together into the right words. I hope you will hear me out."

Ericha stood close to him, and when he looked at her, she smiled. Stefan drew the courage he needed to go on. He cleared his throat and looked into the flames. "The circumstances in my life are . . . difficult, Ericha. I will not pretend that I have anything more to offer you than I do." He reached up a hand to touch her face. "But something changed in me the moment I saw you.

I don't understand it. I can't explain it. But I know I want to be here with you. I wish the rest of the world could just go away, and . . ."

Stefan turned and sighed as he came close to feelings he was not ready to bare. He cleared his throat again and tried a different approach. "I am a man of my circumstances, Ericha. The choices I make now are a result of the life I've lived. And while I try to do what's right, it's difficult for me to draw such boundaries anymore. Doing what I believed was right in the past did not always bring the results I had hoped for."

Ericha felt her heart quicken. What was he saying? While he seemed to want to avoid details, she sensed she was hearing deep confessions. Feeling compassion on his behalf, she touched his face in an attempt to offer comfort. She didn't know him well enough to understand the source of his pain, but looking into his eyes, she could almost feel it.

"I love you, Ericha," he said. His voice turned husky. "I would never want to hurt you. What I'm trying to say is that . . . I can't . . . Ericha, you must not expect me to be strong enough to handle this in your best interest."

Ericha penetrated his eyes, attempting to read the thoughts between his words. After a long moment, he turned guiltily away. Did his thoughts warrant shame?

"And what," she asked carefully, "do you feel would be in my best interest?"

Stefan turned abruptly and motioned toward the door. "Walk away, Ericha. Pretend that you never spoke to me, that we were never foolish enough to speak of love and kiss each other as if the world didn't exist. Just leave and never look back," he almost shouted. Then his voice softened sadly. "It would be far better for you if you did."

"And you?" she asked.

"Me?" He chuckled with a bitter edge. "Sometimes I believe my heart is too numb to know the difference."

Ericha absorbed his words, attempting to feel her instincts. She had many unanswered questions concerning this man, but in that moment she knew it didn't matter. She felt certain there was nothing he could tell her that would make her feel any less for him. The weeks she'd spent longing for him only strengthened her resolve. Nothing could be stronger than this instinctive need she felt to be with him. And it was increasingly evident that he needed her, too.

"I can't leave," she stated. "It's raining."

Stefan looked up at her, wondering what she was trying to say. Her expression was unreadable. A moment later she removed her cloak and tossed it to the sofa. "And even if it weren't, I would stay."

"Why?" he felt he had to ask.

"My mother lived a hard life, Stefan. I asked her once what she would do differently if she could do it over, and she told me—with confidence—she would change absolutely nothing. She told me that she had followed her heart, and in spite of the struggles, in spite of the things that were beyond her control, she had no regrets."

Stefan felt his heart quicken at the implication. He knew little of Ericha's background. But he knew her mother had raised an illegitimate child. He yearned to know what kind of love had brought Ericha's parents together. Just to look at her now, he knew it must have been incredible. *She* was incredible. However wrong certain aspects of her parents' relationship might have been, how could Ericha's existence be wrong?

"My mother taught me to follow my heart, Stefan. My heart has led me here, and I will not deny it."

Stefan shook his head in disbelief. Her wisdom and insight were as remarkable as her innocent beauty. "I believe you remind me of my grandmother," he said.

"I hope that's a compliment." She laughed.

"The *highest* compliment," he replied warmly.

Their eyes met again, and the tension descended freshly. Only the crackling of the fire and the beating of the rain broke the silence. Ericha couldn't bring her mind to focus on anything but the desire to be in his arms. Hoping they had come past whatever had interrupted their last embrace, she gingerly reached out to touch him. She was nearly in awe of the rugged feel of his face, where the dark shadow of a beard was beginning to appear. Growing up with only a mother, she found masculine ways fascinating, and she concentrated on the feel of Stefan's skin beneath her fingertips. She eased subtly closer and was relieved to feel his arms come around her. For a long moment he just held her. She felt more than heard him sigh. He brushed his lips over her brow and tightened his embrace, and relief and contentment washed over her. She looked up at him and couldn't hold back her emotion.

Stefan's brow furrowed in concern when he saw tears glistening in her eyes. "What is it?" he asked softly.

Ericha searched for the words to explain. "Growing up as I did," she began and felt certain he knew what she meant, "I never found the opportunity to really care for anyone in my life beyond my mother. When I lost her, I had no one. Karl has been very good to me since I came to Horstberg, but . . . he has his own life. It's just that . . . being with you fills something in me that was always empty before."

Stefan smiled serenely. "I know exactly what you mean." And then he kissed her. Ericha felt his long fingers push into her hair, pressing against the back of her head. Her lips parted eagerly beneath his subtle power, and she wished that it could never end.

They were both breathless when his lips came away. But like a man in the desert without water, Stefan kissed her again, desperately needing to drink of the comfort she offered. He marveled at her eager response, a delicate combination of trust and passion. She could almost make him believe that he was as innocent as she. Never in his life had he felt the things that Ericha made him feel.

When Ericha knew she could bear no more, she lifted her head to gasp for breath. She couldn't hold back a moan of pleasure as his lips claimed her throat. He kissed her cheek, her eyes, her brow, her mouth again. Thunder cracked, and Ericha gasped. Stefan chuckled warmly and held her close.

With a finger at her chin, Ericha felt Stefan's eyes penetrate her again. He seemed to be searching for something. Then he smiled, as if he'd found it. She felt his sigh brush her skin. His fingers came reverently to her face, then moved gingerly over her throat. But his eyes held hers firmly and she wondered where his thoughts were.

Stefan kissed her once again, surprised by her response. He wasn't sure what he'd expected, but it wasn't this. It was difficult to believe that a woman could express so much emotion in a kiss, and betray so much longing by an innocent gesture. He drew back briefly to check himself, wondering where all of this could possibly lead. Ericha looked up at him with so much trust and wonder in her eyes, he could do nothing but kiss her again. For a moment he just held her while his mind tried to balance reason with emotion. Did she know the crossroads they were at? Did she feel the thinning of a delicate boundary that he had once sworn he would never cross?

Thunder sounded again, and she held to him fiercely. It was a simple gesture, but it made him feel of worth, and he eased her closer, attempting to offer comfort. She looked up at him again, and a thousand reasons tumbled through his mind as to why he should not be with her like this. But her expression pleaded for him to kiss her, and Stefan needed no more permission than that.

Stefan's kiss turned urgent, and Ericha felt a whimper of longing escape her. She gasped as he lifted her into his arms. She wondered where he might take her, but he only moved a few steps and went to his knees on the bearskin rug. With little effort, he sat down and draped her legs over his lap.

"Ericha," he whispered, toying idly with her hair as if he'd never seen it before. "You are so beautiful." Ericha felt the adoration in his words and softened against him. She had never considered herself beautiful, but when Stefan said it, she had to believe him.

"I love you," he whispered and kissed her meekly. "I love you, Ericha." The room darkened, and the rain persisted as he held her and kissed her, over and over, as if each time their lips met was a new and different experience to be savored. Was this what she had longed for since that moment he had first kissed her in the forest?

Ericha felt comfort rather than apprehension as they lay close together. She became absorbed with sensations similar to those she'd felt in the haunting quality of the mountain meadow. The hovering storm lost its threatening hold in the face of Stefan's power. She became nearly hypnotized by his touch, his kiss, his overwhelming presence. While his caress subtly implied an intimacy she longed for, she could feel the evidence of his conscious effort to maintain a distinct boundary. In spite of the desire that was fully evident in his affection, his concern for her was readily apparent. Consumed with a longing for him that she barely understood, she doubted she could bring herself to protest him having his way with her completely. And she felt certain he knew that she wouldn't stop him. Still, his respect for her came through brilliantly as he kissed her, touched her, held her, with a relaxed intensity that made her feel that her life had just begun.

Stefan fought to keep his passion from getting out of hand as her every response made him feel more alive than he had ever felt in his adult life. Even without crossing definitive boundaries, he found himself experiencing an exchange of intimacy that he'd never imagined possible. He felt euphorically detached from himself as he fought to fulfill this starving, thirsting need he had for something Ericha possessed that he'd never known before. It was almost frightening how she formlessly reminded him of something that he loved, something that was a part of him, that he'd lost somewhere in his past. And he was certain he'd not been happy since. When he felt he could bear no more without pressing his affection too close to irrevocable boundaries, he forced himself to relax and eased his arms around her.

Ericha marveled at the incredible reality, certain she had found the answers to her life here in his arms. She lost track of time as she basked in perfect contentment, her head against his shoulder while his hands moved idly through her wind-tangled hair. Shifting just enough to look at him, she saw his eyes smile. In making a comparison, she realized that they were usually quite sad. She brought her hand to his face, marveling over the feelings she had experienced with him. Stefan turned his lips into her palm and kissed her. Ericha moved her hand into the thick waves of hair that moved back from his brow, and touched her lips to his.

Thunder sounded ominously overhead. Ericha put her head to his shoulder and pressed her fingers into his arms.

"The storm frightens you," he stated, and she made no response. "You know," he added, lifting her chin to look at her, "my father used to tell me stories when I was frightened. No one can tell stories like my father."

"I don't have a father," she replied.

"Would you like me to tell you a story?" A smile touched one corner of his mouth.

"But you said no one could tell them like him," she teased.

"I could try." His smile grew, and he kissed her.

"Well then," she lay on her side and looked up at him, "you'd best tell me a story."

Stefan leaned on one elbow and put his head into his hand. "All I know are fairy tales—from the Black Forest. That's the only kind my father ever told."

"I love fairy tales," she said, and he smiled.

"Which one do you want to hear?"

"Your favorite."

Stefan's eyes took on a dreamy look as he began. "Once upon a time there was a cottage—in the Black Forest, of course. It was small but quaint, and surrounded by trees. Down a trail from it was a crystal blue pond. And near that was a grassy clearing, perfect for picnics, with a wild berry patch nearby. And the berries were always sweet and juicy."

Ericha watched Stefan closely, fascinated by the expressions in his eyes as he spoke, the flames reflecting off his face.

"Far, far away from this cottage was a castle—tall and magnificent, with high turrets."

"Like Castle Horstberg," she said eagerly, and he seemed surprised.

"Yes," he said easily, "like Castle Horstberg."

"Did a princess live there?" she asked like a child.

"Of course." He chuckled. "What's a fairy tale without a princess?"

Ericha smiled at him, and he went on. "This princess was very beautiful, with long red tresses," he touched her hair, "full of curls. And there was fire in her eyes. But this fiery princess was taken in by the beguiling ways of her evil cousin, who meant to overtake the kingdom. He wanted to marry the princess so that he could move into the castle and undermine the royal family.

"The king and queen were very upset by this, and forbade the princess to see this man again. But the queen knew the princess well, and she was certain that her daughter was going to run away with the evil cousin. She told the king, and he thought very hard what to do. He was certain that not only was his daughter's happiness at stake, but that of the entire kingdom as well."

Stefan paused to smile at Ericha, who was listening attentively, hardly aware of the storm hovering outside.

"The king was faced with a difficult decision, and it was ironic that he called in the stableboy to assist him. He was tall and thin, with hair like sunshine." Stefan smirked endearingly. "I added that part myself."

Ericha smiled in response, and he continued, "And though he had worked in the stables as long as he could remember, he had always wanted more. When the king offered him a high position in the kingdom if he could kidnap the princess, take her away from the kingdom, and get her to marry him, the stableboy was stunned. He was skeptical that he could do it, but he knew how important it was, and the offer was very tempting.

"But above that, the stableboy knew something that nobody else knew. He had kept the secret in his heart for many years. He loved this princess. He loved her more than anything, and had always wanted to marry her. But he was just a stableboy.

"Now," Stefan said, looking directly at Ericha, "you have to finish the story."

"Did your father always have you finish the story?"

"Of course," he replied. "That's how one learns to tell them."

"Did he tell you that?"

"Of course. So, go on—finish it."

"The stableboy took the princess to the cottage in the Black Forest. And when she realized that he loved her, she forgot about that other man, and the kingdom was saved and they lived happily ever after."

Stefan laughed. "You missed a few details. But that's not too bad."

"Maybe next time I'll do better," she said, but a sadness returned to Stefan's eyes that almost frightened her.

"My mother told me stories," she said, wanting to ignore his expression. "Not often, really. But when she did, they were always sad."

"Didn't they end with happily ever after?" he asked.

"Oh, yes. But she didn't mean it. She didn't believe in ever after. She never said that, but I could tell."

"Why not?" he asked.

"I suppose because she spent her life alone. Everyone knew she had never been married, and I'm certain she faced the brunt of that. I know I did. But I don't think that really bothered her."

"Did it bother you?" he asked.

"No," she said easily, "why should it? It wasn't my fault that my father . . ." She trailed off as her thoughts went briefly to the drawing she'd found earlier today. "Well, I think my mother was just sad, because she was alone."

"What happened to your father?" Stefan asked with compassion.

"I don't know," she said. "Mother never told me. In fact, she never talked about him at all. As far as I know, he just left her. But there must have been more to it than that. She was never bitter—just lonely."

Stefan felt almost sick from her words, a near foreboding

that getting involved with Ericha could somehow cause history to repeat itself.

"Is something the matter?" she asked, noticing the anxious look in his eyes.

"No," he lied, determined to enjoy this time with her while it lasted. There was no telling what tomorrow might bring.

"Are you certain?"

"It's getting late." He rolled onto his back and looked toward the ceiling. "If it doesn't stop raining soon, Karl will be very worried about you."

"Stefan," she moved to lean across his chest, "why do I sense that you are so . . . unhappy, so much of the time?"

"I don't want to talk about that right now," he said soberly. "Perhaps another time. For now, I only wish that it could rain forever, and you and I would never have to leave here and face the realities of life."

Ericha felt something ominous from his words, but she chose to ignore such concerns as she sensed he was. They could not deny the feelings behind their being together now. There was no good in letting reality ruin these moments. She sensed, as she had from the start, that there was something Stefan hadn't told her. But right now she didn't want to know, and she was relieved when he changed the subject.

"Are you hungry?" he asked.

"I don't know," she admitted. "I hadn't thought about it."

Stefan smiled, and he stood up without warning. "Let's see what we can dig up, shall we?" he asked, holding out a hand for her. "I'm not much for cooking, but I do keep enough on hand up here that I won't starve to death."

Ericha took his hand and came to her feet. He embraced her quickly, then led her to the other end of the common room where a little table and two chairs were situated near a small kitchen.

"Have a seat," he said while lighting a lamp. "I'll be right back."

Within minutes, Stefan had laid out a round of dark bread, cheese, jerked meat, and freshly washed apples. While Ericha was slicing an apple, he set two wine glasses on the table. She watched as he opened a bottle of red wine with a corkscrew, sat across from her, and poured.

"We must bless it," she said. He nodded toward her and listened in awe as she offered a brief, sincere prayer over their meal. He marveled at her humble faith, and his love for her blossomed with admiration. Everything about her seemed to remind him of the ideals he'd once had, the life he'd once loved. It was difficult for him to be convinced that being with her was wrong. But deep in his heart he knew it was.

Wanting to know everything about her, Stefan drilled her with questions as they ate. She told him details of her life before she'd come to Horstberg. His mind filled with vivid images of the tiny cottage where she'd grown up with no friends or relations beyond her mother. He felt somewhat relieved to learn that she had caught the attention of more than one young man in the past. Though she admitted the incidents had been brief and shallow.

"Why?" he asked, wishing he might have found Ericha Lokberg in his youth, with no past behind him.

Ericha's eyes turned brittle just before she looked away. "Good people do not want their sons to marry an illegitimate woman."

Stefan winced as he almost literally felt the pain behind her statement.

"But," she added brightly, "I have much to be thankful for. And I have been given a fresh start. The people of Horstberg don't know the truth about me."

"*I* know," he said.

Ericha squeezed his hand across the table. "And you love me in spite of it."

"Perhaps it makes me love you more," he admitted. "Isn't a person made of their life's experience?"

"No," she replied firmly, "a person is what they make of their life's experience."

Once again, Stefan found himself stunned into silence by her wisdom. Wanting to alleviate the tension, he urged the conversation back to her childhood. His heart ached for her as she innocently painted a picture of her separation from the outside world, being raised with only her mother's name. He thought of Johanna's constant harping about the servants, and always needing new gowns and jewels, while Ericha described the sacrifices her mother had made to keep food on the table. And he felt near tears as she told of her mother's death and Ericha's need to sell nearly everything she owned to make the journey to Horstberg so that she wouldn't be alone.

"Your sacrifices have been greatly appreciated, my love, I can assure you."

"I don't understand," she admitted, taking a slow sip of wine as if it were a rare indulgence.

"You have humbled me, Ericha."

She laughed softly. "You don't strike me as the kind of man who would be anything but humble."

Stefan shook his head methodically. "I've tried to be, but I can see now that I've had no comprehension."

Ericha wanted to press him on that, but she had a feeling he would avoid talking about himself. She only prayed inwardly that a day would come when he would open up to her. For the moment, she persisted with her story. "I must admit I was hesitant to come to Horstberg. But I had nowhere else to go." She smiled vibrantly. "I'm happy to say that I've enjoyed being here. I couldn't ask for more."

"Karl has treated you well, then?"

"Oh, yes," she said adamantly. "But it's much more than that." Ericha reached across the table and pressed a hand to his face. "I have found you."

Stefan chuckled tensely. "It is Horstberg that benefits far more from your presence here."

Ericha glanced away timidly, and then she caught something in his eyes that urged her to ask *him* a question. "You told me once that you didn't like Horstberg. Why?"

Stefan cradled his wine glass in both hands and stared into the deep red liquid. "There is little in Horstberg that claims my heart," he stated. Then his eyes shifted to her. "But now that you're here . . ."

Ericha smiled and lifted her glass toward him. "To Horstberg," she said. "She has brought us together. May she thrive and prosper."

Stefan wished he could explain to her this sudden urge he had to just crumble in her arms and cry. Instead he just lifted his glass and touched it to hers. "To Horstberg," he echoed. He took a long sip and set down his glass.

"Do you think it's possible," she asked, "for something inanimate to speak of the past?" He looked puzzled, so she clarified. "The meadow where my mother and father used to meet seemed to speak to me of the past. And I felt that way when I saw Castle Horstberg. My mother had described it so well that I felt like I had seen it before. I have a wooden box with no key that seems to speak to me of the past."

"What does it tell you?" he asked, intrigued.

"Nothing. At least nothing that I could put into words. It's more a feeling." Ericha glanced about the lodge and added, "You say this place has been in your family for generations?"

"Yes."

"Do these walls speak to you?"

"You already asked me that."

"So I'm asking again. Do they?"

Stefan chuckled. "No." She looked at him dubiously, and he added, "But my grandmother has told me things about this lodge that make it very dear to me. I can sometimes sit here alone and almost imagine the happenings that she's told me about."

"Like what?" she asked, leaning toward him.

"Don't you think you could get tired of my telling you stories?"

"Never." She smiled, touching his face with adoration.

Stefan looked at her intently and came to his feet. "Come here." He held out his hand for her. She took it and stood. Stefan kissed her quickly, then pulled her up into his arms and moved toward the stairs.

"Where are we going?" She laughed.

"I want to show you something" was all he said as he carried her up the stairs, kicked open a door, and set her down near a big brass bed. Ericha felt something almost haunting about the room.

"Look." Stefan came to stand near a gabled window with a cushioned seat in it. She stepped beside him and looked out in the direction he was pointing.

"See there," he said.

"What?" she laughed.

"Well," he said, "it is dark, I know, but right down there is a chopping block. I want you to sit right here," he placed his hands on her shoulders to seat her, "and look at that chopping block. I'm going to tell you a story."

She smiled up at him, but his expression was sober as he said, "Don't look at me. Look out the window. Can you see the stable from here?"

"I think so."

"Good. But for now, look at the chopping block."

"I am."

"Once upon a time, there was a beautiful young woman whose pride and joy was a fiery stallion. One night in a blizzard, he broke down his stall, and she followed him up the mountain, through a hidden crevice in a plateau ridge. She slipped and fell, hurting her ankle badly, certain she was going to freeze to death in the snow."

Not recalling the familiarity of a story she'd heard once before, Ericha glanced up at Stefan, sensing something different in his tone than that of the previous story. He pointed to the window and she turned her attention back, trying to imagine this chopping block that she could barely see.

"There was a man who had lived alone in a hidden lodge for three years. He'd been wrongly accused of a crime, and it was his only choice above prison. He heard the woman scream and rescued her. He took her to his lodge, saved her life, and then he didn't know what to do with her. He couldn't take her home. They were snowed in together for the rest of the winter. He'd been alone for so long that he didn't know how to react to her, and he was often sharp with her for no reason.

"But there was a day," Stefan squatted down beside Ericha and took her hand, "when she sat in the window seat, watching him below as he chopped wood."

The intensity in Stefan's voice, combined with her surroundings, made Ericha's heart beat quickly. "He glanced up at her, looking very stern. But she smiled at him and he smiled back. Many weeks later he admitted at last that he loved her. They exchanged vows privately and their commitment was deep, but . . ." Stefan paused and drew a deep breath, attempting to emphasize a point, "They couldn't be together, Ericha, because he was a prisoner of his circumstances."

Stefan stopped abruptly, and Ericha turned to him, sensing deep emotion. She felt certain he was trying to say something personal.

"Ericha," he whispered and touched her face, "I was there when my grandfather died. I heard him say to my grandmother, 'I thought that God sent me to save your life, but I know that God sent you to save mine.'

"You know, Ericha, my grandmother is the greatest lady I have ever known. I love and admire her more than any one person. She's the one who told me that story. When she left the mountain, she was pregnant with his child, not knowing for certain if he'd come for her."

"Did he?" she asked, even though the answer was obvious.

"Yes."

"And the baby?" she asked.

"My uncle."

"Your grandfather must have found a way to escape his circumstances," she stated.

Ericha felt more than saw Stefan's eyes widen in wonder. She sensed a rush of emotion in his aura, but he said nothing.

"Why are you telling me all of this?" she asked.

Stefan glanced down. "That is what these walls say to me."

Ericha rubbed her arms to soothe the tingle of goose-bumps,

and then she kissed Stefan quickly, wanting more than anything to have the opportunity to hear more of his stories, to know his grandmother, his uncle—to be a part of his life.

She moved into his arms. His kiss spoke of his love for her, and Ericha savored it. She easily became lost in his affection that had so quickly become familiar and secure. He urged her to the bed and lay close beside her, kissing her with more fervor than he'd expressed earlier. She felt the evidence of his boundaries weakening, but once again he made a conscious effort to restrain himself and relax, just holding her close. Ericha relished in his nearness, feeling perfectly and peaceably content for these priceless moments.

"Stefan," Ericha whispered, running her fingers idly over his arm.

"Yes, my love," he replied softly.

"Nothing's ever going to be the same again, for either of us."

"Nothing has been the same since the first moment I looked into your eyes," he said. Ericha tightened her embrace and fell asleep in his arms.

Stefan had no trouble staying awake as he held Ericha close to him. He was so amazed by the power behind what they had shared in these hours together. Never had he dreamed that just being with a woman could be so ethereal, that such innocent affection could make him feel so complete. He tried to hold back the emotion. But when he was absolutely certain that Ericha slept, Stefan cried.

Long after his emotion settled into a calm peace, Stefan held her close to him, wondering what his life might be like now if he hadn't been such a fool. Forcing his mind from regret, he relished her closeness and wished only that it could last forever.

Ericha awoke in the darkness as Stefan said close to her ear, "The storm is over. I must take you home."

Ericha felt a distinct sadness as they moved silently together through the plateau ridge and left the mountain lodge behind.

"I think this meadow is haunted," she said quite seriously as he helped her mount again, and she noted the moon showing occasionally from behind swiftly moving clouds.

"Really?" He chuckled slightly.

"Really," she stated.

As Stefan mounted behind her, she realized she was sitting on his horse, and Pegasus's reins were tied to the saddle. Seeming to sense her question, he said, "You came without a saddle. It's a long ride home, and you're tired."

His reasons were perfectly logical, but Ericha believed it was more an excuse to prolong being close as he slipped one arm around her waist and took the reins in the other. The air was cool as they moved into the forest, but Ericha felt warmed by his nearness and relaxed against his sturdy frame.

Stefan rode into the stable and helped her dismount. He unbridled Pegasus and secured him in his stall. Then he walked Ericha partially through the garden, where he left her with one last fervent kiss.

"I love you, Ericha," he whispered against her face. "Whatever happens, you must remember that."

"I will," she whispered, but he was gone.

Chapter Four
THE DUKE OF HORSTBERG

Ericha was glad to find the door unlocked, and she quietly slipped inside. She was nearly to the stairs when Karl stepped into the hall to stop her. She'd never seen him looking so stern, and didn't know how to react.

"Where have you been?" he asked. "It's nearly two in the morning."

Ericha drew back her shoulders, deciding she could handle this. "I was on the mountain when the storm worsened. I knew I couldn't make it home, so I found shelter."

"Shelter?" he asked dubiously. She made no reply, and he stated, "You were with Stefan."

"What is it that you have against him?" she asked sharply.

"I don't have anything against him. He's my best friend."

"Are you saying that I'm not good enough for him?"

"Don't be ridiculous," Karl said with a humorless chuckle. Then his eyes narrowed as he perceived her ignorance. He had to ask, "Just what do you know about him?"

"I know that I love him," she said, certain that nothing else mattered.

While Karl had sensed some kind of intrigue between Stefan and Ericha, he had never stopped to consider that she wouldn't know the obvious. And now it was apparent that he should have taken the time long ago to talk to her about it. He blew out a regretful sigh as he stuffed his hands into his pockets and looked toward the ceiling.

"What's wrong?" she demanded.

"I can't believe he didn't tell you."

"Tell me what?" she insisted as the mysteries surrounding Stefan began to surface with dread.

"But then," Karl chuckled tensely, "I assumed you knew. He probably did too."

"What are you getting at?" she asked warily, feeling her palms begin to sweat.

"Ericha," he looked at her pointedly, and she could see compassion in his eyes, "he's married."

Ericha leaned against the wall, consumed with a sudden weakness. Karl's expression told her this was no joke. "Are you sure?" she asked feebly, not willing to believe it. Of all the possibilities that had flashed through her mind concerning his clandestine attitude, she'd simply never considered *this*.

"Sure?" Karl echoed. "I've known him my entire life. I was the best man, for heaven's sake. Of course I'm sure."

Ericha said nothing, and he added, "I'm sorry. I thought you knew." Numbly she walked toward the stairs.

Hoping to reassure himself that he'd done the right thing, Karl added, "Better that you find out now—before it's too late."

It's already too late, she thought, moving woodenly toward her room. The full impact struck her as she closed the door and leaned against it. Job nuzzled against her in greeting, but she ignored him. A painful knot tightened somewhere between her heart and her stomach. Dazed, she lit a lamp and sat down, fearing her knees would buckle otherwise. Slowly, almost fearfully, she turned to look in the mirror at a woman who had been held and kissed by someone else's husband. Then she curled up on the bed and cried.

For the first time ever, Karl dreaded seeing Stefan at the pub. He both wanted to know what was going on and wished he could remain forever ignorant. Despite how it might hurt Ericha, he couldn't help hoping that she was simply caught up with intrigue, and perhaps Stefan was just humoring her a little. Though it didn't fit with Stefan's character, neither did getting involved with another woman.

"Anybody home?" Stefan asked, startling Karl from his thoughts.

Karl looked up to see that Stefan had arrived without his noticing and was seated across the table. "No, I was out actually," he replied dryly.

"Something wrong?" Stefan asked, taking a long swallow of his beer.

Karl met Stefan's eyes and knew there was no point in pretenses. He wasn't about to let his assumptions come between them.

"You were with Ericha last night," he said quietly. Stefan looked guiltily away. "I thought so," Karl added. "Why?"

"What do you mean, *why?*" Stefan asked with a familiar arrogance that Karl usually found endearing.

"Why were you with her?" he asked with an edge to his voice.

Stefan was silent a moment, wondering what to say. But Karl's expression made it clear that he expected an answer. "I came across her in the lower meadow. It was storming. I knew she wouldn't make it home without nearly freezing to death, so I took her to the lodge."

The explanation rang true with what Ericha had told him, and Karl wondered if he was making something out of nothing. But he recalled Ericha saying that she loved Stefan. Karl felt responsible for Ericha, and he had to know what he was dealing with.

"It seems my cousin has taken a liking to you," Karl said, and Stefan wondered how much Ericha had told him.

"She's a wonderful woman," Stefan replied, wishing his voice hadn't betrayed his admiration so blatantly.

"But she had no idea you were married," Karl added.

Stefan's eyes widened, and a knot gathered in his throat. He opened his mouth to speak, but nothing came out. His mind quickly filed through their encounters, their conversations. Was it possible that Ericha hadn't known? He had to remind himself to breathe when pain began to constrict his chest. He felt sick. When he finally found his voice, it came in a raspy whisper. "Everyone in this whole blasted country knows I'm married!"

"They do now," Karl stated. While Stefan's obvious surprise was somewhat of a comfort to Karl, the intensity of his reaction prickled Karl's nerves all the more.

"You told her." Stefan leaned back and sighed, wishing his stomach would stop smoldering.

"*You* didn't tell her. She had a right to know."

"I assumed she knew," Stefan said, wishing that made a difference. He wondered what Ericha was thinking of him, now that she knew the truth.

"It was an innocent mistake. She'll get over it. No harm done." Karl took a long drink, assuming that should drop the conversation. But Stefan turned away with a guilty sigh. The gesture was so out of character that something about it stabbed at Karl.

"Stefan," Karl drawled, his voice raspy, "don't tell me you . . ." He couldn't bring himself to say it, but he felt sure Stefan knew what he meant. Silence hung tensely. Stefan didn't answer. He wouldn't even look at him. His normally confident manner was completely absent.

"Stefan?" Karl repeated.

Stefan finally gathered the courage to look his friend in the eye. Karl leaned across the table and whispered in astonishment, "You took my cousin to bed?"

"No, I did not!" Stefan retorted. "I was tempted, but I can assure you that what we shared came nowhere near to that point."

Karl's eyes narrowed. In spite of his relief, this was still deeply troubling. "What do you mean by '*what we shared?*'"

Stefan said nothing, but his expression betrayed the truth— that his behavior with Ericha had been out of line and he knew it.

"So you were . . . what?" Karl continued, "Only partially

intimate and not completely intimate?" Stefan's continued silence verified the truth. Karl glanced around to make certain they weren't being overheard before adding tersely, "You arrogant bastard!"

Reminding himself of the conviction that had led to his indiscretions, Stefan met the accusation head on. He couldn't deny what he'd done, but the feelings that had compelled him then gave him strength now.

"If you were anyone but my best friend," Karl said, "I would beat the hell out of you."

"I probably deserve it," Stefan admitted.

"She's not even eighteen!" Karl insisted.

"I know."

"I can't believe you'd—"

"Don't underestimate her," Stefan defended. "She's not a child. In truth, she has a wisdom and maturity that Johanna could not even—"

"Oh," Karl interrupted sarcastically, "and I'm sure you had the opportunity to compare them in many respects."

Stefan drew a deep breath to control his temper. "If you were anyone but my best friend," he said intently, "I'd beat the hell out of you for that."

Karl made no response. He could see the power coming through in Stefan's eyes, and knew he would not be crossed.

"You've known me all my life," Stefan continued. "If you stop to think about it, you will know there could only be one reason that I would do such a thing. I'm not saying that makes my behavior with her right," he added, "but don't go assuming it was something sordid and cheap." Stefan leaned further across the table, and Karl couldn't recall ever seeing him so intense. "I love Ericha," he snarled like some great lion defending his pride. "And she will never—*ever*—be in the same category as Johanna." Stefan took a quick swallow of his beer and slammed the tankard down on the table. "And don't forget it."

Stefan left Karl sitting alone, wondering what he'd done to deserve getting caught in the middle of this. He had to give some credit to what Stefan had said. He was right. Ericha seemed much older than she really was. Surely she could handle this. And Karl knew as well as anyone that Stefan Heinrich was a man of integrity. Karl, of all people, knew how miserable Stefan's life had been. Yet what could possibly be done about it?

Karl paid for the drinks and left the pub, deciding he just wasn't going to get involved. He would be there for Ericha if she needed him. And he would not allow this to come between his friendship with Stefan. The rest was Stefan's problem.

A blessed numbness gradually blanketed Ericha's hurt and anger through a sleepless night and into the following day. She couldn't believe Stefan was married, but she had to admit that it made sense. She understood now Stefan's mysterious actions and the things he'd said that seemed to apologize for his circumstances.

Ericha's emotions were in turmoil as she contemplated seeing Stefan again. She wanted him to take her in his arms and soothe this hurt away, and at the same time to punish him somehow for all this pain she was feeling.

With a heavy heart, she waited for him in the forest as the sun went down. She had no reason to believe Stefan would even come here tonight, only the hope that he would want to see her, and this was the most obvious possibility. Her emotions swept high as she sat contemplating their experience in the mountain lodge. How could she be so hurt and elated at the same time? The confusion surfaced ominously when Stefan rode toward her and dismounted.

Stefan had hoped she would be here, and he'd come prepared to apologize. She had a right to know where he stood. He only wished with all his heart that she had known before. Though he had assumed Ericha was aware of his circumstances, he blamed himself for not having the insight to tell her. Before he had a chance to speak, she gave him a greeting he felt sure he deserved.

"You arrogant bastard!" she spat, sending her hand across his face to enunciate it. Stefan wondered if the title would become permanent. "Who do you think you are?" she went on. "I'm not some easy tramp for you to play with on the side. You have no right to even be with me, and I—"

"Ericha!" he grabbed her wrists and shook her slightly to stop her ranting. "Listen to me."

"There is nothing you can say that will make any difference."

"You're right," he said with force, "but I'm going to say it anyway." He paused, and she sensed a change in his demeanor. "No," he let go of her, "I'm not going to say it. I'm not going to apologize, and I'm not going to try and justify myself. You're absolutely right, Ericha. I *am* an arrogant bastard. And I had no right to even look at you twice. But I did. And you have every reason in the world to be angry with me."

"I'm not angry with you," she shouted. "I'm just angry!"

"You *should* be angry with me," he said in a quiet voice that calmed her. "I assumed you knew. It's as simple as that. In my heart I believed that you were aware of what you were stepping into. But I blame myself for not making it clear."

Suddenly weak, Ericha moved away and sat on the fallen tree. There was so much she wanted to ask him, but her thoughts were spinning so fast she didn't know where to begin. She cursed her heart for the way it quickened as he walked toward her. Saying nothing, he knelt before her, taking both her hands into his, squeezing them with desperation. She could feel stark adoration in the way he pressed his lips to her hands. The gesture alone radiated a sense of humility and regret. Ericha's confusion slipped away as she pressed her hands into his hair. Taking hold of her, Stefan buried his face into the folds of her dress, like a child seeking comfort.

"Stefan," she murmured. He responded by nuzzling closer. "It would not have made any difference."

"I don't understand."

"Knowing you're married does not change the way I feel about you. And knowing it yesterday would not have kept me from following my heart."

Stefan was grateful for the darkness when emotion overtook him so strongly he couldn't speak. Instead he pressed his hands to her back, hoping she knew how much he loved her.

Ericha lost track of the time as her thoughts gradually came together with some order. While she hesitated to break the serenity between them, there were things she needed to know.

"How long have you been married?" she asked.

Stefan almost winced from the question, but he knew she had a right to know. "About five years," he stated.

"Do you love her?"

While Stefan gathered the courage to answer, he had to admit he'd never told anyone the bare truth of his circumstances. "I thought I loved her once."

Ericha stroked his face gently, wanting to dispel the sadness in his voice. "And now?" she asked.

Stefan had no trouble admitting, "I don't love her, Ericha. I don't even *like* her. She is nothing like you. She doesn't resemble you in appearance or character. You are everything she is not. And you are everything I love. Our relationship consists of talk over the dinner table—and even that is filled with contempt."

Stefan lifted his head, wishing he could see more than the shadow of her face. "You must believe me, Ericha, when I say I want to be with you. But I am torn. The scales tell me I have no choice."

"Do you have children?" she asked.

"No," he answered, his tone bitter. "It's not possible for me to . . ."

"What makes you so sure it's you?" she asked, then wondered from his silence if she was being too invasive.

"It's just not possible," he repeated firmly.

Following a lengthy silence, his voice softened, and he laid his head back into her lap. "I should apologize for what happened, Ericha. But I can't. How could I possibly regret even a moment of being with you when you are the most incredible thing that's ever happened to me? Oh, Ericha," he sighed and pulled her closer, wondering if fate would ever cease to torment him.

"Leave her, Stefan," she whispered as if the trees might overhear. "We'll go far away from here and start a new life—together."

Stefan was caught so off guard by her plea that it took him several moments to digest the horrible irony. Unable to find an answer that wasn't heart-breaking, he sat beside her on the fallen tree and pulled her close. He could never expect her to understand how difficult this was for him. "Oh, my love." Stefan pressed his lips into her hair. "If only it could be so easy. If only I could tell you how many times I have wished for just that. If it were possible, I would do it without a second thought."

"Isn't the scandal of divorce worth the—"

"Shh," he whispered, pressing his fingers to her lips. "I would gladly take the scandal. But this is so much deeper and bigger than that. I would give you anything you asked of me, if it were in my power to do so. But this is not within my power, Ericha. It would affect too many lives. You must not ask me."

Ericha felt a power she could never explain coming through the quiet solemnity of his voice. Though everything inside of her protested, the finality of his words put her to silence.

Ericha had felt despair at her mother's death. And the reality sinking into her now was a close comparison. "There is no future for us then, beyond this." It was not a question.

Stefan swallowed hard and pulled her closer. As a new perspective came to light in his mind, he knew it would not be right to ever expect to hold her this way again. Encouraging her to be a part of his life would only prevent her from finding any kind of a normal life without him. Though it tore him to pieces, he knew it was far better to end their relationship now.

"Ericha," he murmured, "what I have done was selfish and completely unfair to you. And what I am about to do is the only possibility of rectifying it. I pray that one day you will be able to forgive me on both counts."

Ericha drew back, wishing she could see his expression. "What are you saying?"

"I will not expect you to be a part of my life, Ericha. I have nothing more to give you."

"What you have given me is—"

Stefan interrupted her protest. "You are a wise and beautiful woman, Ericha. Find a man who can be there for you always."

"I don't want anyone but you," she protested.

"Well, you can't have me!" Stefan shot to his feet. "I am a prisoner of my circumstances."

"Then find a way to escape your circumstances!" she demanded, standing to face him.

"For me there is no escape," he said.

In the ensuing silence, it occurred to Stefan that perhaps she was not aware of his circumstances. If she hadn't known of his marriage, it was possible she had no idea what he was talking about. He wondered if he should tell her but realized it made no difference. He felt certain she would find out eventually, and with any luck, it would only make her hate him. If she could learn to hate him, perhaps she could get beyond what he'd done to her life.

"And that's it," Ericha stated when she could think of no further argument.

"I have no choice," he said with a cold edge.

Her despair deepened. "So this is good-bye." She couldn't help the bitter tone.

"I can't expect you to be a part of my life, Ericha. I have nothing to give you." He nearly hated himself for saying it. Did she have any idea how it hurt him to let her go? She represented everything he wanted but couldn't have. He had freely taken her love and affection—something he wasn't entitled to—but he'd never dreamed the consequences would burn so deep, and so soon. "Forget about me," he insisted. "Find someone who can give you his name."

Ericha bowed her head in defeat, wondering how she would ever deal with these emotions. Stefan reached up to touch her, and she pressed her face into his hand, wanting to memorize everything about him. She eased into his arms and held him tightly, desperately trying to think of a reason to counter his decision. He pressed his lips over hers. The kiss was brief but harsh with reality. And the reality deepened as he stepped back, putting distance between them.

"Will you be all right?" he asked tenderly.

"Somehow," Ericha stated, lifting her chin abruptly.

Fighting the urge to throw herself at his feet and resort to petty begging, Ericha walked away and mounted Pegasus in the darkness. "I love you, Stefan Heinrich," she said and left him standing alone in the forest.

Ericha wanted to cry herself to sleep, but tears would not come to release her pain. She longed for her mother's comfort but resigned herself to seek advice by trying to assess what Kathe Lokberg would have done if this had happened to her. And then she realized that perhaps it had—at least to some extent.

Ericha had certainly wondered what might have happened to her father. But she wondered now more than ever if perhaps he had been married. Had their meetings been secret? Was that why Kathe had left Horstberg to raise her illegitimate child? She couldn't imagine her mother being the type of woman to get involved with a married man, but then, Ericha would have never imagined it of herself, either.

The questions struck a new emotion, but somehow they gave her the courage to know that she could face whatever her mother had. By morning she resigned herself to forget Stefan Heinrich. But just as with her mother, Ericha hadn't predicted the impression this man had left on her heart.

Days passed into weeks. Ericha saw no sign of Stefan, but her thoughts were absorbed with the memories. It became an unwilling habit to stand at the window and watch Karl ride away each day, knowing that he would see Stefan at the pub. She was tempted more than once to follow him, but she knew there was no point.

On a day when she didn't feel well, Ericha felt prone to stay in bed, perhaps looking for a reason to ignore the world. When

Karl inquired repeatedly what was wrong, Ericha tried to evade the question, embarrassed to admit that the problem was of a feminine nature. She was surprised when he sat quietly on the edge of the bed and took her hand into his.

"Ericha," he said gently, "I want you to be honest with me." He drew a deep breath and looked directly at her. "You aren't pregnant, are you?"

Ericha gasped in astonishment. "What makes you think I would be pregnant?" she asked.

"I know you were alone with Stefan and—"

"Nothing happened in that regard," she said indignantly, "I can assure you."

Karl sighed with obvious relief. He chided himself inwardly for doubting that Stefan had told him the truth. "Forgive me," he said. "I just had to be sure."

Ericha became distant for a moment while the memories felt real. Then she turned to Karl, stating abruptly, "No, I'm not pregnant. Quite the opposite, in truth."

Karl apparently knew what she meant, and he didn't seem embarrassed. She was relieved when he left her alone with her emotions. Her thoughts turned to Stefan, and time did not turn them away. Mulling repeatedly over their conversations, new questions rose up to haunt her. While she had no question concerning the validity of his feelings for her, there were things that didn't quite make sense. He had told her that a divorce would affect too many lives. She had assumed he meant children. But then she recalled that earlier he had admitted there were no children. Remembering how adamant he was concerning his circumstances, Ericha began to wonder what kind of life he lived. It almost frightened her to realize how very little she knew about him. While a part of her wanted to probe Karl with questions about Stefan, if only to ease her curiosity, something stronger within her heart didn't want to know the details of his life. Perhaps if she didn't know, it would be easier to let go of these feelings.

Frustrated by questions she couldn't answer, Ericha turned her mind to the happiness she had found with Stefan—however brief. In her musings, she often recalled the stories he had told her in the lodge. Somehow she related to them, and she liked imagining herself a part of them.

Ericha would often look at the picture of her father and wonder what life might have been like if he had been married to her mother. But the thought only provoked further turmoil, and she would end up turning it to face the wall. She liked seeing it there but found it difficult to look at the face.

Feeling little ambition, Ericha mostly remained at home, tatting or working in the garden. But she woke up one morning feeling slightly better than she had in quite some time. With a desire to go out, she first opted to go riding. But realizing it was market day, she decided that buying something new for herself would be just what she needed to perk up.

Approaching the market square, two officers of the Guard passed by. She quickly became aware that they were taking notice of her. Though she gave no response to their subtle flirtations, she couldn't help noticing that one especially was rather handsome. And she couldn't deny the appeal of their uniforms. The incident gave her hope that perhaps she *could* forget Stefan— with time. Surely there were many handsome, eligible men in Horstberg.

As Ericha worked herself back into the old habits of riding regularly and going into town on market day, she found it easier to avoid thinking of Stefan. She began making acquaintances in town and through the neighborhood, and even found a vague interest in a young man who was a blacksmith. He took her to lunch at an inn a couple of times, and she enjoyed their conversations. But in her heart there was no comparison to the feelings she was trying so hard to bury. And in the dark of night, when there were no distractions, Ericha knew she could never love any man the way she loved Stefan. She knew her involvement with him had been impetuous. But that didn't make her love him any less.

On a particularly warm day, Ericha prepared to go into town soon after breakfast.

"Going out?" Karl asked.

"I have business with Frieda," she informed him. "She wants to discuss the possibility of some new lace patterns for a particular . . . Oh, that's not important. After that, I'm . . ."

Karl grinned when she hesitated. "Lunch with your blacksmith friend, eh?"

"Yes, actually," she said without apologizing.

"You haven't even told me his name," Karl said.

"You know, Karl, you don't have to personally make up for my not having a father."

"I just asked what his name is." Karl chuckled and surprised her with a firm embrace. "Someone's got to look out for you," he added. The severity of his tone made Ericha wonder if he'd been concerned about her. She would have liked to tell him everything was all right, but she couldn't bring herself to lie.

Smiling in gratitude for his care, Ericha said simply, "His name is Kurt. And we're just friends."

"Friends are nice," he said.

"I'm not certain when I'll be back," she added on her way out. "I might make a day of it."

"Have a good time," he called on his way into the library to go over some plans for a custom project he was working on. Some time later when he heard the door slam and looked at the clock, he realized it wasn't even noon yet.

"Ericha?" he called, moving into the hall. "Is that you?"

Only the slamming of her bedroom door responded. Karl took a deep breath and hurried up the stairs. He'd tried for the most part to mind his business and let her live her life. But he knew she was struggling, and this was just too blatant to ignore.

"Ericha," he knocked lightly on the door.

"What?" she called.

"May I come in?"

Ericha wiped away the tears and tried to compose herself. Knowing he was just concerned, she couldn't tell him to go away. And in truth, she needed him. He was the only friend she had. Throwing the door open wide, Ericha motioned him into the room.

"Are you all right?" Karl asked, stepping over the dog that was settling himself back down on the rug.

Ericha shook her head, afraid to speak for fear of crying. She eagerly accepted Karl's brotherly embrace. When he urged her head to his shoulder and gently stroked her hair, Ericha wondered if this was how it might be to have a father. His silent comfort squelched her pride and inhibitions, and she cried without restraint.

When she finally calmed down, Ericha eased back to look at him, chuckling with embarrassment. "I'm sorry, I just . . ."

"It's all right." He smiled and wiped at her tears with his fingers. "Do you want to tell me what's got you so upset?" When she said nothing, he asked, "Is it Stefan?"

Ericha almost winced just to hear his name spoken aloud. "Yes," she answered. "I mean . . . no! I mean . . . I've not seen him since . . . well, I'm struggling with my feelings for . . . Stefan." She closed her eyes briefly. It felt good just to let his name pass through her lips. Reminding herself of the present, she clarified. "This has nothing to do with him."

"Kurt?" he guessed, and Ericha nodded.

She sat on the edge of the bed and fidgeted with her hands, wondering where to start. "He doesn't want to see me again." She got right to the point.

Ericha sensed Karl's surprise as he sat down but remained on the edge of the chair, giving her his full attention.

"We've . . . talked quite a bit," she said. "I like him, but . . . I knew it would never come to anything. But still . . ." Ericha bit her lip and forged ahead. "The last time I saw him, he asked me about my parents. I told him."

Karl sighed and leaned back. He could see now where this was headed, and it made him angry.

"I'm not ashamed of my situation, Karl." She looked at him directly. "But maybe I should be. He just told me straight out. Knowing what he knew, he would not be seeing me again."

Ericha stood up and began to pace. "I didn't want to marry him. But even if I had, apparently it would not have made a difference."

"It's not necessary for you to tell others the situation, Ericha. It's nobody's business."

"I know that," she insisted. "And maybe I shouldn't have said anything. But it doesn't take a lot of brains to figure it out. My mother is your father's sister. And I am a Lokberg."

Ericha sat down again. "It doesn't matter anyway. If someone is shallow enough to judge me by that, I don't want to be around them."

"Good girl," Karl said. "You deserve better than that."

"Yes, well . . . my mother deserved better than the life she lived. But some things just can't be changed."

"One day you'll find someone who will love you just because you are an incredible woman. And it won't make any difference."

Ericha couldn't resist saying, "It made no difference to Stefan." She met Karl's eyes, almost hoping he would say something to discredit Stefan, something that might give her a reason to be glad she couldn't have him.

"Stefan's a good man," Karl said firmly. "One of the best, in truth."

Ericha's mind replied with a sarcastic *Thanks. That's just what I needed to hear.*

Karl added quietly, "But some things just can't be changed."

Ericha heard only bits and pieces of the conversation after that. She tried to imagine what Stefan might be doing right now, and she realized she had no idea. She knew absolutely nothing about him—except that he had a wife who was nothing like her.

While Ericha appreciated Karl's friendship, she was glad when he left her alone. It was tempting to sink back into a familiar depression, but she forced herself to go work in the garden. And the next morning, being market day, she went into town, determined to find something worth living for. Moving into the square, Ericha had to admit she felt some semblance of happiness in spite of her setback with Kurt. She was glad she'd made the decision to come out, and convinced herself that there were many good men in Horstberg. She enjoyed looking over the wares and talking to the vendors, many that she had come to know well. With a basket over her arm, already holding her purchases of some cinnamon cakes and cross buns, her eye caught a spread of brightly colored scarves, and she moved closer to investigate.

Ericha was taken with a deep green one and decided it would go well with her coloring. Fingering it carefully, she was about to ask the vendor his price when a deep laugh caught her attention.

Carefully she moved so that she could see across the cart. Peering between the people gathered nearby, Ericha recognized Stefan immediately, even though his back was turned. She might have known it was him by the laugh, except that she had never heard him laugh so completely before.

Ericha's heart raced when he turned and she could see his profile. His hands went casually to his hips, pushing back his jacket enough to show the braces and white shirt he wore. Absorbing the reality of his presence, her mind fled back to moments she had spent in his arms. She wondered what had made her think she could ever forget him. Just seeing him through the crowd kindled a fire in her heart that could never be extinguished—and she knew it with her entire being.

In one moment she blessed the opportunity of seeing him, just to be reminded that he really existed. And in the next she cursed fate for crossing their paths again. It was just her luck. There were thousands of people in Horstberg, and she had to run into Stefan Heinrich. But her thoughts quickly altered when she realized that he was with a woman.

Stefan laughed again as this woman surveyed a collection of handkerchiefs, and Ericha couldn't fight the urge to move closer. She had to get a look at this woman who kept her from having the man she loved.

Stefan had said his wife was nothing like her. He had told her there was nothing left in the relationship. But Ericha knew they must have shared something significant in times gone by, and she wanted to see for herself what his wife was like.

Ericha moved unobtrusively through the crowd until she stood discreetly with Stefan's back to her. Here she could see this woman from the side, and she felt her eyes widen in surprise. She wondered how Stefan could have said they were nothing alike. This woman almost reminded Ericha of herself, at least in her coloring. Yet she was so beautiful, much more comely than Ericha had ever considered herself.

Ericha had never contemplated that Stefan might be a wealthy man. His manner and dress were humble. But this woman's clothes were the finest, and her entire aura suggested refinement and opulence. Surely this wasn't the woman that Stefan had spoken of so distastefully! Ericha felt anger kindle inside as she wondered if Stefan Heinrich had some fancy for women with red hair on the side.

Moving a little closer, she was able to hear this woman say, "Do you think your father will like this one?"

"No doubt," Stefan replied easily, and Ericha noted a happiness in his tone she'd only heard a glimpse of before.

"Well then, that's settled." She laughed gently, and he did the same. "And what about this one for Mother?"

It's his sister, Ericha justified, liking the way it consoled her fears. But Stefan quickly destroyed her theory.

"I'm certain she'd love it. But we'd best hurry, my dear Mrs. Heinrich. Your husband is waiting."

She looked up at him and laughed. "Someone is always waiting for me. It's usually you." She went on her tiptoes to kiss his cheek. As Stefan laughed again, Ericha began to fume.

Stefan had lied to her. It was so obvious. This was not the relationship he had described. Had it all been an acted-out facade to justify the way he'd taken advantage of her? There was no doubt, she decided, looking toward them one more time as he paid for her purchase—Stefan loved this woman.

Hurt and angry, Ericha fought back the burning behind her eyes and moved abruptly away. She bumped into someone and dropped her basket. Grateful the contents hadn't spilled, she willed herself to stay calm and stooped down to pick it up. A hand on her arm stopped her as a familiar voice said, "Let me get that for you."

Ericha fought to keep her feelings concealed as she watched Stefan pick up the basket and hand it to her. She wondered if she was supposed to pretend she didn't know him at all. A quick glance made her aware that they were being watched by those standing about. Had her little accident caused such a ruckus?

"Hello, Miss Lokberg," Stefan said, putting her at ease somewhat. The crowd's attention diverted, and he went on to say, "What an unexpected pleasure this is."

"Indeed," she said, wishing it hadn't sounded so terse. She was contemplating how to get away when Mrs. Heinrich moved beside him.

"A friend of yours?" she asked.

"Uh . . . in a way," Stefan said. "This is Karl's cousin."

"How very nice," she said, nodding politely while she placed her hand over Stefan's arm. Ericha felt consumed with envy and fury.

Her eyes shot briefly toward Stefan, wishing she could give him a piece of her mind. But he smiled easily and said, "Miss Lokberg, I would like you to meet," his voice became subtly intent, "one of the few ladies in my life that make it worth living." Ericha nearly wanted to slap him until he finished proudly, "My mother."

Ericha looked briefly into Stefan's eyes again. Relief washed over her as she undoubtedly caught the same glimmer she'd seen there when he'd said that he loved her. Her assumption had been wrong. She still didn't have Stefan, but she had the peace of knowing that he had been honest with her. It was easy to smile at this woman and take her hand.

"I'm very pleased to meet you, Mrs. Heinrich," she said.

Stefan's mother smiled in response. Ericha was astounded by her youthful appearance, but being face-to-face, she could now see subtle signs of age around her eyes.

"You're not from around here," the woman said, and Ericha thought that Stefan looked briefly embarrassed. She wondered if it was so obvious that she was not from Horstberg.

"No, I only moved to Horstberg in the spring."

"It was a pleasure," his mother said, and then she turned away. Stefan moved close behind her, nodding slightly toward Ericha as he parted. Again she caught something significant in his eyes.

Ericha hesitated a moment, discreetly observing as a tall man with blond hair approached them. Stefan's mother embraced him warmly. He was a little taller than Stefan, but Ericha quickly saw the resemblance in the thin lips, strong cheekbones, and intense eyes. But she could see that Stefan's coloring came more from his mother. Seeing Stefan for the first time in the sun, she realized that his hair was more rust than brown, as it betrayed a great deal of red.

When they had disappeared into the crowd, Ericha turned for home, walking slowly. The lonely ache set into her with fresh pain. She wondered if it was possible to survive without Stefan. She thought of her mother and the frail health that seemed to have no reasoning, which had eventually merged her into death at forty. Ericha was certain now that Kathe Lokberg had died of a broken heart.

The future from that moment was bleak. When Theodor took notice that each Sunday Ericha only seemed more melancholy than the last, he suggested that perhaps she should get out and have some diversion. Whatever was ailing her, for which he'd made no effort to inquire, he was convinced she was spending too much time at home alone and needed a change of scenery.

"Really, I'm fine," she insisted with a phony laugh, and Karl gave her a dubious glare across the table.

"What you need," Theodor said in a tone of light-hearted wisdom, "is to spend more time with me."

Karl laughed. "Oh that should do it." He then looked to Ericha and added with a smirk, "My father can cure anything."

Theodor gave a boisterous laugh. "He's right you know, my dear. Spend a few days with me and life couldn't help but get better. There's room for you in my apartment. It'll be fun."

Karl didn't know if this was good. Knowing well what the circumstances were from both sides, he wondered if Theodor's offer was the right thing. But he reminded himself to keep out of it.

"I'd just be in your way," Ericha protested.

"Nonsense," Theodor laughed, pushing his hand through the air in an elaborate gesture. "Most days I'm not away from the apartment all that much. You can stay there and do whatever you like, and I'll be in and out."

Ericha remained silent while Theodor watched her expectantly.

"Oh, I don't know," Ericha said to break an awkward silence.

"Perhaps," Karl said carefully, "your offer is a bit overwhelming. Ericha loves the garden and feels at home here."

"Well then," Theodor said, taking a less drastic approach, "let's do it this way. Why don't I come and get you Thursday, and you can spend the day? If I do have to go out, it wouldn't be for long."

After a brief silence, Ericha nodded. "It sounds nice. Perhaps a change would do me good."

"That's my girl." Theodor slapped his knee. "I'll see you Thursday then."

As the middle of the week drew near, Ericha had to admit that the idea of doing something different sounded inviting. She was curious to see where her uncle lived and was certain that what little she could see of Castle Horstberg would be exciting.

Thursday arrived with blue skies, and Ericha felt some life come into her as Theodor drove her toward the ominous structure of their destination. She couldn't believe how big it was! In the distance the imposing quality had been lessened. As he drove the trap through the huge gate and into the castle courtyard, Ericha could hardly catch her breath. It was incredible!

Servants in uniformed livery were immediately there to take the trap and care for the horse. Ericha listened to Theodor conversing casually with them, and she realized there were many levels of servants here, and her uncle was close to the top.

Theodor's apartment was among the vast servants' housing in the fortified group of buildings, which were separate from the main residence area and were across the huge courtyard from the keep and the stables. Ericha liked her uncle's rooms, which were small but comfortable. After she'd been shown around, Theodor asked, "Do you know how to play chess, my dear?"

Ericha glanced toward the elaborate chess set that dominated the little parlor, with chairs placed appropriately on either side of the table. "No," she said, "I don't."

"Would you like to learn?" he asked with an impish sparkle in his eyes that reminded her of Karl.

"Is it difficult?" she asked, seriously considering it.

"That's for you to decide." He motioned for her to be seated.

Ericha shrugged her shoulders and accepted his offer, and the Thursday chess game quickly became an established habit.

"You've gotten pretty good at this," Theodor said one afternoon as an autumn wind rustled outside. "Too good, perhaps."

"Nonsense," Ericha stated and stole his knight.

Theodor tried to look disgusted, but he obviously enjoyed her gratification from the game. He concentrated on his next move, and Ericha said in an effort to distract him, "Who did you play chess with before I came along?"

"Mostly the duke," he said tonelessly without drawing his attention away from the board.

"Is he any good?" she asked.

"Hmm," was all he replied.

"Tell me about him," Ericha said.

"He's an ogre."

"Come now." She laughed. "I've heard nothing but ravings of his character from you. He sounds too good to be true, if you ask me."

"So I lied," Theodor stated.

"When you said he's an ogre, or when—"

"Check," he said triumphantly, and Ericha gave a perturbed groan.

Concentrating on her next move, Ericha did well ignoring Theodor as he tried his distraction tactics on her. But the game was interrupted by a knock at the door, and he went to answer it.

A maid in her mid-forties, Ericha guessed, came in with

an elegant black and red uniform hanging over her arm, and a wooden box in her hands.

"What is it, Gretchen?" he asked. She seemed in a frenzy.

"We've got dignitaries arriving within the hour. Apparently the message wasn't received and the duke was unaware of it until just now."

Theodor chuckled and said with easy sarcasm, "Oh, I'll bet he's just thrilled about that."

The maid smiled and continued. "The uniform's been cleaned and pressed, but you're the only one who knows how these are supposed to be pinned on. His Grace insists that I not bother you for more than that."

"No problem," Theodor insisted. "Tell him I'll get it ready and bring it over shortly to help him dress."

"You're a treasure." The woman grinned, then glanced toward Ericha.

"Gretchen, this is my niece," Theodor said proudly.

"Pleased to meet you," she said and bustled off.

"Our game will have to wait," he apologized.

"It's fine." Ericha followed Theodor and watched with interest as he spread the elegant coat over his bed with tender care. He opened the box, which Ericha recognized as being of Lokberg craftsmanship, and proceeded to pin a variety of medals meticulously over the front of the uniform.

"That must be burdensome to wear," Ericha commented lightly.

"I believe many of the duke's obligations are a burden to him," her uncle replied, and Ericha thought briefly about the statement. She had never imagined that someone in such a prestigious position might not enjoy it, but she wondered if perhaps he didn't.

Twenty minutes after Gretchen's visit, another knock came to the door. Theodor was just about finished with his chore. "Straighten that one there," he instructed Ericha, "while I get the door."

Ericha fixed the medal the best she could, eyeing the overall effect and deciding he had done a very good job. She heard voices coming from the front room, then moving down the short hallway.

"I'm sorry to have to disturb you like this. I know how you deserve your time off."

"It's no problem," Theodor replied. "I don't mind. I've got it ready."

Ericha felt a nervous excitement. Was she really going to have the opportunity to meet the duke? She turned to see her uncle enter the room.

Ericha's heart quickened as a voice from the hall spoke. "Well, I thought if I came here, it would save time and you wouldn't have to . . ."

She held her breath and dared not let it go as the Duke of Horstberg entered on an unfinished sentence. Time seemed to stop as she attempted to digest the reality that she had met the duke before.

Ericha read a subtle regret in his eyes. She silently mirrored his expression as Theodor said, "Ah, Your Grace, you must meet my niece."

"Miss Lokberg," he said with a familiar nod.

"Your Grace." Ericha curtsied slightly, and then she brushed past them into the hall, closing the door behind her.

Ericha sat down hard and clamped a hand over her mouth, fighting to keep her composure. She squeezed her eyes shut and tried to absorb what she'd just discovered about Stefan Heinrich. It was difficult to fit everything she knew about him into this new realization, but it didn't take long for everything to make perfect sense. And in a strange way her heart was comforted. He had told her that a divorce would affect too many lives. Had he meant every citizen of Horstberg?

The ironies struck deeply, and Ericha pressed her other hand to her chest, as if it could ease the pain. When she heard the door open, she hurried to appear calm.

Her uncle's voice filtered from the hallway. "Come out here where the light's better, and we'll make certain everything's right."

Ericha tried not to lift her eyes as she became aware of them standing in the room. She didn't give in to the urge to look at him, but her heart nearly went into her throat when she heard the duke say, "Theodor, would you mind going to get the robe from Gretchen? I'd like you to see that it's on properly."

"Very good, sir," he replied, and Ericha found herself alone with the Duke of Horstberg.

There was an unbearable silence before she allowed herself to fully absorb him as the ruler of Horstberg. She began her studied gaze at the highly polished black boots that rose to his knee, with black breeches tucked into them. The red stripe on his breeches merged into the red coat, which was enhanced by black and gold trim, and the medals and adornments Theodor had attached there. She met his eyes briefly to find him staring at her. Then she took in the whole of him. The effect left her breathless. He was incredible: like some mythical prince, capable of conquering the world. He looked so different, yet the regal quality in his eyes had always been there. She just hadn't recognized it for what it was.

"You didn't know," he stated.

Ericha muttered tensely, "I called the Duke of Horstberg an arrogant—"

"You weren't the first," he interrupted, and then his tone deepened. "I deserved it. My position doesn't give me the right to—"

"Why didn't you tell me?" she cut in, not wanting to hear it.

Stefan looked pointedly away. "It made no difference. Who I am does not change the circumstances. It only makes them worse."

"I can't believe it," she whispered.

"What?"

She looked at him straightly. "You're the Duke of Horstberg."

"Yes," he chuckled humorlessly, "I am."

"I thought the duke was blond," she said, still trying to grasp the reality of this. He looked puzzled, and she clarified, "I saw people hovering around a man who—"

He smiled. "Oh. That would be my father."

"But," she paused to scrutinize him, trying to comprehend his father as being the man she'd thought to be the duke, "if your father is alive, then . . ."

Stefan looked sad, perhaps uncomfortable, as he tried to explain. "The bloodline comes through my mother, the Princess MagdaLena du Woernig. My father is Han Heinrich, who was the Duke Regent until I came of age. The people love him. He travels a lot, but when he's around he gets a lot of attention."

"I see," she said, still fighting to perceive all of this. "I hear he's a great storyteller."

Ericha was relieved to see Stefan smile, however faint. "Yes, he is," Stefan said, "but I don't think that's common knowledge."

Ericha recalled meeting Stefan's mother and felt suddenly embarrassed. In ignorance, she had failed to recognize her as royalty. With the same thought, she scrutinized Stefan closely, as if she'd just met him all over again.

The silence became uncomfortable until he said, "I've missed you, Ericha." She looked up to meet his eyes. In an unwilled gesture, Stefan lifted his hand toward her. Ericha hesitated only slightly in taking it. She came easily into his embrace and cried out his name as the comfort of being in his arms left her weak. Their fingers came to each other's faces, and Ericha saw emotion glisten in his eyes.

"My thoughts are with you always," he whispered, as if he dared not admit it too loudly. "I keep hoping that you'll find someone to share your life with, and at the same time I want to die inside to think of you in another man's arms."

"There is no one." She pressed her face against his throat and held him tighter.

"You must find a life without me, Ericha. If you don't, I could never forgive myself for—" Ericha pressed her fingers over his lips to stop him.

"I'm trying," she admitted, looking straight at him, "but . . ." Ericha bit her trembling lip.

"I have dreamed of being free from all of this," he said wistfully. "I lie awake at night and imagine myself asking you to marry me." Ericha's eyes widened. "Ericha," he said, "I'm in no position to ask, but if I were . . . if I could ask you to marry me . . . would you?"

Ericha tried to comprehend the Duke of Horstberg saying such things to her. "I would," she said with no hesitation, and his face showed relief. Again he embraced her, and Ericha was aware of the numerous medals across his chest pressing against her. She glanced down at them as he pulled back, and thought it symbolic of what stood between them.

"Ericha, you must find a life without me; find someone who will make you forget all about me."

"If only it were so easy." She took a step back as reality descended. "Am I supposed to just snap my fingers and forget what's happened between us? Do you think my feelings for you are so trite?" Stefan pushed his hands behind his back and looked down. "If you think I'm the kind of woman who would give such affection to a man I knew nothing about, just for the sake of—"

"Don't you dare say it!" he countered with an authority that made it easier for her to see him as the duke.

"There is no life without you, Stefan," she concluded. "If I'm lucky, I might find someone who will marry me in spite of my upbringing. But I will never—ever—forget you, Stefan. What kind of man wants to spend his life with a woman who has no heart to give him?"

Stefan could find no argument. "You have to try," he stated firmly.

Ericha lifted her chin and penetrated his eyes. Turning the hurt to anger, she said defiantly, "If the duke says it, then it must be."

"The duke is ruled by his circumstances," he came back indignantly, and Ericha had no doubt he was a very powerful man, simply by his aura when he used that tone of voice.

"Don't emotions fit into those circumstances, *Your Grace*? Or is it against the law for the duke to—"

"You have no idea what you're talking about, *Miss Lokberg*." He returned her formality with sarcasm. "You can't possibly live in Horstberg for so short a time and have any comprehension of my circumstances. You have no idea what I—"

"And you have no idea," she interrupted angrily, "how miserable you have made my life. I will never be free of it. I am haunted. You had no right to—"

Ericha stopped abruptly when she heard Theodor approaching, and the door swung open. Stefan passed her a quick glance that she interpreted as a combination of regret and compassion. She wished they'd not wasted those precious moments venting pain and frustration.

Ericha watched silently as Theodor clipped a long, red robe to the duke's shoulders, adding to the regal effect. Then Theodor checked his appearance meticulously. "That should do it," Theodor said proudly.

"Thank you, Theodor," Stefan said warmly. "Could you please get my things from the back room and I'll take them with me now."

Theodor left the room, and Stefan met Ericha's eyes. He took her chin into his fingers and pressed his mouth over hers. His kiss was brief but saturated with emotion.

"Again," he said gently, "I'm sorry."

"So am I." Ericha kept her face expressionless.

"I want you to know," he added, "you're not alone in your misery."

"No," she stated, "but I'm still alone."

Stefan turned away from her just before Theodor came back into the room. And the duke was soon off to meet his appointment. Ericha watched from the window as he seemed to float away across the courtyard, the red robe billowing out behind him.

"Well," Theodor said, "shall we finish our game?"

"Actually," Ericha replied apologetically, "I'm not feeling well. I think I should be going home."

Theodor was obviously concerned, but Ericha felt grateful that he didn't question her further. He walked her to the stable, and Pegasus was quickly saddled for her. Ericha galloped across the courtyard and through the gate, glad to leave Castle Horstberg behind.

Chapter Five

SEPARATE WORLDS

Ericha went straight to Karl's shop once she was home, hoping to distract herself. But he caught on quickly that something was wrong and made a strong point of inquiring.

"I'm fine," she insisted.

"I don't believe you," he retorted.

Ericha looked toward the window. "I met the Duke of Horstberg today."

"I see." Karl sighed. "Well, that explains everything. But I thought you'd already met our distinguished ruler."

"How was I supposed to know it was him? It seems I'm the most ignorant woman in Horstberg."

"I should have told you," Karl said soberly. "I just took for granted that you knew because everyone else does."

"I took a lot of things for granted myself," Ericha said. "I think I'll go lie down," she added. "I'm exhausted."

Karl made no effort to stop her. "Hey," he said before she could leave, "you'll be on your own tonight. I'm having dinner with Luise, and I'll probably stay late. I gave Erma the night off. She's helping her sister with something until tomorrow afternoon. So, I guess that means *I'll* have to cook breakfast."

"That should be an adventure." She managed a smile and walked idly through the garden, trying to sort her thoughts.

Ericha lay down on top of her bed and watched the room grow dark. Long after she heard Karl leave—and Erma soon afterward—she tried to talk herself into getting up. Her stomach growled with hunger, but she felt no appetite. Her mind continually rolled through her past conversations with Stefan as she tried to piece the man she'd come to love into the Duke of Horstberg.

Ericha was startled to hear a distant pounding. Job barked and followed her as she hurried down the stairs, allowing the bannister to guide her through the darkness. Throwing open the front door, she saw no one. The knock came again, from the back of the house. She snarled in frustration as she closed the door and relocked it. A single lamp barely illuminated the long hall, and she nearly ran its distance, wondering if Karl had come back for something and had locked himself out.

Ericha was breathless when she opened the door. All she could see was a cloaked figure moving away down the walk. He turned and came back toward her. Job barked, and Ericha felt briefly afraid, but then the dog moved out the door in apparent greeting.

"Hello," Stefan said pleasantly to Ericha while he scratched Job's head. She wanted to ask what he had to be so cheerful about, and then it became evident he was in the pretense of being a casual acquaintance. "I was looking for Karl. But apparently he's—"

"He's having dinner with Luise."

"Ah," he said, and Ericha wished she could see his expression. "Forgive me for disturbing you. I'll just—"

"You didn't disturb me," she said blandly. "I was just upstairs."

Stefan said nothing, didn't move. Though she knew it was presumptuous, she guessed with a degree of confidence, "You didn't come to see Karl, did you?"

She heard a chuckle of disbelief. "You are unbelievable, my dear Ericha. You can't even see my face, and you can still see right through me."

"I'm sorry," she said in a tone that indicated she wasn't.

"Don't apologize," he said adamantly. "It's one of the things I love about you."

Now Ericha was silent. She was so numb with confusion and longing, she couldn't even think straight.

"The truth is," he said, "I came here with a flimsy excuse to see Karl, hoping I might get a glimpse of you. And I thought if I was really lucky, perhaps I could even talk to you. I was feeling pathetically stupid for what happened earlier, and hoping I could stammer something senseless and ease my conscience . . . just a bit." She said nothing, and he added, "You must forgive me for leaving you in ignorance, Ericha. I am quite unaccustomed to people not knowing who I am."

"Perhaps I shouldn't have been fool enough to be kissing a man I knew nothing about."

"Why did you?"

"You have no business asking me that. You know *why.*"

"Yes," he admitted, "I know why."

Through the following silence, Ericha wondered what to do. She'd lost track of the weeks she'd spent longing to just be with him. And now he was here.

"May I come in?" he finally asked, and she opened the door wide. Whatever his purpose might be, she resolved herself to enjoy his presence while it lasted.

Ericha closed the door and locked it as he sauntered into the hall, Job at his heels. She leaned against the door a moment, trying to think what to do next.

Stefan glanced at the dimly lit hall, with no evidence of light elsewhere. "You must be alone," he said.

"The maid's staying with her sister tonight," she informed him.

The silence grew long, and Ericha reminded herself that this was *her* home, and she was not being very gracious. "Here," she stepped toward him, "let me take your cloak, and . . ."

"Thank you." He flung it off his shoulders, and she hung it on a hook near the door. She wondered now if he wore the cloak in his nightly travels to avoid being recognized.

"I was just going to find something to eat. Would you join me? I mean . . . if I can come up with anything worth eating, or—"

"I've already eaten, thank you. But I would love to join you, nevertheless."

Ericha reminded herself that the Duke of Horstberg was her guest, and she forced herself to her senses.

Stefan followed Ericha into the kitchen, with only a faint glow from the hall lamp guiding them. He watched as she fumbled to find the matches, and she dropped one in her attempt to strike it. She was blatantly nervous, and he wondered why.

"Here," he pressed his hands over hers, attempting to soothe her. "Let me help you." He took the matches from her, noting that she was trembling. With little trouble, he lit the lamp and turned the wick up high, illuminating the kitchen.

"Thank you," Ericha said. "Make yourself comfortable. I'll see what I can find."

Stefan sat down and watched her closely. Job settled himself at Stefan's feet and yawned.

While Ericha forced herself to appear busy, she cursed inwardly for the thoughts catapulting through her mind. Forcing away the reality that the man in her kitchen was the Duke of Horstberg, she had to ask herself: What kind of woman was she that she would actually wish for Stefan to spend the night? She knew it was wrong; she knew it blatantly. She knew the possible consequences of such a decision. But her desire to be with him somehow combined with the ridicule she had endured through the majority of her life. She'd hardly been able to go anywhere in the town she was raised without having adults whisper behind her back, while children openly taunted her for being fatherless. She couldn't count the times she'd been told to her face that the best she could hope for was to be a kept woman, and if she was really lucky she'd get paid for what she had to offer. Of course, her mother had worked very hard to convince her otherwise, but at the moment, her feelings for Stefan made it easy to believe that this was the best she could hope for. He loved her. What more could she ask? Realizing she was fumbling with the task she was about, she forced her mind to the present and scolded herself for having such thoughts. And then it occurred to her freshly: *Stefan was the Duke of Horstberg!*

"Oh, bless her heart," she declared, forcing a steady voice. "Erma loves me after all. Look what we have." She quickly fixed herself a plate of potato salad, fresh sliced carrots, and dark bread with butter. "Are you sure you're not hungry?" she asked, sitting across from him.

"I'm fine, thank you," he said. A moment later he added, "What's wrong, Ericha?"

"Wrong?" she echoed and put a forkful of potatoes in her mouth. "The only thing wrong is that you will not stay nearly long enough. And before you leave, you will probably lecture me on the need to find some wonderful man who can make me forget you."

Stefan shook his head and chuckled. "Besides that."

"Besides that?" She looked genuinely baffled.

"You're treating me differently, Ericha. And don't tell me it's my imagination. I've been feeling this kind of behavior from most of the people in this country for as long as I can remember."

"What kind of behavior?" she asked, setting her fork down.

Stefan leaned forward, and the power in his eyes was almost frightening. "Nearly everywhere I go, beyond my own home, people regard me as if I've just descended from heaven, or something. No matter how ordinary I attempt to behave, they jump quickly to please me, as if I might have them beheaded if I don't get what I want when I want it." His eyes narrowed and his voice lowered. "I make people nervous, as if I carried some kind of plague."

"People are naturally in awe of you," she said. "You're the Duke of Horstberg."

Stefan stood up so fast, his chair tipped over. "Not to you, I'm not!" He pressed his palms on the table and met her face to face. "I'm *Stefan!* Do you hear me? *Just Stefan!* I'm only a man. I eat, and sleep, and breathe. I laugh. I cry. I hurt. I bleed red just like any other man."

Seeing the concern in Ericha's eyes, Stefan picked up the chair and sat on it. Job hardly seemed to notice.

"Forgive me," she said. "I suppose I'm having to adjust. It was quite a shock."

Stefan cleared his throat, suddenly embarrassed for his outburst. "I'm sorry. I just . . ."

"It seems that I hit a nerve," she said when he faltered.

"There you go again." His voice lightened a bit. "Looking into my heart and soul as if . . ."

"As if what?"

"As if you know me better than I know myself," he admitted with piercing eyes.

"Did I hit a nerve?" she asked.

Stefan looked down and tapped his fingers on the table. "It never really bothered me much until . . ." Stefan swallowed hard as he realized once again he was telling her things he'd never told anyone.

"Until?"

"I woke up one day and realized I had given everything to a woman who was in love with family jewels and who had married a title."

Ericha tried futilely to hold back the emotion. Tears burned into her eyes as she saw one more layer of this man.

When Ericha said nothing, Stefan glanced up. But he wasn't prepared for her tears. "You would cry for me?" he asked. She nodded slightly. "I admit that it's tragic," he said, "but nothing will change it—especially crying. My marriage is a matter of political security."

"What about the matter of your happiness?" she asked. "How much does the duke sacrifice for his country?"

Ericha expected him to be defensive, but he sounded sad as he answered, "I'm giving up you. And there is nothing more I can give."

Sick to death of the tragedies of his life, Stefan picked up her fork and began to eat off her plate.

"I thought you weren't hungry." She chuckled, drying her tears with her sleeve.

"Oh, this is much better than whatever I ate for dinner. I think it was something French."

Ericha laughed and watched him closely, allowing his presence to fill her. Thinking back to the way he'd looked in his uniform earlier today, she found it intriguing to absorb the contrast. His blousy white shirt hung loosely over his shoulders. The sleeves were rolled up, a little unevenly. His breeches were common and obviously comfortable. The leather of his boots was creased and thin, as if they had grown to fit over his legs and no one else's. With his ankle crossed over his knee, she could see evidence that they had been resoled at least once. His thumb was hooked casually behind the strap of his leather braces. If not for his regal demeanor, he could pass for a market vendor.

"Are you going to eat it all?" she asked. He held the fork up to her mouth. Something fluttery erupted inside Stefan as he watched her lips slide smoothly over the silver prongs. He cleared his throat in an attempt to clear his head. But something in the way she looked at him seemed to demand that he acknowledge his feelings for her. Those feelings that had drawn him to her in the first place, and only intensified each day he'd been without her.

"Do you want some more?" she asked as she stood up.

Stefan shook his head. "No, thank you." He watched as she bustled around to clear away what little mess she'd made. She paused to lift one of her bare feet and scratch her lower leg. The ruffles of her white chemise disappeared as she set her foot back down and the calico skirt brushed the floor. He concentrated on her delicate fingers as she washed them under the water pump. His mouth went dry as she wiped her damp hands down the back of her skirt, briefly stretching the fabric over her hips.

"I should go." Stefan stood abruptly.

Ericha turned in alarm. "No," she protested, "it's early yet. You said you wanted to talk."

"We've talked," he stated.

"Well, did you ever consider there might be something *I* want to talk about?"

Stefan said nothing. In his present state of mind, he knew he was treading onto thin ice to even stay another minute. He had managed to keep his affection from going too far the last time they'd been together, but he wouldn't deem himself strong enough to be able to do it again.

Ericha picked up the lamp and walked down the hall. Stefan followed. She sat down in the parlor and motioned for him to join her. He took a seat across the room.

"So, talk," he insisted.

"All right." She ignored his terseness. "I have a question for you . . . Your Grace."

Stefan sighed with disgust, but she seemed amused. "You told me once that you didn't like Horstberg. If you are the duke, then—"

"Don't you ever repeat to *anyone* that I said that!" He pointed a finger at her.

"Is that the way you order people about in that grand castle of yours?" she countered in the same tone.

Stefan was taken so off guard he couldn't respond.

"If you don't want me to treat you like the Duke of Horstberg, then don't talk to me like that." Ericha softened her voice and added, "Now, back to my question. Why does the duke dislike his own duchy?"

"I don't dislike it, really," he said quietly. "It's a beautiful place, and it's been good to me in many ways, but . . ."

"But it's a burden?" she guessed, recalling what Theodor had told her.

"Yes," he admitted with a deep sadness that made her realize there were many layers of Stefan Heinrich she had yet to discover. "It is a burden to me."

"That must be very difficult for you," she said.

"At times, yes," he responded, amazed freshly at her perception. Did she have any idea how good it felt just to be understood? "Though, I must admit," he added, "there are aspects of my position that I dearly enjoy."

"Like what?" she asked.

Stefan shook his head. "I don't want to talk about that right now."

Ericha didn't try to hide her disappointment, but she heeded his request and changed the subject. "Well then, I have a question for Stefan."

"I'm here," he said.

"I don't think you'll like it," she warned. "But it's something I have to know. I mean . . . you hinted at it once, but I have to know."

"I'm listening." He nodded warily.

"Do you sleep with her, Stefan?"

She was right again, Stefan thought. He *didn't* like the question. But he respected her for having the courage to ask it. With that in mind, he answered directly. "I stopped going to her bed long before I met you, Ericha—which I consider an important point." Ericha nodded in agreement. "I stopped liking her long before that." Stefan spread his hands for emphasis. "Actually, I have been celibate for . . . Oh, who knows? Seems like forever."

Ericha chuckled, more relieved than anything.

"You find that funny?" he asked. But his indignant tone was tinged with a little smirk.

Ericha forced sobriety into her expression and shook her head. "You don't even kiss her?" she asked.

Stefan snorted. "I'd rather kiss a snake." He showed no sign of amusement, but she couldn't hold back a hearty laugh.

"What?" he demanded.

"It's funny," she insisted, but he only glared at her dubiously. "Do you ever laugh? Did you put out a proclamation or something that the duke is not entitled to laughter?" He said nothing, and she went on. "I heard you laughing when you were with your mother. Beyond that I've never gotten anything but a little chuckle out of you."

"I enjoy being with my mother. She's not around much."

"Well, it's too bad she's not around more—if she can make you laugh."

"How do you know I don't laugh?"

"I only know what I see, and what you tell me."

"Well, I don't find it amusing that my wife is a . . ." He stopped himself abruptly.

"A what?" she demanded, but he didn't answer. "Not only do you not laugh, you don't talk, not about the things you *should* talk about. Have you ever admitted to *anyone* that you'd rather kiss a snake than the woman you're married to?"

While Stefan was tempted to be angry, there was something so genuine in the way she confronted him. Her motives were blatant. She actually cared. "No," he had to admit.

"Not even to Karl?"

"No."

"Do you believe he would think less of you, or—"

"I don't like my circumstances, but condemning and complaining will not—"

"I'm not suggesting you shout it from the rooftops, Stefan. I'm telling you that you should be able to talk to someone you trust, and say anything you like."

"Did your mother teach you that?" he asked.

"Oh, she taught it emphatically." Her voice saddened. "But she didn't live it. She never talked about the things that were hurting her." Ericha pointed a finger at him and added, "But she did laugh!" Her voice took on a dreamy lilt as she mused, "It wasn't easy living without a man in the house. But we couldn't change it, so we learned to laugh about it. We had all kinds of private little jokes about not having to put up with a man snoring, or not cleaning out the basin when he shaved, or . . ." Ericha stopped as a clear image of Kathe Lokberg appeared in her mind. She had shouldered her disgrace with courage and dignity. But Ericha was well aware of the tears her mother shed at night. A deep empathy for her mother's emptiness rose into Ericha's throat. Her eyes turned to Stefan. How quickly he had taught her to feel her mother's pain!

Stefan saw the tears just before she turned away, attempting to hide them. It was evident these tears were not on his behalf, but he wondered if he was the cause.

"Ericha?" he said gently. She only clamped a hand over her mouth and hurried toward the door. Stefan shot out of his chair to block the doorway. She turned her back to him, and he heard her sob. Hesitantly Stefan set his hands on her shoulders, and she immediately responded by leaning her back against his chest.

He pressed his hands down her arms and whispered behind her ear, "Do I cause you so much pain?"

Ericha laid her head back against his shoulder and let the tears fall. "The pain is only as intense as the joy. If I had it to do over, I would do it no differently."

Stefan squeezed his eyes shut. How perfectly she described his own feelings! He pushed his lips into her hair, telling himself he should leave now. He considered himself a disciplined man. He'd been taught to discipline his time, his speech, his attitude. Self-discipline was a job requirement. And his job was his life. But he reminded himself that he was not the Duke of Horstberg now. Just as he'd told her so adamantly in the kitchen, he was nothing more than a man. A very lonely man. Still, he reminded himself, he had to consider Ericha. His selfishness had already brought her much grief. To take it any further could be disastrous.

"I should go," he said, but he didn't mean it.

"No," she protested, much to his relief.

"How long before Karl will be back?" he murmured.

Ericha turned abruptly and looked into his eyes. His hands tightened against her back. She'd nearly expected to see some kind of protest, as if he might be trying to talk himself out of wanting to be with her. But she saw nothing but a reflection of her own desire. Relief filled her. He bent to kiss her, and nothing existed beyond the nucleus of their love. In a single breath, they mutually responded to the weeks of longing. She wanted to laugh and cry as she allowed his kiss to gain fervor. Then abruptly, she stepped back.

Stefan watched her eyes, wondering if she had come to her senses and would tell him to leave. He could see her chest rise and fall with each quickened breath, and he longed to hold her. He'd nearly drawn the courage to ask if something was wrong when she reached a hand toward him, saying gently, "Come upstairs with me."

Stefan watched her pick up the lamp and move into the hall, with Job at her heels, and he followed her up the stairs, while his battered emotions battled with his conscience. As she motioned him through a door, he thought it ironic that he and Karl had played here as children. But he'd not been up here in many years. He tried to tell himself that he could spend this time with her and not compromise her any more than he already had. But he was doubtful.

Job settled himself on the rug as Ericha closed the door and turned the key. She set the lamp down on the bureau near a little wooden box. She turned to look at him, and he knew her heart was beating as hard and fast as his. He wondered over her thoughts but couldn't find the voice to ask her. He was relieved when she said almost lightly, "Make yourself at home."

He sat in a nearby chair, telling himself to get up and leave. But his feet had turned to lead.

"You look uncomfortable," she said. "Relax. Why don't you take off your boots?" When he didn't move, she added, "Here. I'll do it."

Stefan hesitated briefly as a memory caught him off guard. She slapped his knee, and he obediently lifted his foot. He relaxed some as her laughter filled the room while she pulled off his boot and tossed it. "I've never done this before," she said, pulling off the other one.

"How refreshing," he uttered, and thoughts of Johanna fled.

Stefan reached out a hand toward her, and she took it. For a moment he just absorbed her, in awe of his own feelings.

"How is it," she said, "that the Duke of Horstberg loves a woman like me?"

"A woman like you?" he echoed.

"Illegitimate; practically nothing to my name."

"How is it," he countered, urging her onto his lap, "that you loved *me*, not knowing I was the Duke of Horstberg?"

"I love you for who you are, not what you are."

"There's your answer," he stated.

Ericha touched his face, then kissed his brow. Stefan squeezed his eyes shut as the internal battle became unbearable. But the part of him that ached with loneliness and lack of love won out. He urged her lips to his, and passion quickly consumed him.

"Ericha," he murmured and pressed his lips to her throat. He eased her off his lap, telling himself to put some distance between them and get out of here. But he came to his feet to find her immediately in his arms, kissing him as if there was no need to be concerned for tomorrow. And how tempted he was to believe her!

Ericha gasped as he took a step back. Their eyes met, and she feared he would storm out of the room and never see her again. But he kissed her while he fumbled with the buttons of her bodice. There was an urgency in the way he encouraged her dress to the floor. Ericha responded with the same urgency as she pushed his braces abruptly over his shoulders and removed his shirt. He carried her to the bed and lay beside her, making her believe that with his power he could truly make the world go away. The part of her that knew he couldn't, that knew it was wrong and it could likely bring difficulties into their lives, became quickly squelched by something deeper that ached for this seemingly tangible evidence that she was a woman worthy of the love of this incredible man.

In the midst of Ericha's growing response, Stefan squeezed his eyes shut as if he could block out the reality of how far this had come. *Too far.* As she kissed him again, it seemed beyond his ability to ease her away and put a stop to this. But he did it anyway.

"Forgive me," he said, sitting up abruptly. "But I can't do this." His voice was raspy, his breathing labored. "I want you, Ericha, so badly that it hurts. You must know how I do, but . . . I can't do it; not like this."

Ericha wanted to tell him she understood. She wanted to find words to express the relief she felt deep inside that he respected her enough to be concerned with the consequences of such an irrevocable step. But she could only nod and turn away from him before hot tears of disappointment burned into her eyes. Lying on her side, she curled up and wrapped her arms around herself, marveling that unappeased passion could be so physically shocking. She felt herself trembling and resisted the urge to beg him to go on, knowing that once she recovered from these feelings, she would likely be grateful for his discipline. Or at least she knew she should be.

Fearing he would leave her alone with her disappointment and longing, she heaved in deep relief to feel him embrace her from behind and press his lips into her hair. "Forgive me," he murmured.

"I understand," she whispered, proud of herself for the steady tone but unable to hide her disappointment. But it was a disappointment that she knew he shared. And at the same time her respect for him deepened. She wondered how many men, as lonely and deprived as he, wouldn't jump at the chance to have what she was willing to give, and then leave and never look back?

Ericha forced herself to breathe deeply and relax, aware of him doing the same. They lay together in peaceable silence until he murmured close to her ear, "God forgive me for being such a selfish man, Ericha, but I love you."

"I can't help feeling that you are more selfish when you keep us apart."

"I'm concerned for your future," he said sadly. "It's wrong, Ericha. And nothing will change that."

Ericha turned to face him. "But if God knows our hearts, Stefan, don't you think He understands?"

Stefan thought about it. "Perhaps He understands, but wrong is still wrong."

Ericha looked into his eyes, and Stefan could see that she was troubled. He touched her face and attempted to console her, if not himself. "In my heart I divorced her a long time ago, Ericha . . . in every way except one. But it's the only one that matters."

"Not to me," she said.

Stefan kissed her warmly, before urging her head to his shoulder. His next awareness was footsteps in the hall.

"Karl's home," Ericha whispered close to his ear.

"Oh, great," he responded with sarcasm.

"You can sneak out after he's gone to sleep. He'll never notice."

"And do you think he didn't notice my horse in the stable?"

"Good point," she conceded, then she giggled.

"What?" he demanded quietly.

"I don't know," she said, "it's just funny." She pressed her face to the pillow to muffle her laughter. "Admit it, Stefan. It's funny."

"Yes." He chuckled and pulled her close. "It's funny."

He kissed her as if it could somehow compensate for all he couldn't give her, and then he held her until she slept. She didn't stir when the dog jumped onto the bed and curiously investigated Stefan's presence there.

"How you doing, Job?" Stefan asked in a whisper, scratching the dog amiably.

Job settled comfortably at their feet, seeming satisfied that everything was all right. Stefan was well accustomed to the feel of a dog on the bed, and he indulged in the coziness, holding Ericha close.

Restless with his thoughts, Stefan eased away and wandered the room, taking care not to wake Ericha. He tried to convince himself to feel guilty for being with her this way, but it wouldn't come. Still, he felt sure that with the light of day it would. He tried to commend himself for at least stopping before it had gotten completely out of hand, but the thought only saddened him somehow. Again, he told himself he shouldn't even be here. The last thing he wanted was to see Ericha pining her life away for a man she couldn't have—for her sake. But if he didn't stay away from her, she would never get over it.

Watching Ericha sleep, he forced all troubling thoughts from his mind. He moved to the window and unwillingly caught his breath. He saw a perfect view of Castle Horstberg, nestled against the mountainside, illuminated by the moonlight.

He heard a rustle behind him and then Ericha's voice. "It's beautiful," she said, pressing her hands around his chest.

"Yes, it is," he agreed.

"I've stood here and admired it many times, but I never dreamed . . ."

"I'm sorry if I woke you," he said.

Ericha eased into his arms, putting her back to the window.

"I'm not." She relaxed her head against his shoulder. "Are you sad?"

"More . . . afraid," he admitted.

Ericha nearly questioned him, but she sensed he didn't want to mar these moments with anxiety any more than she did.

"Do you want me to tell you a story?" she asked.

Stefan smiled down at her. "I would love it."

"Once upon a time," she said in a wistful tone, "there was a young maiden who came to a faraway kingdom to live with her only remaining relatives. It was quite by chance that she met a man while riding in the forest. But when fate brought them together again, destiny took over. Little did the maiden know that this man she loved was king of this fair country, and . . ."

She stopped abruptly to subdue her emotion, and Stefan lifted her chin with his finger. "Finish the story, Ericha. Use your imagination and come up with a happily ever after."

"You're the one who keeps telling me that's impossible," she stated. "There is no ever after."

Stefan fought the urge to cry, and he pulled her closer, gazing over her head toward Castle Horstberg. He felt as torn, as if he were locked in some ancient torture device.

A pounding somewhere below startled them both. Job let out a bark in response. "What on earth . . ." Ericha murmured.

"I don't know." Stefan lit the lamp and pulled on his boots. "But I'll bet it has something to do with me."

They could hear Karl bounding down the stairs, then distant voices in tones of urgency. Ericha felt a sudden panic, mingled with dread. "Did anyone know you were—"

"I told my grandmother I was going to see Karl. But they wouldn't come looking for me unless it was something serious."

"What constitutes serious?" she asked, pulling a wrapper on over her chemise.

"War, perhaps," he stated, pulling on his shirt, and he gave a little laugh. "Just kidding . . . I hope."

Karl came back up the stairs and knocked at the door. "Stefan, I'm assuming you're in there," he said.

Ericha met Stefan's eyes, wondering how they were supposed to handle this. He appeared completely calm as he pulled open the door, then pulled his braces up over his shoulders. She saw Karl's gaze quickly take in the evidence and wondered if he would ever believe that it wasn't as bad as it appeared.

"What is it?" Stefan demanded. Ericha could see that the duke was now in control.

Karl actually smirked as he said, "There are two of your officers down there, looking for you. I told them we'd had a long evening of poker and you decided to stay. Lucky I noticed your horse in the stable, and your cloak by the back door, or I'd have really duped it." His tone was subtly sarcastic. "Did I do all right, Your Grace?"

"Perfect," Stefan said. "Did they say what's wrong?"

"No," Karl yawned, "I'm going back to bed." He looked at Ericha momentarily, and she felt certain he wasn't happy about this. She couldn't blame him.

Stefan turned to Ericha, his eyes frantic. He kissed her hard and fast, then quickly touched her face.

"Will I ever see you again?" she asked.

Stefan hesitated. "Find someone," he said, as if it were an order, and then he rushed out of the room.

Ericha followed and waited on the stairs, where she could hear but not be seen.

"What is it?" she heard Stefan demanded of the officers.

"Your grandmother sent us, Your Grace."

"That doesn't tell me anything," he retorted, and Ericha could sense the uneasiness in his voice. Was it a family matter—or a national emergency?

"It's your grandfather, sir," was the reply. "The doctor's with him now and . . ."

Ericha heard nothing more beyond the door closing and the galloping of horses on the street. She sat on the stairs and leaned her head against the bannister post. Her most prominent emotion was concern for what Stefan must be feeling. She hoped that his grandfather would be all right, whatever had happened.

"Did you hear what the problem was?" Karl startled Ericha as he sat beside her.

"Something about his grandfather . . . and the doctor. That's all I heard."

Karl sighed. "I hope it's not serious. It would break Stefan's heart to lose Georg."

Ericha felt warmed by the evidence that Karl knew Stefan's life so well, even if she didn't.

"How old is he?"

"Georg? Oh, more than eighty I would guess. He's practically a legend."

Karl put his arm around Ericha's shoulders, and she leaned her head against him. "Is there anything you want to talk about?"

"No," she said easily.

"Ericha, I'll let you live your own life. I'm not going to tell you what to do, but . . . I don't want to see you waste your life away, loving a man you can't have."

Ericha tried not to feel upset. "That's what Stefan said."

"Well, I'll give him some credit for that. I must admit I was a little . . . surprised to realize he was here, and the only room he could possibly be in was yours."

"I was a little surprised myself," she admitted as she stood. "But in spite of how it appeared, he . . ." She hesitated, wondering how to explain without embarrassing herself. Certain that nothing could embarrass Karl, she quickly said, "He kept what happened between us from going too far." He looked dubious, but she simply added, "I'm going to get some sleep."

"Good-night," he said.

"Karl." She paused before adding, "Thank you."

"For what?"

"For covering for him . . . and for not condemning me."

"I don't agree with it, but I will always be there for you . . . both of you."

"Thank you," she said again and went to her room.

For several minutes Ericha just leaned against her closed door and tried to absorb the aura Stefan might have left in the room.

She wandered to the window and gazed at the castle turrets, wondering what was taking place there now. She missed Stefan already, but she felt replenished and somehow more secure in just knowing he loved her.

"The Duke of Horstberg." Ericha said it aloud, just trying to comprehend.

With one last longing glance toward the castle, she crawled back into bed, relishing the memories of Stefan being there. As Job nuzzled close to her legs, she closed her eyes and conjured up a clear image of Stefan floating across the castle courtyard in his regal attire. Trying to imagine Castle Horstberg as his home, Ericha wondered if there could possibly be an ever after.

Ericha was glad to learn through Karl that Stefan's grandfather had only sustained a minor break in his leg when he'd fallen down a few steps. Stefan had told Karl that Georg was as spry as ever and healing well.

Autumn was unusually warm and dry. Ericha kept busy, determined to not let herself slip into the discouragement that had plagued her in the past. But weeks passing made it evident that nothing had changed between her and Stefan. She either had to find someone else or live on the hope that he might eventually come back. But she had difficulty resolving herself firmly to either option.

On a particularly bright morning, Ericha sat quietly eating breakfast with Karl while he perused the weekly newspaper. Erma bustled in to clear the table, obviously dressed to go out.

"Is there anything else you'll be needin'?" she asked. "I'm goin' soon."

Karl peered over the top of his paper. "Why so early?" he asked.

"Today's the parade . . . and the exhibition!" She placed her hands on her ample hips and glared at him as if he were inane.

Karl glanced at the clock. "It doesn't start for hours yet."

"I've got to get a good seat," she insisted and resumed her work. "It's no fun at all if you can't see what's goin' on."

Karl chuckled, and then he apparently noticed Ericha's ignorance as he informed her. "It's the Day of Horst." He waved his hand almost frantically as if he couldn't think how to explain it. "Well, it's like . . . this is the day Horstberg was established officially . . . hundreds of years ago, or something."

"I see," Ericha said, wondering briefly what Stefan might be doing right now. She thought how nice it might feel to walk the streets with him and hold his hand as they watched a parade go by.

"Why don't you go with Erma?" Karl said, startling her.

"What?" Ericha asked.

"Oh, that's a grand idea," Erma said, clapping her hands together. Ericha couldn't recall ever seeing her so excited. "Do come with me, Miss Ericha. It would be such fun. I'll be meetin' my sisters and we have such a grand time. It's our favorite day of the year."

"More than the fair?" Karl asked, seeming appalled.

"Oh, much more!" she insisted.

He made a disagreeable noise and returned to the paper. "Go with her, Ericha. I'm sick to death of you moping around here, day in and day out."

"I have not been moping!" she protested, knowing how hard she'd tried to keep a light demeanor. She saw Karl smirk and believed he was just trying to rile her. "Ooh," she snarled and threw her napkin at him. "Fine. I will go, if only to get away from you for a while."

Ericha moved toward the door, and Karl grabbed her hand. "Hey," he grinned, "have a good time. And buy me a present."

Ericha squeezed his hand and moved along. "If only you could be so lucky," she called from the hallway.

Ericha found it easier than she'd expected to enjoy being with Erma. They walked together into town while Erma chattered almost constantly about the grand things going on today. Arriving at the market square, the evidence of celebration became evident.

There were flags and banners posted all around the square and on the lamp posts lining the main road that led to it. Vendors were setting up in one area, but the square was marked off with ropes.

"That's where the exhibition will be," Erma informed her as she spread a blanket out on a grassy spot at the edge of the square.

"And what exactly is that?" Ericha asked.

"Oh, they have dancers, and jugglers, and musicians, and they'll shoot the cannons, and—"

"I get the idea," Ericha interrupted, pointing toward a striped tent in the center of the park behind them. "What's that for?"

"Oh, that's the art show. They're sellin' all kinds of things that people have made."

"I'm going to look," Ericha said and hurried away.

"Take your time," Erma called, and Ericha enjoyed perusing the paintings, pottery, jewelry, and other odd trinkets. She was taken with a set of wind chimes and bought them, deciding they would be a gift for Karl, and they could both enjoy them.

With her purchase in her basket, Ericha returned to the blanket to find that Erma's sisters had arrived. The three of them looked a great deal alike, and time passed easily as Ericha listened to them chatter. Gertie was married to an officer of the Guard and had a two-year-old daughter, who was toddling around on the grass. Hilde was engaged to a butcher's son.

Ericha watched as people slowly began to fill the perimeter of the square and line the street coming into it. Music played in the distance and the air felt festive. She turned her face to the sun and thought of Stefan. Her heart quickened a little as she allowed her memories to wander into the tender moments they'd shared. She wondered if the duke came to such events, but a quick glance around the crowd made it obvious that running into him was highly unlikely.

Feeling a little hungry, she excused herself and bought some hot pasties from a vendor she knew as Max. She returned to the blanket and shared them with the others, enjoying their ongoing prattle.

"When is this thing going to start?" Ericha asked, realizing by the sun that they'd been there for hours. She was at least grateful that the weather was pleasant.

"Soon, I think," Hilde said. A few minutes later, a distant fanfare was heard and the people cheered. Ericha watched with interest as the parade moved slowly toward the square, like a great colorful serpent. One by one, entertainers of all kinds filed into the square, then moved to the park where they would apparently wait their turn to perform through the day.

As the parade continued, becoming more colorful and vibrant, Ericha intermittently observed the people around her. There were all kinds, and she found the diversity fascinating. She stopped to realize that the man she loved was ruler of all this, and the reality was a little unsettling.

Ericha's attention was drawn to a group of young children who obviously belonged to the same family by their similar dress and appearance. She counted six, the oldest not looking more than ten. The mother seemed to be enjoying herself but was mostly oblivious to the children, who seemed a bit more rowdy than average. Ericha was particularly concerned about a boy she guessed to be around seven years of age. He had a small toy that he occasionally threw into the path of the parade, and then he would slither under the rope and rush out to get it, apparently making a game of being missed by the oncoming horses, carts, and carriages.

Ericha's attention was diverted when she heard Gertie say to Erma, "Look, there's the ducal coach."

"Please, no," Ericha murmured under her breath. Was she so ignorant to think that a parade celebrating a national holiday wouldn't include the country's royalty? While she debated whether to hurry away or hope for a glimpse of Stefan, she realized from the chatter around her that the coach housed only the duchess and the grand duchess.

The duchess? With all the contemplating she'd done over Stefan's position, she'd not connected the title with his wife. She recalled now Stefan saying "she married a title."

As the grand red and black coach moved slowly toward them, Ericha felt a little nauseated. She got a brief glimpse of an older woman who blew a kiss toward the children lining the street. Beyond that, Ericha saw nothing but the back of an apparently voluptuous woman with blonde hair and the sparkle of jewels around her wrist as she waved the other direction.

Ericha wanted to ask Erma where the duke was, but she couldn't bring herself to say it. Within a few minutes, her eye was drawn to a massive red and black formation, some distance up the road, moving slowly closer. She became fascinated by its preciseness, and it took a minute for her to realize it was the Guard, marching in formation at the rear of the parade. As they drew closer, she could hear a distant drum cadence. Ericha felt nearly chilled by the rhythm of hundreds of marching feet on the cobbled street, in perfect tempo with what she now realized had to be several different drums. She became so caught up in the uniformed mass that she gasped aloud to realize a man on a horse was at its head.

Ericha pressed her fingers over her lips to avoid embarrassing herself as emotion crept into her throat. He was still too far away to recognize his features, but the stature alone made her breath quicken. She concentrated on every detail as he moved slowly closer, and she reminded herself of all they had shared. The reality of that was difficult to believe as she absorbed the picture before her. There he was. Stefan Heinrich. The Duke of Horstberg, towering above the mass of men that were in his charge. His stallion moved in a slow, steady canter, as if it had been trained specifically for this purpose.

Ericha took in the bigger picture. The crowds that had been casually enjoying the parade with frequent bursts of cheers and applause were now coming to life. She could almost feel the massive awe of the people as Stefan led the formation into the square.

As he moved closer, Ericha was able to recognize his features, and a giddy lurch erupted somewhere inside. Having seen him in his uniform once before had not prepared her for what she saw now. The red robe hanging from his shoulders fell over the back of the stallion that Stefan rode with perfect ease. His straight back and squared shoulders seemed almost incongruous to his idle demeanor. The reins hung lax in one black-gloved hand, and he looked as comfortable as he had sitting in a chair in her parlor. His rust-colored hair waved back off his face and hung over his collar. His expression was pleasant, almost bored. Most startling of all was the simple gold crown placed low on his brow, circling uniformly around his head.

While Ericha marveled at the incredible picture before her, she became freshly stunned by the reality. *He loved her. He was a king.* She glanced around at the crowds that were enthusiastically cheering their ruler and the force he led. What was she, but one of them? An illegitimate woman, living on her cousin's mercy, dressed in calico and cotton. She felt so small, so insignificant, as the spectrum of their separate worlds fell into place. Even if he were free, could she have ever fit into his world?

Ericha focused on the mass of soldiers as they moved into the square, almost filling it with their numbers. She could see now the six drummers taking up the rear of the foot soldiers, and she noticed several officers on horseback following them. They were men of some higher rank, she reasoned. She noted details of the officers' uniforms, similar to Stefan's but much simpler. Her gaze moved to Stefan. She turned warm as unwilled memories rushed forward.

With no preface, Stefan idly lifted a hand in a seemingly passive gesture. He might as well have been brushing away a fly. But the evidence of his power cemented as the entire force came to a perfect, synchronized halt, and the drummers ended on a perfect beat. Had each soldier's eye been so keenly tuned to his every move? There was a moment of intense silence, and then the crowd went wild with cheers and applause.

Ericha blessed Erma's determination to get a good seat when she was able to see Stefan's subtle smile as he quickly took in the response. He lifted that hand again, and the crowd quieted.

"Guard left!" an officer called. In a split second, the entire force turned with a resounding thud as each boot hit the ground in unison. The same officer bellowed an indiscernible syllable, and a different drum cadence began. Ericha watched in awe as an intricate display of military showmanship erupted. It lasted several minutes, ending with a complex drum cadence. The crowd cheered, then quieted again as three cannons were moved into the center of the square and aimed almost straight up by men in uniform. Stefan rode toward them and dismounted. A soldier held the reins of his horse at perfect attention.

With a great deal of pomp, the duke was presented with a lighted torch by a man who appeared to be the Captain of the Guard by his adornment. Stefan held the torch high, and the people cheered. Ericha noticed people putting fingers in their ears, and she quickly followed their example. The duke lit the fuses of the three cannons, passed the torch back to the captain, then stepped back and covered his ears. Ericha jolted at the *boom, boom, boom!* Then she laughed as a shower of candy poured down, and the children scrambled to gather it up off the ground. Ericha looked up and saw more than heard Stefan laugh as he remounted his horse and turned to look around. He waved his arm carelessly, and the majority of the force dismantled, filtering casually into the crowd.

Chapter Six
FROM A DISTANCE

With apparent purpose, Stefan moved his stallion into a steady trot toward the edge of the square. He slowed and turned, and Ericha realized he was moving around the perimeter. The Captain of the Guard and another officer walked close beside him, like protective shadows. Stefan leaned casually down from the horse with a hand outstretched toward the people who were apparently clamoring to touch him. Ericha stood frozen where she was. Again, she blessed Erma's effort to be here. Without moving a step, Ericha would inevitably come face to face with the Duke of Horstberg. She wondered briefly how she might feel right now if she hadn't known of his position before. Her heart quickened as he moved slowly closer. She felt warmed by his personable manner and the comfortable way he interacted with the people. He seemed so at ease, actually happy. She recalled him saying there were aspects of his position that he truly enjoyed, and she felt certain this was one of them.

Ericha was vaguely aware of the excitement of those surrounding her as the duke moved closer. Erma and her sisters were practically giggling. She caught vague whispers, where the words *handsome* and *distinguished* stood out.

Unobtrusively, Ericha listened as an older woman caught his hand. "Tis good to see you in such fine health, Your Grace," she said in a voice that trembled with age.

Stefan laughed gently and pressed her hand briefly to his lips. "And you, madame. I dare say you're breaking some poor gentleman's heart as we speak."

The old woman giggled like a school girl. Stefan chuckled and moved on. As his attention focused on a man with a child on his shoulders, Ericha thought she would die from trying to conceal her nerves. He ruffled the child's hair, shook the man's hand, then moved on to Erma and her sisters.

"You ladies are looking lovely today," he said and shook each of their hands while they gaped in awed silence.

Ericha kept her hands folded in front of her as his eyes shifted toward her. The vague surprise in his expression was too brief to be noticed. He reached a hand toward her as he smiled more completely than she had ever seen him do before.

"Miss Lokberg," he said as she slipped her hand into his, "what a pleasant surprise."

Ericha was vaguely aware of Erma's increasing gape.

"Your Grace," Ericha curtsied slightly without taking her eyes from his.

"I trust you are doing well," he said. His diplomacy was so genuine, just as it had been with the old woman.

Ericha wished so badly that she could just tell him the truth, that she was trying with all her heart and soul to be happy and content. But her heart was aching for want of his company and the love he gave her. Instead she lifted her chin in a gesture of confidence and replied firmly, "Very well, thank you. And you?"

"I have much to be grateful for," he said as if it held deeper meaning. Then he quickly pressed her hand to his lips. Before he let go, he discreetly squeezed her fingers so tightly that it almost hurt. He nodded once more and moved on, but Ericha felt warmed by the gesture. She had no question that his love for her had not waned.

"What was that about?" Erma asked in an astonished whisper.

Ericha quickly searched for an appropriate answer. "Surely you're aware that he and my cousin are acquainted." She wondered if Stefan's appearances at Karl's home were so rare that Erma would not know the connection.

"Well, of course," Erma admitted, as if she was determined to say nothing more.

At her inquisitive gaze, Ericha added, "His Grace and I just . . . met once." Then she ignored any further probing. She recalled Karl saying that Erma was discreet, and he knew where her loyalties were. Ericha might have understood what he'd meant if she had known at the time his connections with royalty.

Ericha was aware of Stefan passing an occasional discreet glance in her direction as he moved on. When he was too far away to catch her eye, she turned her attention to some kind of entertainment taking place on the other side of the square. She realized Erma and her sisters were preparing to walk through the art show, but since she'd already seen it, she contemplated whether or not to just go home. Now that the thrill of actually touching Stefan had passed, the full gamut of what she'd seen this day was settling in harshly. She thanked Erma and her sisters and told them to go on without her, and then she looked toward Stefan as he approached the final few waiting. She wondered what the remainder of his day would entail. She wished that it might include her. Knowing it didn't, the discouragement began to take hold.

With a deep sigh, Ericha turned to seek out the most obvious route of escape from the crowds. From one eye she saw the ducal coach approaching, and from the other, the daring child toss something into its path before darting out to get it. She gasped as he tripped over an untied shoelace. In the next instant, the horses pulling the coach reared back and sidestepped. The coach swerved and came to an unsteady halt, but not before one wheel went over the child's leg. While everyone beyond the child's mother seemed momentarily stunned, Ericha instinctively rushed toward the howling child.

Stefan heard the commotion and turned to investigate. He wasn't sure what had happened, but as the ducal coach was apparently involved, he heeled the stallion in that direction. He quickly surmised that a child had been hurt, but people were hovering around, and he heard someone say they were going for a doctor. Stefan dismounted and hurried to open the door of the coach.

"Are you all right?" he asked.

"We're fine," Abbi insisted, "but the child is—"

"I'm certain it's under control," Stefan told her. "They've gone for a doctor." He glanced over his shoulder. "From the noise he's making, I doubt it's fatal."

Abbi gave a concerned smile. Stefan's eyes shifted to Johanna, who was examining her fingernails, perhaps fearing she'd broken one.

"I assume you've survived the trauma," he said to his wife.

"I'm fine," she replied tersely, "but I don't know why people can't keep their children out of the street."

"I'll see if I can have the irresponsible parent executed," he said blandly.

Abbi chuckled. Johanna glared at Stefan, apparently disgusted by his humor.

Stefan closed the coach door and called to the driver. "Take them home. I'm certain everything's under control."

The driver nodded, and the coach rolled forward. Stefan observed the gathering crowd of curious onlookers and felt certain the victim didn't need to feel like a sideshow. He was quite accustomed to taking charge and quickly pushed his way into the throng.

"All right," he said with calm authority, "I'm certain everything will be taken care of accordingly. Let's move along and make room for those who can help."

The people eased slowly away, and Stefan looked down to see a young boy with an obviously broken leg. His eyes moved to the concerned mother, whose lap supported the child's head as he wept, more quietly now. Then something fluttered inside of him as he took in the woman who held the mother's trembling hand. Johanna was worried about her fingernails, and Ericha was kneeling on the ground, comforting a perfect stranger. Their eyes met briefly before he squatted down beside the child and took his small hand.

"Looks like it's broken," he said mostly to the child. "But not to worry. My grandfather broke his leg a while back, and he's practically good as new."

Ericha observed the wide-eyed wonder of both mother and child as the Duke of Horstberg gave them his attention.

Stefan wondered how long it would be before the doctor arrived. The tension of the mother and child was evident, not to mention the other children hovering close by that he suspected belonged to the same family. Attempting to ease the wait, he asked the boy, "Have you ever held a real sword, young man?"

The child shook his head slightly. Stefan lifted his hand and barely glanced over his shoulder. The captain pulled his gleaming sword from the sheath at his side and gave it to Stefan. He carefully placed the hilt into the child's hand and helped him hold it safely.

"Now," he said sternly, "since you've gotten so good with a sword, I want you to be very brave, even though it hurts. And I want you to do exactly what the good doctor tells you to do. You need to get that leg healed, and maybe one day *you* can have your own sword, like the good captain here."

The doctor appeared, and Stefan took the sword from the reluctant little hand, returning it to the captain. Stefan knew he could leave now and everything would be taken care of, but he could almost feel the heat radiating from Ericha, though he hardly dared look at her. He concentrated instead on the child's face as the boy endured the doctor's examination. A slight discoloration caught his attention, and he focused on it more closely.

"Why is this child bruised?" he asked the mother.

Her rise in tension was immediate and obvious. He looked her in the eye and wondered if it was the question or his presence that made her look terrified.

"He was just run over by a carriage, Your Grace," she said with a shaky voice.

Stefan tilted the boy's face slightly. "This bruise is turning yellow. It's not fresh." He looked back to the mother as she turned away and glanced down.

Ericha watched Stefan, hardly breathing as she wondered over his purpose. She saw him take hold of the woman's chin and look hard at her face, as she felt certain only a man in his position would dare.

"And this bruise, Madame?" he asked, his voice tightening.

Ericha perceived the implication as Stefan moved perceptive eyes over the other children, then back to the mother. While she sensed Stefan's displeasure, she wondered if he sensed this woman's fear.

"I asked you a question," he stated, kind but firm.

The woman said nothing. Her trembling increased.

"Your Grace," Ericha said, and Stefan was briefly startled by the reminder that she was so close, "perhaps it is better if she remains silent. Perhaps there is fear involved in discussing it . . . with anyone."

Stefan looked back to the woman, her gratitude to Ericha was as blatant as her relief. A far deeper aspect of his suspicions took hold in his mind, and he felt suddenly humbled.

"Thank you, Miss Lokberg," he said, hoping to convey with his eyes how much he meant it. "I'm certain you're right."

When the doctor had the boy's leg secured enough to transport him, Stefan discreetly took him aside. "I want the family examined for signs of abuse. I will cover any expenses. Come straight to me with your report."

"Yes, Your Grace," he said, giving Stefan a look that indicated he would use discretion.

"Captain," Stefan said more loudly, "would you please see that this child is taken safely home, where the good doctor can set the leg properly."

Stefan nodded discreetly to the captain and felt sure the man knew that he was also to be observant in his errand. A minute later, Stefan found himself standing with Ericha as they watched the little family move away with the doctor and the captain. He turned quickly to see that an officer was holding the reins to his horse a short distance away. He turned back to Ericha just as she began to move away.

"Wait," he said and took a step toward her.

Ericha turned hesitantly. By the look in his eyes, she wondered if he wanted to hold her as badly as she wanted to be in his arms.

"Thank you, Miss Lokberg. Your insight is appreciated more than you know."

"What will you do?" she asked, glancing around to be sure that no one was close enough to hear.

"I don't know," he admitted. "My hope is to help the family, but . . ."

"But?" she asked. "That's good, isn't it?"

"I always hope my actions will turn out favorably. But too often there are repercussions that are . . . difficult."

Ericha caught a glimpse of the weight on his shoulders as he glanced away, apparently trying to appear casual.

"I miss you, Ericha," he said without looking at her.

"Don't expect me to respond to that without making a scene," she replied. There was a moment of silence. "You look very handsome, Stefan. I like the crown."

He grunted in seeming dismay but made no response.

"I saw you laugh today," she said.

Stefan looked at her and chuckled. "How many men have been beating down your door, begging to marry you?"

"None that I've noticed," she replied nonchalantly.

"They're all a bunch of fools," he said in a light voice that belied the intensity that passed through his eyes.

"There was Kurt," she said almost flippantly and was not disappointed by the immediate jealousy that filled his demeanor.

"Kurt?" he echoed tersely. His self-discipline quickly softened his expression, but his eyes were tense and alert.

"Oh, it was a while back," she said, thoroughly enjoying this. "I must have forgotten to mention it before. Or since I told Karl about it, perhaps I assumed he might have told you. Kurt is a blacksmith. We had lunch together a few times. I think he was quite taken with me, but . . ."

"But?" he asked sharply.

"How can you stand there and tell me to find someone and

get married, when I know full well that you are raging with jealousy at the thought of my having lunch with a blacksmith?"

Stefan swallowed hard. "Don't expect me to respond to that without making a scene." He cleared his throat and glanced over his shoulder to make certain the officer waiting for him was keeping his distance. "You were telling me about Kurt."

"Ah, yes," she said, "Kurt. The last time I talked to him, he told me that he didn't want to see me again."

Stefan chuckled tensely. Mingled with his relief was shock. How could any man not want to see her again?

"He told me he would not associate any further with a woman who had only her mother's name."

Again Stefan feared responding for making a scene. His pain on her behalf made him want to hunt the man down and throttle him.

Ericha saw the emotion in his eyes. And while it was touching, her own pain suddenly became too much to bear. There he stood, a crown on his head, a robe over his shoulders, surrounded by people who were in awe of his very presence. Here she stood, a woman with nothing—not even a name.

"It seems you have something in common with my father," she said, unable to help the bitter tone.

Stefan felt it coming, but he wasn't prepared for the way it deepened his pain.

"I'm sure he would have *liked* to give me his name, but apparently it was impossible."

Fearing she would either cry or throw herself into his arms, she added quickly, "Good-bye, Stefan. If you'll excuse me, I've noticed a lot of eligible men roaming around here. Some of them look awfully sharp in those uniforms."

Ericha walked away and left him standing, which she had to admit felt much better than watching him leave. She glanced back only once to see him mounting his stallion. A moment later the horse thundered up the cobbled street in the direction of Castle Horstberg. Even in his retreat, Ericha had to admit he was magnificent, with the red robe flying out behind him.

"Heaven help me," she muttered under her breath and walked home.

Stefan looked around his office at the solemn faces of these men who were supposed to keep him informed and see that he did his job right. His secretary. His advisors. His grandfather. The Captain of the Guard. And today, Doctor Furhelm, his family's doctor, whom he had gone to with the evidence of the other doctor's report.

"I'm certain I didn't hear that right," Stefan said, leaning his elbows on his desk.

"I think you did," Georg replied, his leg propped up on a soft chair. He'd been giving the Dukes of Horstberg quiet advice for fifty years, and he did it well.

"Are you saying," Stefan's eyes took in the entire room, "that it is not illegal for a man to beat his wife and children?"

"That's right," one advisor said.

"It's the same in any country, Your Grace," another one informed him. "A man's wife is considered his property and—"

"Not in *my* country!" Stefan interrupted, pounding a fist on the desk. "How can children who are treated that way grow up to be responsible citizens? How can women who are treated that way *raise* responsible children?"

Everyone was silent. Even Georg.

"Doctor?" Stefan nodded toward him. "Tell them what you told me."

The tension in the room mounted as the doctor explained the bruises and welts that had been found on the mother and the children.

"And?" Stefan pressed.

The doctor sighed. "The woman was evidently forced upon . . . multiple times."

At the dumbfounded expressions, Stefan said, "The animal rapes his wife regularly." A long minute later, he added, "Most of you seem terribly uncomfortable." He noted the doctor and Georg seemed to be handling it well enough. "Would you prefer that we just ignore this issue . . . that we pretend we don't know what we now know?"

"Your Grace," one of the advisors said in a tone that indicated he was not pleased, "I'm not sure this law is enforceable."

"Captain?" Stefan motioned toward him. "Do you have a comment on that?"

"Any law is enforceable if the terms are handled correctly," he stated.

"Gentlemen?" Stefan invited other comments.

One of the advisors spoke up. "I wonder how many men would be affected by this, Your Grace. Can you possibly have them *all* arrested?"

"I don't want them arrested," Stefan insisted. "I want them to stop beating their children and abusing their wives."

"If a man considers himself entitled to do with his family members as he pleases, would trying to prevent that be creating enemies within our own borders?"

Another advisor interjected. "Perhaps with the obvious complications here, there are other more . . . important matters that—"

"Nothing," Stefan leaned forward and penetrated each man briefly with his eyes, "is more important than the women and children of Horstberg. That is what we are doing here, gentlemen. If any of you have a problem with that, I will see if I can get you a job in housekeeping. I hear we're shorthanded at the moment."

Stefan heard a subtle snort of amusement from his grandfather. He turned to look at his secretary and asked, "Is it against the law for me to change the law?"

"That's why you wear the crown," Rusty stated. "I wouldn't want to wear it."

Stefan took a deep breath. "I hereby decree that no man . . . No, make that . . . no person shall inflict abuse or cause harm to any family member . . . or words to that effect." He waved his hand carelessly. "Write it up, Rusty. Word it so there's no room for question."

Rusty nodded and scribbled more notes.

"Captain Leichty," Stefan said, "I want that man . . . What is his name again?"

"Bergen Schmidt," the captain answered.

"Ah, yes. I want Mr. Schmidt arrested and a trial date set. I intend to make an example of him."

"I must confess," one of the advisors said, "I admire what you're doing, Your Grace." Stefan nodded, and he went on, "But we must be careful not to press this too hard too fast."

"More specifically?"

"If it was not illegal until now, then has he committed a crime?"

Stefan thought about it. "Good point," he admitted. "So . . . issue him a citation; see that he's informed of the change in the law, and that he is completely aware of its stipulations. And then I want the family checked on. If any more abuse occurs, *then* arrest him. Anything else?" No response. "Good. Then we are adjourned." Stefan came around the desk to shake the doctor's hand. "Thank you for coming. I know how busy you are."

"I'll do all I can. This is something that's troubled me for many years. I see more evidence of it than I care to admit to."

Stefan nodded toward Rusty. "Make a note of that. Doctors' reports could help enforce that law."

Stefan took a moment to thank each of them for their time as they left the room. The tension that had been present dissipated as they exchanged friendly small talk. When they had all gone, Stefan closed the door, glad to have a moment alone with his grandfather.

"How's the leg?" Stefan asked.

"It's fine. No problem."

"You never told me what you were doing on the stairs by Abbi's room in the middle of the night." Stefan's tone was teasing, and Georg's eyes sparkled in response.

"You never told me what you were doing at Karl's house in the middle of the night." Stefan tried not to betray his guilt, but he didn't underestimate Georg's perception. "Karl told the officers you were playing poker. You hate poker."

"I was bored," he said.

"So was I," Georg replied.

They both chuckled, and Stefan relaxed. "You just like to keep the servants guessing," he said.

"That too," Georg admitted lightly.

"So, that's the reason you keep separate rooms? I've wondered, you know."

Georg was slightly more serious as he said, "For obvious reasons, we keep just about everything separate. I married her to make it right before God. What anyone else thinks is irrelevant to me."

Stefan felt a tight knot develop in his stomach as he thought of Ericha, wishing with all his heart and soul that such an option was open to him. He felt compelled to admit, "I envy you, Georg—your relationship with Abbi."

Since Stefan's early childhood, his interest in political matters had made it more convenient to call his grandparents by their given names much of the time. Georg was his father's father, and Abbi was his mother's mother. They were both widowed, and the closeness they'd shared had gradually blossomed into something deeper. Abbi's title and position had prevented her from remarrying, but Georg had found a way to work around it. Legally Abbi had kept her name, her property, her position. Georg wanted nothing but Abbi. They were married when Stefan was ten, and their presence at Castle Horstberg was the only thing that kept it standing, in Stefan's opinion.

Georg said nothing in response to Stefan's comment. But his eyes warmed with compassion. There was simply nothing to say, no consolation to be given.

"Hey," Stefan said, attempting to lighten the mood, "I was just thinking, if a man's wife is his property, do you think I could sell mine?"

Georg said nothing. His expression didn't change.

Stefan laughed. "It was a joke, Georg. Don't you think it's funny?"

Georg shook his head and laughed, though he looked as if

he was trying not to. "Yes," he said, "it's funny. It's just not like you to make jokes . . . especially about things that hit so close to the truth."

"Yes, well," Stefan turned and looked out the window, "I can't change it, so I might as well laugh about it."

"Who told you that?" Georg asked.

Stefan's heart quickened with the memory. He was tempted to lie, but he simply said, "A woman with red hair."

"There's a number of possibilities."

A light knock on the door preceded Abbi's timid entrance into the room. "I saw them leave and knew you were finished," she said, sitting close to Georg and taking his hand.

"We were just talking about you," Stefan said.

"Really?"

"Actually," Stefan clarified, "I was just about to tell Georg that I believe women with red hair are instinctively wise."

"I dare say you're right," Georg agreed.

Stefan turned to look out the window.

"You would be very proud of Stefan," Georg said to Abbi.

"Tell me," she said, and Georg proceeded to fill her in on the details. Stefan continued to stare out the window.

Ericha told Karl about the incident with the child, and a week later he returned from the pub to tell her that the man had been arrested when the abuse had continued after fair warning, and a trial would be held. He explained to her what Stefan had done regarding the law, and her heart swelled with admiration for his courage and his desire to do what was right. Even though it was the same desire that kept her from having him a part of her life.

"The trial is open to the public," Karl said. "I was planning to go. Come with me." She hesitated, and he added, "I wouldn't blame you for not wanting to see Stefan, if—"

"I'd like to go," she concluded. While seeing him always seemed to renew the pain a little, she couldn't help being fascinated by the many facets of his life, even if she only saw them from a distance.

The courtroom was situated next to the keep, just off the castle courtyard. Karl and Ericha found a seat about halfway up, and Ericha was surprised to see how crowded the huge room became. She figured this case was drawing attention because it was bringing an issue to light that had never been dealt with publicly before.

Ericha unconsciously squeezed Karl's hand as Stefan entered the room, escorted by two officers of the Guard and two other official looking men. He wore judicial robes and his demeanor was more severe than usual. She was fascinated by every aspect of the situation being discussed, and impressed with the dignified, straight-forward manner Stefan used in confronting the problem. In the end, Bergen Schmidt was sentenced to ten days in the keep, and he was ordered that the ill treatment of his family members would cease. A doctor would be assigned to make regular checks on the family for a year.

For several days after the trial, Ericha hoped more keenly than usual that she would see Stefan. She wanted to tell him how proud she was of what he'd done. But she saw no sign of him, and weeks passing made it evident that nothing had changed between them.

As Christmas approached, Karl took her along with him to some social events. He introduced her to more than one man that she found intriguing. But in spite of a worthy effort on her part, nothing ever came of it. The winter days became tedious with little to do but make lace and help keep the house in order. An occasional visit to Mrs. Burger broke the monotony a little. But the winter nights were long and cold, and Ericha was lonely.

Karl dismounted and handed the reins of his horse over to the waiting stablehand wearing castle livery. He hurried through the cold to his father's apartment and went in without knocking.

"How cozy," he quipped, making elaborate indications of how cold he was.

Stefan and Theodor barely glanced up from their game of chess to acknowledge him.

"What brings you here?" Theodor asked.

"Ericha insisted." Karl noticed Stefan's eyebrow going up subtly, but he said nothing. Gingerly, Karl pulled a wrapped package from inside his coat and set it on the table beside the chessboard. "Cinnamon buns," he explained. "She knew they were one of your favorites and threatened me with my life if I didn't brave the cold to bring them."

"Ooh." Theodor unwrapped the package. "I do like that girl."

"They're still warm," Karl said, "which is the only thing that kept me from freezing to death on my way here."

"You'd better try one," Theodor said with his mouth full, motioning toward Stefan. "That niece of mine is a fine cook, like her mother before her."

Karl removed his coat and gloves and sat down to peruse the current status of the chessboard. He rubbed his hands together and pretended not to notice the way Stefan picked up one of the cinnamon buns as if it were fine porcelain. He looked at it. He smelled it. He closed his eyes as he took a bite.

"Now," Theodor declared, "is that not one of the finest things you've ever tasted?"

"Undoubtedly," Stefan replied after swallowing.

"Ooh," Karl said, his focus on the chessboard, "you're not doing well here, Stefan."

"He's been a little . . . distracted," Theodor said lightly. "Just as well. I quite enjoy having the duke indebted to me."

"You're betting?" Karl laughed. "Mercy, you people need to get out more!"

Karl helped himself to the food in his father's kitchen while the game progressed. Stefan finally lost after a hard fight, declaring soundly, "You're a shrewd old man, Theodor. It's a wonder I put up with you at all."

Theodor laughed. "No one else could do what I do. And be careful who you're calling old . . . sir."

"Now that you've lost a little more money to this shrewd old man," Karl said, "can we go to the pub?"

Stefan glanced out the window. It was getting late, but he had no desire to return home. "Sure. Why not? I could use some fresh air."

"That's the spirit, Stef!" Karl threw Stefan his cloak. "There's nothing like a good beer to warm your toes."

"I don't know if I'd go so far as to say that," Stefan said, barely showing a wry smile.

They arrived at the pub later than usual and found it crowded. While Stefan generally tried to avoid the crowds, occasionally he enjoyed just observing the people of Horstberg in their everyday activities. He and Karl managed to slip in unnoticed and take a table at the edge.

"You *do* seem distracted," Karl said. "You all right?"

The bar maid set two beers on their table and hurried on.

"Same old thing," Stefan said. "There's nothing to say."

"Then talk about something good. Surely there's *something* good in your life."

Stefan was silent for several moments. He almost didn't dare say it. But feeling a need to verify her existence, he asked quietly, "How is she, Karl?"

"She?" He pretended innocence with a wide-eyed simper that made Stefan chuckle.

"That adorable little cousin of yours," Stefan clarified, leaning over the table. A delightful little tremor erupted inside him just to speak of her aloud. "The one who made those delectable cinnamon . . . what-evers."

"Ah, *that* she." Karl feigned exaggerated enlightenment. "I did notice how you enjoyed those cinnamon . . . *what-evers.* I'll be sure to mention to her that you did."

"Why don't you do that," Stefan said. "How is she?"

"She's still adorable."

Karl watched the reaction in Stefan's eyes and knew this was not the right path to lighten his mood. Instead Karl started in on a story he'd heard that morning from one of his customers. Stefan still seemed distracted, but he made eye contact or nodded his head often enough that Karl knew he was listening.

While Stefan tried to concentrate on Karl's story and keep his mind off Ericha, he became vaguely aware of the antics going on at a nearby table. There were several men, drinking and laughing loudly. None of them looked familiar, but they could have grown up in Horstberg for all he knew.

While these men teased one of the barmaids in a typical way and made some lewd comments, Karl described in detail how an old farmer had shot some poor woman's chicken by mistake. He was trying to avoid the distractions and tune in more to Karl, when the word *duchess* caught his ear. Stefan tried to hear what was being said, but the room was noisy. As he shut Karl's voice out, he distinctly heard the words *duchess* and *bed* in the same sentence.

Stefan discreetly glanced toward the group. They looked mostly like farmers and laborers, and they'd obviously all had one beer too many. They laughed loudly, and one of the men distinctly said something about royal blood being hot.

Stefan felt something sick ooze from the deepest part of him. He was not unaware of his wife's odd habits of coming and going from the castle at all hours. And he knew the reasons, even if she'd never directly admitted it. Karl had once told him he'd heard a rumor filtering around concerning her indiscretions. But hearing the evidence for himself was sickening.

While Stefan was trying to convince himself that he was hearing bits and pieces and getting mixed messages, he caught the phrases *tasty piece* and *not too particular*. And that word *duchess* again.

Karl stopped talking when Stefan held up a hand, apparently indicating that he be quiet. He saw Stefan's eyes shift discreetly, and tried to tune in to whatever he was listening to. Some guy said, "She's a tasty one, all right. And I know it for a fact."

Another said, "You and half the men in Horstberg."

Loud laughter erupted, and then the first man added, "I'd like to get my hands on one o' those emeralds she wears, but she don't take *them* off."

Laughter erupted again, but it came to an abrupt halt as Stefan flew out of his seat and grabbed the guy by the back of the shirt. In one agile movement, Stefan hurled him around and threw a fist into his jaw. Karl's concern over the guy being bigger than Stefan evaporated as the victim hit the floor. Stefan stood for a moment, his legs braced apart, his eyes alert. The room became as silent as snowfall. Karl didn't understand why the Duke of Horstberg was provoking a brawl with some drunk farmer, but he couldn't help but admire the power in Stefan's demeanor. He was like a lion, ready to kill the next thing that moved. But for what?

The man on the floor groaned and spit blood. Stefan hauled him up by the shirt collar and slammed him against the wall. He spoke in a voice that made it evident he intended everyone present to hear, as if he were making some royal proclamation. "Bed her if you like. It matters little to me. But take care that you keep quiet about it."

It became evident this man was either terribly drunk or he didn't know who he was dealing with when he sneered and retorted, "Are you defending the lady's honor, then?"

Stefan slammed him against the wall again. "She is no lady. And she has no honor. But her name—and only her name—I would defend. Take care that you don't defile it."

Stefan let go and hurried out of the pub. In the moment it took Karl to gather his wits and follow, he heard the victim snarl, "Who the hell was that?"

"The Duke of Horstberg, you stupid . . ." The reply faded as Karl stepped outside and hurried to where Stefan had already mounted.

"Have you gone insane?" Karl demanded, riding close beside Stefan. "You're the duke. You can't just go hitting some guy because—"

"What I just did was no different than sentencing a man

to prison for robbery, or ordering an execution for treason. I made an example out of him. I pray that every other man in her web gets wind of it and thinks twice before he starts bragging in the streets."

Karl said nothing for several minutes. Stefan finally broke the silence. *"You* have nothing to say?"

In an unusually serious tone, Karl said, "I can't imagine how it must feel to realize your wife is a . . ."

"Go ahead and say it, Karl. She's a whore."

"I'm not going to say it. The duke would probably have me hung and quartered."

"Funny," Stefan said tersely.

"Since when did *you* start talking about her like that? *You* hardly talk at all . . . especially about such things."

Stefan briefly allowed a warm memory to calm him. "Somebody told me I should be willing to talk to someone I trust about the things that are difficult."

Karl was briefly stunned. "I take you it trust me, then." Stefan made no response, and he added, "And who gave you this phenomenal advice? Your grandmother?"

"Actually, it was that woman who made those delectable cinnamon what-evers."

"I see," Karl said, and they rode slowly in silence. Stefan didn't seemed disturbed by the cold, and Karl endured it, sensing that Stefan needed a friend at the moment.

Hoping Stefan might do some more talking, Karl finally said, "I wish it didn't have to be this way for you."

"I'd divorce her in a minute if I didn't think it would push Horstberg into war. I believe her father knows what kind of woman she is, but having his finger in our pie is something he puts a very high priority on. Sometimes I wish she'd do something just deplorable enough that I could publicly denounce her. But I fear that if I did—even with just cause—the baron would come up with some excuse to press for a piece of what's mine. I wish I could understand what kind of madness made me believe that marrying her was a good thing."

"Don't be too hard on yourself, Stefan. She's a pretty good actress."

"Yes," Stefan replied, "but not being hard on myself doesn't fill the lonely nights."

Karl said nothing more. The subject was pressing a little too close to home.

The following morning at breakfast, Georg said coolly, "I hear you had a little adventure at the pub last night."

Stefan shot his head up. Abbi looked pleasantly curious. Johanna looked like she usually did at breakfast. The years had lessened her grace in covering the hangovers.

"News spreads like fire," Stefan replied in the same cool tone. "What *exactly* did you hear? I could use some good gossip." He wondered what kind of man he was becoming when he found no regret in his actions last night. He glanced at Johanna and felt more like a cat with a mouse to play with. "Wouldn't *you* like to hear some gossip to start the day, my dear?" he asked his wife. She looked almost startled.

Georg smirked as if he too was enjoying this. "I heard you threw a guy twice your size and beat him up pretty badly."

"What?" Abbi exclaimed. Johanna's eyes widened. Stefan laughed.

"Well," he explained, "he was nowhere near twice my size, and I hit him once."

"It's true, then?" Abbi interjected. "Why on earth would you—"

"Forgive me if I have disappointed you, Grandmama," he interrupted, "but what is a man supposed to do when some farmer is spreading *lies,*" he enunciated carefully and shot Johanna a harsh glare, "about his wife?"

"What did he say?" Abbi asked, apparently more calm.

Stefan looked straight at Johanna as he said, "He was bragging that he'd seen the duchess in nothing but her emeralds."

The guilt rose into Johanna's eyes so fast, he was surprised it didn't knock her off her chair. She covered it quickly but said nothing.

Stefan turned back to Abbi and Georg. "So I hit him."

The subject was dropped, but Stefan hoped that his grandparents caught the undertones. He wasn't about to go crying and tattling to them about the injustice in his marriage. But neither did he want them to see Johanna for anything more or less than what she was.

Later that day, Stefan encountered Johanna in the hall. She was unusually sheepish, and he took her arm to keep her from passing. She looked up at him like a timid mouse, and he felt like that cat again.

"Can you imagine," he said quietly, "the nerve of all those men in the pub, insinuating that they had known your pleasures. Do you suppose they all got together and constructed this lie to defame your good character? I wonder how they knew you always wear emeralds on your late-night walks. You can't imagine, my dear, what good it does me to know for certain what you're doing when you spend so much time away from the castle. At least I can stop losing sleep over *that*."

"You've cared nothing about what I do for months," she spat in retaliation. "Why should it concern you now?"

"I *don't* care what you do with your nights, Johanna. But you bear my name. You bear my country's name. Be careful that you don't go dragging that name through the gutter. Or you may end up there with it."

"Don't threaten me, Stefan," she snarled.

Stefan lifted a finger close to her face. "Don't push me, Johanna. There's no telling how far a man will go when he's pushed. Just ask the guy whose jaw I rearranged last night. That is, if you can figure out which one he is."

Stefan let go of her and left her standing. He tried to tell himself it felt good to put her in her place. But deep inside he wondered what kind of man he was becoming.

Karl was hard at work in his shop when Stefan walked through the door.

"Stefan." He smiled. "What's the occasion?"

"Occasion?"

"You mosey out here about once every decade or so. There must be an occasion."

"Actually," Stefan said, "I had some time off."

Karl grinned. "Ah, that is an occasion!"

Stefan gave a slight smile but made no response. He moved aimlessly about the room, examining the projects, and Karl watched him carefully.

"What's up?" Karl asked.

"Nothing," Stefan replied. "Same old thing—day in, day out."

"We should have a war or something and give your life some excitement."

"No, thank you." Stefan managed a smile. "I'm not that bored."

"So what brings you here?" Karl asked.

"Well," Stefan sighed and sat down, "to be quite honest, I couldn't bear the confinement of that wretched castle another minute. I would swear Johanna's entertaining the devil himself by the mood that hangs around her. I've been wishing I could go to the lodge, but it's snowed under. If I went to the pub I'd probably end up drunk. So here I am."

"How flattering," Karl said, but Stefan caught the humor in his eyes.

"You should know by now that you've always been the best cure for me when I'm in need of cheering up."

"Does that make me the court jester?" Karl smirked.

Stefan shook his head and chuckled, toying idly with a tiny chisel.

"It worked!" Karl said triumphantly. "If I can make the king laugh, I must be the court jester."

"Next you'll be wanting wages for your bad jokes."

"Wouldn't hurt. They aren't worth anything otherwise."

Stefan made no further response. His eyes grew distant and a shadow fell over his face that filled Karl with compassion. Something stabbed at him as he thought of Ericha looking much the same way when she didn't know he was watching her. He was wondering what he might say to distract Stefan, when Stefan set aside the chisel and rose to pick up the guitar. He blew dust off of it as he reseated himself, and then he coughed and waved his hand in front of his face. Karl laughed.

"Don't you use it anymore?" Stefan asked.

"I've been busy," he replied. "When I'm not so busy, I use it. Luise loves it when I play."

"So all those lessons I forced you through were worth something, eh?"

"Yes, I admit. But I'll never be as good as you." Stefan picked at it a few minutes, and Karl asked, "Have you been keeping up on it?"

"Actually, yes," he replied. "Every spare minute I get, it's either the music or the oils." He practiced a few minutes, then moved to the edge of his seat and settled the guitar onto his thigh. As Stefan began to play a familiar piece, Karl was freshly amazed at the agility of his fingers—in spite of an occasional missed chord. He never tired of hearing Stefan's music, yet he and Theodor were likely the only ones beyond immediate family who had ever heard Stefan play. Karl often imagined him playing at the pub or in the market square, and thought that it would have suited him far better than being the duke. Stefan gradually seemed to become lost in the music. He occasionally closed his eyes, and Karl saw the burdens of his life briefly dissipate.

Karl was surprised to see Ericha slip quietly through the door. He was glad that Stefan was caught up enough that he didn't notice her. She leaned against the wall where Stefan wouldn't see her and settled herself to watch, and Karl could see plainly what she was feeling.

Ericha had come out to the shop to bring Karl a message that had just arrived for him. She'd paused outside upon hearing the music, and her heart nearly leapt to realize it was Stefan. It seemed she discovered something new about him every time she saw him. For the moment, she let the bitterness of their situation flee, and she was simply grateful for this opportunity. The weeks since she'd seen him seemed like an eternity.

Karl put his work aside and leaned back, placing his feet on the workbench to listen. Ericha became so entranced by the song that she was startled when it ended. Karl applauded as Stefan leaned back, but Ericha remained silent, not wanting to break the spell of watching him while he wasn't aware.

"I may be the court jester," Karl said to Stefan, and Ericha appreciated his not drawing attention to her, "but you should be the court musician. You have the ability to cheer up the king."

"No," Stefan said, setting the guitar aside, "I have the ability to make the king forget for a few minutes here and there. At times the music is no better than getting drunk. It's like a mindless release from the world."

"Except it doesn't leave a hangover," Karl said.

"Not usually." Stefan gave a slight chuckle.

"I really like that song," Karl said. Stefan made no response, and Karl added, "Ericha liked it too."

Ericha glared at Karl, and Stefan turned abruptly in his chair. A sharp tension descended upon the room as their eyes met. Ericha wondered by his expression if he was angry at her for being there, but she didn't care.

"Karl," she forced her attention to him, "this message just came for you."

"Thank you," he said as she crossed the room to give it to him. He opened it and read. "It seems I'm needed." Karl smirked. He glanced at Ericha, then at Stefan. He grabbed his coat and headed for the door, impulsively saying, "I'm turning my job over to my little cousin. I'm certain she'd make a fine court jester."

He was gone before either of them could protest. Ericha hardly dared turn to look at Stefan again. The mixture of emotions was almost unbearable.

"Perhaps I should just—" she began, moving toward the door.

"Please stay," he said quietly. Ericha stopped and turned her eyes toward him. The love in his gaze filled her with relief mingled with a bitter ache.

"I enjoyed the song," she said. "I had no idea."

"When I was a child," he uttered in a wistful tone, "I couldn't decide if I wanted to be a musician or an artist."

"And what conclusion did you come to?"

"I stopped wondering one day before I turned eight."

"That's very young to make such a decision."

"It was made for me. That's how old I was when my father sat me down and told me that I was the Duke of Horstberg."

Ericha didn't know what to say. She had an unbearable urge to just take him in her arms and somehow soothe the hurt. But she only stood dumbly gazing at him, almost wanting to run away.

"Why don't you sit down?" Stefan motioned toward a chair, and Ericha did as he said. "I'm certain you don't want to hear about my troubles. *I* certainly don't. I suppose I'm just feeling sorry for myself tonight. That's why I came to see Karl. He doesn't let me get away with feeling sorry for myself."

"And he has left me in his stead," she said quietly. "What would you have me do for you, Your Grace?"

"Just . . . *be* with me," he said. "Just sit there and let me look at you."

Stefan enjoyed the opportunity to gaze at her openly, in a way he'd never dare in public. Free from having to mask his feelings, he allowed his eyes to drink her in. As usual, she wore a dress of simple calico with a little lace collar as its only adornment. When her hair wasn't hanging loose or braided down her back, it was as she wore it now, plaited and wound against the back of her head. A few straying wisps of red hair surrounded her face. A delicate hand brushed them back, then settled again into her lap. She glanced away, then met his gaze, with green eyes that seemed to see into his soul. He loved her common way, which seemed somehow a stark contrast to an air about her that was every bit as regal as the women in his family who had been raised as princesses.

"You know," he said, "it's not difficult to imagine you in castle courts. You would put them all to shame."

"Me?" She laughed, but her eyes were severe. "No, Stefan," she said, "we belong in separate worlds. You do well at immersing yourself in mine, I admit. But I don't believe I could do so well in yours."

"Don't underestimate yourself," he said with such blatant admiration that Ericha felt nearly chilled.

"It's irrelevant," she insisted. "I will never be a part of your world."

"In my dreams you are," he said. Ericha's eyes showed intrigue, and he leaned forward. "Every time I sit down to eat, I imagine you at the table. And there is a staircase in the castle where . . . well," he chuckled, "actually there are several—too many to count—but this particular one catches me each time I pass it. I have often stopped, just a moment, and imagined you coming down those stairs. There are times in my mind when it seems the most natural thing in the world for you to be there, and I wonder why you are not."

Ericha felt a bitter response slide onto her tongue, but she quickly swallowed it and reminded herself not to let this time with him slip into anger as it had at times in the past.

"Do you ever dream of me, Ericha?" he asked. For a moment she saw the perfect confidence of the Duke of Horstberg recede behind barefaced vulnerability.

"Always," she admitted.

"Tell me," he whispered.

"I have dreamed of stepping onto a train with you, and never looking back. In my mind I see the cottage where we live, and you holding our son while I put dinner on the table."

Stefan discreetly pressed a hand over his mouth as if it could hold back his sudden rise of emotion.

"When I remind myself that you could never leave here,

I am content to dream of simply holding you close at night, knowing you are mine, even if Horstberg must claim you in the light of day."

When she was apparently finished, he said, "I am continually amazed at the way you seem to read my thoughts, my feelings."

Ericha lifted her hand toward him. Stefan looked at it. He touched it. Then he grabbed it as if it were a lifeline. He met her eyes while his thumb moved over the back of her hand, and then he brought it to his lips and let them linger over it.

"When the sun comes up each morning," he said softly, "I look in the mirror and see a man with the weight of a country on his shoulders. I see shadows in my eyes that reflect the miseries of my life, but I do my best to look beyond the shadows and go about my business.

"But at night," his voice lowered to a deep whisper, "the world is different. Alone in my room I can be anything I want, and my mind takes me to a place where nothing deters my happiness." He kissed her hand again, then relaxed his arm against his thigh without letting go of her.

"In your arms, Ericha, I find a solace that words cannot describe. It takes every ounce of strength I have to keep from coming here each night and loving you the way I want to. But in my mind there are no bounds. In my mind I kiss you. I touch you. I hold you. I tangle my hands through your hair."

Stefan slid his chair closer and set his booted feet on either side of her. He leaned toward Ericha, and she held her breath. His eyes were so close they burned through her; his lips so near that his breath touched her as he spoke, barely audible. "And we're together, Ericha, in a place where the world falls away and nothing else matters." He closed his eyes and brought his lips close to her ear. His voice became deep and breathy. "We're together, Ericha," he repeated.

Ericha closed her eyes and tilted her head back. Her breathing became sharp. Her hand tightened in his.

"It's just you and me," he continued. "Just you and me." Stefan came barely closer, and his cheek brushed against hers.

"You beg me to never leave you," he whispered, "and I promise that I will be there forever."

Ericha heard herself sob and felt warm tears rush over her face and throat. "Somewhere in the midst of it," Stefan went on, "I fall asleep. I wake up in the dark, holding nothing but my pillow, breathing your name on my lips, and I . . . I know that I . . ." He bowed his head against her shoulder and his voice returned to normal. "I know that I lied to you. I wasn't there forever. I wasn't even there for tomorrow."

Ericha sobbed again, and Stefan pulled back to look at her. "Think of me, Ericha," he whispered, brushing the back of his hand over her tear-stained face, "as I think of you, and we will be together—every night."

"Stay with me now," she begged, pressing her face to his throat. Stefan put his arm around her and let her weep, while he absorbed her presence like he might drink in water to prepare for a trek through the desert.

When she had quieted, he pulled away. He looked into her eyes, and Ericha read the regret, the empathy, the pain.

A sad smile was his only response to her unanswered plea. He brushed his lips over her brow and reluctantly came to his feet. He squeezed her hand once more then let it drop.

"I love you, Ericha," he said, and left her alone.

Ericha's fingers felt numb from the way he'd held them so long, so tight. She wanted them to never recover as she went up to her room to relive these precious moments with him in her mind, knowing he would do the same.

Stefan returned home to the news that Abbi had ordered an officer to escort Johanna to her rooms. She'd come to the drawing room where Abbi and Georg were having coffee after dinner. Obviously drunk, Johanna started in by complaining about the servants, and gradually worked herself into a rage over everything she considered unfair about living under their roof.

As Georg repeated the story matter-of-factly, Stefan felt sick. "You people must hate me for bringing her into the family," he said.

"You did what you felt was best at the time," Georg said as if he would defend Stefan's honor to the death.

"Yes." Stefan sighed. "Well, obviously it wasn't. I suppose I'd better talk to the shrew and get it over with."

"Your grandmother didn't so much as raise her voice, Stefan. Don't let Johanna tell you otherwise."

Stefan nodded, amazed at how well Georg knew Johanna's ways.

The doors to Johanna's bedroom and sitting room were flanked by officers of the Guard.

"All right," Stefan said severely to one of the young men in uniform, "I'll guard the door. You go in there and have it out with the duchess."

His alarm was so blatant that Stefan couldn't hold back a laugh. "It's all right," Stefan assured him, "I was only joking."

The young officer chuckled tensely and unlocked the door. "You may go now. I'll handle it from here."

Stefan waited until they had gone down the stairs, not wanting to be overheard. He took a deep breath and knocked at the door, then opened it without waiting for a response. The room was rank with the smell of cheap liquor and expensive perfume, and Johanna stood from a chair as he entered, attempting a dignified pose. But the way she teetered detracted somewhat.

"It's about time you got here," she growled without preamble. "Do you have any idea how these people treat me? Your grandmother had the nerve to have me disgracefully escorted away like some kind of criminal, and—"

Stefan moved directly in front of her. "I've already heard the story, and I don't want to hear it again. If you choose to drink all the liquor you can get your hands on, so be it. But you will not afflict my family with your drunkenness. Do I make myself clear?"

"Oh, quite clear," she hissed. "You and your precious family.

It's a wonder you can even walk out the door without your grandmother there to hold your hand."

Stefan felt the anger seethe in him and forced himself to stay calm. "At least my family does not have a reputation for being a bunch of underhanded, powerthirsty fiends."

Johanna slapped Stefan so fast he didn't have a chance to even brace himself. "If my father heard you say that, he'd have you hung out to rot."

Anger tightened Stefan's chest and clenched his fists as he turned back to look at Johanna. He could almost feel the hatred burning through his eyes.

"Or better yet," she raged on, "he could hang your grandmother out with you. Everyone knows that it's she who runs this country." She pushed at his chest with both hands as she said it. "You're not man enough to—"

Stefan backhanded her across the face before he even realized he wanted to. She screamed and reeled back into the chair. Pressing a hand over her reddened face, she turned to look at him with eyes as stunned and afraid as he felt.

Stefan told himself he should apologize or justify. But he knew that any display of weakness would be used against him. Instead he lifted a finger, saying simply, "I will hear no more about it." He turned and left the room, slamming the door behind him.

By the time Stefan got to his own room, he was nearly shaking. He wondered what kind of man she had turned him into. But it wasn't until the middle of the night that he sat up in bed with a stark realization that knotted in the pit of his stomach. *He had just broken one of his own laws.* And if Johanna figured that out, she *would* have him hung out to rot.

Stefan went to his office early without a moment's sleep behind him. He sent out an order to have Captain Leichty come in just as soon as he came on duty. The captain appeared at one minute after eight.

"You sent for me, Your Grace," he stated.

"Yes," Stefan motioned toward a chair, "have a seat. This is between the two us."

The captain closed the door and sat down. His build was average and his coloring fair. But he had a presence about his authority that made it evident why the duke regent had quickly promoted him to captain not long before Stefan's inauguration. They had worked closely together for years, and Stefan appreciated their mutual trust and respect. But he had no idea how this recent turn of events might be perceived by the good captain.

"There is something of a personal nature I need to discuss with you . . . but it is a legal matter as well."

The captain nodded, and Stefan took a deep breath.

"I'm certain you are aware that my wife and I are . . . not on the best of terms."

"I'm aware of it," the captain stated.

Stefan wanted to ask exactly what he *did* know. But he continued with his purpose. "Are you aware of what happened last night?"

"My officers were involved. The incident was reported to me."

Stefan nodded. "Well, to get right to the point. . . after I returned and we were arguing . . . I hit her."

Stefan couldn't tell if the captain was surprised or amused. Or if one was trying to subdue the other. "I would not take you for the kind of man who—"

"I'm *not* that kind of man," Stefan retorted. "I was—"

"That's just my point, sir. She must have goaded pretty hard to push you to something like that."

While Stefan appreciated his understanding, he had to admit, "Nevertheless, I did something that not so long ago I put my neck on the line to make illegal. I don't know if she even realizes it's illegal. I pray she doesn't. I fear she would use it against me and distort the truth. So," he leaned back and motioned toward the captain, "I am putting the matter in your hands. I'm turning myself in, so to speak, before she has a chance to."

The captain said nothing for a full minute, while Stefan wondered what it might feel like to be a fugitive.

"You're putting me in a difficult position, sir," Captain Leichty finally said.

"Yes, I am."

"So, consider it officially reported. If anything comes of it, I'll deal with it accordingly."

"And what about me?" Stefan asked.

"You turned yourself in. We'll just say that I gave you a warning and told you it better not happen again." The captain's eyes hardened on him, and Stefan appreciated the courage he had to put his integrity as an officer first. "I trust it won't happen again."

"It won't happen again," Stefan said firmly. "I can assure you."

"I guess that's settled then," the captain said casually. "Is there anything else?"

Stefan sighed with immense relief. "Not unless you care to put me on probation or something. I could really use some time off."

The captain chuckled and rose to his feet. "If you need a vacation, you're going to have to just take one. It *is* allowed, you know."

As he opened the door, Stefan said, "Thank you, Captain. I appreciate your wisdom and discretion."

"Good day, Your Grace." He bowed slightly and clicked his heels together before he closed the door.

Stefan felt much better, but he had trouble putting the episode with Johanna out of his mind. He wondered why she had the ability to provoke such hateful feelings in him, and why he'd been fool enough to get involved with her to begin with.

Late in the day, Captain Leichty found Stefan thoughtfully dabbing oil onto a canvas.

"What is it?" Stefan demanded when the captain entered through the open door and stood at attention.

"Forgive me for interrupting your personal time, Your Grace, but I thought you should know that Her Grace has reported your indiscretion of last night to me."

"At ease, Captain," Stefan insisted. "And close the door."

With their privacy ensured, the captain relaxed. Stefan set the brush and palette aside. "Out with it," he demanded.

"She came to my office just a while ago. I spoke to her privately. We were not overheard to my knowledge. She showed me the bruise on her face and requested that charges be pressed. Apparently she is well aware of your political moves. I was quite impressed myself with her knowledge of the law related."

"Blast!" Stefan went to his feet and began to pace. He'd feel a lot more comfortable to think of her as being ignorant and foolish. Just his luck she had to keep track of everything he did. She probably told her father every political detail of what went on in Horstberg.

"Go on," Stefan waved his hand impatiently.

"I told her you had already reported the incident to me, and you had assured me it wouldn't happen again." The captain almost smiled. "She seemed terribly disappointed at this. She attempted to argue with me for several minutes. I assured her that everything was taken care of according to the law, and then I politely dismissed her."

"Well done," Stefan said. "You cannot know how much I appreciate the way you're handling this."

Following a moment of silence, the captain asked, "May I speak with candor, sir?"

"By all means."

"I only ask that you be extremely careful. I'm not so much concerned about a repeat of this incident. If it happens again, I'll put you in the keep for a few days and give you time off for good behavior. I *am* concerned at what else she might use against you. She seemed to take great pleasure in having something to hold over you. If I understand the political affiliations with her father well, I believe he would take pleasure in the same."

Stefan stuffed his hands into his pockets and sighed. The captain had just neatly summed up the shackles that bound Stefan and left him helpless.

"Thank you, Captain," he said. "I'll be careful."

The captain turned and left the room, leaving the door open. Stefan walked slowly to the window and looked out toward the valley below. He felt so utterly powerless.

Chapter Seven
THROUGH CASTLE WINDOWS

Winter in Bavaria was beautiful, but it could be harsh as well. Each morning Ericha woke with a conviction to forget Stefan Heinrich, and by evening she longed for him all over again. Months passing only intensified Ericha's loneliness, and she wondered if it would ever end.

Life went on much as before. Ericha filled her time with an occasional visit to Mrs. Burger's cottage, and she produced more lace than Frieda knew what to do with. Despite the cold of winter, Ericha continued to ride habitually. But she avoided places that would intensify her memories. Winter moved into spring as Ericha took Pegasus out daily, and looking back over her first year in Horstberg, she felt a deep mixture of emotions.

Karl was perhaps the key to her sanity during this time. Though he rarely said anything about Stefan, he seemed to know the reason for her melancholy moods and did his best to distract her and keep her cheerful. He continued to make a fair attempt at getting her to meet other men. And Ericha gave worthy effort, hoping to find someone who might ease this ache. But it was futile. She couldn't help comparing every man she met to Stefan, and she always found them wanting. There was one gentleman that she became rather fond of, but inevitably his attitude toward her changed when he learned of her parentage. It seemed that no matter what Ericha did, she was doomed to be alone.

There were days that seemed easier, when Stefan's existence felt distant. There were others when it became unbearable. On a particularly low afternoon, Ericha sat tatting in the parlor, and she was pleased when Karl came in to pass some time with her before going to the pub.

"What is it?" he asked when the small talk was done.

"What do you mean?" she asked, not comprehending her own obviousness.

"More and more you act as though your life is over. I keep thinking you'll get over it, but you don't."

Ericha became briefly distant as she thought of how much Stefan had changed her. She would never be free of him.

"Tell me, Ericha," Karl urged, stretching out his long legs to make himself comfortable.

"What is there to say?" she replied and intensified her concentration on the tatting. All was silent for a moment before she paused and removed the glasses she wore to do the intricate work. With a heavy sigh, she glanced toward the window where she could catch a glimpse of the highest turret of Castle Horstberg glistening in the sun.

"It's pointless, Ericha," Karl said.

She swallowed hard. "I love him," she stated without turning.

"I'm afraid that doesn't make any difference."

"And don't you think I've told myself that? If you only knew how I have tried to convince myself that I can be rid of these feelings. Even if I were to marry, Karl, I fear my heart would always be with him. Is that fair to any man? And I'm not sure there's a man out there who would accept me if he knew the truth."

"What truth?" he asked.

"I'm an illegitimate woman, Karl!" she shouted. "It's what I am. I will never be free of that, any more than I will ever be free of these feelings." She moaned quietly and pressed a hand to her heart, wondering how emotions could cause physical pain.

Karl was silent a moment. His anger melted into compassion. "Ericha, everything he does affects this country. He was a fool to get involved with you in the first place. He should have known better."

Ericha drew back her shoulders. "What if it were Luise?"

"What has Luise got to do with this?"

"Put yourself and Luise into exactly the same situation and tell me if you could live with it. You've told me how much you love her, how you were drawn to her years ago, knowing you couldn't exist without her. What if it were Luise, Karl?"

Karl blew out a long sigh, crossed his ankle on his knee, and leaned back. "You got me there," he admitted. "I know Stefan is a miserable man. I can see it every day, and I feel for him. But for the life of me, I don't know what could be done about it. There is already tension because of his circumstances. Not here in Horstberg really, but between Horstberg and Kohenswald."

Ericha set her shuttle aside to listen attentively, feeling closer to Stefan as Karl spoke of him. "Stefan married her because he believed the Baron Von Bindorf would be more willing to settle differences peaceably if the countries were united by the marriage. Oh, I believe he loved her in a way. He was certainly taken with her. But, well . . . it just didn't work out. And since their marriage hasn't produced an heir, people are starting to get antsy. Horstberg's not worried, really, because Princess Hannah has—"

"Who?" she interrupted.

"Stefan's sister. She lives on her grandmother's estate at the edge of the valley. Her son will be the duke when Stefan's time is done if he doesn't have a son, but Johanna's family doesn't—"

"Who is Johanna?" she asked.

Karl looked briefly stunned. "She's the duchess." Ericha's eyes narrowed, and he clarified, "Stefan's wife."

Ericha glanced away as the name stabbed her. Somehow not knowing her name made her seem less real. Karl went on, "Johanna's family desperately wants an heir that will unite the two countries. Horstberg is bigger, more powerful. As a whole, it has more assets. The Von Bindorf family has always wanted their finger in it, which can be touchy. Nothing serious really, just touchy."

Karl allowed her a minute to absorb the information, and she turned to him and asked, "But is he happy?"

"No, I already told you he isn't."

"How can a man succeed at such an overwhelming struggle if he is not happy?"

Ericha's own question brought something to light in her mind, and hope made her cling to the thought. "What if no one knew?" she asked.

"What are you talking about?"

"What if no one knew that Stefan and I were involved?"

"You couldn't do it. Someone would find out eventually."

"So . . . what if they did?"

Karl looked shocked as he protested. "It could cause problems or . . ."

"Talk?" she finished, lifting her brows triumphantly. "People would say: the duke has a mistress. But dukes have had mistresses before. All through history, dukes and kings have had mistresses. Think of the ridiculous political practices of this world that require people to marry for reasons other than love and to stay in marriages that are a slur to the very idea of marriage. Is it any wonder that people caught up in such things so commonly have relationships outside of those marriages? Of course, I'm certain that many such people rationalize and take full advantage of their circumstances for wicked purposes. But that is not the case for me and Stefan. You see, Karl, by the time anyone figured out that Stefan had a mistress, they would see that a happy man is a better ruler."

"It's ridiculous!" Karl stood and began pacing.

"Is it?" she came back quickly. "As I see it, I have no other choice beyond this. I've done my best to forget him—and it's pointless. No matter what else I did with my life, I would always be wanting him. My mother pined her whole life away longing for the man she loved—and I won't do it! I won't!"

"Ericha!" he shouted. "Have you taken leave of your senses? What you're talking about is wrong, Ericha. Plain and simple. It's wrong."

"No, Karl, it's not plain and simple. It's very complicated. And sometimes right and wrong is not black and white. If Stefan could divorce Johanna, he would. But he can't. He hasn't had a marriage relationship with her for a very long time. Their marriage is a technicality, a political necessity. If we were committed to each other . . . for life, it would be like—"

"You're rationalizing, Ericha, and you know it. It's wrong. The consequences would be inevitable. Eventually, there would be a price to pay."

"Well, I'm willing to pay it!" It was her turn to shout. "And don't stand there and talk to me about right and wrong. You have no idea what it's like to stand where I stand. When you start putting such things into categories of black and white, then my existence is wrong. How can I look at myself in the mirror and believe that good things don't come out of difficult circumstances?"

Karl sighed and looked at the floor. "You're right, Ericha. I have no idea how it feels to be where you stand."

"So, you tell me," she retorted, "what you would do if you were me! What am I supposed to do with these feelings, Karl? I love him! And nothing—*nothing*—will ever change that. I don't care who he is, or what his circumstances are. This is the only chance I've got to be truly happy, and I will take it!"

Karl looked at her sternly, but his words were gentle. "And what kind of life would that be for you? What about the seclusion? You could never be seen in public with him."

"I've always lived a secluded life," she stated.

"There is stigma with that kind of life."

"I've always lived with that, too." She lifted her chin.

"And what about Horstberg?" he asked. "Do you really believe the country would be better off?"

"Yes," she stated with such confidence that he almost believed her.

"I want to see him," she said. "How does one go about seeing the duke?" Karl didn't answer, and she added, "Should I just go to the pub and offer to buy him a drink?"

"No!" Karl said, and then he chuckled. "You're really serious about this."

"Yes," she said, "I am."

Karl stared silently at the floor, his hands in his pockets, and then he sighed and looked up. "I will tell him to meet you."

Ericha breathed relief, but one flaw in her plan rose up starkly. "I'm not certain he'll come. He's so convinced that the best thing for me would be to marry someone else. How do I convince him otherwise?"

"All you can do is try."

Ericha looked deeply at Karl. "And you're behind me in this?"

"It's a difficult line to draw, Ericha. Like you said, some things just aren't black and white. I'm not sure I like it, but I can see you're determined. It's up to you to make your choices. I will be there for you no matter what. What I really want is for you to be happy. And if you ask my help in this, I will do all I can."

Ericha pushed her arms around him in a firm embrace. "Thank you, Karl. Beyond my love for Stefan, you are the best thing that's ever happened to me. I shudder to think what I would have done without you."

Karl pulled back and touched her chin. "If it weren't for Luise, I'd marry you myself."

Ericha smiled. "You're teasing me."

"No." He shook his head. "I admit that my feelings for you are not what I've found with Luise. And I know what you feel for Stefan is that once-in-a-lifetime love. But, Ericha, if circumstances were different, I would make you my wife, and we would be happy."

Ericha was so taken off guard she could hardly breathe. "But we're cousins," she finally managed.

He chuckled and hugged her tighter. "It doesn't matter, not really. Cousins marry."

"They do?"

"It happens." He laughed and stepped back. His expression sobered. "I'll tell him you want to see him."

"Thank you."

"I'm not just doing it for you. I believe Stefan needs you."

Ericha waited nervously in the garden for Karl to return from the pub. But when he rode in at last and dismounted, she knew at once by his expression that it hadn't gone well.

"Tell me," she insisted.

"You were right. He refuses to see you."

"What did he say?" she asked angrily.

"Oh, you know Stefan. He just stares at you with those imposing eyes, says no like he's talking about the weather, and then he changes the subject."

"That's all?" Her anger increased.

"He did say a little later that it would be better for you if he stayed away."

Ericha was thoughtfully silent as they walked toward the house. Karl said as he opened the door, "I don't know, little cousin, maybe it's not right. Perhaps you should reconsider."

"Perhaps it's not right," Ericha stated, "but it's what my heart tells me I must do. There is a fire in my heart, Karl. I must either follow it or let it destroy me."

Karl had to admire her strength, and he put his arms around her with a warm embrace. Ericha returned it and looked up at him. "Karl, you know him. Do you believe he loves me?"

Karl looked at her directly, weighing this carefully in his mind. But he knew he could never lie to her, despite knowing what the repercussions would be. "Yes, Ericha. I have no doubt that he loves you very much."

She smiled completely for the first time in weeks. "You didn't tell him, did you, why I wanted to see him?"

"No."

"I must find a way. I just have to talk to him."

"There may be a way," Karl said, and a light came to his eyes as they walked down the hall together.

"What?" she asked excitedly.

"About ten o'clock tonight," he said with a hint of mischief, "we're going out. Wear something old, and your cloak—the one with the hood."

Ericha felt a rush of excitement that increased steadily as the hours passed. And with the accompanying happiness, she felt certain this was the right decision. Instinctively, she knew she would not regret it. In spite of knowing this was far from ideal, it was simply the best that could be made of the situation under the circumstances.

Karl met Ericha in the downstairs hall just a few minutes before ten. He led the way to the stable and said nothing as he saddled only one horse, then helped her mount. He got on the horse behind her and reached around her to take the reins. They were at a full gallop before they even reached the street.

Karl said nothing, but Ericha's heart quickened as she realized they were heading for Castle Horstberg. She was puzzled when they didn't go up the hill, but rather around it where the mountain rose steeply. He stopped in a thick patch of trees where he dismounted and tied the horse off before helping her down. Ericha was puzzled but kept quiet, except for the gasp she couldn't suppress when he opened some semblance of a door right out of the hillside that had been completely invisible until he did.

Karl reached inside and apparently knew right where to find a torch. When it was lit, he held his hand out elaborately, and she stepped inside, only aware that it was narrow, dark, and perhaps clammy. She heard Karl pull the door shut tightly, and then he eased around her, took her hand, and began walking carefully up a long stone passageway.

Ericha understood now why he'd wanted her to wear something old. She could tell the hem of her dress was getting damp, and she felt eerily overwhelmed by cobwebs. She wanted to ask where it led, but she knew she would find out soon enough.

It seemed they went on forever before they stopped and Karl extinguished the torch. It was so dark that Ericha couldn't see anything but blackness.

"Are you all right?" he asked, and she felt his arm come around her shoulders.

"Yes, I'm fine."

"You wait right here. Don't move. Don't make a sound."

"I won't."

Ericha heard shuffling and could tell Karl was pushing his weight against something. He groaned slightly, and she heard stone grinding against stone, echoing through the tunnel. A crack of light became visible. She heard dogs barking as Karl peered carefully through the narrow space, and then it widened and he stuck his head through. The dogs quieted from a distant order that Ericha couldn't discern.

"Good heavens, man!" She heard Stefan's voice and her heart went mad. "You scared me to death!"

Karl laughed, and she watched him disappear through the space in the wall. "It'll keep you humble."

"Is that why you've shown up in my bedroom? To keep me humble?"

"Uh . . ." she heard Karl chuckle, "not exactly."

"What did you need?" Stefan asked seriously. "It must be important for you to use the dreaded passageway."

"It is important. Now that I know you're here and alone . . . well, hold on, and I'll be right back. Oh, and . . . you'd better put your shirt on."

Karl appeared in the passageway again where Ericha was leaning against the wall with her hand over her heart, trying to suppress the emotions overwhelming her. It seemed forever since she had heard his voice, let alone seen him. She could hardly bear it.

"It's up to you now," Karl whispered. "I'll be outside with the horse. You talk to him. Try to keep it brief." Ericha nodded. "I'll leave a torch burning here. You can make it back through."

"Thank you, Karl." She pressed a kiss to his cheek. Then he urged her through the opening just as Stefan spoke again.

"Hurry it up, Karl. It's been a long day, and I . . ." Stefan's head was down as he buttoned his shirt, and then he looked up and his breath stopped short. His heart quickened as Ericha pushed back the hood of her cloak and the familiar red braid fell over her shoulder.

Ericha had barely stepped into the room when she was approached by two curious hounds. She took a step back, more caught off guard than alarmed.

"Blitzen, Donner," Stefan ordered. "Back. Go sit down." The dogs obeyed immediately, retreating behind Stefan, where they sat side by side.

"Forgive me," she said as their eyes met. "I'm sorry to intrude upon you like this, but I had to talk to you and . . . well, you're not an easy man to find . . . Your Grace."

He continued to stare with no expression, and Ericha felt uncomfortable. She looked away from him to glance about the room, astounded by its size and grandeur.

"I had no idea we were coming to your bedroom." She clasped her hands together to hide her nervousness. "It's very nice. I think it's bigger than the cottage I grew up in."

He only continued to stare at her, seeming stunned. It was evident she had no choice but to get to the point. She knew Karl was waiting.

"Karl and I have been talking about you," she stated, "and I hear you're not doing very well."

Stefan showed his first sign of life and blew out a long, slow breath.

"You will most likely think that what I am about to say is most improper and less than admirable, but I . . ." Ericha stopped, feeling thwarted momentarily, but she drew back her shoulders as she continued. "I need to be a part of your life, Stefan. I have thought it through very carefully, and it is what my heart tells me I must do, and . . ." She paused and sighed in frustration. "How can I say it? What can I possibly do to . . . Well, it wouldn't be so bad. As long as we were discreet. We could treat it much the same as a marriage as far as you and I are concerned. It's the only way, really. You did say you would marry me if you could. But you can't, so . . ."

Ericha watched Stefan as he waited expectantly for her to

finish. He met her eyes with a silent intensity, until they widened in disbelief as he apparently grasped her intent.

"Ericha! You don't mean that you came here because you . . ." He shook his head and made a noise of disbelief. "No! Absolutely not!"

"And why not?"

"Let me get this straight. You are offering yourself as my mistress?"

"You make it sound so sordid."

"It is sordid!"

"Are your feelings for me sordid?"

"No, but . . ."

"But what? Have you got any other options? I already live a secluded life. It's my choice. There is no way that we can be together and be without problems. But at least this way we can glean a certain amount of happiness that will perhaps make up for some of the misery."

Stefan gave a noise of frustration as he turned and pushed his hand through his hair. "I don't think that you have any idea what you're really saying."

"I don't think you realize how miserable I am without you."

"Oh, but I do," he admitted.

"So you see—"

"There is no reason to even discuss it."

"There is, and you will!"

Stefan's eyes widened. It wasn't the first time she'd talked to him like that, but it always took him off guard a little. No one except his father had ever spoken to him that way, and even he had stopped for the most part once Stefan became the duke. It felt good to have somebody else giving orders for a change.

"Ericha," he said softly.

"What?"

"It's good to see you again. I wonder every day if you're thinking of me as I'm thinking of you."

"Constantly." Silence reigned briefly until she added, "We must live while we can, Stefan. This is our chance for an ever after."

"No," he stated, as Karl described, like he was discussing the weather.

"Why?" she asked, more hurt than angry. "Are you concerned about the country and the effect it might have?"

"That's part of it, but I could probably handle it."

"Then what?"

"My marriage is a political obligation, Ericha. It will never change. If I was not the Duke of Horstberg, I would leave her in a minute. But I can't. And that would always leave you alone."

"In a sense," she said, "but if I have you in my life, I will not be lonely."

Stefan looked thoughtful but repeated with conviction, "No."

"That's it then!" she said angrily.

"I have no choice."

"Your choices are what you make them, Stefan. You are choosing to resign yourself to your fate."

Stefan made no reply, but he took her arm firmly, pulling her toward the passageway.

"What are you doing?" she demanded.

"You're leaving."

"I am not!"

"You are!"

Ericha tried to protest, but he led her firmly down the passageway with her arm tightly in his grip and a torch in his other hand.

"Stefan," she said and her voice echoed. "You can't turn me away. You can't do this to me."

"It's for your own good."

"You *are* an arrogant bastard," she said to vent her anger. "You toy with my life, then do nothing but humiliate me and leave me wanting. Do you think it was easy for me to come here?"

Stefan said nothing as they moved steadily on.

"I thought you loved me," she said, and he stopped.

Abruptly he turned her to face him, and their eyes met in the torchlight. "I do love you," he said. "That's why I won't let you do it."

"You can't deny what's happened between us, Stefan."

"I'm not denying anything," he retorted.

"You are denying me the only measure of happiness I could ever hope for." She glared at him. "I will never be content without you. It will either be you or no one. See if you can live with that, Your Grace," she spat, then pulled her arm from his grasp and moved on.

"Ericha!" He stopped her with a firm grip. "You don't understand."

"No," she cried and felt burning in her eyes, *"you* don't understand!"

With little warning, she found her lips beneath his. His free hand came to her back as he drew her against him, and she pushed her arms around his shoulders, relishing in the comfort she absorbed from his nearness. She felt at peace here in his arms and never wanted to let him go.

"I love you," he murmured as his lips went rampantly down her throat. "I love you so much. You are always in my mind, in my dreams, in my heart."

"Please, Stefan," she cried. "We can find a way. We'll just take it as it comes and do the best we can. It would be better than this. I know it would."

Stefan made no reply as he held her, but finally he began to walk again until the door opened out of the hillside and Ericha felt Stefan's grip being replaced by Karl's.

"Take her home, Karl," he ordered.

"Wait," she implored, "I need to know if—"

"And don't bring her back."

"Stefan!" Ericha cried, but he didn't even meet her eyes before he disappeared into the hillside and she found herself alone with Karl, feeling nothing short of shame and despair.

"You realize," Karl said on a late summer morning at breakfast, "that it will soon be Reclamation Day."

Ericha gave a disinterested shrug, and he added, "Come now, my dear. Surely you could show more excitement than that. It's a festive occasion when we celebrate the re—"

"Yes, I know," she said dryly, "to celebrate the day that Stefan's grandfather reclaimed the duchy from his evil brother, and married Stefan's grandmother. Mrs. Burger's told me a hundred times."

"Why does everything have to do with Stefan?" he asked, perturbed.

"I don't know," she stated, "but it does."

"Why don't you just get on with your life, Ericha?"

"Why don't you get married?" she retorted.

"What has that got to do with it?"

"Why don't you worry about you and Luise, instead of worrying so much about me? I can take care of myself."

"You call this taking care of yourself? You're ruining yourself over a man you can't have."

"I'm not ruining myself. I'm fine. Everything is under control."

"Everything except that look in your eyes. I'm getting tired of seeing it."

"I'm getting tired of feeling it," she said, throwing her napkin to the table.

"Then forget about him!"

"I can't!"

Karl said nothing, and Ericha glanced down abruptly, ashamed of herself for acting this way. "I'm sorry," she said. "If you—"

"Ericha," he interrupted gently, "will you come with me to the fair? It'll be such fun. You must be there for the folk dancing at least."

"I'd feel so out of place," she said softly.

"Nonsense." He laughed. "You will fit in beautifully."

He explained in detail about the tradition of the dance and that he belonged to a group, mostly consisting of local merchants, who performed it each year. The group in costume would dance the first set, and then they would split and bring partners from the crowd and so on, until everyone was dancing.

"Say you'll come," he pleaded. "I'll teach you the dance and you can join in right away. You need diversion, Ericha. This would be good for you."

She said nothing, so Karl took her around the waist and started twirling her around the room. "See," he said, "we do this part when the music picks up near the end."

"Karl," she laughed uneasily, "I can't do that."

"Sure you can," he said. "Start here like this." He showed her the simple steps and proceeded to teach it to her without her permission. They spent the morning at it, and Ericha found herself having fun and laughing for the first time in what seemed like forever. When they finally sat down from exhaustion, Karl said, "You see, you know it as well as I do. It'll be great fun."

Ericha asked in monotone, "Will Stefan be there?"

Karl glanced toward her. "I would assume. After all, the whole thing is to honor his forebears. But it will be crowded. I'm certain you can avoid him if you wish."

"I haven't seen him for so long," she said wistfully. "I don't want to avoid him." Ericha smiled at Karl. "I would love to go to the fair with you."

"Good," he said triumphantly.

"Is Luise going?"

"But of course." He grinned. "She's my partner for the first set, and you'll be my partner for the second."

"Sounds delightful," Ericha said, and she left the house to go riding.

Reclamation Day dawned with fair skies. Karl swept Ericha into town with him right after breakfast where Luise would meet them later when her shift was finished at the inn.

The market square was filled with a variety of entertainment, all going on at the same time. There were jugglers, acrobats, musicians, even a group of men twirling fire. Aromas of pastries, sausages, beer, and hot spiced punch lifted through the air. Music filtered from every corner, mingling with the din of voices in all tones, revealing a wide range of enjoyment.

The commoners for the most part were in costume—either folk dance apparel similar to what Karl wore, or a variety of capes and headdresses. Karl told her that at one time it was common for the people to wear masks to the fair. But following Cameron du Woernig's reclamation, he had declared that masks would no longer be worn, to symbolize his coming out of hiding. The fair had a medieval mood to it, and Ericha felt certain that other than the more recent decision to call it Reclamation Day, it had been going on the same for centuries.

Ericha truly enjoyed herself, and she asked Karl as they sat down to eat a hot pasty, "Why didn't you bring me last year?"

"I asked. You didn't want to go."

"Why not?"

"You insisted you were going riding. I tried to convince you."

"Well, you should have tried harder," she said, and they laughed.

Stefan rushed up to his rooms to dress. It seemed his business always made him rush no matter where he was going.

He was grateful for Theodor's efficiency in helping him, and he went straight to find Johanna, certain she'd be ready. He found her sitting quietly in the east summer parlor, admiring the diamonds she wore on her wrists.

"I'm ready," he stated and poured himself a drink.

"Doesn't look to me like you're ready," she said without looking at him. "It would appear that you're having a drink first."

"It won't take long," he said and abruptly set down the empty glass.

"You've been drinking quite a bit lately, Stefan. It doesn't suit you."

"What does suit me?" he asked, pouring himself another.

"Tea with your grandmother, I'd say," she mused, and he

realized that *she* had been drinking. It had slurred her voice and loosened her tongue.

"Too bad she's not fifty years younger. The two of you would make a fine pair."

"You'd best heed that tongue, Johanna. It may get you into trouble."

"Trouble?" she laughed. "Me, in trouble? Never!"

She erupted with that wicked laugh of hers, but Stefan ignored it. "Let's go. We're late. Where's Grandmama?"

"I've decided I'm not going," she said whimsically.

"You have to go," he stated. "It's your duty."

"I'm sick to death of duty," she said. "No. I'm just sick. I don't feel well and I want to stay home."

"I don't care how you feel," he said. "You are supposed to be by my side, and you will be."

"Who do you think you are?" she spat, standing suddenly. "I don't have to do anything! I don't feel well. I'm staying home."

Stefan said nothing as he fought to push away his anger, knowing it would accomplish nothing except perhaps getting *him* into trouble.

"Maybe," Johanna went on with an unnatural lilt in her voice, "I'm going to have a baby."

Stefan gave no hint of the emotion her statement provoked as he briefly speculated over what she was getting at.

"Wouldn't that be something?" she said, and Stefan almost wished she would get pregnant. He felt certain she took precautions to avoid conceiving outside the marriage. But he almost wished it would happen. It was just what he needed to send her crawling back to her father.

"Good thing no one knows we haven't shared a bed in years, isn't it?" Her eyes filled with mischief and Stefan wondered what she was up to. Then he realized he didn't care.

"What makes you so sure no one knows?" he replied, pouring another drink. She looked momentarily distressed.

"Come along, Stefan," Abbi said from behind him. Both he

and Johanna were startled, not realizing she was there. "Let her stay here. We'll enjoy ourselves for a change."

Johanna gave Abbi a sharp glance. Abbi nodded curtly in reply and held out her hand for Stefan. He left the room hastily with his grandmother on his arm, wondering how much she'd heard.

Abbi said nothing about it but quickly changed the conversation with jovial small talk, enabling Stefan to put behind him the ugly scene that was becoming more typical all the time.

Stefan emerged into the courtyard, and Captain Leichty called the troops to attention. Georg was waiting, already mounted. Stefan helped his grandmother onto her horse, admiring her youthful agility. He ordered Johanna's mount taken back to the stables, then hurled himself into the saddle. As Stefan lifted his gloved hand, the captain responded with a command, and the drum cadence started them on their slow trek toward the village.

The royal procession from Castle Horstberg to the market square was enjoyable as usual for Stefan, and he quickly pushed thoughts of Johanna away. This day always made him stop and think about his grandfathers and their accomplishments, and it brought on a mixture of emotions. It was nice to have Georg there with him, receiving the praise he deserved for all he'd done for Horstberg. But he wished Cameron was here as well. He smiled toward his grandmother as the procession moved slowly on, and he knew she was wishing the same.

"Are you all right?" he asked, wondering how she managed to stay in a saddle this long without complaining at her age.

"I've spent my life in a saddle," she insisted as if she'd read his mind. "Don't start coddling me over it now."

"Yes, Grandmama," he said, and they exchanged a knowing smile.

Ericha heard the familiar drum cadence in the distance and knew what it meant. A new bustle of excitement erupted, and she felt her own heart quicken. But her desire to see Stefan suddenly faded. At moments she longed for even a glimpse of him to reassure herself that he was real, but now she feared what seeing him might do to her.

Ericha moved unobtrusively into the crowd, and Karl followed, as if he sensed what she was feeling. He said nothing as they walked down a quiet street, and she appreciated his silent understanding.

"Luise will be off soon," he said. "Let's go and get her."

"You go," she said easily. "I think I'll go home and rest a while. I'll be back for the folk dancing, I promise."

Karl seemed hesitant to leave her alone. But Ericha insisted, and she was grateful to have a moment alone with her thoughts. By the time she returned to the square, she was ready to see Stefan—if he was even still there.

Karl was waiting where he'd said he would be, and Ericha chatted with Luise until it was time for the dance to begin. She found a place to stand where she could easily see, and she felt a rush of excitement as the costumed dancers filled the square and took their places. The music was vibrant in a simple way, as were the costumes with their brightly colored ribbons.

Ericha became enthralled with the dance, appreciating the mood of celebration that had no doubt inspired it. She had almost forgotten about Stefan until she sensed she was being watched. She caught his eye across the square, then turned abruptly away, feeling her heart melt like snow struck by lightning.

Ericha drew courage enough to look toward him again, and she was glad to see that he'd turned his attention elsewhere. How handsome he looked! She could hardly bear it. In one moment she recalled how it had felt to be in his arms, and in the next she was overcome with the reality of him sitting there like a king upon his throne, surrounded by the royal family. *His* family.

Stefan looked toward her again, and she turned away, grateful that the dance had ended as Karl swept her into the square for the second set. The number of dancers had doubled now, and the stomping and clapping in the square had heightened, joined in by whoops and hollers of enjoyment. But Ericha's heart was heavy. Occasionally she glanced toward Stefan and her thoughts wandered. Was he really the same man, she wondered, who had kissed her and held her and whispered tender thoughts to her? It seemed so long ago.

"How many sets are there?" Ericha asked Karl as he danced close behind her, holding her hands high. She wanted to leave but had promised Karl she would stay until it was finished.

"Eight," he said. "On the last I'll be with Luise again."

"Why is that?" she asked, grateful for the diversion.

"After the last set you're supposed to spend the remainder of the festivities with your partner. It's tradition."

"I see," she said, and they eased into a long line for the final steps.

Ericha moved into the crowd to find a partner according to the custom. She did her best to avoid the duke's eyes as the celebration increased and became more enthusiastic each set they danced. It began to get dark, but torches were lit around the market square.

During the fourth set, Ericha fought to push thoughts of Stefan away. She thought of how much she loved Horstberg and its traditions. She thought of her mother and wished she could be here, for many reasons. She started to enjoy herself on the sixth set, and danced with Karl again on the seventh since he insisted. She realized then that Stefan was still seated.

"Doesn't he ever do this?" she asked Karl as they turned close together.

"Not that I recall."

"Why not?"

"No one's ever asked him, I suppose. He usually doesn't like this sort of thing. Probably put out a decree or something that it's illegal to dance with the duke."

"Who's the woman sitting next to him?" she asked.

Karl glanced that way as he moved behind her. "That's his sister, Hannah. Doesn't look like Johanna's there."

"Too bad," Ericha said with no expression.

"Are you going home after the next set?" he asked.

"Probably," she stated.

"Be careful," he said. "I wish you'd stay, but I know you won't. I'll probably be late."

"*You* be careful," she said, and the set came to a close.

Karl moved away to find Luise, and Ericha stood briefly disoriented in the square, wondering if she should just go home now. She had no desire to spend the remainder of the festivities with *anyone*—except Stefan. She turned to watch him as he bent to converse with his sister. In that moment she felt much like ignoring his decrees—all of them.

Ericha moved quickly across the square and was standing directly in front of him before he glanced up and noticed her. Their eyes met, and she curtsied ridiculously deep and held out her hand. "Your Grace should join the festivities," she said with mischief in her eyes.

Stefan showed no expression as he watched her a long moment. She waited, holding her breath, almost hoping he wouldn't accept her offer. She didn't know if she could bear it either way. She wondered briefly if he didn't know the dance, but she thought if he didn't, it was about time he learned.

Ericha's thoughts made her only barely aware that the crowd had become almost silent around her. Everyone seemed to marvel that a common woman would be so bold, and they waited for the duke's response, certain that he would politely decline. A low murmur went through the crowd when Stefan stood and removed the robe from his shoulders, throwing it onto his chair.

"Excuse me, Hannah," he said to his sister. "It seems these people think their ruler is an old stick in the mud. I tend to agree."

Stefan glanced briefly to Abbi. He couldn't see her expression well, but he sensed she was pleased. He took Ericha's hand and walked with her to the center of the square.

Ericha felt emotion from his touch, and something dormant came alive in her when he inconspicuously squeezed her hand, as if to say he felt it too. A hush remained in the air as he escorted her to her place among the women, then moved into position with the men.

"Well," he called with a laugh, "let's get on with it."

Everyone moved quickly into place, and Ericha caught Karl's eye. He grinned proudly at her, and she smiled as the music began. The women joined hands in lines and moved toward the men to curtsy. Ericha felt Stefan's gaze on her as they proceeded. When the lines came together and separated into couples, Ericha's heartbeat quickened. At moments she avoided his gaze, and at others she returned it, always reassured by the love she read there, however discreet.

Ericha caught her breath as his arm came around her waist to turn her. She remained expressionless, as did he, but she could almost feel his heart pounding when he moved close to her. As he came behind and held her hands high, she heard him whisper near her ear, "You look beautiful tonight, Miss Lokberg."

"Thank you, Your Grace," was all she said, and her formality bit at him. He wanted to erase it.

"I'm glad you came," he said. "I've been watching you."

"I noticed."

"I couldn't help remembering," he added, and she turned to meet his eyes. They nearly delved into her, and she knew what he meant.

"It's good to see you, Ericha," he said softly, and she glanced around, grateful that no one seemed to be noticing this discreet conversation. But reality struck her. She was dancing here with the Duke of Horstberg—a man she loved with all her heart, but by his own choice she would have no opportunity to share that love. The unfairness evoked despair, and she regretted her decision to be doing this.

Ericha avoided his gaze, grateful that the dance was coming to an end. Before the last bar, Ericha started to move away, but Stefan caught her arm. "Wait," he said. "Tradition has it that we should stay together the remainder of the evening."

"I can't," she said and tried again to pull away. Stefan held her firmly, and any effort to resist would have brought unwanted attention. He moved with her through the crowd toward where he'd been seated. She panicked, wondering what his intentions were.

People hovered around them with a natural desire to be near their ruler. Stefan remained polite but felt frustrated. He had longed for an opportunity to introduce Ericha to his grandmother, and he wasn't going to let it slip by.

Ericha was grateful for a chance to move away as Stefan became distracted. She nearly ran, pushing her way through the crowd, unable to bear the reality any longer. Despair overpowered her relief as the sounds of the crowd became muffled in the distance. She moved quickly up a side street, longing for solitude to sort out her feelings.

Carefully Ericha moved into a little stable and closed the door behind her. Alone at last, she let the pent-up emotion of the evening overcome her. Sitting in the straw, she pressed her face into her hands and cried.

Less than a minute later, the door opened behind her. She came abruptly to her feet, quickly forcing back the tears and wiping her face.

"Ericha," Stefan said from the darkness. "Why did you leave?"

She made no response. He came closer, but she moved away.

"I wanted to thank you," he said gently, "for sharing that with me. At times I feel so distant from the people. I used to spend more time among them. There are moments when I long to be one of them. Perhaps if I were . . ." He trailed off as the thought seemed pointless. "Ericha, I love you."

Still Ericha remained silent, and he pleaded, "Speak to me."

"You know that I love you," she said softly. "What else can I possibly say?"

"It's nice to hear it. It helps, you know."

"Yes," she said, "it's nice to get together twice a year to establish that we're still in love."

Stefan said nothing, and Ericha felt fresh humiliation, recalling the last time she'd seen him. He moved toward her again, and she backed away. "I can't bear it, Stefan. I shouldn't have done it. I should have just left."

"Why did you do it?" he asked.

"I wanted to be close to you. But I shouldn't have."

"I need to apologize to you," he said. "I was very harsh with you the last time we spoke."

"Yes, you were."

"But I—"

"Had to," she interrupted. "And nothing has changed."

"No," he said, "nothing has changed."

Stefan opened his arms with a silent plea to hold her, and Ericha couldn't find the will to hold back.

"Oh, Stefan," she cried, pressing her face to his throat, "I love you. I love you so much." She looked up at him and found her lips beneath his. Warmth overwhelmed her, and comfort briefly replaced the anguish. She held to him with desperation.

"It can't go on this way," she whispered.

"Don't tell me that now," he said. "Just let me hold you."

He kissed her again, and Ericha's heart quickened as his desires became evident. She gasped for breath and he kissed her harder.

"Stefan, we mustn't," she murmured without conviction.

"I know," he said and kissed her again, making it clear that his passion had taken control.

"Not here," she breathed. "Not like this."

Stefan ignored her, and Ericha gasped again.

"Stefan, please," she insisted, cursing herself inwardly as she responded against her will.

He kissed her again, and she pushed his face away with both hands. Stefan took a step back as if he'd been struck.

"Ericha," he said, his voice husky with unappeased passion.

"Is this what we've come to?" she asked, smoothing her bodice. "A quick tryst in the stable for the sake of—"

"It's not like that," he retorted.

"Then what is it?" she demanded. He didn't answer. "If you want me, it will be on my terms," she said with an authority she'd learned from him. "I will not have you flitting in and out of my life at your convenience, to leave me waiting and wondering month after month. I'm beginning to feel like some kind of cheap tramp who—"

"It's not like that, and you—"

"Prove it." Her voice lowered with challenge.

"Ericha, you know that my circumstances are—"

"To hell with your circumstances! I'm not asking you to change your circumstances. I am only asking for your commitment to something that time has proven is right—in spite of what all the rules, or laws, or decrees might say. Either you have the courage to follow your heart, or you don't. Until you make up your mind, just keep me out of it!"

Stefan remained in stunned silence for several minutes after Ericha left him alone. The dilemma pounded into his head so hard and fast he almost felt dizzy. Groaning aloud, he turned and threw his fist into the stone wall. Reminding himself that he'd left people waiting, he consciously tabled his emotions and walked deftly back to the square.

"Are you all right?" his grandmother asked as he sat beside her. He noticed Hannah had left.

"I'm fine," he lied.

"You're bleeding," she said, taking his hand into hers.

"I hadn't noticed." At least that was true.

"What happened?"

"It's just a little scrape, Grandmama."

Following a long silence while she dabbed at the blood with her handkerchief, Abbi said, "She seemed like a lovely girl, from what I could see. I didn't get a good look at her."

"Who?" Stefan turned, startled.

"The girl you were dancing with. Do you think she knew how good it was for you to get out there and do that?"

"Maybe she did," he stated, his voice distant. "In fact, I'm quite sure of it."

Stefan could see Karl was not in a good mood as he sat down across the table and ignored his drink.

"I don't have much time," Karl said, "but there's something I need to say."

"So, say it," Stefan said, wondering if it had to do with Ericha. He couldn't recall them ever having discord over anything else.

Karl thought this through quickly once more. The idea had come to his mind a few days ago, the morning after the fair when Ericha had come to breakfast looking as if her world would end. He'd let it smolder around since then, and wondered if it might help Stefan see some objective in what was happening here. With firm confidence, he met Stefan's eyes.

"What if I told you that Ericha was engaged to be married?"

Stefan hated the way his heart dropped to the pit of his stomach. It was what he'd been wanting all along, or at least what he'd convinced himself he wanted. It hadn't been so long since he'd seen her, and she hadn't given any indication that her feelings had changed. But perhaps that was irrelevant.

"Is he a good man?" Stefan asked, hoping his voice didn't betray his distaste. Already images of Ericha in another man's arms were flashing through his mind.

"I don't know. You tell me," Karl retorted.

"What do you mean?"

"What if I told you that something had gone wrong between Luise and me? What if I said that Ericha was going to marry *me?*"

Karl got the reaction he'd been hoping for. It was subtle, as it usually was with Stefan. But there was no denying the tightening of his face muscles, nor the contempt in his eyes.

"You wouldn't!" he hissed under his breath.

"Wouldn't I?" Karl leaned back and took a long swallow of his drink. He had to admit he loved the rare moments when he had the Duke of Horstberg hanging by a thread.

"I would take good care of her. We could be happy."

Stefan said nothing, fearing he would fling himself across the table and try to strangle Karl if he even acknowledged this emotion.

"I thought you wanted Ericha to get married," Karl stated.

Stefan forced the emotion down and cleared his throat. "Yes, but . . . you're my best friend. How can you expect me to . . . to . . ."

"To what?"

Stefan didn't answer.

"How can you expect Ericha to live the half life you've sentenced her to?" Karl growled. "There is only one thing I find distasteful about making Ericha my wife."

"And what is that?"

"Her heart would always be with you, and eventually it would make me hate you."

Stefan watched Karl closely while he tried to convince himself that this was what he wanted. He had many times imagined Ericha marrying some fine, young man. But he was always without a face and a name. Could he live knowing that Ericha was giving everything *he* wanted to the only true friend he'd ever had? As the silence grew long, Stefan caught something subtly humorous in Karl's eyes.

"Please tell me you're joking," Stefan said.

Karl leaned back with a self-satisfied smirk. "Actually, I am."

"Damn you," Stefan said with no trace of humor.

"Just to ease your mind, dear friend, Luise and I are as much in love as we ever were. Her father has hung on much longer than we'd expected, but that doesn't change the plans we have for the future. Still, I love Ericha. She's like the sister I never had. And I'm sick to death of seeing her waste her life away because of you!"

He briefly pointed a finger at Stefan, leaning farther across the table. "Joke or no joke, Stefan. I want you to think about the way it made you feel while you self-righteously deem your royal wishes upon one of the most incredible women that you and I have ever known."

Karl watched Stefan silently absorb his words with no expression. "It's your turn to buy," he said and left the pub. Stefan sat there for nearly an hour, unable to move, unable to think. He was shocked and scared and far more humbled than a man in his position ever wanted to admit to being.

Stefan finally headed home, while the scales in his mind tormented him more intensely than ever before. He paused for a moment at the base of the hill and gazed up at the castle. *His* castle. It was as formidable and imposing as the choices that lay before him.

By the time Stefan went to bed, he felt just plain confused. Deep in the night, with no sleep behind him, he got up and stood at the window, gazing into the valley below, wondering how he could possibly come up with an ever after.

Stefan sat behind the desk in his office, more staring at what lay in front of him than doing anything with it. Occasionally his eyes would move toward the huge window, and he'd lose all sense of time. When he realized he'd accomplished nothing for hours, he took off his glasses and stood to look out across the valley.

His grandmother made no effort to enter the room quietly, but Stefan was unaware of her presence until she touched him on the shoulder and startled him. He smiled to greet her before his gaze moved unwillingly back to the window.

"You know," she said gently, "I couldn't help noticing that you spend a lot of time looking out of windows lately."

Stefan wondered briefly if she was teasing him, but she went on soberly, "Every time I'm in a room with you, you end up at the window sooner or later."

"It is a lovely view," he stated.

"Yes," she moved beside him to look in the same direction. "The same view from your bedroom, only one floor below." He looked surprised, and she added, "It was my bedroom for years, you know."

Stefan smiled and put his arm around her shoulders. "What are you up to today, Grandmama?"

"Usual things." She sighed. "I've been up reading to Nik."

"I assume he's as amiable as ever," he said with sarcasm.

"Quite." She smiled wryly.

"Why do you do it?" he asked.

"What better things have I got to do?" she asked. "Besides,

he needs something to enrich his life. If you were confined to bed for the rest of your life, I'd probably entertain you as well."

Stefan chuckled. "I'd like to think so. Nobody else would. But then I didn't bend over backwards to destroy this country. That bed is his prison cell. He deserved his fate."

Abbi du Woernig shrugged the comment off while Stefan continued to be amazed at her goodness.

"And how is this country faring today?" she asked, glancing toward what lay on the desk as if it currently represented her question. Stefan glanced her direction, feeling disoriented.

"You've seemed a little distant from your work for quite some time." She paused for emphasis. "It's been worse since the fair."

He glanced at her sharply, but she quickly became distant. "Your grandfather used to tell me . . ." She lowered her voice to mimic him, and though long in the grave, Cameron du Woernig seemed to come to life through his wife's vivid memories. "'Abbi,' he'd say, 'it is believed that the state of a country is directly related to the well-being of its ruler.' And then he'd ask, 'Do you know what that means, Abbi?'

"And I would say, just for the sake of it, 'No dear, tell me what it means.' And he would say, 'Are you happy Abbi?' And I'd always laugh. 'Of course I'm happy,' I'd tell him."

Her eyes became wistful, and Stefan swallowed. The years didn't make her miss him any less. He could see it in her distant gaze.

"I was always happy with him, Stefan." She smiled and continued her oratory, "That's when he would say, 'I'm happy too. We're all happy. So the country can't help but prosper, right?' And of course I would say, 'That's right, Cameron.'"

Abbi was silent a long moment, lost in her memories until Stefan said, "But we're not happy anymore. Are we." It was not a question.

"I'm happy," she said easily.

"How can you be when—"

"I didn't say I don't miss him. But I have Georg. And I have you. I thank God every day for that. Oh, I could say that it would have been better if it hadn't happened the way it did. But I take what I have and make the most of it. And in my heart, I believe this is how our lives were meant to work out. I believe that the difficulties of life make us stronger—if we let them. And yes, I am happy."

Stefan looked toward the window.

"But you're not," she stated.

"What are you trying to say?" he asked sharply.

"Tell me about Horstberg. Tell me about the state of this country now."

"You know as much about it as I do," he said. "What's the point?"

"Do you want me to tell you?" she asked, and he shook his head. They both knew the present state of affairs. It didn't have to be voiced.

"Stefan," she said, "you manage Horstberg as well as Cameron ever did, in spite of your personal struggles. But it can't go on like this indefinitely. One man can only give so much."

Abbi paused, and he turned to look at her. By the way she drew back her shoulders, he knew she was going to hit him with something hard. "I've also noticed that you've been drinking more. It seems to steadily worsen."

"I'm a grown man," he stated. "Are my habits so—"

"Yes, you are," she interrupted. "And my notice of your habits is only in concern."

"I know," he admitted more softly.

"You have been discreet, and you handle your liquor well. But how will you know when you've crossed the line where that's not possible any longer?"

Stefan glared at her, but she was apparently not affected. "Why are you so unhappy?" she asked gently.

"What reason have I got to be otherwise?" he asked bitterly. "This!" He motioned elaborately toward the valley outside. "This is all mine. And what you're trying to tell me is that this country of mine will slowly dwindle away because I am not happy.

"Well, you're right," he snapped. "You always are. I'm *not* happy. And I find it more and more difficult to even *care* what happens to this country. It shouldn't have been mine!" He hit his fist on the window frame. "If they were still alive, it would not have been mine. I didn't even want it! You're more capable of ruling this place than I."

"Now, that's exaggerating." She laughed slightly, then became intensely serious. "What will you do when I'm gone? I'm your grandmother, Stefan. And I'm not getting any younger."

"Oh, don't say that," he said. "Good heavens. I shudder to think what I would do without you." He gazed toward her wistfully, and a horrifying thought struck him. As he tried to comprehend his life without Abbi, it only took a moment to know he had little he cared about beyond her. Had it come to that?

"Do you know," he admitted, "you are the only thing in my life that is worth living for?"

"There's Johanna," she stated as if to drive home a point. He knew at one time she'd hoped their marriage would somehow recover. But he felt sure she was aware of how bad it had become.

"That's practically blasphemous," he said cynically. "She is—"

"Please don't," Abbi admonished. "It will do no good."

"No," he said, "it won't." He paused, then added, "It's over. There is nothing left between us. I have given to her all I can give."

"I believe you're right," she said, and her eyes filled with wisdom. "You are like a well, Stefan. You give of yourself like the well gives water. What you once gave to Johanna was enough to make most men go dry. Still, you give to me, to Georg, your parents, your sisters. You give to your country everything you can possibly muster. But who gives to you? How much water can a well give before it goes dry?"

"You give to me," he stated. "And so do Mother and Father and Georg and—"

"Is it what you need?" she interrupted. "Your parents are rarely here. Your sisters have lives of their own. And Georg and I are not going to live forever. Do you get what you really need to make you happy, Stefan?" His only response was a bitter and longing look out the window. "Or is what you need to make you happy somewhere beyond the confines of these castle walls?"

Stefan looked at her sharply as she struck a nerve. He'd never questioned her perception, but it was a little unnerving to wonder how much she had figured out.

"My whole world lies within these castle walls," he stated blandly. "That's the way it has to be."

"You are committed to rule this country," she came back, "that is true. You must fulfill the obligations bequeathed to you. But, Stefan, you must also follow your heart."

Stefan tried to ignore the quickening of his blood as she went on. Her voice became dreamy as she embarked on a path of reminiscing that seemed completely out of place in their present conversation. "Did I ever tell you," she said, "how Cameron and I were married privately, long before we exchanged vows before the bishop?"

"I seem to recall something to that effect," he said, urging her on. He'd far rather listen to her nostalgia than discuss the state of his life.

"Of course, we were snowed in together. There was no possible way for us to be married legally. But Cameron felt, and I agreed, that we had to make do with what we had. And we believed that God would understand. So, we exchanged vows, and we were as good as married. Technically, it may not have been right. But it was good enough for us; under the circumstances, it was our only option." Her voice went from dreamy to intense, and he wondered what she was trying to tell him. "Sometimes we just have to make the most of what we have to work with."

Again Stefan's heart quickened as the undertones of her story began to sink in. *What was she saying?*

"I don't know what it is you're longing for," Abbi continued, "and I don't know if your grandfather would approve of the advice I am giving you. But I have thought this through very carefully. I've become terribly concerned for you, Stefan. I'm well aware of the chains that bind you to your marriage, which

I have come to see as nothing more than a technicality that must remain intact in order to keep peace. I have struggled and prayed to find options on your behalf, and as wise as I'd like to believe myself to be, the situation seems futile and hopeless. But hopelessness is the true key to destruction in this life, Stefan. God forgive me if I'm wrong. And of course, you have to make your own choices, and you have to live with them. But I believe that if you thought about it, you would not resign yourself to your fate."

Stefan's eyes narrowed, and his heart beat quickly as Ericha's words seemed to come through his grandmother's lips.

"You must do what is right for you. I know in my heart that you can be the Duke of Horstberg and still be a happy man. Nothing is impossible, Stefan."

Stefan sat down in the huge windowsill. He wondered if she could read his mind. Or did she just know him so well that she could see right through him? *Just like Ericha,* he thought. He wondered if she had any idea the impact her words were having on him.

"Did you know," she said, and her expression told him she was going to say something else about Cameron, "that your grandfather went through a time in his life where his circumstances were not unlike yours?"

Stefan lifted his brows. "You've mentioned it a time or two," he said. "But the Cameron du Woernig I remember was a happy and successful man."

"He became that way. But there was a time when he allowed his circumstances to do him in. The duchy fell into the hands of his younger brother, who nearly destroyed it by his foolishness and greed. And he nearly destroyed Cameron as well. Do you know what saved him—and the duchy?" she asked as if this were a history lesson.

Stefan shook his head slightly.

"Determination," she stated. "One day he found something worth fighting for. He discovered that there are always options. He found a way to make it work. He died a happy man."

Stefan felt a formless peace float into him as he said, "He found you."

"God sent him to save my life," she said wistfully.

"As I heard it," Stefan said, "God sent you to save his. He said it with his dying breath."

Tears brimmed briefly in Abbi's eyes, but she blinked them back and gazed intently at him. "History has a way of repeating itself, Stefan," she said wisely. "For better or worse, life runs in cycles. As rulers of a nation, we are required to understand that, and learn from the past. Take a minute, Stefan, and think what would happen to Horstberg if *you* were not able to fill your position."

"Gerhard," he said more to himself.

"That's right." Abbi's voice became stern. "Your younger brother has never given the family any trouble. But he enjoys his freedom. He cannot even settle down enough to marry. He is very different from you, Stefan, and I wonder if he could handle the power and the responsibility."

She paused to let her words be absorbed. "Cameron had a younger brother, Stefan. Do I need to remind you what happened to Horstberg during Nikolaus's brief reign?"

"No," Stefan insisted. Her point was becoming clear.

"When I met Cameron, he was quite accustomed to allowing his circumstances to rule him, while Horstberg dangled in his brother's greed. It took me a long time to convince Cameron that he was entitled to be happy—and he was capable of making it happen. The state of Horstberg was deeply integrated in his happiness. You are no less entitled or capable."

Abbi's gaze deepened on Stefan, and her expression alone plainly asked if someone had been sent to save *his* life. Stefan felt unnerved by the question and turned back to the window.

After a contemplative silence, she said, "I feel confident that you were raised well to your calling, Stefan. Your parents are good people. Han knew this duchy like the palm of his hand, and he instilled it well into you—just as Cameron asked him to. You're a good man, Stefan. You know what's right and wrong, but you should also know that *sometimes* it's not black and white. The gray areas can be confusing; but gradually it can become defined if we sort it through according to our feelings.

"You know what the consequences might be of any decision that you make. Take the decisions that have been made for you and make the most of them. Then make the choices that are left open to you and find a way to be happy."

Stefan stuffed his hands into his pockets and gazed out the window, feeling something deep settle into him.

"Think about it, Stefan. There is a country at stake."

Abbi left the room quietly while Stefan gazed with longing toward the valley. He was amazed by his grandmother's perception. Through her simple observations she had defined the aching confusion in his heart. He knew his window gazing was nothing more than a longing for something that could make him happy. Yet, he knew that turning his back on his country could never make him happy, a point Abbi had made clearly in her concise analogies. And that was the summary of his confusion.

Idly, Stefan poured himself a drink then sat down and stared at the golden liquid swirling in the crystal. As his eyes became mesmerized by the liquor, he saw a brief vision of the Duke of Horstberg losing himself in the depths of it. A man with a loveless marriage, no children, and the dearest members of his family departed into death. The image consumed him so completely that he wondered for a moment if it might be easier to just take his own life.

Abruptly he set the glass down. Did his grandmother fear it was coming to that? Is that why she had made such a point of discussing the possible results of his absence? Could he take his own life, knowing the duchy that his forebears had fought so hard to uphold would likely dwindle in the hands of those who would allow it to fall?

Repelled by the visions before him, Stefan's eyes turned to the window. His thoughts turned to Ericha. *Ericha.* What was it about her that reminded him of the happier times in his life gone by? Did she know that the fate of a country lay in her hands?

Stefan lost track of the time as he worked it all through in his mind. The sun was setting when he stood abruptly from his chair. His step was brisk as he moved across the office and the door flew open, startling the officers that always stood guard there. The hall seemed longer than usual, and he quickened his pace.

In the dusky light, Abbi saw from a high window the Duke of Horstberg running like a child across the courtyard below and into the stables. She waited until he emerged again on a fiery stallion, and watched him gallop through the high gate toward the valley below. There was a prayer in her heart for him. The situation was precarious at the very least. She hoped that she had done the right thing.

"He is truly like you, Cameron," she said aloud when Stefan had disappeared in the distance. "Your country is in capable hands."

Chapter Eight
EVER AFTER

Karl heard the door of the shop open and close, but he kept his concentration on his work. "It's about time you got here," he said without looking up. "I was getting worried."

"Really, Karl," Stefan said, and the voice surprised him. "I think I can take care of myself."

"Well, look who's here." Karl grinned. "I thought you were Ericha."

Stefan chuckled. "I'm not."

Karl set his work aside and watched Stefan closely as he sat down and crossed an ankle on his knee. He'd not kept their regular meetings at the pub since their last confrontation about Ericha. And Karl had to wonder what was making him close the gap now.

"What can I do for you, my friend?" Karl asked. "I've not seen you here in a long time."

"And I'm certain you know why," Stefan said soberly.

"It wouldn't be that you're trying to avoid my little cousin, now would it?"

Stefan met Karl's eyes, feeling suddenly nervous. But the need for complete honesty—with himself as well as with Karl—urged Stefan on. "Or perhaps avoiding the aspects of myself that she won't allow me to hide from."

"And you've been avoiding me too, I've noticed," Karl added.

Stefan chuckled tensely and leaned his arms onto his thighs. "Perhaps for the same reason."

"I thought it was because my methods were a bit obnoxious."

"That too," Stefan said with a slight smile. His expression turned severe. "That is one of many things I want to talk to you about."

"I'm listening," Karl said when he didn't go on.

Stefan drew a deep breath and leaned back. "I think one of the things that I've always liked about you is the way you make me feel like I'm . . . normal. To you, I'm just a man like any other man. It's always been that way between us, even as children, and I want you to know I'm grateful for that. Looking back, I wonder if you haven't been my link to sanity in more ways than you could ever know."

"Glad I could help." Karl grinned. "But don't go getting all high and mighty and think that my friendship has been purely selfless. You've been there for me through some tough times."

"Glad I could help," Stefan countered, and then his eyes grew distant. "I never realized until Ericha made me see—indirectly I suppose—but nevertheless, she showed me that I step in and out of being the Duke of Horstberg, as if I were changing my jacket."

"I could agree with that," Karl stated.

Stefan nodded slightly, trying to perceive this added validation from a man who knew him well. "I feel sometimes like I am two separate people; like being the duke doesn't allow me to feel . . . or to live . . . or just *be*. Perhaps after I learned the truth about Johanna, I just . . . taught myself to not feel the . . ."

He hesitated, and Karl sensed rising emotion. "Forgive me if I'm being presumptuous, Stefan, but I believe that what happened with Johanna only encouraged you to avoid feelings you'd been avoiding for many years before you ever met her."

Stefan's eyes widened as he tried to digest this. How long had he just been *existing*, and not even aware of it?

"I get the impression you're trying to get to a point," Karl said when Stefan was silent for more than a minute.

"Actually, yes. I have come to a conclusion that still surprises even me. I only know that in spite of everything I've tried to make myself believe, what I am about to do is *right*—even if I don't understand completely why.

"You see," Stefan leaned forward again, "I have been looking at the two sides of myself, and I can see now that one is completely motivated by logic, and the other by feelings. My grandmother said some things to me today that made me realize I cannot expect one side of me to not affect the other. So, while I must live separate lives in a way, I must learn to become one man."

At Karl's dazed expression, Stefan asked, "Are you with me so far?"

"Oh, I'm with you," he said easily.

"Now, to the point," Stefan persisted. "I have come to a decision. I am the Duke of Horstberg. I can't change that. But I can choose what I do with the other part of my life. And I will live it with Ericha."

Stefan watched Karl closely for a reaction, but he was completely unreadable. "Are you asking my permission?" Karl finally said.

"Do I need to?"

"No. I have told Ericha many times that I will let her live her own life, and I will be there for her no matter what her choices may be." When the silence grew too long, Karl asked, "Is something wrong?"

"I keep expecting you to tell me to go to hell or something. What I'm proposing is not . . ." He couldn't find words to go on.

"We're not dealing with ordinary circumstances here, Stefan. Give me some credit for being able to see the full perspective."

A new thought occurred to Stefan. "Perhaps that is what I've been blind to. It seems that those who know me best have come to see something I've been unable to see."

"Perhaps," Karl said. And then he smiled.

"I must be completely honest," Stefan continued gravely, "with you, with Ericha, and perhaps most especially with myself. I've told myself a thousand times that I should have never become involved with her to begin with. And maybe I shouldn't have. I think back to when I made that choice, and I feel as if . . . as if I were outside myself. My feelings for her were more intense than anything I've ever felt in my life. They still are. But . . . it's difficult to act on such feelings rationally, when there are *no* rational options. I've come to believe that every human being has basic emotional needs. And Ericha came into my life when my spirit was starved and shriveled." He chuckled with no humor. "Perhaps it still is."

Stefan took a deep breath and pushed a hand through his hair. "What I'm trying to say is . . . a part of me believes that having a relationship with Ericha is right. I know in my heart that we are meant to be together. Such feelings are simply undeniable. I believe that I made a mistake a long time ago, a mistake that can't be undone. My marriage to Johanna is what stands in the way of what's meant to be for me and Ericha. I see no way to change that from where I stand. I only pray that . . ." Stefan hesitated, suddenly overcome with emotion.

"What?" Karl urged when the silence dragged on.

Stefan sighed heavily. "In spite of what I believe, Karl, I know I'm taking something that—if only in technicality—is not right. I know I'm responsible for the position I've put Ericha into. And while I have every hope that we can live out our lives together with some degree of happiness, I am a man who believes in natural laws. And I believe, that sooner or later, a price will have to be paid. I only pray that *I* will be able to pay that price. And that Ericha will not have to endure hardship because of it."

"Ericha has made her own choices, Stefan. She was young and impetuous when she met you, but no less determined to follow her heart than she is today. She's become a woman with a great deal of insight. Raised as she was, it's impossible to judge her choices. She has an innate wisdom that often leaves me in awe. Whatever comes of this, her strength will carry her through."

"I couldn't have said it better myself." Stefan leaned back in his chair. Having the worst out, he relaxed and found it easy now to talk to Karl openly about this. In spite of things Karl had said in the past, he was amazed at his friend's acceptance of something Stefan had fought against for so long. But now that he was getting used to the idea, it seemed as natural as the sun coming up in the morning. He only hoped that Ericha would see it the same way.

Ericha returned from a late evening ride and found Karl waiting for her in the stable.

"Where have you been?" he asked sharply.

"You haven't been worrying, have you?" she asked as she dismounted.

"Well, not too much." He grinned. "Nevertheless, you really shouldn't be out so much after dark."

Ericha went on her tiptoes to kiss his cheek in gratitude for his concern. "I'm starved. What's for dinner?"

"Dinner's long over, my dear, but," he paused elaborately, "if you're a good girl I'll persuade Erma to bring something up to your room."

"Oh, don't bother," she said. "I'll get something myself."

"No, no," Karl insisted, "I'll take care of it. Hurry up to your room and freshen up."

Ericha looked at him shrewdly, wondering what kind of silly surprise he had up his sleeve. But she only went into the house. Carrying a candle, she moved slowly up the stairs, noting how the flame cast shadows on the walls. She paused on the landing, as she often did, to look toward Castle Horstberg. Then she sighed and moved on toward her room.

Ericha was humming as she came in and set the candle on the bureau. She pulled the pins from her hair, then absently unbraided it. As it fell around her shoulders, she brushed through it in long, even strokes.

"Hello, Ericha," Stefan said quietly.

Ericha gasped as she turned and stood, dropping the brush to the floor. "Good heavens! You scared me nearly to death."

Stefan was silent as she scrutinized him in the candle's glow, sitting low in the chair, his long legs stretched out and crossed at the ankles. Job slept contentedly at his feet.

"Karl let me in," he said at last. "I hope you don't mind. I figured if you could sneak into my bedroom and force me into listening to you, then I could do the same."

Ericha gazed at him, bewildered. With all the time she'd spent longing to be with him, his reality seemed incredible. She felt a mixture of emotions, wondering if he would only stay a short time and leave her, as he'd done before.

"Why don't you sit down?" He motioned with his hand toward the edge of the bed. "Make yourself at home."

Ericha sat slowly, holding her breath in expectation. She sensed something unusual in his mood.

"Ericha," he said, and leaned forward a little, setting his forearms on his thighs, "there is something I need to say to you. But first of all, I must apologize for my behavior with you in the past—most especially the last time we were together."

Ericha's pulse quickened at the memory of his aggressiveness in the stable on the evening of the fair.

"Looking back now, I can see that I've been a very confused man, torn between my heart and my duty. I sincerely apologize for the hurt I have caused you by catching you up in my confusion. And I pray that eventually you will be able to forgive me."

"Believe it or not," she said, "I understand."

"Yes," he agreed, "I believe you do. And perhaps with time, you can help me understand more fully what I am just beginning to see."

Ericha passed over his implication of the future and reminded herself of her boundaries. While she had no question of his love for her, she would not take him in again only to have him turn away and leave her wondering for months at a time.

Stefan felt suddenly nervous and shot to his feet, taking care not to disturb the dog. He walked slowly across the room and back again, searching for the right words. He paused near the bureau and stared for a moment into the candle's flame. Idly he picked up a little wooden box and fidgeted with it. He set it back down but kept his hand on it as he met her eyes.

"I love you, Ericha," he said with strength, "and we will have our ever after."

He waited for a reaction, but her eyes only narrowed slightly. She seemed . . . what? Skeptical? Afraid? He couldn't blame her.

"You must understand." He chuckled tensely in an effort to conceal the vulnerability seeping into him. "My circumstances are difficult to work around. But I've come to believe that nothing is impossible. What I'm really concerned about, Ericha, is you. I'm taking for granted that you still feel as you did the last time we discussed this. If that's the case, I want you to be certain that it's what you really want."

Still she said nothing, and he thought his heart would burst through his chest.

"If I thought about it," he rambled on, "I could fear how this might affect the other aspects of my life. But not nearly as much as I fear what it might do to yours."

Stefan paused and sighed. "I'm following nothing but my instincts, Ericha. But I've come to believe that we must live while we can." Their eyes met strongly in the candlelight, and Stefan could see a sparkle of emotion that gave him the courage to go on. "I even talked to Karl about it. I told him how miserable I've been without you. But as I told you once, it all seems so sordid in a way—for you especially. But Karl told me that it would only be what you and I make it. I asked him to clarify that, and do you know what Karl told me?"

Ericha shook her head slightly, still too moved to speak.

"He suggested that I take you on a honeymoon."

Stefan gave a complacent smile, and Ericha's heart raced. She couldn't believe this was happening.

"You know," he said in response to her silence. "That is one of those vacations that two people who are in love take to spend a lot of time together and get to know each other with no one else around in places where no one knows who they are or cares what they're doing. How does that sound to you?"

Ericha found the will to stand up. She hesitated a moment, then rushed into this arms. "Oh, Stefan," she cried while he held her so tight she could hardly breathe, "it sounds too incredible to be real."

He chuckled and drew back to meet her eyes. "Are you certain it's what you want?"

"With all my soul," she replied, and he smiled.

"Good!" He took a step back but kept her hands in his. "I'll be sending you on a train to Regensberg. You'll be leaving the day after tomorrow. Pack light. I'll buy you whatever you need. From there you're going to a little town on the Danube where you'll be staying in an inn called the *Boar's Den*. I'll arrive there the day after you, and we'll go together by train to Wurttemberg. Karl will take you to the station and have everything you need to get you where you're going. Oh yes, we will be traveling under the name Bruxen. Any questions?"

Ericha shook her head and smiled at him.

"If you change your mind before then," he said carefully, "just let Karl know."

"I won't change my mind."

"There is one thing you should know." The intensity in his eyes deepened. "In all respects, as far as you and I are concerned, this is the real thing. I am committing myself to you—completely—for the rest of my life. We will be as husband and wife in every respect but one. If I could give you my name, I would, but I can't." He gave a slight smile. "You're stuck with me, Ericha. Till death do us part."

She smiled at him again, and he asked, "Haven't you got anything to say?"

"You have just made me the happiest woman alive."

He laughed.

"But I must know," she said, "what made you change your mind?"

"Well," he glanced down at the toe of his boot as it shuffled over the floor, "some things my grandmother said made me take a long, hard look at myself. I looked back over my life and tried very hard to think of everything I'd known that had brought me happiness. The list was quite concise. I have given everything I have to Horstberg. And I will continue to give as long as there's breath in me to do it. But in return I realized that I truly do need you in my life. I deserve this one happiness, Ericha. I only pray that you will not regret this."

"Never," she whispered adamantly. "How can I regret the consequences of the demands of my heart, Stefan? If we truly follow our hearts, doing what we know is right as far as possible under the circumstances, we will be able to face whatever they lead us to."

"You are priceless," he whispered and reached up to touch her face.

"I love you, Stefan."

He smiled. "And I love you."

He gazed at her a long moment before leaving her alone.

Ericha nearly went mad from excitement as she prepared for her journey. And Karl was quick to notice her change of mood.

"I take it you accepted his offer," he said at the breakfast table.

"Did you think I wouldn't?" she replied, wondering how Karl really felt about this.

"Stefan's a good man," he said with conviction. "If it was anybody else, I'm not sure I'd let you do it. I don't think there is a better man alive than Stefan Heinrich. He'll treat you well, Ericha. And you're a good woman. He deserves you." Karl smiled and reached his hand across the table to take hers.

Ericha stood and leaned across the table to kiss Karl on the cheek.

"What was that for?" He laughed.

"For everything," she said. "What would I ever do without you?"

He smirked. "Well, there are advantages in this for me."

"And what's that?" she asked, knowing he was mostly teasing.

"You can't live with Stefan, so you'll have to stay here with me. I can still have the pleasure of your company and have the opportunity of taking care of you a little myself." Ericha looked distressed, and he quickly added, "What's the matter?"

"I didn't stop to think," she said. "You will be stuck with me. I've nowhere else to go. And what will it do to your reputation or—"

"Ericha," he said soberly, "I have never cared what anyone thought of me. And I'm not going to start now."

"Perhaps I should live elsewhere. I'm certain that Stefan—"

"And like I already said," he interrupted, "I want you here."

"Even after you marry?"

"There's plenty of room," he said exuberantly, holding up his hands for emphasis.

Ericha laughed. "Again—thank you for everything."

"It's my pleasure, little cousin." He grinned. "My pleasure."

Stefan came into the dining room and was greeted with expressions of bewilderment. He'd not shown up to eat breakfast with the family for quite some time.

"Well, good morning," his grandmother said. "What a nice surprise."

"Good morning, Grandmama," he replied with the first real smile she'd seen in months. She couldn't help noting his light step and something almost dreamy in his eyes.

Stefan bent to kiss her cheek, then moved toward the opposite end of the table, nodding toward Johanna in a polite greeting, "Good morning."

Johanna nodded curtly in reply and watched him closely as he seated himself. Georg entered the dining room as soon as Stefan was seated. He paused to kiss Abbi's cheek before seating himself at her side. Then he glanced down the long table and grinned to see Stefan sitting there.

"Hello there, my boy," he said.

"Good morning, Georg. How are you today?"

"Couldn't be better," he gave the usual reply, and his eyes turned to Abbi.

Stefan smiled as he observed them. He had many times in the past envied the love that shone in their eyes when they looked at each other. But the prospect of seeing Ericha soon made him feel more like he understood them, rather than longing for something he didn't have.

Stefan thought often that he would give a great deal to have seen Georg and Abbi fifty or sixty years ago. They had been friends since childhood, and Georg had been instrumental in bringing Cameron and Abbi together. Georg had married the same year as Cameron and Abbi, and he became the duke's highest advisor because of his cunning and allegiance in aiding Cameron as he reclaimed the duchy. Their lives had always been connected, yet through all the years they'd shared, Stefan wondered if they could have ever foreseen the relationship they shared now. Stefan loved them both and was grateful for their presence in his life, since most of the family had dispersed from Horstberg in one way or another.

Stefan had one aunt who was his mother's sister, but she lived some distance away and he rarely saw her. His father had been an only child, and in fact, his father's mother had died in childbirth after Stefan's parents had married. Stefan's older sister, Hannah, lived in Horstberg on the Albrecht Estate, which belonged to Abbi. And his younger brother and sisters were scattered about Germany living lives of their own.

Stefan's parents, Han and Maggie, were avid travelers and spent little time in Horstberg since Stefan had taken over the duchy. Which left the residents of Castle Horstberg to be him and Johanna, and Georg and Abbi.

Stefan briefly contemplated the odd circumstances of the foursome surrounding the huge table. Then his thoughts turned to Ericha, and he unwillingly smiled.

"You certainly seem perky this morning," Johanna said, her tone subtly cynical. Stefan noted the rubies she wore.

"I am, thank you," he nodded toward her.

"Why is that?" Abbi asked, and Stefan smiled toward her.

"I've decided to take some time off," he stated. "And I must say I'm looking forward to it."

"What will you do?" Johanna asked, and Stefan caught a brief note of frenzy in her voice.

"I'm going out of town for a while," he said toward her.

"But where," she went on, "and—"

"I'm not certain where, or when I'll be back, for that matter. But I can assure you that I will return. There's no need to fret."

"I think it's marvelous," Abbi said. "You've been working too hard."

Stefan lifted his glass to her and smiled warmly.

"I assume you've made arrangements," Georg said, and Stefan knew he was referring to the business of the duchy.

"I'll have things under control," he said, "and Rusty can handle it. I told him if he needed anything to call on you. I hope you don't mind."

"Mind?" he laughed. "It'll be good to feel like I'm not too old to be useful."

Stefan laughed. "That day will never come."

Abbi smiled affectionately toward Georg, and the gesture warmed Stefan. He paid no mind to the distressed appearance of his wife, until her fork dropped loudly against her plate. He looked up to see that she was obviously upset about something and seemed to be wanting him to realize this. It had been so long since she'd taken any notice of him at all that he wondered if his apparent happiness somehow disturbed her. Realizing he didn't care, he smiled casually and turned his attention to his breakfast.

He broke the silence by saying, "Grandmama?"

"Yes?" she replied, glancing up from her meal.

"It certainly is a good day to be happy, don't you think?"

He saw her eyes sparkle and knew somehow that she was aware of what was happening in his life; though he believed it would never—ever—be verbalized between them. Her outwardly condoning such a thing was unheard of, but he appreciated her silent understanding of the circumstances. And he prayed she would not regret her advice.

"Yes," she said at last, and he felt the contentment for life in her voice, "it is a beautiful day to be happy."

Johanna made a dubious noise. But Abbi smiled at Georg. Stefan's thoughts went to Ericha. And nobody noticed.

Stefan went directly to the office when his meal was finished, longing to be done with his work so that he could get out of here.

"Don't you ever eat breakfast?" Stefan asked lightly when he found Rusty already at work.

"Ate early," he said absently, and he ran his hand slowly through his dark hair, pausing to scratch his head a moment as he concentrated on the papers in front of him. He suddenly seemed finished as Stefan sat behind the desk and pushed up his sleeves.

"Let's get started," Stefan said. "I've got a vacation to get to."

Rusty chuckled. "You could use it. You work too hard, sir."

"I never work as hard as you do," Stefan replied.

"I enjoy it. You don't."

"Ah," Stefan smiled, "it's not so bad."

Rusty seemed surprised by the comment, but he only glanced at the calendar to check the date before beginning. He turned to scrawl it at the top of the page to record today's events, then blinked several times to apparently perceive something in his methodical way.

Stefan was used to Rusty's manner and knew they could probably get done in half the time with someone who didn't think so much about what he was doing. But Rusty's intelligence concerning business matters was unbelievable, which more than compensated for the other. And to Stefan, it was actually quite endearing.

"Is something wrong?" Stefan asked when he paused longer than usual.

"Today's the twelfth."

"Yes."

"My father died sixteen years ago today."

Stefan drew a deep breath, and they were silent several moments before Rusty looked toward him. "Don't look that way."

"What?"

"You always look that way when I talk about him. You shouldn't."

"How should I look?" Stefan asked straightly.

"It wasn't your fault. I've told you a hundred times."

"You still miss him," Stefan said gently. "If only for your sake, I wish he were still here."

"Yes, well, I'm glad *you're* still here."

Stefan glanced down uneasily, recalling the circumstances of Rusty's father's death. Franz had worked as a servant to the duke since the days of Cameron's reclamation. Rusty's mother died young, and Franz and Rusty had always been close to the family.

A few years beyond Cameron's death, Stefan passed out one day in the office, as a dreadful fever came on hard and fast. It was Franz who scooped him into his arms and carried him up to bed. And a few days later, Franz had the same fever. The family feared that Stefan would not make it, and for years beyond it, he had shown signs of frailty as a result. But Stefan survived the fever. Franz didn't.

Stefan knew it was ridiculous to blame himself for Franz's death. He could hardly have protested his assistance when he was unconscious. But still, it tore a little at Stefan's heart when he saw how much Rusty missed his father to this day. The similar loss of a loved one added to the kinship Stefan felt with Rusty, but it made their relationship always a little melancholy. Stefan enjoyed being with Karl for many reasons, but he had a great deal of admiration for Rusty, and perhaps felt a little obligated to see that he was cared for, despite Rusty being three years his elder.

"There you go again," Rusty said in response to Stefan's expression. "Stop it."

Stefan tried to smile, and Rusty resumed his work. Moments later a knock came at the door. Rusty stood to answer it, and Johanna sauntered into the room, wearing emeralds. Stefan wondered what might have happened since breakfast that had made her decide to go upstairs and change her mood.

"Hello, my dear," she said to Stefan with more affection in her voice than he'd heard in months—maybe years. She sat on the edge of the desk and fanned her face with a letter she was holding, touching Stefan's face with her other hand.

"You're looking tired, my love. Are you feeling all right?"

"Yes, fine," he stated, retracting from her touch, which seemed to annoy her more than usual.

"Did you need something?" he asked dryly.

"Just came to see how you're doing, and oh . . . I almost forgot." She sauntered around the desk toward Rusty, who was leaning over the books intently.

"Rusty," she said in a sing-song tone, and he glanced up with wide eyes. Her sultry attention seemed to overwhelm his timid nature. "How are you today?" she asked sweetly.

"Fine," he stated. "Just fine." He cleared his throat, and Stefan chuckled. Johanna's flirtations brought out an endearing nature in him. "And how are you . . . Your Grace?" he asked.

"As good as could be expected," she said, holding the letter in front of his face. "That cute little upstairs maid," she whispered loudly, "you know . . . the one that likes you." Rusty's eyes widened and his color deepened a little. "She stopped me in the hall and told me to give you this."

Rusty took it sheepishly, then stuffed it into his pocket without looking at it. "Thank you," he said shortly, then turned his attention back to his work to avoid further embarrassment.

"Stefan," Johanna said thoughtfully, "I was in the mood to go riding. You know . . . like we used to. Won't you come with me? It would be such fun."

Stefan tilted his head and gave her a sidelong glance, wondering what had brought on this sudden bout of attention.

"I haven't got the time," he stated.

"Oh," she said with a pouty expression. "Some other time, perhaps."

He said nothing, and she left acting a bit sulky.

"We'll never get done with this," Stefan sighed.

"Don't worry," Rusty said. "I'll make sure you get that vacation."

Stefan smiled and turned his mind toward seeing Ericha.

To Ericha, it seemed an eternity before it was time to leave for the station. Karl helped her into the trap, commenting on how lovely she looked, and she nearly beamed.

"I didn't figure it would be a problem for you to pack light," he said at the station, glancing at the familiar valise. She laughed, and he added, "You have a marvelous time, and take care."

"I will," she said, hugging him tightly, "and you take good care of Job for me."

"We'll have a marvelous time, too," he said elaborately.

Ericha felt a combination of emotions as she embarked the train and it rolled forward. But regret was not among them. She contemplated briefly her arrival in Horstberg and the things that had happened since, and then her mind focused on counting down the hours until she would be with Stefan.

Ericha followed his instructions carefully and was treated graciously every step of the way. It was gratifying to finally reach the location where he'd said he would meet her. The first day there she explored the town. But the following day she became tense, hoping for Stefan to arrive. As the day wore on, she wished that he had been more specific about when she could expect him.

Ericha tried to work on her tatting but found it pointless. As darkness set in, she made up her mind that becoming more nervous and frustrated would do no good. She opted to take a long bath in an effort to pass the time and feel at her best when he came.

Ericha felt a fresh excitement envelope her as she relaxed in the soothing water. She tried to comprehend what all of this meant to her. Knowing this kind of life would be difficult, she was counting on Stefan to make up for a great deal. But her faith

in him was endless. Instinctively she knew that his love could
carry her through anything.

Stefan walked through the door of the common room and relief
washed over him. He'd never been so grateful to arrive anywhere
in his whole life. Inquiring of the innkeeper, he was told which
room Mrs. Bruxen was in, then he headed toward the stairs,
longing only to have Ericha in his arms.

"Stefan?" He heard a feminine voice call and turned abruptly.
He felt like a child caught stealing. "Is that you, Stefan?"

"Aunt Sonia," he declared as she swept across the room to
embrace him.

"Of all places," she exclaimed, "imagine running into you
here!"

"Imagine that," Stefan said dryly, grateful that Ericha was not
on his arm at the moment.

"Oh, you've grown up so tall," she added, leaning back to
scrutinize him. "Look how tall he's grown, Rudolf," she said to
her husband as he approached behind her.

"I'm no taller than I was the last time you saw me," Stefan
smiled, trying to act happy to see her.

"How are you, Stefan?" Rudolf reached out a hand, and
Stefan shook it firmly.

"Quite well, and you?"

"The same," Rudolf smiled. "Sonia and I are taking a little
holiday."

"And we're having a wonderful time!" she added.

"What brings you this far from home?" Rudolf asked.

"Uh . . . same reason," Stefan said. "Just needed some time
away."

"I don't doubt that," Sonia said, urging Stefan to an empty
table, where she sat beside him. "Mother writes in her letters how
dreadfully busy you always are. It's a wonder you're still sane."

"That is a wonder," Stefan replied. "How are the children?"

"Fine as ever," Rudolf said.

"And how is Mother?" Sonia asked.

"She's doing very well."

"And I'd ask how your parents are doing, but I doubt you would know."

"From the last letter everything seemed great."

"And where did that come from?" Sonia asked.

"I believe it was Belgium. I think they're going to Italy from there to spend Christmas with the Dormantes."

"I can't imagine why they'd want to be anywhere but Castle Horstberg for Christmas. But then, I hear it's never been quite the same since we lost Father. And I still have trouble believing Erich's gone at times. When I think of him, I almost feel as if I could go back to the castle, and my brother will be there waiting."

"Well, he's not," Stefan said, wishing it hadn't sounded so terse. He was grateful when Rudolf changed the subject.

"Are you traveling alone, Stefan?"

"Uh . . . yes. I am."

"Oh, you must come along with us and—"

Rudolf interrupted his wife. "Perhaps he needs the time alone, my dear."

"Oh, yes of course," she conceded. "Well, you must at least have dinner with us. I do want to hear what's been happening lately. It's been so long since I've been home."

Stefan tried to quickly think how to handle this with the least possibility of trouble.

"That would be nice," he said. "I've got to take care of a few arrangements, then I'll meet you here later on."

Stefan excused himself and left the inn to pass a little time. He was relieved to return and not see Rudolf or Sonia anywhere around, then he quickly made his way up the stairs to Ericha's room.

Ericha was drying herself when a knock came at the door, and her heart beat quickly.

"Who is it?" she called, but no answer came, only another light knock.

"I'm coming, just a minute please."

Putting on her wrapper, Ericha went to the door and opened it just a crack to peer out. At first she could see nothing, and then a face came around the corner with a soft chuckle.

"Hello, love," he whispered.

"Oh, Stefan," she said exuberantly, opening the door wide.

He came in quickly, peered both directions into the hallway, then closed the door behind him.

Ericha laughed as he pulled her into his arms. "I thought you'd never get here," she said. "I—"

"I can't stay just yet," he apologized, and her expression of joy faltered immediately. "You see," he went on quickly to explain, "I walked into the common room downstairs and ran into my aunt and her husband. Quite a coincidence, eh?" he said cynically, but she caught a trace of humor in his eyes.

"Here," he said, pressing a ticket into her hand. "The train leaves at ten in the morning, and I will already be there. I'll meet you at the station. Can you manage?" he asked.

She nodded but asked, "Are you sure you can't stay?"

"I wish I could," he whispered and touched her face longingly. "But I don't dare risk it. You must understand."

Again Ericha nodded, and Stefan took her hand into his, bringing it to his lips with a gentle kiss.

"Until tomorrow, my love," he said and left her alone.

Ericha boarded the train as instructed with no idea where she was going, just anxious to get there. She was surprised by how short the journey was and felt a rush of excitement as she stepped off with her valise. Anxiously she glanced around in an effort to find Stefan, and her heart became heavy with panic. What would she do if something else had come up and he hadn't made it?

Shading the sun from her eyes with her hand, Ericha looked more carefully at the people standing about. She took a sharp breath when she saw him, standing discreetly some distance away.

Their eyes met. Ericha wondered if she was supposed to pretend she didn't know him. When he just stood there, she was unsure what to do.

Unable to bear it any longer, she walked toward him with purpose, keeping her eyes focused on his so that she could read in his expression if she was doing the right thing. When she stood facing him and he remained unreadable, she said with an impish smile, "Excuse me, sir. Could you tell me where I might find the nearest inn?"

Stefan chuckled, and Ericha laughed with relief to feel his arm come around her shoulders. "I can do better than that," he said. "I will take you there personally. And," his eyes sparkled with amusement, "I already have a room there. It's big enough for both of us."

He kissed her quickly on the lips and led her to a hired carriage that drove them into town. Stefan sat across from her with his arms folded over his chest while they silently watched each other, absorbing the reality of being together. There was a tenseness in the air that Ericha became determined to ease.

"Did I ever tell you," she said softly, "about my fondest memory?"

"No," he said with interest, "you didn't."

"It was during a thunderstorm, in a mountain lodge."

Stefan's eyes showed surprise.

"I hate thunderstorms," she said. "Yet that storm was beautiful." She paused. "Will you tell me more stories, Stefan?"

As he nodded, Ericha caught a deeper meaning in his eyes, and she glanced timidly away. The carriage halted, and Stefan helped Ericha out in front of an inn that looked finer than average. He took her bag and led the way up the stairs, where he opened a door and paused.

"Is something wrong?" she asked.

Shaking his head, Stefan set the bag inside the door, pulled Ericha up into his arms, stepped into the room, and kicked the door shut. Ericha laughed as he set her down, but then the air became tense with silence.

"Why don't you freshen up, and we'll have something to eat?" he said. "Then we can go into town and look around."

"All right," she replied.

"Take your time. I'll meet you downstairs."

Stefan left the room, and Ericha wondered if normal honeymoons felt this way. A few minutes later she found Stefan sitting in the common room with a tankard of beer. He rose as she came down the stairs and approached him.

"I ordered for you," he said as they were seated. "I hope you don't mind."

"I'm not fussy," she said. "I'll eat anything." He smiled, and she added, "Well, almost anything." After an uncomfortable silence, Ericha said, "So, did you manage to avoid your aunt?"

"I did. She was traveling the other direction, thankfully. And it's a good thing. She and my mother have few secrets from each other." His gaze delved into her, and he added, "I can hardly believe that we're . . ."

Their food was brought to the table, and Ericha realized she was hungry as the aroma greeted her.

"Will there be anything else, Mr. Bruxen?" the innkeeper asked.

"No, thank you," he said kindly. "It looks delicious."

"Why Bruxen?" Ericha whispered when he had gone.

"My grandmother's maiden name," he replied.

They ate in silence, and Ericha felt both tense and excited to be with him. When they were finished, Stefan made an elaborate point of showing her the town, and he insisted on buying her anything that caught her fancy—or his. It was far past dark when they returned to their room with armloads of packages, laughing carelessly over nothing. But when the door closed and they were alone, that tension descended again.

"You look very tired," Ericha said, noting the weary look in his eyes.

"I must confess," he said, "I had to work long hours to get done so that I could leave. And I traveled straight through."

"You'd best get some sleep," she said easily. "Then when you're feeling rested, we'll see more of the sights."

He smiled warmly at her and sat on the edge of the bed to pull off his boots. Ericha sat by the mirror to take the pins from her hair, and Stefan watched as the long braid unwound to hang down her back. He placed his hands gently on her shoulders, and they exchanged a tender smile in the mirror. He opted to sit in bed to watch her, and when Ericha had finished brushing out her hair, she turned to see the Duke of Horstberg sleeping soundly on one side of the bed.

Ericha smiled to herself, noticing his shirt and breeches on the floor with his boots. After extinguishing the light, she undressed down to her chemise and carefully moved into the other side of the bed. Content and secure from just having him near, she fell asleep.

Stefan awoke in the darkness, feeling disoriented until he became aware of Ericha stirring gently in her sleep. Carefully he moved his arm around her and brought her head to his shoulder without waking her. He fell quickly back to sleep, and his next awareness was a hint of daylight approaching and the reality of Ericha sleeping in his arms.

Stefan realized it was raining, and the familiar mood warmed him as he stared toward the ceiling, aware of Ericha breathing against his neck. Hearing thunder rumble in the distance, he wondered which direction the storm was moving. When it recurred, he knew it was coming closer. But it only added to the coziness of being here, alone at last with the woman he loved.

A bold crack came unexpectedly overhead, and Ericha started from her sleep. She glanced around, briefly fearful, but then she met Stefan's eyes, and his arms moved closer around her. She relaxed against his shoulder, and he asked softly, "Why does it frighten you?"

"I don't know," she replied. But a moment later, she added, "Yes, I do know. It was because of my mother."

"Was she afraid of thunder?"

"I suppose that was it," she said wistfully. "She would always get upset and emotional during thunderstorms. And it frightened me."

Thunder sounded again, and they held each other tighter.

"It won't hurt you," Stefan said, looking down at her. They stared at each other in the dim light, and Ericha's heart swelled with love.

"Will you tell me a story?" she asked as Stefan moved his hand over the side of her face and into her hair.

Stefan answered her with an unblinking intensity in his eyes. He shook his head slightly, whispering, "Later."

Ericha held her breath, expecting him to kiss her. But Stefan's eyes filled with emotion as he took her hand into his, saying gently, "I, Stefan, take thee, Ericha, to be my only love, to have and to hold, to love and to cherish, to honor and to obey, in sickness and in health, in prosperity or poverty, giving myself to thee and forsaking all others, till death do us part."

Ericha smiled warmly, touched beyond words by his sentiment. She absorbed it, then asked, "Do you believe we will part at death?" She could see him pause to deeply consider the question. "By your instinct, where do you believe your grandmother will be when she dies?"

Stefan smiled when he answered. "That's easy. I believe she will be with Cameron."

"Is their love greater than ours?" she asked.

Deep emotion came into his eyes. "I always believed theirs was the greatest love that ever existed. I envied that. But I don't anymore."

Ericha smiled and touched his face. "I, Ericha, take thee, Stefan, as my only love, to have and to hold, to love and to cherish, to honor and to obey, in sickness and in health, in prosperity or poverty, giving myself to thee and forsaking all others—until the end of time."

"Until the end of time," he repeated.

"You may now kiss the bride," she said.

Stefan smiled and did just that, but he found it impossible to stop with a kiss.

"Ericha," he whispered, moving his lips to her throat, "it has been so long. I don't know how I ever lived without you."

"I never knew life without you," Ericha replied, pressing her fingers through his thick waves of hair and over the back of his neck. She was intrigued by the roughness of his stubbled face as she attempted to mingle memories with the present.

Stefan was astounded at how much love and emotion Ericha betrayed as he loved her. He didn't want to, but couldn't help comparing her to Johanna. And it made him realize why he'd been so miserable. He had known nothing with Johanna but a sordid duty. But this! This was love. It edified him and gave him strength. It replenished the well inside him with fresh, vibrant water.

As daylight filtered into the room and the rain ceased, Stefan and Ericha lay close together between the cool sheets, lost in a silent appreciation of being together. The tension had dissipated.

"Ericha," he said at last, leaning on one elbow to look down at her, "where do you want to go?"

"Anywhere, as long as I'm with you."

"I mean it. I'll take you anywhere you want to go. My father always said that seeing the world outside of Horstberg was a glorious experience—as long as you could always go back to Horstberg."

"I like your father more all the time." She smiled. "But let's just stay here," she kissed him, "in bed all day."

Stefan laughed freely. "Well, if you're not going to tell me where you want to go, then you'll just have to go where I take you."

"Sounds wonderful," she declared.

"The first place we're going is the Black Forest," he said with mischief in his eyes.

"The land of fairy tales?" she asked expectantly.

"Precisely. And we're leaving today. We'll stay in an inn tonight, and I'll take you into the forest tomorrow."

"Will you tell me stories?" she asked.

"Later." He smirked and kissed her. But again he found it impossible to stop with that.

Chapter Nine

TALES FROM THE BLACK FOREST

Stefan pushed open the door of their room, and Ericha walked in while removing her hat. He was silent as he set their bags down, then closed the door and locked it. Setting her hat on the bureau and sticking the pin securely into it, Ericha turned to meet Stefan's eyes, and a slight smile passed between them. It was still hard for her to believe not only who he was but that she was here with him like this. And beyond that, it was difficult to grasp the depth of her feelings for this man that she still knew so little about.

She could not look at Stefan without admiring him, and her heart would inevitably swell with emotion. Instinctively she loved him, but she was only gradually coming to realize the reasons why. Stefan Heinrich, with his silent imposing manner, was the Duke of Horstberg—raised to be a king. And he filled the part well. Yet he was a simple man. There was no need for trumpets or banners to declare his power. His power was in his eyes. Those burning, fearless eyes that contrasted so strongly with his humble aura that allowed him to mingle with the farmers and tradesmen that he ruled and not seem out of place.

"It's awfully warm in here," she spoke at last, unbuttoning the jacket of the navy-colored traveling suit he'd bought for her. She moved toward the window and pulled back the drapes to let in the little remaining light of day.

Stefan made no comment as she tried to open the window.

But when her attempts failed, he moved beside her and gave that barely detectable smile where one corner of his mouth did little more than twitch upward. "Let me," he said, and she moved aside, taking a deep breath as the window opened and fresh air penetrated the room.

"You still look tired." She brushed her hand over the side of his face. "Are you feeling all right?"

"I'm fine," he replied. Ericha thought he still seemed tense, but perhaps the farther they got from Horstberg, the more relaxed he would get. She was certain he had been working too hard, for too many years.

"Would you mind," she said, indicating the buttons down the back of her blouse.

Stefan unfastened them, and then he took her shoulders into his hands and kissed the back of her neck. Ericha laughed slightly as she pulled her arms out of the sleeves. She tossed the blouse aside, then unfastened her skirt and let if fall to the floor. Laying her clothes carefully over a chair, she went to the basin to wash up.

Stefan removed his boots and jacket and sat with his legs stretched out, watching Ericha as she freshened up and removed her shoes and stockings. She pulled a few pins out of her hair, and the braid unrolled and fell over her shoulder.

With the room nearly dark, Ericha lit a lamp and impulsively pulled out her tatting. Putting on her glasses, she felt slightly embarrassed, knowing she looked far from attractive in them. But Stefan only smiled. Wearing her long chemise, Ericha seated herself on the floor near the light to work.

Stefan watched her silently for several moments before he asked in a quiet tone, "What are you doing?"

"Tatting," she said without moving her attention from it.

"I've never heard of it," he said.

"My mother taught me," she explained. "She was very good at it. She would sell the lace to fine dress shops. That is how we survived, except for what she made as a seamstress."

"It looks very difficult." He bent forward a little and leaned his forearms on his thighs to get a better look.

"It doesn't seem difficult to me," she said, "but then I've been doing it the better part of my life. I suppose I was raised on it."

"I've noticed the lace you wear," he said tenderly, "but I didn't realize."

"Karl encouraged me to sell it as my mother did," she said, "and I must say it's doing well. I hear it's become fashionable in Horstberg these days."

"I dare say." He chuckled warmly.

Ericha continued to work, unaware of the admiration glowing in Stefan's eyes. Everything he discovered about her made him love her more.

"Come closer," he said, "so that I can watch you."

Ericha moved directly in front of him to work, and Stefan watched, fascinated by the agile way her fingers moved with the tiny shuttle to create the intricate lace.

As Ericha began to tire slightly, she turned and leaned back against Stefan's legs. He relaxed, his hand toying idly with her braid. When she paused and bent her head back to ease the stiffness in her neck, Stefan kneaded her shoulders with his fingers. Ericha moaned pleasurably from its effectiveness.

When her attention turned back to her work, Stefan pulled her braid through his hands, marveling at its thickness. "You know," he said, "I always thought that my grandmother had the most beautiful hair in the world. I do believe it's much like yours."

She gave a soft laugh. "Is hers so unruly and impossible?"

"I don't know." He chuckled. "I'll have to ask her."

Ericha turned quickly to face him. "Your grandmother," she said, "Abbi du Woernig."

"That's right," he said, wondering why it seemed such a revelation.

"My neighbor, Mrs. Burger, told me once that my hair reminded her of Abbi du Woernig's—the grand duchess."

"Well," he smiled, "it seems that Mrs. Burger was right. My mother's hair is similar actually, though not so thick."

Ericha turned back to her work, wondering if Stefan knew

any of the stories that Mrs. Burger was certain she could glean from the grand duchess if given a chance.

Ericha felt Stefan pull the ribbon from the bottom of the braid. Patiently he worked his hands through her hair until it fell in thick waves around her shoulders and down her back. Ericha found her work tedious and set it aside, turning toward him.

"All done?" he asked.

"I can only do so much in one sitting," she said.

He pressed his fingers over the back of her head as she rested it in his lap.

"Where are your thoughts, my love?" she asked quietly.

"Nowhere but with you," he answered. "Actually, I'm enjoying not having to think at all. It seems like most of my life has been spent thinking about my work in one way or another. I'm tired of thinking."

Ericha looked up at him. "You still seem a bit . . . tense."

Stefan smiled genuinely and touched her nose. "My brain is just trying to get used to the idea that it's on vacation. I'm fine, really."

Ericha forced herself to ask the question that she had to admit was haunting her. "Are you having second thoughts . . . about us, I mean?"

His obvious surprise made her feel better already. "Heavens, no," he insisted with a little chuckle. "Once I figured out what was really going on inside of me, I had no doubts. A few concerns, perhaps. But no doubts."

Ericha smiled peaceably and laid her head back in his lap.

"And you?" he asked.

"I am yours, Stefan—heart and soul."

Stefan sighed contentedly and leaned his head back.

"Are you really the Duke of Horstberg?" she asked after a long silence.

"I'm afraid I am," he said a little too seriously.

"Is it really so bad?" she asked.

"There are a lot of things about my position that are not enjoyable. But it's not really such a bad life—now that you're in it," he added with softness in his voice. "It's not so much being the duke that I don't like, as it is the reasons that I became the duke."

Ericha lifted her head to look at him. "I don't understand."

"You see," he rummaged his fingers through her hair as he spoke, "when I was a child, my grandfather, Cameron du Woernig, was the duke. He was a remarkable man. Even in my youth I admired and respected him a great deal—and I loved him. One day he took me to the highest turret of the castle where we could see out over the whole country. He told me then that if my uncle didn't have a son, I would be the Duke of Horstberg. I remember the day very clearly. It's almost as if I sensed even then that it would happen, because I felt afraid in a way."

"Then your uncle must not have had a son."

"He didn't have a chance," Stefan sighed. "When I was seven years old . . ." Ericha watched Stefan closely as a glazed look came to his eyes and he seemed lost in another time. She wondered by the silence if he would go on, but he took a deep breath and said, "There was an explosion at the castle. My uncle was killed and . . ." He paused and cleared his throat tensely. "And my grandfather died from the smoke he'd inhaled, trying to save his son."

Ericha gasped at the news, unable to imagine the horror of such a thing.

Stefan pushed a hand through his hair as the memories became so vivid he could almost smell the smoke. "The next day my father told me with tears in his eyes that I was the Duke of Horstberg. With my uncle gone, my grandfather's last breath left me to this legacy."

He looked directly into Ericha's eyes. "It's painful, Ericha," he murmured, "because there is not a day that goes by when I don't think: If there had been no explosion, they would be alive, and I wouldn't have to be doing this."

Stefan finished his story looking sad and distant. It became increasingly evident to Ericha that Stefan Heinrich had not lived an easy life. After a long silence, she reached up to touch his face.

"You have much happiness ahead of you, my love."

"Not so long ago I would have never believed that."

"Do you believe it now?" she asked.

"Yes," he said with conviction, "I do."

"But you still look sad."

"It's hard to think about them and not feel . . . well, I just miss them. They were both a very big part of my life."

"You know," she interrupted, "when I used to feel down, my mother would sing to me."

Stefan lifted his brows. "What did she sing?"

"It was the same song always," she said nostalgically. "She told me it was a folk song, in a way."

"Sing it for me," he said. She was surprised by his request, but she didn't feel at all uncomfortable as Stefan held her hand while she sang the simple verses.

> *I know a place where snow falls white*
> *That's where I long to be*
> *Where castle turrets strike moonlight*
> *And shine where I can see*
> *I've known my love on mountains high*
> *Where meadows bloom in blue*
> *I know my love is there for me*
> *I know that love is true*
> *There is a place where snow falls deep*
> *And warmth is near the hearth*
> *Deep in my sweetheart's dreams I sleep*
> *There's comfort in this warmth*
> *The world is cold and brash outside*
> *I fear what it imparts*
> *But I know my love is here with me*
> *A fire burns in my heart*

Stefan felt an indiscernible chill run through him as she finished. "That song sounds as if it was written for us," he said, and Ericha felt warmed by his insight.

She took his hand into hers. "Do you still feel sad?"

"I feel," he said, and a tender smile came to his eyes, "that loving you is by far the best thing I have ever done in my life."

Ericha smiled and drew his hand to her lips. "Come to bed." She stood and pulled him to his feet. "It's getting late."

Stefan drew her into his arms, meeting her eyes in the lamp-light. "I love you, Ericha," he whispered.

"I love you," she smiled, "Your Grace."

Stefan smiled in return, then bent to blow out the lamp. In the darkness he felt suddenly awkward. Trying to discern the source of his feelings, he just stood there for an intolerable length of time.

"Is something wrong?" she whispered.

Stefan hesitated answering. How could he tell Ericha the depth of his feelings without sounding trite?

"Whatever it is," she said gently, "you can tell me. There is nothing you cannot tell me."

"Yes," he whispered, "I believe that. I suppose it's just that . . . well, habits don't die easy."

"What do you mean?" She took his hand into hers.

"It's . . . hard for me to say, Ericha, because I . . ."

"You what?" she urged.

"I fear hurting your feelings or . . ."

"Nothing coming from your heart could hurt me. I fear that unspoken feelings might damage you far worse than speaking them would hurt me."

Stefan felt his heart swell. "You have the wisdom of an old woman and the vibrancy of a child."

"I hope that's a compliment." She laughed gently.

"It is indeed."

Ericha whispered with challenge in her voice, "Tell me, Stefan. Give me your feelings, and I'll tuck them safely away."

He reached to touch her face. "I fear," he began then drew a deep breath, "what kind of man I am for you."

"I don't understand."

"I . . . I must admit that I have never known any other woman except . . . my wife. I went into marriage innocent and

willing to give of everything I had. Years later I withdrew myself
from the relationship and realized I had turned into a cold and
sinister man." The timidity in his voice made Ericha realize that
he was speaking of intimate things. She squeezed his hand with
assurance, and he continued. "I was like a different man when I
was with her. I hardened my heart in order to face the fact that
I was supposed to produce an heir. I learned to treat her every
bit as badly as I felt I had been treated." He paused and turned
his head to the side. "Ericha, I fear what the years might have
done to me. I don't want to hurt you."

"Stefan," Ericha whispered, "when you first held me in your
arms, I knew almost nothing about you. Yet my memories of
your affection have given me the determination to find a future
with you. I know nothing of a cold and sinister man." She set her
hand against his chest and eased into his arms. "Give your fears
to me, Stefan, and I will throw them away."

Stefan held her close, realizing she already had. It was
uncanny how Ericha had the ability to make everything seem
right. *Everything!*

He chuckled softly and embraced her tighter. "It seems
bizarre," he said, and she looked up in question. "Here we are,
nearly strangers in some respects, yet you are the center of my
life. I wish I could find words to tell you . . ."

"Just tell me," she whispered when he faltered.

"You have taught me what love is, Ericha. Every moment
with you has been like an awakening, a startling revelation. You
have restored so much in me that I thought I had lost forever." He
kissed her lips timidly, and Ericha felt his heart quicken beneath
her hand.

Impulsively Stefan picked her up and carried her to the bed.
The awkwardness dissipated into passion, and the fears fled with
the desire to become a part of her. He felt as if his life was only
beginning.

Ericha had believed that the affection she had shared with
Stefan in the past was beyond compare. She had treasured each
memory with its evidence of his love for her. But tonight in

Stefan's arms, with the burdens of his life seeming a million miles away, he ushered her through an experience she would have never believed possible. She could almost literally feel his inhibitions flee, leaving in their wake nothing but the heart and soul of the man he was inside. His ability to rule a nation became dwarfed by the way he held her, suspended somehow, in a delicate balance of ecstasy and complete contentment.

Long after it was over, Ericha felt too moved to speak. The surrounding silence blanketed them in perfect comfort. Ericha knew now why she'd become assaulted with discontentment and misery the moment she'd looked into Stefan Heinrich's eyes. It was as if her heart had foreseen this moment, and it would not rest until the full potential of their love was achieved.

Ericha pulled Stefan closer and made no effort to hold back her tears. She had found her ever after.

Ericha was full of excitement as they prepared to set out for the Black Forest. She wore a deep green riding habit that Stefan had bought for her. He'd insisted that green was stunning on his grandmother, and it would no doubt do well for her, considering their similar coloring. Ericha had to admit she was pleased with the result as she pinned a matching hat into place and absorbed her reflection. It was difficult to imagine herself the common woman in calico. And when Stefan entered the room and stopped to obtrusively admire her, she felt a little closer to fitting into his life.

"You are positively the most beautiful woman I have ever seen," he said, his eyes glowing with sincerity.

"Don't be silly." She placed her hand over his arm as they left the room and started down the stairs. "You've probably been surrounded with princesses and ladies all your life."

"Yes, I have. And I can assure you that none of them—"

"Your mother is most beautiful woman I've ever seen."

"She is very beautiful," he admitted with a chuckle.

"What's so funny?"

"She's my mother, Ericha."

They came outside where two saddled mounts and two pack horses were waiting, already loaded.

"How long are we staying?" she asked.

"Not long enough," he replied. The sparkle in his eyes made it evident he was becoming more relaxed.

Ericha was touched by the way he bent his knee below the stirrup of her mount, urging her foot onto his thigh to help her get into the saddle less awkwardly in the heavy skirt.

"Where did you learn to do that?" she asked, settling herself into the saddle as he put the reins into her gloved hands.

"I did a lot of riding with my sisters. They're all rather short." He chuckled, and she thought how good it was to see him this way.

Ericha admired Stefan's lean form as he mounted the other horse. A quiver of excitement rushed through her as they rode away, side by side.

It took much longer than Ericha thought it would to reach their destination. But Stefan stopped often to rest and was continually concerned for her. It became gradually darker as the trees thickened around them. A sense of intrigue settled into her as she thought of the fairy tales he'd spoken of that had blossomed from the Black Forest.

Ericha calculated that it was late afternoon when they stopped at last near a small cottage nestled among the trees. She absorbed the nearly magical quality of her surroundings while Stefan unloaded the horses and took them into the little stable. With their belongings on the porch, Stefan produced a key from his pocket and turned it in the lock of the cottage door.

"Whose is it?" she asked, wondering if he had rented it for their stay.

"It's mine," he said with no expression, as if it should have been obvious. "It could probably use a little cleaning up," he added, searching for a lamp. "This place doesn't get used very often."

"I don't mind." Ericha glanced around with interest as the room became lighter.

She could see now that they were standing in the center of a common room, with a parlor area at one end and a kitchen at the other. In the center, an enclosed staircase went up. Ericha ascended to investigate with Stefan close behind. The bedroom at the top of the stairs was brighter, due to the large windows, and Ericha nearly squealed to see the big bed and the bathtub.

"You like it," he stated, and they both laughed.

"Let's get busy." Ericha removed her hat and set it on the bureau.

"With what?"

"Cleaning it up, of course. And getting unpacked."

"Later." He smiled.

"You're a procrastinator, Stefan," she declared, and he laughed.

"I've got something to show you." He grinned and led her outside. They walked hand in hand down a narrow trail between the trees, until it opened up near a beautiful grassy spot. Ericha began to feel warm and removed her jacket while she took in her surroundings.

"There," Stefan pointed, "are where the wild berries grow. And over there is the pond."

Ericha grasped what he was saying and turned to him in surprise. "It's like the story."

"But of course. This is the very place I was telling you about."

"Where the stableboy with hair like sunshine brought the princess and . . ." Ericha stopped when she saw a serious sparkle in Stefan's eyes. Evidently the story he'd told her was no fairy tale. It had been quite literal.

Stefan knew she had figured it out, but he wanted to say it anyway. "You see," he began, taking her hand and leading her toward the pond to walk its circumference, "my mother fell in love with a man named Nik Koenig, not realizing that he was in actuality her uncle's son. Nikolaus du Woernig had once ruled Horstberg for a span of four years, when he'd managed to frame his brother for a crime of murder. When Cameron returned to prove his innocence and reclaim the duchy, Nikolaus was killed.

"But Nikolaus's son was determined to have what he believed his father should have had. He wanted to marry the Princess MagdaLena, and it became apparent to everyone but her what his motives were. When my grandmother suspected she was planning to run away with Nik, she told my grandfather, and he hired Han Heinrich, who had grown up in the stables, to kidnap the princess and get her to marry him in order to save the country.

"Han brought the princess here, and all anyone knows for certain is that they came back seven months later, not only married but very much in love."

Stefan smiled more to himself. "My father declares it was the magic of the Black Forest that did it. Knowing my father, I think he had some trick up his sleeve."

"Your father sounds like quite a character."

"Yes." He chuckled and sat down near the water's edge, motioning for her to sit beside him.

"And they stayed here for seven months?" Ericha asked.

"Actually, I believe they traipsed around Europe a bit. They've been doing it ever since; well, at least since my father turned the duchy over to me."

"Your family is very wealthy."

"Do you find that distasteful?" he asked cautiously.

"I find it intriguing that a man with such wealth and power can be so good and down-to-earth as you are."

"I was not raised on wealth and power," he stated. "My parents and grandparents made it clear by their example that we are there to serve Horstberg, which is actually a very humble position to be in. Wealth brings responsibility. Power brings more responsibility. To succeed in that takes careful guidance. I was raised on love and kindness."

Ericha looked up at him with admiration. "Yes," she said quietly, "I can tell."

"Actually," he said, "in studying recent history, one sees that the line a ruler sits can be very fine. My family came close to losing it all, not so many years ago."

"When?" she asked, fascinated.

"In 1849."

"Tell me," she urged.

"Nik Koenig gathered a revolutionary force when his original plan didn't work. The family abandoned the castle and all went temporarily to the mountain lodge. I remember it well. My sister was born there, and I recall feeling very frightened, knowing my mother was in labor upstairs, and the whereabouts of my father and grandfathers were unknown. They showed up later, all quite safe, but they weren't certain for a while if their plan was going to work. And they were prepared to leave Horstberg and make a fresh start elsewhere."

"With what?"

"I believe that's when my grandfather buried a substantial amount of money and some of the family jewels in the forest. It's still there, and only five people know the location. It's nice to know it's there in case of an emergency."

"I see."

"I must be boring you."

"Actually, it's fascinating. Who are the five people?"

"Why do you want to know that?"

"I'm just curious who the five most important people in Horstberg are."

"I don't know if I'd put it like that," he said. "It just worked out that way."

"Well, who are they?"

"My father, and his father. My grandmother. My highest advisor, who is also my secretary."

"And you."

"Yes, and me."

"And what happened to the revolutionary force?"

Stefan chuckled. "My father poisoned all of the liquor in the castle before they abandoned it. The entire force died."

"That's amazing. You have a very colorful history, Your Grace."

He shrugged his shoulders, and she asked, "And what of Nik Koenig?"

Stefan betrayed definite irritation as he answered, "He fell into a trap when he tried to take the money and run—literally. It paralyzed him below the chest. He's still alive," he added distastefully.

"You don't like him very much," she stated.

"No." He chuckled tensely. "I do not like him at all."

"I'm not well versed in politics, but if he led a revolutionary force against Horstberg, wouldn't that make him guilty of treason?" she asked.

Stefan's agitation increased, but he answered the question directly. "That's the way I see it. But the case was dropped for lack of evidence. He came up with some story about just being a pawn . . . of being coerced and manipulated. And everyone else involved was dead. In essence, it was concluded that his being paralyzed was his sentence."

"And where is he now?"

Stefan took a deep breath and reminded himself to remain calm. "He's living at Castle Horstberg. Fortunately it's a big place, and I don't have to see him often."

Sensing his annoyance of the subject, Ericha changed it. "What kind of trick do you suppose your father had up his sleeve?"

"What?" Stefan asked.

"You said that your parents came away from here in love. I wonder what kind of trick brings such results."

"Actually," Stefan chuckled, "he declares it was a love potion."

"Whatever it was," Ericha said, "I'm glad it worked."

"Why is that?" he asked.

"Because they had you."

"Yes." He laughed. "Now you know where I came from. Tell me about you."

Ericha glanced down. "There is nothing to tell that I haven't already told you. There are no romantic stories in my history."

"Perhaps there are," Stefan said with a lilt in his voice. "Maybe your mother met a strange man in the forest one day who swept her off her feet and—"

"And then left her," she interrupted.

"But you said there must have been more to it than that. You told me before that she wasn't bitter—just lonely."

Ericha seemed emotional, so he went on to ease the tension.

"She must have made him very happy—whoever he was." He looked directly at her. "If she was anything like you."

"She was nothing like me," Ericha stated.

"Why is that?" he asked.

"She was very beautiful."

"You are very beautiful," he said, and she seemed surprised.

"She had rich, dark hair—that always stayed where she put it."

"But did it have character?" Stefan said, touching the straying wisps around Ericha's face.

"Don't ever leave me, Stefan," she said, and he could see an absence of her normally confident aura. "I swore I would not live the kind of life she had. I don't care about Johanna. She can have your name as long as I can have the rest of you. I don't care about the way people might whisper about me. As long as I have you, Stefan, I can face anything."

Stefan saw a glimmer of tears in her eyes, and he blessed them as he drew her into his arms with a comforting embrace. "Never," he whispered against her face. "I will never leave you."

Stefan kissed her warmly, then abruptly lifted her skirt and pulled off her boots, throwing them to the ground.

"What are you doing?" she laughed.

"I'm taking off your shoes," he smirked as he proceeded to roll her stockings down her legs. Then he laughed for no apparent reason. It was good to hear him laugh.

"I can see that," she said, beginning to discover a side to Stefan she had never seen before. "But—"

"We're going swimming," he stated. "One of my father's favorite stories is the time he pulled my mother into a pond with all her clothes on."

"This father of yours sounds more interesting all the time."

Stefan chuckled, and Ericha could see no sign of tension left in him.

"I dare say," she said, "that there's a little of your father in you."

"Nonsense." He pulled Ericha to her feet. "I'm nothing like my father," he added, and then he casually picked Ericha up and threw her into the water.

"You scoundrel!" She laughed, wiping water from her face.

"Well," he said thoughtfully as he pulled off his boots, "maybe I am like my father."

The days in the Black Forest were truly magical. Stefan found glimpses of the happiness he had lost in his childhood as Ericha filled his life with song and laughter and told him things about Horstberg that even he didn't know. He loved telling her the history of his family, and for the first time since the explosion at Castle Horstberg, he felt some peace over the past.

Ericha found a contentment that she was sure only existed in fairy tales—not unlike the ones that Stefan told her daily. Together they walked through the forest, swam in the pond, and did the work side by side. Ericha was surprised to learn that Stefan's father had taught him to cook a little, and Stefan discovered that Ericha did a fair job at chopping wood.

Stefan came to learn the words to the song Ericha's mother had taught her, and they sang together as they worked and played the days away. Stefan was humming it as he bathed one afternoon while Ericha sat nearby tatting.

"Do you remember," he said, "when you asked me if something inanimate could speak of the past?"

"I remember."

"I feel that way when you sing that song," he said. "I don't know why, but I do."

Ericha smiled at him as he rose from the tub, wrapped a

towel around his waist, and plopped down in the center of the bed.

"When do you want to leave the forest and see some sights?" he asked, adjusting the pillows behind his head.

"I don't want to leave the forest," she stated, still concentrating on her work. "If it's all right with you, I'd like to stay here until we have to return." She smiled toward him. "We can see the sights on our next honeymoon."

"That is more than all right with me," he replied.

Ericha set her work aside and removed her glasses. She had never seen so much of Stefan in broad daylight before, and she couldn't help but admire him.

"You are dreadfully handsome, Your Grace," she said, moving toward the bed.

"I'm glad you think so," he replied, "because you're going to have to look at me for many years to come."

"I can think of no greater pleasure."

Ericha sat beside him on the bed, and he rolled onto his side to place his head in her lap. As the towel fell partially away, Ericha could see a gruesome scar on his thigh that she'd never noticed before.

"What is this?" she asked, touching it gingerly.

He glanced down, then retained his comfortable position.

"It's a scar," he stated.

"I know that!" she insisted, and he chuckled. "It looks dreadful. What happened?"

"I was shot."

"You're joking."

"I'm quite serious."

"Was it an accident?" she asked.

"I seriously doubt it," he replied.

"Well, tell me."

Stefan looked up at her. "Someone was apparently trying to kill me. Fortunately their aim was off." Ericha looked at him aghast. "My uncle saved my life, actually. It was not a good day for either of us."

"But your uncle died when you were just a child," she said.

"Yes, he did. I was seven at the time."

"I can't believe it," she said tensely. "Why would someone want to kill a child?"

"I was an heir to Horstberg, and someone else wanted it at the time. It was all the beginning of that dreadful revolution I told you about before, when the family deserted the castle."

"It must have been terribly frightening for you," she said.

"Oh, getting shot didn't frighten me nearly as much as . . ."

By the way he stopped, Ericha could tell it was something painful. She had come to recognize that tone of voice.

"As what?" she urged.

"I was just recovering from the gunshot when a friend of mine gave me a puppy." He smiled slightly. "That friend would be your dear cousin."

"Karl?"

"None other. He gave me a puppy named Lucky, and the name became quite ironic."

"Why is that?" she asked when he seemed hesitant to go on.

"Lucky died in my stead." Ericha gasped slightly, and Stefan's eyes turned distant as he pushed his arms around her waist to bring her closer. "I remember accidentally tipping over a glass of milk that had been left on my bedside table. Lucky licked it up. The next morning he was dead."

"You mean the milk was poisoned?"

"It appeared that way."

"I can't believe it," Ericha said.

"Neither could my parents." Stefan gave a phony chuckle, attempting to treat it lightly. "But I suppose it's all part of the precarious life of being an heir."

"Did they ever find out who was behind it?" she asked.

"Oh, yes."

Ericha quickly put the pieces together in her mind. "Nik Koenig," she stated.

"That's right," he said. "But they could never prove any of it. And I don't recall my life being threatened since, except maybe when Karl found out that I had become involved with his cousin." Stefan chuckled, and Ericha smiled down at him.

Stefan sobered as he added, "The threats against our lives ended when one of them succeeded." He paused and drew a deep breath. "My father believes that the accident that killed my uncle and grandfather was a result of . . ." He stopped and sat up abruptly. "Talk about something else."

Ericha went to her knees behind him and kissed his shoulder. "Do you want to talk?" She moved her hands over his chest and pulled him close to her. "Or do you want to go to bed?"

"In the middle of the afternoon?" he asked in mock astonishment.

"But of course."

Stefan feigned a yawn and plopped back onto the bed. "I suppose I am tired."

"Very well," Ericha said and moved toward the door.

"Hold on there, Princess." He grabbed her around the waist and pulled her back onto the bed. "If you think I would really turn down an offer like that, you are quite wrong."

Ericha giggled, but her question held a serious tone. "Why did you call me *Princess?*" She couldn't deny the reaction somewhere inside her when he'd said it.

"I don't know. It just seemed . . . right."

"Because you are a prince?"

"No. Because . . . well, my grandfather called the woman he loved Princess."

"And was she?"

"Only after he married her—in a technical sense. But to him, I believe she was always a princess."

"Your mother was born a princess," Ericha said. "Did your father call her Princess?"

"No." Stefan laughed. "He called her all sorts of awful things like . . . well, he always took Your Royal Highness and changed the last word to fit the present situation."

Ericha giggled as Stefan pushed her back onto the bed.

"Let's not talk about my parents right now . . . Princess."

"Very well," she smirked, "Your Royal Handsome Prince."
Then she kissed him.

Stefan never wanted to leave the forest. He often watched Ericha
and marveled at the way she could be comfortable living such a
menial life, yet he could well imagine her in the courts of Castle
Horstberg, easily surpassing the present duchess by her dignity
and natural grace. He marveled at her passion, and treasured the
intimate moments they shared, knowing he could never take this
for granted.

Ericha was surprised one afternoon when Stefan started
moving furniture around in the common room. He ignored her
inquiries, but when the floor was cleared as much as possible, he
took her hand into his as if they were in a grand ballroom.

"Would you dance with me, my lady?" he asked.

She felt briefly panicked. "My mother taught me to dance
some, but . . ."

"It's easy," he said when she faltered. He placed a hand against
her back, holding her tightly against him. Taking her other hand
into his, he moved slowly into a waltz, counting the steps for her,
guiding her carefully.

"See, you're getting it already."

Ericha laughed and tried to concentrate. Stefan continued to
dance with her, not missing a step as he told her of the dance
lessons he'd endured as a youth, since his position required a
great deal of socializing.

"Then one day, I realized I actually enjoyed it," he said.
"Though I've always preferred dancing with my sisters as opposed
to the snooty women who attend those diplomatic socials." He
smiled endearingly. "Still, I don't think I've ever enjoyed it so
much as now."

"Even though we have no music?" she asked as it became
easier to follow his lead.

"If you sing we'll have music."

Ericha began to sing *their song,* as Stefan called it. He joined in after the first few lines, and their dance came to a graceful halt as they finished together, "A fire burns in my heart."

As they stood facing each other in the following stillness, Ericha felt a formless warmth rush over her. By the intensity in his eyes, she could almost believe he felt it, too. He said nothing as he lifted her into his arms and carried her up the stairs, where he made love to her as if he could make it last forever.

Ericha fell asleep and woke up to find Stefan pouring hot water into the bathtub. He smiled as he lifted her into his arms and lowered her gently into the tub. "How many women," she asked, "can say the Duke of Horstberg has prepared their bath?" She laughed when he got in with her and held her close.

"Only two that I can think of . . . besides you." Ericha looked briefly alarmed, and he chuckled. "My mother and my grand-mother. They were each married to a Duke of Horstberg at one time." Ericha smiled and relaxed her head against his shoulder.

"Though it's probably better this way," he said out of nowhere. "I can't help wishing that you and I could have children."

Ericha looked up at him in surprise. "Maybe we can."

Stefan's expression became so sad that she was glad he changed the subject, despite it not being much better.

"I hate to say it, but I'm afraid I should go back soon."

Ericha did her best to not look disappointed. She knew they would have to leave sooner or later. She had vowed to herself before she ever told Stefan she would be his mistress, that she would never complain to him about the circumstances. She knew what it was like to be without him completely, and she would never take for granted having him what little she could.

"It's all right." She smiled toward him. "Life will still be better than it was before."

"Yes," he said gratefully, "it will."

Leaving the cottage in the Black Forest was difficult, and the journey back to Horstberg was far too short. When they parted in order to arrive on different trains, they could hardly say good-bye.

"I will see you as soon as I return," Stefan told Ericha, and then he put her on the train, and they held hands until it moved forward and pulled her away from him. Stefan passed time with the memories of their time together while he waited for the next train to Regensberg.

Ericha was surprised to have Karl meet her at the station, but he said that Stefan had notified him of her return.

"Did you have a good time?" he asked as they rode together in the trap and he noticed the new dress she was wearing.

"Yes." She smiled widely. "I had the most wonderful time ever."

"Good," he said, genuinely gratified, "I'm glad. And you've learned to carry sufficient baggage," he added. "You're coming home with a little more than you took with you."

"Stefan was very generous."

"Back I see," Erma said, apparently in a bad mood as Ericha came through the door with Karl close behind.

"It's nice to see you too," Ericha said, remaining cheerful.

"You'd best treat her good, Erma," Karl said. "She's got some pretty important friends."

A knowing smile passed between Karl and Ericha, and she went up to her room to freshen up. Job greeted her eagerly, looking none the worse for her absence.

The hours dragged by terribly. But Ericha had anticipated this lonely adjustment and worked very hard in the garden the better part of the day. Late in the afternoon she went to visit with Mrs. Burger.

"Did you have a good time, dear?" she asked as they were seated in the parlor.

"Oh, I did!"

"You must tell me all about it," Mrs. Burger insisted.

"It's nothing really exciting," Ericha replied. "I simply met an old friend and we stayed in a cottage in the Black Forest for several days."

"Well, it sounds delightful," Mrs. Burger said, then talk turned to the garden and the plentiful harvest she'd had in Ericha's absence. Ericha realized that Mrs. Burger was assuming this friend of hers was a woman, and Ericha was content to let her think it.

Ericha returned home reluctantly for dinner and spent the evening catching up with Karl. Knowing that sleeping alone would be unbearable, Ericha didn't go to bed until she was too tired to do anything but drift to sleep immediately. She felt relief when the sun came up to know that Stefan would be arriving in Horstberg early today.

Being market day, Ericha left right after breakfast, taking her basket to hold her usual purchases. Wearing a dress Stefan had bought her, she felt the change within herself. Though the dress was simple according to her taste, she felt more like a lady than a simple common woman. It was as if Stefan's royal breeding had begun to rub off on her.

Ericha realized also as she mingled among the people of Horstberg that her closeness to Stefan made her feel indirectly responsible for them. She approached her simple encounters with an added warmth in her heart for each good citizen that comprised Stefan's reign.

Ericha paid little attention to a growing murmur somewhere behind her, until words caught her ear and she realized the reason for the excitement. She turned to see the Duke of Horstberg riding atop his stallion through the crowd, greeting his people amiably, with uniformed men riding on either side of him. He was dressed as commonly as he'd been when she'd left him, but there was no denying the regal quality of his presence.

Ericha's heart beat quickly at the sight of him, and she realized by the whisperings around her that the duke returning from holiday was quite an occasion. Karl told her later it was because the people liked knowing he was alive and well, and everything was going fine—which made sense.

Ericha stood unobtrusively in the crowd as Stefan passed by, feeling the distance that only a mistress of royalty could feel. But she felt elated when he saw her there, and his eyes smiled as they met hers briefly before he moved on. At least she had the peace of knowing that she would be seeing him soon.

Ericha walked home slowly, relishing her memories and feeling content. It was nice when Karl came home from the pub with the news that he'd given Stefan a key to the side door. But as the house became dark and quiet, she wondered when or if he would use it tonight.

As she lay in bed, staring at the ceiling above her, Ericha knew that it would always be this way, hanging on the hope that he could manage to get away from his obligations to see her. And she was certain that the majority of his visits would be paid in the depth of night, when he was least likely to be missed or seen. But still she was content. She knew that he loved her. And even if he wasn't with her, she knew he wanted to be.

Ericha heard the clock strike twelve-thirty, and then it dissipated and left the sound of footsteps on the stairs as its echo. Excitedly she jumped from the bed and opened the door as he approached it. Stefan laughed as she came into his arms, and they smothered each other with kisses as they moved into the room and he closed the door.

"It's been eternity since I saw you, hasn't it?" she asked breathlessly.

"At least." He smiled, and she moved away to light a lamp. When the glow illuminated the room, Stefan sat down to remove his boots.

"You must be exhausted," she said, pressing a hand beneath his shirt to rub the back of his neck. "Have you gotten any sleep at all?"

"I slept on the train, but I am tired. Come here," he added, pulling her onto his lap. "I don't want to sleep. I want to be with you."

"How did Horstberg fare in your absence?" she asked.

"Rather well, actually. I should leave more often." He chuckled. "Rusty does a good job."

"Rusty?"

"He's my highest advisor: my right-hand man, so to speak.

My father had that job until he became the regent. Eventually he hired Rusty, who does the secretarial business as well. People might know more of who he is, but he prefers to remain out of the public's eye. He is one of the most shy men I have ever known. But a good man. And he's been around forever. He and I played together as children, and his father worked for the duke until he died when . . . well, that's a long story."

"Is Rusty his real name?" she asked.

"That's a longer story." He nearly laughed.

"Tell me," she urged.

"When I was a boy," he began, "I picked up the nickname Rusty from my grandfather. He was the only one who called me that."

"Don't tell me," she said. "It's the hair."

"I suppose it is." Stefan smiled and continued. "Well, Rusty's real name is Russell, and he was called Russy. One afternoon we were left to follow the duke around while he entertained the Baron Von Bindorf, who kept getting us mixed up. It was all so comical that it stuck as a joke. When my grandfather died, I didn't want to be called Rusty anymore, so I called *him* Rusty. And it stuck."

"Then the two of you are very close."

"Very," he said emphatically. "And as I said, he's a good man. Horstberg needs him. To see him you wouldn't believe he could run a country, but he does."

Ericha smiled warmly and asked, "Are you hungry?"

"No thank you," he said. "I ate with the family."

"And how is everyone?"

"My grandparents are doing well, and I didn't bother to ask Johanna."

"Did she ask you?"

"Yes, she did," he said smugly, "and I told her I'd never felt better."

Ericha laughed, and then she saw something catch Stefan's eye.

"Why is there a picture on the floor facing the wall?"

"Oh," she said, "that's my father—or at least I believe it is. I found it in the closet. I like knowing it's there, but I don't like to look at it often."

He seemed briefly puzzled by her theory and asked, "May I see it?"

"Not tonight," she said, and he nodded his understanding.

"You look tired," she remarked, touching his face. "Can you stay?"

"I had planned on it." He smiled. "They won't miss me. I rarely show up for breakfast, anyway."

The following morning, Ericha woke Stefan with a kiss. "It's time for breakfast. Meet me in the dining room when you're dressed."

Stefan entered to find Ericha seated at the table with sunlight streaking her hair while she sipped a cup of coffee.

"Good morning," he said, leaning over to kiss her. She pushed her hand into his hair as she returned the kiss with feeling.

"Good morning, Stef," Karl said boisterously, startling them both as he slapped Stefan on the back and seated himself with the newspaper.

"He does come with the bargain, doesn't he," Stefan said with mock disgust, and Ericha giggled. Karl glared at Stefan as he was seated, and then they exchanged a hearty grin.

Ericha smiled at Stefan across the table just as Erma brought breakfast in, mumbling under her breath about having to prepare for guests, as well.

Stefan gazed dubiously at the maid, most likely appalled. Ericha was certain that the duke's servants wouldn't dare show so little respect. But he seemed amused, and the room became incredibly still when Erma set her eyes upon the guest.

"Good heavens!" she exclaimed, dumping the entire cream pitcher into the coffee pot. "Why didn't you tell me we was havin' royalty here?"

Stefan quickly said, "There's no need to upset yourself, miss. But I do prefer my coffee black."

Karl laughed loudly. "All these years I've been meeting you

every day at the pub, and poor Miss Busch looks as though she's seen a ghost when you happen to pop in for breakfast."

"Imagine that," Stefan said coolly, and Erma departed humbly to brew a fresh pot of coffee.

"She's prone to mood swings," Ericha informed Stefan.

"I hope she doesn't gossip," Stefan said soberly.

"I'll bribe her," Karl said with confidence. It was quickly forgotten as Stefan and Ericha mingled their eyes across the table, knowing that even with its obvious complications, life was far better than it had been before.

Chapter Ten
THE BOX WITH NO KEY

awn found Stefan standing with Rusty by his side on the balcony that overlooked the courtyard. While he waited for the officers of the Guard to take their places below, his mind quickly worked over the evidence that had told him this man facing execution was guilty. And his instincts agreed. But still, no matter how many times Stefan did it, giving the signal to have a man executed never became easier.

He was glad to have it over, but every time Stefan closed his eyes, he could see the man fall as the guns were fired. His own position wouldn't be half so bad, he thought, if he didn't have to play chief judge and executioner. But it was part of the job, and he had to live with it.

The day was busy, with hardly enough time to even eat. But Stefan found motivation to get through his work, knowing he had something to look forward to. When the work was completed sooner than expected, and he knew it would be best to wait a while before slipping out of the castle, Stefan went to his music room and toyed with the piano. His mind went to his grandfather as he recalled the countless hours he had spent with Cameron, seated at the piano with his lessons. Music was something Cameron had always enjoyed as a sidelight in his life. But Stefan marveled at the way Cameron had picked up on Stefan's interest at such a young age, and he'd personally taken the time to teach him. In the same respect, it had been his grandmother who had given

Stefan art lessons as a child, and his mother had helped along the way. In spite of the burden left on his shoulders of inheriting a duchy, Stefan was grateful for the inheritance of art and music that enriched his life and had helped him cope through the years.

When it was almost dark, Stefan went to his bedroom to get his cloak, taking a minute to make his bed look slept in. Not wanting to pass the officers always standing guard at his office door, he slipped down a different staircase and through the darkening ballroom. He left the castle by a side entrance to go to the stable, noting it had become a familiar path.

Crossing the courtyard brought to mind the execution he'd been trying so hard to not think about. The night air helped drive away his difficult thoughts as he galloped Fire across the valley to his other home. He unsaddled the horse and left it for the night, then walked through the garden and into the side door.

There was a light on in the parlor as he passed it, and he peeked in to see Karl stretched out on the sofa reading. He glanced up to see Stefan there. They exchanged some trivial small talk, and Stefan resumed his course up the stairs to Ericha's room.

He found Ericha tatting near the lamplight. Her dimpled smile alone made the day worth living. With few words exchanged, he knelt beside her and kissed her warmly, carefully taking her work and setting it aside.

"I need you," he whispered and removed her glasses, setting them aside as well. Ericha smiled warmly from the genuine giving that he betrayed in his affection, and she rose from her chair. Moving into his arms, she pushed the cloak from his shoulders, and the heavy wool billowed onto the floor.

Stefan felt all of his anxiety rush away. Ericha had the ability to erase it all: Johanna's vindictive glances across the dinner table, the sound of executing rifles, the reality of a country on his shoulders. It all washed away in Ericha's love. He felt almost selfish for wanting her for such reasons, unaware that his love only reciprocated those same feelings back to her.

Time passing allowed Stefan's contentment to settle in. He marveled at the way Ericha's presence in his life truly touched *every* aspect of his life. The days were easier to get through, and he realized one morning as he returned to the castle early that he'd not had a drink for weeks beyond a little champagne at social gatherings and the usual wine with dinner.

Stefan entered his bedroom humming, and then he stopped to see Theodor sitting there reading. Stefan glanced toward the bed, then the clock on the mantle.

"The maids are getting more efficient these days," Theodor stated. "Imagine them getting your bed made before seven."

The effort Stefan usually made to mess up the bed had slipped his mind last night as he'd left in a hurry.

"Amazing isn't it," Stefan stated, opening a bureau drawer to look for something.

"But I wonder who cleaned up after you shaved," Theodor said, and Stefan glanced sharply toward him. "That's my job."

"If you've got something to say, Theodor," Stefan insisted, "just come out and say it."

"But you're the Duke of Horstberg. I'm only the valet . . . sir."

"Be serious, Theodor," Stefan slammed the drawer shut. "I've never noticed you holding your tongue before."

"I've never suspected you were having an affair before."

Stefan had to admit he wasn't surprised, but he wondered how to handle the situation.

"You told me to just come out and say it." Their eyes met, and Theodor added straightly, "You should know that you can trust me. I've been with this family a long time, Stefan."

It was rare that Theodor called him by his given name, but it reminded him that Theodor was right. "I know I can trust you," Stefan said, but he wondered what Theodor would think if he knew that the duke's mistress was his niece. "But do you trust my judgment?"

"Are you asking my approval?"

"No," Stefan stated, "but perhaps your acceptance."

"Don't think I haven't noticed the change in your habits. But then, I've also noticed the change in you." Theodor smiled. "It's nice to see you happy for a change."

Stefan sighed. "Do you think anyone else has noticed?"

"To be quite honest, no. But from now on, I'll make the bed look slept in. Just leave it to me to make everything appear perfectly normal, and we'll be a lot less likely to arouse any suspicion."

"Thank you, Theodor," Stefan said. "You can't know how much—"

"Maybe I can. That wife of yours is enough to drive a man to suicide. Better this than that." Theodor rose from his chair and proceeded to mess up the bed, then he stood back to admire his work. "There, that's about how you usually leave it." Theodor grinned, and Stefan felt immense relief. He knew if Theodor was on his side, this would be a great deal easier.

Besides Theodor, Stefan's frequent visits seemed to go unnoticed by everyone but Miss Busch, who was apparently so in awe of the duke that she dared not say anything about her suspicions. And Karl declared that the raise in salary hadn't hurt any.

There were always officers on duty at the castle gates, but Stefan felt sure that with the shift changes, they would simply assume he was prone to late night and early morning rides. And the officers of the Guard were well versed in the requirement of keeping their mouths shut concerning any observance while on duty. There were no servants in the family stables between ten in the evening and six in the morning. No one was there to see when the duke came and went.

Stefan's grandmother was the only one who really seemed to take any notice of his habits. But she said nothing about it until one evening while they were having coffee with Georg.

"I dare say it's good for you to get away from here some at night as you've been doing. You've been in better spirits lately."

"I'm doing well, thank you." He smiled, trying not to betray how her comment warmed him.

"I only wonder where I might find you if you're needed," Abbi added as casually as if she had told him it might rain. Georg was reading a book and appeared to be paying no attention.

Stefan quickly searched for a suitable answer. Abbi *did* need to know where to find him. And he could see no reason to not be honest with her. "Karl has been good enough to let me stay there when I need to get away."

"Ah, that makes it easy," Abbi said. "He's always been a good friend. How is Karl?"

"Doing very well," he replied.

"And it's so nice of him to make you welcome. I know how you enjoyed taking much of your paperwork to the lodge where it was easier for you to concentrate. Karl's home is much closer— and much more accessible in the winter," she added with a little laugh. "It's good of him to give you the space to do it there."

"Yes," Stefan sipped his coffee to avoid smirking. "It certainly is good of him."

Stefan repeated the conversation later to Ericha, and she felt gratified by the evidence that the circumstances of their relationship were settling in well. She continued to gain contentment as her life with Stefan formed a routine. It was rare that he didn't come to spend the night. And though he came late and left early, it was almost like he simply had an occupation with long hours. Which in reality he did.

Little by little, more of Stefan's things were left in her room. And Ericha liked seeing reminders of his existence through the days when he was absent. His razor and other grooming items became permanent fixtures in a particular bureau drawer, and at least one change of clothes usually hung in the closet. It was only when Stefan came with news that he needed to go out of town for a few days that Ericha felt any dismay over the situation at all.

"Even if you were my wife," he said while shaving early one morning, "I would likely not take you with me. It will only be a lot of tedious business that would leave you stuck with a bunch of snooty old women. You'd not enjoy it."

Ericha still felt dismayed. He turned and touched her chin, leaving a trace of shaving soap there. "I used to look forward to any opportunity to leave Horstberg," he said. "It's nice to actually dread leaving, and to know there's something besides my grandparents to come home to." He kissed her, which left more soap on her face. "We'll make up for it when I come back."

The very day Stefan left, Ericha began to feel ill. And two days later she became certain that she was with child. The realization didn't surprise her as much as she knew it would Stefan. Still, she had wondered if conception would be possible, and knowing that she would have children in her life gave her peace. Most women might have feared raising illegitimate children, but Ericha was happy with her life, and she knew that if her mother had succeeded, she could as well.

It was frustrating to realize Stefan wouldn't be back for another day or two. She wanted so desperately to tell him the news. But she passed the time planning how she would let him know and dreaming about this child. She wondered if her pregnancy would arouse talk. But as with everything, Ericha just resigned herself to take one day at a time and deal with it the best she could.

Ericha was tempted to tell Karl, but she wanted Stefan to be the first to know. She decided that perhaps it would be best if she and Stefan talked to Karl about it together, because of the unusual circumstances.

Ericha was lost in thought when Karl seated himself at the dinner table. He waved his hand in front of her face to get her attention. "Yoo-hoo," he said, and she laughed. "Missing the duke, are we?" he added with a smirk.

"Always." She smiled peaceably.

"Well." He leaned back in his chair and grinned. "I know something that you don't."

"What?" she asked blandly, certain he was only teasing her.

"He's back."

"He is?" She sat forward.

"I thought that would get your attention. I saw him at the pub. He'd just gotten off the train. But he asked me to tell you that he wouldn't be by tonight because he'll be catching up business with Rusty until late this evening—and it can't wait."

Ericha sighed with disappointment, aching to tell him her news. When it got late and she found it impossible to relax, Ericha made up her mind that if he wasn't coming to her, she would go to him.

It wasn't quite midnight when she mounted Pegasus and began her ride toward the castle. Despite the snow, she easily found the secluded spot at the foot of the hill where Karl had led her through the passageway. She tied Pegasus off and tried for some time before she found the opening and figured out how to trigger it. She sighed with relief when it came open, and then she groped in the darkness for the torch. She closed the door behind her and moved carefully along, feeling a flutter of excitement at the thought of seeing Stefan.

When she came at last to the end, Ericha set the torch carefully into the bracket on the wall. Then with all the strength she could muster, she pushed against the door with her shoulder, and it moved slowly open.

The dogs started barking, and Ericha winced, but then she heard Stefan order them to be still and they did. She peered around the corner to see Stefan's expectant expression as he waited to see who would emerge.

"These blasted passageways," he teased, sitting in a chair near the fireplace with his legs stretched out. "You never know who is going to show up in your bedroom in the middle of the night."

Ericha smiled and pushed the door closed before she leaned against it and sighed. "If you want me to leave," she teased back, "all you have to do is—"

"Come here." He motioned with his hand. "I'm too exhausted to even stand up."

Ericha laughed as he pulled her onto his lap, and she greeted him with repeated kisses as if it had been months.

"What a pleasant surprise this is." Stefan laughed with her.

"I just couldn't wait to see you." She smiled and kissed him once more.

Ericha stood and took off her cloak, moving nonchalantly around the room while Stefan watched her. The hounds sniffed at her curiously, and Ericha stopped to rub their long ears.

"They're beautiful," she said. "Have you had them long?"

"They were with me before I officially became the duke."

"How do you tell them apart?"

"Blitzen is lighter than Donner. He's also more easily agitated."

As the dogs seemed to accept Ericha's presence and relaxed on the rug, she turned her attention back to her surroundings. "What an interesting painting," she said, tipping her head to examine it more carefully. "Oh, I see now. It's Horstberg. It's a bit abstract, but I like it."

"My grandmother did it."

"Really?"

"It was her first. She has improved since then. But it has great sentimental value. Her paintings are everywhere in the castle. A room isn't complete if it doesn't have one."

"This is a beautiful room," she said. "I mean, I've been here before, but I didn't get a very good look. Is this always the duke's bedroom?"

"Always," he said.

"Then generations of royalty have slept in this room."

"Yes," he replied, "I suppose they have."

"What stories these walls could tell!"

"Indeed." He smirked. "In fact, a murder was committed in this room."

"Really?"

"At least one." He grinned.

"Tell me about it," she said, sitting on the edge of the huge bed.

"My grandfather's first wife was killed in this room by her lover—who was my grandfather's brother."

"Ooh," she said dramatically, rolling to the center of the bed, where she sat to further survey the room. "What a scandalous past you have, Your Grace."

Stefan laughed and nearly jumped from his chair onto the bed, tickling Ericha as he drew her into his arms.

"Hush up," she insisted. "Someone will hear us."

"These walls are very thick," he said with confidence.

"I thought you were tired." She smirked. "That was quite a rejuvenation!"

"You do it to me. I believe you could cure anything!"

With that, he pulled her against him with a hungry kiss, and Ericha teasingly pushed him away.

"Now, hold on," she said. "I came here with some very important information that could be of great interest to the people of Horstberg. Don't you want to know what it is?"

"Later," he grinned and kissed her again.

Ericha laughed and succumbed to his urging, glad to have him back. When their passion was spent, Stefan lay with his head against her shoulder, holding her close in the huge bed.

"I must be dreaming," he said softly.

"Why is that?"

"I can't count the times I have laid in this bed and dreamt of holding you in my arms. And here you are." He leaned up on one elbow to gaze down at her. "You are living proof that dreams come true, my sweet Ericha."

Ericha smiled. "Which reminds me," she said, her eyes glowing with a mischief that made Stefan wonder what she was up to. "I have news."

"Ah, yes." He smirked. "Important information that could be of great interest to the people of Horstberg."

"Do you suppose," she mused, "that the people of Horstberg gossip about you and your family?"

Stefan grunted with humor. "I'm sure they do, but I'm always the last to hear it."

"Not this time," she said straightly. "Because I have some gossip, and *you* will be the first to hear it."

Stefan chuckled. He didn't know what she was getting at, but he loved it when she teased him.

"But first, I wanted to ask you: do you suppose that Johanna has had affairs?"

Stefan's light mood faltered. He really didn't want to talk about that, but he answered her question honestly. "I'm absolutely certain of it."

Ericha made a thoughtful noise, then went on to say, "You know that Horstberg has a few problems."

"Just a few," he stated satirically, wondering where this could possibly be headed. He wasn't catching the connection.

"And some of them can't really be solved. Still, the people might be curious as to—"

"What are you getting at?" he asked impatiently.

"Well, I've figured out the answer to one of the great questions that the people of this country have likely speculated over for years."

"And what's that?" he asked mildly.

"That there is no heir, of course."

Ericha waited patiently for a reaction. She was not disappointed by the unsettled look that rose into Stefan's eyes.

"What about it?" he asked sternly.

"It's Johanna's fault." At his questioning gaze, she added, "It's an easy deduction. If Johanna has had affairs and still has no children, then it's her fault."

"And that's what you came here to tell me?" he asked tersely as he sat up and leaned against the headboard.

"Well," she pressed, tucking the sheet beneath her arms to sit beside him, "isn't that a logical deduction?"

Stefan reminded himself to not take his sore points out on Ericha. He took a deep breath and said firmly, "Forgive me for being so brash, Ericha. But Johanna is a woman well versed in the ways of the world. In spite of her indiscretions, she came from a family where royal blood is everything. I am relatively certain—because she as much as told me—that Johanna would take the necessary precautions to prevent conceiving a child that would potentially jeopardize the binding of two nations, which is the very reason her father wanted her to marry me in the first place."

While Ericha was trying to figure exactly what he meant, she commented, "That sounded like something you'd say in the court room."

"I'm sorry," he said in a voice that indicated he wasn't. "That's the only way I can say it without being crude."

Ericha became distracted from her intent as she began to

fully absorb his implication. She felt incredibly naive as she looked at Stefan, unable to keep from gaping. "Is such a thing *possible?*"

"I can assure you," he stated. When she said nothing more, he asked, "Did you come here to discuss my inability to father children, or are you—"

Ericha pressed her fingers over his lips and smiled. She couldn't have led up to it better herself. She shook her head gently and looked into his eyes. "No, my love," she said, unable to hold back a little laugh, "I came to tell you that you were wrong."

"About what?" he asked blandly. This entire conversation had him frustrated to distraction.

"Your Grace." She took his hand and spoke in a hushed voice that calmed him. "I am with child." She pressed his hand to her belly. *"Your* child."

The silence was finally broken as something between a gasp and a moan erupted from Stefan's throat. "Are you sure?" he asked in a cracked voice, and again she nodded.

Stefan briefly wished that he was alone when tears filled his eyes, but Ericha touched his face with full acceptance as he managed to blink them back before they fell. He pulled her close to him and just held her, while he attempted to comprehend what he could only consider a miracle.

While Ericha played idly with his hair, she asked in a gentle voice, "Why were you so certain it wasn't her?"

"I suppose she had implied so many times it was my fault that I began to believe her. After a while I tried to tell myself I didn't care and forced myself not to think about it. Apparently I should have thought about it a little more."

Stefan tightened his embrace in an effort to express a gratitude that words could not describe. Then Ericha said wistfully, "I believe we can give our children a good life. At least they will know their father."

Her words struck a new reality, and Stefan looked up at her sharply. "Ericha," he said, "when I agreed to this relationship, I was certain there would be no children. I . . . I didn't want such complications for you . . . I . . ." He stopped with a tone of frustration.

"You what?" she urged, sensing that he was somehow angry.

"The child will not be a Heinrich."

"No," she said, "that's impossible."

Stefan said nothing, but she sensed his emotion. "Stefan." She touched his face to make him look at her. "Your children will grow up with you a part of their lives. They will be loved and happy, and we'll make up for the rest with that."

Stefan sighed, freshly amazed at her positive outlook. He reminded himself to follow her example and not be angry over things he couldn't change. How could he not feel joy at the prospect of having children of his own? As always, when he got past his own selfishness, his concern was for Ericha.

"Are you happy about this, my dear?" he asked.

"Happy?" She laughed warmly. "Stefan, I just keep getting happier every day."

"It will be difficult for you," he said.

"It will be worth it," she countered firmly.

"Have you seen a doctor?"

"Not yet, but—"

"See Doctor Furhelm," he said. "I know him well. He'll take good care of you, and he will be discreet."

"All right," she agreed. "And we should talk to Karl about this."

"Yes, we'll do that tomorrow."

Stefan relaxed with Ericha in his arms, trying to suppress the nagging irony of this. Nothing bothered him quite so much as not being able to give Ericha his name. And now she would have a child. *His* child. But he could no more give that child his name than he could give it the moon. Concentrating instead on the wonder of Ericha's news, he drifted to sleep, content and secure.

Just before dawn, Ericha slipped quietly away, leaving the way she'd come. She crawled into her own bed just as the sun was coming up, with a prayer of gratitude in her heart for all that Stefan Heinrich had brought into her life.

While the idea of Ericha having an illegitimate child was difficult for Stefan to accept, Karl was overjoyed by the news. He didn't seem at all disturbed over the prospect of having this child born and raised in his home, and he was willing to support Ericha through all of it.

Stefan insisted that he would support Ericha and the child financially, and he and Karl argued comically about it for nearly an hour. Karl gave in at last, which Ericha knew he'd intended to do all along. She sensed Stefan's need to give her everything he could, and somehow make up for not being able to give her his name. And she knew Karl respected that. He just liked to tease Stefan. Ericha also knew it was not a matter of money for either of them—they both seemed to have plenty. After growing up with next to nothing, she couldn't deny the security in feeling so well cared for; which was something her mother had not been blessed with. She wondered for a moment what her mother's life might have been like if *she* had been loved by a duke.

Stefan sat in the music room, toying idly with the piano while he contemplated the circumstances, wishing with all his heart that this child could bear his name. Was this the pain he had sensed would come by making the decision to take Ericha as his mistress? He admired her for her acceptance of the situation and was inwardly striving to follow her example and accept this for what it was. He knew she was right—that getting upset would make no difference. But still it was difficult.

Concentrating on the good aspects of his life with Ericha, Stefan recalled the song she had taught him, and his fingers picked out the melody. He began to sing the words softly, and they gave him comfort, while the music seemed to soothe his soul. He smiled to himself as he finished it and sighed.

"That was beautiful," Abbi said, and Stefan turned, surprised to realize he wasn't alone. "I wasn't aware you remembered that song. I've not heard it for years."

Stefan's eyes widened, wondering what she meant. "I didn't *remember* it."

"Then where did you learn it?" she asked, sitting beside him on the bench.

Stefan wasn't one to lie—especially to his grandmother. "Karl's cousin taught it to me."

Abbi looked surprised. "I'd heard that the song had filtered through the valley a little. I dare say there are some who have passed it down and still sing it to their children."

Stefan felt curious, sensing she knew something he didn't. "Do you know the song's origin?" she asked.

"No, but I assume you do."

Abbi du Woernig stood and motioned for him to follow her as she went into the hallway and up to her sitting room. With the key that hung around her wrist, she opened a desk drawer, rummaged through some papers, and brought out a yellowed sheet, handing it to Stefan.

Stefan felt emotion overcome him as he sat down and read:

ERICH'S SONG, by Cameron du Woernig, 1817

> *I know a place where snow falls white*
> *That's where I long to be*
> *Where castle turrets strike moonlight*
> *And shine where I can see*
>
> *I've known my love on mountains high*
> *Where meadows bloom in blue*
> *I know my love is there for me*
> *I know that love is true*

There is a place where snow falls deep
And warmth is near the hearth
Deep in my sweetheart's dreams I sleep
There's comfort in this warmth

The world is cold and brash outside
I fear what it imparts
But I know my love is here with me
A fire burns in my heart

Stefan glanced up when he'd finished, and Abbi said, "He wrote it as a lullaby for your uncle. He had a beautiful voice, you know. Oh, how I loved it when he would play the piano and sing to entertain me!"

"He's talking about the lodge," Stefan said, "and the upper meadow."

"Yes, I believe he is."

"It's intriguing that this song would be known by the common people."

"Yes," she said, "it is."

There was a long silence before she added in a different tone, "Things are going much better for you, are they not? You seem happier these days."

"Yes," he smiled, "I believe so. The work seems to be improving."

"And other things?" she asked with a sparkle in her eye.

"I'll never admit to it."

Abbi smiled and quietly slipped the paper back into the drawer.

As Ericha rummaged through her closet searching for something to wear, she wished for the first time in her life that she had more variety. She wanted to look nice for Stefan when he came this evening, and knew he must be tired of seeing her in cotton chemises and calico dresses. He had purchased some fine clothes for her on their vacation, but most of them were suited to traveling and riding. She wanted some things she could wear for everyday use that would make her feel more like a lady.

With that she pulled out one of her mother's old dresses and made up her mind that she would go into town the first of the week to order some new things. Perhaps something more appropriate for the duke's mistress, she thought with a smile. It occurred to her that she would have to take into consideration the way her size would increase in the coming months. What a scandal she was going to cause, she thought with an audible giggle, and then she turned to see Stefan enter her room with Job at his heels.

"What's funny?" he asked.

"I didn't expect you for hours yet."

"I got finished early," he replied, kissing her warmly.

"Good."

"You didn't answer my question. What's funny?"

"I must admit," she said, "I was just thinking of what a scandal I might cause when people realize I'm going to have a baby."

"And that doesn't bother you?" he asked, sitting down to relax.

"I've spent my whole life being looked down upon and whispered about. It can be difficult at times, but I've learned that letting it bother me doesn't make it go away." She looked at him shrewdly. "Does it bother you?"

"Yes," he stated, "but none of this will ever be as difficult for me as it is for you. I am simply grateful that you are willing to do this to bring a measure of happiness into my life."

"It works two ways. I was just thinking," she changed the subject, "that I could use some new clothes. What do you think?"

"Wouldn't hurt." He smiled. Then he lifted a brow comically. "Although you are precious in calico."

Ericha warmed from his obvious affection and proceeded to put on the dress she'd taken out. Before she was dressed, her stomach began to feel uneasy as it often did, and Stefan took notice of her distress.

"What's the matter?"

"Oh," she swallowed hard, "the usual." She took some dry biscuits from her bureau drawer and began to nibble one. "This will help. I've learned to keep them handy."

"Are you sure you're all right?"

"Of course. As long as I get plenty of rest and don't let myself get hungry, I'm fine. The doctor told me it's all very normal."

Stefan looked at her dubiously, wishing he understood even a little bit of what was involved with pregnancy. Ericha smiled at him, and he had to believe she was telling him the truth. He attempted to divert his thoughts.

"What is that?" he asked, and she looked up to see his attention focused on the little wooden box on her bureau.

She laughed. "You've not noticed it until now?"

"I always thought it was a jewel box," he said. "But it can't be, because you don't wear jewelry."

"Would you like me to?"

"No!" Then he added more softly, "You don't need it. Unless you want it, of course," he added as an afterthought, not wanting to hurt her feelings.

"I don't need it," she said easily.

"Johanna likes being the Duchess of Horstberg because of the jewels that go along with it." Stefan rose and picked up the little box, fingering it as he spoke. "Her whole life centers around her jewels. I hate it when she flaunts them like a . . . Well, I doubt the people are impressed by her finery. Quite the opposite, I would assume."

Stefan seemed briefly disturbed, and Ericha felt renewed compassion for his situation. He was a humble man who tried hard to be a good ruler, yet Johanna only seemed to want to defeat his efforts.

"You know," he said more lightly, "I can always tell what kind of mood she's in by the jewelry she's wearing."

"Tell me."

"If she wears her emerald earrings, she's up to mischief or she wants to play. She wears diamonds when she's trying to be elegant. Rubies mean either nostalgic if she wears the simple set with the gold filigree, or depressed if she wears the elaborate ones with diamond clusters around them. If she's really trying to impress me or wants my attention, she wears plain gold because she knows I like the simple things. But if she's trying to impress my family, she wears the family jewels that I gave her as a wedding gift."

Ericha smiled from his rambling. She liked the way he had learned to treat the subject of his wife with near amusement.

"Do the people believe their taxes are paying for such things?" Ericha asked carefully, not wanting to admit that she'd wondered over it herself.

Stefan chuckled in apparent surprise. "I keep forgetting you haven't always lived in Horstberg. Actually, we have made it clear—at least since my grandfather's time—that the du Woernig family is self-supporting. We keep the family fortune invested wisely and use it carefully. Every bit of the people's taxes benefit the people."

Ericha smiled. Stefan held up the box and asked again, "What is it?"

"It's a box."

"What's in it?" he clarified.

"I don't know. My mother gave it to me before she died, saying it contained my heritage. She said it was perhaps better left locked. There is no key."

"Really? How intriguing."

"I suppose."

Stefan returned to his chair, holding the box thoughtfully. He shook it slightly and heard a faint rattling. "Why don't you find a way to open it?"

"Why should I?" she asked.

"I know you want to know who your father is. Doesn't it make you curious, knowing that this box might contain the answer?"

"I suppose it does." She sat on the edge of the bed. "But it frightens me in a way."

"Why?"

"She said it was perhaps better left locked. That implies to me that it could change my life. And I don't want that."

Stefan concentrated on the box as he turned it over in his hands. "If it is truly better left locked," he said gently, "then why did she give it to you?"

Ericha felt a chill rush over her shoulders. She could think of no valid argument.

"It won't change your life if you don't let it," he said. "But perhaps it would help you ease these questions of belonging you've talked about."

Ericha stood and took the box from him. "Maybe you're right," she said, but she put it back where it belonged. "I don't know. I'll think about it."

Stefan laughed slightly, and then he allowed Ericha to coerce him into a stroll through the yard.

"I could use some fresh air," she said, and he followed her outside. There was a sprinkle of snow over the path as they walked hand in hand through the remnants of the garden.

"Winter has been mild so far," she said, stopping to admire some flowers still showing color through the snow. "The stronger ones have survived much later than usual."

"It makes an interesting picture," Stefan said thoughtfully. "Roses in the snow."

They moved to the little bench, and Stefan brushed the snow off before he sat and pulled Ericha beside him, kissing her warmly as he did.

"Oh my," Ericha said as he drew back and she noticed Mrs. Burger out sweeping her walk, making no effort to disguise her curiosity. Stefan looked puzzled, and she clarified, "It seems Mrs. Burger has taken notice of us."

"Who?" Stefan asked just as Ericha returned Mrs. Burger's wave.

"Oh, that is terrific," Stefan said with light sarcasm as Mrs. Burger approached the fence.

"She never goes anywhere, and she's slightly senile," Ericha said. "Maybe she won't know who you are. After all," she smiled, "I didn't."

"Good afternoon, Ericha dear," Mrs. Burger called over the fence. "How are you today?"

"Fine," she called back, "and you?"

Mrs. Burger came around the fence, and Ericha glanced nervously toward Stefan. But he acted as if nothing in the world was wrong as the woman approached them.

"I couldn't help noticing this handsome young man," she said. "You must introduce us."

"Uh . . ." Ericha thought quickly. "This is a dear friend of mine, Mr. Bruxen."

Stefan grinned as he rose and took Mrs. Burger's hand in greeting. "It's a pleasure to meet you, Mrs. Burger," he said. "I've heard nothing but good things about you."

Mrs. Burger blushed like a little girl. "I fear that Ericha has kept you a secret, Mr. Bruxen," she replied. "I should scold her."

"On the contrary, Mrs. Burger, I dare say the two of you have better things to talk about than me. She has told me what a lovely garden you have," he continued, moving toward her yard. "You must show it to me."

Ericha smiled as she followed them. Mrs. Burger was so charmed that she would likely not have any reason to speculate too deeply. Mrs. Burger took Stefan clear through the garden, taking time to explain what it would look like in the summer months.

"I shall have to return next year and see for myself," Stefan said.

Mrs. Burger paused and set a finger to her temple. "I would

swear that you look familiar." She turned to Ericha. "Doesn't he look familiar?"

"Very. He looks just like this man that comes to visit me quite often."

The joke was lost on Mrs. Burger as she concentrated. "Oh well, it'll come to me," she claimed, and Ericha blessed her touch of senility. "My, but it's getting chilly out here. Why don't you come inside, Mr. Bruxen, and I'll see if I've got some cinnamon cakes left. Do you like cinnamon cakes, Mr. Bruxen?"

"I certainly do," he replied, taking Ericha's hand as they followed her into the little cottage.

When they were all seated with wine and cinnamon cakes, Mrs. Burger spoke to Stefan as if Ericha weren't there. "You know, Mr. Bruxen, that Ericha is the sweetest little thing I've ever known. And I'll tell you something, I'm envious of that hair of hers. I've told her before that her hair reminds me of the grand duchess. Have you ever seen the grand duchess, Mr. Bruxen?"

"It seems like I might have a time or two," he replied with a straight face, and Ericha had to fight back a smile.

"What a good woman she is," Mrs. Burger rambled on. "Do you like parsnip wine, Mr. Bruxen?"

"I don't recall ever having tried it."

"Well, the parsnips didn't do so well this year, but when you come back next year, I'll let you try some."

"I'll look forward to it," he replied kindly, but the thought made Ericha a little queasy.

Mrs. Burger continued to regale Stefan with a lot of trivial talk, and he listened attentively, seeming genuinely interested. Ericha marveled as she watched them. Not only did he seem completely comfortable with Mrs. Burger, but he was apparently really enjoying himself. And Mrs. Burger liked Stefan so much that she seemed to overlook whatever speculations she might have had about him.

Ericha felt slightly embarrassed when Mrs. Burger started in again about Ericha's fine qualities. "She's such a sweetheart, much like her mother," she said. "I remember Kathe well. Of course,

Ericha doesn't look anything like her mother, but she's got the same kind spirit, that's for sure."

Stefan smiled warmly at Ericha, touched by her apparent timidity. He could well imagine that her mother had been an incredible woman. He thought back to that little wooden box and an idea occurred to him.

"Mrs. Burger," he said, leaning toward her, "did you ever see any . . . men coming to visit Ericha's mother?"

Ericha's heart began to pound. Why hadn't she thought herself to ask Mrs. Burger?

"Oh," she mused, "I occasionally saw a gentleman caller here and there. But then, I left Horstberg for about a year to stay with my sister. It was about the time of the revolution. I was only going to be away for a few months, but then I got word in letters from a friend about the strange goings on, and I thought it might be better to stay away until things settled. When I came back, Kathe had left Horstberg. Oh, I did miss her. That garden of hers was just never the same—until you came back, my dear."

Ericha just smiled. Her disappointment at Mrs. Burger not knowing anything suddenly made opening that little box a great temptation.

It was past dark when they left Mrs. Burger's cottage and returned to the house. Walking through the garden with Ericha, Stefan said quietly, "I love it when someone has no idea who I am, and still enjoys being with me. There is no better way to get insight to the people I rule than to spend time in one of their homes—like an undercover spy."

He laughed, and Ericha squeezed his hand, her heart swelling with admiration for him.

That night while Stefan slept in her bed, Ericha found it difficult to stop thinking about what he'd said earlier concerning the box. She had told him that she could face anything as long as she had him in her life. Surely she could face the contents of that box.

Ericha finally drifted to sleep, and in her dreams the box contained great riches. But when she awoke it seemed those riches were intangible. The dream intrigued her enough that she felt tempted to take Stefan's advice.

After Stefan left the following morning, she continued to think about it as she walked to Sunday service, wondering if she could be content to leave the box locked now that her curiosity had been sparked. During the service, Ericha's mind wandered to her circumstances. She wondered why it was difficult for her to feel any remorse at being pregnant with the duke's child. Thinking it through carefully, she hoped she was not rationalizing to believe that God would somehow understand. She was willing to face the consequences of her choices, but she could not regret them.

Theodor came for Sunday dinner as he often did. Ericha thought it ironic that he had no idea she was going to have his employer's child. She hoped he would not disapprove of her too badly if he knew. But her thoughts went back to the box, and she inquired of Karl, "Do you suppose there is a way to open that box of mine?"

Karl's brows went up in surprise. Theodor looked keenly interested. Ericha explained, "My mother gave me a box with no key. She said that it contained my heritage. I've been thinking I might like to open it."

"You have no idea, then," Theodor said thoughtfully, "who your father was?"

"No," she said and turned her attention back to Karl. "Do you think we could find a way to open it?"

"Well," Karl said, "the locks are made differently now than they used to be. It would take an old key to open it if you don't want to disfigure the box—which of course you wouldn't." He turned to Theodor. "Haven't you got a bunch of your father's keys that you kept for sentimental reasons after he died?"

"I do," he said. "Why don't you come to my apartment in the morning, my dear, and we'll see what we can do?"

Ericha's heart quickened slightly as she wondered if she should really do it, but something formless urged her on.

"Oh, but wait," Theodor said, "tomorrow will be especially busy. How about Tuesday?"

"That would be fine," Ericha agreed. "I was going into town tomorrow to do some shopping, anyway."

"Good then." Theodor leaned back, seeming almost smug. "I'll look forward to it."

Stefan returned to the castle early Monday morning before anyone but the officers on duty were even awake. He liked the serenity of this time of day, and wandered idly into his music room, searching for some quiet time before the demands of his day settled in. He sat on the piano bench and lazily leaned his head on one arm as he toyed with the keys, picking out the song that Ericha had taught him. His mind wandered as it always did to Ericha. He thought of the little wooden box and wondered what mystery it might contain. He wondered if she would follow through in her desire to open it. He thought of their visit to Mrs. Burger's home, and smiled to himself to recall their ironic conversations. His smiled broadened as he closed his eyes and saw a clear image of Ericha's timid smile as Mrs. Burger had compared Ericha to her mother.

As the conversation flitted through Stefan's mind, something connected with a vague memory. The thought seemed to somehow engage with the melody he was playing—the song his grandfather had written. He stopped playing and shot his head up as if he'd been struck. His heart began to pound before he consciously made the connection.

"Kathe," he said aloud. Voicing the name increased his heart's pace even more. Frantically he thought it out. Ericha had never told him her mother's name. But Mrs. Burger had said it. Kathe. *Kathe Lokberg.*

Stefan pressed both hands to his chest in an effort to ease a sudden painful constriction. "Dear heaven above," he murmured, grateful to be alone. "Could it be possible?" He turned to look about the room as if it might give him the answers. But the silence became suddenly eerie. Was this real? Had he overlooked the obvious? Or were his childhood memories playing tricks on him?

Stefan slammed the cover down over the piano keys and rushed into the hall. He forced himself to keep a steady pace while his mind raced in frantic circles and his heart continued to pound. Taking a deep breath, he knocked at his grandmother's door.

"Come in," she called, and he pushed it slowly open to see her sitting in bed with a book. She smiled when she saw him.

"I was hoping you'd be awake." He closed the door behind him, taking a deep breath to sustain his emotions.

"I woke up over an hour ago." She patted the bed beside her to indicate that he sit down. "I couldn't go back to sleep for some reason."

Stefan sat carefully on the edge of the bed, and Abbi took his hand. "Is something troubling you?" she asked.

"Yes, actually," he said. "I was . . . thinking about . . . well, forgive me for bringing this up, but sometimes I wonder if my memories are clear. I was so young, and . . ."

"Go on," she encouraged when he faltered.

He looked closely at her. "When Erich was killed, did he . . ." Stefan hesitated at the obvious sadness that rose in her eyes. But she squeezed his hand in encouragement, and he went on. "What I was wondering is . . . I seem to recall . . . a woman. He was in love with a woman. She spent a great deal of time here. I remember dark hair, and . . . she was very pretty. But I believe I was jealous of the time he spent with her." He squeezed Abbi's hand. "Did I dream it, or—"

"No." She laughed softly, seeming more at ease. "You didn't dream it. Erich was engaged to be married." Abbi's eyes grew distant with memory, and Stefan watched her closely. This was what he'd hoped for. If he could get her talking, then . . .

"They'd set a date but we had to postpone it, because the revolutionary forces were growing. Erich's life had been threatened more than once, and Cameron said he would not be having a wedding when someone was trying to kill his son. We considered having a private ceremony, but Cameron felt sure she would be safer if she didn't have the du Woernig name. He sent Erich to the lodge. When it was all over, we set a date again, and . . ." Abbi squeezed her eyes shut and Stefan felt her grip tighten. "The funeral was on the day they should have been married."

Stefan looked down and swallowed hard, willing his emotions to stay in control. He knew it took little for Abbi to get upset over the incident still, and he had no desire to provoke *her* emotions. While he was trying to find the words to ask his next question, Abbi continued wistfully, "I've always wondered what happened to her. After the funeral she just . . . disappeared. I'm certain Theodor must know, but he—"

"Theodor?" Stefan shot his head up. In spite of his thoughts, he had trouble believing it could be true. "Why would Theodor know?"

"She was his sister, Stefan." She touched his face and smiled, apparently oblivious to the fresh constricting in his chest and the racing of his pulse. "But of course you were too young to recall such connections. It was Theodor who introduced her to Erich, and . . . Are you all right?"

Stefan could only manage to shake his head.

"What is it?" She leaned toward him. "Stefan, what's wrong?"

"Just . . . the memories," he sputtered, relieved that she seemed to understand. With courage, Stefan swallowed and asked, "Her name?"

"Kathe Lokberg," she stated. Stefan almost winced. "What is it?" Abbi repeated.

Stefan reminded himself that he should know better than to try hiding something from Abbi du Woernig. Quickly he came up with a response that was honest without letting on to what he'd just discovered. It wasn't his place to tell her.

"It's just that . . . well, I know what happened to her, Grandmama."

"What?" Abbi's voice rose so eagerly that it nearly broke Stefan's heart to say it.

"She's dead."

Abbi gasped. "How did you know?" she insisted with a shaky voice.

Stefan struggled for a suitable answer. "Karl . . . uh, he mentioned it. That's all. But I had forgotten the connection . . . until just now."

For a moment Stefan thought she was going to cry. Instead she smiled. With peace glowing in her eyes, Abbi whispered reverently, "They are together, then."

Warmth bathed Stefan's emotions. "Yes." He pulled his grandmother close to him in a firm embrace. "I'm certain they are together." He ached to tell her that Erich had left something very special behind. But with any luck, the secret would be out soon enough.

Fearing his emotions would erupt, Stefan rose quickly and moved toward the door.

"Will you be all right?" she asked. He nodded stoutly and left the room.

Stefan hurried toward the office, knowing Rusty would be there by now. He pressed a hand over his mouth to keep from crying out as the full circumference of what he'd just learned assaulted him again. Calling upon every ounce of self-discipline, he peered into the office, saying to Rusty, "Do what you can without me. There's something I need to attend to. I don't know how long I'll be."

Rusty nodded, seeming perhaps concerned. Stefan closed the door and hurried away, desperately needing solitude. He felt as if he were trapped underwater, and only venting these emotions would give him the air he needed to make it through another minute.

Stefan hesitated before the door, not quite certain why he'd chosen to come here. He'd not been here in more than twenty years. Not bothering to think it through, he took up a lamp from the hall and pushed the door open. It creaked with resistance on long-unused hinges. He stepped through and closed it again. Holding the lamp high, Stefan moved carefully but quickly down the seemingly endless circular steps. While he concentrated on the sound of his boots on the stone, a stifled sob erupted from his throat. He thought of all the times Erich had traversed these stairs. He sobbed again. He thought of the funeral and imagined a woman in black lace, thinking it should have been her wedding day. He wiped a hand over his face, surprised to find it wet with tears. He thought of Ericha and moaned aloud. The ironies were incredible. The tragedy unbelievable.

Stefan came at last to another door. His emotion receded into something closer to fear. He paused, took a deep breath, then pushed it open. The emptiness of the room surprised him. But of course they would have had it thoroughly cleaned out after the explosion. Holding the lamp high, Stefan could see evidence of the damage. The size of what had obviously been a gaping hole was evident by the newer stone that had been laid to fill it in, and the walls surrounding it were darkened, scarred by smoke and flame. Stefan set the lamp carefully on the floor and drew a deep breath. For the first time ever, he tried to imagine the reality of what had happened here. He had felt the loss keenly through the years, but he'd never stopped to contemplate how Erich might have felt coming down here that morning, with no idea that he would never see the light of day again. His thoughts were likely with Kathe. And did he know? Stefan squeezed his eyes shut. A subtle moan rose from his throat. Had Erich known that Kathe was going to have his baby?

"Ericha," he groaned, and the full force of his emotion rose up to choke him. Weakness enveloped him and he fell to his knees, pressing his head into his hands. The emotion exploded, and he made no effort to hold it back. Stefan lost all awareness of time, crying like he hadn't since the explosion had occurred. He mourned the death of his grandfather and uncle, and the torment he'd seen his other family members go through from their loss. He cried for the childhood that had been cut short because of the obligations that had been bequeathed to him at Erich's death. Stefan cried for the disillusionment of a marriage that never would have taken place if he'd not been in such a position. He cried for Kathe Lokberg, leaving Horstberg alone to raise Erich's daughter. And he cried for Ericha. She handled her life with grace and dignity. But did she have any idea of the

blood that flowed in her veins? Did she know the tragedy behind her very existence? *Did she know that what bound them together was far stronger than either of them had ever imagined?*

When the emotion finally ran dry, Stefan sat on the floor, unaware of time passing. Methodically he took his mind through the memories of meeting Ericha and bringing her into his life. What would he have thought if he'd known? A warm chill rushed over him as he realized that perhaps a part of him *had* known. He'd felt affected by her presence the moment their eyes had met. How could he have looked at her that first time and not seen the resemblance? Her hair, her eyes, the shape of her face. *Those dimples.* He thought of things she'd said that had made him feel as if she could read his mind. She'd never even known her father, and yet she seemed somehow drawn to the things that Erich loved, the places he'd been. She was the spirit and soul of Erich du Woernig. And Stefan loved her!

Stefan only wondered for a moment if he should tell her. The answer was easy. If Kathe had not wanted her to know, it was not his business to go against Kathe's wishes. When Ericha felt compelled to discover the contents of the box Kathe had given her, then she would be ready to know the truth. Until then, Stefan would tell no one. While he suspected the knowledge would give her a certain amount of peace, he also knew that having du Woernig blood was more often a burden than a pleasure.

Suddenly feeling the passage of time, Stefan took up the lamp and hurried up the winding stairs. The hall was quiet as he emerged, and the angle of the light told him it was late afternoon. He extinguished the lamp and set it aside, realizing he'd eaten nothing today. Feeling little appetite, he went to the office, wondering what had transpired in his absence.

"We've been looking all over for you," Rusty said when he entered. "I thought you'd left the castle, but your horse was still—"

"I've been downstairs," he stated, sliding into the chair behind the desk.

"Downstairs?" Rusty asked and scratched his head.

"I needed to be alone," Stefan stated in a tone that he hoped would end the inquiries. "What did I miss?"

"It's mostly under control," Rusty stated. "If you'll just sign a few things, we could probably catch up the rest tomorrow."

"Good." Stefan sighed. "Let's get on with it."

Stefan paused mid-signature and pressed a hand over his eyes as the reality struck him freshly.

"You all right?" Rusty asked, startling him.

"Yes, fine," Stefan insisted.

"Maybe you could use a little *more* time alone," Rusty suggested.

Stefan smiled, appreciating Rusty's concern. He finished quickly and went straight to the stable. He needed Ericha. He needed her more than she could ever comprehend.

Chapter Eleven

THE LADY OF HORSTBERG

Mid-morning Ericha set out to Frieda's shop and had a joyous time ordering a wide array of new things. She asked Frieda about a cream-colored gown she'd noticed in the window. But when she was told the price, Ericha decided against it. The gown was most likely too elegant for anything she'd ever need. She knew that Stefan would gladly pay for anything she wanted, and she had enough credit here from her lace to probably pay for today's entire purchase and more. But she could see no point in buying something she would get so little use out of.

They were nearly finished fitting when Ericha felt an ache seep into her lower back. The bell above the shop door tinkled, and Frieda left the fitting room saying, "I'll tell them I'll be finished shortly and be right back." Ericha took the opportunity to sit down.

Frieda bustled back a moment later in a frenzy as she looked through a rack for a particular gown. "Make yourself comfortable, Miss Lokberg. It's the duchess coming to pick up a gown and I cannot let her wait."

It took Ericha a moment to absorb what this meant. *Stefan's wife was here!* While a part of Ericha preferred to remain ignorant, curiosity overruled, and she nearly blessed this opportunity.

After Frieda rushed away to help the duchess, Ericha moved quietly out of the fitting room, despite wearing a dress that had pins tucked across the bodice to fit it.

Ericha was immediately surprised by this flaxen-haired woman who bore Stefan's name. She wasn't certain what exactly she'd expected, but she had to admit that Johanna Heinrich was very beautiful. At first glance she appeared almost angelic by her coloring. But as Ericha studied her, a hardness came through Johanna's countenance that evidenced the truth of all Stefan had said. Her voluptuous figure was accentuated by the tight fit and low cut of a dress that seemed almost garish for shopping. Ericha briefly tried to comprehend Stefan exchanging vows with this woman—and sharing her bed. But she pushed thoughts of the past aside as Frieda showed Johanna the new gown.

"Oh, it does look lovely," the duchess said without enthusiasm, "but I couldn't help admiring that gown in the window."

"It is a lovely piece, Your Grace," Frieda said, "but I dare say that something in more of a true color would suit you better."

"Nonsense," she protested. "Let me try it on."

"But it's not in your size, Your Grace. It would be too small for you."

"Are you certain?" the duchess asked, implying by her tone that Frieda had done something wrong, and Ericha felt angry on her behalf.

"Perhaps I could make you another one in that style," Frieda said with apology, "and in a shade more suitable to your coloring."

"Yes," the duchess smiled, "I would like that. And I'd like it for the social tomorrow evening."

Ericha felt a stab of dismay. If there was a social, Stefan would be involved until late.

"Oh, Your Grace," Frieda gasped, "that's just impossible. I'm truly sorry, but I simply can't get it before then."

"But I want it," the duchess insisted. "I simply must have it."

"But I've just now completed this gown for your social tomorrow evening. I can't possibly do another."

The duchess turned toward the window display with a manipulative sigh. "Oh, well, if you must. Are you sure that color isn't right? I'm certain His Grace would be delighted with it. It's just his style."

Ericha lifted her brows at the mention of this, and couldn't resist speaking up. "I believe you're right . . . Your Grace," she added sweetly when Johanna Heinrich's eyes turned toward her with disapproval. "Although I dare say his uniform suits him better."

Their eyes met boldly for a long moment as the duchess didn't seem to know how to retort to such a statement. She gave a grunt of disgust then insisted that Frieda make her the specified gown as quickly as possible.

When Johanna was gone, Ericha wished that she could have mentioned she was going to have the child that the duchess had never been able to conceive.

Frieda sighed with relief, and her eyes sparkled with amusement as she went back to fitting Ericha's dress.

"Frieda," Ericha said when she was almost done, "what size is that gown?"

"What? The one in the window?"

"Yes," she said, "I too was admiring it when I came in."

"It would probably be about right for you," she said. "In fact, I believe it would do very nicely on you."

"Shall we try it?" Ericha asked, and the amusement in Frieda's expression deepened as she went to get it.

"Oh, it looks grand on you," Frieda declared when it was in place, and Ericha had never felt so elegant. The tiny sleeves enhanced her shoulders nicely, and the skirt flounces added a feminine yet elegant charm that suited her.

"You know it would be so disrespectful," Frieda nearly whispered, "and she's such a sensitive thing . . . but I simply know the style would look atrocious on her. If she weren't the duchess I could tell her that, but she thinks she knows it all. Won't even send anybody else in to pick up her gowns; doesn't trust anybody. Yes, she thinks she knows it all."

"Well," Ericha said slyly, "we know something she doesn't, don't we!"

Ericha laughed out loud, and Frieda merely smiled as if she'd missed something, and then she added softly, "We mustn't be so disrespectful."

"Oh, of course," Ericha said soberly, but a wry smile passed between them.

Ericha took the gown home with her, anticipating the new things that would be ready for her next week. She tried the gown on again in her bedroom and decided she would save it for a special occasion—even if that was nothing more than a nice dinner with Stefan.

Tucking it away in the closet, Ericha felt pleased to have something that the Duchess of Horstberg had wanted. She thought briefly that she would trade the gown for the name any day, but she didn't think Johanna would be willing.

Stefan left his horse in Karl's stable and entered the side door of the house. He immediately saw Ericha working in the kitchen and leaned in the doorframe to watch her. She was up to her elbows in the laundry tub, humming that song. He understood now why Ericha's mother would have known it. It had been written for Erich. The thought warmed him.

She glanced up and smiled. "Oh, it's you. You're here in daylight. It must be a special occasion."

Stefan shook his head, too moved to speak. How could he have been so blind? The resemblance to Erich du Woernig was uncanny.

"Is something wrong?" she asked, wringing water out of something white and lacy.

"No." He smiled. "Of course not." He didn't want her being concerned over things he couldn't tell her. "I'm just a little tired. Why don't you finish what you're doing. If it's all right with you, I'll go upstairs and lie down for a while."

She smiled again. "Does this mean you'll be here for supper?"

"Only if I can eat while I'm looking at you," he said, and she beamed. Stefan moved into the hall, then came right back. Ericha looked surprised as he touched her chin and looked into her eyes. Then he kissed her. "I love you, Ericha."

"I love you, too," she replied.

Stefan entered Ericha's room and closed the door, grateful for the opportunity to be alone here without appearing awkward. His gaze went straight to the framed picture facing the wall. Ericha had said she'd found it in the closet, that she believed it was her father. But she'd seemed hesitant to turn it around, and he'd not pressed her to.

Stefan almost trembled as he went to his knees and slowly turned it. A little laugh of relief escaped him. It was the final piece to the puzzle. This pencil drawing of Erich du Woernig was signed by his mother. Stefan actually remembered watching her do it. The irony was extraordinary.

Not wanting Ericha to catch him, he carefully put the picture back in place and came to his feet. His eye wandered to the little wooden box in the center of the bureau. With new perspective he picked it up, turning it over in his hands as if it could somehow whisper to him of its contents. He both wanted Ericha to open it, and to see it forever remain locked. Either way, the results could be difficult.

Setting the box back where it belonged, Stefan removed his boots and stretched out on the bed. He'd only been there a minute when Job jumped up and joined him. The exhaustion of his weary emotions took hold and he slept quickly. He awoke in the dark with Ericha's lips over his. She laughed as he pulled her into his arms and rolled her onto the bed.

"Once upon a time," she said, "a handsome prince fell asleep for a hundred years. He woke up very hungry and—"

"No, wait. Go back," he said. "He woke up only when a *true* princess kissed him." Stefan's voice turned severe. "The moment he looked into her eyes, he knew she was the one he'd been born to love."

Ericha nuzzled close to him. "Where do you come up with these things?" she asked with a little laugh.

"It's in the blood," he stated and kissed her again.

"Supper is ready, my love," she said. "Are you hungry?"

"After sleeping a hundred years, I'm starving."

Ericha thoroughly enjoyed her evening with Stefan. Karl was with Luise, and Erma had gone visiting. Stefan said little as they shared a meal by candlelight, but the adoration in his eyes said more than words ever could. He complimented her on the meal three times, then insisted on helping her clean the dishes. When the work was done, they went up to the bedroom, and Ericha wished it could always be this way.

Stefan leaned against the headboard and watched as Ericha sat on the edge of the bed and brushed through her hair. He loved watching her do it. That hair was incredible—just like his grandmother and mother before him. He could almost be certain she did it just to please him.

"Guess who I saw today," she said out of nowhere.

"Who?" he asked, grateful for the distraction. He wanted so badly to tell her what he knew that it almost hurt.

"Guess."

"The Queen of England," he said.

"No," she grinned, "but you're close." She lowered her voice to a provocative whisper. "The Duchess of Horstberg."

Stefan lifted his brows dubiously. "So," he said nonchalantly, "I see her every day—unless I can at all avoid it."

Ericha laughed again, then told him every detail of her encounter in the dress shop. Stefan laughed until he nearly cried. Ericha thought it was funny. But Stefan *really* thought it was funny.

"And," Ericha added, "she was wearing pearls. You didn't tell me what pearls mean."

"Oh, that's easy," he said. "Pearls give her power."

"I see," Ericha said dryly. "Power to intimidate the dressmaker?"

Stefan only nodded, wondering what it would be like to have a woman he could be proud of to bear his name.

"So, let me see this magnificent gown," he said.

"Oh, no." She smiled. "I'll save it to surprise you some time. You'll know it when you see it. After all, it's just your style."

Again he laughed, and he couldn't resist asking, "Have you

decided whether or not you're going to open your box yet?" She'd said nothing about it since the last time he'd brought it up.

"Theodor is going to see if he has a key that will fit it in the morning."

It took Stefan a moment to gather his thoughts. He hadn't expected her to act on it so quickly. He wondered briefly how he might have felt to discover the truth from Ericha.

"You're really going to do it?" he asked, feeling somehow concerned. But at least he wouldn't have to bear the knowledge alone.

"Yes," she said with conviction, "I am."

"Are you certain it's what you want to do?" he asked, perhaps to reassure himself more than her.

Ericha thought about it a moment. "Yes," she said firmly, "I think it's time that I know who I really am."

Stefan smiled serenely. "Yes, I do believe it is."

Ericha picked up the box and fingered it longingly, hoping it was not better left locked.

While Ericha slept with her head on his shoulder, Stefan contemplated her encounter in the dress shop. Staring into the darkness above him, his mind wandered back, trying to make some sense of the present situation.

Stefan first saw Johanna Von Bindorf only days after he officially took over as the Duke of Horstberg. The reality had recently sunk in that he was now as good as king of this fair land, and along with that came a duty that caused mixed emotions. He was expected by his people to marry and produce an heir. In a sense it seemed sordid, while aspects of it left him intrigued. He knew from gossip that people speculated over who he might marry, and there were countless young ladies in the valley who would have given anything to become his wife, simply because of his position. Though it had come to his ears that he was considered handsome, it hardly seemed to count for much.

But the reality of marriage hardly entered Stefan's mind— until he saw Johanna. She coyly caught his eye over the brim of her champagne glass. Her flaxen hair reflected the glimmer of the lighted ballroom, as did the jewels at her ears and about her throat. He was actually glad to be the duke in that moment as he approached her and she curtsied deeply before him.

They danced and talked the night away, and through the following weeks, Stefan spent a great deal of time going back and forth between Horstberg and Kohenswald—just to be with her. It seemed that Johanna was everything he wanted, and once his decision was made, he went to his grandmother to tell her the news.

"Grandmama," he said carefully, "I'm going to ask Johanna to marry me."

Stefan was surprised by her astonishment. "You can't be serious."

"Of course I'm serious," he replied.

"Do you love her?" Abbi asked.

"I enjoy being with her," he replied. "I think of her always. I want to share my life with her."

"But do you *really* love her?"

"I suppose I do," he said.

"That's not good enough," Abbi said emphatically. "Not for you, it's not."

"Grandmama," he gave a baffled chuckle, "what are you saying?"

"Trust me, Stefan," she said gently, "when I tell you that her background is not admirable. I have seen little but greed and deceit in the family as long as I have been duchess. I would not trust her to make you happy. It isn't in her blood."

"But she's different," Stefan protested. "If you could see the way she treats me. She's so . . . Oh, I can't explain it. But I feel good when I'm with her and—"

"You're sounding very much like your mother when she wanted to marry Nik Koenig," Abbi stated, and Stefan swallowed hard. "And what of the political aspects?" she continued. "You realize what an advantage such a union would be to Kohenswald. Is that what you want?"

"Wouldn't it be wise? Things have been touchy with them

for years. I believe this would settle our differences and give us a common bond."

"It sounds practical," Abbi said. "Is that why you want to marry her—because it's so practical?" Stefan bowed his head. "Be honest with me," she insisted. "I want to know why."

"It *is* practical," he said. "And I want her to be my wife."

Abbi gazed at him long and hard, and then she stated firmly, "You are a man now, Stefan. You must do what you feel is best. But I don't approve. Why don't you be patient and wait? You're young yet. Wait until you really fall in love. Your grandfather was ten years older than you when he met me. There is no hurry."

"You know, Grandmama, my life has not been full of joy."

She looked toward him sadly. "Yes, I know."

"I am happy when I'm with her," he stated, but still she looked doubtful.

Stefan had always heeded his grandmother's advice before. He didn't know if it was his feelings for Johanna that made him ignore it this time, or perhaps a need to prove that he was indeed a man. He was the Duke of Horstberg now. If he could marry and make a positive political step, surely it was a good thing.

He expected his grandmother to be upset over his decision. But she told him how she felt, and then she let it drop. She set an example for the rest of the family, taking Johanna in with full welcome and doing everything to make her feel accepted.

During the weeks of betrothal, Stefan felt happy, anticipating his marriage greatly. Each moment with Johanna was exciting. She was full of life and happiness, and she said everything just right to make him feel good inside. He believed that she truly loved him. And when he kissed her, it warmed him to the core. Her response urged something in him that made him want to be her husband. He believed he could conquer anything if only he could feel that way forever.

When doubts crept in, Stefan felt certain that marriage would dispel any problems they faced, that somehow they could work it out. His entire future was banked on a good marriage with

Johanna and having her by his side as he ruled the country that had been bequeathed to him.

The day of the wedding was gray and full of clouds, but Stefan felt bright and cheery. He was a little nervous by the pomp and grandeur of the whole thing, but Johanna took it all in and put him at ease. To him the wedding was wondrous. She looked beautiful. He felt warm. Everything was perfect.

There was a look of triumph in her eyes as he pulled back from that sacred kiss. It took him slightly off guard, but he thought nothing of it and concentrated more on the joy he felt as he escorted his wife from the cathedral.

At first when Stefan noticed her subtle flirtations with other men, he passed it off as the gaiety she felt from the day's events. She was the Duchess of Horstberg now, and she felt like celebrating. And celebrate she did. A glass of champagne was always in her hand, and Stefan had to admit that something uneasy nagged at him as she purposely flirted with anything in breeches that came within an arm's reach of her. He credited it to the champagne. She wasn't thinking clearly. But he felt certain that once he had her alone, she would be the Johanna he had fallen in love with. She giggled when he carried her over the threshold of his bedroom, and he felt a fresh hope for his feelings when she turned eyes toward him that betrayed desire.

Stefan felt tense, knowing what would transpire. But he believed that what the two of them would share this night would bind them together irrevocably. Surely this would be the experience of a lifetime. She came to him and lifted her hair, indicating he unfasten her gown, and he did so without hesitation.

"Johanna," he whispered behind her ear, and then he kissed the back of her neck and pressed his arm around her waist. "Johanna, my love," he paused and took a deep breath, "I must confess . . . that I have never done this before."

To him it was right that he had saved himself for his wife. Everything he'd been raised with told him it was. But Johanna turned and looked at him with astonishment. She smiled. Then she laughed.

Stefan had done well in reasoning away all of the little things that she'd done since they'd exchanged vows only hours ago. But he couldn't reason away the shattering reality of her words when she twirled away from him and the wedding gown rustled to the floor.

"So," she laughed again, and to him it sounded wicked, "I've not only conquered the Duke of Horstberg, but I've got myself an innocent child. Well," she added seductively, "I'll teach you a thing or two."

Stefan felt everything inside of him die. He'd just given away his heart and his country to a bewitching little tramp. She had deceived him. She had wanted to marry the Duke of Horstberg for the prestige it gave her in her home country, and she would have married him had he been stout and balding with foul breath.

The shades were torn from his eyes, and he would have far preferred that they had remained. His grandmother's words haunted him as he watched his wife through a shroud of horror. He had to consciously shake his head to make himself believe this was real. It felt like a dream—a very bad dream. Here he was, a virgin man of twenty-one, standing expressionless while his wife undressed. And he didn't even want her. He felt no desire to touch her, let alone make love to her. No, it wasn't love, he thought. Whatever might transpire this night had nothing to do with love.

When Johanna was dressed in almost nothing, she took it upon herself to undress Stefan as well. He coldly allowed her to remove his shirt and push him into a chair to pull off his boots, as if she'd done it a hundred times. He doubted she had gained the practice from her father's boots.

The bright, aspiring young man who had risen from this bed earlier today climbed into it now feeling his heart turn cold and hard. He was grateful when his physical desires reached a point where they took over and made him do what his emotions could not force him to. He felt distant from himself as he kissed her. He felt like a different man as he experienced things that he felt certain should have been beautiful. But all of it made him sick.

What should have felt good wrenched painfully at his heart, and he was so grateful to have it over.

Stefan tried to ease away from her. He wanted to run away. He wanted to be anywhere but here. But Johanna held tightly to him and nuzzled her face against his chest as if he really meant something to her. He might have wanted to run his hands through her hair or trace his fingers over her silken arms. But he could only lay dormant and listen as her breathing moved into a deep, contented sleep. And when he was certain Johanna slept, Stefan cried. He turned his face away from her and let the tears flow into the pillow. Johanna had hit it all very precisely. As much as he hated to admit it, it was true. He was an innocent child.

Stefan had grown up witnessing true love and had wrongly assumed that all marriages were that way. His images of perfect love were nothing but a naive dream. His vulnerability had left his heart wide open to be trampled upon. The reality was painful and humiliating, but it had to be faced. His life with Johanna had only just begun.

It was duty that kept Stefan going back to Johanna's bed. He tried to tell himself that he was as sordid and cold as she, and he was only doing it because it fulfilled some carnal need of being a man. But he knew he could live without it. He hated it. No, it was duty. Once she had a son, he would not go back again.

The years proved his assumptions as the evidence deepened that Johanna was manipulative, tawdry, and greedy. She could cover it so sweetly at times that it nearly sickened him. How could he have been such a fool? The separate rooms suited him fine, as did the length of the dining table. He associated with her enough to keep up the social pretense, and went to her bed often enough that he hoped the odds would eventually find her pregnant and it would be over with.

Only his grandmother knew the truth. Perhaps Johanna knew, but she wouldn't admit it. She upheld the pretenses beautifully. Even when they were alone, she pretended that they were in love, seeming plenty content to pretend.

It was a bitterly cold day when Stefan realized there would

be no heir. Something in him changed when it became evident that more than four years of marriage had not given him a child. Johanna had blamed it on him, but he didn't care. Her fault or his, there was no reason for this sordid business to go on. He knew she'd not been content with him alone all this time. Let her have her way and sleep where she wanted. He simply didn't care—except for that one cold, bitter part of him that wanted to hurt her as badly as she had hurt him, however wrong it might be.

Stefan was waiting in the alcove of a side door just before midnight when she rushed into him and screamed.

"Going out?" he whispered in the darkness, holding her tightly against him.

"I was in need of some fresh air," she said quickly.

Stefan moved her out of the dark alcove and down the hall toward a lamp. He pushed the hood of her cloak away and held her face in the light.

"Emeralds," he said, noting the jewels she wore. "I should have known. Emeralds are appropriate for fresh air. So is that gown. A bit fancy for a midnight walk, don't you think?"

Stefan said nothing more as he pulled her arm behind her back. Not enough to hurt her, but enough to put him in complete control.

"What are you doing?" she protested when he ushered her down the hall.

"I'm taking you where every good wife ought to be," he snarled.

"And where is that?" she asked, obviously upset at his intrusion on whatever her plans had been.

Stefan left her plea unanswered as he moved with her up the stairs and down a long hallway. She looked shocked when they came to the door of his bedroom. Beyond their wedding night, he had always gone to her room.

"Where is that, you ask?" He pushed open the door, then pulled her up into his arms. "In her husband's bed," he said and nearly threw her onto it, and then he brashly kicked the door shut.

Johanna scrambled to sit up, and he caught the uncertainty in her eyes. Briefly he wanted to answer the fear and just tell her to leave. But he reminded himself that for this moment he was the man Johanna deserved: the greedy, power-thirsty tyrant.

Stefan kissed her with the purpose of making her want more, while he remained in complete control. He didn't want *her*. In truth, it was revolting to him. He found a degree of pleasure, only in knowing it was the last time their lips would meet. And then he left her, knowing that in a sense he'd left with the final word.

"No!" she cried from the pain of unfulfilled longing. But did it balance out what he had lived through? "Don't leave me!" she cried.

"I'll see you at breakfast, my dear," he said and calmly left the room, knowing that he'd won.

It was pathetic, he thought as he walked through silent castle halls to find an empty guest room that two people, married to each other, were at this silent battle of hurting. But it was over now. Stefan had won in his own right. Now he would put Johanna behind him and give his heart a chance to heal. He could be content with the life he had, as long as his heart could heal.

The following morning, Stefan felt especially perky as he went down to breakfast. Johanna wasn't there, and he enjoyed visiting with his family without her cynical eyes watching him. He went to his office and set to work until a knock came at the door. Johanna stepped haughtily into the room and dismissed everyone else present. When they were alone, her eyes bored into him.

"You look awful, my dear," Stefan said coolly. "Have a bad night?"

"Quite!" she snapped. "I don't know what you were trying to prove last night, but it was cruel. You must have been drunk."

"I was not drunk," he said proudly. "I wouldn't want such an experience to be wasted on dulled senses."

"You're mad!" she hissed.

"Living with you all this time could make any man go mad," he retorted. "Besides," he went on when she made no response, "it shouldn't make any difference to you. You've still got what you wanted out of the deal."

"And what is that?"

"You conquered the Duke of Horstberg. You've got all of the prestige you could ever hope for and an allowance to keep you plenty happy. So mind your business and be grateful."

Johanna skulked out and slammed the door.

It took little time for Stefan to realize that he was lonely. But then he always had been. And there was little to be done about it. He submerged himself in his work and hoped the discontentment would go away.

At least, he told himself, it was better to be alone and lonely than to be in the same bed with Johanna and feel like a lost child.

And then Ericha had come into his life, and nothing had ever been the same. All those months of trying to convince himself that he could be content without her had been futile. But even now, he felt guilty for the mistakes he'd made that affected her life so greatly.

Carefully Stefan eased away from her and pulled on his breeches. While Ericha slept, he gazed out the window toward Castle Horstberg. The memories never failed to make him feel sick in the pit of his stomach. Cameron and Erich's deaths had nothing to do with him. But it was he who had made the decision to marry Johanna. While the regret deepened, he felt warm hands against his back.

"What is it?" Ericha whispered.

Stefan bowed his head forward with a deep sigh. "I am such a fool," he said quietly.

"And why is that?" she asked lightly, but he turned toward her and his expression was sobering.

"Every time I grasp the reality, I hate myself. It's all so ridiculous. Two women in a dress shop. One bearing my name, and the other my child. At times I have to stop and wonder why it had to be this way."

Ericha wanted to console him. They both knew that

speculating made no difference. But she sensed that he needed to unburden himself and waited for him to go on.

"If I could turn back time, Ericha, I would have listened to my grandmother when she told me not to marry Johanna. She said that true love would find me and I would feel the fire in my heart.

"You see, that is where I made the mistake. It was not wrong of me to fall in love with you, nor to commit my life to you and make you a part of it. No, I made the mistake when I ignored her advice—and I never have since. If I had listened to her, I would not have married Johanna. I would have married you."

Stefan pulled her close to him, wondering what it might have been like if Erich had lived. He and Ericha would have grown up together. It all would have been so different. Reminding himself that regret would not change anything, he held her tighter and whispered, "You must believe me, Ericha, when I tell you that with all my heart I wish you would have been the first for me, as I was the first for you. I wish that I could erase Johanna from my life and have you there instead. It is you paying for my foolishness, and there are some mistakes that simply cannot be rectified."

"There is no need to apologize." Ericha brushed her hand over his face. "I love you now for who and what you are. And I treasure each moment we have. I am only grateful that you are willing to risk so much to share a part of your life with me."

Stefan's eyes showed wonder as his hand moved over her hair. "If only I had more to give you."

"This," she said, pressing his hand to where the baby grew, "is the greatest of all gifts."

"Yet you give it back to me," he whispered.

Their eyes met, and the emotion in his burned through her. "It's all right," she whispered, and he pressed his face to Ericha's shoulder.

"It is all so bittersweet," he said softly. "Everything we share that brings me joy sits on the opposite side of the scale to a bitter reality when I ponder what might have been."

"Stop wondering," she said. "Be content with now. I love you, Stefan. I love you with all my heart and soul."

"Yes, I know. And that is what makes life so good for me."
Stefan kissed her and pulled her close. He smiled and touched her
nose with his. "And yes, life is good for me."

"Come back to bed," she whispered gently.

Yes, he thought as her affection warmed him through, *this is
love.* Comparing this to what he had shared with Johanna was like
comparing heaven and hell. And for whatever price he had to pay
for heaven, he would never return to hell again.

Ericha awoke late to realize Stefan was already gone. She was
barely out of bed when Karl came to her room.

"Are you still going to the castle this morning?" he asked.

"Yes, why?" she asked, brushing through her hair, still wearing
a nightgown and robe.

"Well, I'm going that way. I'll take you, but I have to leave
soon."

"But I just got up."

Karl shrugged his shoulders sheepishly. "I guess you can just
ride Pegasus up."

Ericha normally would have opted for that, but it was cold
out and she wasn't feeling much energy. "Just give me time to eat
something."

"Oh, I know better than to let you go without eating," he
smiled. "Your breakfast is on the table."

Ericha smiled knowingly at him, and he left her to get dressed.

Wearing one of her calico dresses, with her hair hanging
down around her shoulders, Ericha held the little box on her lap
as Karl drove toward the castle. She wondered if she was doing
the right thing. She couldn't deny being curious and intrigued, but
still there was fear. A fear brought on by the way Kathe had never
wanted to speak of it. Ericha wondered why Kathe had chosen
to leave Horstberg rather than stay with her family. And most
of all, Ericha wondered why Kathe had said it should perhaps
remain locked. But on the other hand, as Stefan had pointed out,

if Kathe really never wanted Ericha to see what was in the box, why didn't she keep it to herself or destroy it?

The questions left Ericha confused as they neared the castle. But her mind drifted briefly to Stefan, and she felt pride on his behalf for this beautiful structure that was his home.

Theodor was waiting for her at his apartment.

"So," she said while he rummaged in a drawer, "you said that you have all of your father's old keys. Do you really think one of them will open my box?"

"I'm certain I could find one eventually," he said, "but there's no point." Theodor turned around and handed a key to Ericha.

"What is this?" she asked, taking it hesitantly.

"It's the key to that box." He nodded toward it.

"But how . . ."

"Your mother sent me that key before she died. She figured that when her health finally gave out, you would be in my care, and when you were ready to open that box, you would come to me."

Ericha didn't know what to say. She felt suddenly nervous as it became evident her mother had thought this through very carefully. She wondered briefly if Theodor knew what the box contained.

"I've got work to do," he said. "But you probably prefer to be alone anyway."

Ericha wondered briefly what Theodor's work might entail today. She thought of the time he spent with Stefan each day and felt briefly envious, but the door closing startled her back to the moment. Minutes slipped by while she looked at the little box. By the time she found the courage to slip the key in and lift the lid, her hand was trembling. Inside was a finely etched gold bracelet that looked very old, and some papers rolled up and tied with a ribbon.

Ericha picked up the bracelet reverently, wondering what it meant. She squinted to read the inscription inside, but it appeared to be worn down, and she couldn't make out the words. She didn't recall ever seeing her mother wear it.

Setting the bracelet back where she'd found it, Ericha lifted the papers out and set the box aside. She slid the ribbon off and took a deep breath. Emotion caught in her throat as she unrolled the lengthy letter, immediately recognizing her mother's handwriting. Gathering fortitude, she made herself comfortable and began to read. Any doubt that this was right fled the moment she began.

My dearest Ericha,

I feel certain that one day you will read this, for I believe that when fate makes it necessary for you to know these things, your heart will tell you to find a way to open the box that encloses them. I don't know how old you will be when you open this, but at the time I am writing this you have just turned fourteen.

You are a beautiful girl, Ericha, and you must know that I cannot look at you without thinking of your father. I know that I have told you little, and this is for many reasons—the foremost being that it seems too close to my heart to let it out.

I know that being raised with only your mother's name has been difficult for you, but I've been proud of the way you handle it. That is your father in you, for he was full of dignity and courage. He was a good man, Ericha. I want you to know that. He loved me, as I loved him. It was only a cruel twist of fate that kept you and me, my daughter, from living a life very different from this.

I met your father when Theodor invited him over to dinner. Theodor worked for him at the time and had teased me incessantly that he'd found the man for me. I was astonished to see that he was right, and even more astonished that your father felt it too.

Our love was undeniable, but it was difficult for us to find time alone together. I have told you many times of the meadow where we would often go, and it was not far from there that you were conceived. I have tried to regret that we had not waited until we were married, but it would be impossible to regret having you, Ericha, for you are all that is left of him.

Ericha paused briefly to take a deep breath as she felt a vague relation to her mother's circumstances. But she wondered if this meant her father was dead. Wanting to know the answers, she read on.

Your father's family was very good to me, and it was all like a fantastic whirlwind as we planned the wedding and counted down the days. It was only four days before the date we had set, Ericha, that your father was killed in an explosion.

Ericha felt the anguish in the statement, and it broke her heart to imagine how her mother must have felt.

He was a chemist, and I assume it was amidst some experiment that he lost his life. I remember the rumble of the explosion, for even with the distance between my home and his, it felt like thunder moving through the ground. It was horrifying for me. I believed that my life was over. But within days I realized that I was pregnant.

I considered what to do. I wanted to go to his family and tell them the truth, but not only had they lost him, but his father had been killed in an attempt to save his life, and I knew they didn't need my problems adding to their burden. Theodor wanted me to stay, but worse than the stigma of an illegitimate child was my fear of what my pregnancy might mean politically.

The letter filled Ericha's eyes with mist as she read, and she had to blink several times to catch that last word and absorb it. Her heart beating madly, Ericha read on, feeling the reality of her fear concerning what she held.

You will only understand completely when you have the chance to return to Horstberg and see for yourself the situation. I have told you how beautiful and peaceful it is there. But the year I left, the country had just emerged from revolution, and I feared the instability surrounding my circumstances. I have told you about the magnificence of Castle Horstberg and the way it stirs my heart, but what I haven't had the courage to tell you, my dear, is that it is there you should have been born.

Ericha's hands began to tremble, but she read on frantically.

I am now stating my real intent for this letter, Ericha. This is your heritage. You are the daughter of Erich Cameron Georg Gerhard du Woernig. He would have been the Duke of Horstberg. You should have been a princess, Ericha. It's in your blood, and I know somehow that when you have the opportunity to return, you will feel Horstberg in your soul as your father did.

Ericha's fingers retracted from the letter as if it were hot to the touch, and she watched bewildered as it fell to the floor.

"Oh, no," she muttered and moved her hand over her mouth to suppress a deep moan. Tears flooded forth, and reality struck with harsh blows as it all meshed together in her mind. She thought of all the stories she had heard of the royal family and tried to comprehend herself as a part of it. She had heard of the explosion. Stefan himself had told her of the tragedy.

Stefan. "Oh, Stefan!" she groaned. What did this mean? She was his cousin! They were of the same blood, the same heritage. Is that why they'd been so drawn to each other? But how would he take this?

Ericha's mind ran through the coincidences. She'd been told that her hair was much like the grand duchess. Stefan's grandmother. *Her* grandmother. She remembered meeting Stefan's mother, whose coloring and build had reminded her of her own. That meadow! The lodge! Was that where her life had begun? The truth was incredible. The emotion was overwhelming.

Ericha was grateful to be alone as she wept long and hard. She finally picked the letter back up to finish it, hoping it would give her the strength to face what it had revealed.

I hope that I have done the right thing in this, Ericha. You must know that you are my life. You gave me a reason to live when I lost Erich. You are everything to me, and I only want what is best for you. You must follow your instincts concerning what is best to do with your knowledge. I chose to keep mine in my heart, but it smoldered there and caused me great pain at times. You must follow your own heart.

If you ever are in need, the bracelet enclosed in this box will prove your identity, but not nearly as much as your appearance will. They are a good family, and you must not take advantage of this. I should not even say that, for I know you would not. I trust you will know what to do and I pray that your life will be good, despite what should have been.

With all my love,
Kathe, your mother.

Ericha calmly rolled the letter back up and replaced the ribbon. She put it back into the box with the bracelet, then resolutely turned the key. She felt certain that this secret was better left locked—at least until she could deal with it in her own mind.

Her greatest concern was for Stefan. With the current state of their relationship, she could not even comprehend how he would react to this. In that moment she wished that the box could have forever remained locked.

Ericha was lost deep in thought when Theodor returned and sat quietly beside her.

"How are you?" he asked, and she managed a feeble smile. "You look distressed," he said. "I would have thought you'd be delighted to discover that you're a du Woernig."

Ericha looked up at him sharply. "You knew," she whispered. "All along—you knew!"

"Of course I knew," he said gently, taking her hand into his. "I worked with Erich for years. I introduced him to your mother. I knew her reasons for leaving Horstberg. But she begged me to never tell a soul—and I haven't."

Ericha took a deep breath, still overwhelmed by all of this. She felt Theodor squeeze her hand. "Ericha," he continued, "there is something that I want to implore you to do." She looked directly at him, sensing the severity of his tone. "I know this family very well. They are good people. You must trust me."

Ericha felt unsteady as he led her to the window, pointing out to the residence of the castle. "There is a woman over there right now, who has many times held Horstberg in the palm of her hand. She is the greatest lady I have ever known, and any one of the citizens of this country would testify to that. But, Ericha, one day she lost her husband and her only son."

Ericha caught her breath, and her hand tightened over Theodor's as she began to sense his purpose. "I know, Ericha . . . I know with all my heart what happiness it would give her to know that you exist. You don't know how many times I've had to bite my tongue to keep from telling her something I knew that would give her peace."

"No, Theodor." Ericha backed away. "I don't think that—"

"Ericha," he insisted, "you must trust me."

"But I . . ." she began but couldn't finish. Theodor deftly picked up the box, took her by the hand, and swept her out the door and across the courtyard.

"No," she protested. "I can't. Not now . . . please."

Theodor ignored her completely, and any further protest would have created a scene. Ericha nearly hated him for doing this to her. How could she face the Grand Duchess of Horstberg with this, when she could hardly face it herself?

Theodor entered through a huge door without knocking and pulled Ericha down a long hall. She became briefly distracted at the size and elegance of the place, but she feared what would happen if she ran into Stefan. Theodor opened the door to a room and peered in, and then he ordered her to sit down and wait.

"Theodor," she pleaded again, "I need more time to—"

"To stew over it and lose your courage? I've been waiting for this opportunity for years. I will take the responsibility."

While Ericha was thinking of a response, he looked into her eyes, saying quietly, "Ericha, please trust me. I have honored your mother's wishes. Now, I am honoring your father's."

Ericha was stunned speechless as Theodor left her alone in the elegant drawing room. She sat down and tried to imagine her father here. *Her* father. The reality was beginning to sink in. She knew who her father was. He had a name, an identity.

"Erich du Woernig," she said aloud, and warm chills rushed down her back.

Recalling her reason for being here, Ericha glanced down at herself and groaned aloud. Here she sat, waiting to meet the legendary Abbi du Woernig, wearing an old calico dress, with her hair down around her shoulders like an unruly school girl.

She wondered what this woman would be like. She had heard so much about her. Stefan positively adored her. She couldn't be too bad. He had spoken nothing but admiration for his grandmother. Good heavens, she thought again, it was *her* grandmother, as well. How would she take the news? Oh, how she wished to be anywhere but here!

The door opened, and Ericha stood, fidgeting nervously with the box in her hands. Her first impression of the duchess was surprise at her petiteness. Yet it didn't detract in the least from the regal aura about her as she entered and turned to close the door. Her presence gave Ericha the desire to stand straighter. Her example was inspiring.

There was an obvious length of silence as the two of them stood facing each other. Ericha's heart beat quickly as she first caught the resemblance to Stefan's mother, and then the resemblance to the face she saw in her own mirror each day. Ericha wondered by the way the grand duchess scrutinized her if she had recognized the resemblance. But then, Stefan and his mother had not.

"Theodor told me there was a young woman I must see," she said with a voice both gentle and strong.

"He was quite insistent," Ericha apologized, "I think that perhaps I should have—"

"Please, sit down." The duchess seated herself gracefully, making Ericha feel that her apologies were not necessary. She tried to imagine Stefan having the casual relationship with this woman that he'd spoken of.

"Thank you, Your Grace." She sat carefully.

"Now," she said, folding her hands in her lap, "what is it that I can do for you?"

"I won't take much of your time," Ericha said. "I know how busy you must be and—"

The duchess laughed naturally. "I'm too old to be busy. Please," she said with genuine kindness in her eyes, "go on."

"This box," Ericha said holding it up slightly, "is the reason Theodor wanted me to talk to you." The duchess looked puzzled, and Ericha went on quickly. "My mother gave it to me just before she died, but it had no key. I found the urge—and the means—to open it just today. And Theodor was certain that you would be interested in its contents."

Abbi felt an indiscernible emotion rise in her as she watched this young woman, who formlessly reminded her of something from her past. Her heart quickened slightly as she asked, "What is in there?"

Ericha opened the box hesitantly. "There is a letter to me from my mother. And this."

Ericha reverently held up the gold bracelet. The duchess said, "Bring it here so that I can see it."

Ericha stood and gave it to her, then seated herself again, watching expectantly as the woman bent close to examine it. The fragile hands turned it over carefully, and then they began to tremble. Ericha felt almost frightened when the duchess shot her head up with blatant emotion showing in her eyes.

"Where did your mother get this?" she asked with a combination of authority and emotion.

Ericha drew back her shoulders, but the words came weakly. "My father gave it to her."

There was silence as the duchess bowed her head again. Hoping to ease the tension, Ericha said, "I couldn't quite make out the inscription. It appears to be worn away, but—"

"It was my mother's," she said softly, her head still bowed. "Thank you for returning it. It bears great sentimental value to me. I had wondered what happened to it."

Ericha realized then that the duchess had no idea what this meant. Did she think the bracelet had been stolen or lost and her father had simply come upon it by chance?

"Excuse me, Your Grace," she said, and the duchess looked up. "Perhaps you would be interested to know what my mother wrote to me in this letter." Ericha saw her eyes narrow as she went on. "You see, I never knew my father. I had never known what happened to him . . . only that he never married my mother. This letter has answered the questions I've always wondered over. My father gave that bracelet to my mother." The duchess bowed her head again to look at the piece with nostalgia. "She said that it was proof of my heritage."

Abbi du Woernig shot her head up quickly, and her eyes filled with questions. "What did you say your name was?"

"I didn't."

"Tell me," she said with the authority of a duchess.

Ericha paused, fearing what her reaction might be. "Ericha," she stated. The old woman turned her head to the side but kept her eyes focused intently on Ericha.

"And your mother's name?" she asked, her voice trembling.

"Kathe Lokberg."

"Oh!" the duchess cried softly while one hand clutched the bracelet tighter and the other went to her heart. Ericha hardly knew what to do as the Grand Duchess of Horstberg became overwhelmed with tears.

"Come here, child," she said at last, wiping her face with a lace handkerchief. "Let me look at you."

Ericha moved to her side and felt tears come to her own eyes as the duchess ran her fingers over Ericha's face and a peaceful smile seeped into the midst of her tears.

"Ericha," Abbi whispered, and she put her arms around Ericha with a forceful, warm embrace. Ericha hesitated slightly, but her emotion urged her to return the embrace, and they cried on each other's shoulders.

When the tears were spent, the duchess pulled away, taking Ericha's hand into hers. "There is no doubt. I can see it now. There is so much of him in your face." She laughed softly. "My first thought when I saw you was that you reminded me a great deal of myself—many, many years ago. Yet Erich was so much like his father.

"Oh," she said again, "I can't believe it." She touched Ericha's hair gently with nostalgia in her eyes. "You are an answer to my prayers, Ericha my dear."

Ericha's eyes widened, and she felt the duchess squeeze her hand as if they'd known each other forever. She was surprised to feel the bracelet slide onto her arm.

"You should have this, my dear," Abbi said. "I gave it to Erich to give to the woman he loved. It rightfully belongs to you."

Ericha was too moved to speak. But she felt their bond deepen as the duchess spoke again. "It took time for me to deal with my husband's death, but I have come to terms with it. Yet with Erich it has been different. Would you think me strange if I said that something in my heart made me feel like a part of him had not left? It made it impossible for me to let go of him and accept his death. And now . . . after all these years, I can finally understand my feelings, and . . . Oh!" She laughed. "I can't believe it!"

Again the duchess embraced Ericha, and they both laughed. In that moment, Ericha blessed Theodor and his instincts. Beyond her relationship with Stefan, this was the first real contentment she had ever experienced.

The duchess went into the hall for a minute then returned. A short while later a maid brought a light lunch in on a tray.

"The men are all eating at some dreadful banquet," she said with a little chuckle. "This is much more cozy."

Ericha spent the better part of the afternoon with her grandmother as they each told in detail their side of the story.

"Your mother was a beautiful girl," Abbi mused. "When Erich brought her home I immediately knew it was right. Of course, he must have too. He asked her to marry him the day after they met.

"She was at the funeral," the duchess said, and her hand went to her heart, "but I never saw her again. When I had passed through my mourning enough to think about it, I realized she was gone, and I have worried and wondered ever since. I ordered Theodor to tell me what he knew, but he refused, saying only that Kathe had made him promise to keep her whereabouts to himself."

"Tell me about my father," Ericha said, and tears filled Abbi's eyes again.

"Oh, there was no one like Erich. In one minute he could be laughing like a child, and the next he bore his position with such dignity. He was nearly an exact image of his father—except for the hair." She laughed softly. "He got the red from me."

Abbi touched Ericha's hair again, and Ericha could feel a mutual sense of gratification in finding the final piece to an

elaborate puzzle. Abbi told Ericha stories of the family's history
from a perspective that Stefan could not have known. Ericha
thought many times that Mrs. Burger would have swooned to
know what was happening right now. When the chiming of a
clock made them realize the passing of time, Ericha insisted that
she must be getting home.

"Oh, but you must meet Stefan," the duchess said quickly.

Ericha knew her expression faltered, and her stomach felt
uneasy.

"He is my grandson," she explained. "The present duke. He
loved your father so dearly. I know he would be delighted to meet
you, and—"

"I know who he is," she said softly, "but I . . . well, I look so
unkempt today and . . . I would like to be at my best, and . . ."

"Of course you would," Abbi said with understanding, and
then a light came to her eyes. "You must come back this evening.
We are having a social here. Nothing very significant. But I'm
certain it will be enjoyable. You can meet everyone and—"

"Oh, Your Grace," Ericha said, "I—"

"You must call me Grandmama," she insisted, "as my other
grandchildren do."

"Yes . . . well, Grandmama," Ericha said with a little laugh,
still not believing this was real. "I just don't think that—"

"If you have nothing to wear, I'm certain we can arrange
to—"

"Oh no," she said, "it's not that. I just—"

Abbi took both Ericha's hands into hers and said with a soft
expression, "I don't want to put pressure on you, my dear. You
must decide. But I want you to be a part of the family, and I think
this would be a good place to start."

Ericha was so touched that all she could do was nod in agreement, and they embraced. Abbi walked her to the outside door.
They embraced once more, and then Ericha hurried across the
courtyard to her uncle's apartment. Theodor wasn't there, but she
found Karl stretched out on the sofa reading a newspaper.

"It's high time," Karl sat up and tossed the paper aside. "I've been waiting for—"

"You didn't have to wait for me," she apologized. "I'm certain that your father would have—"

"Do you actually think I would leave here without knowing what in heaven's name is going on?"

It took Ericha a moment to realize he wasn't angry; he was dying of curiosity. She suddenly felt a little weak from the impact of what had happened, and moved uneasily into a chair.

"Well?" he demanded when she said nothing. "Father said you were visiting with someone in the castle. I want to know *who*, and I want to know what it has to do with opening that box. And I want to know *now!*" Karl's mock authority diminished with a chuckle.

"I don't know where to start," she said.

"Well, did you find out who your father is?" he asked more gently.

"Yes."

"Well?" he asked in exasperation.

"You'd better sit down."

"I *am* sitting down."

"Just a figure of speech." She smiled wryly. "How old were you when my mother left here?"

"About seven, I think. I barely remember her."

"Then, obviously you don't remember that she was engaged to be married."

"Obviously," he said, attempting to be patient.

"My father died four days before they were to be wed. He was killed in the explosion at Castle Horstberg." Karl's eyes narrowed as she added, "Do you remember Stefan's uncle . . . Erich?"

"I remember an incident or two, when . . . Merciful heaven above!" he gasped, and his eyes grew wide. "Your father is . . . *Erich du Woernig?*" Ericha nodded. "And you were just now visiting with . . ."

"My grandmother—the grand duchess."

While Ericha had contemplated many possible reactions, she was not prepared for the way Karl rolled back onto the sofa, crippled with laughter. "I don't believe it," he managed to say three times while he laughed so hard tears leaked from the corners of his eyes.

"Is it really that funny?" she finally asked.

"It's the most incredible thing I've ever heard." He finally quieted and mopped his eyes. "I mean . . . you're a *princess*." He surprised her with a firm, warm embrace. "I should have known from the first moment I saw you. If anyone deserves to be a du Woernig, my sweet little cousin, it's you."

Ericha pulled back, tears in her eyes.

"I just wish I could be there to see the look on Stefan's face when he . . . What?" he stopped at Ericha's obvious distress.

"Oh, help! Look at the time. I'm supposed to be back here for a social in . . . Karl. You've got to get me home, quickly. And then I've got to find a way to tell Stefan before . . . Oh!"

Karl chuckled and ushered her out the door. He was obviously enjoying this very much.

All the way home, Ericha recounted the details of the situation to Karl and speculated aloud on the whirlwind of emotions she was caught in. She appreciated Karl's acceptance, as well as his offer to get a message to Stefan. He left immediately for the pub while Ericha went up to her room to get ready. Her nervous excitement was made worse by wondering how she would break this to Stefan. She couldn't possibly show up tonight without his knowing.

Ericha was more than grateful for the insight she'd had to purchase the elegant gown yesterday, and she wondered what Johanna would think when she saw it. The very idea of being at the same social event as the duchess increased her nerves dramatically.

After bathing, Ericha took great pains putting up her hair. She was nearly finished with it when Karl returned and came up to her room.

"Is he coming?" she asked impatiently.

"He wasn't there."

"He *what?*" she asked in a frenzy.

"But I sent a message to the castle. If he can possibly get away, he will."

"But I have to leave in less than an hour."

Karl shrugged his shoulders and laughed. "He'll have quite a surprise."

Ericha glared at him, feeling nothing short of panic. But all she could do was continue getting ready and hope that Stefan would show up before Karl took her back to the castle.

Abbi felt a little disoriented and stunned after Ericha left. *Erich's daughter.* She could hardly believe it, still. It was a *miracle*. A miracle edged with some harsh realities and difficult memories. But a miracle nevertheless. Abbi had spent twenty years wondering about Kathe. She regretted being so caught up in her own grief that she'd not made the effort to draw Kathe in and see that she was cared for. She had believed she'd understood Kathe's desire to leave Horstberg, but she'd never dreamed her reasons might have been due to a child.

Abbi found herself at the balcony overlooking the great hall, while memories and regrets filed through her mind, just as plainly as . . . Her breathing sharpened and her hands gripped the balcony rail so tightly that her knuckles turned white. She closed her eyes, and two decades slipped behind her. The memories became so real she could almost believe the great hall below her was filled with mourners. Noises of emotion and disbelief floated to her ears as the good citizens of Horstberg filed slowly past the two elaborate caskets.

Abbi peered through the black veil covering her face, not amazed in the least at the love and adoration exhibited toward her husband and son. She felt that the distance from where she stood was somehow symbolic of the part of their lives she had always shared with Horstberg. In their lives, just as now, when the light of day was gone, the doors of the great hall were closed, and they were hers alone.

The uniform Cameron wore enhanced the regal aura that he carried with him even in death, as did the crown that seemed so at home encircling his brow. She touched his face and hands, startled by their coldness. But still, she was grateful to be able to touch him. Erich's casket remained closed. The reasons she'd been given were vague, and she couldn't think about it too hard. Instead she concentrated on her husband, unable to grasp that her opportunity to see him this way would be brief. He lay in peaceful dignity, a stark contrast to her memories of his dying in her arms.

The explosion had prompted her to run blindly through long halls and down the stairs, instinctively knowing its origin. There were aspects of the following minutes that were a blur in her memory, while others were too clear to ever forget. She knew Erich was gone. She knew Han was badly burned. But she couldn't recall how she knew. She could only remember Cameron collapsing to his knees, pressing his hands to his chest as he coughed and gasped for breath. He had managed to say something to Han that she couldn't recall. And then he spoke to her, words that she would always hold dear. But in that moment they had brushed past her with the reality that his coughing was taking complete control. She assured him the doctor was coming. She tried to tell him everything would be all right. He took hold of her shoulders as if she could save him. His eyes met hers, filled with some kind of panic. She felt detached, as if she were watching him from a distance. Her own panic began to take hold when he began coughing up blood. She clutched him to her as if she could somehow give him her ability to breathe. And then the coughing ceased. She felt him go limp in her arms. She was vaguely aware of Han easing him away from her, laying him on the floor. Their eyes met, sharing a silent anguish. And then a memory catapulted into her mind with such force that she began to shake. Thirty-two years earlier, before she had even married Cameron, she had dreamt that very moment. But that didn't make it seem any more real. And that didn't make her willing to accept it.

"Cameron!" She took hold of his shoulders and shook him. He'd done this to her before. He'd pretended to be unconscious just to gauge her reaction. "Cameron, this is not funny! Wake up!" She screamed in his face. She slapped him. "Damn you, Cameron du Woernig! Don't you leave me like this." She resisted the hands attempting to pull her away, and the words being murmured close by, trying to convince her that Cameron was dead. "Cameron!" she cried and slapped him again. Then strong hands took her wrists, shaking her slightly. She looked again into Han's eyes, and the reality descended. Then Georg was beside her. She didn't know where he'd come from, but it seemed only right that he be the one to hold her when she crumbled. He'd crumbled in her arms when he'd lost his wife several years earlier. They had shared the best and worst of times. But never had she needed him as she did in that moment.

Abbi didn't recall exactly what made her anguish turn to hysterics. She only remembered Georg forcing her away, carrying her up the stairs against her will, while she screamed and protested. He took her to her bedroom—the room she had shared with Cameron for thirty-two years. She recalled him holding her shoulders, staring into her eyes, insisting that she breathe deeply. She reminded herself of who she was, and the position she had to uphold. Willfully, she eased away from him and turned to look in the mirror. Thirty-two years earlier, she had looked in this mirror to see a newly crowned duchess in her wedding gown. She'd been afraid and uncertain, but she'd reminded herself of her responsibility to behave like a duchess, and she'd made it through. Dozens of times through the years, she had looked at herself in the bedroom mirror and gathered the courage she needed to face another crisis. But today was different. She realized then that it was the reality of Cameron in her life that had given her the strength she needed. By habit, she straightened her hair and smoothed away her tears, but the hollow quality of her eyes reflected the emptiness of his absence in her life. Then her eyes shifted to her dress as she unconsciously pressed her hands over the cream-colored fabric. She met Georg's eyes in the reflection just as her fingers absorbed the blood-stains. *Cameron's blood.* His *life's* blood. She began to shake and turned toward him, crumbling all over again. Georg just held her, lost in silent shock, allowing her to vent her anguish.

Abbi refused to stay in the room she'd shared with Cameron. She slept elsewhere that night, if sporadically merging in and out of anguished consciousness could be called sleeping. And the following day she had her things moved to another room, and the duke's bedroom remained unused until Stefan came of age.

Abbi managed to pull herself together enough to make her public appearances for the sake of the mourners who passed through the great hall. She was grateful to know that the funeral arrangements were being taken care of by others. The entire episode went by in a blur, while she was either lost in a state of shock or consumed by unfathomable emotion.

Abbi couldn't recall how long Cameron and Erich had been gone when she first wondered about Kathe. She actually felt panicked as she searched out Theodor and demanded to know where Kathe was. But he refused to tell her anything beyond the fact that she'd left Horstberg and he'd promised to say nothing more. She felt a new level of grief in realizing that she had lost Kathe as well. They had grown close, and she longed to share this anguish with the woman who loved Erich.

Within a few months, Abbi found a certain peace in the deaths of her husband and son. In her heart she believed it had been their time to go, and she had evidence—intangible as it might be—that validated her feelings. But her peace didn't take away the emptiness. And she knew it never would. Still, peace could go a long way in coping with the reality that life had to go on. Her family needed her. And so did her country.

Abbi went often to the balcony overlooking the great hall. It became a place where she could ponder memories. Bitter as they might be, they were often a blessing, as opposed to the dull emptiness that often prevented her from feeling anything at all. She wasn't surprised to have Georg find her there. But it was the first time since their loss that she noticed stark anguish in his eyes. He'd been there to comfort her. He'd been her strength. But she'd selfishly overlooked the reality of what *Georg* had lost.

"Georg." She looked at him and gripped his hands tightly. "What is it?"

She wasn't surprised at the way he fell apart, expressing the full depth of emotion he'd fought to hold back all these months. But she had trouble believing her ears as he murmured, "I should have seen it coming, Abbi. I should have . . . thought it through . . . I should have kept Cameron . . . from going down there. I . . . I . . . should have insisted that someone else clean out that room and—"

"Georg," Abbi interrupted firmly. "No one could have prevented it."

"*I* could have!" he shouted. "Cameron always told me I had the brains. *I* was the one he expected to keep things straight, to stay level-headed, to . . . to . . ."

"Georg," Abbi interrupted him again. She took his face into her hands and looked directly into his eyes. "No one could have prevented it," she repeated, "because it was meant to be."

Georg gasped and held his breath. "What are you saying?" he asked.

Abbi couldn't hold back the tears as she spoke with conviction. "I dreamt Cameron's death before I ever married him. I felt the reality of that dream when he died. And I . . ."

"What, Abbi?" he urged, his eyes wide. She knew that he respected her gift of dreams. He'd been the one to first validate the gift for what it was.

"I dreamt that . . . the du Woernig name would end with Erich . . . and that . . . Han would wear the crown." Georg gasped again but said nothing. She went on to explain her feelings. "I *know* it was meant to be this way, Georg. Only a short while before it happened, Cameron looked into my eyes and as good as told me good-bye. I believe a part of him knew, even if it wasn't consciously. And I believe Erich knew, as well. We can't begin to understand the full perspective of what these struggles mean to our lives. But I know in my heart that Stefan was destined to rule this country. And his struggles, like those gone before him, will make him strong. And we need to be there for him, Georg. We must find peace and press forward, if only for his sake."

Abbi saw the relief wash over Georg's expression as she shared her deepest beliefs. And then he sank to his knees and cried, holding to her as if she had become the strength to him that he had always been to her.

Cameron had been gone three years when a measure of hope crept into her life. She gazed at the granite stone where her husband's name was carved, oblivious to the heightening wind. It didn't look as shiny as it once had. In the years he'd been gone, it had endured much harsh weather. Pulling her cloak more tightly around her, she wondered if this lonely ache would ever relent. Silent tears spilled over her face, and she turned it skyward, closing her eyes as if she could somehow reach Cameron with her mind. At fifty-three years of age, she felt as if her life was over. She was vaguely aware of the sporadic drops of rain mingling with her tears, but she came abruptly back to the present when a hand came over her arm.

"Why did I know you would be here?" Georg asked gently.

"I don't know, Georg." She looked again at the gravestone. "Why did you?"

"This is where you always are when I can't find you."

"Surely you have better things to do than keep track of my whereabouts."

"Nothing better, I can assure you." He put his arm around her, and she laid her head against his shoulder. Having him close seemed as natural as breathing. He'd always been there. One of her earliest memories was of Georg's comfort when she'd scraped her knee as a child. He'd been as close to Cameron as he was to her, and one way or another, he'd always been a part of her life.

"Come along," he said, urging her away. "It's raining. You'll catch your death."

"How do you do it, Georg?" she asked when they were nearly home. "Elsa's been gone so much longer than Cameron. How do you deal with the loneliness?"

"What makes you think I do?"

Abbi looked into his eyes and saw her own emotion mirrored there.

"A day doesn't pass when I don't miss her. I wonder continually what life might be like if she were still here."

Abbi sighed and fought back the tears. If Georg was still lonely, she wasn't certain she could survive another year alone. As they walked into the castle, Abbi took hold of his chin and looked into his eyes.

"Thank you, Georg." She pressed a quick, sisterly kiss to his lips, just as she'd been doing most of her life. But there was something subtly different in his eyes as she drew back. Briefly contemplating what it might be, she was unexpectedly seized by a wave of butterflies.

"For what?" he asked.

"For looking after me. I don't know what I'd do without you."

"It is I who could not survive without you, Abbi. You have kept me sane all these years."

She smiled subtly and saw him do the same.

"You'd best get into some dry clothes and warm up. I'd better see if Han needs anything. He's having another of those days."

Abbi nodded and watched Georg walk toward the office. She knew what *those days* were like, and it wasn't pleasant for any of them.

Following a hot bath and a good meal that had been brought to her room, Abbi curled up in a chair by the fire, contemplating her loneliness. A knock at the door startled her, but the intrusion was welcome. Even the servants going about their business was a pleasant distraction. "Come," she called, and heard the door open, then close. A moment later she looked up to see Georg.

"Are you all right?" he asked.

"I'm fine," she insisted. "Why?"

"You just . . . seemed so sad," he said.

"Is that unusual?"

Georg sighed. "There are times when you don't hide it so easily."

Abbi swallowed hard, amazed at how well Georg could read her. But unlike in the past, the reality made her uneasy. She watched him as he sat in the chair close by and stretched out his long legs. They had sat together this way countless times, so why did she feel so differently? And perhaps even more startling was the evidence in Georg's eyes that he was equally tense in a situation that had always been comfortable before.

Abbi was accustomed to facing things head on, and she hardly took a second thought before she said, "Georg, have we not been close for more than forty years?"

"Yes," he drawled, giving her a suspicious glance, as if he sensed some deeper motive to her question.

"Then why do I suddenly feel that . . . something has changed between us?"

He lifted his eyes slowly to meet hers. His expression made her heart pound. Then he shot to his feet. He took hold of the mantle and looked down into the flames as if they could somehow protect him from the question she'd just asked. Through minutes of silence, Abbi recognized what her heart had been trying to tell her. But something warm erupted inside her as she realized that Georg's eyes had given her the same message. She rose to her feet and stood beside him, touching his face with tentative fingers.

"Georg," she murmured, and he met her eyes with obvious reluctance, "tell me." Her voice lowered further. "Don't make me be the one to say it."

Georg closed his eyes tightly and held them shut, as if he were engaged in some silent battle inside his head. When he opened them, determination had replaced his hesitancy. He touched her face, just as she'd touched his. Her heart quickened as she realized his hand was trembling. He stepped toward her, moving his lips close to her ear, as if he intended to tell her a great secret.

"Abbi," he whispered, "do you believe in life after death? Do you believe Cameron lives on . . . somewhere . . . somehow?"

Abbi drew back enough to look into his eyes. "Yes, I do."

Georg took her face into his hands. "Do you think he'd understand, Abbi?" His voice became raspy. She didn't have to wonder what he meant as he pressed his lips to hers in a kiss that was anything but the easy friendship they had shared for so long. She took hold of him if only to keep from falling. "Do you think he'd understand," he repeated, brushing her face with his breath, "how I've come to believe you could ease this lonely ache for me, and that I could do the same for you? Do you think he'd know why I'm longing to hold you and . . ." He tightened his grasp. "And kiss you?" He pressed his mouth over hers again. And again. And again.

"Yes, Georg," she murmured breathlessly, "I believe he would understand." She kissed him in return, moving into his arms. "And Elsa would understand, too."

Abbi felt herself spinning into a state of longing that she hadn't experienced since she'd lost Cameron. She was beginning to lose herself in it when Georg stepped back abruptly, putting harsh distance between them.

"We must do this right, Abbi," he said willfully.

Abbi couldn't help the tinge of anger in her voice. "There is no way to do it right, Georg. It is against the law for me to marry again."

"Then we'll change the law," he growled.

"We can't, and you know it. That law is there to protect the people, as well as the family. What if some widowed duchess in the future married away her rights and properties to someone who held no respect for them? We have to abide by that law, Georg."

"Fine," he insisted, "then we will find a way to work around it. You can keep your name, your title, your property. I only want you, Abbi. It's as simple as that. And I'll do whatever I have to do in order to make it right before God."

Georg kissed her again and left her alone. But the following morning he made his proposal official, and Abbi accepted with perfect happiness. At lunch he announced that they were to be married. While the family gaped in silence, he explained the documents his solicitor had drawn up that morning, stating that Abbi retained all legal rights regarding her name, her property, her title and position. He made it clear that it would be better if no one but family and trusted friends knew about the arrangement, simply because most people wouldn't understand all of the implications without explanations that were not any business of the general populace. Abbi and Georg had been seen together in public for decades. No one would think a thing of what appeared to be their ongoing friendship. The servants would continue to believe the same. Georg had always been like a part of the family. They would keep their separate rooms, and whatever transpired between them privately was nobody's business. Of course, the family all agreed.

That evening they were married in the castle chapel, with only family present. And everything had been easier for Abbi since that day. She'd never stopped missing Cameron and Erich, but her only real heartache had come in the uneasiness she'd felt concerning Erich, as if something had been left undone. And now she understood.

Ericha. The thought of making this beautiful young woman a part of their lives soothed away an emptiness in Abbi that had hovered inside of her for twenty years. With fresh enthusiasm and vigor, she hurried from the balcony, wanting only to share the good news, while she counted the minutes until she would see her newly discovered granddaughter again.

Chapter Twelve
THE BINDING OF BLOOD

Stefan sat in his office with Rusty, trying to concentrate on his work and get caught up from yesterday. There were things that just couldn't wait, and he felt frustrated. Taking time out for that dreadful banquet hadn't helped any.

"Oh," Rusty said in a tone that let Stefan know he'd forgotten something, "here's a message for you. Came a while ago. Forgot about it."

"Thank you," Stefan said and leaned back to open it. He read: *It was your turn to buy! Now you owe me two. That mutual friend of ours needs to speak with you immediately! Right now! That means sooner than as soon as possible. K.L.*

Stefan sighed in frustration, wishing with everything he had that he could get away. But he just couldn't. He knew if it was a real emergency, Karl would see to it, so he tucked the note in his pocket and went on with his work.

A few minutes later, a light knock came at the door. Stefan sighed, wondering if they would ever get done. Rusty answered it, and Abbi rushed in full of excitement.

"Stefan," she said, taking him off guard by her tone. "You just won't believe it."

"What?" He chuckled and pulled off his glasses while Rusty gazed on in amazement.

"You know just the other day we were talking about how your uncle Erich was engaged to be married when he was killed?"

Stefan's expression sobered. He could feel it coming. "I remember," he said.

"Oh, Stefan." Abbi's eyes filled with moisture. "Erich has a daughter."

She was clearly disappointed by his lack of reaction.

"Rusty," he said, "would you give us a few minutes?"

"Yes, sir," Rusty muttered, hurrying toward the door.

When they were alone, Abbi said, "What's wrong, Stefan? I thought you would be thrilled to know that—"

"I *am* thrilled, Grandmama—more than you could possibly imagine. It's just that . . . I already knew."

Abbi sat down. Her eyes demanded an explanation. Stefan leaned toward her and put a hand on her arm.

"She has been living with Karl since her mother died. You know I spend a great deal of time at Karl's house. Ericha and I have become friends, Grandmama. But it was only a few days ago that I put the pieces together and realized that she had to be Erich's daughter."

"And you didn't tell me?" She seemed more surprised than angry.

Stefan's voice softened further. "It was evident to me that Ericha did not know who her father was. I figured if Kathe had reasons for keeping it from her, it was not for me to go against her wishes. It was not my place to tell her—or you."

"Did you know about the box?" Abbi asked.

"Yes," he drawled. "I assumed she would feel compelled to discover the truth eventually. And she did." He chuckled, feeling an immense relief. "But I had no idea the news would come to you so quickly."

"Theodor brought her to meet me. I think the poor thing was terrified."

Stefan leaned back in his chair and chuckled again.

"It's incredible," Abbi said, her eyes growing distant. "She just looks like a du Woernig."

"Yes, she does," Stefan agreed. "Which means I have been

blind. I kept thinking she looked familiar, but . . . well, I suppose I wasn't looking for it."

Abbi gave him a comically scolding glare. "I can't believe you've known her all this time and didn't tell me."

Stefan bowed his head slightly and smirked. "You must forgive me, Your Grace. I can assure you that if I come upon any more unclaimed relatives, I shall bring it to your attention immediately."

"I don't think that's possible."

"I certainly hope not," he said a little too seriously. Then he added, "Please don't tell her that I know. I'm not certain how she'd take it."

"I understand," she said. "Well," Abbi stood and sighed pleasantly, "I'll leave you to your work. We have a social to prepare for and—"

Stefan grimaced and caught himself form cursing. He'd forgotten the baron and his family were staying over, requiring him to endure another social. He'd been counting down the hours to be with Ericha, but he had to go to some stodgy dinner party with visiting dignitaries.

"This one won't be so bad," Abbi said, and he felt a little unnerved at the way she could read him so easily. "Ericha will be here." Stefan lifted his brow in surprise, and she added, "I insisted she come. We have so much catching up to do."

"Indeed," Stefan said. "Well, perhaps life in this wretched place has just taken a turn for the better."

"I believe it has," Abbi said and flitted from the room like a woman half her age.

Stefan turned to look out the window as Rusty came back in and situated himself. He thought of seeing Ericha tonight—here, amidst *his* life. Was that why she needed to see him so urgently . . . to warn him? A warm chuckle erupted as he suddenly felt like a giddy school boy.

"Something funny?" Rusty asked, startling him.

"No," Stefan said, still smiling. "Let's just get this work done. I've got a social to attend."

Ericha surveyed her reflection in the long mirror, trying to imagine herself with royal blood. In all her wondering who her father might have been, never would she have guessed him to be the Duke of Horstberg. It was astounding to look back over the simple life her mother had lived and realize that if Erich du Woernig had not been killed, Kathe would have been the duchess—and Ericha would have been a princess.

And Stefan? Stefan would have just been a prince. If Erich had lived, Stefan would be free of this responsibility that he considered a burden. Would he have married Johanna? It was astounding to see the differences in so many people's lives just because of a mistake in a chemistry room.

Ericha took a deep breath in an effort to ready herself for what she would face tonight. She knew now that she would have no opportunity to speak to Stefan, and she could only pray that she could soothe him later. She wasn't certain what to expect, but she feared it would be hard on him. She had visions of him walking away or ignoring her.

But as with everything, Ericha made up her mind to take it as it came. She concentrated more on soothing her nervous excitement while she waited for Karl to come and tell her the trap was ready. Glancing again at her reflection, she was pleased to see that the dress did well hiding the slight hint that she was with child. Recalling the warm acceptance Abbi du Woernig had given her, Ericha decided that she not only felt ready for this but excited as well. As the happenings of this day began to sink in, a part of her was beginning to accept it as being very natural. She truly did possess her father's blood. She felt at peace.

It was rare to see Karl when he was not either joking or distressed. But when he beheld Ericha in the stunning gown with her hair plaited and wound high on her head, his expression was near reverence. He bowed gallantly and held out his arm for her. "Your Highness?"

Ericha giggled and took his arm. Little was said as they drove across the valley, but Ericha could feel her excitement kindling as the castle drew closer. Karl escorted her to the door and left her with a good luck kiss, saying he would meet her back at his father's apartment.

A servant took Ericha's cloak, and she was directed down a long hallway, up some stairs, and down another hallway. The maid curtsied slightly as she opened the door and said, "Her Grace wished to see you alone first."

Ericha nodded and entered to realize she was in Abbi du Woernig's sitting room. The grand duchess turned in her chair and smiled warmly to see Ericha, holding out her hand as she stood.

"Ericha, my dear," she said as they moved closer and embraced carefully. "Oh, you look lovely!" she added, stepping back to eye her with approval.

"I fear I am quite nervous," Ericha admitted.

"Now, there's no need to be," she smiled, urging Ericha to a sofa where they sat close together. "This is actually a casual gathering. Oh, I mean everyone really dresses up. But when you get familiar with all of it, you realize it's just a lot of superficial nonsense to keep relations going well with our neighboring countries."

Ericha smiled, feeling as if her grandmother were fifty years younger. It was easy to see why she and Stefan were so close.

"There will be some diplomats here this evening from Kohenswald, but it's just a formality," Abbi continued, and Ericha appreciated her taking the opportunity to brief her on what to expect. It helped ease her nerves somewhat. If only Abbi could tell her how Stefan was going to react to her being here.

"Now," she went on, "I'll keep you by me all the time if you wish." Ericha nodded firmly. "We'll just mingle, and I'll introduce you around a little. There may be some dancing, but that just depends on if anyone feels like doing it."

Abbi looked briefly concerned, and Ericha said quickly, "Oh, my mother taught me to dance." Though it was true, she could hardly explain that Stefan had given her the confidence to feel that she could handle dancing in public.

Abbi offered a big smile and went on, telling her the titles and courtesies she should use, and then she explained the customary seating for dinner.

Ericha squeezed her grandmother's hand and said, "I truly appreciate your kindness and perception. It does make me feel more at ease."

"There was a time," she smiled, "when all of this was very foreign to me. I woke up one morning with no idea that I would be the duchess by afternoon."

Ericha looked at her with question, but Abbi added, "I'll tell you some other time. We'd best hurry along."

Ericha checked her appearance once more in Abbi's mirror. Together they went down the stairs, then back up a different staircase, and down another hall. They came at last to an enormous stairway that descended into a huge room where guests were already mingling. When Abbi hesitated, Ericha remained at her side, wondering over her purpose. Her heart quickened as everyone stood in respect for the dowager duchess, and she felt all eyes on her in apparent curiosity. But to her relief, Stefan was not there yet. Abbi graciously introduced her to many people, while Ericha kept watching unobtrusively for Stefan. Visions flashed through her mind of his silently leaving the room or disregarding her completely.

Ericha became more at ease as the majority of these people seemed pleasantly surprised to realize who she was. And everyone who had known Erich du Woernig had something sincere and good to say about him. This filled Ericha with added pride in the discovery of her heritage, and she was grateful for Abbi's attitude concerning her birth. Rather than treating it as something scandalous, it was regarded as the result of a tragic occurrence. For the first time in her life, she felt truly accepted.

When Stefan didn't show up after quite some time, Ericha became impatient to have it over with. "Where is the duke?" she whispered to her grandmother.

"Probably finishing up some business," she said easily. "He'll get here eventually."

"What about the duchess?" she added, hoping Abbi couldn't perceive the reasons for her nervousness.

"Oh, she never comes until he does. Etiquette, I suppose. She's no doubt found something to occupy her time while she waits. I believe she's quite used to waiting for him."

Ericha related to that, although thinking of Johanna left her a little queasy.

"Are you all right, dear?" Abbi asked.

Ericha tried to smile, wondering if her distress was so obvious. But she had to acknowledge the combined effect of her condition and all the excitement had left her a little lightheaded.

"Just a little . . . overwhelmed, I suppose. Is there some place that I could rest a few minutes?" she asked.

Abbi graciously escorted her back up the staircase they had entered on, then down a hallway to the first door on the left, where Ericha was told she could rest as long as she needed.

"Thank you," she said, and Abbi smiled warmly.

"You just come back down when you're feeling up to it. I'll be there."

Again Ericha thanked her and went through the door to see that she was in a relatively simple sitting room. It felt good to sit and ease the subtle ache in her back as well as the lightness in her head. But her mind was still in a frenzy over what this night might do to her relationship with Stefan.

Stefan was grateful as usual for Theodor, as he finally made it to his bedroom to change and found him waiting with everything ready.

"I understand you've been keeping secrets from us," Stefan said. He wasn't disappointed by his valet's stunned expression.

"News travels fast," Theodor finally said.

Stefan chuckled. "You've made my grandmother a very happy woman, my good man."

"And you?" Theodor asked cautiously. "How do you feel about having an illegitimate—"

"Ericha's a wonderful girl," he said firmly. "It's no fault of hers that her father couldn't make it to the wedding." He chuckled to ease the tension when Theodor looked as if he might cry. "I think it's wonderful. Next you'll be wanting a raise in wages, since we're practically related."

Theodor chuckled and seemed to relax. "I felt almost like a part of the family before Erich ever met Kathe. I've got no reason to complain."

Just as the robe was being clipped to Stefan's shoulders, a light knock at the door preceded Johanna coming huffily into the room. "Aren't you ready yet?" she insisted. "I've been waiting forever."

"I'll tell you what," Stefan replied, "you run the duchy, and I'll sit around and primp."

Johanna sighed in disgust as Stefan chuckled, and Theodor gave a wry smile that went unnoticed by the duchess.

"All finished," Theodor declared proudly. Stefan thanked him warmly and offered Johanna his arm.

"New gown," he commented as they moved down the hall together, and then his eye caught the intricate lace at the collar. Carefully he fingered it, and she looked surprised at his attention. "This is very nice," he stated, but Johanna missed his complacent smile.

"Oh," she said, "it's the most fashionable thing. Everyone is wearing it these days. It's all handmade. Probably imported from Paris."

Stefan lifted his brows in amusement. "Probably."

When Stefan and Johanna appeared at the head of the stairs, the music stopped and everyone stood as they were announced.

Abbi wished that Ericha was present when Stefan finally arrived. She always enjoyed watching him formally descend the staircase, since it brought back fond memories.

"At last," she said, embracing Stefan as he moved directly to her when the formalities were finished.

"You're looking lovely, Johanna," Abbi said sweetly and was answered with a curt nod.

Abbi waited until Johanna moved away to mingle with people she knew who were visiting from her home country before she pulled Stefan aside and whispered excitedly, "She's here."

"Who is?" he feigned innocence, amused by her excitement.

"Your new cousin."

"Ah, yes." He glanced around with a smirk. "Where is the long lost princess?"

Abbi laughed from his teasing. "She went upstairs to rest for a short while. I think all the excitement has been a bit too much for her."

"I can well imagine," Stefan agreed. "You didn't tell her that I—"

"I said nothing about you. Ah, there she is," Abbi finished when she saw Ericha standing at the top of the staircase.

Stefan was sipping champagne when his eyes moved the direction his grandmother was looking. He coughed when he tried to swallow, then absently set the glass down. His gaze froze on Ericha, and his heart quickened when their eyes met across the space.

"I thought you said that you already knew her," Abbi said in a voice that seemed distant. "You look as though you've never seen her before."

"She never looked like that," he murmured. Abbi squeezed his hand, and he wondered if she sensed his feelings. He hoped that she would credit his affection to Ericha being his cousin. Even from this distance, he could see the vulnerability in her eyes. He reminded himself that she was unaware of his knowledge.

Ericha gripped the head of the bannister tightly as she felt Stefan's gaze on her. She was grateful to see that only Abbi seemed to be paying any attention to what was happening. But everyone in the room turned their attention to the duke as he deftly swept across the room. The music stopped and the crowd hung on a silence broken only by the click of his heels as he ascended the steps with his robe flying behind him.

Ericha held her breath as he stopped on the step below her. Their eyes met as he took her hand into his. Unnerved by the expectancy, she curtsied low before him, saying quietly, "Your Grace."

Ericha stood straight again, wondering what he would do now. She would have given a great deal to know his thoughts. A hint of a smile touched his eyes just before he went to one knee and pressed her hand to his lips. Ericha sucked in her breath and held it as she absorbed the silent awe of those in the room. She suspected it was not common for the Duke of Horstberg to kneel before anyone. She reminded herself to breathe as he came to his feet, and with full acceptance, he took both hands into his and placed a kiss to her cheek. Ericha sighed in relief as their eyes met again briefly, and then he turned and stood beside her, pressing her hand over his arm.

"Ladies and gentlemen," he called in a voice of power and dignity while Ericha watched him, her heart overflowing with emotion. "Allow me to present my cousin: Princess Ericha of Horstberg."

The crowd applauded and the music resumed as Stefan descended the steps with Ericha on his arm. They were too mesmerized with each other to notice the tears of joy in Abbi's eyes, or the seething jealousy in Johanna's.

"You were right, Grandmama," Stefan said. "You can't look at her without seeing she is a du Woernig. As I said earlier, I have been blind." Ericha looked up at him in question. "I told Grandmama this afternoon that you and I were already acquainted. Of course, she knows how much time I spend at Karl's home." He smiled wryly, sensing her relief. "Imagine your being my cousin as well as his. Ironic, isn't it?"

"Yes," Ericha smiled, "it certainly is."

Abbi seemed pleased by the way they were taken with each other, but Ericha wondered what she would think if she knew the truth.

"If you will excuse us, Your Grace," Stefan said to Abbi while his eyes were on Ericha, "my cousin and I are going to dance."

"What a splendid idea," Abbi declared. "You be certain that she's cared for and has a good time, and I'll find Georg."

Stefan smiled and drew Ericha to the center of the floor. Carefully he placed his hand at her back and positioned her against him. The crowd moved away to allow them room.

Ericha found it easy to follow his lead as she recalled dancing around the common room of the cottage in the Black Forest. She expected him to say something about this, now that they were away from listening ears. But he only held her eyes intently, and she found it difficult to decipher what he was feeling.

Unnerved by the intensity in his expression, Ericha said at last, "I thought you'd be angry."

Stefan shook his head slightly. A mere hint of a smile touched his lips, but he said nothing. When the dance ended, Stefan kept Ericha's hand over his arm. He appeared casual and confident, as if this was the most natural thing in the world.

"Champagne?" he asked, handing her a glass from a servant's tray.

"Thank you," she smiled, but her hand trembled as she took it.

"There's no need to be nervous, little cousin," he said. "Everything's perfect."

Ericha glanced around and realized no one was paying any attention. Johanna had her hand over the arm of some man in a blue and gold uniform. He was obviously not from Horstberg. She was caught off guard to be approached by an older gentleman, also wearing a blue and gold uniform, adorned with regalia. On his arm was a woman half his age.

"So this lovely young lady is your long lost cousin," he said to Stefan, eying Ericha in a way that made her uncomfortable.

"She is, indeed," Stefan said with pride in his voice. "Ericha," he added, "this is the Baron Von Bindorf . . . of Kohenswald." His voice tightened subtly as he added, "My father-in-law."

Ericha perceived the hidden message and smiled graciously as the baron took her hand and kissed it.

"This is indeed a pleasure, then," Ericha said.

"The pleasure is all mine, young lady," the baron replied,

holding her hand a little too long, which seemed to perturb Stefan slightly.

Ericha waited for the baron to introduce the woman with him, but he ignored her as if she weren't present. Stefan and the baron exchanged small talk of a political nature that Ericha attempted to follow. When the baron walked away, Stefan leaned close to her ear and said, "You were marvelous."

She tried to act casual. "Who was the woman with him? Why didn't he introduce her or—"

"She is his mistress," Stefan interrupted. He glanced away casually as he said it, which reminded Ericha to do the same.

"But how can he—"

"Because his wife is dead," Stefan stated, but she could hear the subtle edge in his voice. "He chooses not to marry again so that he can change women with the seasons."

Ericha sensed the irony but said nothing. She was relieved to be approached by some official-looking men, who were introduced as the duke's advisors. They graciously introduced their wives and Ericha enjoyed visiting casually with them while Stefan talked and laughed with the men. He seemed much more relaxed than he had been with the baron, and occasionally she caught his eye. The butterflies she felt inside when he smiled reminded her this was not a dream.

The dinner hour was announced, and Ericha was seated at the duke's insistence, to be his companion. She was relieved to note that it seemed traditional for many couples to be separated and mixed in the seating arrangement for the purpose of more stimulating social interaction. This made her being seated with Stefan not appear at all suspicious. Ericha glanced around as the meal progressed, hardly believing the reality of this. It felt good to have a taste of what her life might have been like. But in her heart she longed more for marriage to Stefan than to be included in this social world. It was only her desire to be a part of his life that made this seem appealing. In truth it all seemed very showy and superficial.

She met Abbi's eyes across the table several times, seeing

there a glow of acceptance and understanding. Ericha felt certain that even the grand duchess considered all of this a formality and would have been content without it.

Ericha met Johanna's eyes only once, but she read hatred there. The intensity frightened Ericha enough that she dared not look at her again.

Stefan's public presence was like a soothing balm to Ericha. She sensed strongly the love in his eyes that she was praying inwardly no one else would notice. Glancing around the room, it seemed that no one was taking a second thought to Stefan's attention to her. But then she had to remind herself that his affection was on the basis of her being his cousin—not his mistress. She realized there were many people who remembered her father, and they had known how much Stefan had admired him. It seemed perfectly natural that he would hold some affection for Erich's daughter.

Ericha noticed then the elderly gentleman seated with Abbi, and realized they were holding hands affectionately. She leaned toward Stefan and asked, "Who is that with your grandmother?"

He smiled at her. "Our grandmother, you mean." Ericha smiled shyly, and he said, "That's Georg, of course." She looked puzzled, and he clarified. "I've told you about Georg. He's my grandfather."

"But I thought he died when—"

"Georg is my grandfather. But he didn't become Abbi's husband until I was ten." She still looked puzzled, and he laughed slightly. "Let me put it this way: Georg is my grandfather, not yours. He is my father's father. His wife, Elsa, died before I was born."

"I see," she said, finally enlightened. She watched Georg and Abbi with interest, finding their relationship intriguing.

When dinner ended, Abbi swept Ericha off to visit for a while, and she found the opportunity to get to know Georg a little. Despite his age, Ericha perceived the mind of a genius and a smile that was unforgettable. Though Ericha occasionally caught Stefan's eye across the room, she was pleased to see that they were managing to remain unobtrusive about their deeper feelings.

"I've been thinking," Abbi declared, "and I've discussed it with Georg. I believe that you should move into the castle and live with us."

Ericha was taken so off guard that all she could do was gape. She wondered if Abbi would be so gracious if she knew the truth. It certainly seemed inviting, but Ericha knew it was impossible under the circumstances.

"Oh, no. I don't think that I—"

"Nonsense," Abbi insisted. "You are of our blood. You should be here with us. We will be able to enrich each other's lives."

Ericha wondered how on earth she could convince the most powerful lady in Horstberg that this was not a good idea. But she approached it carefully and said, "I'm very happy living with Karl. I have a garden there that is dear to me and . . ."

Ericha turned when Abbi's attention moved to Stefan as he approached. He took Abbi's hand, and she said, "I was just telling Ericha that I think she should move in with us. What do you think of that, my dear?"

Stefan's brows went up in subtle amusement as he said directly, "It's a splendid idea, Your Grace. It would be so . . . convenient."

Ericha felt almost angry at his insinuation. But Georg said, "It would be good for all of us to have you here."

"I agree wholeheartedly, Georg," Stefan interjected.

"Thank you," Ericha said warmly. But she felt suddenly exhausted as the entire situation overwhelmed her, and she stood quickly. "But for now, I believe I should be going. It really is getting late."

"It has been quite a day for you," Abbi said, rising also.

Ericha nodded then graciously thanked Abbi for everything.

"You think about it," she added as Ericha pulled away from their now-common embrace. "It would be so wonderful for me."

Ericha nodded, then excused herself. Despite many offers to escort her to her uncle's apartment, she insisted on going alone and hurried away. She took a deep breath as she came into the courtyard, so overwhelmed by the evening that she could hardly decipher how to feel. Pulling her cloak tighter around her, she moved quickly to her uncle's apartment. Theodor was out, but Karl was waiting for her. They were quickly on their way home while she told him in detail the events of the evening.

"You won't, will you?" he asked as they came into the stable and he helped her down.

"Move into the castle, you mean? Of course not. How could I?"

Karl seemed relieved. Ericha thanked him with a familiar embrace and went upstairs. She had expected Stefan to come tonight, but she was surprised to enter her room and see right off a familiar regal robe lying across the bed.

Turning abruptly as she closed the door, Ericha found Stefan sitting low in a chair with his legs stretched out. It seemed strange to see him here in his uniform. He was gazing intently at the framed drawing that until now had remained facing the wall.

"He always looked like this," Stefan said as she removed her cloak. "I rarely saw Erich when he wasn't laughing. He used to take me riding. And he liked coursing, which my father didn't, so he'd always take me along. I recall spending hours in his laboratory, and he once declared that he had concocted the love potion that made my parents fall in love."

Carefully Stefan leaned forward, pressing his fingers over the glass that protected the drawing. "I envy his knowledge and wisdom. I admire his strength and courage." His hand moved over the signature near the bottom as he added, "This was done by my mother. She has a knack for capturing expression that I could never grasp."

Stefan sat up straight and turned toward Ericha at last, setting the picture aside. She caught a hint of mist glistening in his eyes. "If you'd have let me turn it around before now, I could have told you that your father was one of the finest men I have ever known."

Ericha took a sharp breath as the ironies descended fully.

"If I were to choose a woman to love," he added, coming to his feet, "it would be the woman who carries the blood and soul of the man whose legacy I bear."

Ericha was touched beyond words. She wanted to cry but felt numb. She took a step toward him and put her fingers to his face the way she'd wanted to do all evening. Not knowing what to say, she repeated her unanswered words from the dance floor. "I thought you would be angry."

"Angry?" He gave a baffled chuckle.

"Well," she justified, "I wanted to tell you myself and—"

"Yes," he apologized, touching her face with reverence, "I got your message, but there was little I could do about it at the time." He glanced down at her gown and added, "You did say you would surprise me when you wore it."

Ericha laughed softly, and their eyes met with deep emotion as he placed his hand to the back of her head. "Tonight was like a dream come true for me," he said gently. "Every time I walk down that staircase, I wish that it was you on my arm. Every time I dance on that floor, I wish it was with you. Every time I sit down to eat, I wish that you were seated with me."

"I love you, Ericha," he whispered and pulled her face close to kiss her. "I wanted to do that all evening." He smiled as he drew back.

Ericha saw his expression falter. "Is something wrong?" she asked.

Stefan motioned toward the chair. "Sit down, Ericha," he said. "There's something I need to tell you."

Ericha felt unnerved by his apparent severity. "Is it to do with my father?" she asked, wondering if there was something about this situation that disturbed him.

"Yes." He began to pace. "You see, a few days ago, I . . . well, it was after Mrs. Burger mentioned your mother's name. I'd never heard you use your mother's name, and . . . the next morning, you see . . . well, I was playing that song you taught me. And . . . it just came to me. I was a child when Erich died, but I seemed to recall a woman, and . . ."

Ericha's heart quickened as she began to see where he was headed.

"What I'm trying to say," his voice betrayed his determination to get this over with, "is that I already knew, Ericha." He stopped pacing and looked at her deeply. "When I put the pieces together, it was so obvious. Erich had been engaged to Kathe Lokberg when he was killed." He chuckled tensely and pushed a hand through his hair. "I couldn't believe it." He sighed. "I'm still not sure I can believe it. I mean . . . I *do* believe it. It's just that . . ."

Ericha saw his distress and couldn't help feeling concerned.

"Ericha." He went to his knees and took both her hands. "It's the most incredible thing." She saw moisture gather in his eyes and felt his grip tighten. "Don't you see, Ericha? It all makes so much sense. The way we were drawn to each other . . . our feelings. It's as if a part of us already knew."

Ericha watched in awe as tears spilled over Stefan's face. It was the first time she had really seen him cry. "He was my mentor, Ericha. My hero. There are days when the only thing that gets me through is knowing that Erich would want me to serve my country well." His voice quivered. "I loved your father, Ericha. I loved him."

Ericha was silently stunned as Stefan pressed his face into the folds of her gown and cried. His emotion gave her a glimpse of how deeply all of this had affected him, and her heart filled with compassion as she gently swept his hair back off his face and held him close.

When Stefan had been silent for several minutes, Ericha asked gently, "If you knew, why didn't you tell me?"

"I needed to respect your mother's wishes," he said. "It was obvious by the way she gave you that box that she wanted to be the one to tell you. I knew that when you were ready, you would open it."

Ericha let out a long, slow breath. "I'm not sure I am ready, even now."

Stefan looked up at her, his eyes sparkling. "My dear, sweet Ericha. You were *born* to this."

While Ericha was trying to absorb what that meant to her,

Stefan came to his feet and pulled her into his arms. "You are so beautiful," he whispered and pressed his mouth over hers, urging her closer.

Ericha felt the medals across his chest press almost painfully into her, and she pulled away, glancing toward them with dismay.

"Sorry." He chuckled. "They can be burdensome at times."

"Is this what Theodor does?" she asked, unfastening his coat.

"Occasionally." He smirked.

"Then I should very much like to have his job." Ericha helped him out of the coat and laid it carefully over the chair. She was amazed at how heavy it was.

"Now it's your turn," she said, indicating the hooks down the side of her gown.

Stefan smiled and did as she requested. "I must confess that doing just this crossed my mind a time or two this evening."

Ericha clicked her tongue scoldingly. "If Grandmama only knew."

Stefan laughed and pulled her into his arms as the gown slid to the floor. "Let's hope she never finds out," he said.

Ericha wondered how she was going to tell her newly found grandmother that she was going to have a baby. But for the moment she was only concerned with responding to Stefan's passion.

"Stefan," she said as he pulled her into the bed with him.

"Yes, my love." He pressed lingering kisses over her shoulder.

"You must promise me something."

"Anything," he whispered.

"Will you tell our children our story—the way you told me about your parents?"

Stefan looked pleasantly surprised by her request. He smiled down at her and replied easily, "It would be an honor, my love, to tell them that their mother is a princess."

Ericha smiled and Stefan kissed her again. There was nothing different in the way he loved her, nor in the way he held her when it was done. Stefan had always treated her like a princess.

"What are you thinking?" Stefan asked, noting Ericha's apparent distance.

"I'm just trying to convince myself that today was real. I've tried to imagine what the castle was like, what your life was like."

"And what did you enjoy most?" Stefan asked with a chuckle.

"Beyond being with you? That's easy. I loved being with my grandmother." She laughed. *"My* grandmother."

"Abbi is incredible," he said with admiration.

"And so is Georg," she added, and he made a noise of agreement. "Why do you call him Georg?" she asked. "If he is your grandfather, then—"

"I don't know. I just always have. I suppose it's difficult to be discussing political matters with someone and call them *Grandpapa*. He's more like a friend to me."

"It seems that your business is very closely integrated with your family."

"It is," he agreed.

"And that's why you could never turn your back on it," she said, and only silence followed.

"Ericha," he said softly in the darkness, "I want you to live at the castle."

Ericha startled him when she sat up abruptly.

"What's the matter?" he asked.

"I can't."

"Why not? It would be ideal."

"Ideal for what? For someone to figure out that you spend more time in my bedroom than you do your own?"

"We would be discreet," he argued, "and careful—just as we have been."

"It's not the same, Stefan. When you're here, you are in a separate world and you can leave it all behind. If I were living there, our worlds would come too close together. It would cause nothing but trouble."

"Ericha," he said, trying to be patient, "it's what Grandmama wants. She'd be so pleased and—"

"Pleased?" she retorted. "When she finds out that I'm going to have a baby? I can't do it, Stefan. I will not bring that kind of stigma into her life."

Ericha couldn't tell if he was hurt or angry as he moved out of the bed and pulled on his breeches. "I hate it," he said, standing at the window, "when you have to refer to carrying my child as a stigma."

"I'm sorry," she said gently.

"Why should you be sorry?" he asked bitterly. "It is I who am sorry. Sometimes I really believe that you deserved better than this."

"Stefan!" she shouted, but he made no response. "Look at me!" she demanded, and he turned abruptly. "How dare you make love to me, then turn around and say that there is something better than this!"

"Forgive me," he whispered. "I love you, Ericha." He moved back to the bed. "I want you to be with me. I want you to live under the same roof, eat meals at the same table. We could see each other so much more."

"You're forgetting something, Stefan. She would always be there. Johanna sleeps under that same roof and eats at that same table. Do you think you can pretend she doesn't exist? Do you think she wouldn't notice?"

"I don't give a damn what she thinks!"

"You *have* to care what she thinks! In spite of everything that's happened, *she is still your wife!*"

At Stefan's obvious distress, Ericha softened her voice. "Did you bother to take notice of the way she was looking at me tonight? Already I believe that she would be willing to kill me if given half a chance. I want to stay here, Stefan, where I can be in control of my life—and my child's. I will not have this child subjected to her. It will already have enough to rise above."

Stefan sighed and attempted to suppress his disappointment. "You're right," he said. "It makes me nearly die inside when I think about the circumstances, but I know you're right. I can't have my cake and eat it too."

"Please, Stefan," she said gently, "don't trouble yourself over what could have been. Just be glad for what we have."

"You always keep me straight, Ericha. How dear you are to

me!" He was thoughtfully silent, then went on, "Do you know what really should have been? You should have been born at Castle Horstberg, and we would have fallen in love over the dinner table."

Ericha laughed and pulled herself close to him. "But Stefan, that doesn't make an interesting fairy tale."

"No," he sighed, "but it has a happily ever after."

Ericha kissed him and added gently, "Happily ever after is only what we make it."

Stefan left while it was still dark, not wanting to be conspicuous in his uniform. But it was long after that when Ericha finally slept. Her mind was in such a whirlwind from the happenings of the day that only exhaustion finally allowed her to rest.

She woke to an irritating knock at the door. She called out an indiscernible grunt, and Erma scurried into the room in a frenzy.

"Oh," she said, "get out of bed. You can't believe it! I can't believe it! I heard the carriage pull up and looked outside and . . . Oh, my. It was the ducal coach! And out stepped the grand duchess herself and—"

"She's here?" Ericha jumped out of bed.

"She wants to see *you*," Erma said in wonderment.

"Oh, my," Ericha said, rummaging through the closet. "Tell her I'll be right down. And be polite, and—"

"Oh, just hurry up!" Erma exclaimed and bustled out of the room.

Ericha entered the parlor, and Abbi stood to greet her.

"I'm sorry to keep you waiting," Ericha said quickly.

"Oh, that's fine," Abbi said as if it were nothing. "I do hope I didn't call at too inconvenient a time."

"Never." Ericha laughed, motioning for her to be seated. "You are more than welcome to call any time."

"That applies for you, as well," Abbi smiled.

"Would you like some coffee or—"

"No, no. Thank you anyway. I just came by to see if you enjoyed yourself last evening."

"Oh, yes." Ericha smiled. "I did. Thank you again for everything."

"It was my pleasure, dear. Stefan seems quite taken with you. But then, he did adore your father. I'm certain it means a great deal to him to have you with us—just as it does to me."

Ericha glanced down uneasily, but the duchess went on. "Georg suggested something to me last night, and I quite like the idea. What would you think of legally adding du Woernig to your name, my dear? It would entitle you to all that your father would have wanted for you. Legally, it would be something akin to adopting you into the family."

Ericha had to force herself to breathe. "Well, I . . ."

"Are you all right, dear?" Abbi asked.

Ericha chuckled tensely. "It's just so . . . overwhelming. But . . . well, I can't think of any reason not to."

"Good." Abbi smiled. "That's settled. We'll take care of it soon." She took a deep breath and went on. "And the more I think about it, the more I would like you to come and live with us, Ericha. Somehow it would help make up for all we have lost, I believe."

Ericha gathered her courage and told herself to face this head on. "Grandmama," she said gently, and Abbi's brow furrowed in concern. "There are reasons why I cannot leave here. You must understand that I don't feel it is right. It's not that I don't want to be with you, or that I don't appreciate all you're doing for me. There are . . . well . . . circumstances that would make my taking your offer very difficult."

Abbi looked concerned as her gaze intensified. Following a long silence, she said, "Perhaps I should apologize. I can tend to let my position make me a little pushy. Perhaps I'm getting senile." She laughed slightly. "I must remember that you have been managing fine until yesterday without me. I must let you live your life."

"Please understand," Ericha implored, "I want to be a part of your life. I want for us to be close. Already you have given me so much acceptance. The last thing I would want is to bring any kind of difficulty into your life. I simply feel that it would be best if I stay here. It's not so very far. We can see each other often—every day if we like."

Abbi did well in swallowing her disappointment. And in a way that Ericha was discovering came naturally, she turned her emotion to concern. "You're not in trouble, are you, my dear? Is there anything you need?"

Ericha was amazed by her perception and glanced down, wringing her hands slightly. "Some might say I am in trouble. But it is nothing that concerns me."

Abbi's gaze told Ericha that she would not insist on being told the circumstances, but it was evident she wanted to know. Not out of curiosity as much as concern. Ericha knew that sooner or later her figure would betray her secret. She decided it would be best to just let her know now and take the consequences rather than dread them.

"You see," Ericha began carefully, "when I first came to Horstberg I met a man. I'm afraid I fell in love with him before I realized that he was married and . . . Well, not that it would have made any difference. I believe I would have loved him no matter what."

Abbi's expression showed no change at all, so Ericha continued. "His marriage is not happy, but I know he would leave her if it was at all possible. The situation is unique for reasons I cannot discuss. Too many lives would be affected if he were to divorce." Ericha took a deep breath. "Grandmama, I must apologize if I disappoint you with my character, but you have a right to know. I am seeing him. We have committed ourselves to each other for the remainder of our lives. He loves me. And he's good to me. And . . . I am going to have his baby."

Still Abbi's expression didn't change, and Ericha couldn't tell if she was going to cry or get up and leave. After several moments of silence, the Grand Duchess of Horstberg leaned back on the sofa and took a deep breath.

"I would like to tell you something," she said, and Ericha expected a lecture. But Abbi's voice was soft and wistful as she went on, "I wasn't much younger than you when fate crossed my path with a man whose life was nothing but a complicated web of problems. But I loved him, and I gave him everything I had with nothing but faith and trust to tell me that I would have him longer than a few stolen moments. I learned much from that experience, but one of the most important things it taught me is this: there is no stronger character than the one who will follow their heart despite the obstacles."

Ericha felt tears brim in her eyes. She would not have blamed Abbi for denouncing her. But her eyes glowed with love and acceptance as she asked, "Ericha, have you ever felt a fire burn in your heart?" Ericha's tears spilled as she nodded with surety. Abbi's eyes clouded as well when she pulled Ericha into her arms and said, "That is because you are a du Woernig. And you can never deny the fire in your heart."

The grand duchess left hours later after sharing brunch and a fresh rambling of stories, with every bit the acceptance for Ericha that she had arrived with. And Ericha was amazed that any woman could be so good.

Ericha could hear shouting in the parlor and couldn't resist investigating. Nearing the bottom of the stairs, she picked up on Karl's voice. But she couldn't make out what he was saying until he opened the door with a boisterous, "It won't happen again because you're fired."

Karl stormed down the hall without noticing Ericha, and she slipped quietly into the parlor to find Erma in tears.

"What's wrong?" Ericha asked gently.

"Oh, go away!" she insisted.

Ericha was tempted to just leave her alone, but she felt compelled to persist. "Please tell me what happened."

"I wasn't meanin' to be rude. I was just so flustered that I . . . well, I don't know what came over me. But Mr. Lokberg found out about it and he . . . he fired me. I . . . I told him it wouldn't happen again, but I . . . I . . . Oh! What am I goin' to do? If I lose this job I'll have nothin' to give my father and . . ." She trailed off with her tears, and Ericha put a gentle hand on her shoulder.

"Now, why don't you settle down and tell me what you did that you didn't mean to do."

"When Her Grace came this morning, I was just so flustered that I did nothin' right."

"I'm sure it can't be as serious as all that," Ericha said.

"Well, how was I supposed to know you was her granddaughter? I'm no mind reader! All I did was ask her why on earth she wanted to see you. As soon as she explained, I apologized, but . . . oh what's the point? I might as well start lookin' for a position elsewhere."

"Let me see what I can do," Ericha said.

"Like what?" she asked cynically.

"I'll talk to Karl. Maybe I can get him to give you another chance."

"Do you think he would?" she asked hopefully.

"Well, let's try it."

Erma followed Ericha out to the workshop.

"Karl," Ericha said as soon as they entered, "don't you think you're being perhaps a bit hasty?"

He glared at Erma and retorted, "No, I don't."

"Really Karl, it's not so—"

"The Grand Duchess of Horstberg calls, and she treats her like the woman next door. She's got no manners. I've had it!"

"And how did you find out?" Ericha asked.

"Stefan told me at the pub. His grandmother went right home and told him she'd never seen a maid quite like this one. It's embarrassing!"

"I would dare say that Her Grace repeated it more from amusement than anything else. You've told me yourself how entertaining Erma can be." The subject's eyes widened at the mention of this. "Even Stefan finds her amusing. Now, be honest. Did Stefan really act disgusted, or was he amused?"

Karl sighed. "He thought it was hysterical."

Ericha gave a slight laugh. "And you know how much better Erma has been doing with the housework," she went on. "Surely you've noticed how much tidier things are these days." Erma looked dubiously toward Ericha. They both knew all of it was Ericha's doing. "Come now, Karl, at least give her another chance. Where are you going to find another maid this close to Christmas? No one can cook Christmas dinner like Erma."

"Oh, very well," Karl conceded, and then he pointed a finger at Erma. "But you'd best mind your manners, and when Her Grace calls again, you show your best behavior no matter what."

"I will, Mr. Lokberg," she said eagerly.

"Thank you, Karl." Ericha kissed him on the cheek, then left the shop with Erma close behind.

"Why did you tell him that?" Erma insisted.

"It seemed like the right thing to do."

"But you're the one that's been doin' all the cleanin'. You didn't have to—"

"Let's just say I owe you a favor."

"You do?"

"Of course. I trust you've been discreet about the things you know about me."

"I've not told a soul about His Grace's visits, if that's what you mean."

"That's what I mean."

"Thank you, Miss Ericha," Erma said as they entered the side door. "Is it true that you're Her Grace's granddaughter?"

"Yes, it is." Ericha smiled. "But I didn't know myself until yesterday."

"And you've been seeing His Grace all this time?"

"Ironic, isn't it."

"He's a very nice man," Erma added. "And from what I've heard about his wife, I can't blame him a bit for . . . well, you know."

"What *have* you heard about his wife?" Ericha asked.

"It's practically common knowledge," Erma stated. "There's more than one man who's been braggin' at the pubs that he and the duchess have . . . well, you know."

"I see," Ericha said. It wasn't surprising, but still it was pathetic. And for what little it was worth, if Ericha had ever felt any twinges of guilt for what she was doing, the reminder that Johanna was doing worse put her concerns to rest. Ericha felt good about the confidence she'd just gained in Erma and figured now was as good a time as any to let her know what she would find out eventually anyway.

"Do you like babies, Erma?"

"I helped my sister a lot when her baby came."

"Good, perhaps you will be able to help me, as well. I'll be having a baby next summer."

"Oh, my!" Erma gasped.

"Now as far as you know, if anyone asks, you have no idea who the baby's father is. All right?"

Erma nodded stoutly. "I wouldn't do anything to cause trouble for you or His Grace. He is such a nice man."

"Yes," Ericha said, "he is. Remember now, you mustn't tell a soul."

"Oh, I won't," she said, holding her hand up in a pledge. Ericha felt confident that her secret was in good hands, and as she turned her mind to the reality that Christmas was approaching, she wondered what might be appropriate gifts for her new family members. The thought warmed her from the inside out.

On Christmas Eve, Stefan came late in the evening, his arms full of packages for Ericha that he insisted she open immediately. There were pretty things to wear and flower-shaped soaps imported from England. There was a box of fine, chocolate candy, wrapped in gold foil, and a pewter model of Castle Horstberg that he declared was to go on the bureau near her wooden box.

Erma warmed up dinner so that he and Ericha could eat together, and then they sat near the Christmas tree, talking far into the night. Stefan carried Ericha up to bed and made love to her by candlelight, and he left before dawn, while Ericha lay pondering how good her life had come to be. She was barely out of bed when Erma came to her door.

"What is it?" she asked, sliding into a wrapper.

"Message just came for you," she said.

Ericha opened it while Erma hesitated curiously.

"Now's your chance." Ericha smiled wryly. "The grand duchess is coming by later this morning to visit. Georg Heinrich is coming with her."

"*The* Georg Heinrich?" Erma gasped.

"I would assume." Ericha laughed, and Erma bustled off nervously.

After the usual exchange of gifts, Abbi announced, "Georg and I are off now to do some visiting. Would you like to come along?"

"Where are you going?" Johanna asked.

"We're first stopping at Ericha's to take her a gift, and then we're going to Hannah's for dinner. Hannah said that we were all welcome."

"I think I'll pass," Johanna said, giving a phony yawn. "I didn't sleep well last night and—"

"I'll come along," Stefan said. "It sounds delightful. I wouldn't want to miss Christmas dinner with my sister."

"Good." Abbi smiled, and he followed her out of the room.

"Have a merry Christmas," Stefan said to Johanna as he paused to close the door. She looked at him dubiously, and he grinned. "I will."

Ericha heard the bell at the front door and checked her appearance in the mirror. She was grateful for the insight she'd had to get a new wardrobe as she hurried down the stairs. She smiled to see Erma curtsying graciously and giving the proper greetings as

Abbi entered the hall with Georg close behind, carrying a very big package.

"Hello, Ericha," Abbi said, embracing her warmly. "Are you having a good Christmas so far?"

"Oh, yes," she replied. Karl took the package from Georg, and Ericha embraced him as well. "How are you this morning, Georg?"

"Couldn't be better." He grinned.

"What about me?" Stefan asked, and Ericha turned in surprise to see him just as he came through the door. "Don't I get a hug from my little cousin?"

"Merry Christmas, Stefan." She smiled, putting her arms around his neck with a sisterly embrace as Karl led Abbi and Georg to the parlor where Theodor rose to greet them.

"Merry Christmas to you, Princess," Stefan said with mischief in his eyes. He gave her bottom a pat when no one was looking. Ericha glared at him, but he innocently stuffed his hands into his pockets.

"New dress?" he whispered, and she nodded. "I like it. You look adorable as always."

"Thank you," she replied with a smile while he eyed her seductively. "Now, mind your manners."

"Yes, Your Highness." He followed her into the parlor to sit down while Karl retrieved the appropriate gifts from beneath the tree.

"This one is for you, Your Grace," he said, handing one to Abbi. "And this is for you, sir," he added, giving a package to Georg.

"Me?" Georg asked in astonishment, looking dubiously at Karl, then Ericha. He tried to protest but couldn't deny that he loved the little wood carving Karl had made. Abbi loved the lace collar Ericha had tatted for her, and she insisted that Ericha not wait another minute to open her gift.

"Your grandmother painted that," Georg said proudly as Ericha pulled away the paper. Stefan watched her closely as she absorbed it, and he felt gratified to see the emotion brimming in her eyes.

"It's beautiful," Ericha whispered.

"The subject was Stefan's idea," Abbi declared. "He came home one day and said that he'd noticed some roses still in bloom with snow over them. He asked me if I would paint it, so I did."

Ericha met Stefan's eyes, hoping he perceived what this meant to her.

"I finished it up just a couple of days ago," Abbi went on, "and I asked him where I should hang it, and he said: 'Why don't you give it to Ericha for Christmas?'"

"That Stefan's a smart one," Karl said wryly, and Stefan gave him a comical glare of disgust.

"I love it, Grandmama," Ericha said, reaching over to kiss her cheek. "Thank you."

Erma came in the room with hot Christmas punch and apple cakes. Ericha gave Karl a knowing smile when she served graciously and did everything just perfectly.

"What a charming maid you have," Abbi said to Karl when Erma had left the room. "She's quite entertaining."

Ericha couldn't suppress a giggle.

"I suppose we should get to Hannah's soon," Georg said.

"It is getting to be that time, isn't it," Abbi added. "Do you have plans, Ericha?"

"Uh . . ." she began, but Georg interrupted.

"What a splendid idea. Ericha must come with us. Hannah would be delighted."

"I couldn't agree more," Stefan said.

"No, she doesn't have any plans," Karl answered for Ericha. "It would do her good to get out."

Karl got Ericha's cloak, and she was ushered out to the carriage on Georg's arm.

"You'd better drop by later," Karl whispered to Stefan. "Ericha and I have something for you. She didn't give it to you last night because I didn't finish it until this morning."

Stefan lifted his brows curiously, and then Abbi called, "Come along, Stefan." And he hurried out to the carriage. He sat beside

Ericha and gave her a quick smile, wishing it could be this way all the time.

"Hannah lives on the estate where I grew up," Abbi told Ericha.

"What about me?" Georg asked.

"Yes, of course." Abbi laughed. "Georg grew up there too."

"I worked for the Albrechts until Cameron coerced me into doing other odd things," he said.

They were greeted at the door by Stefan's elder sister, who was almost as tall as Stefan, with hair more blonde than red. She was full of welcome smiles as she embraced everyone in turn. Then she came face to face with Ericha and paused briefly.

"Oh, Grandmama," Hannah said quietly, "she *does* look like Uncle Erich. What a joy it is to have you with us, Ericha. Do come in."

Hannah took Ericha's hand as if they'd known each other forever. Stefan followed close by her side, and Ericha thought she had never been happier.

Ericha was exhausted by the time she returned home, but she didn't recall a Christmas day that had ever been so full of life and fun. Hannah's children were a delight, and with Stefan present and Johanna absent, Ericha could almost pretend that he was all hers.

With the time it took Stefan to return, Ericha knew he must have gotten out of the carriage at Castle Horstberg and left again within minutes.

"I'm glad you came back," she said as he sat on the edge of the bed. "You have to open this." She plopped a big box onto his lap. "It's from Karl and me, though Karl deserves most of the credit. It was only my idea. But it hardly makes up for everything you gave me last night."

"Everything I gave you last night hardly makes up for what you give me every day of your life," Stefan said, pulling away the bow and the shiny red paper.

"Well, as I said, this is for you, but there is a catch. You already have one of these, so this one is staying here—even though it's yours."

"I see." Stefan chuckled dubiously. He peered into the box to see several things wrapped in white tissue. He took one out and unwrapped it, seeming puzzled. "It's a horse," he stated, and then it struck him and he laughed. "It's a chess set." He looked astonished as he unwrapped a queen, then a knight. "Karl actually carved all of these pieces—for me?"

"It took a lot of bribery," Ericha smiled.

"I'm sure it did. I always told him I envied his father's set, but I never dreamed . . ." He laughed. "I love it."

"Wait until you see the board. It's at the bottom."

Stefan continued unwrapping pieces, setting them carefully on the bedside table. "Your father taught me how to play chess," Stefan said. "He loved it." An idea struck him, and he looked up at Ericha. "Karl doesn't play chess. If I'm leaving it here, then . . ." Ericha grinned. Stefan leaned over and kissed her. "I'd forgotten," he said. "Theodor taught you how to play, didn't he?"

"That's right." He kissed her again, and she added, "Get it unwrapped, Your Grace, and we'll see if you're any good at this."

Stefan set the box on the floor and pushed Ericha back on the bed with a warm kiss. "Later," he said and kissed her again.

A few days after Christmas, Abbi invited Ericha to spend the afternoon with her at the castle. Wearing the green riding habit Stefan had bought for her, Ericha rode Pegasus to Castle Horstberg. A bright sun made the day unusually warm for December.

A maid in the front hall took her cloak, and another maid escorted Ericha to Abbi's sitting room. They exchanged the usual small talk, and then Abbi said she wanted to show her something. They were descending the stairs when Ericha heard male voices. As they moved around the curve, she hesitated to see Stefan coming briskly down the hall, with six or seven other men, all looking very business-like in fine suits.

Stefan stopped abruptly when he saw her. "Move along," he said to the others. "I'll be there shortly."

"Hello, Stefan," Abbi said. "Is everything going well?"

"Business as usual." He smiled. "And how are you ladies this afternoon?"

"Very well, thank you," Ericha said.

While he exchanged small talk with Abbi, Ericha took notice of his apparel. It was somewhere between the common clothing she usually saw him in and the regalia he wore as the duke. The style of boots, breeches, and shirt were familiar. But these were much finer and well-pressed. He also wore a fitted waistcoat, made of an elegant tapestry-like fabric. He looked so handsome her stomach quivered. Realizing the variations in his wardrobe, she wondered how many times a day he changed his clothes. It was no wonder he kept Theodor so busy.

"Well, I should be off," Stefan said reluctantly. "I'll see you later."

I certainly hope so, Ericha thought, watching him walk away.

"He is handsome," Abbi commented, and Ericha cleared her throat gently, wondering if her grandmother had perceived her overt interest.

They went together to a massive library with more books than Ericha had ever imagined existed. But Abbi drew her attention to a section filled with family journals and personal histories. Time passed quickly as they sat near a huge fireplace and read pieces together, discussing their significance to the present. Ericha removed her hat, jacket, and boots, feeling completely comfortable with her grandmother. Together they shared a few tears as they read some segments from Erich's journals concerning his meeting Kathe and the relationship they had shared.

When a clock chimed to tell them it was four-thirty, Abbi came to her feet. "Come along, dear. We have an appointment."

"We do?" Ericha asked, pulling on her boots.

"Leave those," Abbi said, indicating the hat and jacket. "We'll come back here."

Ericha followed Abbi down a section of hallway she'd never seen before. They came to a door where two officers of the Guard stood at attention.

"He's waiting for you, Your Grace," one of them said congenially, and Abbi opened the door.

Ericha caught herself from gasping aloud as she realized they were in the ducal office. It was as large and elaborate as every other room in the castle. But it had a business-like feel that suited Stefan as he stood from behind a huge desk, an enormous window at his back. She felt a giddy lurch inside to see him still wearing that waistcoat. He was also wearing glasses, which she'd never seen before. She was charmed by the way they somehow added to his dignity, and she wondered briefly if the weakness was hereditary. Then her eye was drawn to the two other men seated at one side of the desk. They had not been with those she'd seen earlier in the hall. They rose when Stefan did and greeted Abbi, who graciously introduced Ericha.

"Ericha," Stefan said as they were all seated, "these are my solicitors. Her Grace has asked them to take care of a small matter on your behalf."

Together the solicitors explained to Ericha in excessive detail that she was being officially taken in by the du Woernig family, with Stefan and Abbi acting as her official trustees. While they could not literally correct the problem of illegitimacy, they would consider it something like an adoption. The name du Woernig would be added to her name, rather than replacing her mother's surname. She would automatically begin receiving the standard monthly allowance granted to each family member of single status. Ericha looked at the amount on the paper and gasped aloud. Then she glanced up, embarrassed. Stefan was obviously trying not to smirk. Abbi was positively beaming. She wanted to tell them she didn't need the money, and didn't want to accept it. But the solicitor's oration continued without a pause until he pushed a pen into her hand and showed her where to sign.

Ericha signed the first two papers as Ericha Lokberg. And the next three she signed, according to the solicitor's instructions, as Ericha Lokberg-du Woernig. Stefan and Abbi signed each document as well. She met Stefan's eyes briefly, and the irony struck her deeply.

When the solicitors left, Ericha was the first to speak up. "There is no reason on earth why you should be giving me money. The name I am honored to have, but I did not come into this family for the sake of getting handouts."

Ericha wondered if she had spoken too harshly when Abbi gaped in apparent disbelief. And she couldn't decide if Stefan looked amused or embarrassed.

"It's all right, Grandmama," Stefan said. "I believe she has more than a little of her father in her."

"Proud and stubborn, you mean?" Abbi said.

"That's what I mean," Stefan answered. Ericha glared at him.

"Ericha," Stefan said, removing his glasses, "this ensures that you will never go without again."

"I don't go without. My needs are more than met." Ericha wished she could add that he was personally responsible for meeting many of her needs.

"I know you have a fair income from your lace, and Karl takes very good care of you," Stefan said as he came around the desk. He sat on its edge and folded his arms over his chest. "But that doesn't make up for everything you went without while you were growing up, and—"

"What do you mean by that?" Abbi interrupted firmly.

Ericha nearly wanted to slap Stefan when her grandmother turned to her with eyes that demanded an explanation.

"Go on, tell her," Stefan said. "She has a right to know."

"There is nothing wrong with the way I grew up," Ericha defended, more to Stefan. "My needs were met."

"By the skin of your teeth," Stefan retorted.

"Are you trying to say," Abbi pressed, "that you and your mother lived in poverty?"

Ericha drew back her shoulders and lifted her chin, but she said nothing.

"But surely your mother's father, if not Theodor, would have seen that your mother was—"

"My mother rarely took anything that her family offered her," Ericha explained without apology. "She was determined to make it on her own, and she did until her health began to fail. Even then, we managed to get by."

Abbi turned away and pressed a hand over her mouth as she was obviously overwhelmed with emotion. Ericha glared at Stefan, but he said gently, "We can't change what's past, Ericha. But if we had known, we could have—"

"Apparently that's not the way my mother wanted it."

"Forgive me," Abbi said, taking a deep breath. "It's just difficult for me to think of Kathe struggling on her own all those years, while I was wondering and worrying about her. I wish we would have known; we would have helped her. I'm just grateful to have you here now, my dear. What's done is done."

"Yes, that's right," Ericha agreed. "I've managed fine until now. I see no reason to take your money and—"

"Ericha," Stefan took her hand, "this has nothing to do with money. If you like, we'll put the allowance into a fund. It will be there if you need it."

"That would be fine," she said more softly, not wanting to be ungracious or cause any further tension.

Ericha was invited to share dinner with the family. Stefan showed up in his familiar casual attire, and there was no sign of the tension that had been present earlier in his office. Johanna was absent, which made the meal all the more enjoyable. Not wanting to wear out her welcome, Ericha insisted that she needed to return home when the meal was finished.

"It's dark out," Abbi said. "Perhaps we should—"

"I'll escort her home," Stefan volunteered. "I need to see Karl about something anyway."

Abbi smiled pleasantly. "That's good of you, dear. Have a nice evening."

Stefan helped Ericha with her cloak and walked her to the stables. While their horses were being saddled, she said quietly, "If I had not met you until I discovered I was your cousin, I would have fallen in love with you today."

Stefan smiled warmly at her, fighting the urge to just take her in his arms here and now. Their mounts were brought out, and

Stefan bent his knee to help Ericha into the saddle. After they had descended the castle hill, he rode close to her, saying, "Do you remember when we talked about the things we had fantasized?"

"I remember."

"I realized today that many of them have come true."

Ericha thought about it a minute, and she laughed softly. "So they have."

"I love you, Ericha Lokberg-du Woernig," he said, and Ericha felt certain life could get no better.

A few days later, Abbi asked Ericha if they could go out together, since there was something she wanted to show her. The ducal coach came for Ericha, and she sensed a severity about Abbi as they rode together a short distance. A servant helped the ladies step down, and Ericha was surprised to see that they were at the cemetery.

"I thought you should see your father's grave," Abbi explained as she led the way toward an area surrounded by a high wrought iron fence, where members of the royal family were buried. Abbi said nothing as they entered the gate and came to stand before two nearly identical, elaborate marble stones. Ericha initially concentrated more on Abbi, attempting to comprehend how it must feel for her to stand here and contemplate the loss of her husband and only son.

Abbi nodded toward Erich's stone, saying softly, "We felt the song was appropriate, since Cameron had written it for him."

Ericha absorbed her father's name and the dates of his birth and death. And below them were inscribed the words to the song her mother had taught her. It was difficult to mourn the loss of her father when she had never known him, but emotion came as she contemplated how her mother must have felt to stand in this very spot before she'd left Horstberg, never to return. Ericha reached out to touch her father's name, engraved deeply into the marble stone. She wondered how she might feel to see Stefan's name carved there. The thought chilled her so deeply that she shuddered. And she was grateful when Abbi finally turned to leave.

Following Abbi back to the coach, Ericha contemplated the poignancy of their relationship. She was grateful that her existence was regarded as something joyous to this woman, rather than a painful reminder of what she had lost.

In the coach, Ericha said gently, "I love you, Grandmama."

Abbi squeezed Ericha's hand and smiled with sad eyes. "And I love you, Ericha, my dear. I thank God every day that He sent you back to us."

Ericha sighed deeply and, once again, contemplated the goodness of her life.

Chapter Thirteen

INSIGHTS OF THE DUCHESS

When Mrs. Burger returned to Horstberg after spending Christmas with a sister, she was aghast to see one of the ducal carriages in front of Ericha's house. Not long after the grand duchess left, Mrs. Burger came over, breathless with excitement at having witnessed who Ericha's visitor was. Ericha sat down with her and explained the situation, and Mrs. Burger swore she had never been witness to such a joyous thing. Still, Mrs. Burger didn't reach her height of glory until Ericha arranged for her to spend an afternoon with the duchess. And Abbi more than willingly complied. Mrs. Burger urged some of those stories out of Abbi that she'd been longing to hear, and Abbi became absorbed with nostalgia as Mrs. Burger relayed having been outside the cathedral the day Abbi had married the duke.

Abbi showed genuine interest in Mrs. Burger, and Ericha recalled what Stefan had said about getting a personal insight to the people by spending time with them. As Abbi inquired more of Mrs. Burger and her family, Ericha was surprised by her confession.

"There is something I would like to tell you, Your Grace," she said carefully. "You see, I told you of course, that my son was killed." Abbi nodded. "I am ashamed to say that he was among those who invaded the castle with Nikolaus Koenig in 1849." Abbi's eyes showed compassion.

"I told him then that he was asking for trouble." Mrs. Burger paused, and Abbi said nothing. "Anyhow," she added, "I just thought I'd like to tell you that. Perhaps it helps my conscience rest a bit."

"There is no need," Abbi said gently, "for you to bear the burden of his actions. We regretted the lives that were lost then, but none of us can deny that we are grateful the revolution did not succeed." Mrs. Burger nodded firmly.

"I am only sorry," Abbi went on, "that you have had to live your life without your son. I can assure you I know how that feels." Abbi and Ericha exchanged a warm glance.

"But at least your son died an honorable man," Mrs. Burger said.

"And had he not," Abbi replied, "I would miss him just the same."

Abbi smiled warmly at Mrs. Burger, and her countenance betrayed relief. Mrs. Burger thanked Abbi for coming at least a dozen times as they said good-bye, and she declared that now she could die happy. Abbi made the comment as they walked around the fence into Ericha's yard, "There is nothing quite like spending an afternoon in such a person's home to really feel a kinship with the people."

Ericha smiled to herself, feeling her love for Stefan deepen through her association with Abbi—and vice versa.

Abbi du Woernig came by a habit of visiting Ericha often, and in turn, Ericha went to the castle at least once a week to spend time with her grandmother. Occasionally they would go into town together. And when Ericha took her to sit on the little bench in the park that she had come to like, Abbi declared it was the very spot where she used to meet her father. A wave of goose bumps overcame Ericha as Abbi told her the story of how her father had aided Cameron du Woernig in reclaiming the duchy from his wicked brother. The bracelet Abbi had given to Erich had been a talisman between them that had let her father know Cameron was still alive.

Through her grandmother, Ericha came to know more of the family history, and she enjoyed getting to know other members of the family better. She truly liked Hannah, and on a particular visit to the estate, Abbi spent the day regaling them with stories of her childhood. These heavily involved Georg, and Ericha came to love him as a very important part of the family.

Ericha's favorite story was when Abbi showed her the rose trellis going up to the room that had been Abbi's as a girl. It was overgrown with roses that Abbi declared were a beautiful red when they bloomed. Then she told how Georg had built the trellis so that Cameron could climb to her window when they were meeting secretly in the days before their marriage had been made public.

Later, Ericha teased Georg about it, and he told the story from his side. All of it made the legendary Cameron du Woernig come to life in Ericha's mind. And this was added upon when Georg and Abbi took her to see the family gallery. They spent over an hour looking at the portraits as their history was given. Ericha felt high emotion to see her father's, and she easily caught his resemblance to Cameron.

Ericha could hardly tear herself away from Stefan's portrait. Abbi seemed unaffected by her interest, and Georg just said, "He looks a little bit like everybody, but he gets that nose from Elsa. Don't you think he has Elsa's nose, Abbi?"

"I believe he does," she replied, and Ericha smiled.

That same morning, Abbi took Ericha aside, saying quietly, "There is something else I want you to see. I've been hesitant to show you for reasons you'll understand when you see it, but I think now is as good a time as any."

Ericha silently followed Abbi to a room on the second floor, where she paused at the door and met Ericha's eyes with compassion. Quietly they slipped inside, and it took a moment for Ericha's eyes to adjust to the dim light. The room was large and decorated with a feminine mood that almost reminded Ericha of her own room at home.

"It's a lovely room," Ericha commented when Abbi only stood and looked around.

"It was to be your mother's," Abbi said, and Ericha rubbed her arms to soothe the tingle of irony. "I'm certain we should have cleaned out the memories long ago, but I never stopped hoping she would come back one day." Her eyes turned to Ericha. "In a way, she has come back."

Ericha could say nothing in response. It was obvious that Abbi had loved Kathe Lokberg a great deal. With purpose, Abbi moved to the wardrobe and pulled it open. Just as with the room Ericha now occupied at home, some of her mother's clothes were left hanging there.

"These were things that we bought for your mother in preparation for the wedding," Abbi said, idly rummaging through them. "Some of them were never worn. Perhaps they are a bit old-fashioned for your taste, but they should be yours, to do with as you please."

Abbi pushed these aside and pulled out a gown draped in protective tissue. She lifted the paper just enough to reveal the white satin and lace. Ericha took in a sharp breath.

"This is your mother's wedding gown." Abbi's voice quivered. "She would have prepared for the wedding here, since the procession went from the castle to the . . ." Abbi pressed a hand over her mouth and squeezed her eyes shut. Ericha wondered if their thoughts were the same. How could she not be reminded that the funeral procession had been on their wedding day?

"It's very beautiful," Ericha said, trying to hold back her own emotion, if only to keep things light for Abbi. She put the wedding gown back where it had been, and her eye caught a red evening gown. She pulled it out.

Abbi smiled. "Your mother wore that for the social that celebrated their betrothal. I'll never forget the way she looked in it, dancing with Erich. When they were together they positively glowed . . . much the way you and Stefan looked dancing when . . ."

Their eyes met as Abbi stopped short. By the way Abbi glanced quickly away, Ericha wondered if she suspected the truth about her relationship with Stefan. Whether she did or not, Ericha believed she would never voice it. As long as Abbi loved and accepted them both, Ericha figured it made little difference.

Ericha put the gown back and closed the wardrobe as Abbi

went on with her nostalgia. "Erich gave your mother some jewels to go with the gown. She looked splendid in them. I assume that you would still have them, since—"

"No," Ericha interrupted gently, "but I know what happened to them." Abbi looked toward her in surprise. "She sold them to help pay for our needs."

The revelation seemed painful to Abbi. She turned away, nodding slightly to indicate that she'd heard. Ericha was grateful that she said nothing more. She didn't want a repeat of the tension she'd felt the last time her poverty had come up.

"Perhaps you would like to see your father's room, as well," she offered in a more cheerful tone.

"That would be fine," Ericha complied, "if you're feeling up to it."

"Oh, I'm all right." Abbi laughed softly and moved toward a side door, glancing once more at the room they were leaving. "Perhaps if there is ever a reason for you to stay at the castle," she said, "you would like to use this room—only if you want to, of course."

She proceeded into the next room, and Ericha followed. "This is the sitting room they would have shared after the marriage," Abbi said, attempting to conceal her emotion. She moved quickly through that room and opened another door, motioning for Ericha to look inside but apparently having no intention of entering herself. "They would have shared this room once they were married," Abbi reported, "since it's more spacious."

Ericha took a moment to imagine how it might have been. Would the room Kathe had used eventually have been her own room? She couldn't think about that. Instead she peered through the door to see a larger, masculine twin to the bedroom they'd just come from. Goose bumps rushed over her briefly, and she had a desire to just go in and sit a while. But noting the pallor on Abbi's face, Ericha gently closed the door and ushered her grandmother toward the hall.

"Are you all right, Grandmama?" she asked gently. Abbi turned tear-filled eyes toward her but said nothing. Ericha understood and gave her a warm embrace. Words would have made little difference.

They moved in silence back to the main floor and turned a corner, only to run right into Stefan. Blitzen and Donner followed at his feet. Ericha could tell he'd been outside, and she could see a trace of sweat over his brow.

"How charming," he said cheerfully. "Two of my favorite ladies."

"Did you enjoy your coursing, my dear?" Abbi asked.

"I certainly did." Grasping the mood about them, he touched Abbi's chin, tilting it upward to look in her eyes.

"Is something wrong?" he asked.

Abbi tried to smile and shook her head. But Stefan glanced dubiously toward Ericha, hoping to get an answer.

"She was just showing me my parents' rooms," Ericha provided.

"I see," Stefan said, putting his arms around Abbi in a forceful hug. "You should know better, Grandmama," he said quietly. She only nodded in agreement, then pressed her face to Stefan's shoulder, and Ericha realized she was crying. Stefan responded so easily with comfort that Ericha felt certain Abbi had poured her heart out to him many times in the past.

"Forgive me," she said, managing a smile when her tears were spent. "I always expect it to get easier with time, but I . . . I will never stop missing him."

"I know, Grandmama," Stefan said gently. "We all miss him. But you must—"

"Yes, I know." She smiled up at him. "I must not dwell on it, and you're right. I believe it's nearly time for dinner. Why don't you and Ericha go ahead? I'll freshen up and see you there."

Stefan nodded, and Abbi moved quickly away. Ericha glanced toward Stefan and tried to remember she was here as his cousin, which made her refrain from taking Abbi's place in his arms.

"You should feel privileged, little cousin," he said. "You have just witnessed a side to Abbi du Woernig that few have ever seen. And those of us who do, will see it rarely. I would swear that woman has the strength to lead armies into battle, but inside there is a heart of glass." He paused and sighed. "That is why I love her."

"I *do* feel privileged," Ericha said. "More than you could ever know."

Stefan smiled, and he glanced carefully down both halls before leaning over to kiss her. "It is I who am privileged," he said, and she saw a hint of amusement in his eyes. "I get to dine with my most beautiful cousin, and this evening I have an appointment with my most beautiful mistress." Ericha's eyes turned timid, and Stefan kissed her again. "And I love them both," he added.

"Perhaps we should get to dinner," she said. Stefan smiled and offered his arm.

Ericha was kneeling in the garden when Karl rode in from the pub. After caring for his horse in the stable, he walked idly over to see what she was doing.

"Weeding again, eh?" He chuckled.

"Always," she replied. "Did you have a good time?"

"Always." He mimicked her tone, and she laughed. "Oh." He reached into his pocket and handed her a folded piece of paper.

"What is this?"

"That ogre who rules this dreadful place passed me this note. I don't think it's for me. Although it does sound inviting, I think I prefer Luise's company."

Ericha unfolded the little paper. Her heart quickened to read: *I've got to get out of here for two or three days. Lower meadow, ten in the morning. Bring food.* It wasn't signed.

"Second honeymoon, eh?" Karl smirked.

"You shouldn't be reading my messages," she teased lightly.

"If I didn't read your messages, you would have to stew and fret over how to tell me that you're discreetly leaving for a few days. Look at all the trouble I've saved you."

"Indeed." She laughed. Karl then handed her some money. "What's this for?"

"The food," he said. "The ogre insisted; said he'd look a little conspicuous buying it himself and packing up a hamper. And what he generally manages to steal from the castle kitchen wouldn't suit your purposes."

Karl sauntered into the house, glancing back over his shoulder once with a sly grin. Ericha quickly cleaned up and hurried into the village to get what she needed before the shops closed. A little after nine the following morning, she had everything packed and secured to the horse. Wearing her green riding habit, she told Karl good-bye and headed toward the forest trail. She took the ride at a leisurely pace, knowing she had plenty of time.

Memories stirred Ericha as she came to the meadow and galloped its circumference. She undeniably felt the same haunting quality here that she'd been aware of before. Just when she began to wonder if Stefan would come, he emerged from the forest at a full gallop. Ericha held her breath as she watched him. He drew the stallion to an abrupt halt, and it reared back whinnying loudly. Stefan laughed and patted the animal as if to reward him.

"Good morning, Miss du Woernig," he said. "What a pleasant surprise to come upon you here."

"Surprise indeed, Mr. Heinrich."

Stefan laughed.

"Was that funny?" she asked.

"No one calls me Mr. Heinrich," he said. "It's always 'Your Grace' this, and 'Your Grace' that. It's nice to just be Mr. Heinrich for a change."

He leaned toward her and kissed her long and hard. "I thought the snow would never melt enough to get back up here with you," he said.

By the time they got to the lodge, unloaded the horses, and cared for them, Ericha thought she'd go mad with anticipation. She laughed with relief when he pulled her into his arms and carried her up to the bed.

While they lay holding each other in the peaceful aftermath, a thought occurred to Ericha. The ensuing tingle rushing through her seemed to validate it.

"Stefan," she said, "I believe this is where my life began." He lifted his head to look at her. "Think about it," she added. "Isn't it logical, with everything we know?"

"I'm certain you're right," he said, pressing a hand into her hair. "Do you also realize that this is where your father's life began?" Her eyes widened, and he clarified, "Think about it."

Ericha lay against Stefan's chest, recalling the story of Cameron and Abbi being snowed in together here. The peace that enveloped her was indescribable.

Later that afternoon, they took a picnic to the upper meadow, and Stefan told her that in the summer it would be filled with wildflowers. When they returned to the lodge, Ericha asked, "Has Johanna ever been here?"

"Heavens, no," he insisted. "She knows I have a lodge, but she has no idea where it is. That's what makes it a sanctuary."

"Were things *ever* good between you and Johanna?" she asked carefully.

Stefan pushed down the emotion and just answered the question. "Up until the day we were married, everything was apparently perfect. Beyond that, it was a nightmare. Once we were married, she had what she wanted. There was apparently no need for her to put up her act any longer."

Ericha wanted to press for details, but he obviously didn't want to talk about it.

Their few days together were full of bliss. While it was difficult to return, Ericha felt rejuvenated and replenished. By Stefan's apparent happiness, she knew that he did, too.

"Did you have a good time?" Karl asked when she walked into his workshop.

"I did, thank you. And how are you?"

"Better now." He smiled. "I always miss you. Oh," he added, "your grandmother called for you yesterday."

"What did you tell her?" Ericha panicked. She'd left in such a hurry, she'd not thought about giving Abbi an explanation.

"I just told her you'd left town for a few days when you got a message from a friend who needed you. She didn't seem concerned."

"Thank you," Ericha said, appreciating as always the way Karl covered for her and Stefan. But she wondered if Abbi had connected Stefan's absence to hers.

Stefan and Ericha did well at keeping their secret hidden, and they were certain that beyond Abbi no one except Karl and Erma had any idea they were involved. Theodor remained supportive, but Stefan felt sure that he had no idea who Stefan was involved with.

Ericha was grateful that her figure was slow to reveal the child she carried. And when she admitted this to Abbi, the duchess declared that it was inherited. Abbi too had been able to conceal her pregnancies well for the first several months, and Ericha caught a subtle amusement in her eyes as she spoke of it. Ericha knew she had to be thinking of the time when she'd been pregnant with Erich and unable to make her marriage to Cameron public.

But eventually the pregnancy could not go unnoticed any further. Ericha admitted to Abbi that it was perhaps best she stay away from the castle to avoid scandal falling on the royal family. This didn't seem to disturb Abbi, but she wanted Ericha to feel comfortable. Abbi increased her visits to Ericha, and more than once, she got down on her knees and helped in the garden while they talked.

One afternoon Stefan rode in while the duchess sat with Ericha in the yard, and Ericha became slightly nervous.

"Good day, ladies," he said graciously, as if nothing were out of the ordinary. "I see you're taking advantage of the sun."

"Spring has been beautiful this year," Abbi replied. "Look how wonderful Ericha's got the garden looking."

"Yes, I see," Stefan said. "Is Karl in his shop?"

"I believe so," Ericha answered, and he hurried away.

Ericha was surprised to hear Abbi say, "Stefan used to enjoy working at the lodge. He likes to do what he can in complete privacy. But he's told me now that he comes here often to do his work. It's not as far as the lodge and gives him more solitude—or perhaps a distance from the castle helps. Karl is gracious enough to give him the space to do it.

"I always thought Karl was a nice boy. After his mother died giving birth to him, he would come to the castle with his father occasionally. I suppose that's how he and Stefan became such good friends. But then it was Theodor who introduced your parents, wasn't it?"

Abbi smiled wistfully and turned her face toward the sun as if she thrived on it. A short while later, Stefan came back through the garden, heading toward the stable.

"Still soaking it in?" he asked his grandmother.

She nodded. "You know how I love the sun."

"And how are you feeling, little cousin?" Stefan asked.

"I'm doing well, thank you."

"I'm glad to hear it," Stefan said and hurried toward the stable.

"He's always so busy," Abbi said as Ericha watched him ride away.

As Ericha's time came nearer, she resigned herself to staying at home completely. She became especially grateful for Stefan's visits at night, and Abbi's in the mornings. Stefan was always long gone before his grandmother arrived, but Ericha was surprised one morning to have the duchess call soon after dawn.

Erma woke Ericha, and she slipped out of bed and put on a wrapper, glad to see that she'd not disturbed Stefan. Abbi was full of apologies when Ericha entered the parlor.

"I know I should not have called so early, but I just didn't sleep well and felt the need to get out."

"You mustn't apologize, Grandmama," she insisted. "You know that it doesn't matter when you come. You're always welcome. Is anything particular bothering you?"

"Oh, no," she said, and Ericha sensed something subtly unnatural. Abbi mentioned she'd had a strange dream, then started rambling like usual while Ericha worked on her tatting, hoping for an opportunity to excuse herself and make certain Stefan got out of the house unnoticed.

Ericha panicked when the door came open, but she had no choice but to resign herself to the circumstances when Stefan entered with a jubilant, "Oh, there you are." Of course, he would have no reason to think that anyone would be here so early.

She tried to indicate with her expression that they were not alone. But with his back to his grandmother, Stefan bent over Ericha and kissed her warmly on the mouth, putting his hand against the mound created by the baby. "I woke up and you were gone," he said.

"Uh . . . Stefan . . ." she stammered, and then the duchess gently cleared her throat. Ericha saw Stefan squeeze his eyes shut tightly as his face screwed up in a self-punishing grimace. Carefully he straightened his expression, took a deep breath, and turned to face her with dignity.

"Good morning, Grandmama," he said, bowing slightly. "What brings you out so early?"

When she smiled smugly, Ericha realized this had been a scheme on her part. "I was hoping to see you before you left," she stated. "I suspected you wouldn't be quite so guarded this early in the morning."

Both Stefan and Ericha remained silently aghast as she went on, "I sensed something between the two of you the first time I saw you together. When Ericha told me she was expecting, I put two and two together and knew it had to be you."

"I suppose you're trying to tell us that we underestimated your perception," Stefan said sheepishly.

"Quite." The duchess smiled again.

"It wasn't his fault," Ericha defended Stefan, standing beside him. "It was I who—"

"Ericha," Stefan said gently to quiet her. He took her hand into his and put his arm securely around her shoulders.

"So what's the point, Your Grace?" Stefan asked. "Now you have proof. What do you want us to say?"

"My only point is that I didn't see any reason for the two of you to pretend with me there's nothing going on when I know there is. I can hardly condone your relationship. And once I walk out of this room, you know where my position forces me to stand. I will continue to pretend I don't know, just like the two of you will continue to pretend that it's not happening. I must say you've done well in remaining discreet.

"On the other hand, I can hardly scold or criticize you when I've told each of you that you must follow your heart and find happiness in spite of these deplorable circumstances that have left you with little choice. I simply want to admonish you to be very careful. Listen to an old woman who has seen what the treachery of certain people can do when they find a weak spot and trod upon it."

The three of them were silent until Stefan said at last, "Thank you, Grandmother—for everything you are and all that you have given to us. I'm certain you know this already, but I'm going to tell you, because I've wanted to for so long. I love Ericha with everything I have. She has put soul back into me."

Abbi smiled warmly at them both as she stood. "Stefan," she said quietly, "in more ways than one, Ericha has put soul back into Horstberg."

She nodded regally and left the room. Stefan and Ericha were silent until they heard the carriage drive away.

"I'm sorry," Ericha began, "I should have awakened you."

"Don't worry," he said. "I'm glad she knows. But that will teach me not to walk into rooms unannounced and declare myself."

Ericha nodded in agreement, and they went to the dining room for breakfast.

There came a day when Mrs. Burger realized what condition Ericha was in, and Ericha had no choice but to explain the circumstances the best she could. Mrs. Burger was obviously upset by this, and weeks passing didn't alleviate the tension between them on their increasingly rare visits. A day came when Ericha had to admit that Mrs. Burger wanted nothing to do with her, in spite of her royal connection. Mrs. Burger's disapproval disturbed Ericha, but she swallowed it with dignity and did her best to not think about it.

She was just getting used to the idea when Theodor came to dinner for the first time in several weeks. Ericha had taken for granted that Theodor already knew, and she wasn't prepared for his reaction when she entered the dining room. He stopped talking mid-sentence when he saw her, and his mouth fell visibly open.

"Good heavens, girl," he declared. "You're with child!"

"Perceptive, isn't he," Karl said lightly.

"What on earth have you been doing?" he asked Ericha.

"Surely she doesn't need to explain," Karl added.

"Hush up, boy," Theodor insisted. "I was talking to Ericha."

"I thought you knew," she said quietly.

"If you'd come to dinner more than twice a year you might know what's going on," Karl interjected on Ericha's behalf. "It's not our fault you prefer spending your free time with that Miss . . . whatever her name is."

As long as Karl was doing the talking, Theodor turned the blame to him. "I thought you said you were watching out for her. You go and let her get pregnant?"

"As a matter of fact, I did," Karl said defiantly. "If you would bother to ask, you would realize that she is very happy. She fell in love with a man who is not in a position to marry her, and I give her my full support with the relationship."

"I'm sorry if I've disappointed you," Ericha said quietly. "But Karl's right, I am very happy. It was my decision, and I will take the responsibility. I love the father of this child very much. And he's good to me."

"Who?" Theodor asked, as if he would like to get his hands on the man responsible.

"That is irrelevant," Karl insisted.

"I am your uncle, Ericha. I had such hopes for your future, especially after what your mother lived through."

Ericha quickly worked things over in her mind, and she felt good about her decision to say, "Stefan has told me how supportive you have been. Surely you must understand what this means to us."

Theodor leaned back in his chair and looked as if he might have trouble breathing. "It's *you?*" he said, and Ericha nodded. "I don't believe it!"

Theodor said nothing more about the situation as Ericha sat down and they proceeded with the meal. Ericha sensed that he neither wanted to accept nor disapprove, so he simply said nothing.

That evening as Stefan rushed into his room to change before leaving the castle, he was surprised to find Theodor waiting for him. Stefan looked comically behind him, saying, "Did I miss something? Some banquet or—"

"No, I just wanted to talk to you for a minute . . . if I may."

Stefan sat down. "All right."

"I saw Ericha today for the first time in a long while," he began, and Stefan could feel it coming. "Imagine how surprised I was to learn that she's going to have a baby."

Stefan crossed his ankle on his knee, keeping his eyes firmly fixed on Theodor. "And did she reveal the identity of the scoundrel responsible?"

"Yes," he stated, then said nothing more.

"You are her uncle. You certainly have a right to know. Perhaps we should put the rogue on trial." He paused and deepened his tone. "Or is that what this is?"

"I've known you a long time," Theodor said. "I've been with this family since before you were born. I'm having a difficult time believing that you would treat something like this so lightly."

"If you know me as well as you claim, Theodor, you would know that calling myself a rogue in no way lessens my reasons for doing what I have done."

There was a moment of silence. "I have one question."

"I'm listening."

"Why Ericha? Of all the women in Horstberg, why her?"

It took Stefan a moment to absorb the implication. "Do you think I just made up my mind to have an affair and Ericha just happened to be the first gullible woman to fall in the trap?" Stefan shot to his feet and pushed a hand through his hair. "And you claim to *know* me?"

When Theodor said nothing, Stefan began to pace. "I *love* Ericha with all my heart and soul, and as you said yourself once, I don't have to ask your permission."

"I didn't know it was my niece!"

"And that makes it different?"

"Yes, it does! Do you have any idea how this will affect her life? Did you even consider the stigma or the—"

"You have no idea," Stefan stopped to face him and pointed a harsh finger, "the anguish I went through over just that! Don't you think if I could do it any other way, I would?"

"And what happens when you're finished with her? Then what? What kind of life does she live beyond that?"

"*Finished* with her?" Stefan echoed in disbelief. He forced out a chuckle to keep himself from shouting. "Do you have any idea who you are talking to?"

"Being the Duke of Horstberg does not give you the right to—"

Stefan interrupted in a calm voice of power. "This has nothing to do with the Duke of Horstberg. I am Stefan Heinrich, and like my father and grandfathers before me, I am a man of integrity. My relationship with Johanna ended long before I ever met Ericha. Ericha and I are committed to each other for life. She *is* my life. And don't you ever think of her as anything less than the Duchess of Horstberg. By every right but one, she deserves that title."

Theodor glanced away and folded his hands in his lap with a lengthy sigh. "You're right," he admitted. "I should know you better than that."

Stefan relaxed and took a step back.

"It's just that," Theodor went on, "I had such hopes for Ericha, especially after what her mother went through. I know

now that you were involved before the truth came out about her father, but *I* knew who her father was. In spite of her birth, I had hoped that her connection to the family would bring good things into her life."

"And it has," Stefan said.

"But I wanted her to . . ."

By the way he stopped, Stefan felt certain he was implying a hope for Ericha to marry well. He sat down close to Theodor and looked him in the eye.

"I know you care very much for Ericha. And I want you to know that a day doesn't go by when I don't wish it could be different—for her sake. But she loves me, Theodor. She loves *me*. And I do my best to take good care of her. As long as there is breath in me, I will see that she never goes without. Most importantly, I want you to understand that nothing on this earth could have changed the way we feel about each other, the way we were drawn together. I can't explain it, Theodor, but somehow I know in my heart that she and I would have come together, one way or another. And nothing could have kept us apart."

Theodor said nothing. Stefan finally broke the silence. "So, do you still want to work with me, or would you prefer a position where you don't have to see me every day?"

"You *need* me," Theodor stated.

"Yes, I do," Stefan admitted readily. "But I will not spend every minute in your presence feeling like some kind of criminal. I'm not asking for your approval. But I will demand your tolerance."

"Does your grandmother know?" he asked.

"Yes, but she'll never admit it."

"If she can tolerate it, I will do the same."

"Thank you," Stefan said. "And I trust that your confidence in this is absolute and complete."

"Yes," Theodor said and left the room.

Stefan could feel the tension long after the door closed. But he reminded himself that he should not expect it to be easy. Hoping that time would soften Theodor's heart, Stefan hurried to see Ericha. He found her sitting with Karl in the parlor, her swollen feet propped on the coffee table with a pillow.

"Ah, Your Grace," Karl said, noticing him first.

"Stefan!" Ericha's face lit up, and she held out a hand toward him.

"Hello." He sat close beside her. "How are you feeling?" he asked with a kiss.

"Same as always," she reported lightly, and then she took notice of his expression. "What's wrong?"

"Your uncle is not very happy with me," he said, and Ericha sighed.

"Was I wrong to tell him it was you?" she asked.

"No," Stefan insisted. "I think he has a right to know, and I'm not concerned about his discretion. He just had high hopes for you, and he's not pleased with what I've done to your life. I can't say that I blame him." Ericha looked concerned until he added, "But I told him that you and I were meant to be together."

"Just fire him," Karl suggested.

"Actually," Stefan said, more to Karl, "I told him he didn't have to like it, but I would demand his tolerance."

"Good man," Karl said with a firm nod.

"Your father is a *good man*, Karl. He's just concerned."

"I know that," Karl insisted. "But eventually he'll figure out that this is good; as good as it can be under the circumstances, at least. I did."

Stefan hugged Ericha tightly. She felt concerned for him, knowing he had to work with Theodor every day. But she reminded herself of all that was good, and pressed Stefan's hand over her belly to feel the baby kicking. He laughed with pure delight, and Ericha knew the challenges were worth the joy they shared.

Wanting to get in on the fun, Karl crossed the room and sat on the other side of Ericha. He set his hand close to Stefan's and immediately felt the baby kick. He laughed and said, "Ooh, it's getting stronger."

Stefan smiled wryly. "Don't you have anything better to do

than sit around and play with my baby? Mercy, you need to get out more."

Ericha laughed and listened to them banter while the baby continued its activity for several minutes. She wondered if any woman had ever felt so loved and secure.

As days passed, Ericha did her best to push away the disapproval of those around her and concentrate instead on all she and Stefan shared. She reminded herself often that she had the acceptance of those closest to her. And she was grateful for being able to work in the garden as it was always sanctifying to her. Her increasing size made it a labor to kneel and get back up again, and she couldn't stay in one spot for long. But still she enjoyed it.

Abbi spent a great deal of time with Ericha as it became increasingly difficult for her to do little more than move from one chair to another due to her size. The duchess talked on and on about babies. And when Ericha realized what experience her grandmother had, she implored her to be there when the time came.

"I wouldn't dream of not being with you," Abbi insisted. "I was there when all of Maggie's children were born. In fact, I delivered little Elsa myself, with some help from your father. And not only was I there when Stefan was born, but I helped deliver Stefan's father.

"I want Karl to come and get me just as soon as your pains start. Once I get here, then he can get the doctor," she teased, and Ericha was grateful for her constant kindness and understanding.

Ericha felt an increasing uneasiness as the birth of her child approached. She went to the garden, hoping to distract her thoughts. She was pleasantly surprised to have Stefan come while she was at it, and he sat on the ground to greet her with a warm kiss while his hand moved over the child within her.

Ericha saw Mrs. Burger across the fence, pretending not to notice. And she was grateful that the situation of the yard made it impossible for anyone else to possibly see.

"Perhaps we should go inside," Ericha said, and Stefan helped her to her feet.

"How are you feeling?" he asked gently.

"When I'm not getting kicked in the ribs, it's not so bad," she replied, and Stefan chuckled.

Ericha washed her hands in the kitchen then went to the parlor to work on her tatting with the afternoon sun at her back.

"So, how is business?" Ericha asked Stefan as he sat across the room and put up his feet.

"Nothing new," he stated. Then he watched her intently for several moments before he asked, "What did the doctor say?" Ericha looked up at him, seeming surprised, and he added, "You were supposed to see him this morning, weren't you?"

"Yes, I saw him."

Stefan felt a nervous twitch at the back of his neck. She had always told him the doctor's report without any prodding. "What did he say?" Stefan persisted.

"It could be any day now. He said that it appears the baby is already big and he hopes it will come before it gets any bigger—for my sake."

"You're too little to have a big baby."

"That's what Doctor Furhelm said."

"You're worried," Stefan stated. Ericha glanced up at him, then pushed her thumb and forefinger beneath her glasses to rub her eyes. "I thought so," he said, knowing she did that when she was trying not to cry.

"No," she protested, removing her glasses, "I'm not worried. I know Doctor Furhelm is the best. I'm strong and healthy and there is no reason in the world why everything shouldn't go perfectly fine."

"Then what's wrong?" he asked, moving to sit beside her.

"I'm just scared," she said quietly.

"So am I," Stefan admitted. "You're always in my prayers."

Ericha gripped his hand, and a warm smile passed between them. Then Stefan's expression sobered. "Ericha," he said in a tone of caution, and she realized he'd come to tell her something. "I'm afraid that I have to leave town for a few days."

"Oh, no," she said. "You said you would be here when the baby came. What if . . ." Ericha stopped her complaints when she saw the regret in Stefan's eyes. She knew there was nothing he could do. He certainly couldn't tell his associates that his mistress was having a baby and he couldn't leave. "Hurry back," was all she said.

"I love you, Ericha. You always understand, no matter what. I don't deserve the way you treat me."

"No," she said, "it's the other way around."

Ericha tried to force the tears back, but they pressed out with a gentle sob, and she put her face into her hands. Stefan pulled her close to him, embracing her with conviction. Ericha clung to him and cried on his shoulder.

"I have to go soon," he whispered. "Come upstairs and let me hold you."

Ericha came slowly to her feet and walked within Stefan's embrace up to her room. He helped her to the edge of the bed, then bent to remove her shoes, pausing to gently rub her swollen ankles. Ericha lay back on the bed, and Stefan eased close to her, brushing his lips over her brow.

"Why are you scared?" he whispered.

Ericha only nuzzled closer to him, and the question was left hanging in silence. Stefan moved his hand over the baby within her, feeling evidence of its life. He kissed her warmly, and Ericha longed for the day when bearing this child was behind her.

Ericha fell asleep in Stefan's arms and awoke to find it dark. "Stefan," she said urgently, fearing he was gone. But she felt his arm come around her, and he eased her head against his chest. "I'm glad you're still here."

"I wish I didn't have to go, but my train leaves in an hour." Again he moved his hand meekly over the baby. "You be careful," he whispered behind her ear.

"I think I'll just wait to have this baby until you come back."

"That's a splendid idea. I want a daughter who looks just like you."

"But I want a son who looks just like you."

"That could cause problems around here."

"Yes, it could, but I'll tell you something."

"What's that?"

"It's too late to change your order now."

Stefan chuckled and leaned over Ericha to kiss her. "I'll hurry back," he whispered, and then he left. Ericha prayed that she would see him again before the baby came.

Two days after Stefan left, a heavy rain drizzled down. Horstberg turned gray, and Ericha was lonely. She felt a streak of ambition early in the morning and accomplished more than she had in weeks. But by afternoon she felt tired, and a deep ache settled into her lower back. She went to bed with the hope that lying down would ease the discomfort, but time passing only intensified the pain in regular intervals, and she finally had to admit that this baby was coming.

Carefully she came to her feet and moved into the hall, calling for Karl. When no answer came, she realized he was likely in his shop, and Erma had probably gone into town to get what she needed to cook supper. Slowly Ericha moved down the stairs and toward the back of the house, pausing often to bear the pain of contractions. She was relieved to finally get to the workshop and find Karl at his bench.

"Hello," he said without looking up. "How are you feeling?"

"Karl," she said, then paused too long. He looked up to see the distress in her expression.

"What's wrong?" he insisted, but she didn't answer as her concentration was centered on the pain. Karl moved so quickly to her side that his stool tipped over. She leaned against him, grateful for the support.

"I think this is it," she finally managed to say. With no hesitation, he deftly swept her into his arms and carried her toward the house. "I'm scared, Karl."

"So am I," he admitted. Then he smiled and added, "But everything will be fine, I promise."

With Ericha put back into bed, Karl waited only until Erma returned before he left, giving her strict orders. "Forget about supper for now. You stay with Ericha until I get back."

Erma nodded stoutly, and Karl ran to the stables. He rode to inform the doctor, then went quickly to Castle Horstberg.

Abbi was sitting in the library going over menus with Johanna when Karl burst into the room, and then he bowed graciously as an afterthought. "Excuse me, Your Grace," he said, "but it's time."

Abbi was on her feet before he finished the sentence, and Johanna followed them into the hall, apparently wondering what all the fuss was about.

"Time for what?" she asked.

Both Abbi and Karl ignored her, but Abbi asked Karl if he'd sent for the doctor yet, and he nodded firmly.

"What's going on?" Johanna implored, following them to the door as Abbi threw a cloak over her shoulders.

"Nothing to worry about," Abbi said coolly, and Johanna returned to the library.

"I must see to one thing," Abbi said to Karl and motioned for him to follow her. He watched in awe as she went into the ducal office, scratched out a quick note, then sealed it. She gave it to one of the officers on duty and calmly told him to see that someone ride the three hours to where Stefan was staying and see that he got the message as quickly as possible.

Ericha was increasingly grateful as the hours of the night wore on that she had her grandmother with her. Abbi remained calm and reassuring, and talked enough to make the time move faster.

While Abbi wondered if Stefan would make it in time, she waited for a quiet moment to speak to the doctor. When he didn't appear terribly busy, she brought up something she felt certain he should know.

"Doctor Furhelm," she said carefully, and he looked up attentively, "you're well aware that your father delivered all of my children, and I always felt I could trust him with any confidence concerning them. I feel you have that same discretion."

"I'd like to think so." He chuckled slightly.

"I know from experience that a woman in labor holds nothing back, and I'm certain if you don't know who this child's father is by now, you will before this is over." She paused and added carefully, "Do you know?" He shook his head, and she continued, "This is Stefan's baby."

"Really?" He smiled, seeming more pleased than anything.

"And I trust that your knowledge will not go beyond this room."

The doctor reached over and put his hand over Abbi's. "You know, Your Grace, that I have been with this family a long time. Cameron trusted me during the worst of times, and I assure you that trust remains strong." They shared a long, silent gaze, while Abbi recalled in a matter of seconds how he had attended to both Erich and Stefan through difficult times when their lives had been threatened by revolutionaries. She also recalled how he'd given her something to calm her down and help her sleep following Cameron and Erich's deaths when she had been almost hysterical with grief. With all he had seen this family go through, she knew that he meant what he said, and he could be well trusted. She even believed that he would understand the reasons for the present situation.

"Thank you." She sighed with relief, and their attention turned back to Ericha, who was far too lost in her pain to have noticed their discreet conversation.

As the hours passed, Ericha kept expecting this to end, but the pain only continued to increase.

"How did you do it?" she asked Abbi, who kept a calm vigil at her bedside. "How did my mother do it?"

"Well, for one thing," Abbi said with a little smile, "once you get this far, you don't have much choice. But when you hold that child in your arms, you don't have to wonder why you did it."

Ericha groaned and writhed, attempting to breathe deeply as the contraction gripped her with a pain she would not have thought possible.

"I prayed that Stefan would be here when the baby came," she murmured in the brief interval. The pain overtook her again, even more intense. When it let up, she looked at her grandmother, and tears leaked into the hair at her temples. "Does God answer the prayers of a woman like me, with no name to give my child?"

"The Bible tells us that God looks on the heart. Surely he knows that yours is pure."

Ericha had difficulty believing Abbi as the pain worsened even more. Rather than coming and going, it reached a point of constancy that she felt certain she couldn't bear.

"I'm going to die," she cried, firmly believing that she would. Surely it wasn't supposed to hurt this much.

"You're not going to die," the doctor said gently, and she was reminded of his presence. "I won't allow it. You're getting close now. Soon you can start to push, and we'll work together to get this baby here."

Ericha nodded stoutly, feeling a degree of hope, and then she threw her head back and groaned through clenched teeth as it felt like her body was tearing itself in half. Abbi propped extra pillows behind her head and wiped her face with a cool cloth. "It will be over soon, my dear," she whispered in a soothing voice.

Ericha's surroundings became a blur as the pain worsened still. She thought it was Abbi's hand in hers, and she looked up to see the doctor's face very close.

"Ericha, listen to me," he said. His tone was so severe it frightened her. "This baby is turned wrong." She was hurting too badly to ask what he meant, and she was grateful when he explained. "It is face up, when it should be face down. I have to turn it over before it can be delivered. Otherwise it will be harmful to you and the baby. All you have to do is bear down, like we talked about before. Do you understand?" She nodded willfully. "It's going to hurt, but that doesn't mean anything's wrong. Do you understand?" She nodded again, then clenched her teeth, wondering what it meant to be warned that something would hurt when she already preferred to die over feeling what she felt now.

"Hold tight to me," Abbi said, sitting on the edge of the bed and putting her arms around Ericha's shoulders. "It will be over soon."

Stefan hurled himself off the stallion and ran through the garden. He cursed when he found the door locked, then reminded himself that it was probably five in the morning. He pounded on the door and heard Job barking. It only took a few seconds before Karl pulled it open.

"You're here," he muttered. "Thank God."

"Is she all right?" Stefan asked, hurrying down the hall with Karl close behind.

"As far as I know, but . . . wait." Karl stopped him at the top of the stairs. "You can't go in there."

"Why not?" Stefan demanded.

"You just—" Karl stopped when Ericha's piercing scream broke the night. It was as loud as if there were no closed door between them. Stefan shrugged away Karl's attempt to hold him back. He pushed open the door, then stopped cold. He hadn't paused to think what he might expect. He'd only wanted to be with Ericha. But now he nearly wished that he'd listened to Karl. The room smelled of blood and sweat. In one quick glance he absorbed Abbi's wearied concern and Ericha's oblivion to anything but the pain that made her writhe and groan. She looked as if she'd been to the depths of hell. There were basins with bloody water, medical instruments spread about, and then there was the blood. The bedding beneath Ericha was saturated with deep red.

He'd been witness to gunshot wounds and death. But he'd never seen so much blood. His gaze went to Doctor Furhelm, who was casually wiping blood off his hands with a wet towel. He nearly expected to be thrown out, and almost hoped that he would be. He wondered for a moment if the doctor had known this was his baby, and what the repercussions might be. But the doctor tossed the towel down and said firmly, "Good, you're here. Shut the door."

Stefan did as he was told, leaning against it a moment to gather his courage. His attention diverted to Ericha as she cried out in anguish.

"Stefan," she murmured. "I need Stefan."

Abbi met his eyes, but he couldn't tell if her tears were from relief at his being here or fear related to what was happening. He wondered for a moment if something was wrong. Was Ericha going to die? He'd heard often the story of Georg's wife dying in childbirth. Karl's mother had died in childbirth. And Abbi had nearly died after she'd given birth to Erich.

"Dear God above," he whispered, "don't let her die."

"Stefan," Ericha muttered again, and he rushed to her side.

"I'm here," he said, pressing his face to hers.

Ericha's eyes flew open. "Oh, thank you, God," she cried, and then the anguish overtook her again.

"Take your boots off," the doctor ordered, and Stefan looked up in surprise.

"What?"

"I said take your boots off. She needs help, and your grand-mother has already been with her all night. She needs the strength of a man."

Stefan tossed his boots in the corner, and with the doctor's instructions, he sat behind Ericha, leaning back against the head-board. She leaned back against his chest, and the doctor guided her hands to Stefan's legs at her sides. He then placed Stefan's arms around her, his hands over the baby.

"Now when I say push," he instructed, "push. It's as simple as that."

Stefan nodded. His concentration was distracted by the evidence of Ericha's pain and weakness. He looked to his grandmother, and she sat close to him on the edge of the bed, putting one hand on Ericha's shoulder, the other on his arm.

"Push," the doctor said. Ericha bore down with a cry of agony. Stefan pressed down with both hands, fearing he would hurt her. They went through the process seven times, while Stefan wondered if Ericha would live through this. The evidence of her pain nearly tore his heart out. Just when he thought it would never end, he felt the mound move down a little beneath his hands. A moment later it disappeared and Ericha collapsed. He heard the doctor chuckle, and then the baby's cry broke the air.

"It's a boy," he announced, and a sob erupted from Ericha's throat. Stefan wrapped his arms around her, sensing her relief. He buried his face into her hair as tears burned into his eyes. He couldn't see what was happening until the doctor handed a wiggling bundle wrapped in white to his grandmother. She laughed and tears streamed down her face as she set the bundle into the crook of Ericha's arm.

Ericha laughed and cried as she pushed the blanket back to examine her little son. "Oh, he's beautiful, Stefan. Look at him."

Stefan courageously touched the infant's tiny hand.

"What will you name him?" Abbi asked.

"Cameron Erich," Stefan stated, and his emotion deepened. "Through him they both live on."

"He looks so much like Erich did when he was born," Abbi said, running her fingers over the rust-colored hair. "There are some things a mother never forgets."

While Ericha was absorbed with the baby, Abbi looked deeply at Stefan.

"Are you all right?" she asked.

He nodded but didn't dare speak.

"I remember," she said, and he was grateful that she didn't press him, "when your mother delivered your sister, Elsa. She was born in the lodge. Do you remember, Stefan?"

He nodded again. How could he forget? It was the day they'd nearly lost everything because of Nik Koenig's revolution.

"Erich helped deliver the baby," Abbi said, "the way you just did."

Stefan's emotion nearly choked him as he contemplated the ironies. Abbi wiped a tear from his cheek, then kissed him.

"Your Grace," the doctor said quietly, and they both looked up. His eyes were focused on Stefan. "Your grandmother needs to rest. Perhaps you could see to it while Miss Busch and I put things in order."

Stefan moved carefully off of the bed and helped make Ericha comfortable against the pillows. He paused to touched Ericha's face and kiss her briefly.

"I love you," he said, and another tear leaked out.

Ericha watched Stefan and Abbi move toward the door. She hurt so badly she hardly dared move. But her focus returned to her son—Stefan's son—and she knew that Abbi was right. She would do it all again just to have him.

Karl guided Stefan and Abbi to a guest room that he'd had Erma put in order, anticipating this. Stefan helped his grandmother to the bed as her weariness became increasingly evident.

"You're too old to be staying up all night, Mrs. du Woernig," he said lightly, grateful to be distracted from his intense emotions.

"Don't call me old," she replied just as lightly. Stefan chuckled as he tucked the blanket up over her and sat on the edge of the bed. She took his hand into hers. "If you think I would miss the birth of your first child, you're quite mistaken, young man."

"I didn't expect that you would," Stefan replied. Then more seriously, "Thank you for being there, Grandmama." Tears welled into her eyes, and he quickly asked, "What is it?"

"I'm well aware, Stefan, that I am considered the most powerful woman in Horstberg."

"Beyond a doubt," he said, hoping to lighten her mood.

Abbi's tears spilled as she added, "But I can do nothing to change these circumstances that are so unfair and ridiculous." She squeezed his hand tightly, and he saw a glimpse of the age that she usually hid so well. "He should have been a Heinrich, Stefan. It isn't right that the two of you have to live this way."

Stefan wondered how to console her, when she had just perfectly described the ache in his own heart. But he thought of what Ericha might say and drew strength from it. "Grandmama," he said gently, touching her chin with his finger, "he should have been a Heinrich, but at least he is. At least we have him. And we have each other. That can make up for a lot."

"Bless you, Stefan." Abbi smiled. "I see in you the benefits of teaching one's children well. You return wisdom to me when I'm getting too old and weary to see it myself."

"Ericha is the wise one," he said. "She humbles me."

Stefan's eyes grew distant until Abbi touched his face. "What's troubling *you?*"

"I never dreamed . . ." he admitted, and tears spilled down his face. "I never comprehended what a woman would go through to . . ." He pressed his face against his grandmother's shoulder as the trauma took hold.

"She loves you very much," Abbi said.

Stefan lifted his head to look at her. "God sent her to save my life."

"Yes, I know," she said quietly.

Stefan left his grandmother with an admonition to sleep as long as she needed. He went quietly back to Ericha's room to find that all traces of the ordeal had been cleaned away. He watched Ericha sleeping and contemplated again the enormity of what he had just experienced with her. He thought he had felt it all, but never had he known such a gamut of emotions.

"Stefan." The whisper startled him, and he looked up to see Karl in the doorway, motioning him into the hall.

Stefan stepped out of the room, and Karl shook his hand while they embraced. "Congratulations." He chuckled. "How does it feel to have a son?"

"When I start feeling it, I'll let you know," Stefan admitted.

"Come have some breakfast," Karl said, and they started down the stairs.

"Where's the baby?"

"Erma's washing him up back in the kitchen. She's actually quite good with babies. Seems she's been around them before."

"Good," Stefan said.

Karl pushed open the dining room door, and Doctor Furhelm rose to greet them.

"Ah, Your Grace," he said, "won't you join me?"

"I've already eaten," Karl added. "If you need something, let me know."

The door closed, and Stefan faced the doctor. They'd known each other for years, and had a great deal of mutual respect. But Stefan wondered how this might affect their working relationship.

Doctor Furhelm reached out a hand, and Stefan stepped forward to shake it. "I understand that fine boy belongs to you."

"I must confess," Stefan said as they were both seated.

The doctor poured coffee into Stefan's cup and slid the cream and sugar within his reach.

"I want to thank you," Stefan said.

"I didn't make the coffee, I just poured it."

Stefan chuckled, grateful for the easing of tension.

"For seeing that everything went well. You can't know what it means to know she was in such capable hands."

"The best part of my job is delivering babies," he said. "I quite enjoyed it . . . most of it, anyway."

"Is she . . . going to be all right?"

"Oh, she'll be fine," the doctor said easily. "I've seen women tear much worse than that, and heal up as good as new eventually."

"Tear?" Stefan questioned gingerly.

"The baby was big, and he was turned wrong to start with. She tore a little, but she's all stitched up, and with time she'll be as good as new."

Stefan nodded, feeling a bit queasy.

"Of course, there should be no intimacy . . . for several weeks, at least until she's healed."

Stefan nodded again, feeling a little uncertain to have his relationship with Ericha treated so openly. He was just wondering how to ease his concerns when the doctor said, "If you're worried about my knowledge of your secret, there is no need to be." He put a hand on Stefan's shoulder and looked him in the eye. "Forgive me if I am speaking too candidly, Your Grace. But you are a good man, from a good family, and there are many people who appreciate the way you run this country."

Stefan lifted a brow in pleasant surprise.

The doctor continued. "It doesn't take much to see that Ericha is a wonderful young woman. And I am truly happy for you . . . under the circumstances."

"Thank you," Stefan said. "I can't tell you how much I appreciate that. The situation is . . . touchy, to say the least. I would marry Ericha if I could. But . . . under the circumstances, I have no option."

The doctor nodded with a knowing look in his eyes, and Stefan felt certain he knew something of the difficulties between him and Johanna. He wondered if there was anyone in the country who didn't. But he was surprised when the doctor said, "And in spite of this boy not being your heir, it is a true pleasure to know that you will have the joy of children in your life."

"Yes," Stefan agreed, "it is something I'm very grateful for."

"After the difficulties Her Grace experienced soon after your marriage, I know it must have been a trial for you to . . ."

Stefan wondered if the shock in his expression was so obvious as the doctor stopped, looking downright aghast.

"What difficulties?" Stefan asked.

Doctor Furhelm leaned back in his chair and sighed. "She told me that you knew. She begged me not to discuss it with you, and I just assumed that there were reasons and . . . it wasn't my business to question it or . . ."

"What difficulties?" Stefan demanded, feeling the Duke of Horstberg come to the surface. Doctor Furhelm's expression filled with unmistakable concern. Stefan felt a knot gather in his stomach. When moments passed and he still said nothing, Stefan leaned over the table and said, "Speak candidly, for the love of heaven, and tell me!"

"Stefan," the doctor began and cleared his throat, and Stefan knew this was serious. The doctor had not called him Stefan since he was a boy. "Do you recall, just a few days after your marriage, when Johanna became ill?"

"I remember," he stated, chilled by the memories already.

"She told me that you were well aware of the reasons."

"She told *me* that you said it was nothing, some little virus that would pass."

"She was pregnant," the doctor stated.

"I thought she couldn't . . ."

"At that time, apparently she *could* conceive. Because she was pregnant. I examined her. There was no question."

Stefan's eyes shifted as he frantically thought it through. "But it was . . ." He didn't quite dare say it. Through the years he had come to learn what kind of woman Johanna was. And he'd had his suspicions that it had begun before their marriage. But he'd never wanted to think too hard about it.

"Too soon?" the doctor guessed Stefan's thought exactly. "Yes, it was too soon. She told me that it was your baby, but you didn't want the scandal of having a child born early." Stefan felt his palms begin to sweat as the doctor continued. "I assured her I didn't think that was a problem, since it had happened before."

Stefan's eyes widened as he was briefly distracted. The doctor chuckled. "Surely you knew that Erich was born only four months after the marriage was made public. Cameron reclaimed the duchy while Abbi was pregnant. It was an unusual situation, which my father handled at the time, I believe. As I understand it, Cameron made the knowledge public that he'd been snowed in with her, and then they'd married privately, but . . ."

"Yes, I knew," Stefan said, and then his mind went reluctantly back to the present. There were so many unanswered questions concerning this that he didn't know where to begin. While a part of him felt drawn to anger to learn now how thoroughly Johanna had deceived him, there was something almost comforting in hearing the evidence of what kind of a woman she really was. He felt compelled to explain what he hoped was obvious.

"I did not share a bed with Johanna prior to our marriage. If she was pregnant, then . . ." He couldn't finish.

The doctor continued. "It was quite some time later that I put the pieces together and I was able to see what should have been obvious. But at the time, I felt it was better to—"

"I understand," Stefan insisted. "Go on, please."

"I assumed that for some reason it was important to *her* that the child not be born too soon, and she assured me that you knew. I couldn't imagine you approving of—"

"If she was pregnant," Stefan interrupted as one thought forced its way through all the rest, "what happened to the baby?"

"Well, that's what I'm getting at. Do you remember a few weeks later when she was down in bed for several days?"

"She had a miscarriage?" he asked, while something in his mind wondered why she'd not been pregnant since. He'd certainly tried to get her pregnant, though the very idea made bile rise in his throat.

"She tried to convince me it was a miscarriage, but . . ."

"But?" Stefan questioned firmly when he hesitated.

"That baby was aborted, Stefan, by someone who didn't know what they were doing." When Stefan gaped in disbelief, the doctor clarified, "The pregnancy was terminated by killing the baby."

In one succinct movement, Stefan slid his chair back and pressed a hand over his mouth. He squeezed his eyes shut, trying to comprehend the horror.

The doctor went on. "In all my years as a doctor, I have only terminated one pregnancy. And that was because the mother would not have survived carrying the child to full term. It was a simple procedure and the mother suffered no complications. But with Johanna, there is no question in my mind that this was the reason she never conceived again."

Stefan realized he was shaking as the doctor added, "I'm truly sorry."

"Yes," Stefan managed, though his voice quivered with anger, "so am I."

"Do you want to talk about it?" the doctor asked kindly.

"What is there to say?" Stefan croaked. "I knew the day I married her that I'd made a mistake. I knew she was not inexperienced . . . but to think that she was . . . *pregnant*." Stefan shook his head in disbelief. "And then . . . I can't believe it. Merciful heaven, what kind of shrew did I marry?" He looked directly at the doctor. "What kind of woman is she?"

The doctor countered, "What would you have done? What does a man in your position do when he discovers his wife is pregnant with another man's child, knowing the marriage could make that child an heir?"

Stefan pressed both hands almost brutally through his hair. "I don't know." He shook his head. "I don't know what I would have done. But I never would have wanted her to . . . *kill* it." He shook his head again. "I can't believe it."

"What are you going to do?" the doctor asked.

"Do?" he echoed bitterly. "There's nothing I can *do!* I have to live with it, because our marriage is the only thing that keeps the baron reasonable at all."

"Perhaps I shouldn't have told you, or—"

"On the contrary," Stefan said, "I'm glad you told me."

"Perhaps I should have told you a long time ago."

"Perhaps. But if there's one thing I've learned, regret has no good in it. You did what you thought was best, which is why I married Johanna—at least I think that's why."

"Are you going to be all right?" the doctor asked. "Would you like to—"

He was interrupted as the door came open. Karl entered first, wearing a ridiculous grin. Then Erma, with a blanketed bundle in her arms.

"Come and meet your papa, little man," she said as she crossed the room and laid the baby in Stefan's arms.

Stefan looked up at her, feeling hesitant and awkward. But she only curtsied and said, "He's a fine boy, Your Grace. It'll be a pleasure to help care for him."

"Thank you, Erma," he said quietly and turned his attention

to the infant sleeping in his arms. He looked better now that he'd been cleaned up, and it was uncanny how a family resemblance could be seen in his little, chubby face.

Stefan was oblivious to Erma leaving the room and Karl sitting close by, still wearing a silly grin. The doctor chuckled and leaned back to sip his coffee.

Stefan said without looking up, "Yes, I think I'll be all right." He glanced at the doctor quickly. "He's big, you say?" He chuckled. "He doesn't feel very big to me."

"He'll grow quickly enough. Just enjoy him every day for what that day brings."

Stefan grew more brave and touched the little head, the face, the hands. He stood up carefully and moved toward the door.

"Where you going?" Karl asked with exaggerated disappointment.

"We're going to go see how Cameron's mother is doing," Stefan said, and then he glanced back at the doctor. "Thank you . . . for everything. And we'll keep it between us . . . *all* of it."

"You have my word on it," the doctor said firmly.

Stefan felt as if he were carrying priceless porcelain as he moved slowly up the stairs and into Ericha's room. She was sleeping just as he'd left her, laying on one side. Gently he laid the baby next to her and unwrapped the little blanket to get a better look. Trying to comprehend the reality that this was his son, the memories and emotions came rushing in all at once. How ironic, he thought, that he would witness the miracle of birth the same morning that he discovered the true depth of his wife's indiscretions. While the hurt and anger were strong enough to consume him, the presence of this child far outweighed those feelings with peace. He felt a humble reverence for life that he'd never comprehended. He thought of Ericha's agony, and the healing she had yet to go through, and he was amazed at her selfless love for him and for this child.

Stefan wrapped the baby back up to keep him from getting chilled, and then he bowed his head against the bed, offering a prayer of gratitude for all that Ericha had brought into his life.

Before the prayer ended, the tears came. And before his emotion was spent, he felt Ericha's hand in his hair.

"Why are you crying?" she asked in a hoarse voice as he lifted his head to look at her.

She wiped at his tears while he tried in vain to find the words. There were many aspects to this situation that caused him grief. But he reminded himself that none of that mattered. He touched Ericha's face in adoration as he told her, "I am so proud of you. What you have done for me today means more to me than I could ever tell you." He kissed her warmly. "I love you, Ericha. I love you."

The baby made a squawking noise that turned Ericha's tears to laughter. Stefan watched in awe as she guided the baby to her breast, seeming perhaps unsure of herself but not ashamed. She grimaced slightly as he began to nurse, and Stefan took her hand.

"Are you hurting?" he asked, thinking it was a stupid question. Between what he'd seen and what the doctor had told him, he suspected her pain would not go away quickly.

"I'm trying not to think about it," she said lightly. She touched Stefan's face. "I love you, Stefan Heinrich. Thank you—for letting me be a part of your life, and for letting me have your baby."

Stefan only kissed her, certain he would cry again if he tried to speak.

Returning to the castle and his business, pretending that nothing had changed, was one of the most difficult things Stefan had ever had to do. He was grateful to avoid Johanna, fearing he might strangle her if he was confronted with what he'd learned about her. Instead he concentrated on the reality that he had a son, and he was grateful that he could be open with his grandmother about it.

During a quiet moment in the office with Georg, Stefan brought up something he'd been wanting to bring up for quite some time. "I guess Abbi told you that Ericha had a baby."

"Told me?" He chuckled. "She talks of little else. One of

these days I'm going to have to tag along on one of Abbi's visits and meet the little tyke."

"Has Abbi told you anything about the situation with Ericha? About the baby, I mean?"

"Abbi's no gossip," Georg said.

Stefan shook his head in amazement. It was evident Georg didn't know. "That's for certain," he said. "What *do* you know?"

It appeared that Georg believed he was satisfying Stefan's curiosity. "Abbi said that Ericha told her she was involved with a married man, that she loved him and was committed. And the baby is his. Apparently the relationship started before any of us realized she was a part of the family. That's all I know. But I assumed you knew that much."

"Oh, I did," Stefan said. "But there's something Abbi *didn't* tell you. I doubt anyone would have minded if she had told you. You, of all people, should know."

"I'm listening," Georg said.

"I just thought it was important that you know who the baby's father is."

Georg was quiet a moment. "And how do *you* know who the baby's father is?"

"Well, what do you think?" Stefan asked with a chuckle. "You're a perceptive man. How do you think I would know?"

"Well," he said thoughtfully, "you spend a lot of time at Karl's. Ericha lives there. I assume you must know the man."

"Quite well." Stefan had to admit he was enjoying this moment. It wasn't often that anyone pulled anything over on Georg Heinrich.

"I assume there's a point to this."

"There is." Stefan placed a hand over his grandfather's where it rested on the arm of the chair. "Georg," he said, "the baby is mine."

Georg said nothing, didn't move. Stefan held his breath. "Well, I'll be damned," Georg finally said, and then he laughed.

Stefan laughed with him. "No, I think it's more likely that *I'll* be damned."

"I had no idea," Georg said.

"I know." Stefan became serious. "I wanted you to know . . . because he is *your* great-grandson, too."

Georg was a man of few words, but when their eyes met, Stefan knew that he was pleased. In a rare gesture, he put an arm around Stefan and hugged him with the strength of a man twenty years younger.

"God bless you, Stefan," he said. "You've earned some happiness, I'd say."

The following day, Georg went with Abbi to see the baby, and Stefan managed to drop by, knowing they would be there. Nothing in his life had ever given him such joy as to see Georg and Abbi coddling over his son, while Ericha looked on serenely.

Several days later, Stefan managed to get away late afternoon. He relaxed in the parlor with Ericha while she nursed little Cameron. He tickled the baby's foot then laughed when he kicked and wiggled.

"Stop that!" Ericha scolded lightly. "He's going to sleep."

"I don't want him to sleep *now.*" Stefan chuckled. "I want him to sleep *tonight,* so we can all sleep."

Stefan pressed a kiss to the baby's head, then to Ericha's lips. He caught movement in the doorway and glanced up to see Theodor standing there. Ericha quickly grabbed a lightweight blanket and threw it over her shoulder to retain her modesty while the baby nursed.

"What are you doing here?" Stefan asked with mock authority. "Surely that ogre you work for has something you should be doing."

"He gave me the day off, actually," Theodor stated. "Karl told me if I had any brains I would come and see this baby."

"Karl's right," Stefan said lightly. "Maybe *you* can keep him awake."

Ericha watched Theodor closely as he sauntered in and took a seat. She'd not seen him since the day he'd discovered her pregnancy, and she wondered what to expect.

"He'll be finished soon," she said, "and then you can see him."

Ericha listened while Stefan and Theodor spoke nonchalantly of some incident with a visiting dignitary a few days before. She handed the baby to Stefan and turned away to discreetly fasten her bodice. Stefan laughed and held the baby close to his face a moment before he crossed the room and handed him to Theodor.

"It's just a baby," Stefan laughed. "You don't have to look as though you're going to break it."

"Don't let him talk to you that way, Theodor," Ericha said. "Stefan behaved the same way not so long ago."

"He sure is tiny." Theodor chuckled, seeming mesmerized by the infant in his arms. In a wistful voice he said, "When Karl was this little, I was so preoccupied with having lost Leisl that I hardly enjoyed him."

Stefan instinctively reached out to take Ericha's hand, trying to comprehend how that might feel. "I cannot imagine," Stefan said quietly, "how difficult that must have been."

Theodor smiled toward him, but Stefan could see the evidence in his eyes. He'd never gotten over losing the woman he loved.

"I will never forget," Theodor said, seeming to relax a little as Cameron slept contentedly, "the way Erich stayed with me for hours that day while my father got the baby settled with a wet nurse." He looked at Ericha. "Your father was a good man."

"Yes, I know."

"I think . . ." He cleared his throat. "I think that in spite of everything, he would be proud of you." He glanced at Stefan. "Both of you."

Ericha squeezed Stefan's hand, and they exchanged a warm glance.

"You make a fine great-uncle, Theodor," Stefan said, and Theodor laughed. "But could you please wake the child up?"

Theodor's step toward acceptance urged Stefan's content- ment a little deeper. While he had no choice but to remain committed to his work and keep up the pretenses, he couldn't deny the newfound peace in his life. Each night when he went "home," as he was prone to call it, little Cameron seemed to have changed a bit. He didn't get much sleep since the baby woke every few hours to be changed and fed. But he was grateful to be with him and to have the chance to help Ericha through her healing. The first few weeks were difficult, but with her youth and natural resiliency, she improved quickly once she was able to get up and around on her own. And eventually she was able to walk and sit down without feeling the strain.

As Ericha recovered, she found more fulfillment than she'd ever dreamed possible to watch Stefan with his son. She wondered if any man had ever been so happy to become a father. The child was christened Cameron Erich Lokberg-du Woernig, and once word was out that Ericha had a son, she took herself out of hiding and went for frequent walks with a pram that had been a gift from Abbi and Georg. Little Cameron looked undoubtedly like a du Woernig, but the resemblance was easily credited to Ericha's bloodline. And it was a general assumption in Horstberg that she had gotten herself into trouble somehow. She was pleased to hear through Erma that with the weeks she had spent away from Horstberg in the fall, it was speculated by those who knew her that it had happened then. But Ericha didn't care what people were saying. She was happy with her life, and she would not have traded Stefan and his son for anything in the world.

Chapter Fourteen
THE DUKE'S WIFE

Abbi adored her newest great-grandchild and continued her frequent visits, but she declared one day that it was time Ericha brought him to the castle.

"Is there a reason you don't want to come to the castle?" Abbi asked carefully when Ericha seemed reluctant. "We all love you and—"

"All except Johanna," Ericha interrupted, and Abbi looked immediately concerned.

"You don't suppose she knows or—"

"Stefan is certain she doesn't. I just don't feel comfortable around her for many reasons. I believe she doesn't like the attention Stefan gives me, however seemingly innocent."

"Which is ironic," Abbi said with disgust. "She's hardly given him the time of day for years. Suddenly when he starts appearing happy and secure, she turns into a simpering . . . Oh, I shouldn't talk like that."

"Perhaps," Ericha said carefully, "she senses that she's not well liked and is defensive as a result."

"That could be," Abbi stated strongly, "but she's brought it on herself. From the time Stefan first showed an interest in her, she was given nothing but acceptance and respect from everyone in the family. After they were married and she began doing things we disapproved of, and seemed to put herself above us, we still did our best to accept and love her. To this day I certainly attempt to treat her with respect, in spite of all she's done."

Abbi stood from the sofa and paced as her voice showed subdued anger. "Stefan gave his heart and soul to that woman, and she did nothing but trod upon it. His love for her brought him nothing but pain."

Abbi noted Ericha's expression and composed herself as she sat carefully and finished in a softer tone. "That is why I'm grateful that he has you, my dear—in spite of the circumstances. And that is why you are going to come to the castle whenever you wish. You would be more likely to arouse suspicion if you stay away, I think. We'll all handle it carefully, and no one will be the wiser."

"Are you certain?" Ericha asked warily.

"Of course I'm certain." Abbi smiled.

"Well, I believe I can face anything—even Johanna—if I have you behind me."

"And I always will be." Abbi reached out to take Ericha's hand.

As long as the subject was open, Ericha felt she'd get no better chance to bring up something that she'd felt for a long time needed to be voiced. "Grandmama," she said carefully, "I can't begin to express my appreciation for your unconditional acceptance of me. Your example has smoothed over my circumstances immeasurably. But I'm not so sure the situation can be so easily smoothed over with my own illegitimate child." Abbi's gaze tightened with concern as Ericha went on. "People are well aware that my parents were betrothed, that a war was going on, that his life was in danger. Every citizen of Horstberg knows of his tragic death. The love and admiration these people had for Erich makes my existence acceptable." She shook her head slowly. "But that's not going to be the case with my son. People know nothing of the situation, and assumption will bring stigma. I don't want that stigma to fall on you, Grandmama. You've been nothing but perfectly loving and accepting of me. I do not want my choices to bring difficulties into your life."

Abbi let out a typically thoughtful sigh that let Ericha know she was pondering a careful response. Ericha was surprised when she said, "Did I ever tell you about the man I nearly married?"

"Not that I recall."

"It was Georg's idea. I was married to Cameron and expecting Erich, but Cameron was a fugitive, not certain if he'd survive long enough to reclaim his country and make the marriage public. He needed a visible forum to make the reclamation, and the Captain of the Guard had asked me to marry him. So Georg wanted me to accept the captain's proposal and plan the wedding, and Cameron promised that he would not allow the marriage to take place if he was alive. If he didn't survive, I would at least have a husband and a father for my child. Of course, you know the outcome. Lance . . . the captain, proved to be an honorable ally through a very difficult time. But he proved his devotion more thoroughly through the years. He remained Captain of the Guard, working closely with Cameron, and Lance and I remained close in the friendship we had gained through our . . . *betrothal.* He was an amazing man, and I grew to love him dearly, as Cameron did. When Cameron was concerned about my going anywhere, he would send Lance to be my escort. He knew that this man would lay down his life for me without batting an eye. And he would have. He was by far one of the most honorable, decent men I have ever known."

"What happened to him?" Ericha asked.

"He passed away a number of years ago: heart failure. It was sudden and unexpected, and his wife passed away not many years later. She and I were very good friends, as well." Abbi's eyes shifted from nostalgic to intense in a heartbeat. "At the age of thirty, Lance discovered that his mother had been involved with the duke—Cameron's father—and he was in actuality Cameron's half-brother." Ericha took a sharp breath, realizing now the reason for Abbi's story. "Imagine for a moment, my dear," Abbi continued, "not growing up with the knowledge of being illegitimate, but having it forced upon you as an established adult. He was devastated. But with time he adjusted, and he told me more than once in later years that the experience had taught him many things. First and foremost, he had learned that when people are judgmental and look down upon others, it has a lot more to do with those people than those they look down upon. He also learned that his knowledge had not changed who and what he was inside—what he had always been. Ironically, he married a woman who had been involved with Cameron's brother, Nikolaus, and she had an illegitimate daughter by him. She had been betrayed into believing they were married, but the ceremony had been a farce."

"That's terrible," Ericha said.

"Yes, Nikolaus was very good at doing terrible things." Abbi's eyes softened as she got to her point. "There are all kinds of reasons that children are born into this world when they are not planned or expected, or in circumstances that are less than ideal. But we are all God's children. Whether parents are irresponsible and immoral, or simply caught in a situation that's difficult, every human being has the right to be raised well, and revered and loved." Abbi's voice picked up a severity that Ericha couldn't recall ever hearing before. "I *do not* care what people think or say about you and your son, my dear. He will be loved and revered in this family, Ericha. He is a product of the truest love and the best of intentions, and by heaven and earth, he will live a good life. We will see to that."

Abbi heaved a deep breath, as if she had just relieved herself of a large burden, and then she spoke in a light voice. "Why don't you come to dinner tomorrow? It will be a delight."

Before Ericha had a chance to reply, Abbi's eyes moved away, and Ericha turned to see Karl leaning in the doorway.

"You're just in time," Abbi said.

"Why is that?"

"I'm certain you'd be more than happy to drive Ericha and the baby to the castle tomorrow, now wouldn't you."

"Is that a command, Your Grace?" he teased.

She smiled. "A request," she said easily.

"Yes," Karl sat down across from them, "I'd be more than happy to do that."

"Good," Abbi said triumphantly.

"I suppose it's settled." Ericha laughed, and she had to admit as the time drew near that she was excited with the prospect of returning to Castle Horstberg. It had been a long time, and she truly missed it.

When Stefan came for the night, he was delighted to hear that she would be coming. "Dinner will be a worthwhile event for a change," he said, leaning over Cameron's bassinet to watch him sleep. "And maybe I'll actually get to see my son when he's awake."

Ericha slipped her hand into his and felt compassion for him. Since the baby had started sleeping through the night most of the time, Stefan had hardly been able to even hold him. If for no other reason, she was glad Abbi had talked her into going.

Abbi sat alone in her room and found her mind wandering into the past. The conversation she'd had earlier with Ericha had stirred memories of the abiding friendship she'd shared with Lance Dukerk, but her mind felt compelled to linger on one of the most difficult moments they had ever shared.

The night before Cameron and Erich's funeral, she had gone to the room she had shared with Cameron for three decades. Even though she had already had her things moved elsewhere, she knew she would soon be searched out, and this was where she would be expected to be found. Long after she normally would have gone to bed, she stared into a cold fireplace with a lamp burning low. She had brushed out her hair and removed her shoes and stockings, but she still wore the black dress she'd worn through the day. She knew she would never be able to sleep until this encounter she'd been dreading was seen to.

The Captain of the Guard was one of her very dearest friends, as he had been to Cameron. Through the years, Lance had been as closely affiliated with the family—and the duchy—as Georg had been. The recent revolution of Nik Koenig had been difficult on

Lance and his family, and as soon as the situation had been resolved, he had left the country with his wife and two of their adult children for a brief vacation. He'd not told anyone where they were going, but he'd promised to return the night before the wedding. Abbi kept remembering how he'd laughed and embraced Cameron before he'd gotten into the carriage, insisting that he wouldn't miss Erich's marriage for the world. The wedding should have been tomorrow morning, but instead there would be a funeral. And as of yet, Lance had no idea of what had happened. She knew that as soon as he returned he wouldn't be able to miss the mourning wreaths on the castle gates and doors, nor the black arm bands worn by all of his officers. But she'd given strict orders via Georg that he be sent straight to talk with her, that no one was to deliver the news beyond herself. She didn't want him hearing of Cameron and Erich's deaths through the insensitive tongue of a junior officer who happened to be in the courtyard on duty when he returned.

Abbi felt a sudden panic when she realized that Lance would have to pass by the caskets in the main hall in order to get to her room. With a prayer in her heart that she would not be too late, she rushed down the stairs, past the ducal office, practically running down the long hall toward the main entrance. Approaching the caskets, she slowed her step and paused a moment to be close to them and absorb the reality a little deeper into herself, and then she moved slowly on, knowing she could now avoid having Lance discover the news by such a dreadful means.

Stepping into the courtyard, she realized her feet were bare, but the cold stone beneath them felt good in a way. She ambled slowly toward the officer on duty near the keep and asked him, "Has the captain returned yet?"

"Not yet, Your Grace. It should be soon according to what he told us prior to his leaving. He is nothing if not dependable."

"Indeed," she said. "Thank you." She continued a leisurely stroll around the perimeter of the huge courtyard, lit by occasional torches as it always was. Trying to rehearse what she might say, she wished that Lance had been here when the explosion had occurred, which would have spared her from this duty.

Abbi was nearly back to the main entrance when the carriage thundered noisily into the courtyard and halted. She stood near the door, her hands behind her back. The carriage door opened, and her heart quickened to see Lance step down, his deep voice booming as he asked the officer who stepped forward to greet him according to protocol, "Why the mourning, Lieutenant?" His agitation was evident in the tone of his voice.

"Her Grace asked that she tell you herself, Captain." The officer's eyes moved toward Abbi and Lance's followed. Even from this distance she felt his distress, and she felt certain he perceived the tragedy that her expression couldn't help but betray. She watched him turn with hesitance toward the carriage as his grown son stepped out. "See that your mother gets to bed; she's exhausted. I'm not sure how long I'll be."

Abbi's heart beat in time to his boots on the courtyard as he approached her deftly, his brow furrowed, his eyes filled with dread. When he was standing before her, he asked in a voice that was almost harsh, "What's happened, Abbi? Why the mourning?"

Abbi suddenly lost her voice and motioned him toward the door, both to give her a moment to compose herself and to find a place where they would not be observed. He held the door for her and followed her into the dimly lit hall. They were apparently alone, but she took up a lamp from a little table and led the way into a nearby parlor, not wanting any chance of servants coming upon them. Once inside, he closed the door and leaned against it while she set the lamp down and turned to face him. Their eyes met, and again she struggled to find her voice while she saw him take in the fact that she was wearing black. Watching his eyes, she could well imagine him wondering why Cameron was not here to greet him with the bad news. That's the way it should have been. That was standard protocol when anything went wrong.

"Where's Cameron?" he demanded quietly, and she was momentarily distracted by the thought of how Lance often accused her of being psychic, and how she'd always insisted that it was simply feminine insight.

Abbi resigned herself to not being able to say it without

betraying her emotion. She forced her voice past the lump in her throat enough to say, "He's gone, Lance."

"Gone?" he echoed, his voice croaking. "What do you mean . . . gone?"

Abbi cleared her throat and added with a quavering voice, "He's dead."

"No," he protested weakly.

"Yes," Abbi assured him, feeling her heart break all over again as she considered the love that Lance and Cameron shared. She heard Lance suck in his breath and struggle to let it out. She watched him press a hand to his chest as if he'd been struck with a sudden, tangible pain. He groaned and leaned more heavily into the door behind him, as if it might keep him standing. Instinctively Abbi moved toward him, holding out her hands. He reached for them urgently, as if he believed she could somehow save him from accepting what he'd been told. Holding both her hands in a firm grip, he dropped to his knees and groaned again. She felt his hands begin to shake, and then a sob erupted from his throat. A moment later she was sitting on the floor with the captain's face buried in her lap, weeping openly. She cried silent tears while she held him. They had shared grief before, but never like this.

When the initial shock had evidently subsided and his emotion had quieted, he asked in a raspy voice, "How? How did it happen?"

Abbi squeezed her eyes shut and sucked in her breath. She'd almost forgotten that he only knew half of the reason Horstberg was in mourning. She cleared her throat gently, and at her hesitance, he sat up abruptly and met her eyes. "What happened, Abbi?" he demanded, taking both her hands into his.

"He was . . . trying to save . . . Erich. There was . . . an explosion . . . from the chemistry room and . . ."

"Erich?" he squeaked.

"Erich's gone, as well," she said, and then she was crying in *his* arms.

It took her over an hour to tell him everything she knew in between horrible bouts of emotion, and then they walked together down the long hall to the caskets, where they both cried again. He finally walked her to the door of the room where she was now staying before he returned to his apartment to give the news to his family.

Lance had taken his rightful place in the funeral procession as Captain of the Guard, and as always, he had a public dignity that left Abbi in awe. The day after the funeral, he submitted his official resignation. He insisted that he'd been too old to be captain for years anyway, and he'd only held the position in a mostly supervisory capacity at Cameron's insistence. There were many good officers in place, and one who was an obvious choice to fill the role of captain as Han took over the country. It was someone Han knew well and with whom he shared a mutual trust and respect. Lance moved his family to a home in the country, away from the fine apartment in the castle where he'd lived even before he had met and married Nadine. They had remained in close touch, and he had been an ongoing support to Abbi, as was his wife, Nadine.

Abbi sighed and brought her mind back to the present. Lance and Nadine had both passed on years ago, and she truly missed them. She tried to imagine them being in a better place with Cameron and Erich—and Kathe. Were they all together in another sphere? She liked to think so.

Abbi was grateful when Georg found her and sat beside her, taking her hand into his once he'd greeted her with a kiss. She appreciated the distraction as they talked of the day's events and reminisced of happier times. How grateful she was for his companionship in her life! And he shared her enthusiasm regarding Ericha's pending visit tomorrow. They spoke of the blessing Ericha was to their lives and of their love for the great-grandson they shared. Abbi finally went to bed with the peace of knowing that in spite of many challenges, her life was good. And she was grateful.

When it finally came time to leave for the castle, Ericha surveyed her reflection in the mirror and felt both excited and a little afraid.

She glanced toward the clock and drew back her shoulders, then went downstairs to find Karl laying on the parlor floor with little Cameron on his chest. Karl made a variety of animal noises in an effort to get the baby's attention.

"You're making a fool of yourself, Karl." She laughed.

"That's all right." He grinned as he rose and settled Cameron in his arms to escort Ericha outside to the waiting trap. "He's too little to care, and you'll love me anyway."

"No, Karl," Ericha said, "I love you especially because you make a fool out of yourself for my son."

"Well," he said as Ericha seated herself and he handed her the baby, "he loves old Uncle Karl. What more can I say?"

Ericha laughed, and Karl began rambling about all the fun they'd have when Cameron got old enough to really play. They seemed to arrive in no time, and Ericha drew a deep breath as Karl left her at the main entrance with a good luck kiss.

Before dinner, Ericha visited with Abbi and Georg, who made as much a fool of himself with the baby as Karl had. He adored the child every bit as much as Abbi did, and he commented several times that the resemblance to Erich was uncanny.

When dinner was announced, Abbi called for a servant to take the baby while they dined. Ericha was hesitant, but Abbi assured her that Ruthild had been helping with babies since Hannah and Stefan were born.

Moving down the hall with Abbi and Georg, Ericha nearly caught her breath to see Stefan approaching from the other direction with Johanna by his side. The reality of seeing them together was shocking. Abbi took Ericha's hand to squeeze it, and Ericha was certain she sensed her feelings.

"My dear cousin Ericha," Stefan said immediately, bowing over her hand to kiss it. "I was so pleased when Grandmama told me you'd be coming. It's been a long time."

"It has indeed," she replied coolly. "You're looking well, Your Grace," she added. "And you, Your Grace," she said toward Johanna, who answered with a stilted smile.

"And you," Stefan replied, placing Ericha's hand over his arm to escort her to the dining room. "It appears you've fared well through your ordeal."

"Very well, thank you," she said.

"What ordeal is that?" Johanna asked.

Ericha glanced toward Abbi, who answered calmly, "Ericha had a baby recently."

Johanna looked at Ericha with obvious surprise, but she said nothing.

"You should see the baby," Abbi said as they were seated.

"He must be adorable," Stefan said easily to Ericha. "Grandmama does nothing but rave about him."

"He is handsome," Georg said, and Stefan smiled.

"But of course he is," Abbi said, and then she steered the conversation toward something that would make Ericha less the center of attention.

The meal proceeded mostly with small talk until Johanna said out of nowhere, "It must be a burden to have a child and no husband. For me it's been the other way around."

Ericha glanced up sharply. Stefan leaned forward and his brow furrowed. While the comment appeared innocent, something subtle in Johanna's eyes betrayed that her motives were not.

Ericha was unsure how to reply. Carefully she lifted her chin as an expectancy fell upon the room. "Actually," she said with confidence, "I'm very grateful for my son and don't take his existence for granted."

Abbi discreetly covered her mouth with her fingers to avoid showing the smile spurred by Ericha's reply. Stefan remained expressionless, but Abbi caught the gratification in his eyes as he leaned back and relaxed again.

"It would be nice to have children," Johanna said with a lilt in her voice that passed off Ericha's statement completely. She shot a subtly accusing glance toward Stefan and added, "But I fear we will never have that opportunity. The situation has always been distressing for Stefan—more so than for me, I think, because of his position."

Everyone looked discreetly amazed as she continued. "But of course, I've told him it's just one of those things that can't be helped, and there's no need for him to suffer guilt over it. After all," she added with a sweet smile directed toward Stefan, "we can depend on each other for our happiness. Can we not, my love?"

Stefan felt angry as he silently absorbed her words. But gradually a smile touched one corner of his mouth as he perceived what she was trying to do. "Yes, my dear," he said coolly, "I'm certain Ericha would be pleased to know just how much you and I thrive on each other's company." He said it with such a genuine tone that Johanna seemed to relax as the meal continued. And they were all grateful when the conversation was directed elsewhere.

When the meal was finished, Abbi asked that Ruthild bring the baby to the drawing room where they would have coffee. Ericha was more relaxed once Cameron was returned to her, happy and content. Georg and Abbi coddled over the baby while Stefan sat quietly drinking his coffee. Despite his lack of expression, Ericha knew this was not easy for him.

"Would you like to hold him, Stefan?" Ericha asked, and he looked briefly startled.

He made no response, and Johanna stood suddenly, moving toward Abbi with her arms outstretched.

"May I hold him?" she asked. Abbi carefully gave the baby to Johanna, who seemed somehow taken by the child as she surveyed him closely in her arms. But Ericha couldn't help feeling tense to observe them. She wondered if Stefan shared the feeling when he stood abruptly and, without speaking, gently took the child from Johanna.

"I must admit that he's cute," Johanna said as she relinquished the baby, seeming almost eager to be free of him.

Stefan did his best to observe the baby as if this was the first time. His expression softened naturally as he held him, and then he smiled at the child and moved toward the door.

"Where are you going?" Abbi asked.

"I thought I'd show him around the castle a little," he said lightly, and Abbi smiled toward Ericha.

"You'd best go with him," she said. Ericha followed Stefan out of the room as Johanna declared she was going to bed. Ericha waited until Johanna had disappeared in the opposite direction before she caught up to Stefan.

"Are you all right?" Ericha asked as they walked down the hall and up some stairs.

"Yes, fine," he said easily. "Why do you ask?"

"I know this is difficult for you."

"Any more difficult than for you?"

"Perhaps."

"I'm all right." He smiled subtly. "I'm very grateful for my son and don't take his existence for granted." Ericha smiled shyly, and he added, "You handled her very well. I commend you."

"It's nice to be here with you," she said, "in spite of the dramatics."

"Yes," he agreed, "it is."

Stefan took his son to the family gallery and made quite an ordeal of telling him about his ancestors. They walked through parts of the castle Ericha had never seen before until eventually Stefan led the way up some turret stairs that wound endlessly. When he opened the door at the top, Ericha felt fresh air strike her, and she stepped into a room with a large open window where she could see the moonlit sky. Cameron started to fuss with the change in temperature, but Stefan put the baby to his shoulder and turned his back to the window to shield him from the breeze, and the baby settled right away.

The room was filled with pigeons and little else, and Stefan told her they were used for communication. He explained the method briefly, and Ericha was fascinated to learn they'd been using them for generations.

Ericha stood before the window, astounded by the view that looked out over the forest. Stefan leaned against the sill and brushed his lips over Cameron's wispy hair.

"I wish it could always be this way," he said.

Ericha gave him a peaceful smile that assured him it could be worse, and he bent to kiss her warmly.

"I love you, Ericha," he whispered before leading the way down the stairs to the ballroom. They ascended another set of stairs and turned down a hall that Ericha recognized as where she'd come to rest during the ball. Stefan pointed out the room when she asked about it, then allowed her a peek in the rest of the rooms in this section of hall, most of which consisted of his chambers.

"I recognize this room," Ericha said when he showed her his bedroom, "although I generally use the back door."

Stefan smiled at this and continued on, showing her his sitting room and dressing room as he declared, "It's an awful lot of space for one man."

"And Johanna?" Ericha asked.

"Has equivalent rooms elsewhere—in another wing."

Ericha wanted to comment that his rooms were big enough for her and Cameron to move in. But she knew it would touch too close to a sore spot for Stefan.

They moved on to a door at the end of the hall that Stefan opened and motioned for her to go in, declaring this was his favorite. Along with a grand piano, a guitar, and a mandolin, there was an easel bearing partly finished art, surrounded by the materials that went along with it. This room didn't have the perfect order of the other rooms she had seen. It seemed well used.

"Why is this your favorite room?" she asked.

"This is where I can be me," he stated. "It doesn't get used as much now as it did in the past."

"Why?"

"I spend my free time with you." He smiled.

Ericha returned the smile, then surveyed the room carefully.

"My grandfather taught me to play the piano. My memories of him are very fond. My mother and grandmother instilled my love for art, though they are better at it than I am. I used to have a different room for art, but I found that playing and painting seemed to go hand in hand for me, so I moved it all here."

He stopped and watched her closely. Ericha caught a touch of vulnerability in his eyes that made her realize what he'd just told her was near a confession. This room represented a part of

Stefan that few people knew about. Ericha paused to analyze the work on the easel and had to ask what it was.

"It's a stallion," he stated, "rearing back. I've barely started it."

"Oh, I see now," she said, scrutinizing it again before she moved on. She noticed two completed works leaning against the wall: one was covered, and the other appeared to be the view out of the turret window they'd just seen.

"I recognize that," she said, and he smiled shyly. "It's very nice. You do well."

"It seems to run in the family," he said humbly. "I can take little credit."

"Would you play something for me?" she asked, nodding toward the piano.

Stefan handed Cameron over to her and sat quietly at the bench. Ericha watched him closely as he began a nostalgic piece. The music gradually became more passionate, and he didn't seem at all like the Duke of Horstberg. Here Ericha could see the Stefan Heinrich that she loved: the man behind the obligation of royalty and the facade of an ill-fated marriage.

He finished the song and turned to look at her, placing his hands on his thighs. Ericha met his eyes and tried to grasp that she was the mother of this man's child.

"I had no idea," she said softly, nearly moved to tears. He glanced down with a humble expression, and she added lightly, "It's no wonder I love you so much."

Stefan laughed as he rose and took Ericha's hand to lead her down the stairs to his office, where two officers of the Guard stood at attention near the door.

"Are they *always* there?" she asked when they'd gone in.

"Not the same ones." He chuckled. "But yes, they stand guard twenty-four hours a day."

"Then the contents of this room must be very important."

"Indeed," he said. Cameron started to fuss as Stefan showed her some of the finer details of his job here, and she sat near the desk to nurse him while they continued to talk. She smiled when he put his glasses on, recalling how embarrassed she'd been when he'd first seen her wearing her own glasses. Stefan rummaged through some papers for a few minutes, and then he removed his glasses and leaned back to watch Ericha.

As always, Stefan was enchanted with the domestic scene. He said nothing as Ericha pulled the sleeping baby away and laid him in an overstuffed chair.

Stefan caught Ericha's hand as she went to fasten her bodice. With an aggression that took her breath away, he pulled her onto his lap and kissed her with immediate fever in his lips.

"Ericha," he whispered, kissing her throat, "I love you. I love you so much."

Ericha moved her hands into his hair as he kissed her again.

"Are you coming tonight?" she asked breathlessly.

"I'll be there before you get home," he said, and his kiss became more bold.

Ericha would have been oblivious to someone entering the room, except that Stefan tensed so abruptly it almost frightened her. She turned as Stefan did to see Rusty standing in the doorway, literally gaping to observe their intimate embrace. He closed the door as quickly as he'd opened it, and Stefan cursed under his breath as they were left alone again.

Ericha quickly buttoned her bodice while Stefan opened the door and called in a calm voice, "Rusty, please come in here, if you will."

Ericha picked Cameron up and sat down, wondering fearfully what would result from this. Rusty entered the office sheepishly, avoiding Ericha's eyes. Stefan closed the door and sat behind the desk.

"Sit down," he said sternly. Ericha could see that he was the duke again as his order was obeyed immediately.

Through a minute of silence, Stefan contemplated how to deal with this.

"I apologize, sir, for . . . I mean I . . . well, it's not that . . ."

"Rusty," Stefan said to put an end to his stammering, "there is no reason for you to apologize. I simply have to know that I can trust your confidence in this."

Rusty gave an innocent expression, seeming to portray that he'd seen nothing. Stefan said abruptly, "There is no reason for either of us to pretend that you didn't just see what was happening here. I want to know that you will say nothing to anyone—not anyone."

Rusty's eyes moved briefly to Ericha before he said, "Of course you can trust me, sir. You know I'd have no reason to tell anyone or . . ." He paused and took a deep breath, just now seeming to absorb what the evidence really meant. "Her Grace doesn't know," he stated with wide eyes.

"Of course she doesn't know," Stefan said. "She'd tear me into little pieces if she did."

"Well, she won't hear it from me," he stated with enough conviction that Stefan gave a sigh of relief. "I'll not tell a soul, I swear it."

"Thank you," Stefan said quietly.

Rusty turned to survey Ericha again, and his eyes moved to the baby. He turned to Stefan in question. "He's my son," Stefan said with obvious pride in his voice.

Rusty's eyes widened again as he seemed to grasp the deeper meaning to his confession. "Stefan," he said carefully, and Ericha could tell it was not common for him to use his given name, "maybe I have no right to say it, but you're weaving a tangled web."

"It's already woven," Stefan said soberly. "It cannot be undone." He glanced toward Ericha and added, "I would not want it to be."

Rusty seemed to graciously accept the answer, then stood and moved to the door saying, "Again I apologize for intruding upon you . . . I mean, well . . . as I said, you have my confidence, and . . ." He nodded and sheepishly left the room.

Stefan gave Ericha a weary glance, and she declared, "Perhaps it's time I went home."

"And time I learned to keep my passion under control," he said in a self-punishing tone.

Ericha was silent a moment before saying carefully, "It has

been a long time." He looked at her intently, and she added, "You told me you would be there before I get home."

Stefan smiled and ushered her toward the door. "If you will excuse me, little cousin, I will escort you back to Grandmama. I have an appointment to keep."

Ericha grinned and moved past him into the hall. She arrived home to find him already there, stretched out in the parlor talking with Karl. Ericha visited with them until Cameron's demand to be fed forced her to leave.

"Cameron and I are going up to bed," she declared. "Have a nice chat."

Ericha dressed for bed and lay down to nurse Cameron while her thoughts became absorbed with Stefan. The baby was nearly asleep when Stefan came quietly into the room and sat down to pull off his boots.

"I think he's finished," Ericha whispered. Stefan rose to put the baby in his bassinet, pausing to watch him sleep for a moment before he turned to Ericha. He moved to the edge of the bed and leaned over to kiss her. With gentle purpose he explored every part of her face with his fingertips, and combed them through her hair as if he'd never touched it before. The night was theirs, and here in this room, nothing from the outside world could touch what they shared. Right now, time had no essence.

Ericha quietly worked at her tatting in the east winter parlor of the castle while Stefan toyed idly with the piano. Georg sat on the floor, playing with little Cameron while Abbi looked on with pride. Supper had been especially pleasant as Johanna had claimed to not be feeling well and had eaten in her room. No one had much to say, but the silence had a peaceful quality that Stefan was wishing could be more common. He glanced often toward his son, wondering what life might be like for them as he grew older. Then his gaze turned to Ericha, and he marveled freshly at the love they shared. He had to admit that life was good.

As Ericha's visits to the castle had increased, the situation became more comfortable. But Stefan was careful to save his affection for the times when he was at Ericha's home and there was no chance of betraying their secret to someone who could not be trusted.

Cameron was always the center of attention and was loved by everyone—except Johanna, who was politely uninterested in the child and seemed subtly disgusted by Ericha's immorality. It was perhaps one of the most difficult things Stefan had ever done to pretend this child was not his. But he was at least grateful for the discovery that Ericha was his cousin so that he could justify his interest in the child and have the opportunity to spend more time with him.

Rusty seemed to accept the situation, and Stefan knew without doubt that he would not betray him. Still, it seemed a constant fear that someone was going to figure it out. There were times when Stefan wouldn't have cared if someone did. And other times he felt certain such knowledge in the wrong hands could destroy them. He wondered at times if the true source of their problem was all the deception, but there was nothing to be done about it. For the moment their secret was safe, they were together, and Stefan couldn't help feeling warm inside.

"Ericha, my dear," Georg said, coming to his feet, "would you mind if I took the little man for a walk? I thought I might go to the library."

"I'm certain Cameron would enjoy it," Ericha said, and Georg headed toward the door with the baby.

"Would you like to come along, Abbi?" he turned back and asked.

"I believe I will," she consented, winking at Stefan before she left the room.

Stefan met Ericha's eyes tensely. Being alone with her in the castle tended to make him nervous since Rusty had walked in on them. But he just turned his attention fully to the piano and fought the urge to cross the room and take her in his arms.

"Why is the music so sad tonight?" she asked quietly, and he turned in surprise.

"Is it sad?" he replied. "More thoughtful, I believe."

"Why is it thoughtful, then?"

"Same old things," he said, concentrating on the keys. "You know how it is. I can't help wishing . . ." He stopped abruptly when he sensed more than heard the door coming open. When Johanna eased into the room, he was relieved that nothing appeared suspicious.

"I thought I heard you playing, darling," she said sweetly. "Do you mind if I join you?"

Stefan said nothing. Johanna moved toward the piano, wearing an elaborate dressing gown. Ericha noticed the subtly phony sway of her hips as she moved past.

"Oh, hello, Ericha dear," she said. "I didn't know you were there." Ericha nodded politely. "Where is everyone else?" she added, sitting on the piano bench beside Stefan, who pretended not to notice.

"Georg and Abbi took the baby to the library with them," Ericha replied when it became apparent Stefan wasn't going to.

"Everyone sure loves that baby of yours, Ericha," she said, and only her eyes betrayed anything but sweetness. "It seems even Stefan has taken quite a liking to him. Isn't that right, darling?"

"I can't deny that," he stated tonelessly, trying to ignore the hand she'd placed on his shoulder.

"Like I've said before," she rambled on, "I'm certain Stefan would have liked children of his own. Oh, I would too, of course. But perhaps it's for the better." She sighed.

"Why is that?" Ericha asked.

"I'm not certain that Stefan has the patience for children," she replied, as if it were obvious. Stefan couldn't help the astonished glance he shot toward his wife, and Ericha's eyes widened in surprise.

"I've never seen any lack of patience toward little Cameron," Ericha replied easily. "In truth, it's quite the opposite . . . from what I have observed," she added quickly.

"Perhaps that's because it's not his own child," Johanna went on. "I mean, if—"

"Is there something you wanted?" Stefan asked, pulling his hands abruptly from the keys.

"No," Johanna replied as if his tone of voice only proved what she had been saying about him. "I was just feeling a bit bored and lonely."

She sighed again and pushed her fingers into Stefan's hair. He retracted from her touch, but it didn't seem to affect her as she persisted. Stefan squeezed his eyes shut, attempting to maintain self control. He felt certain any bold defense in Ericha's presence would only make matters worse.

As her hand tugged playfully at his hair, Johanna bent forward and whispered, just loud enough for Ericha to hear, "I was only wondering when you were coming up to bed."

Stefan stood abruptly from the bench and poured himself a drink. He shot a quick glance toward Ericha, and she caught his silent plea for her to understand that this was as difficult for him as it was for her.

"I thought you were ill," he said to Johanna, and he emptied the glass in one swallow and moved to the window. "Why don't you go upstairs and sleep it off?"

Johanna only looked briefly distressed as she moved toward Stefan and whispered something to him that Ericha couldn't discern. She tried to remain unaffected by the seductive glances Johanna gave him and the affectionate way she reached up to touch his face. But everything inside of Ericha wanted to scream as Johanna pushed her arms around Stefan's waist and eased her shapely body against his.

Stefan's hands remained in his pockets. His eyes were cold and hard. But it was easy for Ericha to perceive the intimate relationship they had once shared. And the one harsh reality of the situation slapped Ericha in the face: Johanna was his wife, till death would they part.

"If you will excuse me," Ericha said, proud of herself for the light, calm tone, "I'd best see if little Cameron needs me." Stefan looked distressed as she moved toward the door, but Johanna only smiled, easing a little closer to Stefan.

Once they were alone, Stefan took her hands from behind his back and nearly threw them out of his grasp.

"You're making a fool of yourself, Johanna," he stated and moved back to the piano, setting his fingers onto the keys with hard, strong chords that betrayed his anger.

"Why is that?" she asked innocently.

"You and I both know," he stated, trying to keep his concentration on the keys, "that we've not shared a bed in a very long time. Your insinuating that it will magically change tonight is preposterous, and you know it."

"But surely you don't want your family to know that—"

"I'm certain my family figured out long ago that there is nothing left between you and me."

"But Ericha can't possibly—"

He turned to look at her with hard eyes. "What Ericha thinks of you and me is purely up to her. But I'll not tolerate your play-acting in front of her, or anyone else, for that matter."

Johanna quickly attempted to throw the accusations elsewhere. "I don't understand how she can possibly be so happy with that baby of hers when everyone knows she's never been married. And I don't know how all of you can be so accepting of such a thing. If I were—"

"If you were what?" he interrupted sharply. "I'll tell you what: if you were pregnant and I weren't the father, I suspect that would be acceptable in your eyes, as long as no one else knew. Or is it all right to do that sort of thing as long as you don't get pregnant? If that's the case, you have nothing to worry about."

"What are you insinuating?" she asked haughtily.

"I'm not insinuating anything," he replied calmly. "I am coming right out and saying that I have no doubt what you are guilty of." Stefan glared at her, daring her to deny it. He was almost disappointed when she didn't.

"What would you expect?" she asked, turning away from him.

"When my husband has turned me away, I have no choice but to seek affection elsewhere."

"Are you trying to make me believe you were faithful until that time?" She turned toward him in astonishment, and he added tersely, "Don't bother." He had to bite his tongue to keep from repeating the things Doctor Furhelm had told him.

When it appeared that she was leaving, Stefan turned his attention back to the piano, grateful to have it to release his emotions, otherwise he was tempted to bodily throw her out the window. He tensed visibly when Johanna sat on the bench beside him again and reached up to touch his face. He recoiled abruptly.

"Stefan," she whispered, "what has happened to us?"

Stefan stopped playing and looked toward her dubiously. He chuckled to realize that she was serious.

"Everything was so good," she said quietly, "until that night when you . . . you just turned on me. You were so cruel, Stefan, and then . . . then you stopped paying any notice of me at all."

"The only thing I stopped doing," Stefan muttered, "is coming to your bed. If you think that was all it took to make a good marriage, then you must forgive me—I don't agree. If you weren't so blinded by your ambitions, you would have noticed that what I thought was love disappeared from these eyes the day we married." She looked astonished, and Stefan clarified, "That's right, my dear, this marriage was over the day it began. The only thing you and I ever shared was silent anguish in a cold, dark bed. To you it was ecstasy. To me it was hell."

"I don't understand," she cried, and Stefan believed it was the first time he'd seen genuine tears come from those eyes.

"Maybe you don't," he said from low in his throat, "but I do. I understood it all perfectly on our wedding night when you made it clear exactly why you married me." Her eyes widened. "Don't you remember? Perhaps the champagne dulled your memory. Let me refresh it. You wanted to conquer the Duke of Horstberg. You brought an alliance to your country that will make your name go down in history."

His voice lowered to a hoarse whisper. "You took an innocent heart, enticed it with a deceptive lure of love, and then you threw it on the floor and trampled on it with your victory dance."

Stefan paused to watch her expression. There was no denial there, but perhaps a touch of regret mingling with the tears. But Stefan didn't care. What Johanna felt had stopped mattering to him years ago.

"You are so beautiful," he said, brashly taking her chin into his hand. "Your eyes are bewitching, and everything about you is enticing. But I don't care," he muttered, tossing her face from his grasp. "I find you repulsive, dear wife. So sleep where you want and think what you like. I simply don't care. It's over. That's it."

"You've turned cold and bitter, Stefan," she cried in her defense.

"How observant of you."

"I would have never believed you could be so hateful."

"I would have never believed it myself."

"And what of you?" She lifted her chin saucily. "Are you content to spend your nights alone?"

"Whether I am or not should make no difference to you."

"I don't think you have it in you." She laughed cynically. "A man who is so thoroughly devoted to his country and family couldn't possibly have the nerve to seek pleasure elsewhere."

"If you mean that I would never go tramping around town, looking for any bed where I can discreetly hide from reality, you are quite right. I don't have that in me."

"Do you know what your problem is, Stefan?" she asked bitterly. "You're not man enough to handle a woman like me."

Stefan chuckled tersely. "That's not the impression I got from that last kiss I gave you.Surely you remember how you begged and pleaded for something you never got."

"Damn you!" she spat, lifting her hand to slap him. Stefan caught her wrist and dodged the blow, but she caught her finger-nails against his face, leaving a deep impression in his flesh and a trace of blood.

Stefan twisted her arm behind her back and whispered hoarsely in her ear, "Get out of here, Johanna. Go for one of your late-night strolls and leave me in peace. Or you might find me breaking one of my laws. It would be worth a month or two in the keep to put you in line."

She nearly stumbled forward as he let her go. With a long, defiant glare, she left the room. Stefan drew a deep breath and poured himself a drink, splashing some of the brandy on his face, where it stung until he wiped it away with his shirtsleeve.

Stefan was disappointed to find that Ericha had gone home, but he ignored Abbi's inquiry about the scratches on his face and left the castle, riding as quickly as Fire would take him.

Ericha's thoughts had been filled with anger and resentment, but they fled the moment Stefan walked through the door. His eyes were pained and weary, and anguish seeped through his countenance.

"What happened?" she asked, touching his face. "Did she—"

"It's nothing," he insisted. "I'm sorry," he added, and his arms came around her with desperation. "I love you," he whispered over and over while Ericha just held him. It seemed that everything would be all right as long as she just held him.

Stefan returned to the castle early and went straight to the office to get started. He knew that Abbi had invited Ericha to breakfast, and they would spend the day together. If he worked it out right, he could innocently manipulate himself into their plans and spend some time with his two favorite women—and his son.

Stefan had barely walked into the office when he saw the booted legs stacked in the center of his desk.

"Good morning, son." Han Heinrich laughed. "Just thought I'd see if the old chair still works."

Stefan chuckled and walked around the desk as his father stood. "What are you doing here?" Stefan asked as they shared a hearty embrace.

"I live here," Han said.

"You will never convince me of that. *You* are little better than a gypsy."

"True." Han chuckled, motioning Stefan into the chair he'd just occupied. "But it's better for your mother that way."

"How is she?" Stefan asked as they were both seated.

"Good," Han said, "and how are you?"

"I'm fine," Stefan said with enthusiasm.

"Really?" Han seemed surprised.

"Shouldn't I be fine?" Stefan paused, and then he asked quickly, "And how are you, Father?"

"I'm doing well."

"I'm glad to hear it," Stefan said. "Have you seen your father yet?"

"No. We arrived late. He's still asleep, I believe."

"Well, he'll be here soon. He never sleeps too late."

Stefan put on his glasses and shuffled through the papers on his desk, wondering what he could get started on before Rusty arrived.

He waited for his father to begin rambling about their latest sightseeing, but Han's voice broke the silence with an unusually severe tone.

"I came up to your room as soon as I got in last night. You weren't there. We were up pretty late. You didn't come in."

Stefan reminded himself to not show any defensiveness that might rouse suspicion. "I slept at Karl's house," he said, keeping his attention to the papers on the desk. "I spend quite a bit of time at Karl's these days, if you must know."

"You don't like it here any more?" Han chuckled, but the question was serious, and Stefan knew it.

"You don't," he retorted, looking his father in the eye.

Han leaned back and sighed as Stefan went on. "Give me one good reason—beyond Abbi and Georg—why I should want to be in this blasted castle any more than I absolutely have to be. Do you think I don't know why you and Mother are here so rarely? She can't tolerate the memories, and neither can I. It's easier for me to relax if I get away from here, and Karl's place is a little more convenient than the lodge."

"I just want to know that everything's all right," Han said.

"I appreciate your concern." Stefan nodded slightly and returned to his work. He felt suddenly uncomfortable as a familiar tension descended between them. Han had always been more of a business associate to Stefan than a father. As a young child, Stefan had clung more to Cameron and Erich, simply because he felt more comfortable. Han was a vibrant man, full of fun in spite of his ability to work hard and handle business with a keen mind. But Stefan had always been a more serious child, and he was somehow drawn to Cameron's quiet wisdom and Erich's seeming understanding of Stefan that Han couldn't quite grasp. When Cameron and Erich were killed, Han had become the duke regent, and one of his responsibilities had been to teach his son the business of the duchy. Beyond that day, there had been no laughter between them, only the severity of coping with their mutual loss and restructuring their lives to the duty left behind. To this day, Stefan found it difficult to relax with his father, unless they were at business. He was relieved when Han leaned his elbows on the desk and asked, "So how is our dear country faring this week?"

Stefan told him bits and pieces of the significant events that had happened since they'd last talked. Rusty came in and joined the conversation, managing to get through some paperwork at the same time. He reminded Stefan that his advisory committee would be coming in at ten o'clock to go over some concerns. While Stefan was glad to see his father, he resigned himself to not seeing Ericha until much later. Getting away at all would be difficult under the circumstances. He reminded himself that his parents never stayed more than a couple of weeks, and he would just have to get through it and smile as much as possible.

Ericha got out of bed when Stefan left, soon after dawn. She freshened up and put on a green day dress that she knew Stefan was fond of. She put her hair up carefully and dressed little Cameron as soon as he was bathed and fed. Abbi had invited her to breakfast and afterwards to go into town together since it was Wednesday and the markets would be out. Ericha was looking forward to the day, knowing they would have a wonderful time together as always. And if she was lucky, she might actually get to see Stefan in daylight.

Karl took her to the castle since he had plans to help his father with something at the apartment. Ericha took Cameron to the nursery, and then she went straight to Abbi's sitting room. She knocked but didn't wait to enter, since Abbi had told her long ago it wasn't necessary.

Ericha stopped with the doorknob in her hand. Abbi rose and gave her usual smile. She was wearing a dressing gown, with her hair still down around her shoulders. But Ericha's eyes were focused on the woman sitting across the little table. She too was dressed as if she'd not been out of bed long, with waves of red hair hanging down her back. It only took Ericha a moment to make the connection. This was Stefan's mother. They had met once before.

"Ah, there you are," Abbi said. Ericha closed the door, and they embraced as usual. "You're looking lovely today, my dear. Come, come. Sit down. Breakfast is waiting. You must meet Maggie. She arrived late last night and we've just barely had a chance to visit."

Abbi sat down and motioned Ericha to a chair. "Ericha," she said, "this is my daughter, MagdaLena. But we call her Maggie. Maggie, this is Ericha."

"It is a pleasure," Ericha said, reminding herself that she was part of the family and addressing her by any title in private would not be appropriate in Abbi's eyes.

Maggie nodded, seeming curious. By her expression, Ericha felt certain Abbi had told her nothing. "I believe we have met before," Maggie said. "But I can't recall . . ."

"It was in the market square," Ericha said. "Only for a minute."

"Ah, yes," Maggie smiled, and again Ericha could not believe how beautiful she was. Abbi, even at her age, was an attractive woman. But Maggie had a striking beauty to her features that couldn't be ignored. Ericha thought of her father and realized this was his sister. After all this time, the reality still only settled in a little at a time.

"I remember now," Maggie went on. "Stefan introduced us."

Abbi seemed surprised by this but said nothing.

"He told me you were . . ." Maggie snapped her fingers, apparently trying to remember.

"Karl's cousin."

"Of course." Maggie chuckled, and her eyes turned to her mother in silent question. It was evident by the interaction between Abbi and Ericha that Maggie knew she didn't have the full story.

Ericha also looked to Abbi, counting on her to explain. She was surprised by something close to mischief in Abbi's eyes. "Look at her, Maggie," Abbi said, and Ericha felt uncomfortable as Maggie's eyes absorbed her without reserve. "Doesn't she look . . . familiar to you?"

"Yes, but . . . I can't place it, other than meeting her before, of course."

"Well, it's not too difficult to figure out if you have just a few facts."

"And what facts would those be, Mother?" Maggie seemed subtly irritated by her mother's game.

"Ericha is Karl's cousin, Maggie. She was born in the spring of 1850 . . . to Kathe Lokberg."

Maggie's eyes narrowed on Ericha, and then they widened. She sucked in her breath and put a hand to her chest. "Good heavens," she gasped. "I don't believe it."

Abbi chuckled. "You only have to look at her to know it's true," she said. "Ericha herself didn't know until after she read the letter that Kathe had given her when she died, and—"

"She's dead?" Maggie turned to Abbi in obvious dismay. Then back to Ericha. "What happened? She could not have been more than—"

"She was forty," Ericha explained. "Her health had not been good for quite some time. It was a number of things, really. But I don't think she had much will to live . . . once she knew I could take care of myself."

Ericha was grateful to feel Abbi squeeze her hand when Maggie closed her eyes and tears trickled down her face. Unable to bear the silence, Ericha said, "I have a drawing of my father with your signature on it." Maggie opened her eyes and wiped at the tears without shame. "They tell me the likeness is very accurate. I'm grateful to have it."

Maggie gave a little laugh and reached over to touch Ericha's face. Her hand trembled. "It's a miracle," she whispered. "All these years, and we had no idea that a part of him lived on."

"She has been a blessing to us," Abbi said, a little emotional herself, "in many ways."

Ericha gave Abbi a knowing smile, appreciating her approval beyond words. When the emotion settled, the three women shared a light breakfast. Ericha was fascinated with Maggie as she tried to comprehend her as Stefan's mother and her father's sister. She enjoyed hearing of her father from Maggie's perspective. Erich had teased her and played tricks on her, and at the same time, he had watched out for her as only a big brother could. It was evident that Erich's death had affected Maggie greatly. In fact, her emotion seemed somehow deeper than Abbi's in a way, and Ericha wondered if for some reason she'd not dealt with it well.

A while after the maid had cleared breakfast away, Ruthild brought Cameron to the sitting room to be fed. Ericha was aware of Maggie's surprise as she took the baby, and Ruthild curtsied before scurrying away.

"You're married, then?" Maggie's voice seemed unsure.

"No," Ericha said without apology. A quick glance from Abbi gave her the courage to face this with dignity as she discreetly began to nurse the baby. "I fear I am doomed to live my mother's fate. Although I'm happy to have Cameron's father alive and well. He is unable to marry me, however. And I try to make the most of it. Grandmama has been very supportive," she finished, hoping Abbi would be able to smooth over Maggie's obvious disappointment.

"Unfortunately," Abbi said, "true love does not always come in convenient packages. But Ericha has du Woernig blood in her. How could we not expect her to follow the fire in her heart?"

Maggie smiled, but Ericha sensed she was not pleased. A knock at the door relieved the tension. Ericha adjusted the light-weight blanket over her shoulder when the door opened and a man's voice chuckled as he entered. "So, here you are, sitting about in your nighties half the morning."

"You never change, Han," Abbi said, holding out her arms. Ericha wasn't able to get a good look at him as he embraced Abbi, but he came around the table and hugged Maggie tightly. They kissed, and then their eyes met, and Ericha recognized the love between them. The brief glimpse she'd had of Han Heinrich before now had not prepared her for the reality of his presence. She could see the resemblance to Stefan in his features that she'd noticed before, but they also shared the same commanding demeanor and the intensity in their eyes. She recalled that Han Heinrich had served as duke regent for many years, but it was difficult to comprehend that he'd started out working in the stables, as Stefan had told her. She also took in the fact that Han had been her father's best friend. It was all so strange!

"Good morning, Your Royal Lovely-As-Usual Self," he said to Maggie. She gave him a glare of mock disgust that made him laugh.

Ericha felt Han's eyes shift to her. "And who is this lovely young lady?" he asked diplomatically, bowing slightly toward her.

"This is Ericha," Abbi stated proudly. Then she quickly went on, "Do you remember Kathe Lokberg?"

"Of course I remember Kathe, but . . ."

"This is Kathe's daughter."

Following a moment of silence while he absorbed her overtly, he asked, "Did you say *Ericha?*"

Abbi explained it all again, while Han occasionally shook his head in disbelief. He expressed pleasure at the discovery. But when Cameron finished eating and Ericha handed him to Abbi, she had to explain that again as well. Ericha sensed the same subtle disapproval from Han, but she tried to ignore it. She wondered if it would be better or worse if they knew it was Stefan's son. Good heavens, she realized, these were Cameron's grandparents!

Abbi eased the tension by making a fuss over the baby. "Isn't he the cutest thing?" she said with a little laugh. "At times he reminds me so much of Erich as a baby, I can hardly believe it."

Maggie seemed a little more relaxed as she said, "I was just thinking that he reminded me a great deal of Stefan as a baby."

"It's all in the family." Abbi chuckled with a sly smile too subtle for anyone but Ericha to catch.

With all the extra visiting, Abbi and Maggie were not ready to go into town until it was time to eat again. They decided to leave as soon as lunch was finished, and they had barely begun when Stefan hurried into the dining room. He was obviously tense from whatever his business had been this morning, but Ericha saw his expression soften slightly as he caught her eye. He was dressed nicely, wearing a fitted striped waistcoat over a cream-colored shirt.

As Stefan embraced his mother and talked to her for a minute, it was evident he'd not seen her since her arrival. He greeted Abbi and Georg as usual, then seated himself, smiling toward Ericha.

"Hello there, little cousin," he said. "And how are you today?"

"Well, and you?" she replied.

"Better now," he said, "since I got past that stodgy meeting. I swear sometimes those men are out for my hide, and they're supposed to be working for *me.*"

Han chuckled. "They're supposed to keep you clear on all objectives."

"That they do," Stefan answered with a sigh.

"Where is Johanna?" Maggie asked with obvious disdain in her voice.

"Ah," Stefan actually smiled, "she informed me earlier that she would be traveling home for a few days; something to do with her sister."

"Too bad," Han said with obvious sarcasm. "I don't know what ever possessed you to marry that woman, boy."

Ericha caught the evidence in Stefan's eyes that the statement cut deep. "That gives us something in common," he said to his father.

"I thought *Maggie* was a shrew." Han chuckled as Maggie threw her napkin at him and erupted with a giggle.

"My mother a shrew?" Stefan said more lightly. "Never!"

"Well, she mellowed a little after I finally convinced her that she loved me," Han said, his eyes glowing with amusement.

Stefan watched the obvious love between his parents and glanced discreetly at Ericha. "So," he said, "I see you've met our latest addition to the family."

"You mean Ericha or the baby?" Han asked.

Stefan chuckled. "Both, I suppose."

The attention turned to Ericha as she was asked one question after another about her mother and the means that the discovery had been made. Ericha was glad when the conversation turned more to reminiscing of Erich. Han told stories of the antics he and Erich had come up with as young men, and the closeness they'd shared as friends.

Following the meal, Abbi announced that they were going into the village for the afternoon. Han declared he was coming too, whether they wanted him to or not. Georg declined, since his leg still bothered him if he did too much walking.

"Are you coming, Stefan?" his mother asked. His mind reacted with a silent, *What? I can go into public with Ericha? I wouldn't miss it for the world!* But not wanting to appear too eager, he said, "Well, I don't know if—"

"Surely you can put off a little ducal business to spend some time with your parents," Han insisted.

"Since you put it that way," Stefan said, "it would be a pleasure to come along."

Han and Maggie left the dining room first. Stefan caught Ericha's eyes and saw her smile. He chuckled aloud and followed her into the hall. Ruthild insisted that she would manage fine with little Cameron, and she encouraged Ericha to go and have a good time. At first Ericha felt apprehensive, but once they got out, it felt good to have her arms free and not be concerned over his fussing.

Something warmed inside Ericha to watch Stefan sitting across the carriage from her, next to his father. As the three women sidled close together, Maggie commented, "It's a good thing du Woernig women have narrow hips, or we'd be in trouble."

Han laughed, Stefan chuckled, and Ericha decided she liked Stefan's parents.

"Look at that." Han nudged Stefan with his elbow as the carriage rolled through the castle gate and down the hill. "Three generations of red-haired beauties. You'll never see anything so incredible in the entire world."

"You would know," Stefan said, offering a warm smile in turn to each of these women he loved. It *was* incredible, he thought. He blessed the good fortune that had drawn him to fall in love with a woman who could be a part of his family—even if she couldn't have his name.

When the carriage halted, Han stepped out first, and he turned to help Maggie. Ericha heard Maggie giggling as Stefan stepped out. He helped Abbi down from the carriage, then Ericha slipped her hand into his, absorbing the warmth from his touch as he helped steady her descent.

"Thank you, Stefan," she said. He squeezed and reluctantly let go.

"My pleasure." He leaned toward her and whispered, "Do you have any idea how badly I want to just take you in my arms and kiss you, right here in front of the whole world?"

"Exactly," she replied softly. "But I don't think the scandal would be worth the thrill."

"Not likely." He smirked, and they followed the others into the crowded square.

Ericha felt sure there were few moments in her life when she'd been so happy. It was nice to be part of a family. Her life with Kathe had been good, in spite of the struggles, and she was grateful for the love that Karl and Theodor had given her, but she'd never comprehended the joy of participating in an activity so simple with those who shared the same blood. She felt a deep connection to her father's family that she'd never experienced before. She was reminded of the day she had seen Stefan here with his parents. It seemed so long ago. They'd come so far. Now she was able to see firsthand his interaction with these people who had raised him to be the man he was. He joked and laughed with them, often calling his mother "Mrs. Heinrich" as she'd heard him do before. As they looked over the wares available, Ericha observed the way her new family interacted with the people. In spite of an apparent awe from most who encountered them, the family was humble and respectful to all they met. Ericha could see Stefan's personal interest in individuals, many he likely didn't even know, and he stopped often to converse briefly with villagers. Occasionally he would catch her eye with a knowing smile, and Ericha nearly overflowed with happiness.

While Ericha was looking over an assortment of candles, she noticed Stefan retreat slightly with his mother, her hand over his arm. They appeared very serious for a few minutes, and then he broke into laughter and she touched his face. At the same time, Han took Abbi by the hand as if they were the best of friends. Han was telling her something, using elaborate gestures with his free hand, making Abbi smile. Ericha felt briefly alone, but content nevertheless. She distracted herself by choosing some elegant tapers that would go well in the candle holders in the parlor. She was about to pay for them when Stefan appeared at her side. "Here, let me get that," he said more to the vendor. He handed over some money and added, "Keep the change."

"Thank you, Your Grace."

While he was wrapping the purchase, Stefan said to him, "Have you met my cousin?"

"I've seen her around." The plump man smiled. "Who could miss such a beauty?"

"Hear, hear," Stefan murmured.

"O' course, everyone's heard about Prince Erich's daughter comin' back here, an' all."

"Really?" Stefan said.

"The stuff fairy tales are made of." The vendor smiled again.

"Indeed," Stefan said and glanced unobtrusively to Ericha.

As they turned away to join the others, Stefan placed her hand over his arm. "Isn't this something from a fantasy?" she asked quietly.

"Exactly," he replied, and they laughed.

Chapter Fifteen

DISCLOSURE

They all wandered into a ladies' hat shop on the edge of the square where Han and Stefan sat down casually and pointed to this hat or that one while the ladies tried them on. The flustered shopkeeper stood close by, apparently awed by her royal customers.

"That's atrocious!" Han declared as Maggie pinned on one with a huge feather in it. "Try that blue one, with the flowers on it."

Maggie tried it while Abbi contemplated something mauve, and Ericha simply looked the selections over with little interest.

"Aren't you going to try one on?" Han asked Ericha, almost startling her.

"Try the green one there." Stefan pointed. "It would go well with that dress you're wearing now. And it matches your eyes."

Ericha tried it on, and both men chuckled.

"What?" she demanded.

"Never mind," Stefan said. "It's not you. Try that other green one there."

Ericha pinned it into place, looking in a mirror. She turned for approval, but neither of them commented on the hat. They both seemed a little dazed.

"It's uncanny how she looks like Erich," Han said quietly, though Ericha still caught his words. "It almost makes me want to cry."

"Occasionally I do," Stefan admitted.

Han turned to Stefan in surprise. Ericha looked away, pretending not to hear. "I haven't seen you cry since you were eight years old."

Stefan looked down and cleared his throat. "Well, I made up for it the day I realized that Erich had a daughter. I went to the dungeon and cried half the day."

Stefan glanced to Ericha and felt certain she'd heard his confession by the way she discreetly rubbed her eyes with a thumb and forefinger. Han put his arm around Stefan's shoulders with some semblance of a hug, saying quietly, "Maybe I should try that."

"Wouldn't hurt," Stefan said. Then he spoke more loudly to Ericha, "It's perfect, little cousin. Do you like it?"

She blinked several times, then turned to look at him, smiling brightly as she nodded.

"Good," Han said, "we'll take it."

Maggie settled on the blue one, but Abbi couldn't make up her mind.

"We'll take them both," Han said to the woman eagerly waiting to help them. He paid for the entire purchase, and they moved back into the street, the ladies each sporting a new hat and Han carrying Abbi's extra hat box.

Han treated them all to a hot pasty, and they sat on a park bench to enjoy them. Ericha had nearly finished hers when she thought of Cameron and missed him. She no sooner thought it than a tingle surged into her breasts, leaving her painfully engorged.

"Is something wrong?" Stefan asked.

Ericha was glad to have Han and Maggie out of hearing range when she admitted quietly, "I need to feed the baby."

Stefan rose from the bench and announced, "Ericha needs to get back to the baby. I could take her up and send the carriage back if any of you—"

"Oh, I'm too tired to shop any more," Abbi admitted.

"I've had enough for one day," Maggie added, and they all returned to the waiting carriage.

"Thank you for the hat," Ericha said to Han.

"It was my pleasure," he replied with exaggerated gallantry.

"And you, for the candles," she added to Stefan.

"It was my pleasure." He imitated his father perfectly, and the ladies laughed.

"Maybe you do have some of me in you, after all," Han said to him.

"Maybe," Stefan said. "I've heard occasionally that I'm a scoundrel."

Han glared in mock disgust until Stefan laughed.

Ericha went straight to the nursery, only to find that Cameron was sleeping contentedly with the goat's milk Ruthild had fed him when he had refused to wait any longer. She found Abbi in her sitting room, and she reported that Han and Maggie had gone to their rooms to rest, and Stefan had returned to the office. They exchanged small talk until Abbi apparently noticed Ericha's distress. "Is something wrong, my dear?"

Ericha briefly explained the situation, adding in a whisper, "I've never had this happen quite so badly before. I didn't realize it could be so painful."

"Come along," Abbi said, leading Ericha into her private bathing room. Ericha didn't feel the least bit uncomfortable as Abbi gently coached her on how to express the milk by hand into a basin in order to relieve the pressure. She left Ericha alone to complete the process, and Ericha was grateful for the much-needed advice.

Ericha walked back into the sitting room to find Stefan sitting casually in a chair, while Abbi was busy at her little writing desk. She felt his eyes move blatantly toward her.

"Go ahead and kiss her, Stefan," Abbi said without so much as a glance up from her writing. It was as if she could read their minds. "I won't look."

Stefan chuckled as he held out a hand for Ericha. "You're a shrewd old woman, Abbi du Woernig," he said.

"I was a shrewd young woman," she replied lightly. "And don't you forget it."

"Much like you are," he said more softly to Ericha as he drew her onto his lap. "I must confess that I love the way you can see into my soul."

"Not always," she said as he pressed his face to her throat. He urged her lips to his and kissed her with a hint of anticipation.

"What a delightful day," he said. "I wish it could always be this way."

Ericha put a finger to his lips, then pressed her mouth there in its place.

"What are you writing, Grandmama?" Stefan asked.

"It's only my journal," she said without breaking her concentration.

"Do you write in there about your scandalous grandchildren?"

"Actually, yes," she said, and as if she'd read his mind again, she added, "but I lock my journals up and the key is around my wrist." She turned at last to look at him, seeming to find contentment in the way Ericha was seated on his lap with her head on his shoulder. "When I die, it's up to you to keep them hidden until enough time has passed that it won't matter anymore."

"Do you think that day will ever come?" Stefan asked, holding Ericha more tightly.

"I hope I live to see it," Abbi said, "and then you won't have to worry about hiding my journals." She turned back to her writing and added, "But what is a journal if I can't pour out my every thought and feeling?"

While Stefan was contemplating an answer, Abbi's voice caught a tone of musing. "There was a day when I was rather scandalous myself."

"Would that have anything to do with being pregnant and Cameron nowhere to be found?" Stefan asked lightly. Ericha's attention perked.

"That would be it," Abbi said, still writing as she spoke. "We had exchanged private vows in the lodge, but I was about halfway along before Cameron finally showed up and made it legal. Of course, I had no idea he was the Duke of Horstberg. He wanted me to marry the Captain of the Guard, just in case he didn't make it." She set the pen aside and stared into the distance. "There I was at the front of the cathedral, certain that Cameron was dead and I would spend the rest of my life with a man I didn't love."

"Then what happened?" Ericha asked when Abbi didn't go on. She'd heard the story before but never grew tired of it.

Abbi turned and smiled. "Your grandfather interrupted the wedding—on a horse no less—with a troop of the Guard at his sides. He looked so . . . regal. And before that morning I'd had no idea who he was. He was a common thief, for all I knew." She chuckled. "But in he came. He announced that he was reclaiming the duchy from his brother, that he was prepared to prove his innocence, and that I was pregnant with his child. Our marriage was made public, he crowned me duchess, and in less than an hour, my entire life changed."

"And you didn't regret a minute of it," Stefan stated.

"Not a single minute," she assured them. Huge tears welled into Abbi's eyes before she could turn away in an attempt to hide them.

While Stefan felt a little helpless, Ericha rushed to Abbi's side, putting an arm around her shoulders. Stefan was thinking that he'd like to tell her not to cry, to remind her of all she had that was good. But he learned something by the way Ericha handed Abbi a handkerchief and said, "You miss him, still." Abbi nodded. "It must have been difficult for you, all these years, to be without him."

"Yes, it's been difficult," Abbi admitted with a smile. "But I have much to be grateful for."

She dried her tears and locked away her journal, and they walked together down to dinner. The meal was especially pleasant with Han and Maggie there and Johanna absent. Georg told them some points of interest of the happenings throughout Europe that he'd read in a newspaper he received regularly in the mail. Han and Maggie spoke of their travels, and Han had them laughing as he told of a comical incident they'd encountered in France.

Just before dessert, one of the maids brought Karl to the dining room. He declined Abbi's offer to join them, saying he had plans for dinner.

"I was just wondering when Ericha would be ready to leave. I have the—"

"Oh, you go on ahead," Abbi insisted. "We'll see that she gets home." She added to Ericha, "Is that all right, dear? Do you want to stay?"

Ericha nodded her approval. Karl bowed with ridiculous gallantry, teased Stefan a minute, then left.

They all went to the east winter parlor to have coffee. Ericha went upstairs to nurse Cameron before she took him with her to join the others.

"There's the little man," Georg said with pleasure, holding out his hands to take Cameron. "I get him first."

Ericha turned him over with pleasure, and then she sat by Abbi and turned her attention to Stefan at the piano. She loved to hear him play and noticed that Maggie too was caught up in the music. He apparently finished one song, then moved into another, though he didn't stop playing in between. Ericha quickly recognized the melody as the song she had taught him in the Black Forest. She was surprised when Abbi said, "Oh, that's the song Cameron wrote."

Ericha turned to her in surprise as it seemed to dawn on them in the same moment. "My mother taught me that song," Ericha said.

"And you taught it to Stefan," Abbi replied, and she laughed. "He told me Karl's cousin had taught him. If only I had known . . ." She laughed again.

"Sing it with me, Ericha," Stefan said, motioning her to the piano with a tilt of his head.

Ericha hesitated, but Abbi nudged her with an elbow. She sat beside Stefan on the bench, trying not to get too close. Together they sang the simple lyrics while Stefan played it with an elaborate accompaniment that made it evident he'd spent a great deal of time playing this song.

When they were finished, a reverent hush fell over the room. Stefan glanced around to see that his mother was crying, and his father had his hand over his eyes. Abbi looked lost in another time, and Georg looked downright depressed. He met Ericha's eyes and read his own concern there.

"That bad, huh?" Stefan said, hoping to ease the tension.

"Oh, no," Maggie insisted, "it was beautiful. It's just . . . the memories. I remember Father playing that song when we were children." She turned to Stefan as she wiped her eyes. "I'm so grateful that Father taught you to play. It keeps him closer, somehow."

"I'm grateful for it, myself," Stefan said. "At times the music has saved me."

Stefan glanced toward Ericha, but she turned shyly away and came to her feet. He watched her take Cameron from Georg and suddenly felt a little melancholy himself. Here he sat, his parents and his son in the same room. He wished he could just tell them the truth. But at the same time, he feared what the truth might do to their relationships.

"Would you like to hold him, Stefan?" Ericha asked.

He smiled. "I'd love to." He tried to act like he felt awkward as he took his son into his arms, when in truth it had become as natural as breathing. He'd lost track of the nights he had held and rocked him while Ericha slept.

"He is cute." Stefan chuckled.

"I must say that holding a baby suits you," Maggie said. "I've often wished you could have children of your own."

Stefan looked up sharply, then forced his face into a calm expression. Wondering how his reaction was interpreted, he was relieved when his father said to his mother, "Perhaps that was a bit insensitive to bring up now."

"I'm sorry," Maggie said to Stefan. "I didn't intend to make you uncomfortable, or—"

"It's all right, Mother," he said. "I've dealt with it."

"Perhaps it may still happen one day," she mused. "Miracles do happen, you know."

Stefan felt compelled to make a point. He tried to talk himself out of it, but his instincts told him it needed to be said—for Ericha's sake, if nothing else. "Mother, you should know by now that there is nothing left between Johanna and me."

Maggie's eyes widened.

"Surely you can't be so surprised, my dear," Han said.

"I guess I just hoped that one day—"

"If you were around more, you would know how hopeless it had become," Stefan said, quickly glancing around the room. Abbi seemed calm. Georg was watching Han and Maggie closely, as if he could perceive their feelings. Ericha was staring at the floor. She appeared indifferent, but he knew she hated this as much as he.

"Look at Cameron sucking on that little hand," Abbi said, easing the tension somewhat as all eyes turned to the baby. "I can't believe how he reminds me of Erich."

"I don't know," Maggie interjected. "Like I said earlier, he reminds me of Stefan when he was a baby."

By the look in Stefan's eyes, Ericha recalled he'd not been present when she'd mentioned it before.

A long silence preambled Abbi's next comment. "There is something you should know . . . Han, Maggie."

Stefan's eyes shot to his grandmother. By the determined way she stared at him, he realized her intention. His heart began to pound, and he shook his head adamantly, trying to be discreet.

"You can't keep it from them, Stefan," she said in a calm voice of authority. "They have a right to know, under the circumstances."

Stefan was aware of his parents' attention perking. Ericha looked up at him in alarm, then to Abbi. Georg remained expressionless.

"A right to know *what?*" Han demanded.

Stefan briefly squeezed his eyes shut. It was too late now. There would be no peace until the whole of it was spread out.

Ericha sensed Stefan's panic and wondered if the situation was as it appeared. She saw in his eyes that he was gathering courage, and she resigned herself to do the same. They could do nothing now but trust Abbi's wisdom.

"I'm not sure it's necessary for you to know," Stefan said in one last effort to stop this. "You're not around enough to be affected by any of this as it is." He wished it hadn't come out sounding so bitter. Did he resent his parents' means to escape something that bound him here?

"Abbi is right, Stefan," Georg said. "I know it's difficult, but your parents need to know what's going on."

"What *is* going on?" Han's voice rose impatiently. Maggie put a hand over his arm in an obvious attempt to keep him calm.

Abbi penetrated Stefan with her eyes. "Do you want me to tell them?"

Stefan cleared his throat. "I think I'm man enough to handle it." He rose and stepped toward his mother, holding the baby out to her. "Would you like to hold him?"

She smiled as she took little Cameron, but Han was glaring at Stefan. Stefan stepped back and set his feet close together. He pushed his hands behind his back and took a deep breath. "Cameron looks like me because he's my son."

Maggie gasped. Han showed no reaction beyond a tightening of the muscles in his face. Ericha held her breath, fearing this would not be well received. Wondering what to do, she was grateful for Abbi's nudge. Their eyes met, and Abbi motioned Ericha toward Stefan. She quickly moved to his side and put her arms around him, offering silent support. She could feel his parents absorbing her all over again—this time as Stefan's lover.

While Stefan waited for his father's inevitable eruption, he blessed Ericha's presence at his side. Their eyes met briefly, and he felt her strength fill him. Like a silent pillar of sustenance, she tightened her embrace, and he knew the struggles were worth it. He didn't feel any less confident about his commitment to Ericha now than he had when he'd made the choice to make her a part of his life. If anything, his feelings had only grown deeper.

When the silence grew too long, Stefan tightened his arm around Ericha and attempted to explain. "Ericha and I have been involved for quite some time. We met right after she came to Horstberg. She was pregnant before we knew that she was Erich's daughter."

Stefan felt a little relief to see the way his mother clutched the baby more tightly, in spite of the disbelief in her expression. But it was his father's reaction he feared.

Just when he thought the waiting would never end, Han erupted with a barely controlled, "This is unbelievable!"

"Han," Maggie said as if to remind him to stay calm.

Han abruptly moved a hand over his face as if it could wipe away his obvious anger. "Are you telling me, then, that this young lady is your mistress?"

"If you must put it that way," Stefan said, attempting to control his own defensiveness.

"Well, how exactly would you put it?" Han countered tersely.

"Ericha is a wife to me in every respect but one," he stated firmly.

Han turned away and pressed a hand over his mouth, as if speaking would cause an explosion.

"And what does Johanna think of all this?" Maggie asked.

"Johanna doesn't know," Stefan stated, "and I pray to God she never finds out."

"Oh, that's just marvelous," Han snarled with sarcasm. He fixed his eyes on Stefan with a piercing gaze. "You are the Duke of Horstberg, young man. Do you have any idea what that means?"

"I know exactly what it means," Stefan retorted. "I have lived and breathed this duchy since the day Cameron died, and you know it. I didn't even have a childhood. In return, I deserve this one happiness."

"You're talking about adultery, Stefan," Han shouted, and Stefan winced. "How can there be happiness in that?"

"Hush up, Han," Abbi insisted. "If the servants hear you, we'll have a whole new problem on our hands."

Han barely glanced toward Abbi, and he glared more deeply at Stefan. "Is it or is it not adultery?" Han asked more quietly.

Ericha pressed her face against Stefan's shoulder in an attempt to hide the tears.

"Must you make it sound so sordid?" Stefan retorted, holding Ericha closer.

"Perhaps you should calm down enough to look at the full perspective," Abbi said.

Stefan was grateful for her intervention as Han turned his glare toward her. "And you condone this?" He moved to the edge of his seat and motioned elaborately toward Stefan and Ericha. Before Abbi could answer, he went on, "I cannot believe that you, of all people, would knowingly allow such a thing to go on. Have you taken leave of your senses?"

Stefan interjected firmly, "You are speaking to the Grand Duchess of Horstberg. Be angry with me if you must, but you will show her the respect she deserves."

Ericha glanced up at Stefan, amazed at how the Duke of Horstberg could step in and issue a command to his own father. She was even more amazed when Han didn't question it.

"Forgive me, Your Grace," he said toward Abbi in a controlled voice, tinged only subtly with sarcasm. "Will you please do me the honor of telling me what possessed you to approve of my son having an affair?"

"Before I do that," Abbi said in a voice worthy of her position, "I would like to clarify something. If I thought for one minute that anything—anything at all—was left between Stefan and Johanna, I would *not* approve of it. I have no doubt that Stefan ended his relationship with Johanna before he ever became involved with Ericha. Now, to answer your question, I am willing to admit that I sensed what was troubling Stefan. I had good reason to fear the path his life was taking. I told him to follow his heart and seek out some happiness to compensate for all he gave to Horstberg. And I do not regret that advice. Right and wrong are not always black and white. When Ericha told me she was pregnant, it didn't take much to put the pieces together and figure out that it was Stefan. *I'm* the one who brought it into the open between us. They have been discreet and handled it as well as could be expected. And they are *happy!*"

Stefan's heart surged with love and admiration for his grand-mother as he listened to her acceptance. He turned back to his father. Han was calmer now, but the disapproval in his eyes had not lessened.

In a gentle voice, Stefan said, "I'm not going to tell you that it's been easy. I feel agony every time I think that I cannot give my son a name. I hate having to hide and pretend while Johanna flits around this place like some kind of evil spirit. But I cannot regret the joy Ericha has brought into my life. She has taught me who I am. She has put the soul back into me."

"God sent her to save his life," Abbi stated, and Stefan passed a quick smile in her direction.

"What do you mean?" Maggie asked, seeming suddenly concerned.

While Stefan searched for the words to explain the complexity of his despair prior to Ericha becoming a part of his life, Abbi spoke with a severity that caught him off guard. "He was on a path to self-destruction. I can't explain it, but I know it as well as I know my own name. That woman he married tore his heart into shreds, and one day she would have driven him too far."

Stefan saw his mother's eyes widen as they turned to him. He felt nearly as surprised as she looked to realize that Abbi was right. He'd not consciously felt it then, but looking back, he knew it was true. He'd been dying inside, and there was no telling the desperate measure he might have eventually taken to end his misery—one way or another.

"You must forgive me if I'm a disappointment to you," Stefan said. "I only pray that you can one day come to accept the choices I've made. I should never have married Johanna. It's something I regret every day of my life. But I did. And I can't change it. I would divorce her in a minute if I thought that Horstberg would not feel the repercussions. But the bottom line is simple. I must keep this union in tact because I am the Duke of Horstberg."

"And a fine one at that," Georg interjected, finally adding to the conversation.

"Amen," Abbi said, and Stefan felt emotion burn in his chest. Did they have any idea what that meant, coming from these two people who were practically legends in this country?

"Stefan never wanted this position," Abbi went on, "but he's given it his heart and soul, and he's served his country well."

"Amen," Georg said, and Abbi gave him a warm smile.

"Stefan," Maggie said, easing the baby to her shoulder, "why don't you and Ericha sit down. I want to ask you something."

Stefan moved to one of the sofas, and Ericha sat close beside him, keeping her hand in his.

"Forgive me for being *insensitive* as your father would say, but I feel it needs to be brought up." Stefan nodded his consent, and she continued. "This child cannot be your heir, Stefan."

"I know," he said.

"I know you know, but what I'm getting at is . . . I can't help wondering why there was no heir in your marriage. Is it because you and Johanna were at odds from the start? I guess what I'm asking is . . . did you give it a fair chance? Not that I want you to change what cannot be changed at this point, but . . . I can't help wondering."

Stefan felt Ericha tense slightly and wished she didn't have to hear all of this. But he reminded himself there was no reason to hide anything from her. He simply wondered how to say it without offending her—or his mother. He believed Abbi could swallow just about anything.

"Do you feel your mother's question is inappropriate?" Han asked when the silence persisted.

Stefan could almost feel his father wanting some proof that Stefan had brought all this upon himself, which strengthened his confidence when he stated, "No. In fact, I believe it's a valid concern, and I appreciate her having the courage to bring it up." Maggie seemed to relax slightly as she tenderly patted the baby's back. "I'm just finding it difficult," Stefan went on, "to find the words to say something I've never said aloud to anyone."

Ericha could feel the tension rising in Stefan, and she squeezed his hand, hoping to convey her support.

"The first time that . . ." He cleared his throat unintentionally and pushed a hand through his hair. ". . . That uh . . . Johanna and I were alone . . . after the wedding, she . . . Well, she'd had more than a little champagne, and I guess you could say her inhibitions were absent." Stefan quit stammering as he gained some momentum. "She made it perfectly clear why she had married me. She'd conquered the Duke of Horstberg. She called me an innocent child, and it quickly became evident that she was not innocent at all. I found out much later that she was actually pregnant when she married me."

Ericha was surprised at this but waited for him to go on. She felt fresh tears burning on his behalf and laid her head against his shoulder. He put his arm around her and eased her closer.

Stefan turned to look directly at his mother. He tried to ignore the horror in her expression as he continued in a toneless voice that didn't allow him to feel what he was saying. "I hated her from the moment I learned of her deception. She played upon my innocence like some venomous spider. And I was fool enough to let her. But if there was one thing I knew, it was my duty. For years I went regularly to her bed. But it was no different for me than signing a proclamation or ordering an execution—except that it made me *sick*. And then one day I realized there would be no heir between us. I honestly believed it was me at fault. But I didn't care. I made it clear to her that it was over between us. I tried to hurt her as badly as she hurt me, but I don't think she gave it much thought. I had been aware of her sneaking in and out of the castle at night, almost from the beginning. Karl told me years ago of talk in the pubs about how many men had bedded the duchess. I actually heard it myself one day. I have asked myself a thousand times if there was anything I could have done to make it different. But I know in my heart that she would never change, and I could never forgive her. There, that's the truth of it. I don't expect it to make right what I have done, but in my heart I believe what Grandmama said. Right and wrong are not always black and white. And I believe that God understands, even if He doesn't approve. I ask only the same of you."

Stefan looked around the room at the varied expressions of shock. Was the truth of it so horrible? Yes, he answered himself. It was.

"Stefan," Han said, his voice no less stern than before, "you said that Johanna was pregnant when you married her. How is that possible if all her promiscuity and her years with you have not produced a child? For that matter, what happened to *that* baby?"

As difficult as the rest had been, Stefan hated this most of all. He sighed and began, "That baby was—"

"Wait a minute," Abbi interrupted. "Did Johanna tell you this?"

"No," he stated, "Doctor Furhelm told me . . . the day Cameron was born."

Ericha lifted her head in surprise. She sensed a deep dread in him and wondered why.

"Go on," Han urged.

"The doctor assumed it had been my baby, and that I was aware of the situation. Johanna had assured him that was the case. I can assure you it was *not* my baby. I didn't touch her prior to the wedding, and she showed signs of pregnancy within a few days. She told the doctor that *I* was concerned about having a baby born too soon, and that was apparently how she justified killing it."

"What?" Abbi shrieked.

"I'm only telling you what the doctor told me. But I want nothing more said of it beyond this room. It will change nothing, and I will not have any one of you repeating it to anyone." He took another deep breath. "The doctor told me that she'd had the baby aborted by someone who did not know what they were doing. That's why she was flat in bed with what she explained away as 'feminine problems' a few weeks after we were married. And that's why she was never able to conceive again."

When the silence grew thick, Stefan was grateful for little Cameron's sudden impatience. Ericha rose to take him from Maggie when he began to fuss. Still, nothing was said as she moved slowly away, rocking him gently against her.

"And what about you, young lady?" Han asked, startling them all. Ericha turned to see Stefan's father looking directly at her. "Are you honestly content to live the kind of life this has condemned you to?"

Stefan watched Ericha closely for a reaction. Her opinion mattered to him more than any other. He felt a rush of warm chills by the way she gave his father that soul-searching gaze she was famous for. "I fell in love with Stefan the moment I saw him. The power that drew us together is not something I question. I practically begged Stefan to make me a part of his life, as much as it could be possible. It was nearly a year and half before he was willing to set aside his adherence to duty and make that commitment."

Ericha drew a deep breath and continued. The fire in her eyes only intensified. "My mother taught me to follow my heart. Her life was difficult. She lived with scandal and heartache. But she had no regrets. My existence is proof enough that my parents loved each other, and for that, I can hold my head high. My children will grow up with that same knowledge as their guiding star. My mother's eyes were blazing with love for my father, the very day she died. And I know he loved her." Ericha's voice quivered, but her stance remained strong. "Erich du Woernig would not have chosen to leave us behind if the choice had been his. But by heaven and earth, he loved her. And Stefan loves me no less."

Ericha turned away to choke back her emotion. Maggie shamelessly wiped tears from her face. Han looked stunned. The baby's fussing increased, and Stefan rose to his feet.

"I think we've had enough drama for one evening," he announced, taking hold of Ericha's arm and guiding her toward the door. "I'm taking my family home. Don't expect me for breakfast."

Stefan said nothing on the way home, and Ericha began to fear she had overstepped her boundaries with his father. By the time she had Cameron down for bed, he'd still not uttered a word about this evening's encounter. She found him gazing out the bedroom window toward the castle, as he often did, and she wondered if he continued to feel torn between two worlds.

Ericha was contemplating the words to find out where she stood when he put his arm around her and pressed his lips into her hair. "You were incredible back there," he said. The admiration in his voice was evident.

"I was?" She looked up at him, searching for sincerity.

He chuckled and nodded. "Only a du Woernig woman could silence a man that way." His eyes became serious as he turned back to the window.

"You're troubled," she said, touching his face.

"I'm glad my parents know . . . now that it's over. I don't want to have to pretend with them. It's just that this whole thing with Johanna is so ugly. And sometimes I fear what she may do to me yet."

"Are you afraid she will discover the truth?"

"I have to be realistic enough to accept that it's a possibility."

"But with all she's done . . . the life she lives . . . wouldn't she be willing to turn the other way, just as you have done with her?"

Stefan gave a bitter little laugh. "I was once naive enough to believe such things of her. But I know better now."

Ericha reached up to kiss him before repeating his statement of earlier, "I think we've had enough drama for one evening." She moved her fingers over the buttons of his shirt and urged him to the bed.

As always, Stefan could not measure his gratitude for the love Ericha gave him that put everything else into perspective. She quickly caught him up into a passion so complete, he was briefly able to let go of everything but his love for her.

As they lay peacefully holding each other, Ericha said, "You're still troubled. What is it?"

"That's another thing about du Woernig women," he said. "They can read minds, I swear it."

Ericha laughed softly and nuzzled closer to him. "If I could read your mind, I wouldn't have to ask."

"I was just wondering what my parents are thinking right now.

My father is probably pacing the floor, driving my mother crazy. Whatever they're doing, I know they're not sleeping."

"Maybe they're doing what we're doing," she offered.

"Maybe." He chuckled.

"Do you think they will accept it?"

"My mother will give me acceptance, whether she agrees with it or not. But I'm sure this will only widen the gap between my father and me."

"I'm certain his anger stems from his concern for you, Stefan. Perhaps the difficulties hurt him as they hurt you, but he doesn't know what to do about it."

"Perhaps," Stefan said. "He's a good man, Ericha. We've just always been so . . . different. In some ways, I think I looked more to my grandfather for guidance and comfort as a child. And I always felt most comfortable with Erich. Maybe that's why I've never gotten over losing them."

Ericha tightened her embrace but said nothing. Stefan's next awareness was of the light of day filtering into the room. Ericha was awake beside him, nursing the baby.

"Good morning." She smiled. "Are you in a hurry?"

Stefan shook his head and stretched. There was nothing pressing that Rusty couldn't handle. He usually took his work at a slower pace when his parents were around anyway. Rusty would expect it and keep everything under control.

"I hear Karl in the dining room. Why don't you go get some breakfast, and I'll join you when I'm dressed."

By the time Stefan got downstairs, Karl had gone out to his workshop. But he poured a cup of coffee and helped himself to the food left on the sideboard in covered dishes to keep warm. Sitting at the table, he put on his spare set of glasses he'd learned to keep here, and picked up the local newspaper to peruse it while he ate.

A few minutes later, Erma entered the room and curtsied. "The princess MagdaLena to see you, Your Grace," she said with that stifled awe in her voice that made Stefan chuckle.

"Well, bring her in," he said.

Maggie entered the room wearing a stylish suit he'd never seen before, with the hat Han had bought her yesterday.

"Thank you, Erma," Stefan said as the maid left the room.

Maggie looked briefly startled when Job approached her curiously. "Job!" Stefan ordered. "Get back. Sit down."

The dog retracted to lay at Stefan's feet. Turning his attention back to the paper, Stefan added, "You're looking lovely as always today, Mother. What brings you all the way out here?"

"I was hoping to catch you before you left," she stated.

"You're just like your mother," he said lightly. He tipped the corner of the paper down. "Sit down. Are you hungry?"

"No, thank you. I ate early. But that coffee smells good."

"There's a clean cup on the sideboard," he said, going back to the paper again. "Help yourself."

Maggie sat across the corner from Stefan and stirred a great deal of cream and sugar into her coffee. Stefan sensed she was tense, and he felt her watching him. But he just ate his breakfast and read the paper. If it was going to get opened up again, he wouldn't be the one to do it.

"So, what are you doing?" she finally asked.

"I'm eating breakfast and reading the newspaper," he reported. "I have to keep up on what's *really* happening in Horstberg. I nearly always find out something nasty about myself. Sometimes I read things about the Duke of Horstberg that I never would have known if I hadn't read the paper."

Maggie laughed softly.

"You find that funny?" He bent the paper down and gave her a mock glare.

"Actually, yes," she replied. "I've read a few things about myself in the paper in my lifetime."

"I dare say you have," Stefan said impishly. He scraped his plate clean and read on.

"You can't make everybody happy," she said. "No matter what you do, no matter how hard you try, someone will always disagree with you."

Stefan looked at his mother again, wondering if she was

trying to say something deeper. "I try to remind myself of that," he said coolly. "It's one of the hazards of my position. I'm certain I've made a few enemies along the way."

"Well, I'm not one of them," she said. "So, put the paper down and talk to your mother."

Stefan glanced at her warily. He folded the paper and set it aside, then took off his glasses and leaned back, crossing his ankle on his knee. "What did you want to talk about, Mother?"

Maggie reached out a hand for him, and he took it. "You love Ericha," she stated.

"More than life." Stefan saw Maggie smile, and he relaxed a little.

"Tell me about her," she said.

Stefan glanced away and sighed contentedly. "Where do I begin?"

"Tell me what makes you love her most."

"Oh, that's easy," he said, leaning his elbows on the table. "There was something about Ericha, even before I had a clue who she really was, that filled the emptiness in me. It was as if . . . a part of me had died when Cameron and Erich did. And she put life back into me. Right from the start, she loved me—Stefan— for who I am inside. But even after she found out who I was, she wasn't afraid to put me in my place if I needed it. She saved me. It's as simple as that. And when I realized she was Erich's daughter, everything just made such perfect sense."

Stefan looked at his mother just as she wiped a hand over her face. "Why are you crying?" he asked.

She shook her head and tried to laugh. "I've done little else all night. Oh, it's not what you might think. It's just . . . well, I think it goes way back. I didn't come here to talk about me."

"Enough about *me*," Stefan said. "What *did* you come to talk about?"

Maggie squeezed his hand and looked into his eyes. "Stefan, you must be patient with your father. He loves you very much."

"I know," Stefan admitted.

"He knows that your position has been difficult for you. But we all have some heartache associated with the reason you have had to bear it. It's not easy to talk about. Your father never wanted you to marry Johanna. I wonder at times if he blames himself to some degree for your unhappiness with her."

"I made my own choices," Stefan stated.

"I know that, and he knows that, too. But . . ." Fresh tears pooled in her eyes. "Just be patient with him, Stefan. I believe that with time he will come to accept this, but it *will* take time. That is all I have to say."

"And what of you, Mother?" he asked. "Do you—"

Erma entered the room with little Cameron, freshly bathed and dressed for the day. She handed him over to Stefan, saying, "Miss Ericha asked me to bring him to you while she freshens up."

Stefan chuckled as he settled the baby in the crook of his arm. "Thank you, Erma," he said. She smiled at him as she hurried from the room.

"Oh, let me hold him," Maggie said, beaming as she gazed at the baby.

Stefan handed him over, and she held him up to look into his little round face. "He's so adorable," she concluded. "I *can* see a little of Erich in him, I think. But he does so remind me of you."

Maggie situated the baby on her lap with her hand behind his head. The baby made a happy noise, and she laughed. "Oh, he likes his Grandmama," she said more to the baby. She cooed and smiled at him, while Stefan silently observed. He didn't need to ask the question that had been interrupted. His mother was accepting this child as her grandson. And her love for both of them was evident.

Ericha entered the dining room wearing a dressing gown over her chemise, her hair hanging around her shoulders. She saw Maggie there and hesitated, wondering how she should behave toward Stefan in his mother's presence. She wondered if she should hurry back upstairs and get dressed, but she recalled seeing Maggie much the same way just yesterday morning.

"Good morning, my love," Stefan said when he looked up to see her there. He stood and reached a hand toward her. Ericha felt Maggie's eyes on her as she moved into Stefan's arms and he kissed her quickly in greeting.

Stefan helped Ericha with her chair. Ericha nodded toward Maggie with a smile. "Good morning . . . uh . . ." She hadn't meant to stammer, but she was unsure of what to call her.

"Maggie," Stefan's mother provided easily. "You must call me Maggie. I suppose *Aunt* Maggie would be appropriate." She smiled slyly at Stefan as he walked around the table. "Or perhaps she should call me Mother."

Ericha was briefly alarmed, wondering if Maggie's comment was as light as it sounded, or if there was some cynical undertone. She was relieved when Stefan chuckled comfortably. "Not in public, please. I shudder to think what the newspaper would say about that."

"What brings you out so early?" Ericha asked for the sake of conversation.

"Oh, I just came to see my grandson," she said, smiling at the baby.

"She's lying to you," Stefan said lightly as he served up a plate for Ericha from the sideboard. "She's just like her mother— sneaking in here at the crack of dawn, trying to catch us doing something we shouldn't." He chuckled and set the plate in front of Ericha. "Which isn't terribly difficult, nevertheless . . ."

Ericha looked at the huge helpings in front of her. "You really think I can eat all that?" she asked.

"You're eating for two," he said and poured her a cup of coffee before he sat down.

Maggie seemed to take notice of their interaction, and Ericha said, "There's nothing quite like being served breakfast by the Duke of Horstberg."

"It's something I've enjoyed a time or two in my life," Maggie admitted, concentrating mostly on the baby.

Sensing Maggie's light mood, Ericha felt prompted to tease Stefan a little. "I've noticed that Stefan is prone to disguises." Maggie looked up curiously. "He regularly disguises himself as such common things as a maid or a nanny. He does well in the stable, but then, he learned that from his father, didn't he. My favorite disguise is the musician. But then I like it when he's just Stefan, the common man blending into the crowd."

Stefan gave her a wry smile, and she added, "Well, I don't think he could ever *really* blend into the crowd. There's just something so *royal* about him."

Maggie smiled. "He gets *that* from me."

"You know, Maggie, Stefan disguises himself so well, I actually knew him for months before I realized he was the Duke of Horstberg."

"Really?" Maggie seemed intrigued.

"It took some time to adjust to the shock."

"I dare say it did," Maggie concluded.

"Well, I hate to break this up," Stefan said, coming to his feet. "But I have work to do that can't be put off forever. Mother, are you coming?"

"Thank you, no," she said. "If it's all right with Ericha, I think I'll just stay and visit a while."

"Oh, that would be fine," Ericha said with her mouth full.

Stefan chuckled at her apparent surprise and kissed her as soon as she swallowed. "Have a good day," he said.

Ericha touched his face. "And you."

Stefan held the baby for a minute, then gave him back to his mother before he left. Ericha finished her breakfast while Maggie played with the baby. She was embarrassed to realize she'd cleaned her plate with little trouble. Apparently Stefan had taken notice of her appetite. Quickly she took her plate to the sideboard before Maggie could notice.

"If you have things you need to be doing," Maggie said, "I don't want to keep you."

"There's nothing that can't wait. My days are too long as it is."

"You spend your life waiting for him."

Their eyes met as Ericha admitted, "Yes, I do. But it's not nearly so bad as it used to be. Cameron keeps me very busy."

"Babies have a way of doing that," Maggie said. "Although, Stefan was by far my easiest. He never gave me trouble, not once."

I don't recall ever having to scold him for anything. It was if he knew what was right and did it—from the start. Even as a baby. I worried that he would starve to death because he'd barely give a whimper if he was hungry."

Ericha watched Maggie closely as she sat back down. It took little to realize that this was not idle chatter about babies. The intensity in Maggie's eyes made it evident that she was leading somewhere, and Ericha gave her full attention.

"It wasn't difficult to see that Stefan was an unusual child. While the others played and got into typical mischief, Stefan would sit quietly and draw pictures. He was barely three when we realized that he preferred to be with his father rather than play with the other children. But I think now that was because Han was usually with my father or Erich. He seemed drawn to them both for some reason—in different ways. I think Stefan realized even then that he and his father were very different. Stefan asked his grandfather to teach him to play the piano at four, and I remember them sitting endlessly together on the bench. We were all amazed at Stefan's ability. With his love for drawing, my mother gave him art lessons, and I helped a little here and there. But I wish now that I had helped more."

Maggie moved the baby to her shoulder and rubbed his little back. "Oh, I suppose a mother can't regret being busy trying to raise a family properly. I did the best I knew how at the time. And Stefan was so quiet and content just following the men around, so I hardly gave it a second thought. He was the one I didn't have to worry about."

The way Maggie's expression faltered left little doubt to where her thoughts were headed. Her next sentence confirmed it. "And then we lost them. I wasn't home at the time. But even down in the village, I was stunned by the noise. I felt the rumble move through the ground, like some kind of thunder from hell."

Ericha gasped unwillingly as a thought occurred to her.

"What is it?" Maggie asked.

"It's just that . . . my mother . . . She hated thunderstorms. She would cry and get upset. But I never understood why. I wonder now if . . ."

Maggie nodded as if it made perfect sense. "I saw the smoke billowing up behind the castle. And something inside me crumbled. By the time I got there, the bodies had been moved. I managed to remain calm while I checked on the children. They were a little shaken but fine, except for Stefan." Maggie looked to Ericha as she said with emotion, "Your mother was with him, Ericha. He had watched my father die. He was hysterical. Kathe left us alone, and I held him and cried the rest of the day. The next morning, Han sat him down and told him that he had to be brave, that he was the Duke of Horstberg now. And even though it was hard, they had to work together to see that the country was cared for."

Maggie seemed briefly lost, and she sighed. "I fell apart all over again when I saw my father in the casket. But as hard as it was, I've been able to accept that he was dead. Erich's casket remained closed. It was Han who dragged his body out of the fire. He refused to speak of it.

"Stefan never cried after that—at least not that I saw. He rode his own stallion in the funeral procession, and I remember thinking that already he had learned to bear his position with dignity." She sighed again. "Beyond that day, I ceased being a mother to my children, at least the kind of mother I should have been. I left Stefan to his father and the others to the nannies and governesses. My mother helped compensate, I think. She was stronger than me in so many ways. But I drew myself into solitude and allowed my life to end. Han was always patient, always there for me, in spite of his business. Occasionally he would take me traveling, and a few times we took the children. I would start to feel like I was getting over it, and then we'd go back to Horstberg and it would overtake me again. When Stefan came of age, Han took me away from here, and we've never come back for more than a week or two. To this day, it just doesn't feel right."

Ericha didn't realize she was crying until Maggie glanced up and quietly passed her a handkerchief. She wondered how Maggie could tell such a story with no emotion, but as she pressed closer to what was apparently her point, the tears began to flow.

"It wasn't until last night," Maggie said, shifting the baby to her lap, "that I began to comprehend how all of this had affected Stefan. I had no comprehension of how bad it was between him and Johanna. And somehow I believe if he'd not grown so accustomed to serving his country in spite of his suffering, he would have been able to feel his instincts enough to avoid the marriage. It breaks my heart to think what must have taken place in his young mind. He not only lost his uncle and his grandfather," she choked back a sob, "he lost his mother."

Maggie clutched the baby close to her and cried, as if he somehow gave her solace in her pain. Instinctively Ericha came around the table and sat close beside Maggie. She wrapped her arms around Stefan's mother, and while Maggie wept without restraint, Ericha cried silent tears—for Maggie, for herself, and for Stefan.

When Cameron began to fuss, Ericha eased him away from Maggie. Maggie wiped frantically at her tears with a napkin, then gave an embarrassed chuckle. "Look at me, bawling my eyes out and we hardly know each other."

"We love all the same people," Ericha said, taking Maggie's hand.

"Stefan told me earlier how you have healed him, Ericha. For that alone I owe you a mother's deepest gratitude. But beyond that, I feel for the first time since it happened, that maybe I can come home and not be plagued by the tragedy of losing my father and brother."

Maggie smiled and touched Ericha's face. "It's as if Erich left you behind to heal the wounds of his absence."

Ericha glanced timidly away and Maggie gave a soft laugh. "I've not seen my mother so happy in years. Oh, she always spent her grief in solitude for the most part, but the loss hung around her in spite of her brave smiles. But even before you walked in the room yesterday morning, I knew something had happened to heal her. She is more herself than I have seen in twenty years."

"I fear you give me credit that I don't deserve," Ericha said. "It is being a part of this family that has filled the empty ache in me. My mother never talked about my father; never told me who he was. I always felt as if there was a hole inside of me, not knowing where I'd come from, or why my mother seemed to die of a broken heart. When Stefan took me into his life, I believed I could never be happier. But when I was able to become a part of his family, in spite of the circumstances, it was nothing less than a miracle."

Maggie smiled with contentment. "And it's evident that you are deserving of miracles, my dear girl. Perhaps there are more miracles in store for the two of you."

"Perhaps," Ericha said, but in her heart she could see no possible way for her and Stefan to be together—at least not in this life. If there was life beyond this, then perhaps there was a chance.

Han and Maggie had been there a week when Johanna returned. She was typically cynical at the breakfast table, and Stefan excused himself without hardly touching his meal. Between Johanna's antics and the tension with his father, he felt hard pressed to keep from erupting.

At lunch, Han was absent. Barely into the meal, Stefan asked his mother, "Where is your husband, Mrs. Heinrich?"

She managed a tense smile. "He said there were some things he needed to attend to."

Stefan nodded to accept the explanation. But he felt relatively certain it was more that Han was avoiding the tension of the situation. As soon as Stefan had finished eating, he walked out to the family stable, not surprised to find his father currying a horse. It wasn't uncommon for him to spend time here when he was needing space and solace.

"What are you doing?" Stefan asked, folding his arms over his chest.

Han didn't even look up. "What does it look like I'm doing?"

"We have servants who—"

"I gave him some time off," Han interrupted. "I figured I could still handle this job for a while." He turned toward Stefan and asked, "What might I do for you, Your Grace? Are you needing a mount or—"

"Don't be ridiculous," Stefan insisted.

Han chuckled and turned back to his self-assigned task. "I'll tell you what's ridiculous," he said. "For a stablehand to become royalty is truly ridiculous."

"You always told me that it took knowledge and integrity to be a good ruler. And those things are learned more than bred."

"Then perhaps you would have done well to learn from somebody else." Han's voice became caustic.

"You taught me well, Father." Han looked at Stefan dubiously as he added, "No one could question that."

"*I* question it!" Han shouted.

Recalling what his mother had told him, Stefan clarified, "You are not to blame for my choices—not by any means."

"I'm not so sure," Han snarled, setting his chore aside.

While Stefan was wondering what to say that might bridge this widening gap, Han sat on a bale of straw and pressed his head into his hands. "You know," he said, "there was a day when I wanted more than anything to just get out of this stable and do something worthwhile with my life. If I had known . . ."

"What?" Stefan asked when he faltered. "Are you trying to say you would have chosen not to marry Maggie if you had known the complications it would bring?"

"I would have given my life for your mother, Stefan. Make no mistake about that."

"And that's what you've done, isn't it?"

"Yes, I suppose it is." Han sighed and folded his arms. "I remember the day Abbi made it clear to me exactly what my commitment to Maggie entailed."

While Stefan waited for him to explain, he began to see that what his father was struggling with went much deeper than his disappointment in his son.

"It was after Erich had met Kathe, so it couldn't have been

more than a month or two before he was killed. She told me she'd had a dream. You know how your grandmother has those dreams." Stefan nodded, well aware of Abbi's gift of premonition. "She dreamt that the du Woernig name was lost, and that I would wear the crown."

Stefan's heart quickened at the obvious emotion in his father's eyes. Han chuckled sardonically. "I told her it was preposterous; I was a stablehand, for crying out loud." Han's eyes grew distant. "I will never forget the way she looked over at me when it became evident Cameron was dying, and we knew Erich was already gone. And beyond that moment I was left holding the crown until you came of age. I often wondered what people *really* thought about having a stablehand ruling their country. But I fought hard to live up to what Cameron left in my hands."

Han's eyes turned hard on Stefan, as if to preamble the point he was attempting to get to. "Your mother once told me she'd never marry beneath her. But she did. And there were times when I felt like some kind of actor, filling in a part that wasn't meant for me." Anger began to tinge his voice. "But I fought with everything I had to uphold my responsibilities, and not let them down . . . even though I felt like some kind of *hypocrite*." Han leaned forward a little and his brow furrowed. "The day the du Woernig name died, the son of servants became a king, and the name Heinrich went down in the history books as the royal name of Horstberg."

"And now I've defiled that name?" Stefan retorted. "Is that what you're trying to tell me?"

Han left the question unanswered. "Where did I go wrong, Stefan?" he asked intently. "Was I so determined to teach you to be a good ruler that I overlooked teaching you to follow your heart? I have to wonder what I did that made you believe marrying into that family could possibly be a good thing. And what, for the love of heaven, made you so unhappy and desperate that adultery was your only choice above self-destruction? Did I just take for granted that you would understand matters of the heart? Did I leave you vulnerable to this?"

Stefan absorbed what his father was saying, then responded

in a quiet voice. "As I said, you are not to blame for my choices. You did the best you could under the circumstances."

Han sighed and looked away as if he didn't believe it.

"We were all dealing with a lot of pain," Stefan added. "We were all just trying to cope."

A minute later Han stood up and continued with his chore. "We're still just trying to cope," he said in a tone that made it clear he didn't want to talk about it anymore.

Stefan wandered back across the courtyard and into his office, wishing with all his heart and soul that he could just turn back time and somehow prevent Erich du Woernig from going down to his laboratory that day. It was incredible the hellish circumstances he'd left behind.

Han and Maggie stayed in Horstberg nearly a month. And when they finally left, it was Han who seemed eager to go. Ericha went to the castle with little Cameron to see them off. Han and Stefan embraced, but Ericha could feel the tension between them that had not dissipated since the night Stefan had confessed his involvement with another woman. Han barely acknowledged the baby, but Maggie was reluctant to turn him over to Ericha. Maggie embraced Stefan, then Abbi, and finally Georg. Stefan took the baby while Maggie and Ericha embraced.

"I love you, Ericha," she said. "We've had such fun. I can't wait to come back. You take good care of my . . . of little Cameron, now."

"I will," Ericha promised. Maggie turned toward the carriage, but Ericha stopped her. "Aunt Maggie?" They embraced again quickly. "I love you, too." She added close to her ear, "Mother."

After the good-byes seemed complete and Maggie had stepped into the carriage, Ericha touched Han's sleeve. "Don't I get a hug from you, Uncle Han?"

He hesitated a moment, then embraced her firmly. "He loves you," Ericha whispered in his ear.

Han pulled back and met her eyes. He turned toward Stefan and extended a hand. Stefan shook it firmly. "You take care now, son," he said and disappeared into the carriage.

Maggie leaned out the window, blew a kiss, and waved as the carriage rolled toward the gate.

"I haven't seen her that happy in years," Georg commented. "Maybe they won't be gone so long this time."

"We can hope," Abbi said as she and Georg walked back toward the castle.

Ericha felt briefly disoriented as she turned to take the baby from Stefan. With his mother gone, she had one less excuse to loiter around the castle and be close to him. Trying to be discreet, she followed Georg and Abbi, aware that Stefan was coming a safe distance behind. Only a miracle could close this gap. But in spite of what Maggie had said, Ericha felt certain that an illegitimate woman with an illegitimate child had already received more than her fair share of miracles.

Chapter Sixteen

REPERCUSSIONS

Abbi awoke in the darkness feeling frightened and cold. She drew a wrapper around herself, and with a candle she worked her way down a long hallway. She tapped lightly on the door but didn't wait for a reply. Quietly she opened the door, slipped inside, and closed it again.

"Georg," she called in a whisper, "are you awake?"

"Abbi?"came the startled reply, his voice slurred with sleep. "Is something wrong?"

"I had a dream; a nightmare. I need to tell you."

"Come here," he said with compassion in his voice.

Abbi set the candle on the bedside table and slipped into the bed beside him. Already she felt better when his arms came protectively around her. Given that they both often had difficulty sleeping and didn't want to disturb each other, they had found that they slept better by keeping separate rooms. But she was grateful for the closeness and companionship they shared, especially when one of them might be troubled.

"Tell me," he whispered as his lips brushed over her brow.

"I recall similar dreams," she began, her voice soft with age. "Not that this was the same—but rather the feeling I awoke with."

"And what is that?"

"Cold . . . and frightened. Remember how I told you about the nightmares I had when I was staying in the lodge with Cameron the winter that we met?"

"I remember," he said. She knew that he did, but she felt the need to voice it, if only to validate what she was feeling now.

"Do you remember how I told you that I realized later it had almost been a premonition, because the dreams I'd had were much like what happened the day we married?"

"Yes."

"And then there were the dreams I had before the castle was overtaken when little Elsa was born. And you know I dreamt of Cameron's death before we even married.

"Well, this dream had the same quality," she continued, "but it was more like a memory. Still, it wasn't something I had seen personally. It was something you told me about . . . many years ago."

Georg waited quietly for her to go on.

"I could see Cameron. He looked very young. He was walking down the hall toward the bedroom that was once ours. He went through the door and found Gwendolyn dead on the floor. He pulled the knife out of her, and then the officers of the Guard were in the room. He turned and dropped the knife. It seemed forever that he stood there . . . silent, dignified. But I seemed to realize what turmoil there was in his mind, because I knew him so well. And the . . ." A slight tremor came to her voice and she stopped abruptly. Georg waited patiently for her to continue.

"You remember when that happened to Cameron, don't you, Georg?"

"I remember it well. I fear it's one of those things that even old age won't erase from my mind. It was dreadful."

"In my dream, Georg, as I said, Cameron stood there for what seemed so long . . . looking down at his hands as his wrists were bound. But when he looked back up . . . Oh, Georg, I . . ." The fear overtook Abbi, and she trembled in his arms.

"What is it?" he asked with concern in his voice.

"Georg," she whispered, leaning up to look down at his face

in the candlelight, "when he looked back up, it wasn't Cameron. It was Stefan."

Stefan was surprised when Abbi came to his office and sent Rusty out, requesting that they be alone for a moment.

"What is it?" he asked.

"Stefan," she said carefully, "I came to warn you."

"Warn me?" he asked intently.

"I want you to be extremely careful."

"Why?" He chuckled tensely.

"It may be nothing," she said, "but I've had a dream . . . more than once. And I've had dreams before like this that have been premonitions. There's a feeling about it . . ."

"I understand the nature of your dreams, Grandmama," he said with respect. "Just . . . tell me what you dreamed and I'll promise not to do it."

"I can't," she said.

"Why not?"

"I don't know. I just . . . well, perhaps it's better if I simply tell you to be careful how you react to anything Johanna says or does."

Stefan looked at her shrewdly, sensing this was no small thing. But he simply said, "I'll be careful. I promise."

Abbi seemed relieved and left the office, telling Rusty he could go back in, but Stefan was left feeling uneasy. He was not unaware of his grandmother's gift of dreams, and he couldn't help wondering what horrible event in his future she might have seen. The fact that she had cautioned him concerning Johanna only deepened his concern. But he had to force his concerns out of his mind in order to accomplish his work.

Ericha arrived at the castle just as breakfast was nearly finished, and she found the family in the dining room. Georg and Stefan both stood as she entered, and Johanna made an attempt to look gracious.

"Good morning, dear cousin."Ericha surprised Stefan by kissing him on the cheek, and she was gratified to see that Johanna seemed to disregard it. Stefan grinned as he took Cameron from her and set him on his lap. Ericha exchanged the usual polite nod with Johanna.

"Where is Grandmama?" she asked, moving down the table to greet Georg with a kiss as well.

"She's having breakfast upstairs with Nik," Georg explained as he seated himself again.

"The breakfast conversations must be getting pretty bad if she's resorted to that," Ericha said, and Stefan smiled at her.

"Actually," Johanna said, "she claims he's not doing well and needs more attention. Personally I think he's got her wrapped around his little finger."

"Is he really as bad as he sounds?" Ericha asked.

"You've not met him?" Georg said.

"I've been afraid to." She laughed slightly. "From what I've heard, he's practically the devil himself."

"Could be," Stefan said.

"Well, if you're going to meet him, you'd best do it," Johanna inserted. "They say he'll not live much longer."

"Why is that?" Ericha asked with concern.

It was silent a moment until Stefan said, "What would you expect? The man is paralyzed. He hasn't been out of that bed for over twenty years."

"That's terrible!" Ericha protested. "Not once?"

"Not that I know of," Georg said.

"But why?" she asked.

"Ericha, my dear," Stefan said carefully, "Nik Koenig did everything in his power to destroy Horstberg. And this family, as well. He deserves no compassion."

Ericha was taken aback by Stefan's coldness. "But people make mistakes. Don't you think he's paid for it by now?"

"It wouldn't have happened if he hadn't been toying with things he had no right to toy with."

"But what if—"

"Ericha," Stefan leaned forward, and Johanna seemed to take delight in their arguing, "neither you nor I would be here if he had succeeded in his quest. Nik tried more than once to kill your father, and he nearly killed my father as well in the process. It was Nik's fault my mother lost her first baby, and because of him she nearly lost the second, which would have left her with the inability to have more."

Ericha was left speechless. She wanted to tell Stefan that his resentments would only hurt him, but this wasn't the time. Quietly she said, "I'd like to meet him."

"Fine." Stefan stood abruptly with Cameron in his arms. "Now is as good a time as any."

Ericha followed Stefan down the hall, trying to keep up with his stride.

"Why are you angry?" she asked him.

"I'm not angry," he stated in a hypocritical tone.

"Stefan," she stopped him with her arm, and he turned to face her, "he will be judged by God for his mistakes. It's not your burden to carry."

"Horstberg is my burden to carry, Ericha," he stated. "You have no idea what that man put my family through."

"Your family?" she said.

"Our family," he corrected.

"Nik's family," she stated, and he glared at her. "Well, isn't it?"

"I'd rather not admit—"

"It seems no one cares whether he lives or dies. Is it for us to decide whether or not he deserves to be forgiven?"

"He doesn't want to be forgiven," Stefan snarled.

"Have you asked him?" He made no response, so she added, "Has anyone besides Grandmama given him more than the time of day for the past twenty years?"

Stefan sighed as he looked at the floor.

"It is for us to forgive and be at peace. Then the burden is shifted."

Stefan closed his eyes tightly and turned his head.

"What's wrong?" she asked, and he met her eyes.

"It astounds me," he said, "how I can see in you the wisdom and dignity of Erich du Woernig. And you never even knew him."

"Perhaps I did," she said, and he put his arm around her in a warm embrace before they started again down the hall.

They went upstairs and paused before a door where Stefan knocked lightly, and Abbi called for them to enter. When Ericha's eyes adjusted to the dim light, she saw Abbi sitting near the bed with a book that she had apparently been reading aloud from. Ericha moved her eyes to the legendary villain leaning back against the headboard. Her immediate impression was that he looked far older than Georg, who was at least thirty years his elder. His graying hair and beard were ragged and unkempt. His skin was pale and sallow, his body thin, his eyes lifeless.

"Who's there?" he snapped in a voice both weak and indignant.

"Watch your tone," Stefan said, "I've brought a lady with me, and you'd best act civil or she'll not come back."

"Ah," Nik replied, struggling to lean forward a little in an attempt to get a better look, "it's His Majesty. I hopes it's not that snooty wife of yours with you."

"I'm pleased to say it's not my snooty wife," Stefan replied lightly as he motioned elaborately toward Ericha. "May I introduce my cousin, Ericha Lokberg-du Woernig."

"Cousin?" he said, squinting to scrutinize her. "I thought I'd met all your cousins. Course, she's got the right color of hair. Which du Woernig did you come from?" he asked directly to Ericha.

"My father is Erich du Woernig," she stated proudly.

"Where'd you get the name Lokberg, girl?"

"A little respect," Stefan stated.

"Where'd you get the name Lokberg, miss?"

"It is my mother's name." She moved closer to the bed and gave a smile. "You needn't ask any more questions, Uncle Nik. My father died before he married my mother. I'm not ashamed to admit it. The family has been gracious enough to give me their name in spite of it."

"Ah," he said, "that's right. I don't remember so good these days, but old Erich never did get married. Poor guy. I thought the world had ended when he tried to blow us all up. They say you couldn't even recognize him or—"

"That's enough," Stefan interrupted his ongoing prattle, knowing that Abbi and Ericha were at least equally as affected as he by the subject.

"It's terribly dark in here," Ericha said. "Why don't you let me open the drapes and—"

"If you so much as touch them," he said, "I'll—"

"Oh, nonsense," she uttered and pulled them back abruptly.

Nik squinted and cursed, and Stefan couldn't suppress a chuckle.

"Hush up!" Ericha said, crossing the room. "Your threats don't scare me," she added with a laugh. "What are you going to do? Jump out of that bed and challenge me to a duel?"

"He'll rant and rave until he drives you crazy," Abbi said.

"And I'll go elsewhere," Ericha replied.

Stefan and Abbi both chuckled, but Nik continued his ranting. "She must be related to you, boy. She's a snippy little thing." He turned his attention to Ericha. "This is my room and I prefer it dark, and if you—"

"Don't you realize, Uncle Nik," Ericha said, "that the sun is good for you? It will add years to your life."

"I don't want to live any longer than I absolutely have to."

"Nonsense," she retorted and sat herself on the edge of the bed, much to Nik's dismay. "Don't you want to live old enough to see Cameron grow up?"

"Who's that?" Nik asked with pursed lips.

"My son," she whispered as if it were a secret.

Ericha held out her arms and Stefan gave her the baby. She held him up for Nik to see, and his nose wrinkled slightly.

"What's the matter?" she laughed. "Haven't you ever seen a baby?"

"Not this close," he said, then turned his attention to Ericha. "Where did you get a baby? You can't be married if—"

"Mind your business," she said straightly.

"And your manners," Stefan added.

Nik became unusually silent. Ericha rose to give Cameron back to Stefan, and she took the book from Abbi's hands. "Why don't you run along," she said, "and I'll read to Nik for a while."

Abbi glanced toward Stefan, who nodded and moved toward the door. Late morning, Ericha came down from Nik's room. She found Cameron in the nursery and fed him. She left him sleeping in Ruthild's care and entered the dining room to find the family seated for lunch. They exchanged the usual greetings, but no one asked how it had gone with Nik. Ericha thought it seemed quite out of character for this family she had grown to love so much. They were good, caring people. But the subject of Nik Koenig was obviously difficult—even for Abbi, who was apparently charitable toward Nik.

The meal was nearly finished when an officer of the Guard entered and stood at attention. "Your Grace," he said, "pardon the interruption."

Ericha sensed the immediate tension and assumed that having a meal interrupted was indicative of a problem.

"What is it?" Stefan demanded, coming to his feet.

"There is a woman here, insisting that she see you, sir."

"A *woman?*" he asked. Ericha couldn't tell if he was more surprised or perturbed. "I trust there is a reason that Rusty can't see to it or—"

"Captain Leichty sent me, sir. He feels you should see her personally."

"All right. Bring her to my office as soon as I'm—"

"Excuse me, sir, but that's quite impossible. She just fainted in the front hall, sir, and her children are—"

"Take me to her!" Ericha insisted, leaving Stefan a little stunned as she nearly flew out of the room. Stefan tossed his napkin to the table and followed.

The officer led them to the front hall near the main entrance.

A maid reported that the woman had been carried to a guest room by the captain, but six children were all sitting on the floor, leaning against the wall as if they were terrified.

"I can't get them to talk," the maid apologized. "The poor little things look half starved."

Ericha noted the oldest child glancing up sharply at this. "Get these children something to eat," Ericha said to the maid. "And see that they're cared for."

"Come along," the maid said, but none of them moved.

Ericha realized then that these children looked familiar, one especially. It only took a moment to remember. This was the boy whose leg had been broken when he'd run in front of the coach. She bent down and looked at him, "We'll make certain your mother is fine. And you'll be with her again soon. Right now, I want you to run along with Gertrude here, and she'll see that you get something good to eat."

He came slowly to his feet, and the others followed his example. As soon as they walked away, Stefan said, "Who do you think runs this place, Miss du Woernig?"

Ericha turned quickly in embarrassment. "Oh, I'm so sorry. I didn't think . . ." She stopped when she caught a sparkle of amusement in his eyes.

"She's got a little of her father in her," Stefan said more to the sober officer standing at his elbow.

"Yes, sir," he agreed mechanically, and Stefan chuckled.

As they followed the officer to where the captain had taken this woman, Ericha said softly, "Did you recognize those children?"

Stefan looked surprised. "No, I'm afraid I didn't."

"I believe you made quite an issue over their father's abusive habits."

"Good heavens," he said more to himself as an ominous dread filled him.

The captain met them at the door. "She seems to be feeling a little better now," he reported quietly to Stefan. "I've sent for a doctor, anyway."

"Good. Do you have any idea what this is about?"

"She refused to talk to anyone but you, sir. I know this is far from standard procedure, but . . . under the circumstances . . ."

By the way he left the sentence unfinished, Ericha wondered if the captain realized who this woman was. She also wondered if it would be better for her to just leave this to Stefan. She already feared she had overstepped her bounds a little. As the captain took hold of the door handle, she asked outright, "Would you prefer that I go and leave you to—"

"On the contrary," Stefan said, "this may call for a woman's intuition." Their eyes met, and Stefan fought away the ache. She was born to the calling that Johanna so blatantly ignored.

The captain opened the door and stepped aside, and Stefan entered with Ericha right behind him. The woman stood quickly from a chair near the bed and moved toward him. She was obviously with child, and her face showed the discoloration of fading bruises. While Stefan was choosing his words, she drew her hand back and slapped him hard.

Ericha gasped. The captain rushed to grab the woman's arm. She teetered slightly and leaned into him as if she had exerted her entire strength. "Damn you!" she hissed and strained against the captain's hold as if she'd like to hit the duke again.

"That's quite enough, madame," the captain said sternly. "You are addressing the Duke of—"

Stefan lifted a hand to stop him. Ericha saw Stefan's eyes harden on the woman, filling with that uncompromising power he was famous for. The woman returned his gaze defiantly, in spite of her visible trembling. Ericha tried to comprehend how much courage it must have taken for her to come here and vent her anger on the Duke of Horstberg.

"I trust you are feeling better, madame," Stefan said. "I also trust you will do me the honor of explaining what I have done to deserve such an *amiable* greeting."

"You should have left it alone," she snapped. "We were better off before you started meddling in our lives. Some great hero, you are!" Her voice dripped with sarcasm.

"Is that how you would prefer it, madame?" Stefan asked with no apology in his tone or demeanor. Ericha marveled at the way he remained completely dignified, demanding the respect due to his position without showing any disrespect for this woman. "Are you saying then, that I should blind myself to the beating of women and children in my country?"

"Better that than leaving them abandoned to starve and . . ." A sob caught her voice, and she strained again to break free of the captain's hold. "And to beg in the streets. Would you have me work the farm and . . ." She slumped into the captain's arms as she fainted again, and he deftly carried her to the bed.

Stefan sighed and pushed a hand through his hair. Ericha sensed the dilemma pounding through his mind and discreetly put a hand to his face while the captain's back was turned. He smiled weakly, and she hurried to the woman's side as the captain stepped back.

"I wonder how long it's been since she's eaten anything substantial," Ericha said. Turning to the captain, she ordered, "See that something's brought from the kitchen. I'll stay with her."

He nodded and left the room.

"Now you're ordering my captain about," Stefan said. She turned to look at him, but the light comment had not diminished the concern in his eyes.

"If I am out of line, Your Grace, all you have to do is—"

"You are exactly where I want you," he said. "And don't call me 'Your Grace'; not like this."

Ericha sensed the ache beneath his statement, though his voice lightened as he added, "It would seem you have something in common with Mrs. Schmidt."

"And what is that?"

"You too have slapped the Duke of Horstberg and cursed to his face."

Ericha glanced down, not certain whether she felt amused or embarrassed to recall the incident. Sensing his concern for the present situation, she turned the subject elsewhere. "You handled her well."

Stefan ignored the compliment. "The full picture begins to appear."

"And what is that?"

"The abuse continues. The law closes in. He leaves the country to avoid being arrested. The children starve."

The tone of his voice chilled Ericha. She could almost feel the burden he carried.

"But what I don't understand is—"

A maid entered the room with a tray. She curtsied slightly toward Stefan and set it down.

"Thank you," Stefan said.

"The children are eating and appear to be comfortable," she reported. "Would you like me to stay and help with—"

"No, thank you," Ericha said. "I'll stay with her."

She curtsied again. "The captain asked me to tell you that he's waiting in the hall, should you need him, Your Grace."

"Thank you," he said again, and she closed the door behind her.

"She appears to be sleeping," Ericha commented, and she turned to Stefan. "What don't you understand?"

"There are well-established programs to care for those in need. To my knowledge, every citizen is aware of that and—"

"Every citizen," Ericha interrupted, "or every *male* citizen?"

Stefan sighed and shook his head as her perception struck him deeply.

"Would such a man want his wife to know that she could get along without him?" Ericha added gently. "Or would he—"

She stopped when the woman moaned and opened her eyes. She looked briefly disoriented, then tried to sit up abruptly.

"It's all right," Ericha said, urging her back to the pillow. "We've got something for you to eat. Just relax. Everything will be fine."

"The children?" she murmured.

"They're eating and doing fine," Ericha said gently. The woman seemed to relax until her eyes shifted to see Stefan standing nearby. He caught Ericha's eye and noticed the subtle tilt of her head, indicating that he leave them alone.

"I'll be back," he said quietly and hurried out. He left the captain standing guard at the door and walked quickly to his office. While he calculated the best way to handle this situation, his mind drifted to Ericha. Her wisdom and insight were as impressive as her compassion was touching. How he loved her!

Stefan entered the office to find that Rusty was well aware of the situation. He'd already located census files and property records for the Schmidt family and had come up with a number of possible solutions that he proposed to Stefan.

Stefan returned to the woman's room, hoping to give her some reasonable options. He found Ericha sitting on a chair in the hall. The captain casually stood guard at the door.

"Doctor Furhelm is with her, sir," he informed.

Stefan nodded to acknowledge it, and he sauntered over to Ericha and stuffed his hands into his pockets. "How did it go?"

"She ate a little, but she'll have to take it slow or she'll end up sick. From what little she said, I don't think she's eaten for days. I suspect what little food she had, she's given to the children."

Stefan swallowed hard. "Thank you," he said, hoping she could read in his eyes how much he meant it.

"I'm glad I was here."

"So am I. You seem to have a way with—"

The door opened and Doctor Furhelm emerged. "Ah, Your Grace," he said, and they shook hands. "Good to see you."

"And you. How is she?"

"Everything appears to be fine beyond needing some good nutrition to build her strength up. I told her I'd check back with her at home in a few days." He chuckled and gave Stefan a friendly slap on the shoulder. "And I'll send you the bill."

Stefan chuckled as well and shook his hand again. "Thank you, Doctor."

"I'll check the children before I leave," he said, and Stefan appreciated his insight.

Ericha went quietly into the room with Stefan following. Mrs. Schmidt met his eyes with a combination of fear and defiance.

"You must forgive me, madame," he said. "Apparently there have been some oversights in your situation."

She seemed to relax, and Stefan moved a chair so that he could sit down and face her. Ericha listened as he talked to her for nearly an hour, explaining in simple terms the law that was meant to protect her family and also the laws that provided for the care of those who were unable to care for themselves. He asked her questions concerning her personal abilities to possibly help provide for her family in the future. Then he offered suggestions for some options that she might consider. Ericha thought that he could have easily assigned his secretary or one of his advisors to handle this, but he obviously considered her situation a personal responsibility.

The woman was pleased to realize that her farm land could be leased to someone who was able to work it, and she would not only be free of the burden of caring for it, she would receive some income from the lease. She was also pleased to know that she was entitled to legal help from a solicitor, concerning her rights relating to the abuse and abandonment of her husband.

Stefan asked Mrs. Schmidt if she had any questions, and she shook her head. He took the woman's hand as he came to his feet, finishing gently. "I will see that someone takes you and the children safely home, and that your needs are met. If a problem arises, send word through my secretary."

She nodded, and he left the room. Ericha stayed with Mrs. Schmidt until the officers came to escort her home. Ericha didn't see Stefan before she left the castle, but she went to Karl's shop and told him briefly what had transpired. She also told him about her visit with Nik, then asked him cautiously if he would be interested in making a chair with wheels.

"A bath chair? Whatever for?" he laughed.

"For Uncle Nik," she said, and he smiled wryly.

"You're serious."

"I am."

"Well, sure I can make one."

"Will you then?"

"No problem. When do you want it?"

"The sooner the better."

"Fine," he said easily. "There's some things I need to finish up first, then I'll get right to it. I'll send the bill to Stefan."

A week later, Stefan came as usual to stay the night and reported that Elsbeth Schmidt was doing well. She would be filing for divorce and likely be granted her husband's land in the settlement. Ericha knew he was pleased with the outcome thus far, and she was not surprised when he admitted his wish that a divorce could be possible for *him*. As always, Ericha reminded him of all that was good. Then she distracted him with laughter and happiness.

Following a tediously lengthy meeting with visiting dignitaries, Stefan went to his room to change. Theodor took care of the uniform and left for the day. Stefan was just pulling on his boots when Johanna exploded into his room unannounced.

"Excuse me?" Stefan said. "That door was made to knock upon, Mrs. Heinrich."

"You probably think I'm stupid," she snarled. "And maybe I am. But I'm not blind!"

"What are you talking about, Johanna?" he asked calmly.

"I've been putting some pieces together, and it has become apparent that my husband has a bastard son."

Stefan looked at her sharply and held his breath. It didn't matter how she found out. It was simply her knowing that made him sick. But he swallowed hard and answered coolly, "Better than no son at all."

"You son of a bitch!" she spat like venom. "It's that bastard cousin of yours, isn't it!"

Stefan took a deep breath, forcing himself to stay calm. "You may call me what you like, Johanna. But leave my mother and my cousin out of it."

"I should have known," she hissed, ignoring his attempt to divert the subject. "The first time I saw you look at her, I should have known you'd fall into bed with one of your relatives."

A sharp retort slipped onto Stefan's tongue, but he thought of his grandmother's warning and swallowed it. He reminded himself that she was only trying to bait his anger, and he leaned back and folded his arms. Now that she knew, there was no point trying to pretend.

"Ericha and I were involved long before I knew she was my cousin."

"Lucky for you she wasn't your sister."

"You're pushing me, Johanna. Don't push too hard."

"How dare you humiliate me by flaunting her around here like some kind of prize!"

"I have never flaunted her," he stated calmly, despite the way he was seething inside. He felt like taking her by the throat, but he knew from experience that getting angry didn't make the situation any better. It would only land him in jail if he wasn't careful.

"You flaunt that boy of yours like he's the greatest thing in this world!"

"He is."

"And what do you suppose my family would do if they knew the truth?"

"What truth?" Stefan actually laughed. "That you lost your husband's love because you treated him like a piece of dispensable jewelry; that you couldn't have children, so you manipulated your husband into believing it was his fault to cover yourself from finding other beds to sleep in? Every bit of the bitterness and resentment you feel, you have brought upon yourself, my dear. Just bear in mind that anything you do will come back to you. There is not one rumor you can spread about me or one hurt you can put upon me that will not see you undone in the end. You can destroy Horstberg if you choose, but like it or not, it's your country too. You can't run home to your father, Johanna, so if the ship goes down, you're going with it!"

"If my father knew about this, he would—"

"Johanna," he leaned forward, "your father only cares about one thing. As long as you have *my* name, then he has his finger in *my* pie. Your father has a different mistress every time I see him. He probably has more illegitimate children than servants."

Stefan could see her anger building as he touched truths she obviously didn't want to hear. But now that it was out, he had to admit he was enjoying this.

"I'd wager your father would love to hear what I heard about you at the pub. You owe me one for not telling him that."

A thought crept into Stefan's head so abruptly he was nearly surprised. He told himself not to say it, but the hurt and anger associated plunged it into the open, almost against his will.

"And I'm certain your father would love to hear that you were actually pregnant when you married me."

Johanna's face turned from red to white almost instantly.

"Oh," Stefan's voice rumbled, "if I had known then what I know now, I'd have dumped you back on his doorstep so fast he wouldn't have *dared* cross my borders for a decade. And if being pregnant weren't bad enough, you had to go and kill the child before it even had a chance, which is the reason you were never able to conceive one of *my* children. Oh, you nearly had me fooled on that one. But it looks as if it wasn't my fault after all."

The color gradually came back to Johanna's face while Stefan glared at her, silently daring her to respond to the charges.

"Fine," she finally sneered, as if he'd said nothing at all, "strut around with your little tramp and see if—"

Stefan shot to his feet and pulled Johanna's wrist into his grip. She moaned and tried to squirm away, but he pulled her closer and spoke through clenched teeth. "If you so much as breathe a disrespectful word about her—ever again—or do anything to harm my son, in body or spirit, I will tear you into little pieces and take great pleasure in doing it."

"You don't scare me with your threats, Stefan," she said, pulling her arm from his grasp. "You're not man enough to kill me."

"At least I'm man enough to have a son," he said, "which is something you never gave me credit for."

"That's not fair, Stefan. I—"

"Fair?" he echoed with a bitter laugh. "I used to be fair with you, Johanna. But that's in the past. I've given you all the fairness I can give. You asked for it—every bit of it. And now you're going to have to live with it."

Just before Johanna turned away, he added, "And she is not a tramp. You, my dear, are a tramp!"

It wasn't until Johanna hurried out the door that Stefan realized it was open.

"Damn!" he muttered and pushed a hand through his hair. The walls were thick, but open doors held nothing back.

While a part of Stefan felt some relief in having it out, a tight knot of dread was already forming in the pit of his stomach. He felt certain she would not take the humiliation well of being publicly known as the "The duchess who couldn't conceive the heir." But far worse, something told him he had exposed her too deep and too hard. He knew as well as he knew the sun would set that Johanna would not rest until she considered herself even.

Stefan didn't go to see Ericha that night. He almost felt afraid to leave until the dust settled a little. Johanna was absent at dinner, and nothing seemed out of the ordinary. He went to his music room and stayed there late, hoping exhaustion would dull his nerves enough to enable him to sleep. Still, he laid awake half the night, while bits and pieces of their ugly conversation catapulted through his mind.

He finally drifted to sleep and woke abruptly, sitting up with a gasp. It took a minute to recall the contents of his dream. And with the memory came a cold chill. In the dream he had seen himself lying flat on his back, wearing his uniform, as if he were dead. And Johanna had been floating almost ghost-like above him, laughing wickedly, with triumph in her eyes.

Stefan got out of bed and splashed water on his face. He

wondered why he hadn't gone to see Ericha. If he'd ever needed her, it was now. He tried to go back to sleep but finally got up when daylight came.

Stefan skipped breakfast and went straight to the office with a cup of coffee. A maid informed him that Rusty had gone into the village to do some business, and he was almost relieved that he didn't have to be with anybody right now.

He spent the morning thinking more than working. Just when he thought he could concentrate, disturbing thoughts would burst into his mind. He thought of Ericha. He admired her courage and strength, and she'd never been one to complain. But he knew this was difficult for her. And he dreaded having to tell her that Johanna knew the truth. He suspected the news would frighten her. It certainly had him.

As the oppression settled around him, Stefan found it difficult to avoid wondering if he and Ericha had done the right thing. Whether or not they had, it couldn't be changed. And how could Stefan regret his son's existence? How could he wish away even a moment of the life he shared with Ericha? Still, a deep dread told him the consequences would get worse before this was over—if it would ever be over.

Stefan drew a long sigh and turned toward the window. How many times had he wished he'd just done it differently right from the start? As memories became a blur, he began to question whether his motives had been correct. Had he been too hard on Johanna? Would their marriage have had a chance if he hadn't been so cold and hard with her? And then there was Ericha. Would she have been better off if he had just turned away and never given her a second glance? But she was his cousin, for heaven's sake. Eventually they would have come together, one way or another. And how could he know her and not love her?

Stefan's head began to ache, and he cursed himself for even allowing such thoughts to plague him. He couldn't change it— any of it. All he could do was take the future and make the most of it. Reminding himself to follow that adage, he forced his concentration back to the work spread over his desk. But a short while later, he decided he would get nothing done in this frame of mind. He tossed his glasses to the desk and rose to leave just as a knock came at the door. He pulled it open to see Johanna, looking especially glum. Stefan sighed, wondering if he had to start this all over again. She glanced warily toward the uniformed guards banking the door, then back to Stefan.

"Can I talk to you?" she asked. She almost sounded genuine. Stefan motioned her inside and closed the door. As she came into the room where the light was better, he couldn't help noticing that she looked awful. Her face looked sallow and colorless. Her eyes were blood-shot. She looked as if she'd slept in her clothes and not even put a brush to her hair. As she glanced almost hesitantly toward him, he distinctly saw the discoloration of a fresh bruise.

"What is this?" With little thought he reached up to touch it. She retracted and turned away.

"It's nothing," she insisted. "I just need to talk to you."

"All right." Stefan sat on the edge of his desk and folded his arms. He motioned her toward the chair he usually occupied, but she shook her head and turned to the window. "I'm listening," he said when the silence continued.

"I . . . want you to know that I . . . well, I know that you and I disagree on many things, Stefan. And I know I wasn't always fair. I just . . . never dreamed it would come to this."

"And what did you expect it to come to?" he asked with no trace of malice.

She shot him a harsh look, and then her expression softened and she turned back to the window. When the silence grew too long, Stefan said, "I get the impression something is troubling you. If you want to talk, fine. But let's get on with it."

"I'm just having a hard time believing our relationship has come to this. When I married you, I had every hope that my life would be good."

Stefan swallowed hard, resisting the urge to just tell her to go to hell. She was being civil. Surely he could manage the same.

"What are you in need of, Johanna? More jewels? More clothes? More servants perhaps? Is coming and going as you please at all hours of the night not enough freedom?"

Stefan expected her to get defensive. But she only looked at him with sad eyes and said, "I had hoped we would have children, that we could be happy together."

A brief, sardonic chuckle erupted from Stefan's throat as he contemplated the absurdity of her statement. Forcing his own defenses down, he took it head on. "And what exactly do you feel are the ingredients for this happy marriage, Johanna?"

If Stefan had not lived with this woman so many years, he might have believed the tears welling into her eyes actually meant a softening of her heart. "I love you, Stefan," she whimpered. But his only thought was how pathetically shallow she was.

"Since when?" he asked.

"I've always loved you," she defended.

"You will *never* make me believe that."

Anger replaced her tears quickly. Stefan wondered how he might be feeling right now if he'd actually wanted to believe she felt something for him.

"I should have known you would be cold and hard about it."

"About what?" He almost laughed to see how mechanically she turned on him.

"I was hoping we might have another chance. That maybe we could . . ." She dabbed at her eyes and sniffled.

"Johanna," he said in a firm voice that was not unkind, "some things simply cannot be changed. And sometimes it's just too late."

She looked downright shocked, and he wondered what her motive in coming here had been. Did she possibly believe that he would turn his back on Ericha and try to make things work again between them? The very thought made him ill.

"Johanna, listen to me," he said. "I've looked the other way and let you live life the way you've wanted to. All I'm asking is that you do the same. Is that so much to ask?"

She fidgeted with the rings on her fingers for a minute, then turned to glare at him. "You're a cruel man, Stefan Heinrich," she said and left the room.

For several minutes after she'd gone, Stefan stared at the door, wondering why she'd not driven him to suicide or insanity years ago. He could find absolutely no logic in the way her mind worked—which was perhaps the most frightening thing of all.

"Excuse me, sir," Rusty said, startling Stefan from his thoughts, "I said that it appears this would be the best approach."

"What was that?" Stefan asked distantly. Rusty had returned from his business nearly an hour ago, and Stefan still couldn't seem to concentrate.

"We were talking about the problem with . . . Are you all right, sir?"

"Yes, yes. I'm fine," Stefan insisted. Then he added soberly, "Rusty, what would you do if you were in my shoes?"

He laughed. "I'm not in your shoes. And I must say I'm glad of that."

"Thanks a lot." Stefan chuckled.

"Were you speaking of something particular?"

"Well I—" Stefan began, but a knock came to the door and he sighed.

"Come in," Stefan called, and his grandmother entered the room.

"Would you please excuse us, Rusty?" she said. He nodded politely and left the room.

Abbi glanced around uneasily, and he noted she was wringing her hands. "You've rearranged things," she said. "Wasn't that book cupboard over there before?"

"Servants must have done it," he replied. "Is that what you came to talk to me about?"

"No," she said cautiously. "I was told just now that rumors are filtering among the servants."

Stefan knew what was coming.

"I believe you had an argument with Johanna yesterday."

Stefan turned abruptly in his chair but said nothing.

"I'm afraid it will soon be common knowledge that Cameron is your son." Abbi went on carefully, "And it seems your entire conversation was overheard."

Stefan sighed and looked toward the ceiling.

"You're not saying much."

"What do you want me to say?" he asked. "Johanna came to my room with hellfire and damnation because she'd figured it out. She knows. It's out." He threw his hands in the air. "What am supposed to do about it?"

"Be careful, Stefan," she said quietly, "don't let—"

She was interrupted when Johanna opened the door and popped her head in. "Hello," she said cheerfully, and Stefan wanted to strangle her.

"Don't you ever knock?" he asked sharply.

"Just looking for Rusty," she said easily. "I need to ask him something. Have you seen him?"

"He just left," Stefan stated. "He can't be too far."

"Thank you, my dear," she said as if nothing had ever been wrong. Stefan stood abruptly and went to the window as she left and closed the door.

"Grandmama," he said quietly, stuffing his hands into his pockets. "What am I going to do?"

Abbi met his eyes carefully but left his question unanswered.

Ericha arrived at the castle late morning to meet a lunch appointment with her grandmother. She went straight to Abbi's sitting room carrying Cameron in her arms, but Abbi wasn't there. She inquired of a maid, who eyed her speculatively, then crooned unnaturally over the baby a moment before she told Ericha that Her Grace had gone to the office to speak with the duke.

Ericha felt uneasy as she left the maid and went back downstairs toward the office. She sensed a different mood to the castle but scolded herself for letting her imagination run away with her. She turned into the hall just in time to see Johanna slip out of a room and shut the door quietly.

Johanna looked surprised to see her there, but her expression quickly became complacent.

"Good morning," Ericha said lightly, accustomed to ignoring Johanna's cold expressions.

"Good morning, *Miss* du Woernig," she said with a smirk.

Ericha hurried past her, feeling the uneasiness increase as Johanna glared at little Cameron with a glint in her eye.

Ericha knocked on the office door, and Stefan called out sharply, "What?"

She entered timidly, and he immediately softened his expression, "I'm sorry. I thought you were—"

"What's wrong?" she asked, noting Abbi's expression and the obvious tension that hung in the room.

Stefan got right to the point. "Johanna knows about us." Ericha sat down quickly, holding the baby instinctively close. "And since our argument yesterday was overheard, everyone else either knows or will soon."

"What exactly was said?" Ericha asked.

"Oh, just about everything," he said in a tone of self-punishment. "No matter how hard I try to maintain control with her, she just has a way of . . ." Stefan stopped when he saw the distress on his grandmother's face.

"I should leave the two of you alone," Abbi said.

"No," Stefan insisted, "the last thing we need now is for someone to find us alone together. Please stay."

Abbi nodded, and Ericha asked, "How did she find out?"

"I don't know," Stefan answered. "She said she'd put the pieces together and figured it out. It doesn't matter."

"I would guess it's nothing more than a result of speculations passed between servants and commoners," Abbi suggested. "Even little things don't go unnoticed."

"What are we going to do?" Ericha asked.

"There's nothing we can do," he stated. "I don't know.

Perhaps it's better that it's out. I'm tired of all this pretending and hiding."

"You must be careful," Abbi said intently. "Both of you. Don't let this destroy you."

Stefan shook his head and motioned toward Ericha and the baby. "How can the best thing that ever happened to me have the potential to destroy me? I don't understand that."

"What motivates your relationship is not wickedness or evil, Stefan. Nevertheless, the lines you've crossed inevitably leave a weakness. Evil and wickedness prey upon such weaknesses."

Stefan pressed his fingers to his temples and moaned. He met Ericha's eyes, and she stood and moved into his arms. He took little Cameron and put his arm around Ericha, kissing her brow softly as he whispered, "Everything will be all right."

"I pray," she whispered, and Stefan pulled her closer while Abbi put her hand fearfully to her heart.

Several days passed with little event. Stefan and Ericha decided together that they would continue living as they had and try not to worry. They both felt certain they weren't the first to experience such things, and could only hope that the adverse effects would not be too difficult to handle.

Ericha first felt the repercussions on market day when she took Cameron into town to look over the wares. She'd been doing it since he was born and had been well aware that people knew her child was illegitimate. But being accepted by the royal family had seemed to smooth over many rough edges. She had never felt complete acceptance from people, but with her circumstances she had never expected it.

But this day she knew something had changed. Ericha felt it first as she made a purchase of some cinnamon cakes. She felt the vendor eying her speculatively as she paid for her purchase, then realized there were subtle whispers going on around her.

Ericha did her best to ignore them and almost convinced herself that it was her imagination. She wondered if her knowing that gossip was being spread just made her think she was being talked about. But as she went to the park and sat with Cameron on her lap, she undoubtedly saw heads bent together with eyes turned her way. The glances were subtle, but they pierced Ericha through. She thought of Stefan and wondered if he'd experienced the same, though she felt certain people would not dare be so obvious with the Duke of Horstberg.

Feeling unnerved, Ericha gathered Cameron into his pram and strolled toward home, stopping only at the dress shop to deliver some lace to Frieda that she'd promised today. Frieda was gracious as usual, but she took more interest in the baby than she ever had before. And Ericha noted two other ladies in the shop whispering. She caught the words "duke's child."

Ericha left the shop as quickly as possible and opted to take a side street home, rather than going through the square again. She soon realized that her decision was a mistake as she had to pass by one of the pubs when several men were gathered outside. It took more strength than she'd ever mustered to remain composed when she heard things being said about her that women wouldn't have dared say aloud.

Grateful at last for the safety of home, Ericha forced back the burning in her head and rushed inside with Cameron in her arms. Hurrying toward the stairs, she saw from the corner of her eye that Stefan and Karl were in the parlor. But she ignored them and hurried to her room.

Stefan sensed something was wrong and met Karl's eyes warily before he rushed toward the stairs. "Ericha?" he called, but she moved on even though he knew she'd heard him.

The bedroom door was slammed just before he reached it. He opened it carefully to see her standing before the window, clutching Cameron almost desperately.

"I need to be alone," she said as she placed the baby into his crib and gave him a toy. Stefan ignored her and shut the door quietly.

"What is it, Ericha?" he asked gently, and she put one hand over her mouth in an effort to force back the sob catching in her throat. She shook her head and turned her back to him, but he came behind her and put his hands over her shoulders.

"Ericha," he said gently, "don't try to tell me nothing is wrong. You're practically choking on pain. I can see it."

His voicing of her feelings intensified them, and she turned and slumped into his arms. Stefan was silent as he let her cry against his shoulder, and then she moved wearily into a chair and he knelt beside her.

"Now," he said, "are you going to tell me what's wrong?"

"I'm never going into public again," she said.

"That doesn't sound like the Ericha I know," he replied. Though he sensed the reason, he made an effort to steer her toward her inner strengths.

"Perhaps," she said cynically, "that's because the Ericha you know has never been publicly referred to as the king's whore . . . among other things that I will not repeat aloud."

Stefan leaned back on his feet and squeezed his eyes shut abruptly as if he'd been struck. He swallowed his own pain and touched Ericha's tear-stained face, saying with strength, "It's not true."

Ericha bowed her head forward. "It is true."

Stefan wished he knew what to say. There was nothing that could be done to change the circumstances now. The stigma was there and it always would be. But in his mind, one aspect of the situation stood out strongly. And it did make a difference.

"Ericha," he whispered, lifting her chin with his finger, "I love you with everything I have . . . everything I am."

Ericha sighed and pulled him close to her. She melted into his embrace and felt the comfort engulf her. His lips came over hers and the feeling intensified.

Stefan came to his feet and pulled her up into his arms, carrying her the few steps to the bed. A bittersweetness enveloped them mutually as they sought to absorb the other's pain.

Ericha felt the power of Horstberg melt at her touch. For those brief, inviolable moments, she held the soul of a country in her hands. The Duke of Horstberg was set aside, and Ericha became absorbed with the artist, the musician, the man who followed his heart in spite of the obstacles. Stefan's love filled her with peace, and she knew that somehow they would make it through this.

The high-strung emotion dissipated with their passion, and they lay quietly content in each other's arms with the assurance that if nothing else they had each other.

The peace was broken by Cameron's cries, and Stefan rose to bring him to Ericha to be fed. He lay close beside her, leaning on one elbow to watch her with his son, and he marveled at the beauty. It made him want to paint a picture, but he was certain he would defile the loveliness in his feeble attempt.

"I don't regret it, Stefan," she said, and he met her gaze. "I would do it all over again if I had the choice, and I would change nothing, if only to have you and Cameron in my life."

"But that doesn't make it any less painful."

"No," she replied, briefly closing her eyes, "but I recall a time in my life that was more painful than this."

Stefan furrowed his brow in question. "Nothing was ever so painful for me as being in love with you and believing I could never have you." She smiled and touched his face. "I have you now and I will not regret it."

Chapter Seventeen

A Cup of Laughter

$\mathcal{F}$eeling a need for fresh air, Stefan hurried through his work and announced at the noon meal that he was going coursing. Abbi and Georg agreed it would be good for him to get out. Johanna made no comment.

Stefan tied his horse off and tramped across the meadow through the thin layer of newly fallen snow. Donner and Blitzen romped just ahead of him, sniffing eagerly at the ground. He felt better already as he absorbed the bright sky and the brisk quality of the air. He liked this place and came here often. Memories of Erich washed over him as he recalled their coming here together many times for the same purpose. Now, just as then, Stefan held a shotgun cradled comfortably in his arm. But he had no intention of shooting anything, unless it was especially convenient. Erich had taught him by example that this pastime was more for clearing the head and getting exercise than for diligently searching out any game.

The dogs moved ahead into the trees as they apparently caught a scent. Stefan lost sight of them, but he could hear them not far ahead and followed. His mind turned to Ericha, and he concentrated on all the good she had brought into his life. He tried briefly to comprehend where he might be now without her, but he couldn't come up with any plausible vision that didn't sicken him. So he turned his mind to the present, silently thanking God for sending her to him, in spite of their situation.

Stefan stopped in his tracks when he heard gunshot. He instinctively dropped flat on his chest as a childhood memory took hold of him. How could he ever forget the day he and Erich had been shot while out riding? There had not been attempts against his life since Erich's death, but he didn't have to think twice to know that he likely had many enemies due to his position.

Heart pounding, Stefan looked around carefully, though he could see nothing but trees. He quickly wondered who would have known he was coming here. Rusty, Abbi, Georg, *Johanna.* Stefan stopped himself from jumping to conclusions. He'd told no one else, but any number of people could have seen him leaving the castle with the dogs and a shotgun. He wondered briefly if Johanna would be so low as to actually try having him done away with. But as much as she hated him, he found it difficult to imagine her doing such a thing.

Stefan only laid on the ground a brief moment before he whistled to the dogs. He heard movement and knew they were coming back. Then another shot fired. Then another. And another. Then he heard the anguished yelping of a dog.

"Dear God, no," Stefan murmured and scrambled to his feet. He didn't go far before he found them and he sank to his knees in the snow, oblivious to the possibility that he might be the next target.

"No," Stefan cried softly, momentarily too stunned to even know what to do. Donner was obviously dead, lying motionless in the blood-soaked snow, his eyes open and glazed. Blitzen was bleeding profusely, but his labored breathing startled Stefan to action. He tried not to think about how many years these dogs had been his faithful companions as he scooped the hound carefully into his arms and hurried back toward the horse. Tears burned into his eyes as he rode quickly back to the castle, the dog draped over the saddle in front of him. He had no idea if it would be possible to save Blitzen, but he had to try.

The hurt turned to anger as Stefan wondered who would do such a thing. It was senseless and ridiculous. He reminded himself to be grateful it hadn't been *him,* but instinctively he believed he'd not been the target. Someone had purposely done this to persecute him. Stefan's chest constricted painfully as the only possibility stormed into his mind. *Johanna.* No, she wouldn't be fool enough to try to have *him* killed, or even to harm someone he loved. But she knew his habits, and she knew how to hurt him. Killing a dog wasn't criminal, so no action could be taken—even *if* there was any evidence, which of course, there wouldn't be. But Stefan didn't doubt there were likely many men in Horstberg willing to do her bidding for a price. He cursed her under his breath as he rode carefully into the courtyard.

"Give me some help here," he ordered the officers standing on duty at the cavalry stables. Two rushed toward him. One held the reins of the horse while the other helped support the dog as Stefan dismounted. "Get me the veterinarian," he demanded. "Now!"

"Yes, sir," one officer replied and hurried away. The other followed Stefan toward the door and opened it for him.

Stefan felt consumed with grief and anger as he hurried into the front hall of the castle and laid Blitzen down, kneeling beside him, heedless to the blood spilling onto the carpet. "Get one of the maids to bring me some rags," he ordered the officer. "And get my grandmother."

"Yes, sir," he replied and ran down the hall.

"Hang on, Blitzen," he murmured gently to the dog, pressing a comforting hand over his head. Stefan had kept dogs since his childhood. He'd lost animals to old age and accidents, but he'd never witnessed anything so pathetic.

A maid appeared with an armful of clean rags and gasped at the sight before her.

"Thank you," Stefan said tersely. "That will be all."

She scurried away, and Stefan pressed rags over the wound, hoping to slow the bleeding, conscious of every struggled breath the animal took.

"Good heavens!" he heard Abbi gasp as she approached quickly. He glanced up to see Ericha right behind her. "What happened?"

"Someone shot them," he reported, his voice shaking. "Donner's already dead."

Ericha took a deep breath and willed her heart to stop pounding. When she'd first caught a glimpse of the blood all over Stefan, she had feared it was his.

Stefan briefly explained what had happened, wondering when the vet would get there. Ericha knelt beside him and touched his arm. "You're shaking," she said.

"Yes," he snapped, "I'm shaking."

"Who would do such a thing?" Abbi asked gently.

"That's not difficult to figure out," Stefan retorted.

"You don't really think that . . ." Ericha didn't dare finish.

"I don't have to think, I *know*. I could never prove it, and there isn't a blasted thing I can do about it. But I *know* she had something to do with this."

At Stefan's apparent anger, Abbi felt she had to say, "Be careful, Stefan. Don't let your hatred get you into trouble."

Stefan glared at his grandmother. A biting comeback hit his tongue, but he swallowed it. He knew she was right. There was nothing he could do without causing more trouble. He was going to have to let it go. He centered his attention on Blitzen, wondering if he would be able to make it. A minute later the dog stopped breathing.

"He's gone," Stefan said, and he hesitantly eased back and sat on the floor. "It's just as well," he murmured. "He likely would have died of loneliness without Donner. They've never been apart."

"I'm so sorry," Ericha said. He looked up to see tears on her face. Emotion burned into his eyes, and he pressed the back of his wrists over them, attempting to hold it back without getting his bloodied hands on his face.

Ericha appreciated Abbi's insight when she gently said, "You take Stefan up to his room. I'll send for Theodor to help him, and see to this myself."

"Come along," Ericha said, urging Stefan to his feet. She guided him away just as an officer of the Guard arrived with the veterinarian. Aware of Stefan's rising emotion, she felt certain he would not want the Duke of Horstberg to be seen crying in the hall. She could well imagine how he felt. If she lost Job, it would be devastating. But the means by which Stefan had lost his dogs made it doubly horrible. Ericha said nothing as she helped him to his room. Theodor arrived a few minutes later, and she left him to help Stefan get cleaned up.

Stefan went later with two of his best officers to get Donner and investigate the scene. They found nothing but some horse tracks in the snow that led to a main road and disappeared.

Stefan dug the hole himself to bury Donner and Blitzen side by side at the foot of the castle hill. The carpet in the hall was replaced, and a few days beyond the incident, nothing was said about it. Stefan fought to remember his grandmother's admonition and said nothing to Johanna. But the subtle looks she gave him left no doubt in his mind that she had something to do with it. He knew her too well, and it was evident that she was somehow disappointed he'd not caused a confrontation over the incident.

The loss was deep for Stefan, not only literally but perhaps in its reminder of the precariousness of life and circumstances. He was grateful for the safety of himself and those he loved. And he prayed it would hold out.

Stefan felt light permeate his room and pulled the covers over his head with a groan.

"Sorry, sir," Theodor said loudly, "but it's one of those days when you have to get up."

"I have an idea, Theodor," Stefan leaned against the headboard and squinted to adjust his eyes. "Why don't I help you get dressed, and you can be the duke today?"

"I would if I could."

"Yes, I believe you would." Stefan climbed out of bed and began to shave. "And I think it's a good idea. You can attend to all my duties, and face the brunt of all the gossip."

"Ah, it sounds fun." Theodor chuckled. "Especially the gossip part."

"I shudder to think what they're saying about me these days," Stefan said too seriously. "And then there's Ericha. It makes me sick to think what she must have to face. You of all people ought to beat the hell out of me for that."

"Even I am not so blind that I can't see how happy you've made her."

Stefan stopped and looked at Theodor deeply. He had been tolerant as he'd promised, but under the present circumstances, Stefan was especially grateful for this indication of his acceptance.

"Thank you," Stefan said. "I only wish the rest of Horstberg could acknowledge the same thing."

"It's just talk, you know," Theodor commented. "It will die down once the novelty has worn off. Besides, from what I hear, the talk isn't all bad."

Stefan turned briefly toward Theodor again with a brow lifted in question.

"As far as I know, the general consensus at the pubs is more of amusement than distaste. At least among the men. People aren't blind. They've been watching Johanna flaunt her jewels for years now, and most of them aren't impressed. Your problem isn't the gossip." Theodor handed Stefan a towel as he finished. "Your problem is Johanna."

"All the more reason for you to be the duke today," Stefan said wryly as he threw the towel down and slipped into his shirt.

"Actually, she doesn't seem too upset these days. I doubt she can do much harm."

Stefan thought of his dogs and got a sick knot in his stomach, but he didn't mention it. "As far as the harm she can do, I don't trust her any more than I would a snake. And if she doesn't seem upset, that's all the more reason not to trust her. I know she's upset over it, but she acts too complacent. I don't think she'll rest until she considers herself avenged."

"Well," Theodor assured Stefan as he pulled on his boots,

"I wouldn't worry too much if I were you. She can't do much without getting herself into trouble."

"I hope you're right," Stefan muttered on his way out the door, but he didn't feel convinced.

When Stefan realized Christmas was fast approaching, he felt depressed. What a dreadful time to have a holiday, he thought. Johanna's knowledge of his affair hung in the air like a hovering storm, and the absence of the dogs was a frequent reminder of what his wife could be capable of. Ericha hardly dared go into public for fear of silent persecution. And the business of this blasted dukedom had never seemed so overwhelming and tedious.

Holidays were generally nice for Stefan, though he usually felt indifferent because there had always been an emptiness about them since Cameron and Erich had died. He wondered if that was why his parents never tried too hard to come home. He couldn't blame them. And now the holidays approaching only reminded Stefan of his circumstances. He couldn't really be home for Christmas when his heart was divided. He could only juggle his time between two places and hope that everyone understood.

The work was heavy, and Stefan absorbed himself in it, perhaps hoping to avoid the disconcerting feelings. He didn't realize how absorbed he'd become until a message came for him late one morning, brought by a messenger boy who came frequently to the castle from the village. One of the maids escorted him to the office, saying, "He insisted this was to be delivered personally, Your Grace."

"No problem. Send him in."

"Message for you, Your Grace," the boy said. "From Mr. Lokberg."

Stefan felt the realization of time leaving him behind as he opened it and read: *Will you be coming for Christmas?*

"What day is it?" he asked Rusty as Ericha's handwriting tugged at him. He hadn't seen her nearly as much as he should have lately.

"It's December twenty-third, of course," came the reply, and Stefan felt sick. The past week had slipped by in his work and he'd not seen Ericha once. Had he been so inconsiderate that she felt she had to ask if he would come for Christmas?

Quickly he wrote a reply on the same piece of paper: *Yes.* He handed it to the messenger along with a few coins for his efforts, and said, "If Mr. Lokberg's not at the pub, deliver that to his home."

"Yes, sir," he replied, his eyes wide from the amount of money the duke had just given him. "Thank you, sir," he added and left quickly.

"Let's get this work done," Stefan said to Rusty. "We're taking tomorrow off."

"Sounds like a good idea," Rusty replied. "I would say you've earned a cup of laughter."

"What?" Stefan chuckled.

"Oh, it's just something my father said occasionally. My mother would tell him when he worked too hard that sometimes he just had to stop and drink a cup of laughter."

Stefan smiled at the analogy, then forced his mind to the present. Some time later, Stefan glanced toward the window to see that snow was falling. He watched it several moments, but even as he concentrated on his work, he was aware of the mood that fell with it. A spirit of hope and peace fell over Stefan, and by evening he was anticipating Christmas rather than dreading it.

Stefan had dinner brought to the office, and he and Rusty worked until nearly midnight. Wanting to be done with all that was absolutely necessary, Stefan felt immense relief when he finally crawled into bed, hoping Ericha would forgive him for how little he'd given her lately.

The morning of Christmas Eve came with bright skies and a blanket of white that seemed to coat anything in Stefan's life that wasn't right. His spirit soared as he dressed, and going downstairs, he made up his mind that for today, he would drink his cup of laughter.

Ericha had gone to bed with every hope that Stefan would come before the night was over. When morning came and she had nothing more than one written word to indicate that he still existed, she nearly felt despair. She knew he had been busy, but he had never gone so long without seeing her. Even in her most recent visits to the castle she had not encountered him. She feared that perhaps the occurrences of late had made him keep his distance. Ericha didn't care what people thought. As difficult as the rest was, Stefan's absence had made her realize one thing. She could face any of it as long as he was with her. Without him, life was nothing.

There was a degree of hope in knowing that at least he was coming for Christmas. She didn't expect him until late this evening, most likely. But she looked forward to it and decided she would find something to keep her busy until he arrived. She feared he would be depressed, and she tried hard to lift her own spirits for his sake. But it was difficult to not think of the circumstances. How she longed to just be a part of his Christmas celebration with the family! But she had told him she would not spend any part of Christmas in the same room with Johanna. She'd hardly dared go anywhere near her since the truth had come out.

In search of something to do, Ericha went to the kitchen and found Erma hard at work.

"I thought you were going into town early," she said.

"Oh, I've got to do that too," Erma replied. "But if I don't get this started, we won't have Christmas dinner until Easter."

Ericha chuckled. "Here, let me do this. You go into town and then you can finish."

"Are you sure you wouldn't mind?" she asked.

"Of course not. Now hurry along."

Ericha closed the doors to all of the rooms along the hallway except the kitchen, and left Cameron with some toys so he could crawl up and down to his heart's content. Then she donned an apron and proceeded to finish Erma's pastry dough. She was nearly finished when the bell rang at the front door and she heard Job barking in response.

"Oh, bother!" she muttered, attempting to shake the flour off her hands. She was tempted to ignore it, knowing that no one important ever came to the front door. But the ringing persisted impatiently, and she wiped her hands on her apron and went to answer it. She passed by Cameron, who was banging a wooden spoon on the floor while he chewed on a toy horse at the same time.

Ericha took the apron in her hand to open the door so she wouldn't get flour on the doorknob, and then she stood with her hands in the air, gaping in astonishment.

"Merry Christmas." The Duke of Horstberg grinned.

"What are you doing here?" she asked. Looking past his shoulder, she could see a beautiful sleigh, drawn by four bays, waiting in front of the house.

"Do you want me to leave?" He smirked.

"No!" she insisted, moving aside for him to enter. When the door was closed, he took her into his arms, lifting her off the floor. He laughed as he turned with her, and his cloak flew out around them. "Oh, Stefan," she laughed, "I'm all covered with flour and—"

"I don't care." He set her down and kissed her hungrily. "Today I don't care about anything." He turned toward Cameron and laughed again. "Hello there, little man," he said, pulling the child into his arms. "Did you miss your papa as much as he's missed you?"

Ericha felt elated as she watched them. It was so good to have Stefan here—and happy!

"Get cleaned up, my dear," he said to Ericha while his eyes remained on Cameron, who was still chewing on the horse. "We're going out."

"*Out?*" she asked in astonishment.

"Yes," he laughed, "out."

"But we've never gone *out.*"

"We are today," he stated, looking directly at her. His eyes were shining as he smiled wryly. "Unless of course you don't want to."

"Oh, I do, but . . ."

"Well, don't just stand there. Wash those little hands of yours and change."

"But I . . . I've got to finish the—"

"Fine. Finish it and let's go."

Ericha could do nothing but bustle down the hall to complete her chore as quickly as possible. She cleaned up the mess and washed, then left a note for Erma.

In the hall she found Stefan on his hands and knees following Cameron, who giggled each time Stefan caught his foot and growled.

"You're making a fool of yourself, Your Grace," Ericha said.

Stefan grinned up at her. "I know. Isn't it fun?"

Ericha smiled and hurried up the stairs. While she was changing, she heard Stefan in the next room, which had now become the nursery.

"Where is Cameron's coat and hat?" he called.

"In the bureau next to the crib. Top drawer."

"Aha!" he called back. "These must be his. They wouldn't fit me."

Stefan came in carrying Cameron, all dressed to go out. Ericha smoothed her hair and grabbed her cloak.

"I'm ready," she announced. "Now where are we going?"

"Shopping, of course," he replied, already on his way down the stairs with Ericha close behind.

"You mean, in town?"

He chuckled. "That's the best place."

"But, Stefan . . ."

He stopped on the stairs and turned to face her. "Ericha," he said severely, "I woke up this morning and decided that for today I would set my fears aside. The whole blasted country knows that you and I share a great deal more than the same grandparents.

I don't see any point in trying to hide it." He paused and looked briefly alarmed. "If I'm being a fool, tell me. The last thing I want to do is put you into a situation that would make you uncomfortable." He shrugged his shoulders endearingly. "I suppose we could take Grandmama along, but she's already done *her* shopping."

Ericha smiled. She far preferred facing all of this head on. "It sounds wonderful to me. What are we waiting for?"

Stefan laughed and led the way outside. As soon as they emerged from the house, a servant dressed in royal livery stepped down from the driver's seat and helped Ericha into the sleigh. Stefan sat next to her with Cameron on his lap, and the child seemed in awe of his surroundings.

"I have to ask," Ericha said as the sleigh pushed forward through the snow and she felt a rush of excitement tingle through her, "what brought on this bout of frivolousness?"

"The spirit of Christmas, I suppose." He smiled, but his expression betrayed a brief shadow. "I'm certain there will be hell to pay eventually for us being found out. But the damage is done. We have to live for today. Besides," he smiled again, and Ericha was glad to feel the oppression slip away, "I believe in Christmas. And I believe in the basis of Christmas. If God knows the desires of my heart, He has to know how hard I have tried to be a good man and do what's right. I know that the way you and I live is wrong in a technical sense, but I have to believe that justice is not black and white. Today I celebrate the birth of Christ. If I must pay my dues, so be it. But today we will be happy."

Ericha blinked back her tears and took his hand. "I love you, Stefan, because you are such a good man."

"And I love you," he replied. "I must ask your forgiveness, my dear. I had not intended to neglect you this past week. The business has just been so—"

"I understand," she interrupted. "I'm only glad that you're here now. And," she added emphatically, "I don't want to hear about business today."

He smiled, and the sleigh drew to a halt at the edge of the market square. The bustle of last-minute shopping was halted by an obvious hush as Stefan stepped out of the sleigh with Cameron in his arms. He reached up his hand to help Ericha down, and she felt the speculative glances as she stood beside him.

"Thank you, Frank," Stefan called. "We'll see you later on." The sleigh pulled away, and Stefan sensed the tenseness in Ericha. "We can go home if you like," he offered quietly.

Ericha shook her head and smiled, and then she followed him into the crowds to look over the wares. The aroma of roasting chestnuts and steaming chocolate greeted them, as did the sound of distant carolers. There was a wide variety of greetings from the people they encountered, but Stefan met everyone with a smile and was continually wishing someone a merry Christmas. Ericha's tenseness slowly became replaced by the joy of being with him this way, and she was content to think how natural it felt.

At first Ericha wondered if she should remain aloof from Stefan. It seemed natural to play the part of his cousin. But as Stefan steered her through the crowd, he placed a familiar hand at her back, then took her hand into his. How good it felt to be publicly accepted and acknowledged by the man she loved! When he moved his hand to shift Cameron against his shoulder, Ericha placed her hand over his arm, and he smiled toward her.

Watching Stefan and the subtle awe that people held for him, Ericha doubted that anyone would dare say to him what had been said to her. She felt protected in his presence. His power was evident. But ironically, he preferred to go unnoticed, rather than be treated as a king.

"Good day, Mr. Weisner," Stefan said, approaching a cart where pewter wares were sold.

"Ah, Your Grace," he replied jovially, "I was about to have your order delivered. But I'm glad you're here. I wanted to know how you like it." Taking notice of the child, Mr. Weisner added, "What a handsome boy!"

"Yes," Stefan declared, "he is."

"I can see the family resemblance," the proprietor replied, and he winked at Stefan as if it were amusing. "And this must be your lovely cousin," he added, shifting his eyes to Ericha with approval. And though it was only the approval of one, it warmed Ericha through.

"Yes," Stefan said proudly, "you're smarter than you look."

Mr. Weisner laughed boisterously. "That's not hard."

"How is business?" Stefan asked.

"Very good," he replied. "I think most would agree. This appears to be a prosperous Christmas."

"Good," Stefan said, and Ericha could tell it really meant something to him.

"Well, let's see it," Stefan said and Mr. Weisner bent to pull out something covered in tissue paper. He carefully unwrapped it and held it up, his pride evident. Ericha caught her breath to see the pewter sculpture of a stallion rearing back. Mr. Weisner waited with anticipation until Stefan smiled with approval.

"It's perfect," he said quietly and turned to Ericha. "It's for Grandmama. Do you think she'll like it?"

"Oh, it's beautiful!" she replied. "Is there some significance?"

"You mean she's never told you about Blaze?" Stefan chuckled.

"Not that I recall."

"If she had told you, you would remember. Ask her sometime. You'll not regret it." He turned to Mr. Weisner. "You did well. How much do I owe you?"

"What we agreed on," he replied, rewrapping the little horse. "I'll let the little lady hold this," he said, handing it to Ericha. "It appears your hands are full."

Stefan slapped several bills into Mr. Weisner's hands and declared, "Have a merry Christmas."

"And you, Your Grace," he called as they moved away. Stefan smiled to himself as he imagined Mr. Weisner counting the money and realizing how much was there. Money was a trite way to let people know how he appreciated them, but it made him feel good nevertheless.

"We need to find something for Georg," Stefan said, wandering idly. They paused to listen to a group of children caroling, and when they realized the duke was watching, they did every song they knew. Each one seemed to ring the spirit of

Christmas a little stronger, and Stefan couldn't help putting his arm around Ericha and holding her close as they listened.

"Very good!" Stefan applauded when they were done, and he moved Cameron to his other arm. He reached into his pocket and pulled out a handful of coins, then laughed as he threw them in the air and the children clambered for them as he walked away.

"Merry Christmas, Your Grace," one of them called, and he turned and waved.

They came across an assortment of Christmas candy and other goodies.

"What's your favorite?" Stefan asked, but Ericha's attention was on the children gathered around a huge jar of striped peppermint sticks.

"I'll bet there's a hundred at least in there," one of them said.

"More than that," a younger one replied.

"I wish I had them all," still another said.

"That's 'cause you're stingy. I just want one. Maybe two."

Ericha was amused by the conversation, but it was apparent that none of them had money to buy anything. She was surprised when Stefan said to the vendor, "How much is that?"

"The peppermint sticks?" he asked.

"No, the whole jar."

The children gaped up at him while some sighed with disappointment as he apparently intended to take away their present pastime.

"I . . . I . . . don't really know. I . . . I . . . never intended to sell the . . . whole jar."

"Come now," Stefan smirked, "just name a price. It's exactly what I need. The lady loves peppermint sticks. I want the whole jar."

Ericha looked toward him in surprise. She detested peppermint.

Still the vendor stammered, so Stefan pulled out an alarming amount and slapped it into his hand. "Will that do?" he asked.

"Uh . . . let me get . . . your change and . . ."

"Don't bother," Stefan said. He handed Cameron to Ericha

and picked up the jar, mocking that it was extremely heavy, and Ericha giggled along with the children.

"All right," he said mostly to the children as he pulled off the lid and set it aside, "should we count them?"

"Right here in the middle of the square?" one of them said in astonishment.

"I suppose that would be a little ridiculous," Stefan stated. "Let's do it this way." He pulled one out and handed it to the littlest of the group. "One," he said, and they all gasped. He handed out another and added, "Two." The children's eyes widened as it became apparent they were all going to get one. "Three, four, five, six, seven, eight, nine, ten. Well," he said triumphantly when they all had been taken care of, "we know there's more than ten. Now if you," he pointed to one of them, "will take the lady's package for her, I'll give you another for your efforts. In the meantime, we've got some counting to do."

Ericha handed the wrapped pewter horse over to the child, then fell into step with them as they followed Stefan through the crowds.

"Eleven," he said, stopping an innocent child to give her a piece of candy. "Twelve, thirteen, fourteen," he continued, while young and old alike couldn't help but smile as the Duke of Horstberg delighted every child he could find. Ericha felt so warm and happy as she followed him about that she was certain this was the best Christmas of her life.

"Where was I?" Stefan said to the children following him that had more than doubled in number.

"Fifty-three," several replied in unison.

"Yes of course," he said. "Fifty-four. Fifty-five."

"Hey!" a boy tugged at Stefan's cloak, and he looked down. "You forgot to give one to your baby, sir."

Stefan was caught briefly off guard, wondering if the children of Horstberg accepted Cameron as *his* baby. But it made him smile. "So I did." He turned toward Ericha and held up a peppermint stick. Cameron latched onto it with his little hand, and it went straight into his mouth. Stefan laughed. "I think he likes peppermint," he proclaimed. His merry eyes met Ericha's, and impulsively he gave her a light kiss on the cheek before he turned and moved on.

"Where were we?" he asked.

"Fifty-five," a chorus replied.

They proceeded on and ran out of children before they ran out of candy. "Well," Stefan declared, "I think we'd best get to the shopping." He handed the jar to a big boy that had kept close to him through the entire escapade. "I'm making you captain of the candy jar. Guard it with your life. And you," he pointed to another, "keep a look out for anyone we might have missed. And you," he pointed to another, "remember what number we're on. That's the most important part."

Stefan took Cameron from Ericha and moved forward, requesting jovially, "How about some Christmas carols?"

"Come on," the captain of the candy jar said when the children hesitated, "the duke wants to hear some singin'." He started with a badly pitched "Silent Night," but the children joined in and sang one carol after another as they followed Stefan and Ericha around the square. They bought gifts for Georg, Karl, and Theodor, and something for Stefan's parents to be put away until they returned. Gifts were also found for Hannah and her husband and children. Each package purchased was turned over to a child for safe keeping, until Stefan turned to Ericha and said, "Did we miss anyone?"

"Uncle Nik," she stated.

He looked surprised but said, "Of course. We must buy something for Uncle Nik."

They looked around for quite some time while Cameron fell asleep on Stefan's shoulder.

"I don't know what to get him," Stefan declared. "He's such an ornery old thing, what he needs is a . . ." His eyes turned to the children hovering around, and he got an idea.

"Come along," he said and led the way to the edge of the square where Frank was waiting with the sleigh. "Sorry we were so long, Frank. We had candy to count." Frank lifted his brows, seeming amused by the followers. Stefan took the packages one at a time and set them into the sleigh, and then he helped Ericha in and handed Cameron carefully to her.

Taking the candy jar, he said, "Now where were we?"

"Seventy-eight," the assigned child declared proudly.

"Now to pay off my assistants," he stated, and began handing out a second piece of candy to all those who had stuck with him faithfully. "Eighty-seven," he declared when everyone had one. He peered into the bottom of the jar. "Four left," he said thoughtfully, then he turned and gave one to Frank. "Eighty-eight," he said, and Frank smiled.

"Another for your baby when he wakes up," a child offered.

"Good idea," Stefan said. "When you grow up, I'm going to give you a job."

The children laughed as Stefan handed a peppermint stick to Ericha. "Eighty-nine," he stated.

"One for your lady," another declared, and Stefan smiled.

"Yes," he said, handing her another. "One for my lady. That's ninety. There's one left."

"That one is for you, Your Grace," a child announced.

"I think I could use a peppermint stick," he conceded, pulling it out. He held it up high and called in a voice of royal proclamation, "Ninety-one!"

"Imagine that," he added, "ninety-one peppermint sticks. I think we'd best go tell the candy man. Don't you think he'll want to know?"

They all agreed, and Stefan turned to Frank. "Keep an eye on the lady for me. I'll be right back."

Ericha watched him walk away while the children started singing again, and she silently thanked the power of heaven and earth for sending her such a man.

He returned a short while later with a large package. Ericha looked at him in question as he seated himself next to her and the sleigh started for home.

"It's for Uncle Nik," he stated.

"Well, what is it?" she demanded when he made no effort to show her.

Stefan laughed and slowly pulled the wrapping away, purposely tormenting her curiosity. "I thought it would go nicely on his bedside table," Stefan stated quite seriously. But Ericha laughed when she saw the same candy jar, filled now with a variety of the other treats the vendor had had for sale. "Did I do all right?" Stefan asked.

"It's perfect." She smiled. "He'll love it."

"He'll never admit it."

"No, but he'll love it just the same."

"I love you," Stefan said, reaching his hand out for her.

"And I love you," she replied. "Thank you for a wonderful day."

"It was nice, wasn't it," he stated, leaning back and putting his hands behind his head. "We should do it every Christmas."

"All right." She smiled. "We will."

The sleigh pulled up in front of the house, and Stefan stepped down. Cameron started to cry when Stefan took him and he woke up.

"He's had a hard day," Stefan said, brushing his lips over the baby's brow as Ericha followed him to the door. She expected him to come in, but he stopped in the hall and handed Cameron back to her. "I must get back," he said, "but I'll be here tomorrow, say early afternoon."

"All right," she replied, trying not to sound disappointed. "We'll save dinner."

"Oh, you don't need to—"

"Karl will be with Luise," she interrupted. "I'll wait to eat with you."

He nodded warmly, then bent to kiss her.

"Merry Christmas," he whispered. He tousled Cameron's red curls, then left. Ericha took Cameron upstairs to change him, grateful for this day but wishing she could have Stefan all the time.

"To the castle?" Frank asked as Stefan approached the sleigh.

"No," Stefan said, sitting beside him on the box-seat, "back into town."

Frank looked dubious as he urged the horses forward.

"What did you get your wife for Christmas?" Stefan asked.

"Just a few simple things," he replied. "She likes the simple things."

"What about the children?" he asked. "Did you get a lot of toys?"

"A few." Frank chuckled.

"Well, maybe you should get a few more. And something really nice for your wife."

"But, sir, I—"

"You can buy them with the bonus, of course," Stefan interrupted with no expression. To Frank's questioning gaze he added, "The one you're going to get for going Christmas shopping with the duke."

Frank only smiled, and Stefan did the same. He felt warm to the core.

While Karl was helping Ericha trim the Christmas tree, a knock came at the door and Karl went to answer it. He returned to the parlor holding a large box wrapped in brightly colored paper.

"It's for you," Karl said, and Ericha gasped as she took it from him and just held it. "Come on and open it. I hate anticipation."

Ericha sat down and pulled off the lid. On top of the folded tissue was an elegant card, written in Stefan's hand. *I'll see you tomorrow. Wear this.*

Ericha handed the card to Karl so that he could read it, and then she folded back the tissue and caught her breath. "Oh, look Karl! It's beautiful."

"He does have good taste," Karl declared as she pulled out the green taffeta gown. "But then," he smirked while she held the dress against her, "he hangs around with me."

Ericha laughed. "If you need something to judge his taste by," she said wryly, "just take a look at his mistress."

Christmas Eve was the one night of the year that Theodor slept away from his apartment. Ericha woke him and Karl as soon as Cameron was up and fed, and together they went to the parlor to indulge in the celebrations of Christmas.

"First of all," Karl declared, digging under the Christmas tree to bring out package after package, "let's see what old Uncle Karl got for you, Cameron."

"Good heavens," Ericha exclaimed, "you'll spoil him before he's even learned to walk."

"That's the idea," Theodor declared. "Karl always had more toys than he knew what to do with."

"Does that mean Cameron will grow up like me?" Karl asked proudly.

"I hope not," Theodor said with a smirk.

By the time the gifts were all open, Cameron had a wooden rocking horse that Theodor declared was fit for a prince, and a long toy train, both made by Uncle Karl. Theodor had done the practical thing and given the boy clothes. But Cameron was most interested in the big red bow that had come around the horse's neck.

By mid-afternoon, Theodor had gone to visit some friends, Karl had gone to Luise's home, Erma had left to spend the remainder of Christmas with her sisters, and Cameron was down for his nap. Ericha straightened the house more than once, checked the table to see that it was arranged properly, checked her appearance in the mirror a dozen times, then wandered the house aimlessly, wondering when the real joy of her Christmas celebration would arrive.

As it grew dusky, a light, cold snow began to fall, and Ericha felt so alone. She was grateful when Cameron woke up, and she enjoyed watching him play with his new toys. But she wished that

Stefan was here to see it as well. He missed out on so much that Cameron did.

Ericha's heart beat quickly when she heard a carriage pull up outside. She didn't dare peek out the window, fearing it wouldn't be him. Surely he would come on a horse and use the side door, as always. Job barked at the door until she ordered him to go lie down. Her palms were sweating when the bell rang, and she went to answer it. How relieved she was to see him there on the porch, so overloaded with packages she could hardly see his face.

"Do you still want me?" he asked. Ericha laughed and opened the door wide for him to enter. The carriage rolled away, and Ericha closed the door. Stefan moved into the parlor and set the packages in front of the sofa, and then he turned and Ericha fled into his arms.

"I'm sorry I'm so late, my love," he whispered.

She wondered by his tone of voice if something was wrong, and she pulled back with question in her eyes.

"Johanna," he said bitterly. "She had the decency to sleep late, and we all had a wonderful morning. By the way, everyone positively loved the gifts. Uncle Nik especially." He smirked. "Grandmama and Georg said they'll come by tomorrow. Hannah and her family spent the day and they couldn't very well leave. They have something for you and Cameron. Anyway, I . . ." Stefan's eye caught the green taffeta, and he drew away to absorb her.

"Turn around," he said, and she did. "I knew you would look stunning in it." He smiled. "But I could never have imagined anything so . . . You are so beautiful."

Ericha smiled timidly. "As you were saying?"

"Yes, well, I should get it over with." He took off his cloak, and Ericha hung it for him. "Johanna came down to dinner full of spite and bitterness. She purposely provoked me into an argument. Grandmama tried hard not to be upset, but I knew she was. For a while I wondered if I would ever get away, and then I realized that's what she wanted. She was trying to keep me from coming here. So I . . ."

"You what?" she questioned when he trailed off with a chuckle.

"I sent her home for Christmas. I ordered the maids to pack her things, and I told her that her father would probably be delighted to see her. I personally put her into a carriage and sent it rolling before she could argue. I hope she has a wonderful time."

"Aren't you clever."

"With any luck, she'll decide to stay until next year. No, make it the year after that."

Ericha laughed and kissed him quickly. But Stefan drew her close to him, and his kiss deepened with a betrayal of longing.

"Are you hungry?" she asked as he drew back.

"Starved," he said provocatively.

"Dinner is waiting," she smiled.

"Oh . . . you mean *hungry*." He smirked.

They heard something tear and turned to see Cameron busily attempting to open the gifts on the floor.

"It looks like he's figured out how to do that," Stefan said, sitting on the floor beside his son.

"He had a lot of practice this morning."

"Uncle Karl's been making toys, I see," Stefan said to Cameron. "Tell me, do you like the horse or the train best?"

"He likes the bows," Ericha answered for him, and Stefan grinned.

"As long as you're at it," Stefan went on, helping Cameron with the package he was tearing at, "you might as well get it open. Your papa nearly bought out the toy store last night."

The paper was torn away to reveal a stuffed bear wearing a red suit, and Ericha laughed to see it.

"That bear is as big as he is."

"He'll have someone to play with," Stefan declared.

Cameron crawled over the bear to get to the other packages, and then he grinned up at his father, showing his two and only teeth as he squealed with delight to have found another bow.

"He is so cute!" Stefan laughed.

"He looks like you."

"Nonsense. I have more teeth than that." Stefan's eyes turned serious a moment. "Actually, he looks more and more like your father."

"Really?"

"I can see Erich in him, and it makes me proud."

Ericha squeezed his hand, and Stefan put his arm around her, holding her close to him while he helped Cameron open a toy boat, a ball, and a dozen other things, many of which he could hardly enjoy at this age. But Stefan didn't recall ever feeling such joy as to watch his own son delighted with all the new things surrounding him.

"The rest are for you," Stefan said to Ericha.

"Let's eat first," she said, and he picked up Cameron and led the way to the dining room. Ericha lit candles on the table, and Stefan held Cameron on his lap while they ate, sharing little morsels with the baby of anything that didn't have to be chewed.

When the meal was done, they returned to the parlor, and Stefan declared, "I would swear you have the prettiest Christmas tree in Horstberg."

"You're flattering me," Ericha replied.

"I'm quite serious. It's incredible."

"I just did what my mother always did. We could never afford to buy any fancy ornaments, so she made the tatted snowflakes."

"They're more beautiful than any fancy ornaments I've ever seen," Stefan said, admiring the tree again. He sat on the floor near where Cameron was playing. "Why don't you open your gifts, my dear?"

"Why do you always spend so much on me?" she said, dubiously surveying the pile of packages remaining.

"I don't spend nearly what you're worth."

"Nonsense," she replied timidly.

"This one first." He handed her a large box that contained a traveling suit, dark blue with pinstripes. The next package had a hat that matched, and then she opened gloves and a handbag. Ericha was about to declare that she had everything she needed to leave town, when Stefan brought from his pocket a train ticket, dated for the third week in February.

"It's a little ways off, I know. But I figured it was about time we got away," he said, and Ericha overwhelmed him with an exuberant hug. "I take it you like that idea." He laughed.

"Oh, it will be wonderful! Did you hear that, Cameron? We're going on holiday." Ericha moved to the tree and reached beneath it to bring out four packages. "Now it's your turn," she said, sitting beside him again on the floor.

"But you aren't finished," he said.

"Stefan, I . . ."

He pulled a narrow unwrapped box from the same pocket and held it up for her.

"You must forgive me," he said. "I don't know if it's proper. I don't even know if you'll like this sort of thing. But when I saw it, all I could think was how it would look on you, and how you deserved it. I'm not giving it to you for any other reason than that. Simply because you deserve it." He opened the box in front of her, and Ericha could hardly breathe. "The diamonds are perfect," he said. "Like you. The emeralds remind me of your eyes. The jewels go evenly all the way around the throat—like an eternal circle."

Ericha looked up at him with tears brimming in her eyes. She couldn't bring herself to remove the necklace from the velvet-lined box, so Stefan took it out and fastened it around her throat. He kissed her, then drew back to take in her appearance and sighed. "You should be the Duchess of Horstberg, Ericha."

"From the Duke of Horstberg," she said, "that is the highest of compliments." She bent forward to kiss him. "Thank you. It's beautiful. Everything is beautiful. You are so very good to me." He smiled timidly and kissed her again.

"Speaking of the Duke of Horstberg," she added, "it's difficult to know what to get for such a man. You realize that, don't you?"

"I don't need anything more than what I've got right here." He glanced toward his son, who was playing with his mother's new gloves.

"This one first," Ericha said, handing him a package. "Read the card."

Stefan opened it and read aloud, "To the artist." He smiled. "This must be from someone who knows me well."

"It's something you can always use," she declared as he opened it. "Very practical."

"So it is," he laughed to find the box filled with brushes and oils. "Thank you." He bent forward to kiss her, and Ericha felt anticipation in it.

"Now this," she said, handing him another.

Stefan opened the card on the tiny box and read, "To the musician." Again he chuckled, but his eyes turned serious when he opened it. He looked up at Ericha, attempting to grasp her perception, and then he looked again at the little gold lapel pin, shaped like a treble clef.

"Don't you like it?" she asked.

"Like it?" He laughed. "I love it!" He took it out and handed it to her, indicating she pin it on his waistcoat. "I'd forego all the rest of those wretched medals for this any day."

"I suspected you might." She smiled as she put it in place, then moved back to look at it. "Now this." She handed him another package, and he opened the little card.

"I wonder who this one's for," he said wryly, then glanced at the card, "Ah, I know him. This one is for the Duke of Horstberg. Would you like me to deliver it to him? I don't believe he's here tonight."

"You open it and you can give it to him later," Ericha insisted.

Stefan opened the gift and looked briefly puzzled by the odd array of little toys. "I think these must be for you," he said to Cameron, who paid no attention.

"Oh, no," Ericha said, "I got the card right. They are for the Duke of Horstberg."

"Toys?"

"Precisely." Ericha looked him straight in the eye, and her voice warmed with empathy, "They are for the little boy who lost his childhood one day before he turned eight."

Stefan bowed his head and was silent for several moments. He choked back his emotion and set the box aside as he pulled Ericha into his arms and held her tightly, wanting to convey just how precious she was to him.

"You're not finished yet, Stefan," she said, and he pulled back, looking surprised. She laid another package into his lap, and he hesitantly opened the card. *To Stefan,* it said. He opened it to find a little carved box and smiled. "I bet I know who you talked into making this."

She smiled knowingly. "Read the top."

Stefan looked closely to see the little heart carved in the center, and the words around it that read: *A fire burns in my heart.*

"From the song," he said aloud.

"Now be careful when you open it," Ericha said.

Stefan lifted the lid carefully and peeked inside. The lining was red velvet beneath tatted lace, but the box was empty.

"There's nothing here," he said.

"Of course there is," she replied. "Close it and try again."

Ericha put her hands over his and closed the box. She held it near his face and whispered, "Now close your eyes." Together they opened the box, and Ericha leaned close to his ear. "Do you feel the warmth?" she whispered. "Can you hear it filling the air around you? Can you feel it beating?"

Stefan opened his eyes to see her face close to his. "You see," she whispered, and her breath warmed his skin, "the box holds exactly what it says on the top: the fire in my heart."

"I feel it," he whispered, setting the box aside. He pulled her against him and brushed his fingers over her throat. "I feel the warmth." His hand pressed meekly over her heart. "And I can feel it beating." He kissed her hard and drew her into his arms, laying with her on the floor, kissing her over and over. "Oh, I've missed you so dreadfully," he murmured, pressing his lips over her throat.

Cameron started fussing, but Stefan only looked over at him and laughed. "I suppose he gets you first."

"It's nice to be so popular with the men in my life," Ericha said.

Stefan helped unfasten the hooks over her shoulder, and she eased her arm out of the gown so that she could nurse Cameron. Stefan extinguished the lights in the parlor and added some wood to the fire, and then he lay near Ericha while Cameron drifted to sleep. The candles on the Christmas tree scattered shadows about the room, illuminating the piles of discarded gift paper, the bows Cameron had feasted on throughout the day, and the array of gifts that didn't begin to tell of the love present in the room.

Chapter Eighteen
THE VILLAIN AND THE VICTIMS

Stefan tucked Cameron into bed and set the new bear in the corner of the crib. He kissed the child's head and watched him for several moments before he slipped into Ericha's room to find her taking down her hair.

"I've missed you," she said to Stefan as she came to her feet and the green taffeta rustled to the floor. Stefan put his mouth over hers as his arm came around her waist, and then he nuzzled his face into her hair. How he loved her hair! He loved to thread his hands through it and bury his face in it. It was incredible!

Ericha marveled at the love she felt for Stefan and briefly wondered if Johanna had ever known the same man that she knew. In all honesty, Ericha believed that Johanna had no idea what kind of man she was married to. If she had known, she never would have taken him so much for granted.

"I am the luckiest woman alive," Ericha murmured.

"Why is that?" he asked absently while his lips teased her eyelids.

"Because I know a man," she whispered, "who holds a country in awe of him." Stefan pulled back, surprised by her words. "He's not even aware of the aura of power that surrounds him. He is a king in his own right, with a country in the palms of his hands." Ericha's voice cracked and mist filled her eyes. "Yet he comes to me and gives everything he has to give." She kissed him and pressed the side of her face to his. "You see. I am the luckiest woman alive."

Stefan felt a rush of emotion that he momentarily tried to hold back. But it got the better of him. He cried out Ericha's name, then kissed her as if he never had before. He loved her more than words could ever describe. How could he possibly tell her that in truth she held the power over him? It was Ericha who held a country in the palms of her hands.

A few weeks into January, Ericha came awake abruptly in the middle of the night to Job's barking. She ordered him to be quiet, fearing he would wake the baby. Then she realized someone was pounding on the front door. Hurriedly, she put on a wrapper and went to answer it, but Karl got there first. He took a message from someone and closed the door to lean upon it and read.

"What is it?" she asked, noting his furrowed brow.

"I'm not certain," he replied, absently handing it to her.

Ericha opened it as Karl rushed away to finish getting dressed. The paper simply read: *I need you. Luise.*

Ericha found it difficult to go back to sleep, and she was relieved to hear Karl returning just before dawn. Quickly she checked on Cameron, then went down to meet him in the hall.

"Is anything wrong?" she asked with concern.

"Luise's father just died," he stated, lumbering toward the parlor. Ericha followed.

"I'm so sorry," was all she could think to say.

Karl plopped onto the sofa and set his booted legs on the table.

"It's a difficult thing," Karl said, "but actually Luise is quite relieved. Not that his absence isn't hurting her already, but he has been in very poor health for years. His body has been doing him little good. I suppose it was time he laid it aside."

"I understand," Ericha said quietly.

Karl looked directly at her. "We'll be getting married soon. She's no longer tied at home, so there's nothing to hold us back.

We've talked it over, and as soon as the funeral is taken care of, we'd like to get married quietly—probably here at the house."

"Are you happy about that?" she asked.

"Yes," he said emphatically, "I most certainly am. It's high time she moved in with me."

"Then I'm happy for you." Ericha smiled.

"Of course, you are one of the lucky few who will be invited."

"I'm honored."

"In the meantime," Karl rose and stretched, "I'm going to get some sleep."

He left the room, and Ericha went upstairs, dreading Karl's wedding. She was already certain who else would be included in the lucky few, and it was likely to be a difficult day for them both.

Ericha went with Karl to the funeral, but as he hovered near Luise offering comfort, Ericha felt alone. Theodor came with a lady friend. Abbi and Georg came, but they remained close together in quiet reverence. Stefan arrived late, but his presence intensified her loneliness, as it seemed proper for them to remain aloof for such an occasion.

A few days later, Abbi invited Ericha to a social at the castle. She'd been invited to most of them since she'd been taken into the family, and she had chosen to attend now and then. But for the most part, she simply didn't enjoy them, in spite of the opportunity to be with Stefan. Since Johanna had discovered the truth, however, Ericha had declined altogether. But Abbi assured her that the people attending this gathering had nothing to do with Johanna, and since the duchess was absent, it would be ideal.

Ericha enjoyed the event, especially the opportunity to dance with Stefan. She wore the taffeta gown and necklace he'd given her for Christmas. She felt beautiful and couldn't deny the discreet admiration in Stefan's eyes. At moments she could almost pretend she was his wife, but there was always an invisible wall that stood between them with boundaries that could not be crossed by a woman who did not bear his name. She said nothing about her feelings to Stefan, but she sensed that he was well aware of them. There was no denying the little cloud of sadness that always hovered over their relationship in spite of all they had been blessed to share.

When Stefan came the next evening, nothing was mentioned about the upcoming wedding. He avoided speaking of anything that was occurring at home, but Ericha felt the tension in him. He stood over the crib watching Cameron sleep for a very long time, and then he sat on the edge of the bed, saying little.

"What is it?" Ericha asked gently. He made no response, but she kneaded her fingers at the base of his neck, and he gave a pleasurable moan. "Tell me," she whispered behind his ear.

"There is nothing to tell," he said, lying back on the bed, "that hasn't already been said before."

"Is Johanna still away?"

"Yes, thank heaven. But she won't stay too much longer. Perhaps that's part of the problem."

Ericha leaned over him to touch his face, and he became lost in her eyes. "Distract me," he whispered. Ericha brought her lips close to his with a timid kiss, and he closed his eyes. A second kiss ignited his emotion into passion. It ended as quickly as it had begun, and they lay close together while Stefan kissed her throat and brushed wisps of hair away from her face.

"Now," he said gently, "there is absolutely nothing in the world wrong."

Ericha kissed his brow and silently agreed. But something deep inside couldn't deny a formless dread.

Ericha had felt moments of reality many times since she had met Stefan. But the distance had never seemed so great as when they mutually observed Karl and Luise exchange marriage vows. The lump in Ericha's throat was so tight that she hardly dared look at Stefan. But after he handed Karl the ring, she looked up to meet his eyes and couldn't bring herself to look away. The pain was etched so plainly in his expression that she was glad no one else paid any attention. The lump in her throat deepened, and she felt moisture gathering in her eyes. She tried to will it back, but the tears fell. She was at least grateful that women were expected to cry at weddings.

It was a relief when Karl and Luise left for a brief honeymoon, but an emptiness enveloped Ericha as the reality deepened. In her heart she began to feel bitter for these circumstances, but there was no one to blame the bitterness on.

Late afternoon, a message arrived bearing the ducal seal, and Ericha went to her room to read it. All the bitterness fled as the words leapt from the page.

Get that traveling dress ready, little cousin. I'm counting down the days. I love you with all my heart.

Ericha knew everything would be all right.

Ericha left Cameron with Ruthild and went to the duke's office.

"Come in," Stefan called when she knocked, and he looked pleasantly surprised as he rose to greet her. In Johanna's absence, Ericha had resumed her frequent visits to the castle. He enjoyed having her around as much as he dreaded Johanna's inevitable return.

"Good afternoon, dear cousin," she said, and Rusty gave a shy smile before he turned his attention back to his work.

"Good afternoon," Stefan replied. "What can I do for you?"

"I have a request to make on behalf of Uncle Nik."

Rusty shot his head up in surprise as Stefan motioned for Ericha to be seated.

"Would it be possible," she began right away, "to move him permanently to a room on the main floor?"

"For what purpose?" Stefan asked.

"I'm just asking if it's possible," she stated.

"I suppose that would be fine," Stefan conceded.

"Good," she said and rose quickly. "I'll have the servants take care of it if you don't mind. And in the meantime, could I borrow two strong men—from the Guard perhaps—and your valet as well?"

"What are you up to?" he asked with a baffled chuckle.

"You'll see," she said.

He shook his head. "Fine. Just take over the duchy. I don't care."

"No, thank you." She smiled and left the office.

Stefan looked toward Rusty who shrugged his shoulders innocently, and they continued their work.

Ericha followed a newly acquired habit that accompanied her visits to Castle Horstberg. Without knocking, she paraded into Nik's room where she opened all the drapes, argued with him for a few minutes, then sat where she usually read aloud whatever he requested.

"We're not reading today," she announced.

"Why not?" he asked, his lips pursed tighter than usual.

"We're going out."

"Out?" He laughed.

"Well at least I got a laugh out of you. You must be the most miserable man I've ever known in my life. But we're going to change that. You just watch and see."

Nik grunted dubiously, and Ericha went on.

"Do you trust me?" she asked.

"Why should I?"

"I have an honest face," she stated.

"Huh!" he said with a sneer. "I've heard about you." Ericha's expression faltered slightly, and he added in a biting tone, "Servants talk, you know. Shouldn't I believe them when they tell me that baby of yours belongs to His Majesty himself?"

Ericha looked toward the floor and said nothing.

"I've hurt your feelings." His voice held no compassion.

Ericha lifted her chin and drew back her shoulders. "I'm certain it would give you great pleasure to hurt my feelings, but

I'll tell you something, Uncle. I'm not letting anything deter me today."

"It's true then," he said.

"And if it is?" she asked.

"I'd say you're a pretty spunky little thing to think you can take on Horstberg and win. I tried that once and lost."

Ericha became thoughtfully silent, but her mood seemed to affect Nik. He didn't argue nearly as much as she thought he would when she insisted that Theodor help him shave and dress, and then he was carried downstairs to the waiting bath chair that Karl had finished before the wedding. Theodor had brought it to the castle early that morning.

"You must be insane, girl," he ranted. "I'm not getting in that thing!"

"You most certainly are, and there is nothing you can do about it."

The protests gradually lessened as Ericha pushed him through the halls of the castle, rambling about anything she could think to say to keep him from talking. He ranted about being tired and wanting to go back to bed when Ericha rotated and backed her way out a door, pulling him with her. As Nik realized he was outside, he took a sharp breath. Ericha turned him around to see a perfect view of the castle gardens. Even covered in snow, the view was beautiful.

"It's cold out here," he said.

"Don't worry," she replied, "we're not going much farther than this. But I figured it was about time you had some fresh air. It will put some color back into that nasty old face of yours."

Nik grunted but said nothing as she came beside him and pointed toward the scene. "It's beautiful in the summer. When the roses are in bloom, I'll bring you out here and we'll explore every path." He looked up at her dubiously, but she ignored him and continued. "The white roses are my favorite," she mused. "They remind me of new, pure life—and the chance to start again."

Nik looked abruptly into her eyes, but he said nothing before he turned back to look at the view.

"So," she repeated, "how are you doing?"

Carefully he took her hand from where it rested on the arm of the chair, and Ericha looked up to see the legendary villain of Horstberg crying silent tears.

"Nik," she said, "I have something I want to tell you. I like you and I want to confide in you, but if we're going to be friends, I want you to confide in me too."

He nodded, seeming at ease as Ericha apparently ignored his emotion. The situation was as Ericha had hoped. She believed from what little she'd gotten to know about him that the desire to be free of his pain was strong and close to the surface, and Ericha had hoped to bring it out.

"You were right. The baby is Stefan's. But I love Stefan, Nik. I could never put into words what he means to me." She paused and met his eyes straightly. "Nik, Stefan told me that you did some awful things to the family." Nik's eyes widened. "Is it true?"

Nik bowed his head forward but said nothing.

"He told me that you hurt his mother and—"

"I loved Maggie," he said, leaving his head bowed. "But I was a fool. I wanted power more. All my feelings for her became lost in my vision for power and glory, and—" He paused a long moment and looked up to meet Ericha's eyes. "Yes," he stated, "it's true."

Ericha reached up to touch Nik's face, and his eyes softened with her acceptance.

"Do you regret it?" she asked carefully.

"Ericha," he said, "every day for over twenty years I have stared at the ceiling and longed with everything I had to be able to live my life over."

"And how would you change it?" she asked.

Nik Koenig smiled and turned his pale face toward the sky. He took a deep breath and began, "I wouldn't want to change Maggie's marriage, because I know that Han is a better man than me. And I know how much she loves him. But there was a cute little maid who worked at the castle. And if I could do it over,

I would have asked her to marry me and been grateful for what Cameron du Woernig was willing to give me, and I would have minded my own business."

Nik's tears came again, and he squeezed his eyes shut as he cried aloud, "I was such a fool! One day I thought I had it all. I thought I had succeeded with my quest. I was going to be the Duke of Horstberg."

His voice softened, and he leaned his head forward. "The next day everyone that meant anything to me was dead—my friends, my mother, that pretty little maid. And it was my fault. Their faces have haunted me for twenty years."

"They don't have to anymore," Ericha said gently.

He narrowed his eyes in question, and she went on. "All you have to do is forgive yourself and start over. You could have many good years ahead if you'd only have a desire to live them."

"It was not myself that I wronged."

"Who would you like to forgive you?" she asked.

Nik sighed and stated, "Cameron du Woernig foremost—and he is gone."

"His wife is not," she said, and his expression betrayed that he was perceiving her intent.

"Erich du Woernig," he stated.

"I will speak on my father's behalf."

Nik silently absorbed her meaning a long moment then said, "I believe your grandmother would forgive me. She's a good woman. If not for her, I'd have gone insane. And I believe you would forgive me, too. You're a good woman like her. But," he paused and looked at her directly, "could Horstberg forgive me for trying to destroy it?"

"You could start by asking the duke. I can testify that he's really a very nice man."

Nik looked thoughtful, and Ericha added, "Either way, I was thinking it would be nice if you would come and have dinner with the family. I've already arranged it, but only if you want to, of course."

Nik smiled unwillingly and said, "It would be nice to look the

Duke of Horstberg in the eye if I was going to start eating at the same table. Do you think he's terribly busy right now?"

Ericha stood and wheeled Nik into the house. "He's never too busy to see me."

Nik laughed, and the sound of it touched Ericha as she wheeled him toward the duke's office.

"You know," he said as they went along, "for the first time since I woke up in that bed with no feeling below my chest, I'm actually glad to be alive."

"It's about time," Ericha said, then knocked at the office door. She received the usual answer then peered inside. "Could I bother you for a moment . . . alone?"

Stefan nodded toward Rusty, who immediately rose to leave. Ericha opened the door wide and wheeled Nik into the office. Stefan rose and his expression was unusually readable as he practically gaped at what he saw.

"So, this is what you were up to," he said to Ericha.

"Uncle Nik has something he would like to ask you."

"Fine," Stefan said, seating himself again.

"Do you want me to go?" Ericha asked Nik.

"No, no. Please stay," he said, and she sat in a chair nearby.

"Your Grace," Nik said with the utmost respect in his tone, "because you are currently the ruler of this fair country, I would like to ask you something on its behalf. And at the same time, perhaps you would do well to represent your family—at least those who have passed on."

Stefan nodded regally. Nik glanced warily to Ericha, who gave him assurance by her expression.

"I would like you to know, Your Grace, that I have come to sorely regret my mistakes, and I . . . would like to ask your forgiveness."

Stefan was silently aghast. Ericha sensed Nik's nervousness, but she felt certain Stefan would not disappoint her. Carefully he rose and came around the desk, where he leaned against it and folded his arms.

"Why?" he asked, looking Nik in the eye.

"Not because I deserve it, but because it would give me a chance to perhaps make something useful of what little is left of my life."

Stefan remained thoughtfully silent but left his imposing eyes resting upon Nik. He finally said, "I don't think it's within my power to forgive you. The things you have done go far beyond my realm of judgment."

Ericha felt a nervous twitch at the back of her neck. Nik's hopeful expression faltered, and Stefan went to the window.

"No," he said tonelessly, "I can't forgive you."

"Stefan!" Ericha came to her feet. "What are you saying?"

"I'm saying that I can't do it," he stated firmly.

"It's all right, Ericha," Nik muttered, "I understand. You mustn't—"

"I *don't* understand!" Ericha persisted, meeting Stefan face to face. "I would have thought that you, of all people, would have the heart to—"

"Ericha," Nik interrupted quietly, "let's go. It's not worth the trouble."

"It *is* worth the trouble!" she insisted, and she took a step toward Stefan and asked, "Why?"

Stefan gave a quick glance toward Nik, whose head was bowed with his hands folded in his lap. His eyes came back to Ericha's, and he said with a voice that pierced Ericha through, "He killed your father, Ericha."

"I know he made attempts against his life. We talked about that and—"

"He killed Erich," Stefan interrupted, "and Cameron died as a result."

Ericha gaped at him as she tried to make sense of this. "But . . . it was an accident. In the letter, my mother told me it was—"

"Tell her, Nik," Stefan shouted, and the old man's head shot up. "If you want to make amends, you're going to have to start by admitting to the truth, which is something you've been hiding from since it happened. Don't expect her to become your advocate when she has no idea what *really* happened. Tell her!"

Ericha gazed at Stefan in amazement. She had never seen him so angry. Nik glanced toward Ericha, then his eyes turned guiltily away. Stefan grabbed Ericha's wrist to get her attention. "He killed your father, Ericha. He might as well have held a gun to his head and pulled the trigger. It was cold-blooded murder. If there was any way on earth to have proven it, he would have been dragged before a firing squad and executed twenty years ago. If I could prove it now, I'd do it in a minute."

"I went on trial for that a long time ago," Nik stated with a caustic edge. "If I had been guilty, they would have shot me."

"It was dropped for lack of evidence," Stefan retorted. "But that didn't make you any less guilty. Do you think I don't know the stories you told in that courtroom, how you put the blame on those who were already dead?"

"You were a child," Nik snarled. "You have no idea what you're talking about. I *wanted* to be found guilty. Execution would have suited me far better than the hell I've lived in all these years."

"Well, at least we agree on that," Stefan snapped.

"If I were dead," Nik said, and Stefan looked toward him, "would you forgive me?"

The question hung uncomfortably for a long moment before Stefan left the room, leaving Ericha to try and repair the damage.

"I'm sorry," she muttered helplessly. "I never dreamed that he would—"

"Believe it or not," Nik said, "I don't blame him for feeling the way he does."

Ericha wheeled Nik back to his new room on the main floor. The silence between them grew uncomfortable as Ericha tried to comprehend what Stefan had said. Her father, *murdered?* Nik responsible? Aware of the growing tension, she quickly came to the conclusion that whatever had happened, it didn't change Nik's desire to put it behind him.

As they entered the bedroom, she rambled about its advantages, as opposed to the old one. She got him settled in with a little help from Theodor. And when he was comfortable in the bed, Ericha noticed his eyes turning wistful. Then he closed them.

"I should let you get some rest," she said.

He ignored her. "It's true, you know," he said quietly. "I did kill your father."

Ericha held her breath. She thought of the life her mother had lived—that *she* had lived—because of Erich du Woernig's untimely death. She thought of Stefan's anguish in losing his loved ones, in bearing the burden of the country, his lost childhood.

Nik went on. "I have little doubt the explosion that killed him was a result of something I had set up. It was not done by my hand, but it was done at my insistence."

"Tell me," she said. While a part of her didn't know if she really wanted to hear it, she had to agree with Stefan as far as needing to know the whole truth. She also believed that talking would help Nik face up to it. She doubted anyone else would be willing to listen. And she could hardly blame them.

Nik kept his eyes closed tightly, as if he couldn't bear to look at her. "I was not very old when my mother told me that she had been secretly married to Nikolaus du Woernig. That makes me a du Woernig, you know—officially. But unlike with you, no one's ever seen fit to let me use the name. I can't say that I blame them.

"Before my father could make the marriage public and somehow dissolve his betrothal to some princess, he was killed. My mother told me daily that I was born to rule Horstberg, and she would see that I avenged my father's death and claimed what should have been his. It wasn't until I'd been paralyzed for about ten years that I realized my mother was a very bitter, unkind woman."

Nik took a deep breath and continued. "The plan was for me to marry one of the princesses, move in with the family, and figure out a way to work my way to the top. Han foiled that plan when he took Maggie away from Horstberg. So, I followed my mother's admonitions and did my best to do away with any possible heir to Horstberg that might stand in my way. But it had to look like an accident. I never actually did the dirty work, but there were many willing to do just about anything with the promise of prestige and power when I took over the country."

Ericha listened with growing horror as all the bits and pieces she'd heard in the past began to come together. She recalled Stefan telling her how he'd been shot as a child, and very nearly poisoned. She wondered what other things had happened during those years.

Nik cleared his throat tensely, and she saw his fists clench against the bed. "I knew that Erich went down to that dungeon of his to play with his chemicals nearly every day. It was the perfect way to be almost certain the accidents that were set up would happen to Erich."

Ericha pressed a hand over her mouth to keep from crying out. She was grateful Nik still had his eyes closed.

"There were a couple of pretty close calls, but in the end, I lost. And I lost hard. While I was laying in that bed, trying to face up to the fact that I had come away with nothing, and I would never walk again, I knew they were planning the wedding."

He paused, and Ericha felt tears trickle down her face as she thought of all the people she'd come to love who were affected by this. But most of all, she thought of her mother, preparing to marry the heir to Horstberg, with no comprehension of how her life would be shattered.

Nik's voice began to crack with emotion as he added unsteadily, "I also knew that a bottle of liquid explosive had been discreetly left among the other chemicals in that room. I don't know what it was, but the person who got it for me said it was powerful. And I had the bottle put where there was a strong possibility of it getting knocked over. But I said nothing. Even when the duke demanded to know if there was anything left undone that was potentially dangerous, I didn't tell him what I knew."

Nik said nothing more. Ericha cried silent tears until she realized he was watching her. She quickly wiped them away and cleared her throat.

With tears showing in his eyes, Nik asked, "Do you suppose it's possible to be forgiven of such a thing?"

In spite of her emotion, Ericha had to admit, "I believe that anything is possible."

"And what about you, Ericha? Can you forgive me for such a thing?"

Ericha's heart was warmed by his humility and the courage she knew it must have taken to make his confession.

"It's affected my life, yes," she admitted. "But it can't be changed. It is not my place to judge you for anything but what you are now. The man who did those things is not the same man I see before me." She took his hand into hers. "Not only do I forgive you," she bent to kiss his brow, "I love you, Uncle Nik." She pulled back and saw fresh tears in his eyes. "And with any luck, Stefan will come to see my reasoning."

Ericha moved toward the door until Nik stopped her. "Ericha, don't let it come between the two of you."

"Nik," she smiled, "with what Stefan and I have been through, I know one thing for certain. Nothing can come between us." He smiled, and she added, "Would you like to come to dinner?"

"Not just yet," he said. "Let's give it some time."

Ericha nodded and left him alone. She felt like finding Stefan and getting to the bottom of this, but in her heart she knew it would be better to wait until his anger cooled. In the nursery she found Ruthild just changing Cameron.

"Ah, there's your mother now," she cooed. "I was just comin' to find you, miss. I think young Cameron is ready for a feeding."

"Thank you, Ruthild," she said, and impulsively took the baby to Abbi's sitting room, where she found her painting at an easel near the window. While Ericha nursed little Cameron, she told Abbi of her experience with Nik.

"You've made astounding progress with him," Abbi said, "and I'm proud of you for your efforts. But you must be patient with Stefan. His wounds are deep."

In spite of what Nik had told her, Ericha couldn't help wondering how Abbi perceived all of this. "It's true, then, that Nik killed my father."

"Oh, yes," Abbi said, looking briefly at nothing, "it's true."

"Then, in a sense, he killed your husband, as well."

"Yes," Abbi said quietly.

"I look at Nik now and hardly find it possible."

"Oh, he has changed considerably. There was a day when Nikolaus Koenig du Woernig strode into the castle, full of arrogance, and he told Cameron exactly what he wanted. He was handsome and charming, just like his father before him, and he would have stopped at nothing to succeed in his quest."

"Which was?" Ericha tested, perhaps to see if Nik's story rang true.

"He wanted to be the Duke of Horstberg. There were three things standing in his way. Cameron, Erich, and Maggie's son."

"Stefan."

"Exactly."

"Long before Stefan was born, Maggie lost a child as a direct result of one of Nik's escapades. Erich was shot in the shoulder and was fired upon again more than once. Han nearly lost his life in an accident that had been intended for Erich, and Maggie would have lost Hannah, and perhaps her own life, if we had not been very alert.

"Things quieted down for a few years, but when it started again, it was every bit as awful. At that time Stefan was at a very impressionable age. He was an intelligent child, and well aware of what was going on. I still can hardly comprehend how he must have felt, at the age of seven, to realize his life was in jeopardy because he was heir to something he didn't even want.

"After repeated attempts against his life, the family abandoned the castle. When we thought it was all over at last, we returned to Horstberg and Cameron set a date for your parents to be married. The wedding had already been postponed because of the problems. But it was four days before the wedding that . . . well, it was horrible. That's all there was to it. Nik had had someone tampering with the chemicals in your father's laboratory, and when he went down to clean it up, he . . ."

Abbi became briefly distant, then she looked toward Ericha and said gently, "Stefan saw it all, Ericha. He knew who was behind it. His pain goes very deep."

"As does yours."

"Yes, but . . . well, it is in the past."

"Have you forgiven Nik?"

"I have," she said with no hesitation, "but it took me many years and a great deal of effort."

"Why do you suppose it's so easy for me to let it go? I care for Nik. I want to see him happy."

"Even though you were directly affected by the things Nik did, you were not aware of them until now. Despite the difficulties you were raised with, you have been content with the circumstances and would not have known otherwise had you not been told. You lived your life without Erich, and yet you never knew him. It's different. It's easier to accept. Stefan lost so much that day, and those of us who should have been there for him to lean on were so lost in our own pain that I'm certain he was brushed aside.

"You see, Ericha," Abbi turned to look at her, "you are the first real happiness Stefan has known since that day. You must not let such a thing as this come between you."

Ericha smiled. "That is what Nik told me."

Abbi gave a soft laugh, and the pain of her previous words dissipated. "Yes, he has changed."

"It appears that Cameron is finished," Ericha said, setting him on the floor to crawl while she fastened her bodice.

"It's nearly time for dinner," Abbi said. "I assume you'll be staying?"

"I'd love to," Ericha agreed and hurried to pull Cameron out of exploring Abbi's things. "I guess that means Cameron goes back to Ruthild."

"I'll take him," Abbi said. "Run along and I'll see you there."

Ericha went slowly to the dining room, thinking over the things Abbi had said. Rather than being angry with Stefan for his reaction, she felt a fresh compassion for the life he had lived, and she wanted only to somehow soothe his hurt.

Entering the dining room, Ericha stopped. Not only had Johanna obviously returned, but Ericha had inadvertently walked in on an argument. She paused at the door and swallowed hard, realizing they were unaware of her presence. While Stefan's anger earlier had caught her off guard, she had never seen him so blatantly bitter.

"It's nice to have you back, my dear Mrs. Heinrich," Stefan said with acrid sarcasm. "You could at least say hello before you start spitting venom."

"But surely you missed me," Johanna retorted with a wicked laugh as she leaned against the dining table, near where Stefan was sitting.

"If only you knew how—" Stefan began, then stopped as his eye caught Ericha standing near the door.

"Ah," Johanna said, swirling a glass of brandy in her hand, "look who's here. It's that wench you sleep with."

Ericha wondered if she should just turn around and leave. Stefan rose from his chair and leaned across the table. He grabbed Johanna's arm so abruptly that the glass fell to the floor and shattered.

"If you so much as breathe another disrespectful word while I am in this room, you will regret ever coming back here. Do I make myself clear, Mrs. Heinrich?"

Johanna glared at him as she pulled her arm from his grip. Her eyes turned harshly to Ericha, and it was tempting to turn and run from the gleaming hatred. If it wouldn't make her look like a coward, she would have done it. The tension was broken as Abbi and Georg came into the room, apparently unaware of what was happening.

"I couldn't find Ruthild right off," Abbi said, "so I brought Cameron with me."

"He might liven things up a little," Georg said, and Ericha moved quietly to her chair.

The maid came in to serve, and Johanna pointed to the broken glass. "Tell someone to clean that up," she insisted before sitting in her usual place.

Cameron's presence was the only thing that seemed to keep the room from exploding with tension. Ericha realized immediately that Stefan was angry, not only at Johanna, but at her as well. Was he still upset over what had happened with Nik?

As the meal progressed, Johanna seemed to take notice of the way Stefan was regarding Ericha, and she looked calmly smug over it. Before dessert was served, Cameron became restless and was no longer content to sit on Georg or Abbi's lap. Ericha rose to rescue them from Cameron's squirming and fussing. But Stefan came to his feet, walked the distance of the long table and took Cameron into his arms. His anger was set aside as he settled Cameron on his lap to share dessert, but Johanna was apparently displeased by the situation.

"I don't have to do this!" she declared without preamble.

"You'd best watch your tongue, Johanna," Stefan cautioned. "You say things better left unsaid when you've been drinking."

"Someone ought to say it," she insisted. "I'm sick to death of sitting here while you coddle that child as if he were the greatest thing on earth."

"I've told you before," Stefan replied calmly, "he is."

"Well, he won't be the Duke of Horstberg," Johanna retorted. "You can coddle him all you like, Your Grace. You can flaunt him to the world," she shouted, "but he will still be a bastard, just like his mother."

"Johanna!" Abbi rose to her feet. "That kind of behavior will not be tolerated in this household."

"But you'll tolerate that?" Johanna pointed to Stefan.

"The child is his cousin's son. There is nothing but gossip to make us believe otherwise."

"You're blind!"

"I am tolerant," Abbi retorted, "which is something you have never been."

Johanna came to her feet and leaned her palms on the table to glare at Abbi. "You are a—"

"Johanna!" Stefan said sternly, and she turned her eyes to him. "When you are speaking to the Grand Duchess of Horstberg, you will speak with respect or you will not speak at all. If you are unable to share dinner with the family and remain civil, you are advised to remain in your rooms."

"Are you banishing me, Your Grace?"

"I am warning you."

"And if I don't obey," Johanna's voice turned cynical, "what will you do? Put me in front of a firing squad?"

"Don't tempt me," he answered through clenched teeth.

There was a moment of silence, and Abbi sat down, apparently calm. Johanna held Stefan's eyes, and the hatred between them made Ericha sick.

"I can't believe you would—" Johanna began again, but Stefan interrupted with a voice more stern and angry than Ericha had ever heard.

"Johanna! Enough! Either sit down and be quiet—or leave!"

Cameron began to cry, apparently frightened from Stefan's unusual behavior. But Ericha was grateful for an excuse to leave. She rose quickly and took the baby from Stefan, avoiding his eyes as she left the room.

A mixture of anger and fear hovered with her as she left the ugly scene behind and took Cameron to the nursery. Ruthild was there, but Ericha remained with the baby a while, absorbing the calming effect of his presence.

When Ericha became restless, she left the nursery and wandered down to the drawing room, hoping to find a place to be alone. The room was empty and she extinguished the lights. She added wood to the fire until it blazed, casting eerie shadows across the tapestried walls.

Leaning back into a soft chair, Ericha's thoughts tumbled wildly through every aspect of the present situation. She wondered if it could possibly get any better, or if this tension would only intensify with time. Her mind swam with a montage of concern for Uncle Nik, fear of Johanna's wrath, compassion for Abbi being caught in the middle, and a lack of understanding for the depth of bitterness she had seen come to the surface in Stefan just today. It made her wonder about, and almost fear, the parts of him she didn't know.

Ericha came to her feet abruptly when she heard someone enter the room. Johanna didn't look at all surprised, and Ericha wondered if she'd been looking for her. They stood silently facing each other until Johanna moved across the room to pour herself a drink.

"Isn't this quaint?" she said, sweetly cynical, plopping into a chair with her glass of brandy. Ericha said nothing, and the room hung tensely until Johanna added, "Come now, surely you and I must have a great deal to talk about. We have much in common, you know."

"We have nothing in common," Ericha muttered, moving toward the door.

"Oh, you mustn't leave, dear Ericha." Ericha paused but felt apprehensive. "You see, we have something very important in common. You and I are the only two women who really . . . *know* the Duke of Horstberg."

Ericha could see little point in trying to deny the truth. "On the contrary," Ericha replied, "I don't believe you know him at all. If you did, you wouldn't treat him the way you do."

"I wouldn't *what?*" she asked, her voice catching anger. "How on earth would you know how I treat him? Would you like me to tell you how he treats me?"

"No, I wouldn't."

"Well, perhaps you should. What will you do one day if he decides to turn on you? And I couldn't help noticing how displeased His Grace was with you this evening." She laughed wickedly. "What did you do to displease him, Ericha?"

"That is my business. I can assure you it will be settled."

"Oh, will it? Well, you know, there was a time when Stefan loved me. He treated me like a queen and—"

"And what did you give him in return?" Ericha asked calmly. "I will not lose Stefan's love, because I reciprocate it back to him."

"Oh, yes," she said sarcastically, "just because you're lucky enough to have his son. If I had—"

"That's not what I was speaking of."

Johanna set down her empty glass and came to her feet. Ericha felt instinctively afraid as she realized the distance to the door, with Johanna standing between.

"You have a lot of nerve," Johanna stated, and Ericha heard

bitter hatred in her voice, "coming here out of nowhere, moving in like you belong, and destroying my marriage."

"The way I heard it," Ericha replied, proud of herself for the cool tone, "your marriage was long over before I even came to Horstberg."

"I'm sure he told you that," she snapped. "He'd probably tell you anything to—"

"I have no doubt that Stefan has been completely honest with me."

"You're very gullible." She chuckled. "And naive. What else did Stefan tell you?"

"I refuse to discuss this any further with you. It's pointless."

"You can't refuse me!" she nearly shouted. "I am the Duchess of Horstberg, *Miss* du Woernig, which is something you will never be. And if I want to talk about the way you've lured my husband into hating me, we will talk!"

"You're drunk, Johanna."

"You're a bewitching little tramp, and I will not tolerate you or your bastard son in my house any longer."

"I don't think you have as much say around here as you'd like to think you do." Ericha fought to remain calm on the surface. "You're lying to yourself, Johanna. You're misconstruing the truth to suit yourself. Why don't you just face the reality?"

"Why don't *you* face reality?" Johanna's voice raised a pitch. "You've deluded yourself into believing that he's yours. Well, he's not! He's mine. You will never have his name! You will never have his title!"

"You will never have his son . . . or his heart. And everyone in this country knows it."

"Damn you!" she spat, impulsively lifting a vase off the table beside her. Ericha realized her intentions and held up her arms in defense as Johanna drew back to throw it. Ericha heard the crash, quickly uttered thanks for not being struck, then lowered her arms.

"That was an heirloom," Stefan said, releasing his grip on Johanna's arm. She turned to glare at him in spite. "I'll take it out of your allowance."

Johanna swung to hit Stefan, but he caught her arm again and urged her toward the door. Ericha could feel that his mood had not lightened. She knew he would not be crossed. "I think that's enough drama for one evening, my dear. Go drown yourself in some hot coffee and mind your business or you might find yourself in trouble."

Johanna opened her mouth to protest, but Stefan only had to lift his finger in front of her face to silence her. "Enough!" he whispered authoritatively. "Get out of here."

Johanna left the room, but the bitterness didn't leave Stefan's eyes. The length of silence became intolerable, and Ericha moved to leave as Stefan poured himself a drink.

"Don't leave," he said without looking at her. "I want to talk to you." It sounded like a command.

"And what did Your Grace wish to talk to me about?" she asked, unable to avoid the caustic tone.

"Oh, not you too!" he said sharply. "The last thing I need is a battle from both directions."

Ericha felt herself seethe with anger. "The last thing I need is to be put into the same category with that fiend you are married to. If you want to talk, fine! We'll talk when you can treat me with more civility than you do your wife!"

"Don't be absurd!" he muttered, setting down his drink abruptly.

"I am *not* being absurd." She lowered her voice to drive home a point. "Today I have seen a bitter, hateful side of you that I don't understand, and I will not come against it."

"Ericha!" he shouted, grabbing her arm as she moved toward the door. The unfamiliar scorn in her eyes made him hear the bitter echoes from his own voice. She glanced toward his hand, and he released his grip and looked toward the floor, recalling vividly the day he'd once struck Johanna. What was wrong with him? Johanna had called him a hateful and bitter man and he hadn't cared. But hearing the words come from Ericha's lips forced him to take a long, hard look at himself. He knew she was right.

"Ericha," he cried in a whisper. Her shoulders came into his hands and he buried his face against her neck. "Don't go," he pleaded. "I need you. We have to talk."

Ericha sighed and held him against her, grateful to feel the Stefan in her arms that she knew and loved.

Chapter Nineteen

CAMERON'S FATE

"Forgive me," Stefan whispered, and Ericha could see the sincerity in his eyes as they reflected the firelight. "It's just that today has been so . . . I don't know, Ericha." He turned away and pushed both hands through his hair. "I will admit that what happened today with Nik took me completely off guard. And then with Johanna returning, I—

"Forget it," he interrupted himself, throwing his hands in the air. "There is no excuse for treating you that way, and I'm sorry. We've always been able to talk things through. Why not this?"

"I don't know," she replied softly. "Why not this?"

Ericha let silence give him time to settle the question while he stood near the fireplace, gazing distantly into the flames. He turned to look at her, and she saw the pain and fear in his eyes.

"There is nothing you can't tell me," she said, and he believed her, but still it hurt. "What is it?" she added, sitting on the edge of a chair.

He gave a tense, phony chuckle. "I feel as if a Pandora's Box is opening inside of me, and I fear what it contains."

"Give the fears to me," she whispered, "and I will throw them away."

"Yes," he said, "I believe you could do that." He looked again into the flames, and Ericha saw him take a deep breath and draw back his shoulders. "You're right, Ericha," he began, "I am bitter. I *hate* that man!" He hit his fist against the mantle. "I believe I have hated him more every day for more than twenty years. You can't know what self-restraint it takes to even be in the same room with him. I hate him!" he finished through clenched teeth, and then his voice softened as he leaned both hands against the mantle.

"I believe I was in shock after Cameron and Erich died. Within days after it happened, my brother and sisters acted as if nothing were any different. I remember watching them play and wondering why they couldn't see the pain and feel the emptiness. Everywhere I turned it was there. I drifted in and out of rooms completely unnoticed, like some kind of ghost, and all I could see was pain.

"I found my father crying more than once, and my mother became a shadow. She had a new baby to care for, but she barely managed. She turned pale and her eyes looked distant. But she wasn't nearly the shadow that Grandmama became. It was as if her heart had been torn right out of her. She would lie for hours just staring at nothing. She hardly ate or slept. At times she looked as dead as Cameron had.

"I felt the pain myself. Erich was the best friend I had ever had. And my grandfather had kept me under his wing from the moment I was born. Sometimes I believe that he instinctively knew I would be his heir. I missed them dreadfully, and I had seen how tragically they had lost their lives, but I didn't really understand why or how . . . until the day my mother came to her senses enough to comprehend the reality."

Stefan stood straight and squeezed his eyes shut. "I remember it as if it were yesterday. She tore out of her room almost hysterical, and I followed her, wondering what could possibly be wrong. She stormed into Nik's bedroom, screaming at him. I've never seen such rage. She cursed him and threatened him. She called him a cold-blooded killer and told him he would rot in hell for killing them. Before I knew what was happening, she had her hands around his throat.

"It took both Georg and my father to pry her away. I honestly believe she would have killed him if they hadn't come in time." Stefan turned his back to the fire and stuffed his hands deep into his pockets. "In the years since, I have often imagined myself doing exactly the same thing. I have wanted so badly to let all my inhibitions go, tell him exactly what I think of him, and strangle him right to death."

Stefan slumped into a chair and put his head into his hands, as if the confession had taken all of his strength. Ericha wondered if he was finished, but he looked up at her and continued. "Of course the years have softened everything. My mother actually apologized to Nik some years later. My father has accepted it all. He actually claims that he likes Nik. Georg has come to terms with it, and Grandmama . . . well, the woman is a saint. It took time, but I believe she has put it behind her."

"And what about you?" Ericha asked gently.

"Me?" he chuckled humorlessly. "I will never come to terms with it. I can't even look at him without seeing vivid images of my grandfather dying in his wife's arms. She screamed at him. She slapped him. She told him if this was some kind of joke she would kill him. Then I saw the change in her eyes when she realized it wasn't a joke. He was gone.

"I look at Nik Koenig and recall the body they dragged up from the basement, covered with sheets. That was when Georg had to carry Grandmama up the stairs. She went mad when they wouldn't let her see Erich. My father said she wouldn't recognize him."

Ericha squeezed her eyes shut and felt tears spill out, and she tried to comprehend the seven-year-old boy who had witnessed it all.

Stefan looked directly at Ericha. "When I see Nik Koenig I think about you—raised in poverty without a father's name. I think about me, stuck with ruling this duchy when I know that not only would Erich have done a far better job, he would have enjoyed it. He wanted it. And then I think of us—stuck here in this madness—and I want to die inside. I have no doubt whatsoever that if you had grown up here the way you should have, I would not have married Johanna, and she would not be here, standing between us, tormenting us every time we turn around."

A long moment of silence followed, and Stefan finally leaned back and crossed his ankles. "So, there you have it. That is why I hate Nik Koenig, and no, I cannot forgive him. I can only hope that you won't let it come between us."

"You have one thing in common with Nik."

"What is that?"

"He told me not to let this come between you and me."

Stefan looked surprised but said nothing.

"I won't expect you to forgive him, Stefan. That is your decision and I will not interfere."

"Thank you," he said, his voice betraying relief.

"But I want to ask one thing."

"What is that?"

"If you can't find forgiveness, perhaps you can find tolerance."

"Clarify that."

"He has lived under this roof all these years and only today has come out of that room. Let him make this his home, Stefan. Let him share meals with the family. If he isn't completely polite and agreeable you can banish him to his room. But give him a chance. That's all I ask."

Stefan didn't want to consent. He didn't want to look at him across the dining table every day, or happen to come across him in the hall at any time. But Ericha had backed down on her plea for his forgiveness, and he knew how badly she wanted peace between them. Surely he could give this much in return.

Stefan was silent, and Ericha feared that he would refuse even this. She almost wouldn't blame him. But still she uttered a silent prayer that he would consent, and perhaps time would prove to Stefan how penitent Nik had become.

"I think I could tolerate him," he finally replied, "as long as he's agreeable."

"I love you, Stefan," Ericha said, coming to her feet, trying to keep her joy concealed.

"I love you too, Ericha," he replied softly.

"May I ask you one question?" she asked.

"Of course."

"I was just wondering . . . when was the last time you saw my father alive?"

"Oh, that's easy," he mused. "That day at lunch he told me we would go riding as soon as he finished cleaning out the dungeon. Too bad I didn't go down with him, then old Nik could have—"

The door came open, and Ericha turned abruptly, grateful for the intrusion on Stefan's thoughts.

"Ericha, is that you?" Abbi called softly.

"Yes, I'm here."

"I've been looking for you. It's very late. Ruthild already has Cameron down for the night, and I sent a message to your home that you would be staying until morning. I've had the room east of the nursery prepared."

"Thank you," Ericha replied.

"Are you all right?" Abbi asked, moving into the room.

"Yes, of course. I'm fine."

"I hope you're not upset by the things Johanna said at dinner. You know she can be—"

"Really, I'm fine," Ericha interrupted.

Abbi was silent a moment, then asked, "Have you seen Stefan? I was wondering perhaps if he'd left for the night or—"

"I'm right here," Stefan answered out of the darkness. He came to his feet and stretched. "But I was just leaving."

"If the two of you need to talk . . ." Abbi began.

"Such conversations are better left unfinished," he said and moved toward the door. "Good-night, Ericha." He bent to kiss her on the mouth. "Perhaps I'll be fortunate enough to see you at breakfast."

"Good-night," she whispered.

"Grandmama." He kissed her cheek. "Sleep well."

"And you," she said.

He left the room, and Abbi turned a questioning gaze to Ericha.

"He'll be fine, I think," Ericha answered. "Come along, Grandmama, we'd best get to bed."

Ericha wished she could explain the apprehension in her that continued to deepen. She had trouble sleeping that night as the ugly moments of the day kept storming through her mind. She ached for Stefan and thought how easy it would be to go unnoticed through the darkened halls of the castle and be with him. If it weren't for needing to be near Cameron, she decided she would have done it. But the baby was restless, sensing he was in a different bed, and more than once she had to go into the nursery and soothe him back to sleep.

Hoping Cameron would stay asleep this time, Ericha returned through the darkness to her room and crawled into bed. There was a different mood to the castle at night, and she wondered briefly how it might have felt to grow up here.

"Don't move," Stefan's voice made her gasp. She could barely see his shadow as he stood from a chair and moved toward the bed. "There's a scoundrel in your room, Miss du Woernig, and I'm absolutely certain his intentions are not honorable."

"Would that be the same scoundrel who once coerced me into meeting him in the forest?"

"Precisely," he replied, kneeling on the bed.

"Then let him have his way," she said, reaching up to touch his face.

Stefan pressed his mouth over hers with immediate passion.

"Aren't you worried that someone will find you here and . . ."

"And what?" He almost laughed. "Is there *anybody* in Horstberg who doesn't know we're lovers?"

"Good point," she said and allowed herself to become caught up in his kiss.

Stefan returned to his room before dawn. Though Ericha didn't get much sleep, it felt good to know that everything was as it should be between her and Stefan—in spite of the difficulties going on around them.

Cameron's cries urged Ericha out of bed early, and she fed him and left him with Ruthild. She went straight to Nik's room where she announced he was coming to breakfast with her.

"Do you think I should?" he asked with apprehension. "I mean . . . won't His Grace—"

"Stefan and I had a long talk. He has a great deal to come to terms with. Perhaps he never will. But he did agree to this, as long as you remain perfectly civil and polite—which I know you will."

"Of course I will." He laughed, and Ericha wheeled him up to the table.

The meal began tensely, but Georg and Abbi began talking with Nik and soon had him at ease. Johanna remained silently indifferent to her surroundings, apparently suffering some degree of a hangover, which suited everyone else just fine. Stefan politely ignored Nik, but Ericha caught his eye more than once and felt peace to see no sign of bitterness, only the love that was familiar to her. She wished Johanna would have noticed.

Ericha returned home soon after breakfast and was surprised to find that Karl and Luise had returned from their honeymoon late the previous evening. It took little time to realize that it wasn't easy to observe them sharing their newly married life. Both Karl and Luise made obvious effort to make Ericha feel included, but she went to her room as soon as dinner was finished, feeling somehow out of place. She was about to go to bed when a knock came at the door.

"Come in," she called, pulling on a wrapper.

Karl peered through the door. "Are you all right?" he asked.

"Of course I'm all right," she insisted. "Why wouldn't I be?"

"I know this isn't easy for you. But we'll all adjust in time, I believe."

"I'm sure we will," she said. "Now stop worrying about me and enjoy being a newlywed."

Karl lifted his brows in amusement and backed out, pausing only to say, "If you need anything, please let me know."

"I will," she said, appreciating his concern. What would she ever do without Karl?

Stefan came through the side door shortly after eleven and closed it quietly behind him. Just past the kitchen, he literally collided with someone in the hall and a feminine voice cried out.

"Luise?" he said in surprise. "Is that you?"

"Oh, my . . . Stefan. I mean . . . Your Grace. I . . ."

"Stefan would be fine. I didn't think you were due back until next week."

"We weren't, but well . . . it's just that . . . oh, never mind. Karl is asleep. If you need to see him I can . . ."

"Let him sleep," Stefan said and moved past her toward the stairs, while Luise headed on toward the kitchen.

Stefan slipped into Ericha's room and found it dark. Quietly he undressed and slipped into the bed, easing as close to her as he could without waking her. She immediately turned over and drew him into her arms.

"I'm sorry," he whispered. "I didn't mean to wake you."

"I was awake," she said. "Besides, why would I want to waste all of the time I spend with you by sleeping?"

"Good point," he chuckled and kissed her warmly. "Is something wrong?" he asked, sensing a subtle tension in her.

"Nothing really," she replied. "It's just that . . . well, Karl and Luise came back early from their honeymoon."

"Yes, I know. I just ran into Luise downstairs. I think I scared her half to death." He heard Ericha sigh and added, "So, what's the problem?"

"It's just . . . difficult: the situation, I mean. I don't feel comfortable with . . ."

She faltered, and he pulled her closer. "I think I understand," he whispered.

"Good, because I don't want to try and explain it."

"I'm certain you will all adjust to the changes with time."

"That's what Karl said."

"Then there's nothing to worry about."

Ericha wanted to tell him there was more to her feelings than that, but there was nothing he could do about it, so she let it drop.

Stefan came downstairs the following morning to find Ericha

sipping a cup of coffee while Cameron played on the floor nearby. He bent to kiss Ericha, then took a sip of her coffee before pulling Cameron onto his lap.

"Ooh," Ericha smiled, running her hand over his face, "it feels so nice freshly shaven."

Stefan chuckled and kissed her again, then turned his attention to Cameron. "Good morning, my boy. Why don't you tell Papa what you dreamed about?"

"He would if he could talk," Ericha said just as Karl and Luise entered the dining room, both giggling like a couple of children.

Luise's laugh was cut short while Karl slapped Stefan on the shoulder with a jubilant, "Good morning, Stef. Did you miss me?"

"Have you been gone?" Stefan smirked, and Karl laughed boisterously as he was seated. Only then did everyone notice Luise's stunned expression.

Before she could speak, Erma bustled into the room with more coffee and some hot rolls. She served Stefan first with a jovial, "Good morning, sir. I baked your favorite."

"Thank you," he replied with a smile. "You're a dear as always."

When Erma left to get the rest of their breakfast, the tension descended again.

"Is something wrong, Luise?" Karl asked. "Why don't you sit down and—"

"You spent the night!" she said accusingly to Stefan.

Stefan glanced toward Karl, puzzled by her apparent ignorance. Then he nodded politely and replied, "Yes, I did."

Her eyes moved with purpose to the baby on his lap and the way he held Ericha's hand across the table. Enlightenment filled her expression and she turned astonished eyes toward Karl.

"I don't believe it!" She chuckled tensely. "I knew he had a mistress, but . . . I . . . I don't believe it! Right here! In this house."

"Come on, Luise," Karl said, attempting to soothe her, "you knew that Ericha had a baby, and—"

"Yes, but—"

"Luise, the whole blasted country knows that Ericha is—"

"Well, I didn't! And you obviously didn't bother to tell me. You just move me in here and expect me to—"

"I think it would be best if we discussed this privately," Karl interrupted, glancing apologetically toward Stefan and Ericha.

"Fine!" Luise retorted. "Now would be a good time."

Luise left the room and Karl followed, leaving the tension of a hovering storm lingering behind.

Stefan met Ericha's eyes and saw tears brimming there. Before he had a chance to gather his thoughts, they spilled over her face. He set Cameron free to play with his toys and pulled Ericha into his arms.

"It's all right," he whispered.

"It's not all right!"

"We knew it wouldn't be easy." He lifted her chin and kissed the tears away. "Now listen, I will talk to Karl. We're leaving on holiday soon, right?" She nodded. "We're going to have a glorious time, and when we come back, I'll get you a place of your own. I've been contemplating doing that anyway. Now seems a good time. I think it will make things better for all of us now that Karl is married." He kissed her and smiled. "Will that be all right?"

Ericha nodded, feeling a degree of relief. But she couldn't fight the inner voice that kept telling her the situation was only going to get worse.

Stefan awoke in his own bed, as he did rarely these days, and his thoughts went immediately to Ericha. The passing of time had done little to ease his worry over the common knowledge of their involvement. What would it do to the country? To him? To Ericha? He sighed and turned over, then sat up abruptly.

"What the . . ." he said sharply, realizing that Johanna was sitting in bed next to him with the sheet pulled up beneath her arms, and obviously wearing nothing underneath it.

"Good morning, dear husband." She smiled wickedly. "Did you sleep well?"

"What are you doing here?" he demanded.

"I'm just being where every good wife ought to be—in her husband's bed."

Stefan got out of the bed and pulled on his breeches.

"I don't know what you're up to, woman," he said angrily, "but it's not going to work."

She laughed and a knock came to the door. He looked tensely at Johanna as she immediately called, "Come in please."

A maid timidly entered the room, seeming to take great notice of the situation. "Breakfast as you ordered, Your Grace," she said, setting the tray down.

"Thank you," Johanna said complacently, and the maid left the room.

"Damn you," Stefan growled, and then he pulled her clothes off the floor and threw them at her. "Get out of here! Do you hear me? Get out!"

"Now, Stefan, my love," she said coolly, moving out of the sheets to casually get dressed while he looked blatantly away from her, "you mustn't upset yourself. I'll not have people saying that my husband has turned me away for some common woman."

"She's got as much royal blood as you do," he defended.

"Huh!" she laughed. "She's a bastard just like her son. Won't she be surprised to hear where you were this morning, as will everyone else?"

"Get out of here!" Stefan insisted, but she only laughed again.

Abruptly he scooped up her remaining clothes and opened the door, throwing them into the hall. Then he took Johanna by the arm and all but pushed her out the door in her chemise and petticoats.

"What are you doing?" she protested.

"I'm making it clear," he said loudly, hoping the servants would overhear, "that I don't want you in my room, and if you come here again—ever—you will sorely regret it."

He glared at her, then slammed the door and locked it.

She stood outside his door shouting at him while he dressed, then he came out and pointed his finger at her, saying low in his throat, "That kind of behavior will not be tolerated from the Duchess of Horstberg, my dear. And if you choose to continue it, I will see that you are properly disciplined."

"Still considering putting me in front of a firing squad?"

"Don't tempt me!" he said, moving past her and down the stairs.

"You're not man enough to kill me!" she shouted.

He quickly told Rusty that he needed to go somewhere, and then he nearly ran to the stables. He needed Ericha. She could help him see the light through all this madness. He found her dressed to go out and apparently upset over something.

"What's the matter?" he asked after greeting her with a kiss.

"Oh," she said, "I had an appointment at the dress shop and Erma promised she'd be here to watch Cameron. Now she's run off somewhere and forgotten about it, and—"

"I'll watch him," Stefan offered easily.

"Oh, you can't do that—"

"And why not?" he asked. "My father and grandfather were always about the ducal business with a child on their lap. I can take care of him that long."

"Are you sure?" she asked. "It's not that important. I can—"

"Nonsense," he insisted. "You never get out. Now go!" He pushed her toward the door. "Have a good time! Get out of here!"

Ericha laughed and opened the door, but he stopped her with his arm. "Wait," he said softly, then kissed her hard, with desperation.

"Something's wrong," she said when he pulled away. "What is it?"

Stefan smiled warmly. "We'll talk when you get back."

He urged her out the door before tugging Cameron's coat over his tiny arms, placing a hat on his head, and taking him out to walk in the garden. He was grateful that Luise was still working long hours at the inn since she'd hardly said a civil word to either him or Ericha in the few days since she'd discovered their involvement.

He noticed Mrs. Burger across the fence and shuddered from the cold glare she gave him. He was well aware that she had completely stopped speaking to Ericha long ago. And he felt certain she'd realized by now that he had deceived her in pretending to be someone he wasn't.

Ericha returned to find Stefan and Cameron sitting on the bench outside. She overheard Stefan telling the baby a fairy tale.

"He can't understand you," she said.

Stefan turned and smiled. "Sure he can. You weren't gone long."

"I did what I needed to," she said. "Thank you."

"My pleasure," he said and kissed the top of Cameron's head as he played with the buttons on his father's jacket.

"You came to talk," Ericha said, sitting beside him on the bench. "Is something wrong?"

"Yes," he said coolly. "But there's little to be done about it. I just wanted to let you know what's going on before it reaches your ears through some other source. I think that's what she wants to happen."

"What did she do?" Ericha asked intently.

"Oh," he chuckled satirically, "it was all very amusing to her. I woke up this morning to find her in my bed."

"What? What could she possibly hope to accomplish?"

"That's easy," he said. "She won't fight straight out. She does it one little step at a time. Very subtly she weaves a web like some kind of vindictive spider, and waits for me to fall into it.

"My guess is that she just wants to make me look bad. If the servants think I'm sleeping with her and have a mistress as well, it makes me look like a . . . well, you know what I'm saying. Who knows what her next move will be. I believe I've wounded her pride and she's out for nothing but vengeance. Our affair has proven that in many ways she's been lying to me. But look at me. I haven't got a lot of room to talk."

Ericha glanced down and swallowed hard, but Stefan lifted her chin with his finger.

"Now don't go blaming yourself for this," he said gently. "I am responsible for my actions and I will face the consequences. I need you to be here for me with that conquering smile and hopeful eyes." She gave the expression he'd just described, and he kissed her softly.

"Besides," he said, leaning back and repositioning Cameron on his lap, "I can handle Johanna. I know how she works and I won't let her destroy me. At least I don't have to lie and pretend anymore. And neither do you. Even if no one will talk to us."

Ericha gave a subtle smile and leaned against his shoulder.

"I love you, Stefan Heinrich," she said.

"I love you, Ericha du Woernig," he replied, and she looked up at him and smiled.

"Are you packed yet?" he asked.

"No," she smiled, "but I'm working on it."

"Good!" He grinned. "I'm counting down the hours."

"I'm afraid packing light isn't as easy as it used to be. It's amazing how much it takes to care for a baby."

Stefan chuckled. "I'm certain we'll manage."

"Where are we going?" she asked.

"I don't care," he replied. "Just as long as we're together," he tousled Cameron's red curls, "and we can leave all these wretched problems behind."

Stefan stayed for brunch, then left late morning with a promise to return the following afternoon.

"Our train leaves at four," he said before mounting his stallion. "Be ready."

"I will," she promised. He bent down to kiss her and then galloped away.

Stefan spent the following morning in the office with Rusty, certain everything was under control enough for him to leave for a lengthy vacation. He was relieved when Rusty said he had an appointment and needed to go for a while.

Stefan escaped to his music room and took out his frustrations on the piano keys. He recalled his mother often playing the piano to release her emotions, and he suddenly missed his parents dreadfully, wondering what country they were in now.

After finishing a passionate piece that was one of his favorites, he played idly a few moments, allowing his mind to wander. Hearing something unusual, Stefan stopped playing. He heard it again, and his heart quickened. A woman's scream. Johanna? He was contemplating going to investigate when he heard the shot. Undoubtedly a gunshot. He moved into the hallway, but he didn't see anyone, so he ran to the head of the stairs and looked down. There was no one in sight. Haphazardly, he threw open the doors to all the rooms in this short length of hallway, feeling a dread come over him. Then he realized the only room he hadn't looked in was his bedroom.

With panic, he opened the door. Everything inside of him screamed with horror when he saw the splatter of blood on the wall. He moved his eyes to the floor where the gun lay—not far from Johanna's body.

His first instinct was to see if she was alive. But as he knelt and scooped her into his arms, her head fell back limply to reveal the mass of blood soaking her flaxen hair, oozing from the bullet hole behind her ear, which was clipped with an emerald earring. He noticed a number of fresh bruises on her face and wondered who had done this to her.

"Johanna," he whispered, briefly feeling heartache for a time long gone by when he had loved her and wanted the best for them. But his sadness was quickly overridden by a short-lived guilt. He felt little remorse for her death as he realized that this left him free to marry Ericha. And the thought was joyous.

Carefully he laid the body back down, and with the confidence of innocence and being the Duke of Horstberg, he stood and picked up the weapon, knowing it would help as they investigated who had done this. He was surprised to realize it was his own pistol that had been kept in the bureau drawer. And as far as he knew, no one else was aware that he kept it there.

Stefan was briefly startled when several officers of the Guard came running through the door that he'd left open. He stood waiting for them to do something, until their silence struck like a knife through his heart. Stefan felt his eyes widen as he looked down at the gun in his hands, and the blood on his shirt. He swallowed hard and somehow knew it wouldn't do any good to tell these men he hadn't done it.

None of them seemed to dare speak. Stefan met Captain Leichty's eyes. He almost looked like he was going to cry. He could almost imagine the captain mentally battling between his respect and knowledge of his ruler's character and the evidence that Stefan Heinrich hated his wife. The fact that Stefan had a mistress only added to his motive. The captain finally said, "Please drop the gun, Your Grace."

Stefan did as he was told. He knew it only made him look more guilty, but he was too numb to do anything else. He wondered if the brief ray of hope that he might have a real life with Ericha had only been a vain and bitter farce. His hope shattered as his wrists were bound in front of him and he was led quietly from his bedroom to face the judgment of a murderer.

Descending the stairs with guards on every side, Stefan's mind clicked through all of the executions he'd witnessed. He wondered if he'd ever sent an innocent man to his death. At least he would have a trial, he thought. But would it make any difference?

"Captain," he said as they came to the foot of the stairs.

"Yes, sir," he replied, and Stefan could tell this was difficult for him.

"Would you please let me talk to my grandmother a moment before we go?"

The captain nodded and clicked his heels before he sent one of his men to get the duchess while they all waited at attention in the hallway.

A moment later, Rusty stepped out of the office saying,

"Captain, did you—" He stopped abruptly when he saw Stefan there, and then he turned his gaze away and went back into the office. Stefan felt sick inside.

Abbi was far enough away from the duke's chambers that she'd been unaware anything was amiss until an officer entered the library, stood at attention, and said without looking at her, "Your Grace, the duke wishes to see you at once. If you'll come with me please."

"What's happened?" she asked as the memory of a recurring dream struck her forcefully. He made no reply, and she fled down the hall in a frenzy. "Where is he?" she asked the officer who could barely keep up with her.

"At the foot of the stairs near the duke's office, Your Grace," he replied, close behind her as she moved briskly with the worst kind of fear gripping at her heart. The last time she'd felt this way was the day Erich and Cameron had been killed.

When Abbi came around the corner to see Stefan with his head bowed and surrounded by officers of the Guard, she cried out and pushed her way through them, wrapping her arms protectively around him.

"What happened?" she insisted, glancing quickly to his bound wrists and the blood on his shirt.

Stefan waited momentarily, hoping that someone would volunteer the information. When it became apparent they weren't going to, he spoke softly, "Johanna's dead."

"Oh, no!" Abbi cried, putting her hands to her face.

"Please," he whispered, taking her hands the best he could. In spite of his trembling hands, he managed a steady voice. "You must listen to me. You must send for Father." Abbi nodded. "Rusty can handle things until he gets here. And Grandmama, please . . . make certain that Ericha and Cameron are safe. I think you know what this could mean."

Again she nodded and bit her lip fearfully.

"One more thing," he said, and she saw the sincerity in his eyes as he stated, "I didn't do it."

Abbi nodded and started to cry while Stefan was escorted

across the courtyard and into the keep, where the duke's cell was no different from the lowest thief.

Through her experience as duchess of fifty years, Abbi du Woernig was a doer. After crying her heart out on Georg's shoulder, she employed his assistance to gather everyone together who was in the castle at the time. The Guard had sealed off the gates immediately, and no one had come or gone since the crime was committed. With that much certain, she explained what had happened and demanded that if anyone knew anything, now was the time to speak up.

With members of the Guard present, including Captain Leichty, the facts were derived that the shot was heard by Rusty, who was in the duke's office, one floor below the bedroom. And by two maids, one who was dusting a hall stand just outside the office, near the foot of the stairs that led up to the hall, the other who was in the ballroom working below the other set of stairs that led to that section of the house. No one saw anyone go up or down those stairs after the shot was heard. And there was no other way to get to the duke's rooms.

It was Rusty who summoned the Guard when he heard the shot, and no one else was aware that anything had even happened. The Guard reported that each room on that floor had been thoroughly searched while Stefan was being arrested. Apparently he had been the only one on that floor. After the servants were dismissed, Abbi spoke with Georg and the captain.

"Georg," she said, "there is another way to that bedroom."

"Yes," he said hopefully, "there is."

"Captain," the duchess said, "Georg will go with you to see if a passageway has been used. Your knowledge of it is to remain confidential." He nodded. "I also want you to send men to Miss Ericha's home. They are to wait for her to pack her things and she is to come here with the child for an indefinite period of time."

Again the captain nodded, and she added, "And I want anyone entering or leaving the castle grounds to be monitored and questioned. That will be all for now. Keep me posted on everything."

Georg went with the captain and left Abbi alone, wondering what had happened to leave Stefan to face Cameron's fate. It had taken Cameron years to prove his innocence. What would this do to Stefan?

Ericha had just gotten Cameron down for his nap when an incessant banging came to her door, and she opened it to face Erma, irritated that the knocking might have awakened the baby.

"What is it?" she asked.

"I wish I knew," she said, seeming unusually perturbed. "There are three men downstairs . . . from the Guard. They want to see you."

"Me? Whatever for?"

Erma answered with an indiscernible grumble as she moved down the hall. Ericha had little choice but to go downstairs and find out what was going on. She had almost not believed Erma, but there certainly were three men standing in the entry, wearing the uniform of the Guard. They gave her little chance to wonder what their purpose was as one of them spoke directly.

"You're to come with us, Miss du Woernig. We have orders to bring you and your son to Castle Horstberg immediately for an indefinite period of time."

She briefly wondered if this was some kind of joke on Stefan's part, but there was a sense of foreboding that squelched the idea.

"For what reason?" she asked.

"Protection, miss," he stated.

"From what?" she asked, astonished.

"I only know that you're to come with us. Those were our orders."

"Who gave the orders?" she asked.

"The duchess," he paused and clarified, "du Woernig."

Ericha could do little but what they'd asked. A fearful knot tightened in the pit of her stomach as she did her best to think clearly. She was mostly packed for their holiday, and quickly tried to think what else they might need, while the men waited at the foot of the stairs. Her fear became so tangible that she jumped when Karl came into the room and startled her.

"Oh, Karl." She could see something in his eyes. "What's going on?"

He paused too long. "Uh . . . well, I was at my father's apartment and . . . we were playing chess. And . . . the duchess called together everyone in the castle for a meeting. I had to go, of course, and . . . oh, Ericha . . ." He ran his hand through his hair, and she noticed he looked pale.

"What?" she insisted as her blood quickened with dread.

"Johanna's been shot."

Ericha's mind raced with a thousand questions, the foremost being: Why did that mean she had to go to the castle?

"She's dead, Ericha. And Stefan was caught holding the gun."

Ericha's heart wrenched, and she felt suddenly weak. She sat carefully on the edge of the bed to absorb what she'd just heard.

"He didn't do it," Ericha stated in a calm voice that belied the turmoil gurgling inside her.

"I know that."

"Where is he now?" she asked, her heart aching for him.

"He's in the keep," he replied soberly, "where every prisoner waits for a trial."

"Heaven be merciful," she whispered, then pressed a hand over her mouth as emotion threatened to choke her. Suddenly panicked, she frantically started throwing things into the nearly packed trunk.

"I assume they're here to take you to the castle," he said.

"It appears that way." She realized she was shaking. "I don't know why, but . . ." She couldn't finish as she looked around in a frenzy, wondering what she might need.

"I would guess they fear what fanatics might do under the circumstances. Or at least that's Her Grace's excuse to have you under her wing where she knows that you're well."

Ericha only nodded and numbly finished packing, feeling more afraid than she ever had in her life.

Abbi and Georg went together to Stefan's cell to tell him the results of their efforts. He sat with no expression while they stated all they knew, adding that Georg was certain, considering a recent snowstorm, that the passageway had not been used for several days at the very least. Captain Leichty had carefully traversed the length of the passageway and found nothing, while the duke's bedroom had remained guarded. No one could have possibly been hiding there. It appeared from all points that no one went out of the bedroom after the shot was fired.

Abbi then insisted to hear Stefan's side of the story, and he repeated it very carefully, ending with the humble statement, "I didn't do it."

They were all silent for several moments, and then Stefan asked, "Where is Ericha?"

"I've sent for her and the baby to be brought here for protection until this is settled."

Stefan nodded, then looked down solemnly.

"We will postpone any trial until your father gets here," she added. "I've sent messengers out already with his most recent letters. But who knows how long it will take them to find him."

"He'll probably kill me himself," Stefan said, and Georg chuckled to ease the tension.

"No he won't. I won't let him."

Stefan attempted to smile gratefully at Georg, then at Abbi. And they left him alone.

Ericha arrived at the castle overcome with dread and uncertainty. She was grateful to immediately have time alone with Abbi, but as she explained the circumstances, Ericha's dread increased.

"How is Stefan reacting?" Ericha asked.

"Outwardly he is calm and has every bit the dignity you'd expect. But I know he is tormented. It doesn't look promising. And he knows it."

"Can I see him?"

"Come along," Abbi said. "We'll arrange it now. My position doesn't allow me to change the laws, but I can stretch visitation rights."

It was past dark when Ericha followed an officer across the courtyard and into the keep. The mood was cold as they entered, and Ericha felt her heart sink further as she followed him down a long hall lit dimly by a few wall sconces. He turned a key in a squeaky lock and pushed the door open with effort.

"Your Grace," the officer stated tonelessly. "A visitor for you."

"Thank you." Stefan's voice came from the darkness, and Ericha could only see his outline on the far side of the tiny room from the bit of moonlight coming through a small barred window.

The door was slammed and locked. Ericha winced, trying to comprehend how it must feel to be confined here with no freedom.

"Stefan," she whispered, and he moved to sweep her into his arms. He said nothing, but pressed his lips over hers, and then he buried his face against her throat, holding her tightly against him.

"Are you all right?" she asked gently.

"I am now," he said.

"Are they treating you well?"

"As well as can be expected."

Stefan sat down on the narrow cot and urged Ericha to sit close beside him. "Thank you for coming," he said. "I need you. We should have been gone from here by now."

"I know," she said, running her fingers over his face. "What are you feeling, Stefan?"

"I don't know what to feel." He chuckled humorlessly. "In one moment I was glad she was dead, and in the next I was being led away and cursed her for dying and leaving me to this."

He touched her face meekly. "We should have left the country yesterday."

Ericha felt like crying, but she held her tears back, not wanting to burden him further. "Surely they will find a way to prove your innocence," she said adamantly.

"Don't talk about that now," he whispered. "Just let me hold you. They won't let you stay long. I need to hold you. Is Cameron all right?"

"Yes, he's fine. He was asleep when I left. Georg is with him."

"Ericha," he said, "when this is over, we will marry. I have a name to give you now, my love. And I will."

"Yes, Stefan," she said with hope in her voice, "when this is over."

Chapter Twenty

THE DUKE'S REGENT

ericha's attempts at sleep were futile. The realization of the present circumstances left her with such an onslaught of emotions that just trying to decipher them left her wound up, tense, and afraid. Knowing that rest was impossible, Ericha took up a lamp and went quietly into the hall. She had to think carefully on just how to get to the family gallery and felt pleased with herself when she found it. The castle was so huge.

One by one, Ericha held the lamp high to illuminate the portraits of her relations, and she tried to remember all that she'd been told about them. She felt a rush of goose-bumps encompass her when she looked into the eyes of Cameron du Woernig, and she had to wonder what it would be like if he were still alive. But then, if he were alive, Erich would be too. The thought was astounding.

Coming to her father's portrait, Ericha sighed and attempted to imagine what he might have been like. In her mind she could easily envision him and Kathe together, and it gave her comfort. But Ericha's emotion became unbearable when she approached Stefan's portrait. Tears burned into her eyes to think of him alone in a cold cell. It was all so horrible. Was this the kind of thing she had rationalized away when she'd made the decision to become his mistress?

Deciding there was no room for regret, Ericha said a prayer in her heart for him, then impulsively decided to go to Stefan's room in an effort to feel close to him. Carefully she made her way through the halls, down the stairs and back up again, liking the mood of the castle at night as the lamplight cast eerie shadows in the darkness.

Ericha opened the door to his bedroom and stepped inside, feeling briefly unsettled to realize Johanna had been killed here. But from what Stefan had told her, she wasn't the first to be murdered in this room. She could see no evidence of the crime, except that one of the rugs was missing. She knew that Johanna's body had already been taken to Kohenswald, and the funeral would be held there. Abbi and Georg were planning to attend.

Ericha sat on the bed a moment, recalling fond memories here, and she prayed there would be more good times ahead with Stefan. It crossed her mind that perhaps he *had* killed Johanna. But the thought was quickly passed off as an absurdity. Though she could understand why he'd want to be free of her, Ericha knew Stefan would never do such a thing.

Going through the sitting room and into the hall, Ericha tried to remember which door was his music room. She felt pleased when the first one she tried was right. Emotion rose again as she set the lamp down on the piano and touched the keys, recalling vividly how well he could express himself with his music.

Ericha turned and looked about her, wishing with everything she had that Stefan was free from this and she could be with him now. Her heart ached for him, and the dim light of the room added a haunting quality to her emotion. What would happen, she had to wonder, if they didn't prove him innocent? Would she ever be able to bear it?

Ericha forced her thoughts elsewhere and took up the lamp to get a closer look at his paintings. She noted that he'd worked some on the stallion since she'd last seen it, then she glanced toward the one leaning against the wall, of the view from the high turret. Scrutinizing it closely, she read at the bottom: *Stefan 1869.* Then her eye caught another painting that was covered, and she recalled seeing it here before.

Ericha stood for several moments, wondering if she should invade his privacy and look beneath the cloth. She almost talked herself out of it, but impulsively, she set down the lamp and knelt beside it to carefully lift the cloth away. The work was large, and she had to move the light to grasp what it depicted.

"It's beautiful," she said aloud, and then she wondered if the woman with red hair bent over a garden of flowers was her. The face wasn't visible, but the dress and hat were clearly her own, and his accurate depiction of the garden was uncanny.

"Oh, Stefan," she said as she ran her fingers gingerly over the textured oils, and tears brimmed in her eyes. Moving her gaze to the signature, she felt emotion deepen in her heart. *Stefan 1867*. The year they had met, she thought, but it wasn't until the autumn of sixty-eight that he had come to the decision to share his life with her. It touched Ericha to know that during a time when she had been aching with thoughts of Stefan, he had been thinking of her too. And with the present situation, it gave her comfort.

"I love you, Stefan," she said aloud to the empty room, and then she carefully covered the painting and retraced her steps to check on Cameron, who slept peacefully in his little bed in the nursery, completely unaware of the events that were molding his life.

Han Heinrich stepped down from the carriage into the castle courtyard, and he reached up to help his wife. His stride was long and determined as he moved deftly down the hall with Maggie following close behind. They were both in a panic to know what had happened. The messengers would tell them nothing more than he was being summoned back to act as duke regent. They knew there would be no reason for such drastic measures unless Stefan was unable to see to his duties personally.

Abbi was sitting in the drawing room with Ericha, while little Cameron played on the floor. They both jumped slightly when the door flew open. Ericha held her breath as Han Heinrich rushed into the room, Maggie close behind.

"What happened?" he demanded.

"Now calm down, Han," Abbi insisted, coming to her feet. "How about hello first? It's been a long time."

"Is Stefan hurt?" he asked with his hands on his hips. Ericha recognized where Stefan had gained his natural authority.

"No," she said carefully, "Stefan is not hurt. Now, how about hello?"

"Hello, Mother," he said curtly, bending to kiss her cheek, and then she held out her arms to embrace her daughter.

"Oh, Maggie," she said gently, "it is always so good to see you."

Ericha rose to embrace Maggie, feeling warmed by the strength she felt from Maggie's arms. "It's so good to see you, Ericha," she said.

"And you," Ericha replied, trying not to betray her present state of mind.

Han barely acknowledged her with a nod as the women were all seated. "Now," he insisted. "I want to know what's going on."

"Sit down," Abbi said, and he did. Ericha saw Abbi take a deep breath, and she wondered how the subject would be approached. "Well," she said, "I'll get to the point. Johanna's been killed."

"Good heavens!" they said almost in unison, and Maggie added, "What happened?"

"That's the problem, really. We don't know, but . . ." Abbi seemed thwarted and glanced toward Ericha for support. Ericha had none to give.

Han questioned abruptly, "Where is Stefan?" Abbi answered him with a blank expression as she searched for the right words. He shot to his feet and shouted, "If Stefan were able to—"

"Calm down, Han," Abbi insisted. "Anger will not do any good. The situation here is bad. We don't need your temper to make it worse."

Han took a deep breath but remained standing, and Abbi just said it. "Stefan has been arrested for suspicion of killing Johanna."

Han sat down. Maggie went pale. Ericha rose to get Cameron out of mischief.

"I believe he didn't do it," Abbi said gently. "But the evidence is not good. It's been nearly three weeks, and nothing has turned up to give any proof otherwise. But we simply must be determined that he is innocent and find a way to prove it."

Abbi stated all that she knew about the circumstances of the crime, and then Han stood quietly to leave the room.

"Where are you going?" Maggie insisted.

"To talk with my son," he said sternly and slammed the door.

Ericha felt tension in the room and wished there was something she could say to ease it.

"And how are you?" Maggie asked Ericha.

Ericha was so touched by her genuine concern that she nearly cried. But she choked back the emotion and tried to smile. "Afraid," she said, "but I guess we're holding up."

"Oh, look at my sweet little Cameron," Maggie said, her arms outstretched. "He's growing so quickly. Come to Grandmama," she cooed, and Ericha handed him over. Cameron became interested in Maggie's brooch.

"How is Stefan?" Maggie asked while she openly admired the baby.

"As long as we keep him busy," Abbi said, "he seems to manage. But you know Stefan. He bears his grief well."

Maggie pressed her fingers between her eyes as if she could hold back a sudden rush of emotion, but tears leaked out of her eyes in spite of the effort.

Abbi went on in a brave voice that belied the endless days they'd endured since this nightmare had begun. "At least they've modified his cell somewhat. He's actually keeping up on his paperwork. But I think if he couldn't be doing that, he'd go insane. He's not accustomed to sitting still for long."

Maggie dabbed at her eyes with a handkerchief, and then she removed one of her earrings for Cameron to play with. Ericha unwillingly began to pace, wringing her hands. It had become a common habit these past few weeks, while she could almost feel Stefan's confinement.

"Are you able to see him?" Maggie asked.

Ericha realized the question was being directed at her. "Not nearly enough."

Maggie shook her head solemnly.

"I hope Han isn't too hard on him," Abbi said.

"He can be an ogre at times," Maggie said mostly in humor, "but he'll get past it."

"He's most likely more hurt than angry," Ericha said, and Maggie almost smiled. She reached a hand toward Ericha and she hurried to take it, sitting close beside her. Maggie pulled Ericha close to her with a tight embrace, and they held each other and cried. Abbi looked on with tears streaming over her face, while little Cameron contentedly examined his grandmother's jewelry.

Stefan became alert when he heard steady footsteps coming down the hall. He knew before the door opened that it was his father. No one had a stride like Han Heinrich.

He entered alone, and the door was locked behind him. Stefan waited like a child to be punished while Han stood with his hands on his hips, glaring sternly at his eldest son.

"Go ahead," Stefan insisted, "get it over with."

"All right, I will. The last time I came home, I was let in on the secret that you have a mistress and an illegitimate son. Now I—"

"It's no secret, anymore," Stefan interrupted. At Han's questioning look, he clarified, "It's been common knowledge for quite some time."

Han shook his head in disbelief. "And now," he went on, "I am summoned home to find out that you are on trial for murdering your wife . . . with enough evidence to have you shot right now. It would take a miracle to prove you innocent. You're the Duke of Horstberg, Stefan!" he shouted. "Did you think twice about what this would do to the family—the country?"

There was silence until Stefan answered calmly, "Yes, I did."

"Do you have any idea what this means?"

"Yes, I do."

"Is that all you can say?"

"What do you want me to say, Father?" Following a miserable silence, Stefan went on, "You've told me many times about the intense love you felt for Mother, and that nothing could make you deny it. I followed my heart, Father. And even sitting in this forsaken little cell, wondering if I will ever see daylight again before the day I'm shot, I am a happy man. I have a son. And there is a woman who loves me. Do you have any idea what that means to me? Have you stopped to think about that? Or are you still angry because I'm not man enough to carry a country on my shoulders without some love and happiness to sustain me?"

Han maintained his silent, imposing expression, and Stefan went on. "Father, I didn't kill Johanna. I despised her with all my soul, but I would not have taken her life for any reason. I'm not asking you to approve of my choices, but I'm asking you to acknowledge Ericha as the woman I love, and Cameron as your grandson. And I'm asking for your help."

Stefan nearly cursed aloud when his voice cracked with emotion. The only good thing about being alone in this wretched cell was not having anyone around to see how many tears he'd cried in helpless anguish. "I need you," he managed. "I'm not ready to die, Father. I have too much to live for."

There was an uncomfortable length of silence before Han reached over and slapped his son's shoulder. "I know you didn't kill her," he said gently, and Stefan sighed with relief. Han moved toward the door and added, "I'll see what I can do and keep you posted."

"Father," Stefan stopped him, "it's good to see you again."

Stefan stood, and Han moved back across the tiny room to embrace him.

"I should go back," Han said, and a smile touched his lips, "but I'll return later."

Stefan nodded, grateful to know that his life was in capable hands.

Stefan had just finished what these people called breakfast when he heard visitors approaching.

"I guess being royalty pays off," the officer on duty said in good humor as he turned the key in the lock. "I've never seen anybody get so much company."

Stefan looked up to see Karl enter the cell, and he couldn't help but smile.

"You call this company?" Stefan asked his jailer lightly. "I call a woman with red hair company. This is more like torture."

The officer laughed and locked the door. Karl stuffed his hands in his pockets and said, "I'm glad to see you're being your old normal self."

Stefan's expression sobered as he sat on the narrow cot and said, "If I didn't make jokes with these people, I'd go insane."

"I've heard the keep's never been so lively. They say since the duke's been here, it's a regular party."

Stefan gave a humorless chuckle and asked, "How many fingers did they cut off to let you come in?"

"None actually," Karl said. "I knew someone who could pull some strings. My cousin. Have you met her?"

"Not recently," Stefan said. "Actually, I haven't seen *my* cousin for several days. It seems taboo to let a man's mistress into his cell more than once or twice a week."

"She seems to be holding up, if you were wondering."

"I was, actually."

"I brought Job up this morning. She was glad to see him. It seems she's staying. Now that your grandmother's got Ericha here, I don't think she'll let her go."

Stefan nodded to acknowledge the news, silently grateful to know that Ericha was here and in Abbi's care.

"Oh, I hate this!" he said strongly as he rose and moved to

596 Elizabeth D. Michaels

the window. "The waiting is torture. The boredom is unbearable. And then I have to sit here and wonder if I'll make it through."

"You can't be serious," Karl said dubiously. "They'll find out who did it. They have to," he added as if he couldn't comprehend accepting anything less.

"And if they don't?" Stefan asked, turning to lean against the wall.

Karl met his eyes, then looked away uncomfortably.

"I have a feeling," Stefan said quietly, "that this is the end for me."

"Don't even say it!" Karl insisted. "You're barely twenty-eight. It's too—"

"There's no good in telling the jury I'm too young to die. They'll just say Johanna was too."

"Who do you suppose did it?" Karl asked.

"I wish I knew." Stefan gave that dry chuckle again. "But that's the big question, isn't it? If we knew, I wouldn't be in this forsaken place." He paused and looked straightly at Karl. "If I don't make it through this, Karl," he stated, "you must look out for her. She loves you, you know."

"I love her, as well," Karl replied, "and I must say I miss her these days. But I'd far rather have her move in with you than be without you."

"It's not in your hands."

"I know, but—"

"She'll need you . . . even if she lives at the castle, you've got to keep touch with her."

"She'll never get over it."

Stefan cleared his throat slightly and turned away. "I'm certain you didn't come to talk about my last will and testament. What's up?"

"As a matter of fact, there is something I thought you should know. I talked to your father about it and . . . well, he didn't think I should tell Ericha. He's probably right."

"What?" Stefan insisted.

"A small mob broke into the house last night."

Stefan said nothing, but his eyes revealed an astonished horror.

"There was very little damage. Luise and Erma are a bit ruffled but . . ."

"What did they want?" Stefan asked, fearing he already knew the answer.

"They were looking for your mistress, of course," Karl stated calmly. "Though the terms they used for her weren't quite so polite."

Stefan's jaw tightened, and Karl saw his fists clench. "What did you do?" he asked.

"I told them she wasn't there. They didn't believe me, so I took them on a guided tour of the house with full cooperation and inspections of every closet. I told them a few jokes and sent them on their merry way."

Stefan sat down carefully and ran both hands through his hair. "Are people in this country really so brash as to—"

"I dare say there are people like that in any country, but these people weren't from Horstberg."

Stefan shot his head up abruptly.

"They're from Kohenswald. They made that very clear."

"Ah, of course," Stefan said satirically, "that quaint neighboring country that I once made a fair alliance with, one that I will never cease to regret. I got nothing but a tramp and a handful of problems. And now I suppose they're bent on some sort of warped revenge or something."

"Probably," Karl said, seeing no point in arguing.

"Too bad I missed the funeral. I would have liked to do a little dance on the coffin."

Karl chuckled. "That would have gone over well with the baron."

"Indeed." Stefan managed a little laugh.

"There's something else," Karl added severely, and Stefan's brow furrowed. "The ring leader was someone I recognized. It took me a while to place him, but I'm relatively certain it was the man you had on trial for beating his wife and kids. I believe Bergen Schmidt was his name."

Stefan shook his head and moaned in frustration. "What a world we live in. No matter how hard a man tries to do the right thing, something always comes back to slap him in the face." He thought of his encounter with Elsbeth Schmidt and almost chuckled from his unintended pun.

"Blast!" Stefan began to pace almost frantically. "I feel so pathetically helpless!"

Seeing Karl's stunned expression, he calmed slightly. "I shouldn't take all of this out on you," Stefan said apologetically.

"If you need to talk," Karl said, "feel free."

"Thank you," Stefan said, turning again to the window, "but what I need is a miracle."

Early the following morning, Stefan's cell was opened and Captain Leichty entered.

"Good morning, Your Grace," he said as if they were sitting down for a meeting in the office. "My men are treating you well, I trust."

"As well as could be expected," he replied. "But we've got to do something about the food." The captain chuckled, but Stefan was quite serious. "If I ever get out of here, Captain, remind me to take care of that."

"You said yourself once, sir, that being in prison was not intended to be a pleasant experience."

"Did I say that?" Stefan managed a chuckle. "Well then, I should be shot for that alone."

The captain looked at the floor as if he didn't know how to respond. He cleared his throat tensely, then said, "There's someone here to see you. This visitor's not family, but I approved it under the circumstances. I just wanted to be certain you were decent. She came to me personally."

"She?" Stefan asked dubiously.

The captain stepped back into the hall where guards stood at the door, and motioned with his arm. He stood aside, and Elsbeth Schmidt stepped timidly into the room. He wanted to tell her he'd recently been thinking about her. The captain turned his back but hovered in the doorway.

"Your Grace," she curtsied slightly, apparently very nervous.

"Mrs. Schmidt," he nodded slightly, wondering what this was all about.

She held out a basket toward him. "Some things for you," she said. "The captain said it would be all right. It's not much, really, but I . . ." Stefan hesitated, and she took a step forward, holding it closer. He took it from her and realized she was trembling as she went on. "I wanted to apologize for my behavior when I saw you last. I was . . . well . . ."

"I understand," he said to ease her stammering. "Truly I do. There is no need to apologize."

"You're very gracious, I must say. I wanted to thank you . . . for everything. Things are much better for us now."

"I'm glad to hear it."

"But I . . . well, I read in the paper just this morning that my husband . . . I mean, he's not anymore, but . . . well, that he was involved in some things that could cause trouble for you . . . for Horstberg; one and the same, I suppose. And I . . . we, the children and I, wanted you to know that we hoped everything turns out all right." She nodded toward the basket. "The children helped with the baking. The cookies taste better than they look."

"I'm certain they will be wonderful." Stefan smiled, fighting the urge to cry. "Thank you. Your offering is more appreciated than you know. And tell the children thank you . . . for me."

Stefan saw tears form in her eyes, and she bit her lip. Her voice cracked as she said, "I bless the day that carriage broke my son's leg, Your Grace. You have saved us. God bless you, sir."

"And you," he said.

She turned to leave, and the captain stepped aside, then she hesitated and added, "Your cousin, Princess Ericha, is a fine lady, Your Grace."

"Yes, she is," he agreed eagerly.

"She was very kind to me, as you were. I pray that all will be well for the two of you in the end."

"Then there is hope for me yet," he said. She smiled, seeming surprised somehow, and the captain escorted her into the hall and the door was locked.

Stefan sat down and stared at the basket in his hands for several minutes. He wondered if Elsbeth Schmidt had any idea how much her kindness meant to him, in this, his darkest hour. He could never put his feelings into words, but somehow her offering was evidence that God was mindful of him, in spite of his shortcomings. Reverently, he folded back the gingham napkin and smiled at the assortment of home-baked treats. Her family's humble contribution warmed him, and he leaned back and tried to forget about reality while he relished in the simple pleasure of savoring every bite—and refusing the dreadful breakfast they brought him a while later.

Chapter Twenty-One
AN ACT OF TREASON

Abbi contemplated and prayed deeply through the night. They needed time. Actually, she thought, they needed a miracle. But for now, they needed time—time to prove Stefan's innocence. Something just had to turn up.

She pondered over her dreams and shuddered to realize that she had known this was going to happen. She might have felt guilty in wondering if she could have prevented it. But in looking back over the years and how her dreams had guided her, she realized that they were more for the benefit of preparing her rather than allowing her to change something that simply could not be prevented. And Abbi wasn't one to wallow over the past. It was Stefan's future that concerned her now, and her entire being was absorbed with finding the answers.

The similarity of these circumstances to what Cameron had gone through astounded her. She wondered if Cameron would have the answers if he were here now. As she pondered deeply on the struggles he'd endured, a hopeful peace settled over her. A part of her almost believed that he *was* there with her. If Stefan had suffered Cameron's fate and Cameron had survived it, then surely the answer to Stefan's problems were the same as Cameron's. At least it would buy them time.

Abbi was so excited that she hurried to tell Georg her idea. Before she reached his room, however, she thought of how discouraged he'd become lately, and her heart filled with compassion. Impulsively she changed her mind and went instead to see Han.

"Good morning, Mother," he said solemnly as she entered the office. "Is there something I can do for you?"

"Not for me," she said, "for Stefan."

"Any ideas?" he said elaborately.

"Not exactly," she said, "but I can't help thinking that perhaps we could find some time for Stefan by recalling what Cameron did in the same situation."

"Then you *do* have an idea."

"My idea," she said, and he caught a sparkle in her eye, "is that you should go to your father for an idea."

Han's eyes widened. "Surely he doesn't want to be burdened with—"

"His mind is as sharp as it has ever been, Han," she stated. "He's been helping do what he can, but in many ways he feels useless. Yet sitting upstairs is the man whose genius saved this country when Cameron was in very similar circumstances. Go talk to him, Han. Let him know that we need him. Ask him what to do."

Han smiled warmly at Abbi and came around the desk to kiss her cheek. "You, Your Grace," he said with sincerity, "are unbelievable. I shudder to think what any one of us would do without your insight and courage."

"Nonsense!" She laughed humbly. "Now run along. Time is precious."

Han smiled, but Abbi could see the deep concern in his eyes. "What is it, Han?" she asked, setting a hand to his face.

Han looked away and blinked several times. "I wonder," he admitted solemnly, "where I went wrong."

"I don't understand."

"Was I so caught up in raising him to be the duke that I overlooked teaching him the most important thing of all?"

"And what is that?" she asked gently.

"It's a difficult thing to explain," he went on. "But when I look back at my own choices, I know that although my concern for Horstberg ran deep, the reasons behind what I did were only because I loved Maggie. I believe what fully rooted the concept for me was the day the castle was overtaken and Cameron said that he would not see his family torn apart—even for Horstberg." His gaze deepened on Abbi. "Did I not teach my son that he was entitled to love and be loved? Not in spite of Horstberg, but because of it?" Before Abbi could answer, he added, fire in his eyes, "Then why did he marry that miserable little tramp to begin with?"

"You mustn't blame yourself for Stefan's choices, Han. Stefan's pain runs deep, and that's something none of us had any control over. I can assure you, however, that Stefan knows now, beyond a doubt, that he is entitled to love and be loved—not in spite of Horstberg, but because of it."

Han sighed, and his chin quivered. He pushed his arms around Abbi and hugged her tightly, and then he left the office, going directly to his father's room. He knocked and entered to find Georg seated near the window with a book.

"Good morning, my boy," Georg said, seeming surprised to see him here.

"You're looking awfully spry this morning," Han said.

Georg made a dubious noise, and Han chuckled.

"Is there something you needed?" Georg asked, and Han sensed that he was doubtful. He blessed Abbi's insight all over again. Why hadn't he seen that his father needed a purpose?

Han sat near his father and leaned his forearms on his thighs, looking directly at him. "How are you feeling these days?" he asked.

"Fine. Why do you ask?"

"I need help," Han said with sincere humility. "Father, they're about to put my son on trial for a crime that I believe he didn't commit. But there is no proof. We need time. Somehow we've just got to have more time. But for the life of me, I don't know what to do."

Han paused thoughtfully and could already see his father's expression changing.

"Can you help me?" Han added, lowering his voice to a plea. "Tell me what to do, Father. Stefan's life is at stake."

Georg was thoughtfully silent a moment, then said, "Give me a while. Let me think about it."

Han nodded and patted his father on the shoulder, and then he left him alone. He had only been in the office for a matter of minutes before Georg came in and sat down in the big chair behind the desk, pushing up his sleeves. Han smiled, waiting to hear what he would say.

"The way I see it," Georg said, "we must consider first things first."

"And what is that?" Han urged.

"We have to take into consideration that he might not make it through this, which makes the most important thing obvious."

"What?" Han asked impatiently, frustrated by his father's calmness.

"The boy needs to get married," he stated and seemed gratified by Han's reaction. Abbi was right. Georg Heinrich was a genius. Han had been so concerned with the problems that he had overlooked something very important.

"The way I see it," Georg went on, "we don't want to leave Ericha to suffer her mother's fate. Stefan needs to give her his name, and then whatever happens, the family rights will be secure. In the same respect, we need adoption papers for the child drawn up immediately, and Stefan's will should be changed."

"That all sounds good," Han said, "but you act as though Stefan's life is over. Isn't there anything else we can do? Didn't Cameron face some similar problems that—"

"You get Stefan married," Georg said as he stood with purpose, "I'll take care of the rest."

"All right," Han said.

"Oh, yes," Georg went on, "I want a statement sent to Kohenswald immediately to let them know you've returned and we're doing everything we can to take care of this. Make it sound very humble and diplomatic. And," he lifted his finger for emphasis, "send Captain Leichty with it personally. No one else. And tell him to spend the night. I believe he has relations there. He could probably use some time off."

Han nodded, briefly puzzled over the instructions but more than willing to do as his father asked. He shook his head in wonder and nearly laughed as his father left the room with the vigor of a man thirty years younger.

Soon after little Cameron went down for a nap, Ericha wandered to Abbi's sitting room. While Abbi aimlessly dabbed oils onto a canvas, Maggie rambled about some of her most recent encounters in their travels. Ericha just looked out the window toward the keep, her heart aching.

All three of them were startled by a loud knock at the door, and then Han strode into the room without waiting for an answer.

"Good afternoon, ladies," he said brightly.

"What have you got to be so cheerful about?" Maggie asked sourly.

Ericha didn't give him a chance to answer. "Have you found something?" she asked. "Will we be able to prove that—"

Han's expression sobered as he shook his head. "No, I'm afraid nothing has changed." He met her eyes briefly, and Ericha wondered if he would ever come to accept her as Maggie had. "Nevertheless, there is something important that my father has brought to my attention." He winked discreetly at Abbi. "And I need your help."

While they waited for him to go on, he stepped slowly toward Ericha. She was surprised when he took both her hands into his, looking at her closely with smiling eyes. "My dear Ericha," he said, "you are well aware that this situation has troubled me. I want you to know now that I am grateful for the love you have given my son that has made up for so much we were unable to give him."

Ericha was so touched she could neither move nor speak.

"I am now taking the liberty," Han went on, "to ask you something on his behalf." Han's eyes nearly glowed as he went down on one knee, and Ericha gasped. "Ericha," he said, "will you marry Stefan . . . today?"

Ericha sucked in her breath so fast she nearly saw stars. A little noise erupted from her throat, something between a laugh and a sob.

"Does that mean yes?" Han chuckled, coming back to his feet. Ericha threw her arms around him and felt gratified by the tight, eager embrace he returned.

The day flew into a whirlwind. Kathe's wedding gown was pulled out of the closet, and after the three women had a good cry over it, the fit was declared near-perfect. While the circumstances hadn't changed, Ericha couldn't deny that she had been blessed with a miracle.

The duke's solicitors were called in, and all the necessary documents were drawn up or altered. Captain Leichty was sent out as requested, seeming appreciative to have some time away. All those involved were sent for, including the Bishop of Horstberg.

With all of that done, Han let Theodor know that the duke would be needing his assistance, and then he summoned four officers of the Guard to accompany him to Stefan's cell.

"Get up, boy!" Han shouted before they reached the door, and Stefan wondered if they'd just decided to shoot him and get it over with.

The door was unlocked, and Han motioned elaborately for Stefan to exit. He hesitated only slightly, then moved out of the cell and walked next to Han down the hallway with officers in front and behind.

"Where are we going?" Stefan asked.

"You're going to get cleaned up a little." Han waved his hand comically in front of his nose. "You're not going anywhere smelling like you've been in the keep for a month."

Stefan wondered if his father's pleasant mischief was an attempt to mask how bad the situation really was. Wherever they were going, it was obvious that Stefan still did not have his freedom.

"Being in the keep has not prevented me from bathing regularly," Stefan retorted, "I can assure you."

Stefan squinted when they came out into the courtyard. He'd forgotten how bright the sun could actually be. He was led into the main entrance of the castle, then up to his bedroom.

"Make yourself presentable," Han said. "I'll be back to get you shortly."

Theodor was waiting to help him bathe and dress while two guards stood outside in the hall, and two in the sitting room.

"Do you have any idea what's going on, Theodor?" Stefan asked while Theodor efficiently trimmed his hair.

"Can't say I do," he replied, "but I was threatened to not let you out of my sight until you're presentable."

"Why do I have to wear that thing?" Stefan asked with disdain as he was helped into his uniform.

"Your father said it was official."

"Oh, great," Stefan said with sarcasm, "they probably have the firing squad waiting."

Theodor chuckled but said nothing. When Stefan was ready, Theodor slipped away, and Stefan nearly went mad, pacing the floor and staring out the window.

When Han returned, Stefan was escorted by his guards down the stairs and through a series of hallways. He was surprised when they came to the door of the castle chapel, and he looked at his father sharply. "What is this? Last rights?"

Han only pushed open the door. Stefan entered hesitantly. A quick glance told him that nearly everyone that mattered to him was here. Abbi and Georg. His parents. Hannah and her husband. Karl and Luise. Rusty. But where was Ericha? Was this something she couldn't be a part of? He turned to his father in question. Han only motioned him toward the front of the chapel, looking especially sober.

As Stefan moved down the aisle, he was aware of all eyes on him, and the bishop rose to greet him. He could only figure this was some kind of religious service regarding his impending doom. While Stefan had attended a Sunday service in this chapel every week for as long as he could remember, and he regularly consulted with his religious leaders on certain matters, he was having difficulty at the moment in wanting much to do with religion. Perhaps he felt like God had let him down one time too many. Or more likely, he was wondering if God would intervene on behalf of an adulterer.

Stefan went briefly down on one knee before the bishop in greeting as he always did. He wondered if they were perhaps hoping he would confess to the crime and save them all a lot of trouble. As Stefan came to his feet, he heard the chapel doors open behind him. He turned to look over his shoulder, noticing first the four officers standing guard there to remind him of his imprisoned state. He glanced quickly at his loved ones, wishing he could just put his arms around them each in turn.

Theodor stepped through the door, and then Stefan turned and became aware of Karl standing at his side. He discreetly leaned over and whispered to Karl, "I wish someone would tell me what the hell is going on."

"Watch your language," Karl whispered back. "Remember where you are."

Stefan caught a subtle sparkle of amusement in his eyes. He glanced around again and realized that nobody looked terribly glum. Then his eye caught movement at the door.

"Merciful heaven," he murmured.

"Now, that's more like it," Karl said wryly.

Stefan's breath quickened and his heart began to pound. He met Ericha's eyes, and she smiled serenely. The elaborate white gown and flowers in her hair could only mean one thing, and his vision of her blurred as moisture burned into his eyes. Karl nudged him with an elbow and whispered, "It's about time you married her, don't you think?"

Stefan couldn't suppress a breathy chuckle. He blinked and discreetly wiped away his tears as Ericha moved forward with Theodor. There was no music to guide them up the aisle, no flowers, no pomp or grandeur. But Stefan's heart swelled with an emotion mirrored in Ericha's eyes as Theodor placed her hand into his and they knelt solemnly before the bishop to be married.

Karl produced a ring at the appropriate moment, and it slid easily onto Ericha's finger. Ericha cried when he kissed her to seal their vows, and they embraced desperately.

Stefan felt hard pressed to keep his emotion under control as everyone present offered congratulations and tearful embraces. The family did well in expressing their joy over the event, but there was a dark cloud hanging over them, knowing it wouldn't be done this way if Stefan was not a wanted man.

They all went to the drawing room for champagne, and the four guards hovered magnetically near Stefan. Little Cameron was brought in, and Stefan laughed with tears in his eyes as Ruthild took the baby straight to him. Cameron was fascinated with all the shiny things attached to his father's uniform. Ericha remained close at his side, trying not to think about anything beyond this moment.

When it had quieted somewhat, Karl and Luise approached them. "I want to tell you," Luise said gently, "both of you, how sorry I am for the way I reacted when . . . well, you know. It just caught me off guard, and . . ." She smiled. "I just wanted to say that."

"I understand," Ericha said, giving her a warm embrace. "Really, I do. It's forgotten."

Han interrupted to say, "We have business to attend to."

Ericha panicked, not wanting to let Stefan out of her sight. She was relieved when Han motioned toward her. "It involves you, as well. Come along."

Maggie took little Cameron and embraced Stefan desperately. Little was said as he shared an equivalent embrace with Abbi and Hannah. He shook Karl's hand and their eyes met. He touched little Cameron's face and hurried away, Ericha at his side, guards in front and behind.

Han led them to the office where Georg was waiting. The

guards waited outside the door, and they were all seated around the huge desk. Han slapped a paper in front of Stefan and stuffed a pen into his hand.

"Sign it!" he insisted.

"What is it?" he asked, putting on his glasses.

"Adoption document." Stefan looked briefly puzzled, and Han clarified comically by pointing to certain words on the page. "See here. It says: Cameron Erich Lokberg-du Woernig will become Cameron Erich *Stefan* Lokberg-du Woernig *Heinrich*—as you sign it."

At Stefan's questioning gaze, he added, "Ericha approved the adding of your name. By tradition, it honors his bloodline."

Stefan turned to smile at Ericha, and she laughed as he scrawled his signature across the document. After three more signatures on various documents, Han put a lengthy one before him and said, "This is the last one."

"And what is it?" Stefan asked.

Han hesitated, then said soberly, "It's your will." All was silent until he added more lightly, "It leaves nothing to the family Von Bindorf of Kohenswald, and everything to your wife and son, who will be heir to Horstberg by double lineage."

Stefan sighed and signed the document, and then he threw the pen down on the desk.

"Now what?" he asked, setting his glasses on the desk. "Have they set a trial date yet?"

"No," Georg said soberly, "though we can't put it off much longer."

"But," Han added jubilantly, "not to worry. Eat, drink, and be merry, for—"

"Han," Georg said sternly, "that is a very poor choice of cliches."

"Yes," he said, "I must admit, but . . . well, come along. Dinner for two is waiting upstairs. We've made arrangements for you to spend tonight in your own bedroom."

Han grinned when Stefan and Ericha smiled at each other with obvious relief at having some time together. "After all," he added, "it is your wedding night. Of course, the doors will be guarded, but you can stay until nine in the morning."

"Wait," Georg said as they stood to leave the office. "Ericha, why don't you go on upstairs. I'd like a word alone with Stefan."

Han and Ericha left, and Stefan wondered what Georg wanted to discuss that he wouldn't with Han present.

"Sit down," Georg said, and he did. "I want you to know that we are doing everything possible to prove your innocence. But it doesn't look good. What we need is time, and we haven't got it. We are torn in wanting to spare your life, and doing what is politically necessary. You must understand."

Stefan nodded firmly.

"What I have to say to you, Stefan, must never be uttered to anyone. Not Abbi. Not Ericha. Not your parents. No one. Do you understand?"

Stefan nodded again, feeling his heart quicken.

"If they have no knowledge of this, they will remain genuinely innocent, and there is no chance they can be accused of treason."

"What are you saying?" Stefan asked breathlessly.

"I'm saying this—and I will say nothing more. The doors to your bedroom will be guarded, but the room holds secrets that you're well aware of." Stefan's eyes widened. "Captain Leichty is the only official who is aware of those secrets, and he is gone for the night. He left before anyone knew you would be out of the keep tonight. We've been blessed to have a light winter and an early thaw. I sent your friend Karl to the lodge this afternoon with enough provisions to last a few weeks. It took him a while to dig out the pass, but he managed. We'll send more supplies if necessary."

Georg finished abruptly, and Stefan hardly knew what to say. "Why?" he asked feebly.

"We need time," Georg stated. "This is the only way we'll get it. Your judgment can't possibly be any worse than it is now. It's what Cameron did. And it worked."

"But what about you, Georg? This is treason."

Georg laughed like Stefan hadn't heard in years. "At my age, Stefan, the game of treason for the sake of my grandson's life could be very exciting." He lifted his finger and added, "No one else must know . . . for their sakes."

Stefan nodded again. He embraced his grandfather and thanked him.

"God go with you," Georg said with strength, and Stefan was escorted to his bedroom.

Ericha turned abruptly from the window when Stefan entered the room. He leaned against the door with a sigh, and they watched each other silently for a long moment.

"Is something wrong?" she asked.

Stefan shook his head while he unhooked the coat of his uniform. "I was just trying to comprehend it. We are married, Ericha."

"Yes," she smiled brightly, "I am Mrs. Stefan Heinrich. Do you have any idea what that means to me?"

"Yes," he smiled in return, albeit sadly, "I believe I do. It's nice to be alone with you and not feel like I'm doing something wrong."

"That's all in the past now."

"The past." He chuckled humorlessly, throwing his coat over a chair. "Our blemished past together is likely *all* we'll have together."

Ericha wanted to protest, but she didn't know what to say. Stefan glanced around the room. He chuckled satirically and sat down. "It's just like her; even dead, she keeps me bound to her like a plague upon my soul. She's getting her revenge, isn't she?"

"Stefan." Ericha said gently, but he didn't look at her. "You must not destroy yourself with resentments. She's gone now, and it will only hurt you further." He turned toward her. "You said you would not let her destroy you. Let's not waste this precious time with—"

"Yes," he interrupted, his voice still bitter, "this is likely the last night you and I will ever spend together as husband and wife."

"You're innocent," she said calmly, fighting to hide her fear, for his sake, "and they'll find a way to prove it. But whatever happens, Stefan, you must come to terms with it. You must find a way to be at peace."

Stefan sighed slowly. "That almost sounds like Abbi du Woernig talking."

Ericha smiled humbly, and they sat down to share the meal that had been brought up for them. They ate mostly in silence while Ericha attempted to comprehend the reality that she was his wife. She refused to even think about the other realities they were facing. When they'd finished eating, she asked, "Do you need to talk?" Watching him closely, she sensed a great deal of pent-up emotion in him.

Stefan set his finger thoughtfully to his chin and sighed. "Later," he said. "Come here, Ericha Heinrich."

She laughed at the sound of her new name, and he stood to greet her as she came toward him. The way he kissed her reminded Ericha of that first time in the forest. She felt the same desperation and urgency, as if this were the only moment they would ever share. He loved her with the same urgency, and afterwards held her so close she felt a part of him.

Ericha fell asleep and woke to see that it was dark, but a lamp had been lit. Stefan was sitting at the foot of the bed playing with Cameron, and she wondered when Ruthild had brought him in.

"I was just about to wake you," he said when she sat up. "I think he's hungry." Ericha smiled, and then she nearly cried.

Stefan held his son against his shoulder, squeezing his eyes shut in an effort to block out the pain of wondering if he would ever have the opportunity to do this again. Stefan handed Cameron over to his mother and watched with intrigue as she nursed the child and he gradually fell asleep.

"Ericha," Stefan said as she laid Cameron carefully on the bed.

"Yes, my love."

"Ericha . . . whatever happens, I love you. You must remember it."

She gazed up at him fearfully. "The last time you put it that way, I believe you had no intention of ever seeing me again."

Stefan looked away like a guilty child, and Ericha was certain he knew something she didn't.

"What's going on?" she insisted.

"Nothing is going on," he replied almost sharply. "I'm wanted for murder! The trial can't be put off. There are few choices left to me. That is what's going on!"

"I love you, Stefan," she said gently. "Whatever happens, you must remember it."

"I'm sorry," he whispered, moving into her arms. "Don't let me take these fears out on you."

"What are you afraid of?" she whispered.

"I'm not so much afraid of dying," he replied, "as I am of losing you. Our time together has been so brief. I feel like I've been cheated. Even Grandpapa got to see his children grow up."

"You admitted once that you believed he would be with Abbi again someday. Surely if God exists," she whispered reverently, "He will give us an opportunity to be together again. You must turn your fate over to Him."

Stefan lifted his head to look at her, his eyes wide with intrigue. He kissed her warmly and felt peace seep into him as she slept again in his arms.

The lamp burned itself out while Stefan stared toward the ceiling, wondering what would become of his life. Even if he did succeed tonight in getting away, he couldn't run and hide forever. His grandfather's example had taught him that. There was no life for his wife and son that way. *Ericha is my wife,* he reminded himself. In spite of it all, he was grateful for that. But if he couldn't be with them, what was life worth for him?

The clock on the wall chimed three, and he knew he had to get out of there. Hesitantly, he drew himself away from Ericha, pausing to ponder her face in the darkness before he kissed her gently on the brow. He dressed quietly and gathered some extra clothes into a bundle that he tied onto his back before he donned his hooded cloak.

Gently he ran his fingers over little Cameron's wispy hair, and then he kissed Ericha again and quietly opened the passageway, lit a torch, then closed it again. His heartache deepened as he moved stealthily through it. He thought briefly that it seemed more drafty in here than usual, but his mind was too caught up in what he was leaving behind to think further on it.

Stefan doused the torch before stepping out into the night air. He hadn't known for sure what to expect but was glad to find a horse tied there. Georg never missed a detail, he thought as he mounted. Carefully he glanced in all directions before breaking into a gallop toward the forest trail.

Before Ericha was completely awake, she shifted in the bed, searching for a familiar warmth. She found Cameron sleeping close beside her and moved the other direction, only to find the bed empty and cold.

Abruptly she sat up and surveyed the room. Nothing. "Oh no!" she whispered and jumped up to search further. But her eye caught something tacked to the mirror frame, and she knew there was no need. With a stark contrast of emotions, she pulled the paper down to read: *Forgive me, Stefan.*

Ericha wadded the paper in her fist and choked back the tears that burned in her eyes. Her joy that he might have really made it out of here was overridden by fear of what would happen if he was caught. And then there was the pain in wondering if she would ever see him again either way.

A knock at the door startled her. Thinking quickly, she pulled on a wrapper and scooped little Cameron into her arms before she answered it.

"What is it?" she asked the two guards before her.

"Twenty minutes," he said politely, "before His Grace needs to return."

Ericha knew there was no point in pretenses. And she knew it could cause trouble for her if she didn't appear cooperative with the law. Even Stefan with all his power could not alter the law.

"I fear he has already left," she stated, and one of them barked orders as they all burst into the room through every door.

"What happened?" one of them insisted.

"I woke up and he was gone," she stated with little emotion. "He told me nothing."

Ericha didn't wait to hear their cursing or see them tear the room apart in their search. She went directly to her grandmother's sitting room and entered in a flurry.

"What is it?" Abbi asked, standing quickly from her breakfast.

"Oh, Grandmama," she cried, "he's gone."

"What?"

"He escaped in the night."

Ericha saw in Abbi's eyes a brief contest between the Duchess of Horstberg and Stefan's grandmother. But it was the latter who put her arms around both Ericha and little Cameron as she whispered, "God go with him."

When they were dressed, Ericha followed Abbi to the office, carrying little Cameron with her. They arrived just after the captain had been informed that the duke had escaped. Ericha had to fight to keep a sober expression as Abbi burst in unannounced and nearly shouted at Han, "What is the meaning of this? Why wasn't that passageway guarded?"

Han shrugged his shoulders sheepishly and replied, "I just didn't think about it. I didn't realize he even knew it was there."

They continued to argue in front of the captain, and Ericha knew it was all for the sake of appearances. They could not outwardly condone Stefan's escape, and Ericha knew that's why Stefan had most likely told no one of his plans.

Georg came into the office to cease the drama and excused Captain Leichty with some stern-sounding orders.

When only family was present, Abbi whispered, "I can see it in your eyes, Georg. You had something to do with this."

"Who me?" He all but smirked. "Nonsense! I'm too old to be

up to such mischief. By the way, Han, I've had an urge to spend some time with the pigeons. Great hobby. I was just up there as a matter of fact. In the tower, I mean. We received the strangest message."

He smiled and held up a tiny note between his fingers. Abbi grabbed it and read silently, before handing it to Ericha, and a knowing smile was passed around the group. It read simply: *Here and all is well,* written in Stefan's hand.

"Destroy it," Abbi said, and Georg nodded. She lifted her finger and added, "We will keep up the proper appearances and pray that he can stay hidden until this is over."

They all nodded, and it seemed that things were looking up.

Han took the baby from Ericha and started to play with him on the desk while Georg and Abbi talked over some things of little interest to Ericha. Han was still playing when Georg and Abbi excused themselves, so Ericha made herself comfortable and watched, enjoying the opportunity to be with Stefan's father.

So far they had exchanged very little personal conversation, and though the events of yesterday had seemed to put estrangements behind them, she wasn't sure at times how to take him. She sensed he still saw her more as the other woman in Stefan's life rather than Erich's daughter. She smiled as Han sat Cameron in his lap and pulled the chair close to the desk.

"Now," he said authoritatively, "this is where it all happens. You're never too young to learn the trade. This is a pen. No, you're not supposed to eat it. You're supposed to write with it. You act more like your father every day.

"Now pay attention! There's a lot of paperwork involved here, and the secretary can't do it all, so if you want to be duke someday, you've got to get on the ball. Are you listening to me?"

Han chuckled a little and pulled up his sleeves in an elaborate gesture to indicate he was really getting down to business in training this child here and now. Ericha noted something unusual on Han's left arm. Before she recognized it as scars, a feeling hit her so strongly that she caught her breath aloud.

"What's the matter?" Han said quickly.

"Nothing," she said breathlessly. "It's just that . . ." Their eyes met, and he urged her on by the intensity in his expression.

"Well, before I realized who my father was, I would sometimes feel certain things that I credited to be a vivid imagination, until I realized when Grandmama told me stories from the past that what I had been feeling was, well . . . I can't explain it."

"I think I understand," Han said easily, but there was still question in his eyes.

"I felt that way just now," she said. "And I have to wonder if it's just my imagination or if . . . Would you think me rude if I asked how your arm became scarred?"

Han glanced toward the arm, and then his eyes shot to Ericha and widened. His expression softened, and he leaned back in the chair, resetting Cameron on his lap. "The scars are from burns." He paused, and his eyes penetrated her. "My shirt caught fire when I was pulling your father's body out of the room where he died."

In the following silence, Ericha felt the sensation within her deepen. "Tell me about him," she said gently.

Han chuckled with a distant look in his eyes. "He was incredible. Life has just never been the same without Erich. Over twenty years and there still isn't a day when I don't wish he was here."

Han began his next discourse with an "I remember the time when . . ." and Ericha stayed in the office until it was time to eat, discovering a side of her father that she'd never heard from Stefan or Abbi. To Han, Erich was the funniest man in the world. Their life together as friends had been full of fun and laughter in spite of the struggles they'd endured.

Ericha was touched by Han's affection for her father, and appreciated this opportunity to know him better. Before they left the office together, Han embraced her warmly. She could almost believe a part of her father was with them.

Abbi sat up abruptly, bringing herself out of sleep as if thunder had cracked overhead. She felt cold and clammy, and her breath was short and labored. Her dream had been so real that fresh fear enveloped her in remembering it, a fear that only intensified with the realization that many such dreams had come true.

"Oh, no," she said aloud, going instinctively to Georg's room. She needed him.

Georg's presence was a comfort to her, but telling him about the dream only intensified the fear she felt. "The surroundings were vague," she said, "but I could see clearly that Han was holding a gun, and I seemed to realize it was pointed at Stefan." Georg looked surprised, but he said nothing, so she went on.

"He drew back his arms slightly. He was hesitating. He felt afraid. But he seemed to gain courage and pointed it directly again, then cocked it. Again he withdrew slightly, then pointed again. Stefan was expressionless as Han pulled the trigger. Smoke came from the barrel, and I woke up."

Georg pulled Abbi securely against him and reassured her that it was only a dream. "Han would never do anything to hurt Stefan," he said gently. "You know that as well as I."

Abbi justified in her mind that he was right, but the following night brought the same dream. Again she woke up before Stefan fell, but somehow she knew he fell.

Chapter Twenty-Two
AT THE HANDS OF JUSTICE

It took little time for word of Stefan's escape to filter not only through Horstberg, but to Kohenswald as well. The family Von Bindorf became furious that justice for Johanna's death had not been met, and then Horstberg became seized with something that even Georg had not predicted.

The first sign of it came as a roaring howl in the depths of the night. The fanatics of Kohenswald were quick to prey upon the weak-minded in Horstberg, and an angry mob became determined to see that justice was met. The name Stefan Heinrich became blasphemous to these people. They were convinced that more could be done to hunt the killer down, though they themselves were as ignorant as the Guard in where to find him. They took out their barbaric vengeance by swarming around the castle gates, relentlessly inflicting their roaring and ranting upon the Guard and the royal family.

The Guard succeeded repeatedly in temporarily dispersing the groups, but inevitably they returned, their numbers increased, their anger more heated. It was evident they had rationalized enough to believe that if the duke was responsible for his wife's death, he was also responsible for every other problem in their lives, political or not, and Stefan's blood became a symbol of some fantastically higher life that they might achieve by shedding it.

Georg called the family together to discuss the situation. Hannah was there as well, since he'd sent for her family to come to the castle at the first sign of trouble. He explained that history was full of such mobs. It typically happened when the right—or rather the wrong—ingredients were mixed. He wasn't sure how to handle it, and no one seemed to have any suggestions that would make any difference. It appeared that, unlike with Cameron, Stefan's escape had not been the answer.

They agreed it was most important to keep Stefan well hidden for now. But Georg said, and they knew he was right, that if this continued, time would eventually run out. The responsibility to the people of Horstberg was something that had to be weighed. There were already homes and shops that had been troubled with vandalism as a result of this. And they knew it was likely to get worse.

"We must find a way to prove Stefan's innocence!" Abbi insisted, but all was silent in response.

Han felt obligated to say, "I fear that's not possible."

"Are you implying," Abbi asked sternly, "that he *did* kill Johanna?"

"Whether or not he did makes little difference at this point. Those people want blood, and the evidence is just too strong against Stefan."

All was silent again, and Ericha sank deep in her chair as despair overcame her. She felt suddenly uncomfortable and looked up to see a room full of empathetic eyes turned her way.

"There is no way of knowing what will happen," Abbi stated. "We can only pray for a miracle and hope that time will lessen their vengeance rather than deepen it. In the meantime, Ericha should be with Stefan."

Ericha looked up with hope filling her expression, but the faces greeting her were severe. She knew Abbi was saying that Stefan's days were numbered.

Nevertheless, arrangements were made quietly, and Ericha's heart filled with joy to think that she would be able to see him again. She and Abbi had a long talk alone the evening before she was to leave, while murmurings from the mobs filtered through the high windows. With Abbi's advice, Ericha made up her mind to be cheerful and positive for Stefan, and do her best to make this time memorable and happy for him. With courage, she set herself to do this, trying to ignore her fears that she would be a widow before the month was out.

In the deepest hours of the night, Ericha moved carefully down the passageway, holding a torch high while Han walked just ahead of her, carrying little Cameron in his arms. At one point she felt a subtle breeze brush her, and the flame wavered slightly. She was going to comment about it to Han, but he was moving on ahead and she hurried to keep up with him.

It was a relief to come into the open air, and she wasn't surprised to see horses waiting, already loaded with their things. Ericha mounted and Han gave her the baby, and then he mounted himself and rode slowly ahead.

The trek up the mountain seemed slow, but it couldn't be helped when traveling with pack horses and a baby. It seemed forever before they arrived at the lower meadow, and she was grateful that Han was there to carry little Cameron through the ridge.

Ericha felt flutters of excitement at the prospect of seeing Stefan again. They approached the lodge quietly, and Han took the baby so that she could dismount again. He whispered, "This ought to give him a good scare."

Han returned Cameron to his mother, pulled a key from his pocket, and turned it in the door. He pushed it open loudly and shouted, "Stefan, wake up!"

Ericha hesitated behind Han, but she caught a glimpse of Stefan running onto the landing as he called back, "What on earth are you doing here?"

Han laughed, and the indication that nothing was wrong made Stefan slump against the rail with a sigh of relief.

"You scared me to death," he added. "I was sound asleep forty-five seconds ago." He had apparently slept in his clothes.

"Just testing your reflexes, boy." Han grinned. "Actually, I thought you could use some cheering up, so I brought you a bottle of wine."

"Oh," he replied sarcastically, "just what I need. I'll get drunk and let them—"

"It's not to get drunk on," Han said. "It's to celebrate with."

Stefan wanted to ask what was worth celebrating, but Han stepped aside and Ericha moved into the common room, pushing back the hood of her cloak.

"Hello, Stefan," she said softly in response to his widening eyes. He nearly flew down the stairs to take her in his arms, and little Cameron became consumed by his parents' embrace.

"Ericha. My Ericha," he whispered, "I wondered if I would ever see you again."

Han cleared his throat in mock disgust, then excused himself to unload the horses.

"Grandmama insisted," she said gently. "She said that we should be together."

"Why?" Stefan asked, his eyes narrow.

"You know," Han said breathlessly, coming into the lodge with an enormous armload, "babies sure take a lot of stuff!"

"You should know." Stefan laughed.

"Yes, I should," Han replied as he set it down in one heap on the floor. "I was hauling stuff around for you once. You can hug her later. Right now let's get her moved in."

Stefan laughed to realize she was staying for more than a little while, and he went to help his father. When that was done, Han sat them down with brief but careful instructions. He embraced them both, then coddled over Cameron for a minute or two, and left in order to return before dawn.

When they were alone, Stefan watched Ericha silently across the table where they sat. Quietly he said, "Once again, you are an answer to my prayers."

"What have you been praying for?" she asked.

"A chance to live out my days with you—however few they may be."

Ericha bit her lip and looked down.

"I love you, Ericha," he said with strength.

She looked up at him and smiled, trying to be happy for him. "Haven't you heard?" she said, holding up her left hand to admire the ring. "I'm Mrs. Heinrich."

Stefan laughed. "Yes, I believe I heard something to that effect . . . but only briefly."

She smiled, but he added soberly, "Why did Grandmama insist?"

"You know Grandmama," she said airily as she stood to put some of the baby's things away in the kitchen.

"Ericha," he followed, "you're evading the question."

"Yes, I am," she said cheerfully.

"Why?" he asked.

"Because I did not come here to dwell on our problems. You know how Grandmama is. There's no need to explain."

"Yes," he said, leaning against the counter and folding his arms, "I know how she is. She wants us to be together because she's afraid this is the only chance we'll ever have."

Ericha looked up at him sharply, confirming his assumption.

"That's what I thought," he said with a breathy, humorless chuckle. "What's going on?" he asked, but she made no response.

Stefan threw his hands up, then pushed them through his hair. "Every message I get says: 'We're doing all we can. Everything's fine.'" Ericha stepped back as his voice raised angrily. "Why won't anyone tell me what's going on?"

"Because there's no point in it," she retorted.

Stefan grasped the deeper meaning fully, and he sat down. His brow creased. He swallowed hard and took a deep breath.

Ericha sat near him and searched deeply for encouraging words. "No one will ever find us here," she said with a note of jubilance in her voice. "The family will make certain we have everything we need. We have each other. We can be happy."

Stefan's expression didn't change. "So, that's it," he stated. "I have received my sentence. Guilty. Banished for life." Stefan tugged at his hair with his hand. "I have to wonder why I am only allowed so much in my life. First I had everything except you, and I was expected to be content. Now I have you and nothing else."

They watched each other for a long moment. There was so much to say, so many emotions that needed venting. But Ericha didn't know where to begin. She couldn't console him. He was right. He had lost everything. She could tell him that at least they were together. They were married. They had little Cameron. He was alive. But words seemed trite. She couldn't convince him to be happy or content with this, so she only reached out and took his hand, trying to convey with her eyes all she felt.

"There is a scale," he said. "On one side is you, and on the other an enormous weight, centered with my dominion." He paused and sighed. "I will take you. And yes, you are right. We can be happy."

He smiled, but still his eyes were sad.

Days went by peaceably for the little family in the mountain lodge, but there was an ever-increasing foreboding as Stefan sensed that his valley was not at peace. He thought often of his grandfather being here for those years when the situation was not unlike this. He recalled the stories well but wondered if Cameron du Woernig had felt this kind of internal anguish.

Most of the time it was easy to pretend that everything was all right, and he treasured each moment he could spend with his wife and son. But there were moments when reality hit him in the pit of his stomach, and he had the urge to sit down and cry like a child. With these feelings, he wondered again: did his grandfather ever know them?

Stefan's nights were often sleepless, but he was grateful for Ericha's nearness and the silent comfort she offered. It had seemed well to avoid the subject as Ericha had insisted, but a night came when Stefan couldn't bear it any longer. Realizing Ericha was awake as well, he pulled her close to him and whispered his innermost fears. She comforted him with gentle words then gave him solace with her love, but it didn't erase his fear that a time would come when those fears would have to be faced. He knew he hadn't killed Johanna. But he had committed adultery. Hadn't he known the consequences could be severe? Yet he'd never comprehended that the decision might cost him his life. In desperation, he pulled Ericha against him, knowing that she was worth it, and he blessed the day she had come into his life.

"Stefan," she said gently, "let's leave Horstberg. We could go to the Black Forest—anywhere. We'll change our names. We'll start a new life . . . together. I have all that money put away. Georg could get it to me. We could manage somehow. I know we could."

Stefan said nothing for a full minute. While he was trying to protest the idea, he couldn't deny his intrigue with it. He leaned up on one elbow to look down at her through the darkness.

"What of Horstberg?" he asked.

"Horstberg has already lost you," she replied.

"Do you think we could leave our family behind?"

"What are they if you are dead?" she countered.

"Do you think our pictures would not be in every newspaper in Europe?" he asked. "Wouldn't we always be fugitives?"

"Stefan," she touched his face, "we would be together. We'll be careful. With time it will die down."

Stefan became thoughtful again, until he said in a whisper, "Keep talking, Ericha. Talk me into it."

Ericha pulled him close, feeling a surge of hope. "We'll think about it," she said, "and plan carefully what to do."

Stefan nodded against her shoulder and willed his heart to calm down. He never would have dreamed that he'd be forced to choose between Horstberg and his life. But at least he had a choice.

Little Cameron awoke in the dark hours of the morning, and Ericha rose to change him. She was surprised to feel Stefan's hand come to her shoulder as she laid the baby back down. He turned his attention to his son, and with reverence and admiration, he caressed the child's head while his eyes betrayed the ache he felt inside.

"Come along," Ericha said gently. "I'll fix some coffee, and we can talk."

Stefan followed her to the common room and sat silently at the table while Ericha poured out the steaming liquid into two cups and sat across from him. She knew how he felt and longed to tell him that everything would be all right, but in her heart she wondered if it would be. She felt hope in the possibility of leaving Bavaria together, but even that had such a bitter loss.

Stefan pushed the cup aside and put his head against his forearm in a gesture of despair. Ericha reached out to take his hand, but a loud knock came to the door. Her heart quickened as Stefan shot his head up fearfully.

Stefan knew how it felt to be a fugitive as he met Ericha's eyes and they both wondered if he had been found. He nodded toward her and she knew what he wanted her to do.

"Who is it?" she called.

"It's me, Rusty."

Stefan's body nearly slumped in relief, and Ericha called, "Are you alone?"

"Yes," he called back, "yes, of course."

Ericha went to the door and unlocked it, moving aside for Rusty to sheepishly enter the room.

"What on earth are you doing here?" Stefan insisted as he stood. "You nearly scared me to my grave." He wanted to scold Rusty, but he had to admit it was good to see him.

"I'm sorry, sir," Rusty said, fidgeting with his hat, then moving it to one hand in order to scratch his head. "I just took a chance that you would . . . well, be here. It is important. I . . . well, I felt certain there was something you should . . . well, something you should know, and . . ."

Stefan was used to waiting for Rusty to spit out his thoughts, but he felt particularly impatient as he and Ericha were both seated again and Rusty stammered on.

"I would have never believed you'd get into this kind of situation, sir. I mean that . . ." He looked embarrassed by his choice of wording. "It really is too bad that things went this way and . . . well, it's not something that . . ."

When Stefan realized he was stammering more than usual, he felt a prickly sensation at the back of his neck and couldn't help the sharp tone, "Out with it, man! It's barely daylight and it's already been a long day."

"Yes, of course. Like I said, I'm sorry to catch you off guard this way. Perhaps I should have gone to your father with this but . . . well, I thought I could talk to you more easily and . . . You know, we have known each other for so long and . . ."

Stefan sighed, and Rusty looked down guiltily. As if he was trying hard to muster the courage to get something out, he drew back his shoulders. "You see, sir, I know that . . ."

Hearing a noise outside, Stefan's expression turned fearful, and Rusty stopped, looking around expectantly. They all heard something again, and Stefan insisted quietly, "Are you certain you came alone?"

"Yes," he said with panic in his voice. "Of course. I would never—"

Ericha cried out as the door flew open, and it took only seconds for eight uniformed officers to file in and surround Stefan, taking his arms firmly.

"You fool!" Stefan exclaimed to Rusty, who nearly cowered from his tone of voice. "You let them follow you!"

Ericha gripped the back of a chair, and her knuckles turned white as Stefan met her eyes.

"The lodge is surrounded, Your Grace," Captain Leichty informed him. "You will need to come with us."

Stefan angrily glanced toward the hold on his arms and insisted, "I can go of my own accord."

The captain nodded toward the two men who held him, and they released their grip. Ericha saw the change in Stefan's eyes as he resigned himself to his fate. The hope of any life together beyond this crumbled before them.

Stefan was barely aware of Rusty lumbering out of the lodge before he met Ericha's eyes and unbearable emotion passed between them. "A moment with my wife," Stefan said to the captain, who nodded in reply. He held out his arms, and Ericha flew into them.

"We will find a way," she whispered, touching his face desperately. Stefan tried to smile from her encouragement, but despair seeped into her from his unleashed kiss. A moment later she was alone.

Ericha felt no panic to realize she was alone with little Cameron. She knew that Han would figure it out soon enough and make certain they were well. It was Stefan her heart ached for. She truly wondered if his life was over.

After Stefan was escorted carefully through the ridge that had once guarded a secret harbored for generations, he was ordered onto a horse and his wrists were bound behind him. The troop of more than a dozen men remained silent as they rode single file down the forest trail toward Horstberg. Stefan wondered if it was as humiliating to these men to have to hunt down the man who had once ruled them as it was for him to be in this situation.

Emerging from the forest, the captain immediately gave orders to surround the prisoner in a tight-knit circle as they rode, and be prepared for the worst. Fear crept into Stefan. He wanted to ask the reason, but he knew it was probably one of those secrets the family had been keeping from him. And he figured his knowledge probably made little difference at this point.

Riding through the edge of town toward the castle hill, Stefan became aware of people's interest, and he did his best to remain at attention, as did the Guard around him. The situation was far too humiliating to do anything else. But he was well aware of the wide variety of expressions greeting them. There were all degrees of compassion or sympathy, which contrasted strongly to those that held none at all. Gradually a crowd began to gather and follow. Rallied on by a bold few, they became louder and more brash as their numbers grew.

Stefan briefly squeezed his eyes shut in an effort to block out the ranting aimed at him, where the terms adulterer, traitor, and murderer were the gentler ones.

Stefan knew the situation of his country and his people well, and it was easy for him to figure where the basis of all this had come from. But he wondered how far out of hand it would get. He was aware of Captain Leichty whispering something to the man at his side, who galloped off immediately toward the castle. Knowing common procedures, Stefan was certain that he'd gone to get more men. Was this situation really going to get that bad? Stefan only had to think it and several men came in unison beneath the horses' bellies of those who protected him, and suddenly all was chaos.

Without use of his hands, Stefan was completely helpless as the mob overran the surrounding Guard and he was dragged from the horse onto the ground. There was no way to describe the fear he experienced as his life began to drown in a pool of angry eyes, a chorus of resentful chants, and blow after blow of self-appointed justice. He wondered what he had done to deserve having these people believe he was responsible for all of their problems, and that killing him was going to solve them.

Stefan became oblivious to his surroundings. The murmurings of the crowd were muffled and distant, consumed by the throbbing ache that encompassed his entire body. He felt blood run into his ears and tasted it in his mouth, while dizzy images of the people he loved swam through his mind.

Stefan heard voices that seemed more comforting than angry. He opened his eyes to see the ground about to swallow him up. By someone else's effort, he rolled over to face the sky, and the sunlight hurt his eyes. He wondered briefly if he was dead, but being brought to his feet, he was overcome with enough pain to prove that this body of his was still existing.

It was a relief to feel a saddle beneath him, and with help he leaned forward to wrap his arms around the horse's neck. Drifting in and out of consciousness as they rode, Stefan was barely aware of his surroundings. But he knew they were at Castle Horstberg when the hooves of a hundred horses rattled on the stone of the courtyard. It was a familiar sound, and he took comfort in it.

Trying to tune in his senses, he realized that the mob had not let up easily, and they were just now being held at bay as the gates to the fortress were closed with great effort.

Abbi opted to eat breakfast in her sitting room and was pleased when Georg came to join her. It had been difficult having both Stefan and Ericha gone. As the situation only seemed to worsen, along with persistent disturbing dreams, she felt on the verge of insanity. But Georg was a comfort to her, as he always had been. It was only his easy-going attitude that allowed her to keep her reason.

They were both alarmed to hear commotion from the courtyard below, and moved to the window to see what appeared to be the better part of the force of the Guard hastily leaving the castle in regimental order.

"What on earth could be happening?" Abbi asked fearfully, and Georg took her hand with reassurance.

"Whatever it is, I'm certain they'll be able to handle it."

Abbi tried to be consoled, but she felt uneasy as they returned to their meal. A short while later, the murmurings of battle floated faintly to their ears. Abbi moved to the sill and sat in it to push open the huge window. Georg came beside her as the force returned to the courtyard in a disorderly manner. They said nothing as they witnessed for the third time this week the Guard managing to keep a frenzied mob from entering the castle gates.

Abbi feared their blood-thirsty, seemingly inhuman ways, but she was at least grateful that the quest of their irrational vengeance was tucked safely away. She was about to voice her thoughts to Georg when her eye caught, in the midst of the sea of red uniforms, a tattered white shirt bent low over a horse, and the sunlight glanced off familiar rust-colored hair. She took Georg's arm in a fearful grip, and he quickly grasped the reason as they both saw the weary form nearly fall from his horse into soldiers' arms.

"Stefan!" she cried and ran with youthful vigor down the stairs and into the courtyard with Georg close behind. Georg couldn't help but feel an awe that he was accustomed to when the petite figure floated across the courtyard in a satin wrapper, her wild hair flying behind. As her presence became realized, every man in the courtyard, all of them at least a head taller than her, came to perfect attention and moved easily aside for her to be near the wounded prisoner.

Captain Leichty was just giving orders for the surgeon to be summoned at once when Abbi approached him. Another officer was kneeling beside Stefan, minus his jacket, which was rolled beneath the duke's head. Abbi went to her knees beside him and choked back the sob that caught in her throat to see her grandson's face so distorted with blood and bruises that she could hardly recognize him. The only acknowledgment that he knew her or Georg was a very slight, crooked smile.

Abbi looked up to the captain and demanded, "What happened?"

He explained the circumstances efficiently, and Abbi felt something dying inside of her. Stefan had to face it now. There was no way out.

Georg went to find Han and see to getting Ericha back, but Abbi remained with Stefan as he was moved into the keep and attended to by the surgeon. She was grateful that nothing appeared to be permanently damaged except for the broken nose. She was assured that with careful stitches, the cuts would heal with slight scars, and the broken ribs would mend eventually.

Gradually Stefan became more coherent as he was attended to. When the surgeon was finished, Abbi requested to be left alone with Stefan in the little cell.

"How are you feeling?" she asked gently, running her hand over his swollen face.

"Where is Ericha?" he said as if his mouth was full of cotton. "Don't let them hurt Ericha. The baby. Don't . . ."

"It's all right," she soothed. "Your father has already gone to get them. They'll come back in the night and go unnoticed. We'll make certain they're fine."

He looked up feebly. "I thought I'd never see you again."

"I'm here," she said strongly.

Stefan tried to smile. "Do you think I'll be able to stand up straight when they shoot me?"

Abbi wanted to scold him for saying such things, but she only put her face to his shoulder and cried.

Stefan ignored the pain it caused to put his arms around her and cry with her. When their emotion subsided, Abbi pulled away to look at him and dabbed at his tears with her handkerchief.

"A man my age shouldn't be crying," he stated.

"A man your age shouldn't be facing this."

He paused a long moment. "It's over."

She said nothing.

"Tell me, Grandmama. I want to know where it stands."

Abbi bit her lip slightly, but she knew he had a right to know. Courageously, she sought the right words. "The people of Kohenswald have filtered into the valley, stirring up mobs. So far they have done little more than make threats and try to get into the castle without success. They ranted outside the gates for a day and a half when they realized you had escaped.

"In their weak minds, these people seem to be willing to follow a thirst for power that they will never achieve, even if they do accomplish what they've set out to do. But they've gone mad. They want vengeance. It's come down to . . ."

Abbi stopped in an effort to sustain her emotion, but Stefan urged her to go on. "Please," he said, "I have to know the truth."

Abbi drew back her shoulders and said with a trembling voice, "It seems that Horstberg will have no peace until you are dead."

Stefan closed his eyes and sighed. "Then it must be."

"I will not let you go that easy," she insisted. "You will not resign yourself to martyrdom yet."

"I'm no martyr." He tried to laugh. "I'm getting what I deserve."

"You don't deserve any of it!"

"Do you know what they called me back there?" he asked. "I am no murderer. But I have to wonder if I'm a traitor. And I know that I'm an adulterer."

"And you never wanted anything but to do what was best for you and this country."

"But I failed."

"Circumstances have caused this, Stefan. In regard to Ericha, I would not want you to do things any differently if you were to do them over again."

Stefan smiled feebly at her. "Well, that makes two of us."

Abbi laughed softly to see the lack of regret in his eyes.

"Take care of them," he implored. "And please grow old enough that my son will be able to know and remember you."

"I'll do my best," she whispered. "But you can save your last will and testament for another time. It's not over yet. Rest now. I'll come back later to see how you're doing."

Stefan smiled at her as she got up to leave, and then he turned his mind to humble prayer.

The surgeon returned and gave Stefan something to help ease the pain. As it took affect, he drifted in and out of coherency while bizarre dreams and troubling memories sifted through his mind. A formless anguish knotted deep inside him, tightening slowly like a vise with every reminder that his life was coming to an end. He had told Ericha he wasn't afraid to die. He knew now that he was. While pain and bitterness and hatred swarmed inside of him, he became terrified of having to carry them on through eternity. The anguish within became as intense as the pain of his battered body, until he nearly wished that hell would just swallow him now and get it over with.

Chapter Twenty-Three

ABSOLUTION

As the medication began to wear off, Stefan's eyes burned if he tried to hold them open. But the rest of him hurt so badly that he could hardly attempt to sleep. His mind kept going to his grandfather, and for some formless reason, he wished that Cameron du Woernig was with him now.

Turning his mind inward, away from the pain, memories came so vividly to Stefan that he could almost hear Cameron's voice, his laugh. It became so clear that if he concentrated, he could believe the veil between heaven and earth was momentarily thin enough that he was almost with his grandfather again.

It was just like that day in the office. Stefan sat quietly in the huge windowsill, working on the sketching assignment his mother had given him. He ran into a problem with the mouth and wished that she hadn't gone into town so that she could help him.

Stefan paid little attention to the things his father and grand-father were discussing as they hovered over the huge desk. His mind was more on the clock. Uncle Erich had promised to take him riding as soon as the basement was cleaned out. He knew Erich would be getting married in a few days, and hoped that their time together would not cease.

Pausing to watch Han and Cameron, Stefan briefly wondered what was so important to take that much work and concentration. The ducal technicalities always surrounding him were tedious to a seven-year-old boy. He far preferred his lessons, of which art and music were his favorites. Perhaps because they were taught to him by some of the people he loved the most. Hannah and Gerhard liked other lessons better, and they preferred to remain in the nursery or play in the gardens. But Stefan liked being here.

He looked up from his sketch pad with interest when his father made a deliberate pause in the work to tell Cameron a joke he'd heard at the pub. Stefan laughed when they did, not because he understood the joke, but because it was amusing to see his grandfather fall into hysterical laughter that left him nearly weeping.

That laugh! It rang like music through Stefan's ears.

"All right," Cameron said, mopping his eyes and trying to suppress further chuckles. "Back to work. We've got a wedding to get ready for."

Cameron pushed his curly hair behind his ear and tried to sober himself, and then he broke into fresh laughter and they all became hysterical again for no apparent reason.

Stefan was suddenly gripped with fear as an overwhelming rumble moved through the floor like thunder. The laughter stopped abruptly and was contrasted strongly by the fear and panic that Stefan read in his grandfather's eyes. Han pulled Stefan protectively into his arms as the windows rattled, the chandelier swung, and mobile objects fell to the floor.

Cameron muttered a frenzied prayer as he nearly flew from the office with Han close behind. Stefan could do nothing but follow, as did the officers who had been standing guard at the office door. Cameron and Han seemed to know what was going on and where they were headed, and the dread and uncertainty Stefan felt made him instinctively stick close to them. Cameron came first to the door that Stefan knew led down to Erich's chemistry room, and he began to guess what had happened as the smell of smoke assaulted them. Cameron moved to descend, and Han stopped him. "Let me go. One of you has got to—"

"Don't say it," Cameron uttered.

"Your Grace," one of the officers took his arm firmly. "Please, let me go and—"

"No," was all Cameron said as he pushed the officer away, leaving him stunned. Cameron disappeared with Han and the officers close behind. Han called over his shoulder, "Stefan—get help!"

Stefan wasn't certain who to get, but instinctively he went toward his grandmother's sitting room. She was the one he always went to for help when his parents weren't available. He met her on the stairs, as she was evidently coming to investigate the rumbling. Her expression was already filled with panic. She seemed to already sense his purpose, so Stefan said nothing. He followed her back to their destination, pausing only long enough for her to order one of the servants to send for a doctor.

Abbi apparently intended to go to the basement herself, and Stefan wasn't about to be left alone. But she had only gone a few steps when she heard Han and Cameron coming up and she retracted into the hall. Stefan stood back and leaned against the wall, astonished to see his father emerge first, blackened with smoke, half of his shirt gone into ashes, and a mass of burned skin over his shoulder and arm.

Cameron came close behind, nearly crawling up the stairs with a great deal of assistance from Han. Abbi quickly went to her knees, pulling Cameron against her. He took hold of her shoulders and coughed from deep in his chest while Abbi watched him fearfully, before glancing toward the door as if she expected someone else.

"Erich?" she said close to Cameron's face. "Where is Erich?"

"He's gone, Abbi," he barely managed to say, and then he buried his head against her shoulder, and Stefan couldn't tell if he was coughing or crying. Most likely a lot of both. Abbi cried with heaving sobs, and Stefan began to comprehend what this meant. He glanced toward his father, hoping for an explanation, but Han was apparently in so much pain that Stefan hesitated. He wanted to run away. He wanted to hide. He wanted to be in his mother's arms. But all he could do was stand there. His legs wouldn't move and the rest of him was numb.

Cameron's coughing steadily worsened, and he pressed his hands to his chest, groaning painfully. "The doctor will be here soon," Abbi muttered, and Cameron nodded, then looked up and saw Stefan there. It was only Cameron's outstretched hand that willed Stefan to move. He squeezed his grandfather's hand and felt it reciprocated, while Cameron said something to him that he couldn't understand. He only nodded in response and stepped back as Cameron turned to Han, instructing him through intermittent coughing about raising Stefan properly.

Han and Abbi both seemed to grasp in the same moment what Cameron was trying to say. Han ignored his own pain and moved on his knees toward Cameron as the coughing became more intense. Cameron barely managed to whisper those words to Abbi that Stefan would never forget, and then he coughed into his hands and blood oozed between his fingers. Stefan saw the panic in Cameron's eyes as he looked at Abbi, unable to speak as the coughing became constant and his life slipped away, but his expression pleaded for more time. It was as if his heart was breaking to realize that he was going to leave her.

"Cameron!" Abbi cried, holding to him tightly. "Don't go," she whimpered. "Don't leave me!" She pulled his head to her shoulder and threaded her hands through his hair while he coughed and gasped incessantly against her. Then with no warning, the coughing ceased. And Stefan knew Cameron was gone.

As memories became too much to bear, Stefan forced his mind back to the laughter. He could still hear the laughter, so close, so comforting. He shifted, and the pain brought him back to the reality of the present. The laughter was only in his imagination, and the rest was etched too deeply into his memory for him to ever be free of it. He tried to think of something else, but the scenes only became more vivid.

He heard himself moan, then felt his head being lifted slightly. A cup was pressed to his lips and cool liquid ran down his throat. His eyes focused on a uniformed officer, but it took him a moment to recognize the face.

"Captain," he managed to say, "surely you have better things to do than—"

"Don't talk, Your Grace," the captain said with every bit the respect he'd always had. "I regret that this had to happen. I should have been better prepared."

"I should have stayed in the keep where I belonged."

"I wish it didn't have to be this way," the captain said quietly. "I've never disliked my job . . . until now." He helped Stefan drink a little more, then gently laid his head back on the pillow. "Is there anything you want me to do, Your Grace? If it's within my power, I'll do it."

Stefan took the captain's hand in the firmest grip he could manage. "Just promise me," he said, "that when the time comes, I will be able to go with dignity."

"I pray it doesn't come to that," the captain replied.

Stefan managed a slight nod, and then he closed his eyes against his will. When he opened them again, he was alone.

Ericha was relieved when Han arrived at the lodge even sooner than she had expected.

"Hello, my dear," he said solemnly as he entered and embraced her. "Are you all right?"

"Yes, fine," she replied, "considering."

"I have some bad news," he stated, and her eyes widened fearfully. Han motioned for her to sit down and he sat close beside her, taking her hand in his. "Stefan's been hurt."

"How?" she insisted. "What happened?"

"He's going to be all right, I believe. But he's in pretty bad shape. The entire situation is not good." He paused and sighed. "He was overrun by a mob on the way to the castle."

"Good heavens! How badly was he hurt?"

"It's bad enough. But as I said, he'll be all right."

"He will have to face a trial now," she stated softly.

"Yes, I'm afraid he will. But not until he's back on his feet, which gives us a little more time." Han stood and pushed his hands into his pockets abruptly. "It's all so blasted unfair!"

Ericha agreed with him emphatically, but she felt desperate to see Stefan and set to gathering her things.

"Come along . . . Father," she said with a gentle smile, and Han returned it.

"You're no doubt your father's daughter," he said and took her hand to squeeze it.

They returned to the castle deep in the night and immediately got some much-needed sleep. Ericha shared breakfast with Abbi in her sitting room, where she was given all the details of the situation that Han hadn't told her. Then Han made arrangements for her to spend some time with Stefan.

Captain Leichty himself escorted her down the hall of the keep. "We've had someone sitting with him most of the night, but I don't think he's been very coherent. The doctor has checked him regularly, and we've tried to keep him as comfortable as possible."

"Thank you, Captain," Ericha said, appreciating his compassion. But then, Stefan had worked closely with Captain Leichty for years. The situation was ironic.

He turned the key in the lock, and an officer came to his feet from a chair near Stefan's bed.

"Come along," the captain called. "We'll let the lady sit with him for awhile."

"Thank you, Captain," Ericha repeated, and the door was locked behind her. By what little light that came through the small window, Ericha pulled the chair close to the narrow bed and sat down.

"Oh, my love!" She gasped to see his face. "What have they done to you?" She had assumed he was asleep, but at the sound of her voice, he groaned and tried to lift his head.

"Ericha." He opened his eyes with great effort and reached his hand toward her. "Is that you, Ericha?"

"I'm here," she whispered, placing her hand into his and pressing a kiss to his brow.

"I prayed you would come," he said, and his voice sounded dry. She glanced around and found some water that was apparently there for him. Carefully she lifted his head and pressed the cup to his lips. He drank with difficulty, and Ericha set the cup aside and moved onto the bed, carefully placing his head on her lap. Stefan nuzzled close to her and gave a contended sigh.

"Does it hurt much?" she asked.

"Like hell."

"Is there anything I can do? They told me I could stay a while."

"That's all you can do," he replied, looking up at her. "Just be with me."

Ericha could see the pain in his eyes, and she knew there was something he needed to say. "Tell me, Stefan," she whispered.

"It's over, Ericha."

"Not yet," she replied gently, fighting to keep her emotion under control. "Right now you and I are together."

"But it won't be long," he stated, and Ericha made no response. "Do you know what is really stupid?" he asked.

"No, what?"

"They're trying to heal me so I can stand up when they shoot me. Why don't they just come and shoot me now and put me out of my misery?"

"Because you deserve a trial, and perhaps the time will help us prove your innocence."

"Face it, Ericha. This much time hasn't given them a clue. Nothing is going to change. It's over."

Ericha choked back her tears, not wanting him to see them. She knew he was right, but what could she possibly say? "Let's talk about something else, please," she said gently.

"There is something I wanted to tell you." His tone lightened.

"And what is that?"

"All through the night I kept having these vivid memories roll through my mind . . . of the day it happened . . . the explosion, I mean, and I remembered your mother very clearly."

Ericha felt her heart quicken with emotion as he went on. "I have vague memories of her being with Erich on different occasions. I seem to recall walking into the drawing room one after-noon to find the two of them kissing on the sofa." Ericha smiled at this, and Stefan seemed pleasantly distant as he added, "They were really kissing." His eyes focused more clearly on Ericha. "If I had any strength I would demonstrate."

Ericha smiled, and he went on, more sadly, "But my clearest memory of her came when I recalled standing there in hall, watching my grandfather die." He nuzzled closer to Ericha and gave a subtle moan. "I was numb, realizing he was gone. And Erich was gone. I didn't know what to do. I wanted to run away, but I couldn't move. And then she was there. Her arms came around me and I remember the comfort and relief I felt. She must have been dying inside, but she was giving me comfort."

Stefan's eyes delved into Ericha as they mutually tried to absorb the years and the ironies between them. "Ericha," he whispered, and his tone betrayed emotion, "you would have been with her then." Ericha felt tears burn behind her eyes. "We were so close." He reached up with effort to touch her face. "If only I could have known."

An emotional silence hung over them until Stefan whispered, "Come here, Ericha. I want you to lay beside me."

"I'm afraid I'll hurt you," she replied.

"I don't care how much it hurts," he insisted, attempting to sit up and groaning from the pain. Ericha moved beside him and urged him back to the bed, easing carefully onto the narrow cot as he turned to his side to make room. "I'm going to die, Ericha, and I want to hold you."

Ericha cried silent tears against his shoulder while Stefan held her close, until she was told she had to leave.

Nearly a week after Stefan's encounter with the mob, Ericha began to feel on the verge of insanity. She was too nervous to do tatting without making a mess of it. Cameron stayed in the nursery most of the time, simply because he wanted to be where he could crawl and play. Since she had recently stopped nursing him, it was easier to let Ruthild manage him while she tried to deal with her nerves.

Ericha thought that if she were still at Karl's house, she could work in the garden. Then she decided that she would do it anyway. She was the wife of the Duke of Horstberg, and if she wanted to pull weeds in the castle garden, so be it. She put on an old dress and her straw hat and spent the afternoon at it, while Job lounged lazily in the sun close by. She even had a nice chat with one of the gardeners, who had been at Castle Horstberg since before Cameron du Woernig became the duke.

Ericha rinsed her hands off under an outside water pump and came back inside, drying them on her skirt. She was on her way up to Maggie's sitting room, with Job at her heels, when she nearly bumped into someone on the stairs. She took a step back and felt herself being appraised by one of the most conventionally handsome men she'd ever seen. He glanced at Job with apparent disdain, and then his focus turned to Ericha.

"What is this?" he asked with a roguish smirk. "Since when do the servants use these stairs?"

As he smiled fully, Ericha had no question that this man had Heinrich blood in him. And since Han was an only child, that narrowed it down. She pulled off her hat, and with no apology or embarrassment over her attire, she stated, "I *live* here, thank you very much."

Apparently impressed with her spunk, he took her hand and said lithely, "How quaint." He fingered her wedding ring and nearly scowled at it. "Married, eh?"

"Quite," she stated, pulling her hand away.

"And who is the lucky man?"

"If I didn't know better, sir, I would think you're flirting with me."

He chuckled and made a ridiculously innocent gesture. "I was simply wondering—"

"My name is Ericha Heinrich," she said, loving the way it felt just to say it. His eyes widened as she added the obvious, "I am married to the Duke of Horstberg."

He looked more amused than embarrassed. "You must forgive my impudence, Mrs. Heinrich."

"You must be Gerhard," she stated.

"Very good." He chuckled. "Do I remind you of my brother?" he asked impishly.

"Not in the slightest," she stated. "But you look a great deal like your father."

"So do you," he said, gazing at her openly. He chuckled again. "So, you're the woman who lured old Stefan away from that vixen he married. Mercy, but you must be something."

"What makes you say that?"

"I've just spent the past hour and a half hearing nothing but your fine qualities."

Feeling suddenly uncomfortable as his flirtatious attitude had not lessened with their introductions, Ericha moved on up the stairs. "If you will excuse me, I'm certain we'll have plenty of time to get better acquainted."

"I'm counting on it," he said, and she was aware of him watching her from behind.

Later that evening, after the family had eaten, they all went to the east winter parlor for coffee. Ericha hated sitting through meals with Stefan's chair empty, almost as much as she hated being in this room without having him at the piano. Much of the evening had been spent with Gerhard regaling them with tales of his travels. He'd recently returned from India and had been settling in for a long stay in Italy when he'd received word that he needed to return home.

They'd not been seated long when Gerhard said, "So, what's the truth of it, Father? I know Stefan's about to get shot for killing his wife, and all, but—"

"He did not kill his wife," Maggie interrupted.

"I just said he was going to get shot for it," Gerhard retorted, and Ericha cringed at his apparent callousness. "I know you didn't make me come all the way back here just so I could see the execution, and—"

"Gerhard," Han said gently, "would you please not be so graphic in front of the ladies?"

Gerhard glanced innocently at his mother and grandmother,

then to Ericha. His smile unnerved her. "I am so sorry," he said. He turned back to Han. "So what's the truth of it? What am I doing in this forsaken place?" When Han didn't answer right away, he added, "If you think that I'm going to take his place, you can think again."

"That's the way it has to be," Han stated.

"Like hell it is!" Gerhard erupted from his seat. "You're the duke regent. You're the one who—"

"You're the rightful heir in Stefan's absence," Han interrupted. "If you are able to fill the position, then—"

"I'm not able to fill the position," Gerhard countered. "And I won't do it. If you think I'm going to hole myself up in this wretched place for the sake of duty or honor, or whatever damnable thing you—"

"Like it or not," Han interrupted again, "it's in your blood, and you—"

"Let it go, Han," Abbi said firmly. All eyes turned to her, but her focus was on Gerhard. "If he doesn't want it, I will not allow it to be forced upon him."

"Thank you, Grandmama," Gerhard said. "You're a saint, as always."

"Are you saying, then," Han asked Abbi, "that it's up to me to fill the position?"

"For the time being, yes," she stated. "Hannah's son will be of age in a few years. He will need proper training. You're the only one who can do that."

Han sighed and pushed a hand through his hair. Ericha became so unnerved by the tension in the room, she got up to leave for fear she'd scream otherwise.

"What is it, Ericha?" Maggie asked as she reached for the door.

"You're talking about all of this as if Stefan were already dead. I realize we have to be prepared, but I don't have to listen to it."

Ericha hurried into the hall before anyone could see her tears. She went outside where she could cry unnoticed, and then she wandered to the keep, wondering if she might be able to see

Stefan. Telling herself to be firm and confident, she decided the worst they could do was tell her no.

She stepped inside, and two officers came to attention. "Good evening, Your Grace," one of them said. The title took her off guard. She had not officially been crowned duchess, but she *was* married to the duke. It was still difficult to believe.

"Good evening," she replied. "I wonder if I might see my husband. It is important."

Ericha was amazed at how quickly she was led down the hall to Stefan's cell. As the officer opened the door, she got a brief glimpse of Stefan, leaning on one elbow on the narrow bed, a lamp burning low.

"Her Grace to see you, sir," the officer announced.

Stefan sat up carefully, expecting to see his grandmother. When Ericha walked in, he smiled. "So it is," he said, holding a hand toward her as the door was locked again.

Ericha took it and sat beside him, burrowing her face against his shoulder.

"How are you?" he asked, pressing his lips to her brow.

"I want to die with you, Stefan. Don't leave me here alone without you. I can't bear it."

Stefan swallowed hard. "You won't be alone," he whispered. "You have a family now. And you have a son who needs you."

"He needs *you,*" she cried. *"I* need you."

"What's happened to upset you?" he asked gently.

Ericha wanted to tell him it was a stupid question. Her husband was going to be executed for a crime he didn't commit, and he was wondering why she was upset. But she knew he could sense her feelings, so she simply answered him. "Your father and Gerhard were arguing about—"

"Gerhard?" he pulled back, alarmed. "He's here?"

"Yes, I met him this afternoon when—"

"Blast!" Stefan eased away from her as he became suddenly distracted. "If Horstberg falls into his hands, everything I've worked for will—"

"Grandmama said she wouldn't allow it."

"Oh, thank God," he murmured with obvious relief.

"She wants your father to act as regent until Hannah's son comes of age."

Stefan met her eyes and saw the sorrow there. He understood now why she was upset. "Ericha," he said, "there is someone who takes precedence over Hannah's son. His reign will be only temporary. *My* son will be the Duke of Horstberg when he comes of age. You must teach him, Ericha. Raise him the way your mother raised you."

Ericha shook her head, and fresh tears spilled down her cheeks. "I'm not giving up yet, Stefan. I believe in miracles, and I'm not letting you go that easily."

"Oh, my love," he whispered and pulled her close, ignoring the pain it caused. A few minutes later, she was told she had to go.

On her way back across the courtyard, Ericha met Gerhard. "And how is the duke this evening?" he asked flippantly.

"As well as could be expected," she snapped.

Gerhard chuckled. "You're a fiery little thing," he said. "You remind me a bit of my mother that way."

"Thank you," she said, wishing he'd let her pass.

"You know," he almost whispered, taking hold of her arm, "being the Duke of Horstberg might not be so bad if it meant having you as the duchess."

Ericha wrenched her arm free. "Go to hell," she snarled and hurried on.

Not long after Ericha left, Stefan heard someone else being ushered down the hall. He didn't bother to get up, already fearing it would be his brother.

"How's it going, Stef?" Gerhard asked as soon as the door was locked behind him.

"Great," Stefan said with sarcasm, "and you?"

"Not too bad, considering I'm in Horstberg. Nothing can make a boy long to be home like fighting my way through mobs and listening to talk of murder and execution over the dinner table." He rocked on his heels and looked around the room. "Nice little place, considering."

"Did you want something particular," Stefan asked, "or did you just come to annoy me with your flippant prattle?"

"Always the duke, eh?" Gerhard said snidely. "And that's quite a duchess you've got there. The two of you make a fine pair. She just told me to go to hell."

Stefan suppressed a chuckle. "She has a way of putting arrogance in its place."

"Well, then," Gerhard said, "she must keep *you* in line."

"She does, actually."

"So," Gerhard sat down and crossed his ankle on his knee, "tell me the truth, brother. Did you really shoot your wife in the head?"

"What do you think?" Stefan retorted.

"Well," he chuckled, "I would have thought, you being a man of such impeccable morals, sworn to duty and all, that you would never do such a thing. But then, who would have guessed that *you,* of all people, would go out and get yourself a mistress? So, who knows? Maybe I don't know you as well as I thought I did."

"Imagine that," Stefan said tersely.

"Now if it were me, I would have shot Johanna years ago."

"Why is that?" Stefan asked, sensing an unusual seriousness in Gerhard's tone.

Following a lengthy pause, he said, "Well now, I guess that's what I wanted to talk to you about, Stefan." His severity increased, and Stefan wondered what was coming. "Johanna was the reason I left Horstberg when I did. She was trying to play me against you, Stefan." Gerhard hesitated, looking perhaps nervous. "Now, I'll admit that you and I have very little in common, except that we grew up in a very depressing home. You became depressed like the rest of them. I learned to laugh it off. I know I'm impertinent and obnoxious. But the truth is, Stefan, I would never do anything to hurt my family. That's why I won't try to pretend that I can take your place and let everyone down when I can't do it. And that's why I left Horstberg. You and I had enough tension between us without having Johanna there. So, I left."

Stefan tried to absorb this. He wondered if anything short of facing death would have brought him and Gerhard to such honesty. "Did you sleep with her?" he asked.

Gerhard said nothing.

"Come on, little brother. If we're going to get it all in the open, let's do it. Do you think I don't know what kind of woman she was? Did you or didn't you?"

"Yes," he admitted. "But to this day, I don't know how it happened. I think I was half drunk. She was like some kind of spider, weaving this little web around—"

"You don't have to explain it. I know exactly what you mean."

"Forgive me, Stefan," he said, and Stefan couldn't recall ever seeing him so humble. "I won't let you die with something like this between us."

"Thank you," Stefan said with genuine warmth. "It's in the past."

Gerhard sighed visibly with relief. "You are a good man, Stefan," he said. "I want you to know that. Growing up, I always resented the attention you got because you were the heir. Then after I'd been away for a couple of years, I realized that you resented it, too." He chuckled. "I guess that's one thing we have in common."

"We have many things in common, Gerhard."

"Like what?"

"We love all the same people, and we would never want to hurt them."

"That's true."

Stefan chuckled. "And we both wanted to shoot Johanna."

"But neither of us did," he stated firmly.

"No," Stefan admitted, "neither of us did."

"And you're willing to die for something you didn't do?"

"I'm willing to die to keep Horstberg in peace, if that's what it takes."

"You're a better man than I," Gerhard said.

"You have no idea how I have envied you all these years. Your freedom. Your ability to enjoy life. But I never envied you so much as when I met Ericha. I wanted nothing more than to take her away from here and never look back."

"But you didn't."

"No, I didn't."

"And this is what it's come to."

"I'd do it again."

"You would die for a woman?" Gerhard asked incredulously.

"For *that* woman, yes. Gerhard," Stefan leaned forward and met his eyes, "if you only remember one thing about me, remember that I told you this. When you find a woman who makes you stop and wonder how you ever lived before you found her, take hold of her. If she makes you see things about yourself you never considered before, listen and learn. Move heaven and earth to have her, to keep her, and give everything you have to make her happy."

Gerhard chuckled warmly. "Maybe I already have."

Stefan lifted a brow in question.

"Her name is Felicia. She lives in Italy, and—"

Their conversation was cut short as Gerhard was told he had to leave. Stefan lay staring at the ceiling long after he'd left, trying to absorb the healing that had just taken place with his brother. The peace warmed him. He didn't blame Gerhard for whatever had happened with Johanna. He knew well where the blame belonged. He only had to think of her, and that bitter, hateful knot tightened inside of him. If only it was possible to find peace with *that* before he had to face death! He was not prepared to spend eternity feeling this way.

It was nearly dusk when Abbi walked alone across the courtyard toward the keep. Her word was quickly adhered to when she requested to see Stefan, and she followed the officer down the narrow corridor between the cells.

Stefan came carefully to his feet when the key turned noisily in the lock, and Abbi moved past the officer saying, "Thank you. Leave us alone, please."

Stefan said nothing as his grandmother embraced him gingerly and took his hand. He glanced briefly toward the books she held, wondering what they were. "How are you?" she asked gently.

"I seem to be healing," he stated, "if that's what you mean."

"Is there a light in here?" she asked, and Stefan lit one.

Abbi scrutinized his face carefully, lightly touching the reminders he bore of the mob's brutality.

"It is looking better," she stated, "but how are you feeling?"

"How should I be feeling?" he asked scornfully as he moved to the tiny window and gazed toward the darkening sky.

"I've brought you something," she said, and he turned to look again at the books she held. In the light he noted that the bindings looked worn and old, but he didn't recall ever seeing them before.

"What are they?" he asked.

"Sit down," she said, and he did. "Before I tell you what they are," she muttered in a tone that brought a childhood memory to Stefan, "I want you to tell me about Cameron du Woernig."

"What could I possibly tell you that you don't already know?" he asked, barely chuckling.

"You can tell me the impression he left on a seven-year-old boy."

Stefan sighed. "My memories are of a man who seemed to have it all. I don't think there was anything that could have come against him that he couldn't have handled." Stefan closed his eyes briefly. "I truly loved and admired him. Something in me died when he did."

Silence ruled in the tiny cell as Stefan's words seemed to put Abbi briefly in another time. "I dare say," she said at last, "that your memories are very accurate. I find it interesting to compare him to the Cameron I met. There is quite a contrast. This man was apparently cold and hard with no sensitivity whatsoever, and beneath his cruel facade, he was uncertain, afraid, and felt sure his life was over. He was a broken man."

Stefan's expression intensified as she went on. "I know you've heard all of this before. But you are much like him in many ways. I think you might find this worthwhile."

Abbi handed him the books, and he took them almost hesitantly. "What are they?"

She nodded slightly, and he opened the cover of the first to
read in a left-handed script: *Memoirs. Cameron du Woernig.*

Stefan glanced up at her in question, and she stated, "I've
never shown them to anyone before, so you must know it is not
something just to pass the time with."

"Then what?" he asked.

Abbi gave no reply. She only bent to kiss Stefan's swollen
cheek, then called for the officer to unlock the door.

Stefan sat alone with the first book in his hands for several
minutes before he found the courage to turn the page. He had
always been in awe of his grandfather, and somehow feared
having one he adored brought to a humble reality.

The book began with an explanation that this was not a daily
diary, but rather a place to write when there was something worth
writing about. Scanning through the entries, Stefan noted that at
times there would be several over a period of weeks, and sometimes months or even years in between entries.

It took little time to realize why his grandmother had seen fit
to let him read this. Stefan felt a grain of comfort as Cameron's
writings began with an explanation of how it felt to realize as a
youth that he would be the Duke of Horstberg when he came
of age, because of his father's death. Stefan related to the feelings, though the circumstances varied in many respects. Emotion
sparked as Cameron spoke briefly of his marriage to Gwendolyn
Dukerk, and a brief entry four years later stated, *I look at my wife
and wonder at times what it is I ever felt for her. Would anyone ever believe me
if I told them how she has played upon my weaknesses and subtly destroyed
my faith in love and happiness?*

The simple statement struck Stefan deeply, and with interest
he read on. There was a section on a political uprising that
Stefan found interesting, and he briefly forgot about Cameron's
personal circumstances, until the following entry changed the
mood abruptly. *One day I was the ruler of a prosperous nation. The
next, I was nothing.*

Stefan swallowed hard. Again the circumstances varied, but he felt astounded to read how Cameron du Woernig felt sitting in a prison cell, accused of a crime he did not commit. With the comfort of relating these words to himself, Stefan blessed Abbi for putting this book into his hands. Feeling close to Cameron in spirit, he read the account of Georg Heinrich's careful maneuver in helping Cameron escape and securing him away in the mountain lodge.

Georg had made it appear that Cameron was dead, with intentions to bring him back when they were prepared to prove his innocence and restore him to the throne. But time filled Cameron with despair. The entries during the three years of solitude were few. He said in them that there was little of interest to write, but Stefan grasped the broken man that Abbi had spoken of.

He found it interesting that nothing was written about Abbi's appearance in his life until a few days before they exchanged private vows. And again Stefan related to his grandfather. After Abbi left the mountain, he spoke of the torment of waiting to return to Horstberg so that he could be with her and reclaim his duchy. In his loneliness, he related the story of saving this woman's life, and what had transpired during the winter they had shared in seclusion.

Cameron finished the entry with a statement that rang closely to what Stefan had heard him say just before he died, and reading it made those moments come back vividly.

In those first weeks when Abbi was with me, I felt quite proud of myself for having saved her life. I felt perhaps she owed me something for being there at the right time. But her presence has humbled me. When a man has to sit down and admit that he is desperately in love with a woman he was determined not to love, he has to face a lot of other things as well. Abbi made me realize that I was hiding from my responsibilities as the Duke of Horstberg, and that even facing death is far better than the torment I have dealt with in knowing that there are things my heritage makes mandatory for me to face. I can see now that in the distortion of solitude, I questioned myself in ways that Abbi has forced me to face realistically. I can see now that I

have been the instigator of this intrinsic civil war taking place inside
of me, and the man I grew to think I should be is not the man I am
inside. Abbi has given me peace with my conscience and the desire
to live again. In a word, she has given me everything. If I die now,
it will be in peace, and if I live, it will be in gratitude for a second
chance, and retribution for the mistakes I made. And I will never,
ever, forget that the credit belongs to Abbi. She has given me motive
to live. She has given my life back to me. I thought that God sent
me to save her life, but I know now that God sent her to save mine.

Stefan blinked repeatedly to clear the mist away so that he
could read the last paragraph, and then he read it again, replacing
Abbi's name with Ericha. He felt a degree of the peace he'd been
seeking come over him, and knew that if retribution meant his life
was to be given for the sake of his country, he would go in peace.
And if he too was granted a second chance, he had Cameron du
Woernig's shining example as a ruler who had gone through the
worst of circumstances and come through victorious.

With a different attitude, Stefan chose to forego sleep and
read through the night about Cameron du Woernig's astounding
return to power in 1817 and the experiences of the years beyond.
There were more details of the births of his children and stories
of their youth than there were accounts of political happenings.

Stefan knew as the remaining pages grew less, and the events
recorded spoke of his children as adults and the coming of his
grandchildren, that Cameron du Woernig's life would end soon.
He dreaded reaching that point. His death was so unexpected and
tragic; this book would surely seem left unfinished.

Cameron told of the failed revolution of 1849, and how
Han's ingenuity had saved Horstberg in a way that filled Stefan
with pride for his father. Stefan was well aware that Cameron
died very soon after that revolution, and he repositioned himself
on the tiny cot, drawing a deep breath before beginning the last
entry, dated less than a week before Cameron's death. But he was
almost pleasantly surprised as he read.

I feel moved today to stand back and look over my life, and
I realize my regrets are few. Those regrets I have felt in the past

have been dealt with in one way or another, and I cannot say that I would do it any differently. This evening at dinner I looked down that dreadfully long table we have, and I am embarrassed to admit that I was almost moved to tears.

Everyone was here, of course. They've all come home for the wedding. And it was astounding. There sat Abbi, as beautiful as ever, and I marvel at the joy she has given me. And nearby is Georg, of course. What would I have ever done without Georg? He won't ever let me admit to anyone that he's the brain behind this duchy, but he is. Han and Maggie still act like a couple of children, and yet they have four of their own. Sonia was there with Rudolf and their four children as well. What beautiful daughters I have! And I can see that they are happy.

And then Erich. How can I possibly say what a joy he is to me? It brings something to life in me to see the look in his eyes when he is with Kathe. And I love her as well. I can look at her and almost believe that without her knowing it, she will bring about the means for Horstberg to be saved again.

Stefan closed his eyes, and his breath escaped him. "Ericha," he whispered aloud, wondering if Cameron had known the significance of what he wrote. He sighed and read on.

It seems that Horstberg comes close to the edge every so many years. But it always manages to recover, and I am grateful. How blessed I am! My life has been full, and God has been with me and my loved ones. Of this I am certain.

Stefan turned the page, wishing it wasn't blank. Then he cried silent tears . . . tears full of a hundred emotions. But the most prominent was comfort. Comfort to know that perhaps Cameron's death had not been quite so tragic; somehow he seemed to have sensed his time had come. And comfort to almost feel his grandfather's presence with him as he wondered if his own time had come. Whatever lay ahead, the words of Cameron du Woernig gave Stefan the strength to know that he could face it with courage and dignity. And he would!

Stefan fell asleep with the last book in his hands and awoke startled to feel a certain desperation. Something in him had changed. Han came to his cell right after breakfast just as he did every morning, and Stefan didn't give him a chance to speak before he blurted, "I want to see the bishop—immediately."

A few hours later, the Bishop of Horstberg was let into his cell. He looked so ordinary without his clerical robes. But his aura of peace, and the wisdom in his aging eyes, was evident.

"I've been wanting to come and see you," he said. "But I felt it was best to wait until you wanted to see me."

Stefan felt a little unnerved at having his actions predicted. He knelt and took the bishop's hand, but the older man urged Stefan to his feet.

"It's just you and me, Stefan. Sit. Let's talk."

The bishop sat on the chair as Stefan took the edge of the bed. Through the following silence, Stefan realized it was up to him to start.

"You know about . . . Ericha and me."

"Yes. She's a good woman. She has softened your heart."

Stefan was surprised but went on with his purpose. "I wonder if I should regret what we did, but I love her. I can't explain it, but somehow I know that God sent her to save me from destroying myself."

"And God knows the desires of your heart, Stefan."

"I'd like to believe that."

"And you have married her now. The situation is rectified as much as it can be. It's up to you to find peace with it and forgive yourself."

"Forgive myself for what?" Stefan asked, wishing it hadn't sounded so sharp. "For loving her? For wanting some measure of happiness in my life?"

The bishop leaned forward and set his forearms on his thighs. "Stefan, my son," he began in a voice that chilled Stefan, "you should know that whatever the desires of our hearts, there are some things that are simply wrong, and no amount of justification will ever make them right."

Stefan bowed his head and squeezed his eyes shut. "Yes, I know."

"Adultery is a serious thing," the bishop said, and Stefan winced inwardly. "It often has far-reaching repercussions that can be devastating. You've married her and made it right. But it is important for you to find restitution in your heart, to know for yourself that God has forgiven you—and then you can forgive yourself."

"Is such a thing possible?" Stefan asked.

The bishop smiled serenely. "With God, nothing is impossible." He penetrated Stefan with his eyes and added, "What's *really* troubling you, my son?"

It took Stefan a minute to come up with an answer. "Is there really life beyond this?" he asked.

The bishop's expression warmed with a peaceable smile, but he only said, "Look inside yourself, Stefan. Search your feelings. What do you think?"

Stefan thought about it, and the bishop allowed him the time to do so. He was surprised at how easily the answer came. And the firm resolve behind it. "I believe there is."

"Does that make what you are facing easier . . . or more difficult?"

"Both perhaps." Stefan realized they were getting down to the core of what he'd really wanted to talk to the bishop about. "You see," he began carefully, "there have been many things in my life that have caused me grief . . . for different reasons."

The bishop nodded his understanding, and Stefan went on. "There are times when I think of those things, and it's as if something inside of me threatens to explode. I feel as if the pain will somehow ooze out and destroy me." Stefan leaned closer and whispered, as if the walls might overhear. "My deepest fear is spending the life after this feeling that way."

"Feelings are a very big part of our human existence, Stefan. When we acknowledge our feelings and act upon them, in balance with what we know is right, we can find peace."

Peace. The very word struck something in him. "How do I find peace, Your Grace?" Stefan asked. There was something humbling, almost warm, about sharing the same title with a man he held in such high esteem. "If I'm going to die, I have to go with peace."

The bishop intensified his gaze. "There is only one way to be completely at peace. And that is through our Lord and Savior. He paid the price for our sins and our grief, Stefan. And when we sort through all of our suffering, there comes a point when He will lift it from us. When you are at peace with yourself, you will be at peace with Him."

Stefan was speechless. He'd been hoping for some simple answer, a formula to find what he was seeking. In a way it was simple. But it wasn't easy. He knew in his heart that he had a great deal of soul searching to do in what little might be left of his life. And there were places in his soul he had no desire to search.

"Is there anything else you wish to talk about?" the bishop asked.

Stefan shook his head slowly. "But will you come back? Before the trial?"

"I will," he promised. "And you send for me if you need me . . . any time."

Stefan nodded. He expected the bishop to leave, but he remained seated. "I wonder if you would be interested to know how the good citizens of Horstberg view what is happening in your life?"

Stefan managed a chuckle. "I don't know. Do I want to hear it?"

The bishop smiled. "Of course, you know of the mobs. Every period of history has its weak minded . . . those who fall prey so easily to the anger and deceit of Lucifer's influence. But from what I have seen and heard, and what those of the clergy tell me, the good people of this country believe you are innocent. They are praying for you, and for your good wife."

Stefan squeezed his eyes shut and bowed his head. He couldn't recall ever feeling so humbled. "Tell them, as far as it's possible, that their prayers are very much appreciated."

"I will," the bishop said gently. "And I will tell them that I am certain they're right, that you *are* innocent."

Stefan looked up abruptly. "How do you know that?"

The bishop gave that peaceable smile. "How did you know that God sent Ericha to save you?"

Stefan caught his breath and held it.

"There are some feelings that just can't be explained with mortal words."

The bishop prayed with Stefan, then left him with a warm embrace. He ate nothing of the food they brought him the remainder of the day, and told them when he was hungry he'd let them know. For the first time since he'd been brought to the keep, he was grateful to have no visitors. In his solitude, Stefan reflected deeply on all the bishop had said. He prayed in his mind for the courage to sort out his feelings and search his soul. Somewhere deep in the night, he began to uncover that part of himself he'd dreaded finding. It was the man who hated Johanna enough to *want* to kill her. The man who hated Nik Koenig for what he'd done to his family, and refused to forgive him for it. He found the raw, festering part of him that oozed with the grief of seeing loved ones die, the pain of lost childhood and disillusioned marriage, and the regret of choices that couldn't be undone. And he found the part of him that had willfully sinned, however justified he might have felt in doing so. Lying alone in a darkened cell, Stefan experienced a harsh, physical pain at the very core of his heart and soul. As it continued relentlessly, he felt as if the darkness would close in and devour him. He bit into his hand to keep from crying out. He groaned into his pillow to muffle the sound. He prayed with everything inside of him that he could only be free of his anguish and face his death in peace.

Somewhere in the midst of his agony, Stefan drifted into an exhausted, tormented slumber. He awoke with the sensation that it was late in the day, by the way the sun's rays angled through the tiny window. And then he felt it. He reached a hand up into the beam of light as if he could somehow touch it. Something had changed in him. Everything made sense. It was easy for him to look at his feelings for Johanna and know that they had been warranted, but it was not for him to mete judgment upon her soul. It was out of his hands. And he knew in his heart that he *had* been forgiven.

Stefan heard the key in the lock and sat up abruptly. The door opened, slowly and quietly.

"You're awake," the officer said. "Your father came earlier, but he didn't want to disturb you. Are you hungry yet?"

"Yes," he admitted, "but while I'm eating, I want a message taken to my father, immediately. Tell him I want to see Nik Koenig—just as soon as possible."

"Yes, Your Grace," the officer replied and left him alone.

Stefan took a deep breath and looked out the window toward the sunlight. He smiled. Then he laughed. *He was at peace.*

The evening meal was interrupted by an officer of the Guard.

"What is it?" Han demanded.

"His Grace asked that I tell you something immediately."

"So, he finally woke up, eh?" Han said. "Has he eaten anything yet?"

"He is now, sir."

Ericha breathed a sigh of relief. When she'd heard that he was refusing to eat, she had feared what state of mind he might be in.

"So, what's the message?" Han asked.

"He wishes to see Nik Koenig, as soon as possible."

Ericha and Abbi exchanged a questioning glance. Han looked confused but said, "I suppose that could be arranged."

"Very good, sir," the officer said and left the room.

"What do you suppose that's all about?" Han asked, focusing on Nik at the far end of the table.

Nik just shrugged his shoulders. They'd all become accustomed to his quiet, polite manner as he shared most meals with the family. But he kept much to himself beyond his interaction with Ericha and Abbi when they would come to his room or take him for walks in the garden.

"Well," Han said, returning to his meal, "I guess you'd better get over there as soon as you're finished."

Nik nodded and met Ericha's gaze. In her heart she hoped this was what it appeared to be.

Stefan had barely finished eating and cleaning up when he heard commotion in the hallway and realized Nik was being wheeled toward his cell.

The first thing Stefan noticed as they brought him in was how much better Nik looked. His new lifestyle was suiting him well. They were left alone for several moments before Nik responded to the silence by saying, "Here I am."

"Yes, well . . ." Stefan cleared his throat. "This is not easy for me. I've been thinking a lot about the day Ericha brought you into my office, and I . . ." He hesitated, and Nik leaned forward.

"Believe it or not," Nik said, "I understand how you feel, and I don't blame you a bit for feeling it. I've done some deplorable things that even time will not erase, and I know how greatly you've been affected. Don't think that I haven't thought a lot about that the last twenty years."

"Yes," Stefan said, folding his hands together, "I believe you have. So have I. It's embarrassing to admit, but the position I am in now has perhaps humbled me enough to make me see things differently." Stefan cleared his throat again and tapped his fingers together nervously. "I know I told you that I'd never forgive you, and I apologize for that, because that is what I want to do right now."

Stefan looked into Nik's eyes and said straightly, "I want you to know that I have forgiven you for all you have ever done against my family and myself, and I would ask that you forgive me for taking so long to get around to it."

Stefan saw tears forming in Nik Koenig's eyes and felt emotion rising in his own throat.

"You really mean it, don't you, boy?" Nik said, betraying a tone of relief.

"Of course I mean it." Stefan chuckled tensely. "A man doesn't say things he doesn't mean when he's going to die any day now."

"You can't know what this means to me," Nik added.

"Well," Stefan stood and turned toward the window, "I don't know how other men feel when they come this close to dying. But if nothing else, I have realized that I don't want to be carrying selfish judgments with me into the grave. It is not my place to judge. It is my duty to forgive. In truth, how can I expect to be forgiven of my own sins, if I am not willing to forgive? So you see," he chuckled in an attempt to lighten the mood as he turned back to face Nik and leaned against the wall, "I'm doing it for purely selfish reasons." Nik smiled, and Stefan added, "I only wish I could be around long enough to get to know you a little better. I know you've changed. It would be nice to just start over."

"Perhaps there is hope yet," Nik offered on a light note.

"I fear it's too late for that," Stefan admitted.

"You didn't kill her, did you?" Nik asked.

Stefan was surprised. "And what do you think?" he retorted.

"Nah," he chuckled, "you didn't kill her. I've no doubt of that." He smiled mischievously. "But I might have if I'd have been you. Good thing I wasn't you."

Stefan chuckled, wondering why he found this amusing, and Nik continued. "I don't know what made you marry her, but I don't think I've ever seen such a woman in all my life. Lightning may strike me for saying it, but she got just what she deserved."

"Amen," Stefan said, and then he chuckled and pointed a finger at Nik. "Don't you ever repeat that I said that!"

Nik held up his hand in a gesture of promise, and his eyes lightened merrily. "Now on the other hand, that cousin of yours has got to be the most remarkable woman I have ever met. But then, most du Woernig women are. Would you believe that woman has put life back into me?"

"Yes," Stefan said nostalgically, "I would believe that. I believe that Ericha could do anything."

"Now don't turn sad, boy," Nik said. "It won't do any good. Besides, she's sad enough for both of you." Stefan looked toward him abruptly. "Oh, she tries to hide it, but I know it's there. That girl's heart is breaking. Although she did look pleased when they said you wanted to see me. Do you suppose she knew what it was about?"

"She probably did," Stefan stated distantly. "I believe she knows me better than I know myself."

"Maybe that's why she doesn't want you to know about the baby."

Stefan's heart began to pound. "What baby?"

"The baby Ericha is going to have. I would assume it's yours."

"Of course it's mine!" he insisted, and Nik chuckled.

"I know that."

"How did you find out?" Stefan insisted.

"I figured it out," he said proudly. "You know how pregnant women are. She looks a little green in the mornings, always tired, eats too much, and cries every time she turns around."

Stefan felt a combination of heartache and joy as Nik went on. "So, I asked her. She told me it was true, but she didn't want anyone else to know . . . under the circumstances, she said. I told her it was something you might want to know—under the circumstances—but she said it would only make things more difficult for you. But I didn't agree. I was hoping she wouldn't make me promise not to tell you, and she didn't. So I'm not breaking any promises. I'm telling you because I think you ought to know."

"Thank you," Stefan said distantly.

"I was right, then."

"Yes, you were right. I am glad to know, though it doesn't make leaving any easier."

"I didn't expect it would, but then . . ." A key was turned in the lock, and Nik seemed disappointed. "Looks like I have to go now."

"Nik," Stefan said before he was taken away, "I'm expecting you to be there for her. She'll need you, I think."

"I'll do everything I can," he replied.

Stefan held out his hand, and Nik smiled as he shook it firmly. "I'll remember you in my prayers," Nik added, and he was wheeled away.

Long after little Cameron went to sleep for the night, Ericha felt restless and uptight. She wandered to Stefan's music room, wanting to feel close to him somehow. Idly she set a lamp on the piano and sat at the bench. With reverence she touched the keys, the same way she would touch Stefan if he were with her now, and she longed for the ability to bring them to life with music the way Stefan could. She closed her eyes and conjured up a clear image of his hands. She loved his hands.

"Shouldn't you be in bed?" Gerhard's voice startled her.

"I don't sleep much these days," she said warily as he sauntered toward her, one hand in his pocket, the other cradling a glass of brandy. She'd not encountered him beyond meals with the family since their unfriendly chat in the courtyard.

Ericha came to her feet. "Perhaps I should—"

"Don't let me scare you off," he said gently. His normally insolent manner was completely absent. "Please, sit down," he added. "I'd like to talk to you. I promise to behave myself."

Ericha sat down slowly, watching him with caution. Gerhard sat on the stool Stefan used to paint. He took a long swallow of his drink and eyed the partly finished canvas with a tilt of his head.

"You probably don't like me much," he began. "Most of the family doesn't. I mean . . . they all love me, I'm certain. But I'm not always pleasant to be around. The truth is, they just don't understand me."

Ericha listened for several minutes while Gerhard summed up his status in the family. As a child he'd wanted nothing but to play and get into mischief. He admitted that it was likely with the motive to get his parents' attention. As a youth he had resented Stefan and convinced himself he'd hated his brother. Gerhard had inherited his father's wit and laughter, and he'd taught himself to use it as a defense against the misery in his home. As an adult, Gerhard admitted that he respected Stefan, he loved his family, and he was grateful that he would not be forced to take Stefan's position. And he was gradually learning to set aside his flippancy when it was necessary.

"But what I really want to say," he concluded, "is that I'm sorry for the way I behaved toward you before. You're obviously a wonderful woman, Ericha, and I'm truly glad that my brother has you. I only pray that he will live beyond this."

"Thank you," was all Ericha could think to say.

"Do you play?" he asked, nodding toward the piano.

"Heavens, no," she said, touching the keys gently. "If only I could, perhaps I wouldn't miss him so badly."

"Well," he chuckled, "I did learn a thing or two from all those dreadful lessons my mother forced me to endure."

"You play?"

"My dear Ericha, when you grow up in Castle Horstberg, you learn to play the piano." He motioned toward it. "May I?"

"By all means," Ericha said. She slid to the end of the bench as Gerhard set his drink on the piano and made himself comfortable. It only took a minute to realize that his skill was comparable to Stefan's, but the music he played was nothing the same. Ericha quickly felt Gerhard's personality coming through in the light-hearted, whimsical nature of his talent. He played her every song he knew, intermittently telling her funny stories of his travels and a few jokes. Ericha listened and laughed, briefly forgetting her heartache. Then without hardly realizing it, she began to tell him how she had met Stefan, unaware that he was the duke, and unaware that she was Erich's daughter. He held her hand when she started to cry, and he walked her back to her room a little before three in the morning. The way he kissed her cheek before he left reminded her of Karl.

"Thank you, Gerhard," she said as he walked away.

He turned and blew her a kiss. "You keep smiling, Princess," he said. "It's not over yet."

Ericha managed a little laugh, but in her heart she found it difficult to believe him.

Chapter Twenty-Four

A COUNTRY AT STAKE

Ericha awoke to the rumble of a mob outside the castle gates and cringed inside as she thought of Stefan at their mercy and how he must have felt. She saw to little Cameron's needs, then had breakfast with Abbi in her sitting room while they tried to ignore the continuing roar outside.

Ericha left Cameron in Abbi's care and went to the office to speak to Han, needing to know where things stood. Since Stefan had regained his strength, they were restricting his visitors considerably, and she hadn't seen him for several days.

Han greeted her warmly, but she had barely sat down in the office when the door flew open and Han stood abruptly from behind the desk. Captain Leichty entered, obviously very upset, and threw a sword with a note attached to it onto the desk.

"What is this?" Han insisted.

"My stables were burned to the ground this morning just before dawn," he said bitterly. "That was stuck in the tree outside my front door!"

Han picked it up as Ericha moved to his side, and they read together the red ink, made to appear like blood: *THE KING MUST DIE!*

"That's it!" the captain said. "The trial cannot be put off another day. I can't hold them off any longer!"

Han motioned Ericha out of the office so that he could speak with the captain. She scurried into the hall, and panic and dread pierced her to the very core. At least she had gotten what she'd come for. She knew exactly where things stood.

Ericha was granted a brief visit with her husband that evening. While there were a thousand things she wanted to say as she was let into the darkened cell, none of it seemed relevant with what little time they had. She held him close and urged her lips over his. The desperation in his kiss provoked the emotions she was trying so hard to keep in control. Impulsively she leaned into him. His momentary surprise vaporized into obvious desire as he pressed his hands to her back and kissed her harder.

"We must hurry, Stefan," she whispered. He hesitated only a moment before he lowered her back onto the narrow bed. Their passion erupted quickly, edged with a harsh desperation.

"I love you, Ericha," he murmured against her face. And then he just held her until they heard footsteps in the hall. She eased away and discreetly adjusted her skirts before the door came open. She pressed her mouth over his once more, and walked away. Stefan winced as the door was slammed and locked. He felt certain he had just experienced the last real pleasure he would ever know. And even that was tainted with pain.

Stefan was brought fresh clothes and some water to clean up with, and then he waited quietly in his cell until four officers came to escort him to the courtroom, Captain Leichty being one of them.

"Are you sure you don't want an advocate?" the captain asked.

"Why?" Stefan chuckled tensely. "There is absolutely no evidence in my favor to present, and I certainly doubt that attempting to establish my good character at this point would do much good."

The captain made no further comment, which told Stefan that he agreed.

Ericha stood close beside Abbi and Maggie as Stefan was escorted in, and then everyone was seated. She could still see some evidence of the mob's cruelty on his face, but she wondered how he could look so dignified and calm when she knew his anguish closely matched her own.

Stefan briefly took in those present. The room was packed as tightly as it could be, mostly with curious citizens from Horstberg, he concluded, although he recognized some dignitaries from Kohenswald seated near the front that were there officially to represent their country's interest in the case. Also close by were his family, as well as Karl and Luise. He exchanged a quick glance with each of his loved ones, then rested his eyes on Ericha with empathy. She looked so beautiful, he thought. He recalled their brief lovemaking last night and his heart quickened a little. Why hadn't she told him she was going to have another baby? A hush fell tensely over the room as Han took his place to act as judge, and Stefan felt sure that even those who believed he was guilty couldn't help but sense the irony in the situation.

Stefan remained expressionless as the testimonies began. The two maids who had heard the shot established that no one had left the floor where the duke's rooms were located, and officers of the Guard testified of a thorough, immediate search that verified no one else was on that floor at all.

Captain Leichty testified that the passageway leading from the bedroom was not used the day of the murder, and Rusty told of hearing the shot from the office and immediately summoning officers to investigate its source.

The jury then established that it appeared Stefan was the only one in the area at the time. Which brought them to the subject of motive. Abbi and Maggie each gripped one of Ericha's hands tightly as the evidence continued to mount against Stefan, and hope slowly filtered away.

Through the testimony of various servants, a distasteful image of Stefan and Johanna's relationship was brought to light. It seemed that arguments were common, and it was suspected they had not spent a night together in a very long time. Stefan couldn't believe how many nosy people with eavesdropping skills he had working for him. The only thing established in his favor was the evidence that Johanna had been having various affairs for several years, and the general opinion of her character was avid distaste.

Stefan was wishing they'd just hurry and get this over with when another maid was called to the stand. She told plainly of overhearing Johanna accuse her husband of having an illegitimate son, and that he didn't deny it.

"And was anything said beyond that point?" the prosecutor asked.

"Yes, sir," she replied.

"Could you tell us what, please?"

"The argument became more heated, and . . ."

"Please go on," he urged when she hesitated.

"He threatened to kill her."

Stefan leaned his face into his hand as a low murmur went through the courtroom. The maid was asked to return to her seat, and Stefan sighed, hoping this was all. But another servant was brought forward, and he swallowed hard to recognize the maid that had brought breakfast into his room the day before Johanna was killed. This was the moment he'd been dreading.

She stated what she saw when she entered the room, seeming to think it was obvious they had shared a bed as man and wife. As she left the room and immediately heard them arguing, she lingered curiously. Her interpretation of the conversation was that the duke feared his mistress would discover that he'd been sleeping with his wife.

Stefan glanced sharply toward Han, wanting so badly to say that it had been distorted—mostly for Ericha's sake. But his father's eyes told him that it had to wait. In his heart Stefan knew that what little he had to say in his defense would make no difference.

When it became apparent that there was more than enough motive, Stefan held his breath as Ericha Heinrich was called to testify. Her expression told him that she had not been forewarned of this, and panic filled her eyes. She glanced toward Stefan, wondering how to approach this. He met her eyes with assurance and nodded firmly.

Ericha knew she must speak with candor. With dignity she stood and moved forward, her tenseness increasing as the prosecutor began his questioning. He first established that she had married Stefan Heinrich since his wife had been killed. Stefan was grateful for Georg's insight when she was asked if she had knowledge of Stefan's escape, and she was able to answer that she didn't.

"Your son was born several months before your marriage," the prosecutor stated.

"Yes," she replied simply.

"Could you tell us who the child's father is?"

"My husband is his father."

"Are you certain?"

"Of course," she replied, trying not to sound indignant at the insinuation.

"And how long have you known Stefan Heinrich?"

"I met him soon after I came to Horstberg. It was the spring of 1867."

"About three years then."

"Yes."

"And tell us the circumstances concerning your affair."

Ericha glanced toward Han, wanting to protest that this was not necessary. But he nodded firmly, and she had to go on.

"We met by coincidence several times and came to love each other. It was my idea to carry on the relationship. Stefan fought the idea because of his obligations."

She paused and the prosecutor asked, "What made him change his mind?"

Ericha lifted her chin slightly and stated, "An unhappy man does not make a good ruler."

"And was he unhappy?"

"I believe that has been established."

"And then?"

"We began seeing each other regularly, and things seemed to go better for him."

"Except his marriage."

"It was a difficult situation," she said, fearing what her words might imply.

"One last point," he said, and Ericha felt relief that this was almost over. "Do you feel that your husband has always been honest with you?"

"Always," she said with strength.

"And what has he told you concerning the situation of his first wife's death?"

Ericha took a deep breath and thought over her answer briefly before she stated, "He has admitted his animosity toward Johanna but told me repeatedly that he could have never killed her, and he didn't."

"That will be all," he replied, and Ericha returned to her seat where Abbi and Maggie squeezed her hands tightly.

Doctor Furhelm was called to the stand. Stefan felt some hope as he repeated what he knew of Johanna's pregnancy and abortion early in the marriage. But then he was questioned specifically on his examination of Johanna's body after the death. He told of several fresh bruises, mostly on her face, indicating that she had been hit numerous times before she was shot.

Stefan was then called to speak in his defense, and Ericha's heart beat quickly. He calmly stated his side of the story, beginning with the argument the day she had discovered his affair, up to his discovering the body. He was asked about his feelings for Johanna and admitted that he believed she was manipulative and insensitive. He tried to illustrate this by repeating what he believed her intentions were the previous morning when he woke to find her in his bed.

"And why do you suppose," the prosecutor asked, "she was in your bedroom when she was killed?"

"She was up to mischief," Stefan stated.

The prosecutor lifted his brows, and Stefan realized that hadn't sounded good.

"Explain please," he stated.

"When I found her body, she was wearing emeralds. She always wore emeralds when she was up to mischief. If she had come there to impress me or argue with me, she would not have worn emeralds."

The statement seemed to be taken lightly, and Stefan sighed, wishing he hadn't even mentioned it. In his own mind it affirmed his innocence, but to the jury it probably sounded like a feeble attempt.

He was beginning to believe it could get no worse when the prosecutor asked, "Did you ever physically strike your first wife?"

Stefan wanted to explain the way Johanna provoked and pushed him. He wanted to beg the jury to understand that it was a mistake and he had regretted it. But he could only swallow and answer the question. "Yes," he said, glancing toward Captain Leichty, who was looking at the floor. "But only once," he added, fearing it hadn't been heard as a low murmur went through the crowd. Though it was subtle, he caught the astonishment in the women he loved—Ericha especially.

Stefan hoped to be asked questions to fill in the specific details on that, but the prosecutor only said, "One last question. Did you kill Johanna Heinrich?"

Stefan said firmly, "No, I did not."

"That will be all," he said, and Stefan returned to his seat.

Silence ruled in the courtroom as the jury came to their decision, and Stefan's mind became distant as he sensed the inevitable. He thought deeply about his grandfather's journals and drew comfort from the things he had read. And he was grateful for the personal peace he had come to. The bishop's visit early this morning had helped confirm that.

Stefan and those who loved him held their breath as the jury's decision was handed to Han. Stefan swallowed hard when Han squeezed his eyes shut with a bitter expression. He cleared his throat and said carefully, "The jury of this court deems Stefan Cameron Han du Woernig Heinrich . . . guilty as charged."

Stefan showed no emotion when his father sentenced him to death by firing squad to be carried out the following morning at sunrise. He scanned the eyes of those in the room for reactions. Those of his family were various degrees of distress; others in the room varied from smug and triumphant to piteous. And Rusty wouldn't even look at him. This was all so horrible, Stefan thought.

When the sentence was given, Abbi leaned against Ericha and pressed a handkerchief to her mouth to suppress a weak moan. Ericha put her arm firmly around Abbi's shoulders to offer support as they watched Stefan escorted out of the room. Abbi nearly fell apart with her emotions. It was uncharacteristic of her, especially in public. Ericha and Maggie moved her quickly away where they could be alone.

"What is it, Mother?" Maggie asked when solitude only expounded Abbi's tears.

"I understand it now," she said.

"What?" Ericha asked, trying to blot out of her mind the trial they had just witnessed and what it meant.

"My dream," Abbi sobbed.

"Which one?" Ericha insisted, trying to remain calm.

"With Han . . . the gun . . . and . . ."

"Yes," Ericha said, urging her on.

"Don't you see?" Abbi whispered. "By right of authority, Han must give the final signal for execution."

Ericha met Maggie's eyes, and her heart sank as she perceived Abbi's realization. The three of them cried together in an effort to release their despair. Ericha thought she would die inside. She missed him so much already.

Later that day when the first opportunity arose to be alone, Ericha found herself in Stefan's bedroom, pondering the situation. She thought of the wedding night they had shared here and it seemed like a dream. Abbi had suggested that she could use this room now, since she was Stefan's wife. But Ericha couldn't bear the thought of sleeping here without him and had chosen to stay in the room she had been using near the nursery.

Sitting on the edge of the bed, Ericha's arms ached with loneliness, and she folded them tightly around her. She thought again that this was the room Johanna had been killed in. But combined with her present frame of mind, that realization suddenly meant something more. Was it possible that anything had been missed? Could there be a grain of hope left? She moved carefully around the room, trying to think like a murderer would.

Stefan was in the hall as soon as the shot was fired, so no one left this room. They had to have gone out the passageway, but they knew that no one had come out of it at the other end. She wondered if other passageways existed in this room, but a diligent search of the walls proved that theory wrong.

Using simple deduction, she decided the answer must lie in the passageway, and she ventured to explore it more carefully. She lit a torch and moved carefully through it. She'd been in it so many times that she almost felt certain there was nothing here that would mean anything, but her mind churned with possibilities. She became angry to think how easily something could be overlooked that could cost a man's life. Her thoughts were absorbed with this when the torch flickered slightly, and she stopped, breathless.

"Of course," she said aloud, realizing that in her visits before Johanna was killed she couldn't recall a breeze, but coming through with Han, she'd been aware of it.

Holding the torch high, Ericha surveyed the wall on both sides of her. She was dismayed to see nothing but stone, just like the rest of the passageway. She almost gave up, but the torch flickered again, and she brought it closer to the breeze to see a narrow crack that went the length of the wall.

Ericha's heart beat quickly as she ran her fingers over the wall, searching for something—*anything*. It could mean Stefan's life!

She didn't know what triggered it, but Ericha caught her breath sharply when the opening widened. She held up the torch to see that another passageway had opened before her. With her heart beating madly now, she moved carefully into it.

It was different than the other, which descended gradually like a tunnel. This immediately moved into stairs that went down steeply. Ericha held to the wall and stepped carefully, wondering what she might discover. She was surprised that it ended quickly. The wall before her was much like the end of the passageway that led into the bedroom, so she probed around carefully and was not surprised to have it open in front of her.

Hesitantly she pushed her shoulder against it, and with great effort it opened further. She poked her head through the opening and gasped. Ericha hadn't known what to expect, but it hadn't been to come into the duke's office—right where the book cupboard used to be.

Gratefully the room was empty, but she heard footsteps in the hall and quickly doused the torch and closed the wall. Han came in the room and looked surprised to see her there.

"Did you need something?" he asked, noting her expression.

"Uh . . . no. I was just . . . wandering."

Han looked at her intently as if he sensed that it was more. Ericha knew she should tell him what she'd discovered, but she felt it was important to tell Stefan first.

"Uh . . ." she said, "will I be able to see Stefan . . . again?"

"They will allow him a few minutes with each of his family members later this afternoon. I'm afraid I can do no more than that."

Ericha nodded her understanding, and Han's eyes filled with compassion. "Why don't you go get some rest and I'll let you know when it's time."

She nodded again and left the room, wondering if she was handling this right. The officers guarding the door didn't seem to notice that she had come out when they hadn't seen her go in. Perhaps there had been a recent change of shift for the officers. She scolded herself for not telling Han what she had discovered. But she knew who had been in the office right after the murder, and to her it didn't make sense. Knowing how Stefan felt about Rusty, she felt she had to tell him first. She only prayed her decision was not a mistake.

The hours dragged by slowly. She was grateful for a lengthy visit from Karl, and he did well to keep her distracted. He and Luise had managed to get through the mobs with the help of several officers in order to be there for the trial. He wasn't allowed to see Stefan, but they would be staying with Theodor until this was over.

When Karl returned to his father's apartment, Ericha became so anxious to see Stefan, she could barely sit still. But then, she didn't want to see him, knowing that once she did, that would be it—unless something came of what she had discovered. Perhaps it could at least stall for time.

Throughout the evening, Stefan was visited in turn by each of his family members. Embraces and tears were shared abundantly, but very few words were spoken. It was difficult to face saying good-bye to all of them, but his brief time with Abbi was almost unbearable. She sat close beside him on the narrow cot with her head against his shoulder while he held her silently. He knew she was trying to be brave, but her aura betrayed her anguish.

"Everything will be all right," he whispered, but they both knew he was lying. She wanted to offer him comfort but could think of nothing to say. When she finally left him alone, Stefan felt empty.

Han and Maggie came in together, and Han leaned against the door while Maggie pulled her son fiercely into her arms and just held him. She touched his face and hair while tears spilled over her face, and Stefan felt his heart being torn into little pieces.

"I love you, Mother," he said quietly. "You have given me so much."

"I remember," she tried to smile, "the day you were born. I was so proud to have a son, and you never failed me. Your father used to accuse me of spoiling you. He was probably right. But you never took advantage of that, Stefan. You were always so good."

She laid her head against his shoulder and sobbed helplessly. "Don't cry, Mother," he whispered. "A part of me will always be with you."

Han urged her away and held her against him while he reached out to put his other arm around Stefan's shoulders.

"She's right, you know," he said quietly. "We couldn't have asked for a better son."

Stefan looked humbly toward the floor, wondering how they could feel that way when he was dying with such disgrace. But Han embraced him, and his love and acceptance were genuine.

When his parents left, Stefan knew the only one left was Ericha. He wondered how they could possibly attempt to make up for a lifetime in the few minutes she was allowed to be with him. He turned from the window as the door to his cell opened and Ericha entered. As the door closed again behind her, she moved into his arms and they held each other desperately.

"Ericha," he whispered, "our time is so brief, and I—"

"Nonsense," she smiled. "Perhaps it's not over yet."

"What are you thinking?" he asked. "You're up to something. I can see it."

"Stefan," she whispered, "you're not going to believe this, but . . . I just found a branch off the passageway from the bedroom." Stefan's eyes widened with a hope that faded quickly as she finished. "It leads to the office."

Stefan drew back, and his eyes narrowed intently. He was stunned. Carefully he sat down and ran his hands through his hair.

"But Rusty was the only one in the office after it happened," Stefan stated tensely. "It's impossible!" No one would understand, but to Stefan this was almost worse than taking the blame himself. "It can't be," he whispered as if he were alone. "What reason could he have possibly had to . . ." Stefan's eyes shot to Ericha. "He wouldn't have done it!" He said adamantly. "And even *if* he had, he wouldn't let me take the blame. It's impossible."

"Stefan," Ericha protested quietly, "it's the only thing that makes sense. It should at least be looked into."

"No," he said. "He wouldn't have done it. And I won't accuse him of it."

"It's not an accusation. It's evidence. Look at the facts, Stefan. What do you suppose he came to the lodge to tell you?"

Stefan's eyes narrowed, and he turned toward the window. In his mind he pieced it together. "The only reason he would have killed her is to protect me, but I still don't believe he did it."

"What makes you so certain?"

"I know, Ericha," he pointed a finger at her. "I *know* he would not let me die for something he had done. He wouldn't!"

Ericha felt her hope starting to dwindle. "It means your innocence can be proven. You don't have to die."

"Oh, but I do," he stated. "It's gone beyond Johanna's death. It's me they want. I know those people, and I know they will rationalize anything to have my blood. So what's the point in ruining Rusty's life when I have to die anyway?"

Ericha couldn't believe what he was saying. "So," she said indignantly, "you're just resigning yourself to martyrdom. Leave me a widow for the sake of pride!"

"Ericha," he insisted, taking her arm, "it is for the sake of my country! I have no choice. I don't want to die. I've got something to live for!" He took her into his arms. "But it has gone too far. If Rusty doesn't confess to it, I'm not going to accuse him. And neither will you. You will say nothing of your knowledge. And I mean it—emphatically. You must trust me, Ericha. You must!"

"How can I possibly stand by and let you die when you are everything to me?"

"Because I ask you to," he stated.

"I can't do it!" she cried. "I can't!"

"You have to!" he insisted, and Ericha felt anger well up, momentarily drowning the hurt and fear.

"How could you?" she cried, hitting her fists against his shoulders. Her efforts to stay in control were lost, and she sobbed helplessly while he grabbed her wrists to keep her from hitting him again. "How can you die and leave me alone? I don't understand how you could do this to me! I don't!"

"Ericha," he said gently, attempting to calm her down. "Ericha, please don't!" She gave little response, and Stefan felt their precious time slipping away. With desperation, he put his mouth over hers and kissed her hard.

Ericha wilted into his arms, sobbing in the midst of his kiss, longing for it to last forever. She felt crushed against him, consumed by his strength.

"Ericha," he whispered, "I love you. I love you!"

"Please," she cried, "let me talk to your father and—"

Stefan put his fingers to her lips, and she squeezed her eyes shut. "Ericha," he said, and the softness of his tone distracted her fears, "do you know how it felt to ride through this country—*my country*—in bonds, while the people looked on with everything from pity to disgust? Do you know what they called me? A traitor!" He paused and his voice turned gruff. "An adulterer."

Ericha swallowed hard and felt compassion for him. She recalled moments when they had contemplated what their affair might do to the country. But neither of them could have comprehended such a thing as this.

"I remember," he said, "my grandfather's attitude toward this duchy. Horstberg was his whole life—except his family. The responsibility bequeathed in my blood is not something I can take lightly. I have disappointed my people, and I'm not certain they would ever accept me as their ruler again. Perhaps I made a mistake," he said humbly, "but dying with courage will let me die with something that most men never possess. I must turn it over to fate. Don't think of my dying as a martyrdom for my country. Ericha, my dying is a declaration that I love you, and I don't regret the decision I made to make you a part of my life."

Ericha's tears welled up again, and Stefan kissed her, doing his best to completely consume her, as if he could somehow bring her inside himself and take her along.

"I love you, Stefan." She sighed, resigning herself to the reality that this was their last moment together. She looked at him deeply, wanting to memorize every detail of his presence. "You have given me so much happiness."

He smiled. "You, Ericha, have given me life." His eyes delved into hers. He hadn't intended to ask, but he had to know. "Is it true, Ericha?" he whispered and pressed his hand to her belly.

"How did you know?" she whispered breathlessly.

"Nik told me, but you mustn't be angry with him. I—"

"I didn't want you to know. I was afraid it would only be harder for you, and—"

"Ericha," he interrupted, "I'm glad to know. I'll admit that it adds to the regret of my not being here, but there is a degree of comfort in it. Again, you're making it possible for my life to go on without me—and I am grateful."

They heard the key turn in the lock and held to each other tightly. "I love you, Ericha," Stefan whispered with panic seeping through his voice. "You must remember it."

He kissed her one last time while they barely heard the officer say something apologetic. Ericha felt a gentle arm urging her away from Stefan, and she made no effort to hide her emotion as she was ushered from the cell.

Stefan squeezed his eyes shut when the door was locked. "I love you, Stefan," he heard her cry as her voice became distant, and then silence fell over him like a plague. Impulsively he turned and slammed his fist into the stone wall, ignoring the pain that couldn't compare to what he felt inside.

Ericha was numbly going through the task of putting Cameron down to bed when Han slipped into the nursery.

"Don't put him down just yet," he said, taking Cameron into his arms and throwing a blanket around him.

"Where are you going?" she asked when he headed toward the door.

"I'm taking him to see his father," Han said, and Ericha put her hand over her mouth to suppress her emotion. She had done little but cry for hours.

"Wait," she said, and Han turned back slightly. Ericha pulled open a bureau drawer and brought forth the little box she had once given Stefan. He had kept it at her home, and she had packed it when she'd come here. "Give him this," she said, "if they'll let you, of course."

Han nodded and went into the hall. "And tell him I love him," she added, then closed the door and sat down to cry.

Captain Leichty entered the cell with a lantern, and Stefan came to his feet.

"It goes against regulations, but I gave into a bribe so you could have one last visitor." He smiled. "I doubt he'll give us much trouble."

Han stepped into the cell with little Cameron in his arms, and Stefan smiled. "Thank you, Captain," he uttered, pulling his son into his arms. Han and the captain stood back while Stefan turned away to share a few quiet moments with little Cameron, who was innocently unaware of what all of this meant.

Their time was over quickly and Stefan had to give the child back to Han, but he was grateful for the opportunity to have seen him. "Thank you, Father," he said quietly. Han held out his free arm, and he and Stefan embraced. "Take good care of my children, now." Han lifted his brow in question, but the captain moved toward the door with an indication that he had to leave.

"Is there anything you want me to do, any . . . last wishes, so to speak?"

"Yes," Stefan said, "whatever happens, I want you to be certain that Rusty is in his usual place for the execution—right beside you on the balcony."

"That's it?" Han asked. There was no time to question his motives.

"That's it," Stefan stated dryly.

Han began to turn away, then added hastily, "Oh, Ericha asked me to tell you she loves you—and to give you this." Stefan took the little box reverently. "The captain already inspected it for escape devices," Han added lightly, and a moment later he was gone.

Stefan sat down and held the box close to the light, tracing his fingers over the words carved there. "A fire burns in my heart," he said aloud. He remembered well the night Ericha had given it to him, and how she'd told him to open it slowly so the love wouldn't escape.

Stefan glanced around the little cell. He was alone now. No more visitors; only a long night ahead with no point in sleeping. The minutes of his life were numbered. He followed Ericha's instructions now and opened the box very slowly. Then he stared helplessly at the red velvet beneath the delicate, tatted lace, feeling a knot gather in his throat.

It seemed he stayed motionless for hours, just staring at it, and then he heard words come from his lips that felt as if someone else were saying them, giving him comfort. "The world is cold and brash outside. I fear what it imparts. But I know my love is here with me. A fire burns in my heart."

Stefan finally set the box down, but he couldn't bear to close it. He doused the light, turning his mind to prayer in an effort to prepare himself to meet what lay beyond tomorrow's sunrise.

Ericha lay helplessly awake, so full of fear and emotion she thought she would die inside. Instinctively she wanted to fight for Stefan's life and rush to tell Han what she knew. But she kept recalling the words she had committed herself to Stefan with— not only in the castle chapel more recently, but long ago when their relationship had just begun.

She had promised to love, cherish, honor, and obey him no matter the circumstances. Ericha pondered long over the words, realizing how sacred a marriage covenant was in that respect. She didn't understand Stefan's reasons for wanting to keep her knowledge quiet, but she trusted him and could do nothing but respect his decision. She wished briefly that she had known this before she'd been questioned in court. She would have had to reveal her knowledge. But it was too late now. Stefan had turned himself over to fate. His life was in God's hands.

Ericha resigned herself to accept that this was the end, and she tried to concentrate on her gratitude to have with her his name, his son, and the child she carried, and to be a part of the family he loved. And then she prayed, wondering if God might see fit to grant them a miracle.

Abbi called the family to come together before dawn. Karl was also present. When they were all seated, she drew back her shoulders to speak. "I was thinking in the night about the days when I was falling in love with Cameron du Woernig—with no knowledge of his identity. I had no idea I was to be the Duchess of Horstberg until the day that it came about. I have never regretted loving Cameron despite the burden that being his wife has put on my shoulders at many times in my life.

"Even now, I will not forsake his memory by wishing that my life had been different. I would not blame any of you at this moment for wishing to have been born under any circumstances other than these. In all the trials I have suffered over the fifty years or better that I have been at Castle Horstberg, nothing has grieved me as much as what we must face today. This day could only be comparable to the day we lost Cameron and Erich, yet still this anguish seems more severe by the methods that must be carried out."

Abbi glanced around to see the tear-stained faces of her posterity and knew they were depending on her to know how to deal with this. She felt her heart breaking inside but knew that she had to be strong.

"We must depend on each other to make it through this," she implored gently. "We will mourn. We will never forget. But we will not forsake what it is that he is sacrificing for our peace as a country. I will tell you what he told me. He begged me to not be sad over his death, but to always remember the soul of Horstberg and what it means to us."

Abbi could think of nothing more to say that would make any difference, so she asked the family to kneel together so they could ask God to help them through this day, and those ahead with the emptiness they would bear. In a circle of grasped hands, Georg took his natural place as patriarchal leader of the group and offered thanks to the Unseen Power for all their lives had been blessed with, and he asked that the happenings of this day would not destroy their spirit. He asked for comfort to be with Han as he faced what he must inevitably do, and especially for comfort to be with Stefan.

There was a tearful mutual *amen,* and as Georg and Han left the room to attend to their duties, Abbi was certain she felt Cameron's arms come around her in comfort.

The cell was still very dark when the door opened and light shed in from the hall. Stefan sat up as Theodor entered the room with two officers carrying all he needed. Nothing was said as Stefan stood and lit the lamp. His clothes were laid over the bed and water was poured into a basin for him to shave as the door was locked.

"You're not saying much, Theodor," Stefan said when he couldn't bear the silence any longer.

"I wasn't sure you wanted to talk," he stated.

"I don't. I want *you* to talk, Theodor. Talk about normal everyday things."

Theodor met his eyes, and Stefan felt certain he was on the verge of tears. He turned away and blinked several times before he cleared his throat and started talking about the evening he'd spent with a lady friend and the chess game he'd played with Karl the other day. He mentioned how the garden at Karl's house had suffered since Ericha had moved to the castle. But he could see that Karl and Luise were very happy. Luise was expecting a baby, and he was excited about being a grandfather, even though he didn't want to admit to being that old. When Theodor apparently ran out of things to say, Stefan was dressed in full uniform. Nothing was said as the robe was clipped to his shoulders.

Stefan glanced down at his chest and managed a chuckle. "It's a shame to put a hole in the uniform. Why don't they just bury me in it?"

Theodor stopped momentarily as if he'd been frozen. He resumed his work and said in a raspy voice, "You have more than one, Your Grace. I'll see that you look as good then as you do now."

"Thank you," Stefan said almost lightly.

Figuring they were finished, he was surprised when Theodor said, "One more thing." He opened a box that had been left on the bed and reverently picked up the ducal crown.

"Is that necessary?" Stefan asked, feeling somehow hypocritical.

"Necessary and appropriate," he insisted.

It was tradition that he kneel whenever the crown was put onto his head. While he thought it was a bit silly, Abbi had told him it was a reminder of the humility in bearing such a position. He took a deep breath and went down on one knee, wondering if this was as difficult for Theodor as it was for him.

As Stefan came to his feet, adjusting the crown slightly, he realized the room was filling with predawn light. His heart quickened, but he took a deep breath and reminded himself to be calm. He thought of the peace he'd found within himself and knew he had nothing to fear. He thought of Cameron and Erich, and Kathe, and his grandmother Elsa, and wondered if they might be waiting to meet him. The thought assuaged him with an added measure of peace.

As the door was unlocked, Stefan felt a brief panic, but he fought to subdue it. Theodor gripped his forearm firmly, then gave him a quick embrace. He said nothing. As Theodor left, taking Stefan's belongings with him, the bishop entered, wearing his clerical robes. The door was left open. Four guards stood at the opening, their backs turned. Stefan met the bishop's eyes briefly, and then he went down on his knee, taking the bishop's hands. He didn't realize he was trembling until he tried to let go and couldn't. He was relieved when the bishop began to pray aloud on his behalf, and his inability to come to his feet went apparently unnoticed.

When the prayer ended, the bishop helped Stefan to his feet. Their eyes met. The bishop squeezed his hands in calm reassurance before he stepped aside and stated, "It is time."

The guards parted, and Stefan stepped into the hall, taking a deep breath and falling into step with them. He imagined his stallion waiting for him in the courtyard for a procession of celebration through the village. But as he stepped outside, there was only a firing squad, already waiting at perfect attention. He thought how only one of those rifles was loaded with the real bullet, and no one knew which man would fire the fatal shot. As he was escorted across the courtyard, he felt the panic hit. It took every inkling of self-control to maintain his dignity as everything inside of him screamed in horror. Something was wrong, he thought. He wasn't supposed to die now, not for a crime he didn't commit. He wished he'd let Ericha tell his father of the evidence she'd discovered. He didn't want to die. He wasn't ready to die! *Dear God,* he prayed, over and over in his mind, *don't let me die.*

Stefan was positioned against the wall, and he knew it was too late. Concentrating on the peace he'd felt earlier, he resigned himself to this—panic or not. He glanced up to see the women he loved huddled close together in a high window. He prayed they would have the sense to move away before it happened. And then he just prayed.

Han stopped before the door that led out to the balcony over the courtyard. He turned to his father. "I can't do it," he said. "I can't."

Georg put his hands gently on Han's shoulders and urged him out the door, standing close behind him to offer support.

As the duke regent stepped into view, the Guard came to attention, and the twelve gunmen moved forward into position.

Ericha gripped the windowsill, with Maggie, Abbi, and Hannah close to her. She was vaguely aware of Gerhard and Karl hovering in the room behind them. The women held their breath as Stefan was escorted from the keep into the brightening court-yard, wearing his full uniform and ducal robe. And his crown.

"What he must be feeling," Ericha whispered. Abbi and Maggie both gripped her hands firmly as Stefan moved into place against the wall. He stood with dignity and his stance spoke of courage. Slowly he turned his head, and for too brief a moment, he met eyes distantly with each of the women he loved, ending with a long gaze toward Ericha.

Stefan turned to face the gunmen and lifted his chin, and then his attention turned toward the balcony where his father stood. Even from the distance, Ericha saw the change in his expression. He looked briefly distressed, and then solace filled his eyes, and Ericha felt her heart beating madly. She was certain that when his life ended, she would feel something literally die inside of her.

Han waited expectantly for Rusty to arrive in the appointed spot. He remembered Stefan's request and was determined to do as he'd asked. He almost wished Rusty wouldn't show up because then he could have a good excuse to put this off. But he felt a painful relief when Rusty nervously came out to stand beside him. Han saw Stefan's eyes set on Rusty, then move to meet his own. Han felt himself die inside as Stefan nodded firmly toward him, indicating that he was ready. He found himself recalling the story from the Bible of Abraham and Isaac, and he knew now how it felt to be called upon to sacrifice a son. But he doubted that God was going to intervene now and call it off like He'd done for Abraham.

Han gripped the rail firmly and saw Stefan's eyes move back to Rusty. Han tipped his head back and swallowed hard, and he was grateful to feel his father's hand come over his shoulder. It took more courage and strength than he'd ever had to find in his life to bring his head forward and give the signal for the captain to order his son executed.

When the signal was finished, Han felt Rusty slip back through the door behind them, and wanted more than anything to follow.

His eyes went to Stefan. And though the courage had not failed, he seemed distressed by Rusty's sudden absence. But Stefan's eyes shot quickly forward as the captain's voice called clearly, "Ready!"

Stefan drew back his shoulders and lifted his chin, bringing his hands behind his back in a resigning gesture.

Abbi moved away from the window, imploring the others to sit with her where they couldn't see. They held to each other desperately, and a painful burden fell mutually over them as they heard clearly through the open window, "Aim!"

Han wanted to turn away, not wanting the tormenting memory of seeing his son fall. But Stefan caught his eyes, and Han did his best to offer an expression of love that might go with him. He was surprised to see Stefan give a comforting smile. Already he blessed the gesture; even now it softened what lay ahead. He concentrated on that smile in his mind as Georg stood close beside him and they leaned against each other for support.

Ericha kept repeating in her mind the final words: *And fire. And fire.* She knew those words would torment her, and when she heard the first of the order, she cried out a frenzied prayer that muffled the sounds following.

The women all slumped in tears. But Gerhard hurried to the window, saying, "Wait. There was no shot."

They paused to listen and heard the captain call, "Retract the arms."

Ericha moved to the window with the others. She felt Karl's hand in hers and cried out in joy to see that Stefan was still standing. He caught her eyes briefly. It seemed that only the captain knew what was happening, as his attention seemed distracted by something in the courtyard.

"He didn't do it!" a voice called from below, and Han looked skyward, disbelieving but grateful that perhaps he had been granted the blessing of Abraham after all.

"He didn't do it!" Rusty repeated, moving swiftly toward the captain. "And I can prove it."

Ericha laughed tears along with Abbi and Maggie and the others. Stefan had been right, she thought. Rusty wasn't going to let him die. Stefan showed no expression as he watched what was happening.

Han gripped his father's arm in hopeful expectation until the captain looked toward him, questioning what to do. The words came from Han's lips without tone, but in his heart they shouted for joy. "The execution will be postponed until we have the opportunity to survey new evidence. We will convene in court immediately."

Ericha saw Stefan close his eyes and bow his head. Even from the distance, she could see his shoulders move with a sigh of relief. Abruptly he looked up at her, and the sunlight caught a glisten of emotion in his eyes. He was led away by the Guard toward the door that entered the courtroom, and Abbi pulled the others away from the window.

"Come along," she said, "we must be there. Let's try to look presentable."

As Stefan was escorted into the courtroom, a different kind of tension descended. He briefly caught a glimpse of the women he loved, sitting close together, looking weary with swollen eyes. Did they love him so much? The same officials from Kohenswald who had been present to witness the execution were now seated in the courtroom, looking angry. Voices in the room buzzed quietly while they waited for what seemed like forever while the original jurors were brought in, and Han took his place, wearing the judicial robes.

Stefan felt his palms sweat as Rusty solemnly took his place to testify of this proof. Expectancy hung thick in the air. Even with what Ericha had told him about the passageway from the bedroom into the office, he could not comprehend Rusty committing murder. He prayed that this *proof* led the guilt elsewhere.

Rusty met Stefan's eyes briefly, and then he looked mostly toward the floor. The prosecutor approached the stand and said to Rusty, "Will you please tell us this evidence that you say can prove His Grace's innocence?"

"Perhaps I should start at the beginning," Rusty stated, and Stefan was surprised by his lack of stammering; it was as if his words had been carefully thought through and memorized. "Her Grace and I were having an affair. It had been going on for years."

A murmur went through the room, and Stefan had to blink several times to be sure this was real. He was stunned. He wondered if he should have felt betrayed, but he didn't. If anything, he resented Johanna playing upon Rusty's weaknesses. He knew Rusty was a good man, and most likely he either had loved Johanna or had been made to believe that he did. Only Stefan could fully understand Johanna's vindictive ways, and he felt sick with empathy and grief as Rusty relayed a story that put Stefan in shock.

"Looking back, I realize," Rusty continued, "that I was being used to come between her and Stefan, er . . . His Grace. It was after she had discovered her husband's affair that she began making plans to have him framed for treason." Stefan shifted uneasily at the mention of this, wondering what might have happened if she had lived. "I kept trying to tell her she was being a fool, and to just live her life and let him live his. But she was crazy with vengeance.

"On the day Her Grace was killed," Rusty continued, "she showed me a passageway that went from the office to the duke's bedroom, and while we were in his room, she started telling me her plans to do him in. She had purposely provoked one of her lovers in the village until he had hit her several times. She intended to put the blame on His Grace, but she wanted me to back her up and say that I had evidence it was true. Her plan was to weaken her husband's position with this, and then bring forward accusations of treason. There were people both in Kohenswald and Horstberg that she had lied to, convincing them that His Grace was involved in treasonous activities. I told her she was mad and I had no intention of helping her. She turned on me. She told me she would destroy me along with her husband. She said she would tell him everything that had happened between us, and her rendition of it was so distorted . . . and I couldn't bear the thought.

"I panicked. I knew Stefan kept a gun in his room." He drew a deep breath and said with effort. "I killed her. I dropped the gun and went back through the passageway to the office. I think I've been in shock ever since."

Rusty finally turned to look at Stefan. "I never dreamed you would get blamed for it," he said as if they were alone. "And if I had believed it would go this far, I would have come forward long ago. I feel like such a coward." He bowed his head. "I only pray you can forgive me." Rusty apologized publicly for his weakness of character, and while Stefan felt a mixture of emotions, he found it difficult to be disappointed in Rusty.

When Rusty's testimony was apparently finished, the Captain of the Guard took three officers with him to investigate the passageway, in order to verify Rusty's testimony. The waiting seemed torturous while the room remained almost deathly silent. When they returned, the captain testified under oath of what they had discovered. There was more waiting while the jury left the room to discuss the new evidence. Finally the jury turned in their verdict, and Han stated, "I hereby declare, in regard to the murder of Johanna Von Bindorf Heinrich, that Stefan Cameron Han du Woernig Heinrich is not guilty."

Stefan squeezed his eyes shut in silent gratitude, trying to swallow his emotion. He could hear behind him the evidence of relief from his family. But he was well aware that the representatives of Kohenswald were not necessarily pleased with the outcome.

Stefan's mood quickly descended again as Han had to condemn Rusty to the fate that Stefan had nearly met. Even those who were most grateful for Stefan's release could not help but feel regret. But by Stefan's request, the execution was postponed one week to allow time for Rusty to put his life in order, both in business and matters of a personal nature.

All was quiet as Rusty was led from the courtroom, and then Captain Leichty turned to Stefan and showed a genuine smile. "It is a pleasure, Your Grace," he bowed slightly, "to release you from our care."

Stefan laughed as they shook hands. "I'd like to say it's been a pleasure being in your care, but . . ." They laughed together, and he added more seriously, "I must say that I'm impressed with your abilities. Keep up the good work." Stefan lifted a finger. "But we must do something about the food."

Captain Leichty nodded and left his side, as did the other officers. Stefan turned slightly and felt disoriented. For a moment he wasn't certain what a free man was supposed to do, but he didn't contemplate it long before his father approached. The embrace they shared could not begin to express the emotion the two of them had experienced in the past hours. Before Han set his son free, the family overwhelmed them. Stefan laughed freely as he received a jubilant greeting from each in turn, until Ericha pushed her way through the group. She was crying so hard she couldn't speak. They held to each other tightly while Stefan realized he was shaking. Emotion hovered in his throat in a tight knot. He nearly wished he *could* cry, but he felt numb. He dreaded the moment when his mind fully perceived how close he'd come to dying. The family huddled together in the courtroom long after everyone else had left, laughing and crying tears of joy. They all went back to the drawing room where they had met earlier that morning and knelt together in grateful prayer for what they considered nothing short of a miracle.

Chapter Twenty-Five
THE COURIER

Stefan spent the following hours looking at his world through different eyes. Everything he touched, or saw, or heard only made him appreciate life. He pondered the boundary he had come so close to passing and wondered what lay beyond it. He spent time alone in the chapel, thanking God for this second chance at life, and then he shared time with the people he loved, grateful that yesterday's good-byes had not been necessary.

Holding Ericha close through the night, Stefan fingered the wedding band on her finger and again thanked God for miracles. He rose before dawn and walked out to the courtyard to watch the sunrise, grateful just to have lived one more day. He felt a kinship with this day in his chance to begin again, and just like his grandfather before him, he would live each day to its fullest.

Ericha awoke to find Stefan gone and briefly panicked. But he entered the room only moments later, and she felt so grateful just to see him and know he was alive.

"Good morning, Mrs. Heinrich," he said warmly, kneeling on the bed to kiss her.

"Good morning," she replied, and he kissed her again. "Where have you been already?"

"Oh," he laid back and put his hands behind his head, "I just thought I'd watch the sun come up." He turned to look into her eyes. "And it was beautiful."

Ericha laid her head on his shoulder and sighed peaceably.

"And I talked to Rusty," he added. She leaned up to look at his face, sensing emotion in his voice.

"What did he say?"

"He was full of apologies and such, but I set him straight."

"How is that?"

"I told him that I owed him my life, and I only wished there was some way I could keep him from facing this." Stefan looked toward the ceiling.

"It wasn't easy talking to him," she perceived.

"No, it wasn't." He touched Ericha's face. "I only wish I could tell him how I really feel. Not only did he save my life yesterday, but he gave you and me a life together. I know it's an awful thing to say, but I'm glad she's gone and we are together the way we always should have been. To me, it's a miracle. I only wish he didn't have to die for it."

Stefan's thoughts switched tracks when he noticed Ericha looking uneasy. "Is something wrong?" he asked.

She swallowed, and the brief wave of nausea subsided. "Nothing that a good breakfast wouldn't cure."

"Well then, little mother," he said, sitting up, "let's get you some."

Ericha pushed him back onto the bed and kissed him with fervency. "Later," she said, and he didn't argue.

Though Stefan had predicted as much, it was dismaying to realize that even the statement of the court did little to deter the mobs. Word had it that they believed Rusty had constructed a lie on Stefan's behalf, and because he had no family, he was willing to sacrifice his life for his beloved duke. It was Stefan's life they wanted, and the assurance that Johanna's killer was set to be executed gave little ease to the mob's constant efforts to get into the castle and pursue their vengeance.

When Stefan managed to ignore the ongoing threat, it felt

good to be running his duchy again. In truth, with Ericha there as his wife, he could easily admit it wasn't such a bad position after all.

If not for the persistence of the dreadful mobs. Karl and Luise were still staying with Theodor for fear of getting home safely. Hannah's family and Gerhard weren't eager to try leaving the castle for the same reason. Stefan was grateful to have ample supplies of food and water within the castle to sustain its occupants for quite some time yet. But the entire situation was so ridiculous.

Han was glad to relinquish the duchy back to his son for many reasons and declared he could use a vacation.

"Not until this wretched mess is cleared up," Stefan said, pointing a finger at his father. "You're not going anywhere until it's safe to walk the streets of Horstberg again."

"Yes, Your Grace," he bowed in mock humility, and Stefan shook his head and laughed, grateful to be alive.

Stefan rose three mornings after he'd become a free man with his mind made up to put a stop to this nonsense once and for all. Even if it meant having the Guard finally just use brutal force to disperse the mobs. He only prayed it would not result in war.

He left Ericha sleeping and went to tell his father of his decision but realized when he got to the office that things were unusually peaceful. Captain Leichty came in moments later to inform him that the mobs had dispersed on their own in the night, and even their encampments below the castle hill were completely gone. A sense of relief fell over the castle throughout the day, but something uneasy kept teasing at Stefan's mind, telling him they'd given up too easily. After dinner, he called Han and Georg into the office, and they were quick to agree that they could not take for granted that this was over.

"I've been thinking seriously about this," Stefan said authoritatively, "and I believe we should send out a courier."

"Who are we relaying messages to?" Han asked, pretending he didn't know what Stefan meant.

"Ourselves of course," he said in mock disgust.

Han laughed. "Quite a boy, isn't he!" he added proudly to Georg, who shook his head. Han had passed fifty and still acted like a child at times.

"If you all agree to this," Stefan said, "I'll take care of it from here."

"Sounds good to me," Han said, and they discussed the plan a little further.

"Who are you sending?" Georg asked.

"I've got someone in mind," Stefan said with no expression as he stacked some papers on his desk. "As I said, I'll see to it."

Stefan went to his bedroom to find Ericha just putting little Cameron to bed. He pulled her into his arms with a hungry kiss. "Ah," he said, "it's so nice to have you here with me. And it's nice to be alive, too."

"You've been saying that quite a lot lately."

"Isn't it true?" he asked wryly.

"Very," she smiled and blew out the lamp, drawing him with her to the bed.

When Ericha lay sleeping against his shoulder, Stefan slipped quietly away from her and dressed in his oldest clothes. He went into the sitting room to write a note for his wife, then left it on the bureau and donned his reliable hooded cloak. Carefully he kissed Ericha and his son, then slipped out into the hallway. He went straight to the high, east turret and climbed the winding stairs where he removed the cloak and put on a waistcoat that hung there. With the cloak back in place, he reached into the high cote and pulled out one of the most reliable pigeons, tucking it into the specially designed pocket inside the waistcoat. He put writing materials into the other pocket, then went quietly back down the stairs and out to the cavalry stables. The men on duty looked surprised to see him there in the middle of the night, but no comment was made when he requested a fast, sturdy horse.

With purpose, Stefan rode away from Castle Horstberg into the night, knowing that a man in his position had to earn the right to serve his people again. He hoped that this would prove him sincere.

In the few days since Stefan had been back to share this room with Ericha, she had gotten used to waking alone since he usually left early to see to his business. She nuzzled against his pillow, relishing the subtle trace of a masculine scent that told her Stefan had recently been there.

Cameron's cries finally urged her from the comfort of her bed. Only then did she see the note lying on the bureau. She nearly cursed aloud before she even picked it up. Hurt and anger flooded through her as she read it.

Ericha, my love. Again I ask you to forgive me. There is something that must be done that could possibly put all of this to an end. And for reasons that I cannot explain on paper, I feel I must see to it personally. I must go now or I fear no one would let me. I love you, Ericha. Give Cameron and Grandmama a good morning kiss for me, and with any luck I'll be back before supper. All my love, Stefan.

Ericha took the message to Han and he *did* curse aloud. "Has he taken leave of his senses?" he shouted. "He told me he was going to send out a courier; said he had somebody in mind. When I get my hands on him, I'll strangle him personally."

"Where has he gone?" Ericha asked fearfully.

"Kohenswald," Han stated, throwing the note scornfully onto the desktop. "And if they discover who he is, they'll kill him in a minute."

The family was seated at supper when a young officer nearly ran, unannounced, into the room.

"Sir," he said directly to Han.

"What is it?" Han asked, standing to take the paper held out for him.

"On the pigeon, sir. Just now."

Han scanned it quickly, then ordered the officer, "Tell Captain Leichty to meet me in the office immediately. Send criers through the valley. Close up the gates and get every man into position."

"Yes, sir," he said and left as quickly as he had entered.

"What is it?" Abbi asked fearfully.

Han sat back down as he slowly reread it aloud. "'Be prepared for attack at any time. Troops are numerous. Desire to gain total control of Horstberg. No small thing. Way out of hand. Don't underestimate. Got to go. Fear they're onto me. Love you, Ericha. God be with you all.'"

A hush fell over the room until Ericha stood and demanded, "Someone has got to go find him!"

Han met her eyes with empathy and walked out of the room, leaving her plea unanswered.

Ericha couldn't relax enough to even close her eyes. She prayed until her head hurt, wondering if she and Stefan had come this far only to have death come between them now. Her mind filled with horrible images of Stefan being discovered by his enemies and beaten to death by their hot-blooded hatred. And if that weren't bad enough, there was no ignoring the activity in the courtyard. Even in the dark of night, when it was usually calm and quiet, she could hear distant noises to indicate the military preparation for battle.

Ericha knew that by now the entire country had been alerted. The villagers would be prepared with weapons ready, women and children hidden safely away. Every officer of the Guard was stationed to protect the borders, specific areas throughout the country, and the castle gates. Some time before dawn, she began to hear the sounds of warfare rising up from the valley. She screamed when cannons fired from the castle battlements. Was it really getting that close?

Cameron awoke from the noise. While she tried to soothe him, Ericha's mind worked frantically. What would happen to them if Horstberg lost this battle? Instinctively Ericha dressed herself and the baby, and bundled together a few of his things. She hurried to Abbi's rooms. If nothing else, she would wait it out with her grandmother.

Ericha found Abbi and Maggie calm but equally prepared. The sun came up while the cannons continued to fire at regular intervals. The sounds of battle came closer, and the women gradually became more tense. Ericha was just wondering where Han and Georg were when Han erupted into the room. "They're penetrating the gates," he announced. "You've got to get out of here."

"Where's Georg?" Abbi demanded.

"He's helping see that the servants get into the cellars."

He was gone as quickly as he'd come, but Abbi seemed to know what to do. Ericha tried to imitate her calm example as she and Maggie followed Abbi quickly down the hall. She went into a room Ericha had never been in before, and it was too shadowed to see much of anything. The next thing Ericha knew, Abbi was putting a revolver into Ericha's hand.

"Do you know how to use it?" she asked.

"Ye-es," Ericha stammered, "my mother had one."

Ericha tucked it carefully into the bundle with Cameron's things while Maggie loaded a double-barreled shotgun as if she'd done it a thousand times. They hurried down the hall again, and Ericha realized they were headed back to the duke's bedroom.

The passageway, she thought, recalling the story of how the family had fled through there to the lodge in the revolution of 1849. But as they entered the room, the door into the tunnel was already open. They stood silent for a long moment, just staring at it.

"Mother," Maggie finally said in a whisper, "would Han have—" She screamed as a man stepped out from behind the draperies. He laughed triumphantly, and a sickening dread formed in the pit of Ericha's stomach. It hadn't been so long since she and Cameron had been alone in this room.

"Well, if it isn't *the* ladies of Horstberg," he said snidely.

"How did you get in here?" Abbi demanded, apparently unruffled.

"Well now, everyone knows by now that this castle has this remarkable passageway, what with that glorious court case that put your murdering duke back on the streets." He grinned, and Ericha felt his eyes more on her. He looked familiar, but she was having trouble placing him in her memory.

"Of course," he went on, "it would be impossible to find where to enter from the outside if you didn't know. Lucky for me, your former duchess, may she rest in peace, showed it to me."

Ericha could almost feel Abbi seething with anger. How much grief was one woman capable of unleashing on this family? Even dead, Johanna continued to haunt them.

"Drop the guns, ladies," he said, pulling a pistol from the back of his belt.

Ericha gave Abbi a quick glance, hoping she could pick up on her advantage. While Maggie and Abbi's weapons were in plain sight, Ericha's was tucked into the bundle wedged between herself and Cameron. While she had both arms around the baby, it was impossible for this man to see the gun.

Maggie and Abbi both dropped their guns to the floor. The man smiled, and Ericha remembered where she'd seen him. It had been in the court room, a very long time ago. This was Elsbeth Schmidt's ex-husband, who had abandoned his family when he'd become wanted for his continued abuse. It began to make sense. Had Johanna sought this man out, knowing his obvious hatred for Stefan? Was he part of her plan to frame Stefan for treason?

"Well, now," he said, putting his gun back in his belt as he stepped toward them, "there's no reason for all of you to get hurt." He focused on Ericha. "This is the one we're looking for." He touched Ericha's face and eyed her lewdly. She retracted but tried not to move too boldly and upset him. "This is the one who caused all the trouble. Pretty little thing, I must say. Of course, we'll need to take the baby, too."

Ericha instinctively tightened her grip on Cameron, discreetly moving one hand higher on the baby. She was beginning to think she was completely in control when he grinned again and said, "You might like to know we already got that murdering husband of yours." She heard Abbi and Maggie gasp, and her heart fell into her stomach. "But then," he went on, "you don't *really* want to be married to a man who murdered his wife. It might be you next."

He laughed, and Ericha's hurt and anger seethed through her. She fought to remain calm, knowing it might be her only chance.

"But not to worry about him. I fired the shot that got him myself; fool that he was to come traipsing where he didn't belong. If he—"

In one agile movement, Ericha drew the revolver, cocked it, and fired. Cameron screamed and tried to squirm free. Mr. Schmidt took a step back, stunned as the shot hit his shoulder. Ericha felt Maggie pull the baby from her arms as she saw the intruder reach for his gun. She cocked and shot again, hitting him square in the chest. Cameron screamed louder.

"Damn you!" Ericha shrieked as the reality of what he'd said about Stefan took hold. She fired again. And again. He hit the floor in a pool of blood. "Damn you to everlasting hell!" she cried, shooting him again. And again. The empty cartridges clicked as she continued to cock and fire until Abbi put a gentle hand on her arm.

"I think he's as dead as he's going to get, my dear," she said gently.

Ericha dropped the gun at that word *dead*. She'd just killed a man. *The man who had killed Stefan.* She turned to look at Abbi and saw tears streaming down her face. But she calmly said, "We must go, before someone else finds their way in here."

Ericha turned to take her screaming child from Maggie, who looked as pale as a sheet. Maggie and Abbi picked up the guns and hurried into the hall. Cameron calmed quickly in his mother's arms, but Ericha was shaking. She wondered where they would go now. She guessed that they would join the servants in the cellars, but as they descended the stairs near the office, it was evident from the sounds of fighting close by that they would never make it down that hall unnoticed.

Abbi glanced both directions, took up a lamp, and opened an apparently rarely used door.

"Oh, Mother, no!" Maggie whispered.

"I was hoping to get to the chapel, but we have no other choice," she replied softly. "Be careful now," she said to Ericha as they slipped through the door and she closed it behind them. "The stairs are steep. Take it slow."

Ericha wondered where they were going as they seemed to go endlessly downward in a slow spiral. Cameron drifted to sleep in her arms as they went. When they reached the bottom, Abbi and Maggie had to push together against a squeaky-hinged iron door. They eased into a room and closed the door. Then they just stood there. Ericha was aware of Abbi and Maggie being more tense than they had been upstairs. The room was completely empty.

"Where are we?" Ericha demanded when the silence became eerie.

Abbi cleared her throat tensely. "This used to be Erich's chemistry room," she stated, holding the lamp high to illuminate the smoke-darkened walls and a huge section of newer stone where an obvious, gaping hole had once been.

"Merciful heaven," Ericha breathed, grasping the full implication. *This was where her father had been killed.* Then she thought of Stefan. The entire drama made her suddenly weak, and she sat against the wall, moaning from the anguish. Abbi and Maggie sat on either side of her, huddling close together. Nothing had to be said to know they shared the same anguish. They cried. They prayed. They waited.

Cameron woke up after a long sleep. He quickly became fussy, not pleased with his surroundings and wanting something to eat. Maggie had stuffed a biscuit from the breakfast tray in her pocket and gave it to him, which helped for a little while. But his crankiness only increased as time slipped by.

Finally Abbi said, "One of us has got to sneak up there and see what's going on. We can't stay down here forever."

"I'll go," Ericha said. She was amazed at how courageous she felt, knowing that her husband was dead. They were just discussing a plan when they heard noises on the other side of the door.

"Oh, please, God," Abbi prayed aloud, "don't let them find us."

They doused the lamp and huddled in the darkest corner. Ericha whispered soothing words to Cameron, grateful that he was being quiet. But as the door came open, he started to cry. Maggie stepped forward, the shotgun poised firmly toward the door as light shed through the opening.

"Put that thing away, woman!" Han exclaimed, and she nearly collapsed. He set down the lamp and pulled her into his arms where she sobbed uncontrollably. He looked over her shoulder toward Abbi, apparently baffled by the depth of Maggie's emotion.

"We've reason to believe that Stefan is dead," she reported tearfully. Ericha just rocked Cameron back and forth, feeling dead inside herself.

Han squeezed his eyes shut and held Maggie tighter while Abbi explained what had happened. When Maggie quieted down, Han told them that everything was over. Because of Stefan's warning message, Captain Leichty had sent word out to three different countries that were allies to Horstberg. Just when it looked as if they'd lost everything, armies rode in from the east and the south and sent Kohenswald into a hasty retreat. The borders were being patrolled, and the damage assessed.

Along with the others, Ericha breathed immense relief to know that Horstberg was safe and secure. But when Han finished his report, she felt compelled to ask the question that apparently no one else dared, "But what about Stefan? Where is he? What happened to him?"

"We already have men out looking for him," Han said. "They'll find him eventually . . . one way or another."

Stefan opened his eyes, and an ominous brightness immediately made him squint. An unexplainable feeling of peace and serenity enveloped him, and he wondered if he was dead. He didn't feel dead. But then, he'd never died before, so how would he know?

The light became suddenly shadowed, and he opened his eyes fully to behold a woman's face. Her features were shadowed as light streaked from the window behind her, shining around her head like a halo.

"Ericha," he whispered. She moved closer, and his heart beat quickly.

"No," a gentle voice replied, and he felt a hand come over his arm, "I'm not Ericha. Whoever she may be, I'm certain she's dreadfully worried about you."

Memories filtered back, and Stefan tried to sit up. "I've got to—"

"Calm down," the woman interrupted, and gentle hands urged him back against the narrow bed where he lay. "You're in no shape to be doin' that. Just relax and I'll tell you all you want to know. Unless of course you start askin' about the great mysteries of the world. I'm not well schooled. But I could tell you what you're doin' in my bed."

Stefan's eyes followed the woman as she moved to the opposite side of the room, wiping her hands on an apron. He noted a slight limp as she walked, and he realized his surroundings were humble. She looked somewhere between his mother and grandmother's age, with hands and eyes that betrayed many years of hard work.

"Your horse," she said, "wandered into my garden lookin' for somethin' to eat. You fell off, bleedin' all over the place.

"I would assume," she went on, working at something on her lap as she talked, "that a bullet went through your shoulder. Holes like that don't come from runnin' into trees or the like. I would have to assume as well from the looks of you that you are either wanted, not well liked, or just poor like me."

She looked toward Stefan with no expression, waiting intently for a reply. He said hoarsely, "All three perhaps."

"Thought so," she stated, and silence reigned for several moments.

"The shoulder should heal well," she said. "I'm not so bad at doctorin'. Are you hungry? You should be. Been in that bed for three days."

"Three days?" he asked, sitting up abruptly. Pain shot through his chest and arm, and he moaned, repositioning himself carefully.

"If you had any appointments, you missed 'em."

"Where am I?" he asked.

"In my house," she stated.

"Which country?"

"Which one did you *not* want to be in?"

He made no response, and she rambled on. "Things have been pretty unsteady around here. But it seems that since you got shot, it's settled a bit. I hear there was quite a battle. Pretty gruesome. They say a lot of people died. I guess that makes you lucky."

Stefan's heart beat madly, but his voice was toneless as he asked, "Who won?"

"It wasn't us."

"Who is us?"

"Full of questions, aren't you?"

"Who is us?" he demanded, and she looked at him sharply. "I need to know," he asked in a softer tone, and she smiled.

"You're a spy."

"What makes you think so?"

"Pigeon hold in the waistcoat," she stated, and Stefan glanced down to realize he was covered with nothing but the blanket that lay over him to the waist. He said nothing as he tried to decipher his senses enough to figure out if he was a prisoner of war or simply the beneficiary of a charitable woman.

"Please," he said at last, "tell me what you know."

She set her basket aside and stood, placing her hands on her hips. "Horstberg was . . ." she paused and nearly smiled, and he sensed she was teasing him, "victorious."

Stefan closed his eyes and sighed.

"Somehow I knew that would be important to you," she said.

"Now for what I know. I know that you are not in your home country. But no need to worry. I won't let them get you. I know that right now you are goin' to muster up enough strength to eat a hearty dinner, and before you know it you'll be strong enough to go home to Ericha . . . whoever she may be."

Stefan laughed, and true to her word, this charitable woman cared well for him until he had the strength to ride. He discovered little about her. She seemed more apt to talk of him. But it was only as he mounted to leave that she bothered to ask, "Who are you, anyway?"

He smiled slightly and replied, "Only a man . . . grateful that my horse wandered into the right garden."

She grinned endearingly, and he added with warmth, "Thank you. And if you ever are in need—and I mean it—feel free to call on me."

"Where do I call?" she asked.

"Castle Horstberg," he stated with a wry smile.

She looked at him sideways, with a humorous suspicion in her eyes.

"Does that disappoint you?" he asked.

"I heard the Duke of Horstberg was missin', but you're far too kind and too common to be the man I've heard talk of all this time."

"You can't believe everything you hear," he said. "Maybe I'm just a spy." He winked at her, and she smiled.

"Tell me one thing," she said. "Who is Ericha?"

Stefan smiled and took the woman's hand. He bent down and pressed it briefly to his lips, squeezed it, and smiled.

In a loud whisper he said, "Ericha is the Duchess of Horstberg."

He smiled again and started the horse toward the road, pausing only to say, "Thank you again, madame. God will surely bless you for your kindness and mercy."

It took a few minutes for Stefan to adjust to riding with only his left hand at the reins, but he soon grasped the idea and focused his concentration on where he was headed. *Home!*

He caught his breath when the high turrets of the castle came into view, and he unwillingly heeled the stallion to quicken his pace.

Ericha moved to the window for the tenth time that day and sighed at the stillness below.

"He'll come back," Abbi stated. "Eat your breakfast."

"How can you be so sure?" she asked.

"I've told you a hundred times, my dear. Han said there was no indication from Kohenswald that they knew where Stefan was, and if there was a body, the Guard would have found it. He's alive, I tell you. I just know it. Stefan is a part of us. If he were dead, we'd feel it."

"I used to believe that, Grandmama," Ericha admitted. "But I'm so numb I can't feel anything anymore. It's been ten days. What could he be doing for ten days, if he *is* alive?"

"He'll come back," she repeated. "Eat your breakfast."

Ericha played with her food more than ate it. She was vaguely aware of Maggie doing the same. Eventually she gave up and returned to the window.

"Stefan used to do that," Abbi said wistfully, and Ericha wondered if she was going senile. She hadn't seemed as well since the battle.

"Do what?" she asked distantly.

"Stand at windows. He was always looking out the window. He was looking for you, you know. I told him to stop looking out the window and go find you."

"I wish you could tell me the same."

"He'll come back."

Ericha wanted to cry. It all seemed so futile, so hopeless. She closed her eyes with a silent prayer that Abbi du Woernig's instincts were not suffering with age.

Ericha wasn't aware of the lone rider moving stealthily up the road to the gate, nor the steady trot of the stallion as it thundered into the courtyard. Stefan saw her seated in the window before she realized that her prayers had been answered.

"Ericha Heinrich!" he shouted as he dismounted, and a stable servant was immediately there to take the horse, grinning broadly.

Ericha's eyes shot toward him, and her heart raced as Abbi and Maggie rushed to the window, gripping her arms.

"Oh, Grandmama!" she cried. "Oh . . . I can't believe it! Oh!"

Stefan met their eyes from below, and a mischievous grin absorbed him as he called, "Your husband is home! How about a . . ."

He didn't bother to finish since they had disappeared from the window. Instead, he hurried toward the door, his heart beating quickly, more from excitement than from the weakness of his ordeal.

Ericha ran into the hall with Abbi and Maggie close behind. She flew down the stairs, her heart racing with joy, and Stefan took three steps at a time until they met on the middle landing with an embrace that twirled them both from the force of their meeting.

"Stefan," she whispered tearfully, touching his face, his hair, the sling that held his right arm. "Oh, Stefan," she cried, "you're hurt."

"I'm alive." He laughed, and she overwhelmed him with a vibrant kiss.

He laughed again as Abbi and Maggie pushed their arms around them both. "I told you he'd come back," Abbi insisted.

"How did you know?" Stefan asked with an endearing grin.

"I had a dream," she whispered. "I knew you would come back."

After supper that evening, the family gathered in the drawing room for coffee. Ericha sat close beside Stefan while he was filled in on the details of what had happened in his absence. Hannah and her family had returned to the estate days ago. And Gerhard had left for Italy, insisting that word be sent as soon as there was news of Stefan. He'd said there was a woman he had to catch up with, and if things went well, he'd be bringing her back to meet the family before long. Han reported the casualties of the battle soberly. And Stefan, like his forebears gone by, wondered why such pointless fighting had to even occur. He was relieved to hear that everything was well now, and it seemed that Kohenswald had given up their ridiculous quest.

"The only real problem is," Han said with seriousness, but Stefan caught a subtle contradiction in his eyes, "that in the heat of the chaos, somebody went through the keep and opened all the cells. We were holding a number of Kohenswald's citizens arrested over the past weeks. But now," Han shrugged his shoulders, "everyone is gone."

"Everyone?" Stefan asked, lifting his brows.

"Everyone," Han replied.

"Ironic, isn't it," Georg piped in. "They were seeking this overblown vengeance for Johanna's death, and it was they who set the killer free."

"Yes." Stefan sighed. "Ironic. Was he pursued?"

"Of course," Han said emphatically. "But I'm sorry to say that they've not found a trace of him."

"Funny thing," Georg said. "You recall the little emergency stash we had buried in the forest. You'll remember, Abbi . . . how Cameron had it put there when we left the castle in 1849."

"I remember," she said with a warm smile.

"On a hunch we went to check it out," Georg continued, "and there was a fair amount of money missing."

Stefan's eyes narrowed, feeling a mixture of emotions. "How much?"

A very subtle smirk passed between Han and Georg before Han stated, trying to sound distressed over it, "Just a little less than the salary we owed him, and the bonus due to him next month."

Stefan said nothing, but he uttered a silent prayer of gratitude in his heart that Rusty had been given a second chance, and Horstberg could not be held responsible for setting a murderer free. In his opinion, it couldn't have worked out any better than that.

"As long as we're all together," Stefan said in a grave voice that caught the attention of his family members, "there is something I need to say."

Glancing at the faces of those he loved most, Stefan realized this was more difficult than he'd expected it to be. He cleared his throat carefully and forced himself to the point. "I want you to know that I made a mistake. It was wrong of me to get involved with Ericha the way I did, and . . ." He hesitated when he saw the alarm in her expression, but he squeezed her hand tightly with a silent assurance. "Don't get me wrong. I do not regret the love I felt for her, nor the determination I found to share my life with her. The problem was that . . . well, I should have channeled my determination in a different direction. I should not have taken something that I had no right to take. Ericha was young and impetuous when we met, and in my heart, I know I took advantage of that. I should have had the strength to do right by her from the beginning."

"Perhaps," Abbi interjected, "you're being too hard on yourself. Your spirit was battered when you met Ericha. You simply weren't strong enough to see the full perspective. I don't see any need for you to keep punishing yourself for—"

"I'm past punishing myself, Grandmama. I know in my heart that God has forgiven me for what I've done. But it's important for you to understand what I have learned." Again he absorbed the expressions of his loved ones before glancing down briefly. "My feelings for Ericha were right and good. The way I acted upon them was not. I should have had the courage to make it right from the beginning. I should have—"

"Forgive me, Stefan," Abbi interrupted again, "but I don't see that you had any choice. You told me once that it was difficult to act on something rationally when there were no rational options."

"Oh, but there *were* options, Grandmama. I was just too blinded by fear to see them. That's what I'm trying to say. I should have had the determination to make a life with Ericha the *right* way. And I should have had faith to know that by doing what was right, God would have shown us a way. There was only one thing that kept me from denouncing Johanna and divorcing her. And that was fear. I was afraid her father would resent it . . . that he would find an excuse to use it against me, and Horstberg would end up in war." Stefan met the eyes of each person in the room, one by one. "Could it have been any worse than what we have lived through now?"

The hushed silence that came in response made it evident that he'd made his point with impact. He looked directly into Ericha's tear-filled eyes as he continued. "The past is in the past. What's done is done. I am forever grateful that Ericha came into my life, proving to me that love truly does conquer all. I only hope that you," he glanced around the room, "each of you, can forgive me for the hardship I have brought upon my family and my country because of my poor choices and my weak spirit."

Following another taut silence, Georg spoke with a gentle voice. "Stefan, my boy." He looked into Stefan's eyes as if they were alone. "I'm reminded of Cameron." Stefan glanced briefly to Abbi as his thoughts turned to the journals she'd brought to him that had given him so much strength. But her focus was on Georg, her eyes glowing with love and admiration.

"There was a time," Georg continued, "when Cameron too was confronted with the reality of his choices. And I'll tell you what I told him. Sometimes hardship just has to happen in order to make us stronger, better people. If he had not been framed for a crime, put into exile for four years, and forced to claw his way back to the throne, he would have only been a mediocre ruler, without the conviction to meet the requirements of his position effectively. But Cameron emerged from that with a great deal of wisdom and strength. He carried this country successfully through some tremendous difficulties, and he raised a good family."

Georg was oblivious to the tears coursing down Abbi's cheeks as he leaned his forearms on his thighs and penetrated Stefan with a gaze he would never forget. "Now, I want to share something with you that I think you're ready to hear. A few months after Cameron and Erich were killed, the reality finally settled in for me that they were gone, and I . . . fell apart.

I was filled with regret, certain that I could have—or should have—done something differently, and they would still be alive. But Abbi shared something with me then that has had a deep impact on my life. Only indirectly however. As I have watched this drama unfold between you and Ericha, contemplating where it all began, I have often pondered the words Abbi told me that day." He glanced toward her and quickly pressed her hand to his lips in a gesture of consummate adoration.

Georg turned back to Stefan with purpose. "She told me that she knew in her heart it had been their time to go. And that *you* were destined to rule this country, and the struggles of your life would make you strong."

Stefan unconsciously squeezed Ericha's hand more tightly as his heart reacted to what Georg was saying. But the impact only intensified as he went on.

"That's the most important point, Stefan. I've wondered why one or the other of them couldn't have survived. I've wondered why Kathe couldn't have been married to Erich, to spare the hardships of Ericha's life. But she, just as you, has a mission to fulfill in this life. Together, I believe the two of you will accomplish things far greater than any generation gone before you—because you have the strength to do it. And you have that strength because of all you have suffered. So learn from your mistakes. Become wiser. Press forward. But don't regret the sorrows that have made you what you are. I believe future generations will revere you for accomplishments that you've not yet encountered."

Stefan felt briefly embarrassed when he realized tears were streaming down his face. But a quick glance around the room assured him that everyone else was doing the same. Several minutes of silence made it clear that no one had anything else to say on the subject, but it was even longer before Stefan found his voice enough to speak. Since he'd brought them into this conversation, he figured it was up to him to take them out of it.

"I was thinking," he said, and glanced lovingly toward Ericha, "that as of yet my lovely wife has not been officially crowned duchess of this fair land."

"I was thinking the same," Abbi said, seeming eager to have the tension broken. "I mentioned it to Georg just the other day. We must do that soon."

Ericha said nothing, suddenly overwhelmed, not certain what that entailed. Stefan smiled warmly at her and winked just as Han said, "Not only that. We must have a cathedral wedding."

"What a splendid idea," Maggie said. "You know Stefan, if nothing else, your father is clever."

"Yes," Stefan chuckled, "he is that."

"Perhaps a little senile," Ericha inserted lightly, and Han laughed.

"If he's senile," Georg said, "what does that make me?"

"I don't want to know." Abbi laughed. "Now don't change the subject. I think a cathedral wedding is just what we need."

"But we're already married," Ericha protested.

"That's all right," Han said. "Maggie and I eloped, but we had a cathedral wedding. If we had to do it, so do you."

Stefan laughed loudly. "What's funny?" Ericha asked.

"Good heavens!" he exclaimed. "It's a great day to be alive!"

Stefan declared the next morning at breakfast that he had one item of business that needed to be taken care of before their public wedding took place.

"And what is that?" Georg asked.

"I will be visiting the baron this afternoon."

"You're not going *there?*" Ericha was appalled, if not concerned.

"Oh, yes I am," Stefan said. "But I will be taking an army with me if I must."

"I think I know where you're headed with this," Han said, "but what specifically are your intentions?"

"Well," Stefan leaned back in his chair, "I've had a lot of time to think lately." He almost smirked, actually feeling grateful for all those weeks stuck in seclusion. "And something occurred to me," he went on, "that I'd never considered before. I realize now that I've always felt a little intimidated by the baron, perhaps because he was a powerful man even when I was a child. He always seemed to look down on me, as if I were *still* a child. I've wondered if I might have handled the situation with Johanna better from the start if I had not allowed myself to feel intimidated."

"You can't go regretting such things," Maggie interjected.

"No, I can't," he agreed. "And when I see how all of this has worked out, I am grateful to see many miracles in my life, in spite of my faults and weaknesses." He smiled at Ericha. "I can't go back and change the past, but I can learn from it and make the future a little better. I intend to make it clear to the baron *exactly* how I feel about the things he's allowed to take place here, and how I *really* felt about his daughter."

"Be careful that you don't get him riled up all over again," Abbi cautioned.

Stefan smiled. "I'll take Ericha with me," he said. "She'll make certain I stay in line." He winked at her, amused by her gaping astonishment. "But I can assure you, by the time I get through with the baron, he wouldn't *dare* breathe down my neck for as long as he lives."

"I'd like to see this." Han smirked.

"Good." Stefan lifted his glass toward him. "I was wanting to take you along as well."

A few minutes later, Stefan said, "Mother, do you still have that suit, the one you wore for my inauguration? And a few times since, I believe."

"Of course I do. Why?"

"I was wondering if it might fit Ericha. I would like her to wear it for our little jaunt to Kohenswald."

Maggie smiled. "I'll see that it's aired out as soon as we're finished here."

Stefan smiled and met Ericha's eyes. She seemed a trifle nervous, but there was a familiar conquering look in her eyes that let him know she could take on anything. And for him, she would.

Stefan sent out a messenger with military escort to inform the baron that he would be coming. While Theodor was helping him dress, Ericha swept into the room, wearing the suit he'd requested. It was a near-perfect fit and still looked as good as new. Designed much like a riding habit, the skirt was black with red piping around the hem. The jacket was red and black, a feminine version of the military uniform. The black hat had an elaborate veil trailing down her back. She looked like a queen.

Ericha became briefly mesmerized by the adoration in Stefan's eyes as she walked into the room. She was surprised when he went down on one knee, saying with reverence in his voice and a sparkle in his eyes, "You are beautiful, Your Grace."

"Oh, get up off the floor." She laughed softly. He stood and kissed her. "I'm not the duchess yet."

"You're married to me. And that's good enough. That other is just a technicality. But then, to me, you were always the duchess."

When Stefan was ready, he placed Ericha's hand over his arm and walked with her out to the courtyard. "This is a dream come true," he admitted as he pushed open the door and they stepped outside.

Ericha caught her breath as the troops came to attention. Stefan helped Ericha mount Pegasus, and then he and his father mounted their stallions as well. The men accompanying them all mounted horses at the captain's order and started down the hill, Stefan and Ericha in the lead, with the captain and Han directly behind. The ride to Kohenswald was pleasant, but Ericha began to feel nervous as she saw their destination approaching.

"Are you all right?" Stefan asked.

"I'm not sure if I'm . . ." She didn't finish, unable to explain her apprehension.

"You were born to this, Mrs. Heinrich," he said gently. "All you have to do is stay beside me, look your dignified and beautiful self no matter what is said, and clear your throat or nudge me or something if I get out of line."

Ericha chuckled. "So, that's what a duchess does?"

He smiled. "It's one of many duties that your predecessor did not handle well."

She knew he was talking about Johanna, and Ericha turned her attention to the road ahead, knowing it was Johanna's home country they were entering. Immediately Ericha felt a difference between Horstberg and this place. There was a beauty and peacefulness absent here as they rode through the village and toward the castle. Although the structure itself was awesome, it lacked the unique aesthetic quality of Castle Horstberg. Ericha felt pride for her home and country in comparing them.

Ericha absorbed the reactions of people as they rode, and she began to perceive a degree of Stefan's motive in making his visit with so much pomp. He was letting these people know by his fearless appearance that he had triumphed over their country's persecution, and he would not cower or hide, no matter what they believed.

There was a cool terseness about the way they were received at the castle. When she and Stefan were finally escorted to see the baron, along with Han and the captain, Ericha could see immediately that he was not pleased.

"You have some nerve coming here like this," the baron spurted. Ericha had nearly forgotten what he looked like, and she was struck now by his cruel eyes and commanding presence. There was a goodness about Stefan in the way he ruled that was absent in this man.

"I would have come to the funeral," Stefan retorted, "but I was a bit tied up at the time. The cell keepers have a little problem with allowing their guests to have time off for funerals."

"Which is where you should still be, or if I had my way, you'd be hanging from my highest battlement."

"It's a pleasure to see you, as well, Baron," Stefan said, putting his hands behind his back. "I can see you want to get right to the point, so I'll do that. I have something to say to you, and I wanted to say it face to face. I know that losing Johanna must be very difficult for you, and I am certain it's equally as difficult for you to lose your assets in Horstberg. I married your daughter in good faith with every hope that our nations could be united in peace. But if I had known then what I know now, I would have dumped her back on your doorstep the day after the wedding."

The baron nearly turned red with anger, but Stefan leaned a little closer, apparently not intimidated in the slightest. "She was pregnant with some other man's child when she exchanged vows with me, and then she had the pregnancy terminated and ruined her chance for ever giving me an heir."

"It's a lie, and you'll—"

Stefan leaned closer still. "Believe what you want. She's gone now, and it is irrelevant as far as she is concerned. But I have proof enough. Just as I have proof of her whoring about Horstberg at night and persecuting my family through the days with her drunkenness and her vixen tongue. She disgraced my name. She disgraced my family. She disgraced my country. And she disgraced you. But I didn't kill her. There were times when I was angry enough that I nearly wanted to. But the trap that killed Johanna is one that she set for herself, and I'll not apologize to you for her death."

"If you are quite finished denouncing my daughter with your lies and—"

"I'm *not* finished," Stefan interrupted firmly, but not with malice. "I only wish I'd had the courage to denounce her years ago. Then perhaps she'd be alive today, and you would have the pleasure of her company with you still. But she's gone, and neither you nor I, with all our power, can bring her back."

Stefan took a deep breath, and his eyes caught that imposing quality which Ericha knew from personal experience could be very intimidating. "I have only one thing more to say." He lifted a finger. "Know this, Baron, if you so much as breathe down my neck with the intent of doing harm to myself, my family, or my country, Horstberg will give you a fight you will never forget. The scars will be upon this land for decades to come."

"Are you threatening me then, young man?"

Stefan took a step forward. "Yes," he said, "I am. A lot of

good people lost their lives in this pathetic power struggle that oozed out of the sewers of Kohenswald—both in my country and in yours. Innocent blood is too high a price for whatever you were trying to prove, or whatever you may wish to gain. And I'll not stand for it. I will tell you what I told your daughter. You let me live my life in peace, and I will do the same for you. But she just couldn't leave well enough alone. Learn a lesson from her death, and leave well enough alone. That is all I have to say."

A moment of silence made it evident the baron had no immediate retort. Stefan turned on his heel, and his robe flew out around him. He put a hand to Ericha's back and guided her to the courtyard where their horses and the military escort were waiting.

When they had passed the castle gates, Stefan leaned toward Ericha and said, "You didn't nudge me or make any noise, my lady."

She smiled. "I didn't need to."

He took her hand and kissed it quickly before they rode on.

Stefan directed them onto a side road where he lifted his hand and the group came to a halt. He nodded toward the captain, who seemed to know what was going on. He dismounted and went to the door of a small farm house. The woman who answered the door looked stunned as the captain apparently explained something to her. He handed her what appeared to be an envelope, then motioned toward Stefan, who nodded and smiled warmly.

The woman waved exuberantly, apparently recognizing him.

"Thank you again, madame," he called. "And God bless."

"And to you, kind sir. Is that Ericha?"

Stefan nearly beamed as he took his wife's hand. "It is indeed."

The captain mounted, and Stefan signaled the group into motion. He waved again, then turned to smile at Ericha.

"She is the woman who saved my life," he said in response to Ericha's questioning gaze.

"Then I owe her *my* life," Ericha said. Stefan only smiled. "And the envelope?"

"Ah, it was nothing really." He shrugged his shoulders. "She's getting on in years and has no family to care for her. It's just a little something to help her get by."

Ericha sensed he was nearly embarrassed to admit to his deed. She simply smiled and enjoyed her return to Horstberg with her husband at her side.

Chapter Twenty-Six

AT PEACE

Ericha heard the drum cadence begin in the courtyard below and hurried to the window to watch as the procession started out the castle gate, with Stefan at its head. She barely caught the gleam of his crown as the sun reflected off of it.

"Come along, child," Abbi insisted, bustling into the room with Maggie right behind her, "we must go."

"Do I look all right?" Ericha asked, turning for her approval.

"Perfect," Abbi said.

"Your parents would be proud," Maggie added. "Come along. We must go."

Ericha carefully lifted the long train of her mother's wedding gown over her arm as she hurried down the stairs. Han was waiting to help the women into the open carriage, draped with wedding streamers and bells, with six white caparisoned horses at the harness. Ericha was seated with her back to the driver, with Abbi and Maggie facing her. Han mounted and rode behind them through the castle gate. Ericha knew that in the three carriages going before them were other members of the royal family, including Gerhard, who had come back for the wedding, bringing his new bride Felicia along. And there was Hannah's family, who had taken charge of little Cameron, and Stefan's other sisters and their families as well. And of course, Georg.

Ericha thought about her parents as the carriage rolled toward the village. She could well imagine her father's funeral procession taking this same route to the cathedral, shrouded in black, while her mother contemplated what her wedding day might have been like. Turning her mind to the present, Ericha felt certain that her parents were with her in spirit this day. In a way, she felt as if she and Stefan were able to live the life that Erich and Kathe could not.

Stefan felt a joy he'd never known as he rode at the head of his wedding procession into the village. As the people lining the streets cheered and threw flowers and streamers, he felt their love and acceptance, in spite of all they had struggled through on his behalf.

At the cathedral, he rode by tradition on his stallion, up the aisle between the throngs of people. At its head, Karl waited, looking positively smug. An officer took the horse, and Stefan turned to see the bridal party enter at the rear. The music rose and reverberated off the high walls as Ericha moved slowly up the aisle on her uncle's arm. *It is a miracle*, he thought as her hand was placed into his and they knelt before the bishop to be married— even if this time it was only for show. But Stefan loved it. He knew it was important for the people to feel a part of this and be able to witness it in order to accept Ericha as their duchess. The bishop gave him a knowing smile as he proceeded with the ceremony. The people cheered when he kissed her, so he kissed her again.

Ericha realized this wasn't over as a young officer stepped forward, holding a carved box she'd never seen before. Stefan opened the box and lifted out a crown: a smaller, simpler version of the one he wore.

"Please kneel," Stefan said with the authority of a duke. Ericha knelt before him and bowed her head.

Stefan's voice rang loud and regal through the cathedral as he spoke. "Let it be known upon the records of this land that I, Stefan Cameron Han du Woernig Heinrich, being of sound mind, and by the power vested in me as the reigning Duke of Horstberg, do hereby pronounce thee, Ericha Katherine Lokberg-du Woernig Heinrich," he paused and drew an emotional sigh, "Duchess of Horstberg. And with the sustenance of thy husband, the approval of thy people, and the blessings of God, I place this crown upon thy head that thou might reign with nobility as duchess of this land for all the days of thy life."

Ericha felt the crown slide easily over her head, and warmth seemed to permeate from it. She saw Stefan's hands come down in front of her, and she put her hands into his. He squeezed them gently as he helped her to her feet. Then he kissed her again and the crowd cheered. Stefan turned to thank the bishop before escorting Ericha down the steps and helping her mount his stallion. He mounted behind her while she pulled the train of the elaborate gown over her arm to keep it from dragging. With one arm around her waist and the other holding the reins, Stefan guided the horse slowly through the line of uniformed men who fell into step behind them. The crowd continued cheering as they approached the huge cathedral doors.

Emerging into the open air, they laughed to see that the crowds had increased. Ericha wondered if there was anyone in Horstberg still at home. She thought of Mrs. Burger and wondered if she might have wandered out of her home to witness this glorious event, so much like Abbi's wedding more than fifty years ago. Stefan laughed easily and tightened his embrace. She felt certain there were no two people happier than they in the entire world.

Abbi felt memories absorb her as she observed the public marriage of her grandchildren. Georg was there beside her, just as he had been on that day when she had married the Duke of Horstberg. She felt Cameron close to her in spirit and pressed her hand over Georg's arm as they exchanged a warm smile. She knew he still longed for Elsa after all these years, just as she did Cameron, and it made her love him all the more for being with her now.

Abbi started to cry when Stefan and Ericha knelt together before the bishop to exchange vows, but Georg put his arm around her as the joy inside her swelled. She could hardly contain her happiness when Stefan placed the ducal crown onto Ericha's head. She felt Georg had read her mind when he whispered in her ear, "Cameron would be proud."

Abbi's joy increased as she observed the traditional folk dancing in the square. But amidst the wedding festivities afterward at the castle, she began to feel especially tired, and she asked Georg if he would walk her to the garden. He gladly complied as always, and they sat together, reminiscing of days gone by and marveling over the more recent events that had led to this day.

"We did it again," she said triumphantly.

"What's that?" Georg asked.

"Somehow Horstberg always manages to come through. No matter what we come up against, we always manage to come through."

"Yes," Georg said thoughtfully, "it seems we do."

"Why do you suppose?" Abbi asked.

"That's no problem to figure out," Georg said with wisdom in his voice. "Horstberg is beautiful—through and through. It's a good country because we've worked hard to make it good. God could not help but see that and bless us for our efforts."

Abbi was briefly moved to silence from his reply but finally said, "I believe you're exactly right.

"What do you suppose," she said in speculation, "would have become of us if I'd not lost myself on the mountain?"

"Many lives would have been very different," Georg stated with a smile. "I'm glad you did."

"Yes," she nearly laughed, "so am I."

"It all seems so long ago," Georg mused.

"It was," Abbi said, and they laughed. "I was just a girl. And how young and strapping you and Cameron were back then!"

"Some things do change." Georg chuckled.

"I will never forgive you," she said in mock disgust, "for the way you tried to tell me that Cameron was only patronizing me."

"All for a good cause." Georg smirked. "But I know you're lying. You forgave me as soon as I apologized—on my knees, if you'll recall."

"Still," she insisted with a sparkle in her eyes, "I will never forgive you.

"You know," she added with a different mood to her voice, "I had the strangest dream last night."

Georg looked concerned but only said, "Tell me about it."

"I dreamt that I got into bed and went to sleep, like I always do, and I woke up young again. I seemed to hear Cameron calling my name, and I walked out into the courtyard to find him. The day was especially bright, but when my eyes adjusted to the light, he was there, sitting atop Blaze, looking much the way he did the winter I met him."

Abbi stopped and looked distantly toward the mountain with nostalgia in her eyes.

"Was that all?" Georg asked.

"No," she stated. "He took my hand and pulled me into the saddle with him, and then he put his arms around me and we galloped away from the castle into a snow-covered meadow. Though it wasn't snow really; it was different."

Georg watched her closely as she seemed to be finished. He noted the tired look about her that was growing permanent and found that he felt much the same way. She turned to him and laughed slightly. "Isn't that funny?" she asked with a lilt in her voice.

Georg took her hand and gave a sad smile. A sense of peace filtered over him as their eyes met. Then Abbi turned her face skyward, and the sunlight caught the green in her eyes.

"Yes," she said easily, "you're right, Georg. But then, you always are. I forgave you long ago."

Stefan watched silently as Ericha unwound her hair and pulled out the weaving. His thoughts turned to the feelings he'd experienced in that moment when he had faced a firing squad, and he blessed the opportunity to be with her like this. He'd faced death twice and triumphed. How could he deny the miracles in his life?

With a grace and dignity that he was certain only a du Woernig woman could bear, Ericha removed her wedding gown in the firelight and slipped between the sheets to be near him. She kissed him warmly, but he laughed and whispered in her ear, "Later." She looked at him in question and he said, "First I'm going to tell you a story."

"Oh, please do," she said, leaning on her arm to watch him. "What's it about?"

"That's easy. It's about a princess who didn't know she was a princess until after she'd fallen in love with a prince, whom she didn't know was a prince."

Ericha laughed, and he asked, "So how does the princess feel, being the Duchess of Horstberg?"

"I'll tell you later," she said. "First the story."

"All right." He made himself comfortable. "This one is for Cameron . . . both Camerons."

"Does it have a happily ever after?" she asked, her green eyes sparkling in a way that reminded him of Abbi.

"Oh, yes." He smiled and kissed her. "It's the stuff that fairy tales are made of."

ℰlizabeth D. Michaels began writing at the age of sixteen, immersing herself ever since in the lives created by her vivid imagination. Beyond her devotion to family and friends, writing has been her passion for nearly three decades. While she has more than fifty published novels under the name Anita Stansfield and is the recipient of many awards, she boldly declares *The Horstberg Saga* is the story she was born to write. *Through Castle Windows* completes the five initial volumes, but she has a follow-up series planned.

Michaels is best known for her keen ability to explore the psychological depths of human nature, bringing her characters to life through the timeless struggles they face in the midst of exquisite dramas. For more information, please visit Elizabeth's author page on WhiteStarPress.com.

www.ingramcontent.com/pod-product-compliance
Lightning Source LLC
Chambersburg PA
CBHW051053030726
47504CB00006B/1605